N-SPACE

TOR BOOKS BY LARRY NIVEN

N-Space
Playgrounds of the Mind
Destiny's Road
Rainbow Mars
Scatterbrain
The Draco Tavern
Ringworld's Children

With Steven Barnes

Achilles' Choice
The Descent of Anansi
Saturn's Race

With Jerry Pournelle and Steven Barnes

The Legacy of Heorot
Beowulf's Children

With Brenda Cooper

Building Harlequin's Moon

With Edward M. Lerner

Fleet of Worlds
*Juggler of Worlds**

*Forthcoming

N-SPACE

LARRY NIVEN

A TOM DOHERTY ASSOCIATES BOOK
NEW YORK

This is a work of fiction and nonfiction. All of the characters, organizations, and events portrayed in the stories and excerpts from novels in this collection are either products of the author's imagination or are used fictitiously.

N-SPACE

Book design by Jaye Zimet

A Tor Book
Published by Tom Doherty Associates, LLC
175 Fifth Avenue
New York, NY 10010

www.tor.com

Library of Congress Cataloging-in-Publication Data

Niven, Larry.
N-space / Larry Niven.
p. cm.
ISBN-13: 978-0-7653-1824-4
ISBN-10: 0-7653-1824-5
I. Title.
PS3564.I9N18 1990
813'.54—dc20

90-38888
CIP

First Hardcover Edition: September 1990
First Trade Paperback Edition: August 2007

Printed in the United States of America

0 9 8 7 6 5 4 3 2 1

CONTENTS

N-SPACE

INTRODUCTION

THE MAKER OF WORLDS BY TOM CLANCY

Some years ago, when I was still dreaming about becoming that special breed of cat called "author," I had a birthday coming up and my wife was out of ideas. I told her to check out the bookstores for any book by Larry Niven except the three I'd already acquired. I don't remember how many Wanda returned with, but I do know that I still read them periodically.

One of the bad things about being a writer (and there are many) is that when writing a novel, you often find it impossible to read someone else's novel. Some evil agency inside your brain takes note of the fact that you are *reading* instead of *writing* and forbids you to read more than thirty or forty pages. So, often you go back to vegetating in front of the TV because you can only write so much in a day, and the reason you picked up that book in the first place is to get your mind off what you were doing that morning. Writing is, therefore, both a form of compulsive behavior and, I frequently tell people, a self-induced form of mental illness. Those few writers who don't start off by being a little nuts soon get that way as a direct result of their vocation.

When I find myself in desperate need of removing my mind from THE PLOT so that I can look at it just a little more objectively the next day, my helper and pshrink is Larry Niven. For some reason, my brain does not recognize him as a threat to my compulsion.

The scope of Larry's work is so vast that only a writer of supreme talent could disguise the fact as well as he does. He doesn't just set up a cute little story of ETs or interplanetary war. Not Larry—he builds a complete universe. Oh, sure, he keeps the galaxy pretty much as we know it (or think we know it), but he peoples it with whole sets of civilizations, some active, some extinct, all interrelated somehow or other. Now, that's a pretty tall order, and if you're not careful how you go about it, the reader would soon be overwhelmed by the background and have trouble catching on to the story itself. But not with Larry. With little more than an occasional *oh, by the way* he sets all the scenery in place and then gets on with his tale, which is always a story with an interesting point and a fairly tight focus embellished by the scenery instead of being dominated by it.

And this ain't easy. Trust me, I write for a living, too.

All authors get fan mail, some good, and some not so good. There are two kinds that really matter. The stuff you get from kids is very special. Kids who read for recreation, and then have the audacity actually to write a letter to the author (I never did) are something that always touches you. These kids will go on to accomplish things, and it's rather nice to think that you've influenced them a little bit. Next best is the mail you occasionally get from fellow writers. To be read by someone in the same line of work—and the worst thing about being a writer is that it really murders your reading—is rather like being a fighter pilot and having a beer handed to you by another fighter pilot. Your basic good feeling. I expect that Larry gets a lot of such letters. In the times when I need to escape from inside my head and relax, Larry's the guy who relaxes me. As I suspect he does with a lot of others. Thanks, pal.

• • •

ON NIVEN

The first time I met Larry Niven I accused him, in a jocular way, of stealing some of my best ideas and publishing them before I had even had them. For instance, I read PROTECTOR about a year after I'd had the idea about why immortality in an individual would never make sense. There happen to be powerful Darwinistic reasons for people to die and get out of the way and stop breeding. However, Larry had already taken this notion, explored it so thoroughly that, in effect, no one could ever explore that territory again without tipping his hat to Larry. This is actually a fairly rapacious thing to do. If you think that the territory of notions is limited, then the hard sf writer is like a wildcat miner drilling out resources that are shrinking. For whatever it's worth, some people think that way. A lot of sf writers aren't writing hard science fiction because they think most of it has been written. If their reasoning is true—and I don't think it is—one of the reasons is that you have writers like Larry Niven out there mining out whole veins and leaving nothing left for the rest of us to explore.

In hard science fiction originality is especially prized. If you're the first to explore a certain idea, a new technology—black holes, neutron stars—you get a fair amount of acclaim. But for Niven it's not enough to be the first. He has to also be last. That is his attitude, and in a sense it is a very aggressive attitude.

So in the end we writers revere Larry Niven, even though he makes our jobs harder. He not only mines all these marvelous veins of ideas, he mines them to exhaustion.

—David Brin

I met Larry in the mid-1960s, when he was just starting as a writer. Like many of us he began shakily, unsure of many aspects of his craft, but absolutely firm in the realm of ideas. He knew what he thought and felt a solid assurance.

I saw in him then a facet I've witnessed since in many university students: a love for the scientific worldview, but an impatience with the humdrum daily grind of science itself as universities too often present the field. Larry always liked the big picture, the supple intersection of ideas. After Cal-Tech and his mathematics degree, he seemed to feel an urge for larger landscapes.

I suspect many sf writers encounter such a moment, which becomes the launching point for careers. Poul Anderson finished his degree in physics and then turned not to ornate calculations but to a typewriter. This desire to sing rather than walk the pedestrian pathways of science is all to the good: we need our bards. Indeed, perhaps we need them more than we need more careful but closed thinkers.

Many science fiction readers are similar sorts. Larry was a breath of Campbellian clarity in the New Wave murk, and he is the natural voice of a whole segment of the scientific-technical community, irreplaceable and golden. Long may he sing!

—Gregory Benford

The first time I read Larry Niven? It was in college just before a chemistry exam. I discovered these Larry Niven books and read straight through them instead of studying for the exam.

I eventually got to meet him, and I've known Larry ever since—about fifteen years now (longer if you count knowing him through his books). I think my favorite thing about Larry personally is that he always has time for people. If you show an interest in him or what he does, he's always ready to listen to you—I mean listen intently. You never feel as if you have just a little bit of his attention. He puts his whole self into listening and talking.

There are a lot of science fiction writers who frighten fans. Fans are actually scared of them. Larry's never been that way. Never.

—Wendy All

Larry is probably the most beloved pro in the science fiction fan world. Panels in which he is participating, parties at which he is likely to appear, are thronged. With good reason. He says wonderful things. He is truly congenial (which few science fiction pros are). People like to be around him.

—John Hertz

About 11 years ago I'd done a lot of writing but the only payment I'd received was something like ⅕ of a cent a word or payment in contributor's copies. Still I considered myself a writer.

So one day I'm in the club house of the Los Angeles Science Fiction Society, and Larry Niven walks in. When Larry walks in, you understand, he is completely surrounded by the people there. It's like he's a god, and this is his domain.

I walked up to him and said: "Hello, Mr. Niven, my name's Steven Barnes, and I'm a writer."

He took a puff on his pipe, looked at me and said: "Okay, tell me a story."

I just about died. But it so happened I'd sent out a story earlier that day about a compulsive gambler who pawns his pacemaker, and somehow I stumbled through it.

After that we started talking. He seemed kind of reserved, but even then I could see he was still in touch with his child-personality. I could especially see it in his eyes. In some ways it was as if the beard and pipe were props to convince you that, yes, these are the badges of adulthood. But back there were these little boy's eyes.

I asked him if he'd read a story, and he said he would, and the next week I gave him an envelope containing three. I saw him the week following and asked if he had read them, and he said, yes, Jerry Pournelle and he had both read them. He said he was intrigued and asked me whether I'd be interested in looking at a story he'd tried writing ten years before and hadn't been able to complete to his satisfaction.

Thank God the problems with the story had nothing to do with astrophysics or any of the technical things that Larry is a master of. They had to do with the way the human beings were relating to one another, and I was able to fix it.

We've been collaborating ever since.

The imperative for men in our culture is that they must go out and create—work, produce, change the land around them. Now people often think that it's easy when you have a lot of money handed to you as a kid, as Larry had. All that does is say to you that the chances are very good you'll never live up to the man who created all that wealth.

But Larry created a career separate from anything his family had handed him. He could have taken their money and lain by the side of the pool and vegetated or put it into land or condominiums and made a lot of money. And, indeed, he has made money off the money his father handed him. But the most important thing Larry did was to go out and define a whole new world. If his world in California had already been conquered, then Larry would create new worlds to conquer and people them with his own creations.

—from a conversation with Steven Barnes

Since I happened to be the lucky editor who published Larry Niven's first story, I've been asked to tell a little bit about him, which I'm glad to do. Let me tell you about that first story . . . but forgive me if I start by explaining something about my own editorial practices.

When I was editing *Galaxy* and *If* in the 1960s I had made it a condition of employment that no one was to expect me to spend much time in the office of the publishing company. I was willing to appear now and then—one afternoon a week wasn't objectionable—but that was as far as I would go. Between times I had an assistant to sit at a desk in the office for the purpose of answering the telephone and dealing with whatever routine things had to be dealt with. (For most of that time my assistant was a young woman named Judy-Lynn Benjamin, later Judy-Lynn del Rey, who went on to considerably better things later on—Del Rey Books is named after her.) One of Judy-Lynn's jobs was to go through the week's accumulations of unsolicited manuscripts by unknown writers (unflatteringly called "the slush pile") for me. She wasn't to read them—I have always read everything that was submitted to me myself, on the grounds that, as Frank Munsey once said, no magazine can survive the mistakes of more than one person—but Judy-Lynn took the stories out of the envelopes they arrived in, clipped rejection slips on them, put them in return envelopes with postage attached and stacked them up, unsealed, for me to pick up when I came in. Then, in the smoking car of the train back to the Jersey Shore each week, I read the fifty or a hundred stories that had turned up in that week's slush. There would generally be a handful that required some sort of letter to the author, and, if I was very lucky, one or two that I could actually buy. All the rest I sealed up and dropped into the mailbox at the Red Bank train station, and that was the end of that. One doesn't expect much out of the slush, you see. One is generally right about that, too.

So it was on just such a train ride, somewhere between Newark and Matawan, that I pulled out of its envelope a slim little manuscript called "The Coldest Place," by some previously unknown person who said his name was Larry Niven.

That manuscript didn't get mailed back. "The Coldest Place" wasn't a *great* story. But it had a number of good things going for it. It started with a clever science-based idea—the "coldest place" of the title, paradoxically, was on the dark side of the very hottest planet in the solar system, Mercury—and the writing was competent enough, and besides the story was beautifully *short*. (I was always particularly looking for short stories, because—since we paid by the word—all those savvy professional writers had learned early that they ate better if they wrote long ones.)

So I kept that story out, and wrote a letter to the author saying I would be happy to buy it (for very little money, to be sure), and asked him a few questions about himself. And by return mail he answered that he'd take the offer and, yes, he had never sold a story before so I could call it a "first." I put the check through, and marked it up for the printer, and all was well.

Or so I thought.

You never know, though, do you? There was a wholly unexpected development. Just at that time some busybody scientists, who should have found some more productive use for their time, were conducting radar studies of Mercury. They came up with the surprising (and just at that moment really unwelcome) information that the planet did not always present the same face to the Sun, as everyone (including Larry and I) had always thought. The damn thing *revolved*. It didn't *have* a "coldest place."

It was evident that Larry Niven read the same journals as I did, because a day or two later I got a worried letter from him to say that he'd just discovered his story had turned out to be scientifically wrong, and should he give the money back?

By then I had been giving the question some hard thought at my end. There was a kind of moral question involved. I believe that science-fiction writers have a duty to be careful about the science in their stories (and over the years I rejected a good many otherwise good stories, most of which sold elsewhere, because of scientific flaws).

On the other hand, I don't believe that science-fiction writers have to be *more* right than the scientists themselves are. Larry had done his homework. At the time he had written "The Coldest Place" the science in it was fine; it wasn't his fault that the scientists had changed their minds. (We can still read, for instance, Edgar Rice Burroughs's Barsoom stories with as much pleasure as ever, in spite of the fact that the Percival Lowell picture that he based them on of a somewhat habitable Mars turned out to be all wrong.) Besides, for any writer his very *first* sale is a major landmark, and I didn't have the heart to ask him to unsell it.

In any case, the story was already well along in the assembly line, and so I let it go through and it appeared as written. No one seemed to mind.

The key thing that struck me about Larry was that he not only wrote well, he had gone to the trouble of getting his science right, and even of making the science an important part of his stories. He still does. Larry is a member of that sub-class of the class of science-fiction writers which

I particularly admire: He doesn't just like science fiction, he likes science, and he even does his best to keep up with and understand it.

Finding somebody like Larry Niven was a delight for me, because I could suggest science-based story ideas to him, and rely on him to make the most of them. He was a natural. Writing science fiction asks more of an author than getting the science right; the characters have to be good, the settings have to be imaginative, the societies and psychologies involved need to be worked out carefully and consistently. Larry was fine in all those ways.

For instance: Neutron stars were a new discovery in the 1960s, so I suggested he write a story about a neutron star. He sat right down and wrote it, and he put into it some grand picaresque characters with intriguing plot problems. Between us we thought of a wonderful title for the story about the neutron star—we called it "Neutron Star"—and it won him his first Hugo the following year. A little later Freeman Dyson, at the Institute for Advanced Study in Princeton, came out with his suggestion that a truly advanced civilization would want to capture all the energy radiated from its parent star by building a sort of shell around the star to trap it for their use—what came to be called a "Dyson sphere." And of course I immediately asked Larry to write me one of those.

I'm sorry to say that I never got to print that one. The magazines I edited were sold to another publisher around then, and I didn't want to go along. Actually, the story never quite got written quite the way Dyson had in mind, either, because when Larry got down to serious thinking about it he redesigned the concept. Instead of a sphere, the artifact became a sort of hula-hoop around the star, peopled with Larry's always intriguing aliens. He called the story that came out of it RINGWORLD, and it remains one of his best novels.

I think I did one other important thing for Larry Niven around that time. I wanted to encourage his interest in science—not that he needed much encouragement—and, most of all, to make it easier for him to keep in touch with the up-to-the-minute developments, even the developments that hadn't quite happened yet, by getting a chance to talk with some of the actual scientists who were doing the latest research. So I suggested to him a couple of research establishments he might want to visit, and in particular recommended he go and talk to some of my friends in the Artificial Intelligence labs at MIT.

I suspect that that was Larry's first encounter with the MIT people, which led to coming to know the MIT Science Fiction Society . . . which led to his meeting a member who chanced to be a pretty young female fan called "Fuzzy Pink." A few years later I was delighted to be an usher at the wedding which transformed Fuzzy Pink into Mrs. Marilyn Niven—a marriage which still sturdily survives and shows every sign of having been made in heaven.

You will have noted from the above evidence of one of the great character flaws shared by almost all editors: They love to brag about the writers they have "discovered," and the ways in which through their fond parental guidance and instruction the writers attained success.

Partly that's jealousy; a successful writer generally winds up with a lot *more* success than the editor who buys his stories. Editors have expense accounts, but writers have more fun. (That's the main reason why, years ago, after decades of being a split personality as both editor and writer, I finally gave up editing entirely and went straight.)

The fact is that editors aren't always as important as they think they are. Actually, very few good writers *need* to be discovered. They discover themselves. They *write*. They keep on writing. They do their best to get better at writing with everything they write, and they send out what they have written to people who may want to publish it; and they keep on doing those things, no matter what. They may have to endure periods of accumulating rejection slips and unrewarded effort, but if they are any good at all somebody or other, sooner or later, will notice, and publish, and then they're on their way.

And yet it may be that, to some small extent, Larry Niven was an exception to that general rule.

The special circumstance in Larry's case was that his family were quite important to him. They were also quite hard-headed about what sort of careers their offspring chose to devote their lives to, and they didn't really thrill to his fascination with science fiction. They had viewed with no great pleasure his devotion to reading all those crazy science-fiction stories from an early age, and they took active alarm when he told them he had decided to make a profession out of writing the stuff.

So when he proudly showed them that first tiny check for "The Coldest Place" they were probably moderately pleased, but they certainly were not greatly impressed by the amount. Fortunately, things soon began to get better. As it happened, the second story I bought from Larry was a little longer and I was able to up the rate a bit, so the check was several times as big as the first . . . and the third also got a rate raise and was a good deal longer still and thus the payment check grew accordingly . . . and, all in all, it turned out that he was getting better paid by an order of magnitude or so with each new sale.

Well, that didn't go on forever. Still, it had its uses. "That sort of growth impressed them," he told me later. "From then on I didn't have to worry as much about opposition from my family, and so I could get on with writing in a more supportive environment."

As it happens, that subject came up again just a few months ago. I didn't bring it up. Larry did. We were on a panel in Pasadena, California, discussing the future of space exploration; we had all just been spending a wonderful weekend at the Jet Propulsion Labs to watch the pictures from the flyby of Neptune come in. We were accordingly all juiced up and, for once, happy about the way the world was going—and, during a lull in the debate, Larry leaned over to me and whispered, "You know something, Fred? I think you're entitled to about half the credit for my whole career."

I whispered back, "Thank you. Does that mean half the money, too?"

"No, no," he said, "just half the *credit*. But thanks."

—Frederik Pohl

● ● ●

DRAMATIS PERSONAE

• •

Frederik Pohl. The Famous Writers School taught me how to know when I was a writer. I knew it when I saw the check.

It was signed by Frederik Pohl.

Fred bought my first four stories, and many others, for the *Galaxy* chain. The third was a novella called "Relic of Empire." He retitled it "World of Ptavvs," got Jack Gaughan to do a stack of interior illos for it, and paid in peanuts. He also took it to Betty Ballantine (the science fiction arm of Ballantine Books) and suggested that it could become a novel.

Fred has figured large in my life.

He was an usher at my wedding.

At my first science fiction convention I was a lost neofan; but a writer too, because Fred Pohl knew me.

Early on, he suggested that I write stories about odd astrophysical domains: very hot and cool stars, hypermasses, Hal Clement's kind of thing; we'd pair them with articles on the same, and paintings . . . That notion fell through, but he set me to looking for the odd pockets in the universe.

When Fred left the *Galaxy* chain, someone should have warned me to go with him. His replacement, Ejler Jakobssen, was a recycled editor from "pulps" days. Ejler rejected a story months after "buying" it (saying he'd take it, but not sending a check). He "bought" THE FLYING SORCERERS as a four-part serial, demanded references for all of the Tuckerized friends in the book (which ruined all the jokes for me), then rejected the first section! *Then* rejected the rest. I'd heard horror tales about the days of the pulps. I got to live through them.

Milford Writers' Conferences. Tradition says that a novice writer learns nothing from a writer's conference.

I knew this. I attended the Milford Conferences hosted by **Kate Wilhelm Knight** and **Damon Knight**; but for fear of losing my ability to write, I skipped every other year. Presently I dropped out, or was dropped; my memory won't tell me which.

The Milford conferences were serious. Each attendee brought several copies of at least one manuscript. During the day the others would read it. The attendees would gather in a Vicious Circle to offer comments, criticism, suggestions.

Of three stories I took to Milford (and Madeira Beach, when the Knights moved there) only one was improved. That was "For a Foggy Night."

It's still true that the Milford Conferences were *different*. My urge to write did not die because I went to Milford. On the contrary, I always enjoyed myself; I always went home inspired, one way or another; and I met people I'd wanted to know since I was a little boy.

James Blish brought the first section of a novel, *A Torrent of Faces*, and described what he had planned for the rest. An asteroid is due for collision with Earth . . . an Earth inhabited by a trillion people, with no margin of error for any such catastrophe. Bombs are placed to blow away pieces of the rock; lasers fired from the Moon are to boil away some of the surface; but too much of it will touch down . . .

My turn. "Suppose you fire those lasers at just one side of the body? Boil one side. Vapor pressure, law of reaction. Couldn't you cause it to miss the Earth?"

Blish said, "I hope not."

It took me a moment to join the laughter . . . to realize that I'd suggested a way to shoot down the plot for his novel!

But Blish did what a professional would do (and I learned by seeing what he did). He made the laser just powerful enough to shift the impact point of the meteoroid from Chicago to a place not so heavily populated . . . and it still destroyed too much.

Arthur C. Clarke brought a Questar telescope and set it up on the Knights' porch. It was early afternoon and we all took turns looking at Venus.

Many years later, during a radio interview in Los Angeles, Arthur was asked, "Who's your favorite writer?" You know the answer to that, surely. You can't name one, or many; you'll offend all the rest.

He said, "Larry Niven." And apologized to Jerry Pournelle that night at a Pournelle party.

But Jerry tells a similar tale, and in fact lots of us can do so. Arthur Clarke is the kind of man you want to kill someone for, just so he knows.

I'd discovered **Lester del Rey**'s juveniles at the same time as Robert Heinlein's. Here he was in the flesh, generating wicked arguments on every possible topic.

I met **Piers Anthony** at the Madeira Beach avatar of KnightCon, but we never got to talking. We got a dialogue going many years later, because I sent him a fan letter after reading *Omnivore*.

Gordon Dickson and others talked about working for an agency for reading fees. He spoke of a novice writer whose wonderful characters never got involved in anything like a story, and another who mistook funny hats for characterization. They never got the point, and the readers-for-hire never stopped caring . . . and were not allowed to tell anyone to quit.

Harlan Ellison wanted unqualified praise. Any suggestion that a story could be improved was met with verbal vitriol. The circle of critics saw a lot of that. This grated. If a story didn't need fixing, why bring it?

Then again, he brought very good stories, and his suggestions for improving others' stories were pointed and useful.

Years later, my whole attitude flipflopped.

I sent ''Inconstant Moon'' to Damon Knight for *Orbit*. He rejected it.

Damon Knight was then one of the foremost critics of speculative fiction. The other was James Blish. Judith Merril was taking a break; Algis Budrys was making a reputation; Spider Robinson didn't exist. And *Orbit* was definitive: it was the literary end of the spec-fic spectrum throughout the New Wave period.

What I write was never New Wave; but there's never been a time when I didn't want to expand my skills. I thought I'd made it this time. A solid study of character; no visible hardware; a love story. ''Inconstant Moon'' was New Wave for sure, even if I was writing in complete sentences.

I recently unearthed Damon's long rejection letter. He made a good deal of sense, more than I remembered. Even a Hugo Award–winning story can be improved.

At the time I was furious. I questioned his critical skill. This story was perfect, and only an idiot would have questioned etc.

Maybe a writer needs that much arrogance. Else he'll never send out his first story, never make his first sale.

Judy-Lynn del Rey. Judy-Lynn Benjamin entered the field as an editor under Fred Pohl at *Galaxy Science Fiction*. When Fred quit, she continued with Ejler Jakobssen for awhile. She wound up at Ballantine Books and became one of the most powerful editors in the field.

She was a dwarf. One got over noticing that. She was charming, intelligent, enthusiastic, competent. She was tactful within limits: she generally wouldn't lie to an author.

She liked stuffed animals. When I introduced her to the cat-tail (see WORLD OUT OF TIME) which Takumi Shibano had brought me from

Japan, she fell in love with it. Takumi got me another, and I passed it on.

She wanted to chop hell out of THE MOTE IN GOD'S EYE. Jerry and I wouldn't have that, so the book wound up with Simon & Schuster and Bob Gleason. In later years her comment on that decision was, "I don't want to talk about it."

She never bid on books at auction. Thus she lost FOOTFALL to Fawcett Books . . . and got it back when Ballantine bought Fawcett!

Let me tell you about the last time I noticed her height.

We were walking along a Philadelphia sidewalk, talking: me and Marilyn and Judy-Lynn and Lester, who is kind of short himself. Suddenly I was sitting on the sidewalk, dazed, hurt, looking up, with blood dripping down my nose from a wedge-shaped notch in my forehead. I saw something massive and metallic hanging over the sidewalk at eyebrow height.

In Philadelphia they put construction equipment where it can bite pedestrians. If I hadn't been looking down I'd have seen it. As it was, I had to go into the construction site and borrow Kleenex and a Band-Aid.

William Rotsler. Bill was part of the LASFS crowd when I joined. He's easygoing, curious about his fellow man, easy to get to know. His life follows his whims.

He collects epigrams for what will someday be an enormous volume; meanwhile he sometimes sends them to *Reader's Digest*. ("Everything starts as someone's daydream." Larry Niven, fifty bucks for five words.)

He's a photographer . . . of "fumetti," of bottom-budget movies, of naked ladies. (Of models, that is. Naked ladies? "She gets the benefit of the doubt, just like you, dear.") At science fiction conventions his tendency was to escort supernaturally beautiful women, "Rotsler women."

If things get dull at a science fiction convention banquet, look for the cluster of interested, amused, excited people. Bill Rotsler has gotten bored. So he's started drawing . . . on his notepad, the tablecloth . . . When things were slow to start at a banquet some years back, Bill began illustrating the butter dishes. The restaurant must have been dismayed at how many butter dishes went home with the guests. Mine was a dialogue:

> *"What does a collaborator do?"*
> *"He adds his name to a work which would not otherwise have the luster."*

But I didn't grab my favorite. It's "The Memorial Vincent Van Gogh Coffee Cup," with the handle for an ear and a bandage drawn on the other side!

Once upon a time his whim had him making badges. He made a great many. Some were for sale, for charities. Some, personalized, were for friends. So there were badges labeled *Not Larry Pournelle* and *Not Jerry Niven*. I wore *Jerry Pournelle's Voice Coach* for awhile, and when I'd got my fair share of fun out of that, I gave it to Jerry's wife. I wear *LARRY NIVEN, Friend of the Great and Near-Great* to conventions. (Which are you? Well, if you're standing close enough to read the badge . . .) I no longer wear *Have Sex Outside My Species* because it's been too long since THE RINGWORLD ENGINEERS, and because I once forgot to take it off when I left the hotel.

You can identify inner-circle fandom by the Rotsler badges.

Tom Doherty. I met Tom Doherty by walking into the Ace party at the World Science Fiction Convention in Miami Beach, Florida, Labor Day weekend 1977. Tom had just taken over at Ace Books.

He met me at the door. He knew my name. He had a good smile and (I tend to notice) an impressively large head, roomy enough for the brain of a blue whale. He was talking to Adele Hull of Pocket Books, and he started to tell me how good she was . . . and caught himself. It occurred to him that he shouldn't be praising the opposition in front of a solid author.

I said, "I have to tell you, it probably will never cost you a nickel."

"Why not?"

Oh my God. He didn't know! And I realized that I was going to have to tell him. Who else would?

So I did. "Nobody deals with Ace Books unless all the other choices are used up. Nobody expects royalties; the advance is *it*. Overseas money is never reported . . ."

Tom Doherty is a careful businessman. He didn't take over Ace without checking first. He checked back for two years and found no complaints lodged against Ace . . . not because there weren't any, as he thought, but because no writer ever expected to get money due from the old Ace Books.

The encounter with Larry Niven was his second awful shock of the day. He had already met Jerry Pournelle that afternoon.

"I'm Jerry Pournelle, President of the Science Fiction Writers of America, and we want to look at your books!"

Tom wound up paying several hundred thousand dollars in back fees to authors.

After he and James Baen parted company with Ace, Tom formed his own company, Tor Books. Then Jim dropped away and formed Baen Books. In this field we tend to train each other.

I see Tom fairly frequently. Once we met at a Boskone (annual Boston convention) and he took Marilyn and me off to Loch Ober, along with his editor, his wife and his daughter. He talked four of us into ordering lobster Savannah.

The lobster is cut open along the back; the meat is cooked, chopped and mixed with herbs, then put back. Lobster Savannah looks like it could *heal*. These beasts ran three pounds each. I started talking to my dinner:

"Doctor McCoy will see you now."

"The Federation doesn't think you can defend yourselves without our aid."

"Now, wretched bottom-feeder, you will tell us of your troop movements!"

By dinner's end I had arranged a mutual defense treaty with the baked Alaska. And by the time we reached the hotel, I had been dubbed *Speaker-to-Seafood*.

The last time Marilyn and I were in New York, I came to realize that Tom had bought me five meals! Though he was only present at two!

I was told early: when you eat with an editor or publisher, that's who pays the check. It's surprisingly easy to get used to such a tradition . . . but enough is enough. Hell, I'd never even sold him a book.

This book started with a phone call from Bob Gleason, one of my favorite editors. He and Tom had got to talking over a dinner . . . and it emerged that Larry Niven was going to have been a published author for twenty-five years, real soon now. Why not publish a retrospective volume? So Bob called.

It sounded good to me.

In May 1989, Tom Doherty and Bob Gleason stayed at my house for a few days before the SFWA Nebula Awards. We did a fair amount of work on the book. And I fed Tom Doherty by *cooking* several meals.

I even picked up a restaurant check once, by previous negotiation. He tried to back out afterward, but I wouldn't let him.

We called **Don Simpson** the Eldritch Doom because of the things he kept in his room. He's an artist and inventor, of that breed that never gets rich, because he invents new art forms. By the time anything could become successful, he'd be on to something else.

He had a wonderful time with some glass engraving equipment.

I'd been leaving Michelob beer bottles all over the clubhouse: the old lovely vase-shaped bottles too tall to quite fit in a refrigerator. At my fanquet (the banquet given for a LASFS member who has made a professional sale) Don presented me with a beer bottle engraved with Jack Gaughan's illustration of one of my aliens. I got him to do two more for me, then a Baccarat decanter and some Steuben crystal . . .

He was in the LASFS then. Later he moved to San Francisco, but I don't think he gave up his habits.

Frank Gasperik was an oddity. When I met him he was a biker and a hippie and a science fiction fan. Among bikers he carried a guitar and called himself The Minstrel. At science fiction conventions he sang filk.

Jerry and I put him in LUCIFER'S HAMMER as "*Mark Czescu.*" We put his song in too. He makes a good character . . . though he tends to take over a book, like kudzu.

We put him in FOOTFALL too, as "*Harry Reddington*," and commissioned a ballad from him. By then Frank had been through major changes. He'd been rear-ended twice within two weeks while driving two different cars, neither of which had headrests. His insurance company was giving him the runaround and his lawyer told him he'd look better on a witness stand if he didn't get well too quick. So he was avoiding major efforts to walk normally. It's all true . . . and Jerry and I screamed at him separately and together until we made him see that he wasn't being paid enough to stay sick!

We were working near the end of FOOTFALL at my house when Frank phoned about another matter. I told him, "We're at the poker table deciding Hairy Red's fate."

"Give me a heroic death," he said. So we killed him.

Dan Alderson. Dan is classic. At Jet Propulsion Laboratories they called him their "sane genius." He designed a program used by most of the Free World countries for deep space probes. Computer nerd, sedentary, white shirt with infinite pens and pencils in a plastic holder in the pocket. Diabetic.

Characteristic cry: "Weep! Wail!"

From Dan came the germ of a short story, "There Is a Tide." He worked out the exact instability of the Ringworld; it took seven years. I went to him for numbers for the Ringworld meteor defense. He was "Dan Forrester" in LUCIFER'S HAMMER. The list of what Forrester would need after Hammerfall is his, because Jerry asked him. He's the hero of one of Jerry's tales of asteroid colonization.

He likes Known Space. He's published intricately plotted outlines for stories that would vastly extend Known Space if they were written. I've described his multiple Ringworld system elsewhere. His extended outline requires putting the Warlock on the Ringworld at one point. When I killed off the Warlock in THE MAGIC GOES AWAY, Dan had to include the Niven-Pournelle INFERNO in his background, in order to bust the Warlock out!

NOREASCON, 1989: LOUIS WU'S BIRTHDAY PARTY

For twenty years Boxboro Fandom threw parties at the Boston regional conventions. Their themes were strange; their promotions imaginative. Now they've self-destructed, but they did it with a bang. Their swansong was a tremendous party at the Boston World Science Fiction Convention.

They sequestered the entire second floor of the Hilton Hotel for Friday night. They decorated the halls and rooms to fit environments real and imaginary, with doors designated as displacement booths: a teleport network running world-wide and then some. They called it "Louis Wu's Birthday Party."

The advertisements were movie ads altered by Niven quotes. They were everywhere.

They photographed me for an ID badge: RINGWORLD ENGINEER. I smiled a wide-eyed, toothy maniac's grin for their camera.

The Convention had booked Marilyn for a late panel; but I was at the party the whole time. It was full but never crowded . . . because the Hilton kept it that way, and the crowds waiting to get in reportedly ran around the block.

The Mad Tea Party included a croquet match with stuffed birds for mallets. A chef served vegetable sushi at the Japan site. There was a band, and dancing, in Paris. A kzin wandered about: Drew Sanders in the costume Kathy Sanders made for the 1984 Masquerade. There were several Pierson's puppeteers in the Kzinti Embassy; one was Kathy's costume, without Kathy in it, and one was a wonderfully baroque portrait. The Map Room was covered with Ringworld maps and Niven quotes.

And now I've got a T-shirt that says they're too tired to do it again.

At the Boskone convention last Sunday (February 1990) two perpetrators recognized my Ringworld Engineer badge and its maniacal grin. They told me stories:

The Hilton people loved them. Several asked if the Friday party would be repeated Saturday.

Boxboro's Hotel Liaison was a straight-looking guy who never raised his voice or appeared without a tie: a proper gent. And heck, they were taking the whole second floor! So the Hilton Manager was cooperative. She signed the thick contract without really noticing a clause near the end.

Getting the prop walls for the Kzinti Embassy into the hotel was tough. They'd measured the largest doors—the *front lobby* doors!—but hadn't measured them *open*. Open, they were too small. Boxboro considered taking them off their hinges, with and without permission. They considered junking the props. They were sure the prop walls wouldn't come apart; but someone tried it, and they did.

Still, the only feasible way to get them *out* after the party would be to hack them apart with a chainsaw! That would also allow the debris to fit into a dumpster. So they put it in the contract.

"I can't believe I let you use a chainsaw at four in the morning!" the Hotel Manager wailed. But she didn't stop them. It was in the contract.

● ● ●

• • •

"The point is, diving straight into a sun is a rare thing in the Service. It doesn't happen every trip. I thought someone ought to tell you."

"But, Mr. Whitbread, are we no about to do exactly that?"

THE MOTE IN GOD'S EYE, 1974

FOREWORD

PLAYGROUNDS FOR THE MIND

When every page has been read and the book has been put down, is the story over?

Some stories flow onward through the reader's imagination. Some authors leave playgrounds for the reader's mind. That was what charmed me about Andre Norton's stories: all the endings were wide open. I could close the book and continue moving further into the unknown.

As I grew older I began demanding endings.

As a writer I learned that endings are not so easy. They do make better art; at least most critics would say so. Poul Anderson is king of the powerful ending . . . but when his story is over, the playground remains.

Something should be left behind at the end of the story. There are characters unkilled, and actors who never reached the stage. Esoteric technologies. Alien ecologies. Worlds. The laws by which the universe behaves. **The playground.**

I knew it long ago: I'm a compulsive teacher, but I can't teach. The godawful state of today's educational system isn't what's stopping me. I lack at least two of the essential qualifications.

I cannot "suffer fools gladly." The smartest of my pupils would get all my attention, and the rest would have to fend for themselves. And I can't handle being interrupted.

Writing is the answer. Whatever I have to teach, my students will select themselves by buying the book. And nobody interrupts a printed page.

I knew what I wanted when I started writing. I've daydreamed all my life, and told stories too: stories out of magazines and anthologies, aloud, to other children.

One day my daydreams began shaping themselves into stories. I wanted to share them. Astrophysical discoveries implied worlds weirder than any found in fantasy. I longed to touch the minds of strangers and show them wonders. I wanted to be a published science fiction writer. I wanted a Hugo Award!

Money formed no part of that. Science fiction writers didn't get rich. (Robert Heinlein excepted. Kurt Vonnegut excluded.) I used royalty statements to keep score: how many minds had I reached?

I had my Hugo Award three years after I sold my first story. Among science fiction fans one becomes a Grand Old Man fast. Now what?

Now: become a better writer. I'll always have things to learn. In my earlier novels almost nobody got old or sick. I still have trouble writing about the things that hurt me most.

But I'm learning.

I used to get allergy attacks. Alcohol, dry air, lack of sleep, or any combination could cause me to wake up blind and in pain, with deep red eyes and puffy eyelids. I had to use a humidifier, or go to sleep with a wet towel.

I stopped smoking in August of 1987, and the allergy attacks went away.

And they'd be none of your business if I hadn't made it all public. I gave the allergy to Gavving in THE INTEGRAL TREES and Rather in THE SMOKE RING, for story purposes, and I had to nerve myself up to it. I still have trouble writing about what hurts me.

Also, parts of my life are private. My computer erases my early drafts, and that's fine. My mistakes are not for publication.

Writing is the ideal profession in many ways. It's not always easy, but—

You set your own hours.

You're being paid to daydream.

In psychoanalysis you would hire a professional to listen to you. You'd have no idea whether he was seriously interested. You'd operate on *his* schedule. The most you could expect from him is that he'd force you to face the truth about what you're saying.

But a writer has several tens of thousands of psychoanalysts. He knows they're listening because they're paying him for the privilege. Writer and reader both set their own hours. And he will seek the truth within himself, because more realistic writing is more convincing.

This feedback to the author: it's rare outside of fantasy and science fiction.

A few years ago, while the Citizens Advisory Council for a National Space Policy was in session in my living room, I snatched a moment to read my mail. Then I ran in to announce, "Hey, I just got a love letter!"

It sure was. A woman in Britain wanted me to write a congratulatory letter for her husband's birthday. He was a fan, and she was in love.

Hard science fiction in particular is a game played with the readers. They try to spot my mistakes. I see mathematical treatments of the dynamics of neutron stars, design alterations for the Ringworld, detective story outlines for Gil "the ARM" Hamilton. I get a constant flow of letters from strangers to keep me current on transplant technology, Bussard ramjet possibilities, black holes, magnetic monopoles. There are songs about the Motie Engineers and Lucifer's Hammer, sculptures of Pierson's puppeteers in every conceivable medium, and paintings of the Ringworld.

All of this is proper use of playground equipment. A reader need not be satisfied just to read the book. He paid his way in; he can stay as long as he likes.

I know where to go to talk a story over, to be admired, to get criticism, to meet my peers, even to do some business. There's always a science fiction convention going somewhere.

I was never sane until I became an established writer. So why do some writers go crazy?

There *are* occupational hazards.

It's lonely. How many professions are there such that you spend most of your working time alone with the door locked? (Terrorist, maybe. Does Stephen King qualify as a terrorist?) A nice view from your window is a liability. An interruption from your loved ones can break a valuable chain of thought.

Collaborations? Not everyone can stand to share a dream, and nobody in his right mind would collaborate with a novice, not even another novice.

Writing is a collaboration with the readers. I sensed that long before I wrote my first real collaboration. It goes like this: Somebody out there, thousands of somebodies, are entertained by the same things I am. They like to play in their heads, and I'm out to help them. I'm writing a dialogue between me and the paying public. *I'm not really alone in here.*

The money is lousy. After you've got a few books in print, and if they're any good, you'll be paid for them forever via royalties and foreign sales. But you really need to be born with a trust fund to survive the first several years.

Gene Wolfe says that what an aspiring writer generally wants is to quit his job. Gene argues that his job frees him to write what he likes, and spend as much time as he likes on any story—which to Gene is important, as he's the world's prototype nitpicker—and he can do it without worrying about deadlines.

I wouldn't know. I was born with a trust fund. And now I don't need it, but I lived off it for the first ten years of my career.

Marijuana is death on writers. I've seen several go that route. Typical behavior for a long-time marijuana user is as follows. He gets a story idea. He tells his friends about it, and they think it's wonderful. He then feels as if he's written it, published it, cashed the checks and collected the awards. So he never bothers to write it down.

Alcohol can have the same effect.

The suicide rate is high among writers. Maybe you have to be neurotic to write and sell your first story. H. Beam Piper's agent had neglected to send him a check. Piper may have felt that his work was no longer popular, since he thought his story hadn't sold, and he needed the money, too. For us, love and money may be nearly indistinguishable.

"I suppose I'll say this again sometime," Steve Barnes said, "but I just *love* being a writer!" We were finishing up "Achilles' Choice," a novella, "the story we were *born* to write." And yeah, it was fun.

Too many would-be writers are really would-be authors. They want *to have written*.

But a writer can pay moral debts by dedicating a book. He can put friends in his stories, changing them to suit his whim. The feedback can be wonderfully soothing to the ego. There's the opportunity to sound off without being interrupted . . .

I suppose there was always a fanatic inside me, demanding to be let loose; but I was lazy. I didn't get fanatical about anything until the organ transplant problem entered my soul.

If organ transplants become easy and popular, who are the donors? Condemned criminals have already donated their eyes and such to hospitals. The Red Cross must ultimately see the obvious, that a man on death row could donate five quarts of blood as easily as he faces the gas chamber.

The problem is this. While Jack the Ripper has five quarts of healthy blood in him, and a working heart, lungs and liver and kidneys, the same holds true for a political dissident, or a thief, or for a man who gets caught running six red traffic lights within the space of two years. You can go too far with this!

I wrote "The Jigsaw Man" two years before the first successful heart transplant. It seemed to me that nobody else had seen the problem, nobody else was worrying about it, and I had to sound off. Then came the heart transplant in South Africa, and suddenly a dozen doctors' groups were studying the ethics of the situation.

Maybe I was worried needlessly. We could have been executing criminals by exsanguination for these past ninety years, and we haven't done it. I've had to find other things to worry about, and when I find them, I sound off.

Nuclear power plants! Do they scare you? Are you afraid they're shooting out atoms at you?

Look: I write books with a man who is afraid of heights. Jerry Pournelle can tough it out if he knows what's coming. I've followed him along a ledge no wider than our feet, with fifteen Boy Scouts following me, and our backpacks unbalancing us toward a twenty-foot drop.

I asked him afterward, How? He said, "You just do it."

But . . . Bob Gleason took us to the top of the World Trade Center for a drink. Self-involved, I didn't notice Jerry's unnatural silence in the wavering elevator. We got to the top, got out, and moved down some shallow steps toward floor-to-ceiling picture windows. I turned from admiring the magnificent view to see Jerry frozen in place.

"Go ahead," he said, "I'll be right with you."

He joined us in a few minutes. He said, "I remember being at the top of the Statue of Liberty, and being terrified. Now there I was looking down on the Statue of Liberty like a toy!"

I have never once heard Jerry suggest that people should be forced to stop building skyscrapers.

Nuclear is the safest power source we've got—with two exceptions, neither of which is being built. If some folk are terrified of unseen death by radiation, then let 'em deal with their own neuroses, instead of forcing us to stop building the atomic plants.

Hence the nuclear plant in LUCIFER'S HAMMER, defended by the heroes and attacked by environmentalists who have turned cannibal. We've been accused of *preaching* in that book. I'm shocked, *shocked*, that you would accuse us of such a thing.

We preach for a viable space program, too. Of all the excellent reasons why we should be going into space, the danger of a Lucifer's Hammer is not even the best. But—When I was growing up, the mystery of the dinosaurs had *everybody's* imagination. They had ruled the Earth for about thirty times as long as mankind. Then, *poof*. I remember a certain contempt on the part of the popularizers. The dinosaurs couldn't hack it. Something changed, and they lay down and died.

Okay, they lay down and died. But what hit them, apparently, was a medium-sized asteroid, a nickel-iron mountain nine kilometers across . . . or else a much larger comet nucleus, mostly ice, carrying the same tonnage of nickel and iron and rock. Picture Lucifer's Hammer, only big.

What have we got that the dinosaurs didn't? We've got telescopes to see it coming. We have the potential to control the solar system, to push the dinosaur-killer out of our path. And we've got William Proxmire, and NASA.

Then again . . . now and again, I could be wrong. It's one reason I wouldn't tell—for example—Ralph Nader to shut up, even if I could make it stick. It takes a lot of people to hold civilization together; some of us are only here to ask the right questions.

● ● ●

• • •

The comet's nucleus is bathed in light. The tail and coma trap sunlight throughout a tremendous volume and reflect it, some to Earth, some to space, some to the nucleus itself.

The comet has suffered. Explosions in the head have torn it into mountainous chunks. Megatons of volatile chemicals have boiled away. The large masses in the head are crusted with icy mud from which most of the water ice has boiled away.

Yet the crusts retard further evaporation. Other comets have survived many such passages through the maelstrom. Much mass has been lost, poured into the tail; but much of the coma could freeze again, and the rocky chunks could merge; and crystals of strange ices could plate themselves across a growing comet, out there in the dark and the cold, over the millions of years ... if only Hamner-Brown could return to the cometary halo.

But there appears to be something in its path.

LUCIFER'S HAMMER, 1977

From WORLD OF PTAVVS

This was my first novella *and* my first novel. The first few thousand words were written in longhand during a trip through Europe. I took my time over it. When I thought it was ready I sent the novella to Fred Pohl, who had already bought two stories from me.

Fred chose the title. My choice was "A Relic of Empire." I liked it well enough to recycle, hanging it on a short story. Jack Gaughan sketched various of the alien life-forms in "Ptavvs," and I first felt the terrific ego-kick of seeing something from my own mind rendered visible.

Fred used the novella to get the attention of Betty Ballantine at Ballantine Books. On the strength of that, Betty sent me a contract for a novel. I would not have thought of that. I was a poor businessperson in those days . . . but I recognized an opportunity when Fred hit me in the face with it.

WORLD OF PTAVVS established some patterns that have persisted throughout my career, more or less. Optimism. Logic problems. Bizarre technology derived from esoteric physics. Aliens with depth to them. (Algis Budrys, writing as a critic, said that telepathy in most current novels felt like something from Ma Bell; that in PTAVVS, it didn't.) In particular, I taught myself to enjoy playing games with astrophysics.

I played such games throughout PTAVVS and many that followed. The excerpt is from near the end, as Kzanol and Larry Greenberg (carrying Kzanol's memories) are about to land a fusion spacecraft on Pluto. I would hate today to defend the thesis that the planet Pluto can catch fire, but it made some great scenes.

• •

Kzanol/Greenberg swallowed, swallowed again. The low acceleration bothered him. He blamed it on his human body. He sat in a window seat with the crash web tightly fastened, looking out and down.

There was little to see. The ship had circled half the world, falling ever lower, but the only feature on an unchanging cue-ball surface had been the slow creep of the planetary shadow. Now the ship flew over the night side, and the only light was the dim light of the drive, dim at least when reflected from this height. And there was nothing to see at all . . . until now.

Something was rising on the eastern horizon, something a shade lighter than the black plain. An irregular line against the stars. Kzanol/Greenberg leaned forward as he began to realize just how big the range was, for it couldn't be anything but a mountain range. "What's that?" he wondered aloud.

"One hundredth diltun." Kzanol probed the pilot's mind. The pilot said, "Cott's Crescent. Frozen hydrogen piled up along the dawn side of the planet. As it rotates into daylight the hydrogen boils off and then refreezes on the night side. Eventually it rotates back to here."

"Oh. Thanks."

Evanescent mountains of hydrogen snow, smooth and low, like a tray of differently sized snowballs dropped from a height. They rose gently before the slowing ship, rank behind rank, showing the tremendous breadth of the range. But they couldn't show its length. Kzanol/Greenberg could see only that the mountains stretched half around the horizon; but he could imagine them marching from pole to pole around the curve of the world. As they must. As they did.

The ship was almost down, hovering motionless a few miles west of the beginning rise of the Crescent. A pillar of fire licked a mile down to touch the surface. Where it touched, the surface disappeared. A channel like the bed of a river followed below the ship, fading into the darkness beyond the reach of the light.

The ship rode with nose tilted high; the fusion flame reached slightly forward. Gently, gently, one mile up, the *Golden Circle* slowed and stopped.

Where the flame touched, the surface disappeared. A wide, shallow crater formed below the descending ship. It deepened rapidly. A ring of fog formed, soft and white and opaque, thickening in the cold and the dark, closing in on the ship. Then there was nothing but the lighted fog and the crater and the licking fusion fire.

This was the most alien place. He had been wasting his life searching out the inhabited worlds of the galaxy; for never had they given him such a flavor of strangeness as came from this icy world, colder than . . . than the bottom of Dante's Hell.

"We'll be landing on the water ice layer," the pilot explained, just as if he'd been asked. He had. "The gas layers wouldn't hold us. But first we have to dig down."

Had *he* been searching for strangeness? Wasn't that a Greenberg thought slipping into his conscious mind? Yes. This soul-satisfaction was the old Greenberg starlust; he had searched for wealth, only wealth.

The crater looked like an open pit mine now, with a sloping ring wall and then an almost flat rim and then another, deeper ring wall and . . . Kzanol/Greenberg looked down, grinning and squinting against the glare, trying to guess which layer was which gas. They had been drilling through a very thick blanket of ice, hundreds or thousands of feet thick. Perhaps it was nitrogen? Then the next layer, appearing now, would be oxygen.

The plain and the space above it exploded in flame.

"She blows!" Lew crowed, like a felon reprieved. A towering, twisting pillar of yellow and blue flame roared straight up out of the telescope, out of the pale plain where there had been the small white star of the *Golden Circle*. For a moment the star shone brightly through the flames. Then it was swamped, and the whole scope was fire. Lew dropped the magnification by a ten-factor to watch the fire spread. Then he had to drop it again. And again.

Pluto was on fire. For billions of years a thick blanket of relatively inert nitrogen ice had protected the highly reactive layers below. Meteors, as scarce out here as sperm whales in a goldfish bowl, inevitably buried themselves in the nitrogen layer. There had been no combustion on Pluto since Kzanol's spaceship smashed down from the stars. But now hydrogen vapor mixed with oxygen vapor, and they burned. Other elements burned too.

The fire spread outward in a circle. A strong, hot wind blew out and up into vacuum, fanning great sheets of flame over the boiling ices until raw oxygen was exposed. Then the fire dug deeper. There were raw metals below the thin sheet of water ice; and it was thin, nonexistent in places, for it had all formed when the spaceship struck, untold eons ago, when food yeast still ruled Earth. Sodium and calcium veins; even iron burns furiously in the presence of enough oxygen and enough heat. Or chlorine, or fluorine; both halogens were present, blowing off the top of Pluto's frozen atmosphere, some burning with hydrogen in the first sheets of flame. Raise the temperature enough and even oxygen and nitrogen will unite.

Lew watched his screen in single-minded concentration. He thought of his future great-great-grandchildren and wondered how he could possibly make them see this as he saw it now. Old and leathery and hairless and sedentary, he would tell those children: "I saw a world burning when I was young. . . ." He would never see anything as strange.

Pluto was a black disc almost covering his scope screen, with a cold highlight near the sunward arm. In that disc the broad ring of fire had almost become a great circle, with one arc crawling over the edge of the world. When it contracted on the other side of the world there would be an explosion such as could only be imagined. But in the center the ring was darkening to black, its fuel nearly burned out.

The coldest spot within the ring was the point where the fire had started.

• • •

The fire had slowed now. Most of the unburned hydrogen had been blown before the fire, until it was congested into a cloud mass opposite on Pluto from the resting place of the *Golden Circle*. Around that cloud bank raged a hurricane of awesome proportions. Frozen rain poured out of the heavens in huge lens-shaped drops, hissing into the nitrogen snow. The layers above nitrogen were gone, vaporized, gas diluting the hydrogen which still poured in. On the borderline hydrogen burned fitfully with halogens, and even with nitrogen to form ammonia, but around most of the great circle the fires had gone out. Relatively small, isolated conflagrations ate their way toward the new center. The "hot" water ice continued to fall. When it had boiled the nitrogen away it would begin on the oxygen. And *then* there would be a fire.

At the center of the hurricane the ice stood like a tremendous Arizona butte. Even the halogens were still frozen across its flat top, thousands of square miles of flourine ice with near-vacuum above. Coriolis effects held back the burning wind for a time.

Alexei Panshin wrote a savage review of PTAWS. I wish I had a copy, but I tore the fanzine up in a rage, and I don't remember the name or even the editor. I was fool enough to write an answer to that review! I learned better later. Meanwhile Alexei had used PTAWS in an essay on writing, as a textbook case of how not to write science fiction.

The editor, Ghod bless him, persuaded both of us to bury our respective submissions.

My memory says that that issue included Panshin's reviews of a dozen books. He considered them all failures, even Heinlein's THE MOON IS A HARSH MISTRESS, with but a single exception. Ted White's THE SECRET OF THE MARAUDER SATELLITE entirely lived up to Panshin's standards.

• • •

• • •

God was knocking, and he wanted in *bad*.

FOOTFALL, 1985

BORDERED IN BLACK

"Bordered in Black" is a nightmare vision.

If a vision were enough, it would have been sold at once. I wrote it as a vignette. Ed Ferman's comment (months before my first story sale) was that it looked like an outline for a story. So I set it aside, and tackled it again a few years later. The version that appeared in *F&SF* was much changed.

If I wrote it today it would be changed again. A story needs more than the original idea . . . but the nightmare still shows through.

• •

Only one figure stood in the airlock, though it was a cargo lock, easily big enough to hold both men. Lean and sandy haired, the tiny figure was obviously Carver Rappaport. A bushy beard now covered half its face. It waited patiently while the ramp was run up, and then it started down.

Turnbull, waiting at the bottom, suppressed growing uneasiness. Something was wrong. He'd known it the moment he heard that the *Overcee* was landing. The ship must have been in the solar system for hours. Why hadn't she called in?

And where was Wall Kameon?

Returning spacers usually sprinted down the ramp, eager to touch honest concrete again. Rappaport came down with slow, methodical speed. Seen close, his beard was ragged, unkempt. He reached bottom, and Turnbull saw that the square features were set like cement.

Rappaport brushed past him and kept walking.

Turnbull ran after him and fell into step, looking and feeling foolish. Rappaport was a good head taller, and where he was walking, Turnbull was almost running. He shouted above the background noise of the spaceport, "Rappaport, where's Kameon?"

Like Turnbull, Rappaport had to raise his voice. "Dead."

"Dead? Was it the ship? Rappaport, did the *ship* kill him?"

"No."

"Then what? Is his body aboard?"

"Turnbull, I don't want to talk about it. No, his body isn't aboard. His—" Rappaport ground the heels of his hands into his eyes, like a man with a blinding headache. "His grave," he said, emphasizing the word, "has a nice black border around it. Let's leave it at that."

But they couldn't, of course.

Two security officers caught up with them near the edge of the field. "Stop him," said Turnbull, and they each took an arm. Rappaport stopped walking and turned.

"Have you forgotten that I'm carrying a destruct capsule?"

"What about it?" For the moment Turnbull really didn't understand what he meant.

"Any more interference and I'll use it. Understand this, Turnbull. I don't care any more. Project Overcee is over. I don't know where I go from here. The best thing we can do is blow up that ship and stay in our own solar system."

"Man, have you gone crazy? What *happened* out there? You—meet aliens?"

"No comment.—No, I'll answer that one. We didn't meet aliens. Now tell your comedian friends to let go."

Turnbull let himself realize that the man wasn't bluffing. Rappaport was prepared to commit suicide. Turnbull, the instinctive politician, weighed changes and gambled.

"If you haven't decided to talk in twenty-four hours we'll let you go. I promise that. We'll keep you here 'til then, by force if necessary. Just to give you an opportunity to change your mind."

Rappaport thought it over. The security men still held his arms, but cautiously now, standing as far back as they could, in case his personal bomb went off.

"Seems fair," he said at last, "if you're honest. Sure, I'll wait twenty-four hours."

"Good." Turnbull turned to lead the way back to his office. Instead, he merely stared.

The *Overcee* was red hot at the nose, glaring white at the tail. Mechs and techs were running in all directions. As Turnbull watched, the solar system's first faster-than-light spacecraft slumped and ran in a spreading, glowing pool.

. . . It had started a century ago, when the first ramrobot left the solar system. The interstellar ramscoop robots could make most of their journey at near lightspeed, using a conical electromagnetic field two hundred miles across to scoop hydrogen fuel from interstellar space. But no man had ever ridden a ramrobot. None ever would. The ramscoop magnetic field did horrible things to chordate organisms.

Each ramrobot had been programed to report back only if it found a habitable world near the star to which it had been assigned. Twenty-six had been sent out. Three had reported back—so far.

. . . It had started twelve years ago, when a well-known mathematician worked out a theoretical hyperspace over Einsteinian fourspace. He did it in his spare time. He considered the hyperspace a toy, an example of pure mathematics. And when has pure mathematics been anything but good clean fun?

. . . It had started ten years ago, when Ergstrom's brother Carl demonstrated the experimental reality of Ergstrom's toy universe. Within a month the UN had financed Project Overcee, put Winston Turnbull in charge, and set up a school for faster-than-light astronauts. The vast number of applicants was winnowed to ten "hypernauts." Two were Belters; all were experienced spacers. The training began in earnest. It lasted eight years, while Project Overcee built the ship.

. . . It had started a year and a month ago, when two men climbed into the almost luxurious lifesystem of the *Overcee*, ran the ship out to Neptune's orbit under escort, and vanished.

One was back.

Now his face was no stonier than Turnbull's. Turnbull had just watched his work of the last ten years melt and run like quicksilver. He was mad clean through; but his mind worked furiously. Part of him, the smaller part, was wondering how he would explain the loss of ten billion dollars worth of ship. The rest was reviewing everything it could remember about Carver Geoffrey Rappaport and William (Wall) Kameon.

Turnbull entered his office and went straight to the bookshelf, sure that Rappaport was following. He pulled out a leather-bound volume, did something to the binding and poured two paper cups full of amber fluid. The fluid was bourbon, and it was more than ice cold.

Rappaport had seen this bookcase before, yet he wore a faintly puzzled frown as he took a cup. He said, "I didn't think I'd ever anticipate anything again."

"The bourbon?"

Rappaport didn't answer. His first swallow was a gulp.

"Did you destroy your ship?"

"Yes. I set the controls so it would only melt. I didn't want anyone hurt."

"Commendable. And the overcee motor? You left it in orbit?"

"I hard-landed it on the Moon. It's gone."

"That's great. Just great. Carver, that ship cost ten billion dollars to build. We can duplicate it for four, I think, because we won't be making any false starts, but you—"

"Hell you wouldn't." Rappaport swirled the bourbon in his cup, looking down into the miniature whirlpool. He was twenty to thirty pounds lighter than he had been a year ago. ''You build another *Overcee* and you'll be making one enormous false start. We were wrong, Turnbull. It's not our universe. There's nothing out there for us.''

''It *is* our universe.'' Turnbull let the quiet certainty show in his politician's voice. He needed to start an argument—he needed to get this man to talking. But the certainty was real, and always had been. It was humanity's universe, ready for the taking.

Over the rim of his cup Rappaport looked at him in exasperated pity. ''Turnbull, can't you take my word for it? It's not our universe, and it's not worth having anyway. What's out there is—'' He clamped his mouth shut and turned away in the visitor's chair.

Turnbull waited ten seconds to point up the silence. Then he asked, ''Did you kill Kameon?''

''Kill Wall? You're out of your mind!''

''Could you have saved him?''

Rappaport froze in the act of turning around. ''No,'' he said. And again, ''No. I tried to get him moving, but he wouldn't— Stop it! Stop needling me. I can walk out anytime, and you couldn't stop me.''

''It's too late. You've aroused my curiosity. What about Kameon's black-bordered grave?''

No answer.

''Rappaport, you seem to think that the UN will just take your word and dismantle Project Overcee. There's not a prayer of that. Probability zero. In the last century we've spent tens of billions of dollars on the ramrobots and the *Overcee*, and now we can rebuild her for four. The only way to stop that is to tell the UN exactly why they shouldn't.''

Rappaport didn't answer, and Turnbull didn't speak again. He watched Rappaport's cigarette burning unheeded in the ashtray, leaving a strip of charred wet paper. It was uncharacteristic of the former Carver Rappaport to forget burning cigarettes, or to wear an untrimmed beard and sloppily cut hair. That man had been always clean shaven; that man had lined up his shoes at night, every night, even when staggering drunk.

Could he have killed Kameon for being sloppy?—and then turned messy himself as he lost his self-respect? Stranger things had happened in the days when it took eight months to reach Mars.—No, Rappaport had not done murder; Turnbull would have bet high on that. And Kameon would have won any fair fight. Newspapermen had nicknamed him The Wall when he was playing guard for the Berlin Nazis.

''You're right. Where do I start?''

Turnbull was jerked out of his abstraction. ''Start at the beginning. When you went into hyperspace.''

''We had no trouble there. Except with the windows. You shouldn't have put windows on the *Overcee*.''

"Why not? What did you see?"

"Nothing."

"Well, then?"

"You ever try to find your blind spot? You put two dots on a piece of paper, maybe an inch apart, and you close one eye, focus on one dot and slowly bring the paper up to your face. At some point the other dot disappears. Looking at the window in overcee is like your blind spot expanding to a two-foot square with rounded corners."

"I assume you covered them up."

"Sure. Would you believe it, we had trouble finding those windows? When you wanted them they were invisible. We got them covered with blankets. Then every so often we'd catch each other looking under the blankets. It bothered Wall worse than me. We could have made the trip in five months instead of six, but we had to keep coming out for a look around."

"Just to be sure the universe was still there."

"Right."

"But you did reach Sirius."

"Yes. We reached Sirius . . ."

Ramrobot #6 had reported from Sirius B, half a century ago. The Sirius stars are an unlikely place to look for habitable worlds, since both stars are blue-white giants. Still, the ramrobots had been programed to test for excessive ultraviolet. Sirius B was worth a look.

The ship came out where Sirius was two bright stars. It turned its sharp nose toward the dimmer star and remained motionless for twenty minutes, a silver torpedo shape in a great, ungainly cradle studded with heavy electromagnetic motors. Then it was gone again.

Now Sirius B was a searing ball of light. The ship began to swing about, like a hound sniffing the breeze, but slowly, ponderously.

"We found four planets," said Rappaport. "Maybe there were more, but we didn't look. Number Four was the one we wanted. It was a cloudy ball about twice the size of Mars, with no moon. We waited until we'd found it before we started celebrating."

"Champagne?"

"Hah! Cigars and drunk pills. And Wall shaved off his grubby beard. My God, we were glad to be out in space again! Near the end it seemed like those blind spots were growing around the edges of the blankets. We smoked our cigars and sucked our drunk pills and yakked about the broads we'd known. Not that we hadn't done *that* before. Then we slept it off and went back to work . . ."

• • •

The cloud cover was nearly unbroken. Rappaport moved the telescope a bit at a time, trying to find a break. He found several, but none big enough to show him anything. "I'll try infrared," he said.

"Just get us down," Wall said irritably. He was always irritable lately. "I want to get to work."

"And I want to be sure we've got a place to land."

Carv's job was the ship. He was pilot, astrogator, repairman, and everything but the cook. Wall was the cook. Wall was also the geologist, astrophysicist, biologist, and chemist—the expert on habitable planets, in theory. Each man had been trained nine years for his job, and each had some training as backup man for the other; and in each case the training had been based largely on guesswork.

The picture on the scope screen changed from a featureless disk to a patterned ball as Carv switched to infrared. "Now which is water?" he wondered.

"The water's brighter on the night side and darker on the day side. See?" Wall was looking over his shoulder. "Looks like about forty percent land. Carv, those clouds might cut out enough of the ultraviolet to let people live in what gets through."

"Who'd want to? You couldn't see the stars." Carv turned a knob to raise the magnification.

"Hold it right there, Carv. Look at that. There's a white line around the edge of that continent."

"Dried salt?"

"No. It's warmer than what's around it. And it's just as bright on the night side as on the day."

"I'll get us a closer look."

The *Overcee* was in orbit, three hundred miles up. By now the continent with the "hot" border was almost entirely in shadow. Of the three supercontinents, only one showed a white shoreline under infrared.

Wall hung at the window, looking down. To Rappaport he looked like a great ape. "Can we do a reentry glide?"

"In this ship? The *Overcee* would come apart like a cheap meteor. We'll have to brake to a full stop above the atmosphere. Want to strap down?"

Kameon did, and Carv watched him do it before he went ahead and dropped the overcee motor. *I'll be glad to be out of here*, he thought. *It's getting so Wall and I hate the sight of each other*. The casual, uncaring way Kameon fastened his straps jarred his teeth. He knew that Kameon thought he was finicky to the point of psychasthenia.

The fusion drive started and built up to one gee. Carv swung the ship around. Only the night side showed below, with the faint blue light of

Sirius A shining softly off the cloud cover. Then the edge of dawn came up in torn blue-white cloud. Carv saw an enormous rift in the cloud bank and turned ship to shift their path over it.

Mountains and valleys, and a wide river . . . . Patches of wispy cloud shot by, obscuring the view, but they could see down. Suddenly there was a black line, a twisting ribbon of India ink, and beyond that the ocean.

Only for a moment the ocean showed, and then the rift jogged east and was gone. But the ocean was an emerald green.

Wall's voice was soft with awe. "Carv, there's life in that water."

"You sure?"

"No. It could be copper salts or something. Carv, we've got to get *down* there!"

"Oh, wait your turn. Did you notice that your hot border is black in visible light?"

"Yah. But I can't explain it. Would it be worth our while to turn back after you get the ship slowed?"

Carv fingered his neatly trimmed Vandyke. "It'd be night over the whole continent before we got back there. Let's spend a few hours looking at that green ocean."

The *Overcee* went down on her tail, slowly, like a cautious crab. Layer after layer of cloud swallowed her without trace, and darkness fell as she dropped. The key to this world was the word "moonless." Sirius B-IV had had no oversized moon to strip away most of her atmosphere. Her air pressure would be comfortable at sea level, but only because the planet was too small to hold more air. That same low gravity produced a more gentle pressure gradient, so that the atmosphere reached three times as high as on Earth. There were cloud layers from ground to 130 kilometers up.

The *Overcee* touched down on a wide beach on the western shore of the smallest continent. Wall came out first, then Carv lowered a metal oblong as large as himself and followed it down. They wore lightly pressurized vac suits. Carv did nothing for twenty minutes while Wall opened the box out flat and set the carefully packed instruments into their grooves and notches. Finally Wall signaled, in an emphatic manner. By taking off his helmet.

Carv waited a few seconds, then followed suit.

Wall asked, "Were you waiting to see if I dropped dead?"

"Better you than me." Carv sniffed the breeze. The air was cool and humid, but thin. "Smells good enough. No. No, it doesn't. It smells like something rotting."

"Then I'm right. There's life here. Let's get down to the beach."

The sky looked like a raging thunderstorm, with occasional vivid blue flashes that might have been lightning. They were flashes of sunlight penetrating tier upon tier of cloud. In that varying light Carv and Wall stripped off their suits and went down to look at the ocean, walking with shuffling steps in the light gravity.

The ocean was thick with algae. Algae were a bubbly green blanket on the water, a blanket that rose and fell like breathing as the insignificant waves ran beneath. The smell of rotting vegetation was no stronger here than it had been a quarter of a mile back. Perhaps the smell pervaded the whole planet. The shore was a mixture of sand and green scum so rich that you could have planted crops in it.

"Time I got to work," said Wall. "You want to fetch and carry for me?"

"Later maybe. Right now I've got a better idea. Let's get the hell out of each other's sight for an hour."

"That is brilliant. But take a weapon."

"To fight off maddened algae?"

"Take a weapon."

Carv was back at the end of an hour. The scenery had been deadly monotonous. There was water below a green blanket of scum six inches deep; there was loamy sand, and beyond that dry sand; and behind the beach were white cliffs, smoothed as if by countless rainfalls. He had found no target for his laser cutter.

Wall looked up from a binocular microscope, and grinned when he saw his pilot. He tossed a depleted pack of cigarettes. "And don't worry about the air plant!" he called cheerfully.

Carv came up beside him. "What news?"

"It's algae. I can't name the breed, but there's not much difference between this and any terrestrial algae, except that this sample is all one species."

"That's unusual?" Carv was looking around him in wonder. He was seeing a new side to Wall. Aboard ship Wall was sloppy almost to the point of being dangerous, at least in the eyes of a Belter like Carv. But now he was at work. His small tools were set in neat rows on portable tables. Bulkier instruments with legs were on flat rock, the legs carefully adjusted to leave their platforms exactly horizontal. Wall handled the binocular microscope as if it might dissolve at a touch.

"It is," said Wall. "No little animalcules moving among the strands. No variations in structure. I took samples from depths up to six feet. All I could find was the one alga. But otherwise—I even tested for proteins and sugars. You could eat it. We came all this way to find pond scum."

They came down on an island five hundred miles south. This time Carv helped with the collecting. They got through faster that way, but they kept getting in each other's way. Six months spent in two small rooms had roused tempers too often. It would take more than a few hours on ground before they could bump elbows without a fight.

Again Carv watched Wall go through his routines. He stood just within voice range, about fifty yards away, because it felt so good to have so much room. The care Wall exercised with his equipment still amazed him. How could he reconcile it with Wall's ragged fingernails and his thirty hours growth of beard?

Well, Wall was a flatlander. All his life he'd had a whole planet to mess up, and not a crowded pressure dome or the cabin of a ship. No flat ever learned real neatness.

"Same breed," Wall called.

"Did you test for radiation?"

"No. Why?"

"This thick air must screen out a lot of gamma rays. That means your algae can't mutate without local radiation from the ground."

"Carv, it had to mutate to get to its present form. How could all its cousins just have died out?"

"That's your field."

A little later Wall said, "I can't get a respectable background reading anywhere. You were right, but it doesn't explain anything."

"Shall we go somewhere else?"

"Yah."

They set down in deep ocean, and when the ship stopped bobbing Carv went out the airlock with a glass bucket. "It's a foot thick out there," he reported. "No place for a Disneyland. I don't think I'd want to settle here."

Wall sighed his agreement. The green scum lapped thickly at the *Overcee*'s gleaming metal hull, two yards below the sill of the airlock.

"A lot of planets must be like this," said Carv. "Habitable, but who needs it?"

"And I wanted to be the first man to found an interstellar colony."

"And get your name in the newstapes, the history books—"

"—And my unforgettable face on every trivis in the solar system. Tell me, shipmate, if you hate publicity so much, why have you been trimming that Vandyke so prettily?"

"Guilty. I like being famous. Just not as much as you do."

"Cheer up then. We may yet get all the hero worship we can stand. This may be something bigger than a new colony."

"What could be bigger than that?"

"Set us down on land and I'll tell you."

• • •

On a chunk of rock just big enough to be called an island, Wall set up his equipment for the last time. He was testing for food content again, using samples from Carv's bucket of deep ocean algae.

Carv stood by, a comfortable distance away, watching the weird variations in the clouds. The very highest were moving across the sky at enormous speeds, swirling and changing shape by the minutes and seconds. The noonday light was subdued and pearly. No doubt about it, Sirius B-IV had a magnificent sky.

"Okay, I'm ready." Wall stood up and stretched. "This stuff isn't just edible. I'd guess it would taste as good as the food supplements they were using on Earth before the fertility laws cut the population down to something reasonable. I'm going to taste it now."

The last sentence hit Carv like an electric shock. He was running before it was quite finished, but long before he could get there his crazy partner had put a dollup of green scum in his mouth, chewed and swallowed. "Good," he said.

"You—utter—damned—fool."

"Not so. I knew it was safe. The stuff has an almost cheesy flavor. You could get tired of it fast, I think, but that's true of anything."

"Just *what* are you trying to *prove*?"

"That this alga was tailored as a food plant by biological engineers. Carv, I think we've landed on somebody's private farm."

Carv sat heavily down on a rainwashed white rock. "Better spell that out," he said, and heard that his voice was hoarse.

"I was going to. Suppose there was a civilization that had cheap, fast interstellar travel. Most of the habitable planets they found would be sterile, wouldn't they? I mean, life is an unlikely sort of accident."

"We don't have the vaguest idea how likely it is."

"All right, pass that. Say somebody finds this planet, Sirius B-IV, and decides it would make a nice farm planet. It isn't good for much else, mainly because of the variance in lighting, but if you dropped a specially bred food alga in the ocean, you'd have a dandy little farm. In ten years there'd be oceans of algae, free for the carting. Later, if they *did* decide to colonize, they could haul the stuff inland and use it for fertilizer. Best of all, it wouldn't mutate. Not here."

Carv shook his head to clear it. "You've been in space too long."

"Carv, the plant looks *bred*—like a pink grapefruit. And where did all its cousins go? Now I can tell you. They got poured out of the breeding vat because they weren't good enough."

Low waves rolled in from the sea, low and broad beneath their blanket of cheesy green scum. "All right," said Carv. "How can we disprove it?"

Wall looked startled. "*Dis*prove it? Why would we want to do that?"

"Forget the glory for a minute. If you're right, we're trespassing on somebody's property without knowing anything about the owner—except that he's got dirt-cheap interstellar travel, which would make him a tough enemy. We're also introducing our body bacteria into his pure edible algae culture. And how would we explain, if he suddenly showed up?"

"I hadn't thought of it that way."

"We ought to cut and run right now. It's not as if the planet was worth anything."

"No. No, we can't do that."

"Why not?"

The answer gleamed in Wall's eyes.

Turnbull, listening behind his desk with his chin resting in one hand, interrupted for the first time in minutes. "A good question. I'd have gotten out right then."

"Not if you'd just spent six months in a two-room cell with the end of everything creeping around the blankets."

"I see." Turnbull's hand moved almost imperceptibly, writing, *NO WINDOWS IN OVERCEE #2! Oversized viewscreen*?

"It hadn't hit me that hard. I think I'd have taken off if I'd been sure Wall was right, and if I could have talked him into it. But I couldn't, of course. Just the thought of going home then was enough to set Wall shaking. I thought I might have to knock him on the head when it came time to leave. We had some hibernation drugs aboard, just in case."

He stopped. As usual, Turnbull waited him out.

"But then I'd have been all alone." Rappaport finished his drink, his second, and got up to pour a third. The bourbon didn't seem to affect him. "So we stood there on that rocky beach, both of us afraid to leave and both afraid to stay . . ."

Abruptly Wall got up and started putting his tools away. "We can't disprove it, but we can prove it easily enough. The owners must have left artifacts around. If we find one, we run. I promise."

"There's a big area to search. If we had any sense we'd run now."

"Will you drop that? All we've got to do is find the ramrobot probe. If there's anyone watching this place they must have seen it come down. We'll find footprints all over it."

"And if there aren't any footprints? Does that make the whole planet clean?"

Wall closed his case with a snap. Then he stood, motionless, looking very surprised. "I just thought of something," he said.

"Oh, not again."

"No, this is for real, Carv. The owners must have left a long time ago."

"Why?"

"It must be thousands of years since there were enough algae here to use as a food supply. We should have seen ships taking off and landing as we came in. They'd have started their colony too, if they were going to. Now it's gone beyond that. The planet isn't fit for anything to live on, with the soupy oceans and the smell of things rotting."

"No."

"Dammit, it makes sense!"

"It's thin. It sounds thin even to me, and I *want* to believe it. Also, it's too pat. It's just too close to the best possible solution we could dream up. You want to bet our lives on it?"

Wall hoisted his case and moved toward the ship. He looked like a human tank, moving in a stormy darkness lit by shifting, glaring beams of blue light. Abruptly he said, "There's one more point. That black border. It has to be contaminated algae. Maybe a land-living mutant; that's why it hasn't spread across the oceans. It would have been cleaned away if the owners were still interested."

"All *right*. Hoist that thing up and let's get inside."

"Hmph?"

"You've finally said something we can check. The eastern shore must be in daylight by now. Let's get aboard."

At the border of space they hovered, and the Sun burned small and blinding white at the horizon. To the side Sirius A was a tiny dot of intense brilliance. Below, where gaps in the cloud cover penetrated all the way to the surface, a hair-thin black line ran along the twisting beach of Sirius B-IV's largest continent. The silver thread of a major river exploded into a forking delta, and the delta was a black triangle shot with lines of silvery green.

"Going to use the scope?"

Carv shook his head. "We'll see it close in a few minutes."

"You're in quite a hurry, Carv."

"You bet. According to you, if that black stuff is some form of life, then this farm's been deserted for thousands of years at least. If it isn't, then what is it? It's too regular to be a natural formation. Maybe it's a conveyor belt."

"That's right. Calm me down. Reassure me."

"If it is, we go up fast and run all the way home." Carv pulled a lever and the ship dropped from under them. They fell fast. Speaking with only half his attention, Carv went on. "We've met just one other sentient race, and they had nothing like hands and no mechanical culture. I'm not complaining, mind you. A world wouldn't be fit to live in without dolphins for company. But why should we get lucky twice? I don't want to meet the farmer, Wall."

The clouds closed over the ship. She dropped more slowly with every kilometer. Ten kilometers up she was almost hovering. Now the coast was spread below them. The black border was graded: black as night on Pluto along the sea, shading off to the color of the white sand and rocks along the landward side.

Wall said, "Maybe the tides carry the dead algae inland. They'd decay there. No, that won't work. No moon. Nothing but solar tides."

They were a kilometer up. And lower. And lower.

The black was moving, flowing like tar, away from the drive's fusion flame.

Rappaport had been talking down into his cup, his words coming harsh and forced, his eyes refusing to meet Turnbull's. Now he raised them. There was something challenging in that gaze.

Turnbull understood. "You want me to guess? I won't. What was the black stuff?"

"I don't know if I want to prepare you or not. Wall and I, we weren't ready. Why should you be?"

"All right, Carver, go ahead and shock me."

"It was people."

Turnbull merely stared.

"We were almost down when they started to scatter from the down-blast. Until then it was just a dark field, but when they started to scatter we could see moving specks, like ants. We sheered off and landed on the water offshore. We could see them from there."

"Carver, when you say people, do you mean—people? Human?"

"Yes. Human. Of course they didn't act much like it . . ."

A hundred yards offshore, the *Overcee* floated nose up. Even seen from the airlock the natives were obviously human. The telescope screen brought more detail.

They were no terrestrial race. Nine feet tall, men and women both, with wavy black hair growing from the eyebrows back to halfway down the spine, hanging almost to the knees. Their skins were dark, as dark as the darkest Negro, but they had chisel noses and long heads and small, thin-lipped mouths.

They paid no attention to the ship. They stood or sat or lay where they were, men and women and children jammed literally shoulder to shoulder.

Most of the seaside population was grouped in large rings with men on the outside and women and children protected inside.

"All around the continent," said Wall.

Carv could no more have answered than he could have taken his eyes off the scope screen.

Every few minutes there was a seething in the mass as some group that was too far back pulled forward to reach the shore, the food supply. The mass pushed back. On the fringes of the circles there were bloody fights, slow fights in which there were apparently no rules at all.

"How?" said Carv. "How?"

Wall said, "Maybe a ship crashed. Maybe there was a caretaker's family here, and nobody ever came to pick them up. They must be the farmer's children, Carv."

"How long have they been here?"

"Thousands of years at least. Maybe tens or hundreds of thousands." Wall turned his empty eyes away from the screen. He swiveled his couch so he was looking at the back wall of the cabin. His dreary words flowed out into the cabin.

"Picture it, Carv. Nothing in the world but an ocean of algae and a few people. Then a few hundred people, then hundreds of thousands. They'd never have been allowed near here unless they'd had the bacteria cleaned out of them to keep the algae from being contaminated. Nothing to make tools out of, nothing but rock and bone. No way of smelting ores, because they wouldn't even have fire. There's nothing to burn. They had no diseases, no contraceptives, and no recreation but breeding. The population would have exploded like a bomb. Because nobody would starve to death, Carv. For thousands of years nobody would starve on Sirius B-IV."

"They're starving now."

"Some of them. The ones that can't reach the shore." Wall turned back to the scope screen. "One continual war," he said after awhile. "I'll bet their height comes from natural selection."

Carv hadn't moved for a long time. He had noticed that there were always a few men inside each protective circle, and that there were always men outside going inside and men inside going outside. Breeding more people to guard each circle. More people for Sirius B-IV.

The shore was a seething blackness. In infrared light it would have shown brightly, at a temperature of 98.6° Fahrenheit.

"Let's go home," said Wall.

"Okay."

"And did you?"

"No."

"In God's name, why not?"

"We *couldn't*. We had to see it all, Turnbull. I don't understand it, but we did, both of us. So I took the ship up and dropped it a kilometer inshore, and we got out and started walking toward the sea.

"Right away, we started finding skeletons. Some were clean. A lot of them looked like Egyptian mummies, skeletons with black dried skin stretched tight over the bones. Always there was a continuous low rustle of—well, I guess it was conversation. From the beach. I don't know what they could have had to talk about.

"The skeletons got thicker as we went along. Some of them had daggers of splintered bone. One had a chipped stone fist ax. You see, Turnbull, they were intelligent. They could make tools, if they could find anything to make tools out of.

"After we'd been walking awhile we saw that some of the skeletons were alive. Dying and drying under that overcast blue sky. I'd thought that sky was pretty once. Now it was—horrible. You could see a shifting blue beam spear down on the sand and sweep across it like a spotlight until it picked out a mummy. Sometimes the mummy would turn over and cover its eyes.

"Wall's face was livid, like a dead man's. I knew it wasn't just the light. We'd been walking about five minutes, and the dead and living skeletons were all around us. The live ones all stared at us, apathetically, but still staring, as if we were the only things in the world worth looking at. If they had anything to wonder with, they must have been wondering what it was that could move and still not be human. We couldn't have looked human to them. We had shoes and coveralls on, and we were too small.

"Wall said, 'I've been wondering about the clean skeletons. There shouldn't be any decay bacteria here.'

"I didn't answer. I was thinking how much this looked like a combination of Hell and Belsen. The only thing that might have made it tolerable was the surrealistic blue lighting. We couldn't really believe what we were seeing.

" 'There weren't enough fats in the algae,' said Wall. 'There was enough of everything else, but no fats.'

"We were closer to the beach now. And some of the mummies were beginning to stir. I watched a pair behind a dune who looked like they were trying to kill each other, and then suddenly I realized what Wall had said.

"I took his arm and turned to go back. Some of the long skeletons were trying to get up. I knew what they were thinking. *There may be meat in those limp coverings. Wet meat, with water in it. There just may.* I pulled at Wall and started to run.

"He wouldn't run. He tried to pull loose. I had to leave him. They couldn't catch me, they were too starved, and I was jumping like a grasshopper. But they got Wall, all right. I heard his destruct capsule go off. Just a muffled pop."

"So you came home."

"Uh huh." Rappaport looked up like a man waking from a nightmare. "It took seven months. All alone."

"Any idea why Wall killed himself?"

"You crazy? He didn't want to get *eaten*."

"Then why wouldn't he run?"

"It wasn't that he wanted to kill himself, Turnbull. He just decided it wasn't worthwhile saving himself. Another six months in the *Overcee*, with the blind spots pulling at his eyes and that nightmare of a world constantly on his mind—it wasn't worth it."

"I'll bet the *Overcee* was a pigpen before you blew it up."

Rappaport flushed. "What's that to you?"

"You didn't think it was worthwhile either. When a Belter stops being neat it's because he wants to die. A dirty ship is deadly. The air plant gets fouled. Things float around loose, ready to knock your brains out when the drive goes on. You forget where you put the meteor patches—"

"All right. I made it, didn't I?"

"And now you think we should give up space."

Rappaport's voice went squeaky with emotion. "Turnbull, aren't you convinced *yet*? We've got a paradise here, and you want to leave it for —that. Why? Why?"

"To build other paradises, maybe. Ours didn't happen by accident. Our ancestors did it all, starting with not much more than what was on Sirius B-IV."

"They had a *helluva* lot more." A faint slurring told that the bourbon was finally getting to Rappaport.

"Maybe they did at that. But now there's a better reason. These people you left on the beach. They need our help. And with a new *Overcee*, we can give it to them. What do they need most, Carver? Trees or meat animals?"

"Animals." Rappaport shuddered and drank.

"Well, that could be argued. But pass it. First we'll have to make soil." Turnbull leaned back in his chair, face upturned, talking half to himself. "Algae mixed with crushed rock. Bacteria to break the rock down. Earthworms. Then grass . . ."

"Got it all planned out, do you? And you'll talk the UN into it, too. Turnbull, you're good. But you've missed something."

"Better tell me now then."

Rappaport got carefully to his feet. He came over to the desk, just a little unsteadily, and leaned on it so that he stared down into Turnbull's eyes from a foot away. "You've been assuming that those people on the beach really were the farmer's race. That Sirius B-IV has been deserted for a long, long time. But what if some kind of carnivore seeded that planet? Then what? The algae wouldn't be for them. They'd let the algae grow, plant food animals, then go away until the animals were jammed shoulder to shoulder along the coast. Food animals! You understand, Turnbull?"

"Yes. I hadn't thought of that. And they'd breed them for *size* . . ."

The room was deadly quiet.

"Well?"

"Well, we'll simply have to take that chance, won't we?"

• • •

• • •

Primary colors streamed up from beneath the Warlock's fingers, roiled and expanded beneath the beamed roof. Heads turned at the other tables. The clattering of table knives stopped. Then came sounds of delight and appreciative fingersnapping, for a spell the Warlock had last used to blind an enemy army.

THE MAGIC GOES AWAY, 1978

CONVERGENT SERIES

I hold a doctorate, but it's honorary, a D. Litt. The rank I *earned* was a bachelor's degree in mathematics.

I haven't used my math training much. This story is as close as I get to pure math.

One Chris Silbermann wants to make a movie out of it.

• •

It was a girl in my anthropology class who got me interested in magic. Her name was Ann, and she called herself a white witch, though I never saw her work an effective spell. She lost interest in me and married somebody, at which point I lost interest in her; but by that time magic had become the subject of my thesis in anthropology. I couldn't quit, and wouldn't if I could. Magic fascinated me.

The thesis was due in a month. I had a hundred pages of notes on primitive, medieval, Oriental, and modern magic. Modern magic meaning psionics devices and such. Did you know that certain African tribes don't believe in natural death? To them, *every* death is due to witchcraft, and in every case the witch must be found and killed. Some of these tribes are actually dying out due to the number of witchcraft trials and executions. Medieval Europe was just as bad in many ways, but they stopped in time . . . I'd tried several ways of conjuring Christian and other demons, purely in a spirit of research, and I'd put a Taoist curse on Professor Pauling. It hadn't worked. Mrs. Miller was letting me use the apartment-house basement for experiments.

Notes I had, but somehow the thesis wouldn't move. I knew why. For all I'd learned, I had nothing original to say about anything. It wouldn't have stopped everyone (remember the guy who counted every *I* in *Robinson Crusoe*?) but it stopped me. Until one Thursday night—

I get the damnedest ideas in bars. This one was a beaut. The bartender got my untouched drink as a tip. I went straight home and typed for four solid hours. It was ten minutes to twelve when I quit, but I now had a complete outline for my thesis, based on a genuinely new idea in Christian witchcraft. All I'd needed was a hook to hang my knowledge on. I stood up and stretched . . .

. . . And knew I'd have to try it out.

All my equipment was in Mrs. Miller's basement, most of it already set up. I'd left a pentagram on the floor two nights ago. I erased that with a wet rag, a former washcloth, wrapped around a wooden block. Robes, special candles, lists of spells, new pentagram . . . I worked quietly so as not to wake anyone. Mrs. Miller was sympathetic; her sense of humor was such that they'd have burned her three centuries ago. But the other residents needed their sleep. I started the incantations exactly at midnight.

At fourteen past I got the shock of my young life. Suddenly there was a demon spread-eagled in the pentagram, with his hands and feet and head occupying all five points of the figure.

I turned and ran.

He roared, "Come back here!"

I stopped halfway up the stairs, turned, and came back down. To leave a demon trapped in the basement of Mrs. Miller's apartment house was out of the question. With that amplified basso profundo voice he'd have wakened the whole block.

He watched me come slowly down the stairs. Except for the horns he might have been a nude middle-aged man, shaved, and painted bright red. But if he'd been human you wouldn't have wanted to know him. He seemed built for all of the Seven Deadly Sins. Avaricious green eyes. Enormous gluttonous tank of a belly. Muscles soft and drooping from sloth. A dissipated face that seemed permanently angry. Lecherous—never mind. His horns were small and sharp and polished to a glow.

He waited until I reached bottom. "That's better. Now what kept you? It's been a good century since anyone called up a demon."

"They've forgotten how," I told him. "Nowadays everyone thinks you're supposed to draw the pentagram on the floor."

"The floor? They expect me to show up lying on my *back*?" His voice was thick with rage.

I shivered. My bright idea. A pentagram was a prison for demons. Why? I'd thought of the five points of a pentagram, and the five points of a spread-eagled man . . .

"Well?"

"I know, it doesn't make sense. Would you go away now, please?"

He stared. "You *have* forgotten a lot." Slowly and patiently, as to a child, he began to explain the implications of calling up a demon.

I listened. Fear and sick hopelessness rose in me until the concrete walls seemed to blur. "I am in peril of my immortal soul—" This was something I'd never considered, except academically. Now it was worse than that. To hear the demon talk, my soul was already lost. It had been lost since the moment I used the correct spell. I tried to hide my fear, but that was hopeless. With those enormous nostrils he must have smelled it.

He finished, and grinned as if inviting comment.

I said, "Let's go over that again. I only get one wish."

"Right."

"If you don't like the wish I've got to choose another."

"Right."

"That doesn't seem fair."

"Who said anything about fair?"

"—Or traditional. Why hasn't anyone heard about this deal before?"

"This is the standard deal, Jack. We used to give a better deal to some of the marks. The others didn't have time to talk because of that twenty-four-hour clause. If they wrote anything down we'd alter it. We have power over written things which mention us."

"That twenty-four-hour clause. If I haven't taken my wish in twenty-four hours, you'll leave the pentagram and take my soul anyway?"

"That's right."

"And if I do use the wish, you have to remain in the pentagram until my wish is granted, or until twenty-four hours are up. Then you teleport to Hell to report same, and come back for me immediately, reappearing in the pentagram."

"I guess teleport's a good word. I vanish and reappear. Are you getting bright ideas?"

"Like what?"

"I'll make it easy on you. If you erase the pentagram I can appear anywhere. You can erase it and draw it again somewhere else, and I've got to appear inside it."

A question hovered on my tongue. I swallowed it and asked another. "Suppose I wished for immortality?"

"You'd be immortal for what's left of your twenty-four hours." He grinned. His teeth were coal black. "Better hurry. Time's running out."

Time, I thought. Okay. All or nothing.

"Here's my wish. Stop time from passing outside of me."

"Easy enough. Look at your watch."

I didn't want to take my eyes off him, but he just exposed his black teeth again. So—I looked down.

There was a red mark opposite the minute hand on my Rolex. And a black mark opposite the hour hand.

The demon was still there when I looked up, still spread-eagled against the wall, still wearing that knowing grin. I moved around him, waved my hand before his face. When I touched him he felt like marble.

Time had stopped, but the demon had remained. I felt sick with relief.

The second hand on my watch was still moving. I had expected nothing less. Time had stopped for me—for twenty-four hours of interior time. If it had been exterior time I'd have been safe—but of course that was too easy.

I'd thought my way into this mess. I should be able to think my way out, shouldn't I?

I erased the pentagram from the wall, scrubbing until every trace was gone. Then I drew a new one, using a flexible metal tape to get the lines as straight as possible, making it as large as I could get it in the confined space. It was still only two feet across.

I left the basement.

I knew where the nearby churches were, though I hadn't been to one in too long. My car wouldn't start. Neither would my roommate's motorcycle. The spell which enclosed me wasn't big enough. I walked to a Mormon temple three blocks away.

The night was cool and balmy and lovely. City lights blanked out the stars, but there was a fine werewolf's moon hanging way above the empty lot where the Mormon temple should have been.

I walked another eight blocks to find the B'nai B'rith synagogue and the All Saints church. All I got out of it was exercise. I found empty lots. For me, places of worship didn't exist.

I prayed. I didn't believe it would work, but I prayed. If I wasn't heard was it because I didn't expect to be? But I was beginning to feel that the demon had thought of everything, long ago.

What I did with the rest of that long night isn't important. Even to me it didn't feel important. Twenty-four hours, against eternity? I wrote a fast outline on my experiment in demon raising, then tore it up. The demons would only change it. Which meant that my thesis was shot to hell, whatever happened. I carried a real but rigid Scotch terrier into Professor Pauling's room and posed it on his desk. The old tyrant would get a surprise when he looked up. But I spent most of the night outside, walking, looking my last on the world. Once I reached into a police car and flipped the siren on, thought about it, and flipped it off again. Twice I dropped into restaurants and ate someone's order, leaving money which I wouldn't need, paper-clipped to notes which read "The Shadow Strikes."

The hour hand had circled my watch twice. I got back to the basement at twelve-ten, with the long hand five minutes from brenschluss.

That hand seemed painted to the face as I waited. My candles had left a peculiar odor in the basement, an odor overlaid with the stink of demon and the stink of fear. The demon hovered against the wall, no longer in a pentagram, trapped halfway through a wide-armed leap of triumph.

I had an awful thought.

Why had I believed the demon? Everything he'd said might have been a lie. And probably was! I'd been tricked into accepting a gift from the devil! I stood up, thinking furiously—I'd already accepted the gift, but—

The demon glanced to the side and grinned wider when he saw the chalk lines gone. He nodded at me, said, "Back in a flash," and was gone.

I waited. I'd thought my way into this, but—

A cheery bass voice spoke out of the air. "I knew you'd move the pentagram. Made it too small for me, didn't you? Tsk, tsk. Couldn't you guess I'd change my size?"

There were rustlings, and a shimmering in the air. "I know it's here somewhere. I can feel it. Ah."

He was back, spread-eagled before me, two feet tall and three feet off the ground. His black know-it-all grin disappeared when he saw the pentagram wasn't there. Then—he was seven inches tall, eyes bugged in surprise, yelling in a contralto voice. "Whereinhell's the—"

He was two inches of bright red toy soldier. "—Pentagram?" he squealed.

I'd won. Tomorrow I'd get to a church. If necessary, have somebody lead me in blindfold.

He was a small red star.

A buzzing red housefly.

Gone.

It's odd, how quickly you can get religion. Let one demon tell you you're damned . . . Could I really get into a church? Somehow I was sure I'd make it. I'd gotten this far; I'd outthought a demon.

Eventually he'd look down and see the pentagram. Part of it was in plain sight. But it wouldn't help him. Spread-eagled like that, he couldn't reach it to wipe it away. He was trapped for eternity, shrinking toward the infinitesimal but doomed never to reach it, forever trying to appear inside a pentagram which was forever too small. I had drawn it on his bulging belly.

• • •

• • •

She thrust herself into the sky, naked; waved her arms and yelled. The Dark shark froze. A window came open in a nearby cluster of cubes. The beast charged.

Rather didn't have his wings. He called, "Sectry! Dark sharks aren't funny!"

... "Are you nuts?" he bellowed, and she laughed. Then the Dark shark burst through in a shower of leaves and splintered wood.

... The predator snapped its teeth at them, raging and impotent. Sectry murmured in his ear. "Gives it a kick, doesn't it?"

THE SMOKE RING, 1987

ALL THE MYRIAD WAYS

A quarter of a century has passed since I first read "Sideways in Time," by Murray Leinster. He wasn't the first to write of alternate time tracks—that was O. Henry in "Roads of Destiny," unless someone beat *him*—but Leinster codified the idea and gave science fiction a whole new playground.

Wholesale theft is the sincerest form of flattery, as someone once said. Your novice writer begins his career by writing the story to end all stories about the basic themes, the ones that never seem to wear out: deals with the devil, three wishes, the locked room mystery, solipsism, the sun going nova, the little shop that sells wonders . . . and alternate histories.

There are a lot of them. Some are unforgettable classics. Phil Dick's *The Man In The High Castle* opens decades after the Axis won the Second World War. The world of Ward Moore's *Bring The Jubilee* diverged at the Battle of Gettysburg. There's a scholarly retrospective on Abraham Lincoln's life following his recovery from that gunshot wound, called "The Lost Years." Norman Spinrad's *The Iron Dream* had Adolf Hitler migrating to the United States after the First World War, to become a hack science-fiction writer.

Many are good entertainment. Some are simple cribs from history, with little of ingenuity or original thinking, the dance of ideas that hooks us before our teens. But Keith Laumer, H. Beam Piper, Poul Anderson, and Fritz Leiber took Leinster's idea a step further, giving some worldlines the vehicles that allow travel between the lines, for trade and conquest.

What if? Like other worlds, like the past and future, like worlds where magic works: a younger reader sees playgrounds for the mind. Mature readers and novelists sees more. Alternate timelines are a background on which one may play games of political theory, refight old philosophical or military battles with altered rules, and explore the many ways of being human. If it hadn't happened *that* way, how would it have happened, and how would we be living now?

I finally decided I hated the whole idea.

Don't misread that. I could live with a handful of parallel universes, or a hundred, or a million. They'd make life more interesting. Many stories do restrict the proliferation of the timelines, via doubletalk. It's *the whole idea* I dislike, taken honestly and without modifying it for story purposes.

Take it from quantum mechanics: the idea is that every time an elementary particle may zig instead of zagging, it does *both*, and the universe splits in two. When an observer gets around to looking ("the collapse of the wave function"), he sees only one state of things; but all other states are just as real. Similarly, every time you've made a decision in your life, you made it all possible ways. I see anything less than that as a cheat, an attempt to make the idea easier to swallow.

A thought-experiment, then. Let's play a game with loaded dice. There are thirty-six ways a pair of dice can fall. That implies thirty-six universes every time we roll, 1296 universes for two rolls, 46,656 universes for three rolls, 1,679,616 universes for four rolls, etc. Your chance of finding your*self* in any one of these universes is the same, *whether or not the dice are biased.* In practice, however, the bias can be seen to affect the roll. Therefore the theory doesn't hold.

Does the argument hold? Probably not. Branching histories in all their horrible multiplicity have come to be accepted as basic to quantum mechanics. (Then there are all those universes where it is regarded as nonsense . . .)

My real grievance is that I spent time, sweat, effort, and agony to become what I am. It irritates me to think that there are Larry Nivens working as second-rate mathematicians or adequate priests or first-rate playboys, who went bust or made their fortunes on the stock market. I even sweated over my mistakes, and I want them to count.

But that's my problem, not yours. I wrote my story to end all alternate-timeline stories long ago, and of course it didn't. It never does.

I wrote one myself, afterward. The idea has a fascination.

Breathes there a history student with soul so dead, that he has not wondered what would have happened *if? If* the South had won the Battle of Gettysburg, what would the world be like today? We'd like to know.

Why?

We can't get there from here. Travel between the lines isn't like space travel; it's not an achievable ideal. No assertion in *Bring The Jubilee* can be proved, even in principle; and in principle all assertions are true somewhere in the megauniverse of the timelines.

Bring The Jubilee and all its cousins are fantasy without fantasy trappings. In fantasy, more than in other forms of literature, the obligation is to teach something universally true about the human condition.

• •

There were timelines branching and branching, a megauniverse of universes, millions more every minute. Billions? Trillions? Trimble didn't understand the theory, though God knows he'd tried. The universe split every time someone made a decision. Split, so that every decision ever made could go both ways. Every choice made by every man, woman and child on Earth was reversed in the universe next door. It was enough to confuse any citizen, let alone Detective-Lieutenant Gene Trimble, who had other problems.

Senseless suicides, senseless crimes. A city-wide epidemic. It had hit other cities too. Trimble suspected that it was worldwide, that other nations were simply keeping it quiet.

Trimble's sad eyes focused on the clock. Quitting time. He stood up to go home, and slowly sat down again. For he had his teeth in the problem, and he couldn't let go.

Not that he was really accomplishing anything.

But if he left now, he'd only have to take it up again tomorrow.

Go, or stay?

And the branchings began again. Gene Trimble thought of other universes parallel to this one, and a parallel Gene Trimble in each one. Some had left early. Many had left on time, and were now halfway home to dinner, out to a movie, watching a strip show, racing to the scene of another death. Streaming out of police headquarters in all their multitudes, leaving a multitude of Trimbles behind them. Each of these trying to deal, alone, with the city's endless, inexplicable parade of suicides.

Gene Trimble spread the morning paper on his desk. From the bottom drawer he took his gun-cleaning equipment, then his .45. He began to take the gun apart.

The gun was old but serviceable. He'd never fired it except on the target range, and never expected to. To Trimble, cleaning his gun was like knitting, a way to keep his hands busy while his mind wandered off. Turn the screws, don't lose them. Lay the parts out in order.

Through the closed door to his office came the sounds of men hurrying. Another emergency? The department couldn't handle it all. Too many suicides, too many casual murders, not enough men.

Gun oil. Oiled rag. Wipe each part. Put it back in place.

Why would a man like Ambrose Harmon go off a building?

In the early morning light he lay, more a stain than a man, thirty-six stories below the edge of his own penthouse roof. The pavement was splattered red for yards around him. The stains were still wet. Harmon had landed on his face. He wore a bright silk dressing gown and a sleeping jacket with a sash.

Others would take samples of his blood, to learn if he had acted under the influence of alcohol or drugs. There was little to be learned from seeing him in his present condition.

"But why was he up so early?" Trimble wondered. For the call had come in at 8:03, just as Trimble arrived at headquarters.

"So late, you mean." Bentley had beaten him to the scene by twenty minutes. "We called some of his friends. He was at an all-night poker game. Broke up around six o'clock."

"Did Harmon lose?"

"Nope. He won almost five hundred bucks."

"That fits," Trimble said in disgust. "No suicide note?"

"Maybe they've found one. Shall we go up and see?"

"We won't find a note," Trimble predicted.

Even three months earlier Trimble would have thought, *How incredible*! or, *Who could have pushed him*? Now, riding up in the elevator, he thought only, *Reporters*. For Ambrose Harmon was news. Even among this past year's epidemic of suicides, Ambrose Harmon's death would stand out like Lyndon Johnson in a lineup.

He was a prominent member of the community, a man of dead and wealthy grandparents. Perhaps the huge inheritance, four years ago, had gone to his head. He had invested tremendous sums to back harebrained, quixotic causes.

Now, because one of the harebrained causes had paid off, he was richer than ever. The Crosstime Corporation already held a score of patents on inventions imported from alternate time tracks. Already those inventions had started more than one industrial revolution. And Harmon was the money behind Crosstime. He would have been the world's next billionaire—had he not walked off his balcony.

They found a roomy, luxuriously furnished apartment in good order, and a bed turned down for the night. The only sign of disorder was the clothing—slacks, sweater, a silk turtleneck shirt, knee-length shoesocks, no underwear—piled on a chair in the bedroom. The toothbrush had been used.

He got ready for bed, Trimble thought. He brushed his teeth, and then he went out to look at the sunrise. A man who kept late hours like that, he wouldn't see the sunrise very often. He watched the sunrise, and when it was over, he jumped.

Why?

They were all like that. Easy, spontaneous decisions. The victim/killers walked off bridges or stepped from their balconies or suddenly flung themselves in front of subway trains. They strolled halfway across a freeway, or swallowed a full bottle of laudanum. None of the methods showed previous planning. Whatever was used, the victim had had it all along; he never actually went out and *bought* a suicide weapon. The victim rarely dressed for the occasion, or used makeup, as an ordinary suicide would. Usually there was no note.

Harmon fit the pattern perfectly.

"Like Richard Cory," said Bentley.

"Who?"

"Richard Cory, the man who had everything. 'And Richard Cory, one calm summer night, went home and put a bullet through his head.' You know what I think?"

"If you've got an idea, let's have it."

"The suicides all started about a month after Crosstime got started. I think one of the Crosstime ships brought back a new bug from some alternate timeline."

"A suicide bug?"

Bentley nodded.

"You're out of your mind."

"I don't think so. Gene, do you know how many Crosstime pilots have killed themselves in the last year? More than twenty percent!"

"Oh?"

"Look at the records. Crosstime has about twenty vehicles in action now, but in the past year they've employed sixty-two pilots. Three disappeared. Fifteen are dead, and all but two died by suicide."

"I didn't know that." Trimble was shaken.

"It was bound to happen sometime. Look at the alternate worlds they've found so far. The Nazi world. The Red Chinese world, half bombed to death. The ones that are so totally bombed, that Crosstime can't even find out who did it. The one with the Black Plague mutation, and no penicillin until Crosstime came along. Sooner or later—"

"Maybe, maybe. I don't buy your bug, though. If the suicides are a new kind of plague, what about the other crimes?"

"Same bug."

"Uh uh. But I think we'll check up on Crosstime."

Trimble's hands finished with the gun and laid it on the desk. He was hardly aware of it. Somewhere in the back of his mind was a prodding sensation: the *handle*, the piece he needed to solve the puzzle.

He's spent most of the day studying Crosstime, Inc. News stories, official handouts, personal interviews. The incredible suicide rate among

Crosstime pilots could not be coincidence. He wondered why nobody had noticed it before.

It was slow going. With Crosstime travel, as with relativity, you had to throw away reason and use only logic. Trimble had sweated it out. Even the day's murders had not distracted him.

They were typical, of a piece with the preceding eight months' crime wave. A man had shot his foreman with a gun bought an hour earlier, then strolled off toward police headquarters. A woman had moved through the back row of a dark theater, using an ice pick to stab members of the audience through the backs of their seats. She had chosen only young men. They had killed without heat, without concealment; they had surrendered without fear or bravado. Perhaps it was another kind of suicide.

Time for coffee, Trimble thought, responding unconsciously to dry throat plus a muzziness in the mouth plus slight fatigue. He set his hands to stand up, and—

The image came to him of an endless row of Trimbles, lined up like the repeated images in facing mirrors. But each image was slightly different. He would go get the coffee *and* he wouldn't *and* he would send somebody for it *and* someone was about to bring it without being asked. Some of the images were drinking coffee, a few had tea or milk, some were smoking, some were leaning too far back with their feet on the desks (and a handful of these were toppling helplessly backward), some were, like this present Trimble, introspecting with their elbows on the desk.

Damn Crosstime anyway.

He'd have had to check Harmon's business affairs, even without the Crosstime link. There might have been a motive there, for suicide or for murder, though it had never been likely.

In the first place, Harmon had cared nothing for money. The Crosstime group had been one of many. At the time that project had looked as harebrained as the rest: a handful of engineers and physicists and philosophers determined to prove that the theory of alternate time tracks was reality.

In the second place, Harmon had no business worries.

Quite the contrary.

Eleven months ago an experimental vehicle had touched one of the worlds of the Confederate States of America, and returned. The universes of alternate choice were within reach. And the pilot had brought back an artifact.

From that point on, Crosstime travel had more than financed itself. The Confederate world's "stapler," granted an immediate patent, had bought two more ships. A dozen miracles had originated in a single, technologically advanced timeline, one in which the catastrophic Cuba

War had been no more than a wet firecracker. Lasers, oxygen-hydrogen rocket motors, computers, strange plastics—the list was still growing. And Crosstime held all the patents.

In those first months the vehicles had gone off practically at random. Now the pinpointing was better. Vehicles could select any branch they preferred. Imperial Russia, Amerindian America, the Catholic Empire, the dead worlds. Some of the dead worlds were hells of radioactive dust and intact but deadly artifacts. From these worlds Crosstime pilots brought strange and beautiful works of art which had to be stored behind leaded glass.

The latest vehicles could reach worlds so like this one that it took a week of research to find the difference. In theory they could get even closer. There was a phenomenon called "the broadening of the bands." . . .

And that had given Trimble the shivers.

When a vehicle left its own present, a signal went on in the hangar, a signal unique to that ship. When the pilot wanted to return, he simply cruised across the appropriate band of probabilities until he found the signal. The signal marked his own unique present.

Only it didn't. The pilot always returned to find a clump of signals, a broadened band. The longer he stayed away, the broader was the signal band. His own world had continued to divide after his departure, in a constant stream of decisions being made both ways.

Usually it didn't matter. Any signal the pilot chose represented the world he had left. And since the pilot himself had a choice, he naturally returned to them all. But—

There was a pilot by the name of Gary Wilcox. He had been using his vehicle for experiments, to see how close he could get to his own timeline and still leave it. Once, last month, he had returned twice.

Two Gary Wilcoxes, two vehicles. The vehicles had been wrecked: their hulls intersected. For the Wilcoxes it could have been sticky, for Wilcox had a wife and family. But one of the duplicates had chosen to die almost immediately.

Trimble had tried to call the other Gary Wilcox. He was too late. Wilcox had gone skydiving a week ago. He'd neglected to open his parachute.

Small wonder, thought Trimble. At least Wilcox had had motive. It was bad enough, knowing about the other Trimbles, the ones who had gone home, the ones drinking coffee, et cetera. But—suppose someone walked into the office right now, and it was Gene Trimble?

It could happen.

Convinced as he was that Crosstime was involved in the suicides, Trimble (some other Trimble) might easily have decided to take a trip in a Crosstime vehicle. A short trip. He could land *here*.

• • •

Trimble closed his eyes and rubbed at the corners with his fingertips. In some other timeline, very close, someone had thought to bring him coffee. Too bad this wasn't it.

It didn't do to think too much about these alternate timelines. There were too many of them. The close ones could drive you buggy, but the ones further off were just as bad.

Take the Cuba War. Atomics had been used, *here*, and now Cuba was uninhabited, and some American cities were gone, and some Russian. It could have been worse.

Why wasn't it? How did we luck out? Intelligent statesmen? Faulty bombs? A humane reluctance to kill indiscriminately?

No. There was no luck anywhere. Every decision was made both ways. For every wise choice you bled your heart out over, you made all the other choices too. And so it went, all through history.

Civil wars unfought on some worlds were won by either side on others. Elsewhen, another animal had first done murder with an antelope femur. Some worlds were still all nomad; civilization had lost out. If every choice was cancelled elsewhere, why make a decision at all?

Trimble opened his eyes and saw the gun.

That gun, too, was endlessly repeated on endless desks. Some of the images were dirty with years of neglect. Some smelled of gunpowder, fired recently, a few at living targets. Some were loaded. All were as real as this one.

A number of these were about to go off by accident.

A proportion of these were pointed, in deadly coincidence, at Gene Trimble.

See the endless rows of Gene Trimble, each at his desk. Some are bleeding and cursing as men run into the room following the sound of the gunshot. Many are already dead.

Was there a bullet in there? Nonsense.

He looked away. The gun was empty.

Trimble loaded it. At the base of his mind he felt the touch of the *handle*. He would find what he was seeking.

He put the gun back on his desk, pointing away from him, and he thought of Ambrose Harmon, coming home from a late night. Ambrose Harmon, who had won five hundred dollars at poker. Ambrose Harmon, exhausted, seeing the lightening sky as he prepared for bed. Going out to watch the dawn.

Ambrose Harmon, watching the slow dawn, remembering a two-thousand-dollar pot. He'd bluffed. In some other branching of time, he had lost.

Thinking that in some other branching of time that two thousand dollars included his last dime. It was certainly possible. If Crosstime hadn't paid off, he might have gone through the remains of his fortune in the past four years. He liked to gamble.

Watching the dawn, thinking of all the Ambrose Harmons on that roof. Some were penniless this night, and they had not come out to watch the dawn.

Well, why not? If he stepped over the edge, here and now, another Ambrose Harmon would only laugh and go inside.

If he laughed and went inside, other Ambrose Harmons would fall to their deaths. Some were already on their ways down. One changed his mind too late, another laughed as he fell. . . .

Well, why not? . . .

Trimble thought of another man, a nonentity, passing a firearms store. Branching of timelines, he thinks, looking in, and he thinks of the man who took his foreman's job. Well, why not? . . .

Trimble thought of a lonely woman making herself a drink at three in the afternoon. She thinks of myriads of alter egos, with husbands, lovers, children, friends. Unbearable, to think that all the might-have-beens were as real as herself. As real as this ice pick in her hand. Well, why not? . . .

And she goes out to a movie, but she takes the ice pick.

And the honest citizen with a carefully submerged urge to commit rape, just once. Reading his newspaper at breakfast, and there's another story from Crosstime: they've found a world line in which Kennedy the First was assassinated. Strolling down a street, he thinks of world lines and infinite branchings, of alter egos already dead, or jailed, or President. A girl in a miniskirt passes, and she has nice legs. Well, why not? . . .

Casual murder, casual suicide, casual crime. Why not? If alternate universes are a reality, then cause and effect are an illusion. The law of averages is a fraud. You can do anything, and one of you will, or did.

Gene Trimble looked at the clean and loaded gun on his desk. Well, why not? . . .

And he ran out of the office shouting, "Bentley, listen! I've got the answer . . ."

And he stood up slowly and left the office shaking his head. This was the answer, and it wasn't any good. The suicides, murders, casual crimes would continue. . . .

And he suddenly laughed and stood up. Ridiculous! Nobody dies for a philosophical point! . . .

And he reached for the intercom and told the man who answered to bring him a sandwich and some coffee. . . .

And picked the gun off the newspapers, looked at it for a long moment, then dropped it in the drawer. His hands began to shake. On a world line very close to this one . . .

And he picked the gun off the newspapers, put it to his head and
fired. The hammer fell on an empty chamber.
fired. The gun jerked up and blasted a hole in the ceiling
fired. The bullet tore a furrow in his scalp.
took off the top of his head.

● ● ●

• • •

Grendels wandered around outside the fences, gorged on meat, their bellies full. They watched one another suspiciously. Something happened— Cadmann, watching with professional interest, still couldn't tell what sparked it, but two grendels blurred into *speed*, passed each other, curved back in a mist of pink blood, attacked like a pair of enraged buzz saws.

THE LEGACY OF HEOROT (with Jerry Pournelle and Steven Barnes), 1987

From A GIFT FROM EARTH

Hank Stine and I were budding writers together. We planned to write GIFT together, but other projects forced him to drop out. Matt Keller's peculiar psychic power was Hank's idea. He forced me to face the implications, the social and sexual problems of a man with "Plateau eyes."

Hank may therefore be responsible for "Man of Steel, Woman of Kleenex" and other horrors including the "organ bank problem." Following the implications of an assumption is a science fiction writer's basic skill. If you predict the automobile, you must predict the traffic jam too.

Hank and I did collaborate nonetheless. There was a story I couldn't sell. I showed it to Hank Stine and asked if he could do something with it. He could: he put an ending on it and called it "No Exit," and sold it to Ted White at *Amazing/Fantastic*, for what he says was the grubbiest, filthiest check he had ever seen.

In Plateau my optimistic tendencies were already showing. Observe the environment! Houses grow themselves. Carpets ("indoor grass") renew and clean themselves. Crops don't need tending. Things are not what they seem: the center of government is not just a big building, but two landing craft embedded in architectural coral. There are serfs and lords—crew and colonist—but the colonists have civil rights and access to technology and news from other worlds.

As for the organ bank problem, Earth has *already* sent them the solution!

A GIFT FROM EARTH is about revolution in fairyland.

Graduates of Cate School in Carpinteria, where I attended high school, will recognise scenery and events on this alien world. The fogs are common on the Mesa. I saw the shadows and the rainbow halo one midmorning in eleventh grade. The apple juice incident is notorious.

Why is a second novel harder to write than the first?

You can take forever to write the first novel, and some do; it's only a damn hobby. But the first novel makes you a *writer*, and then you expect yourself to *produce*. GIFT had me worried. There *are* one-shot novelists.

It's the last time, so help me, that I ever started a novel without an ending in mind.

• •

Later, they stood at the edge and looked down.

Often Jesus Pietro had watched groups of children standing fearful and excited at the void edge, looking down toward the hidden roots of Mount Lookitthat, daring each other to go closer—and closer. As a child he had done the same. The wonder of that view had never left him.

Forty miles below, beneath a swirling sea of white mist, was the true surface of Mount Lookitthat the planet. The great plateau on Mount Lookitthat the mountain had a surface less than half the size of California. All the rest of the world's surface was a black oven, hot enough to melt lead, at the bottom of an atmosphere sixty times as thick as Earth's.

Matthew Keller had committed, deliberately, one of the worst of possible crimes. He had crawled off the edge of the Plateau, taking with him his eyes, his liver and kidneys, his miles of blood tubing, and all twelve of his glands—taking everything that could have gone into the Hospital's organ banks to save the lives of those whose bodies were failing. Even his worth as fertilizer, not inconsiderable on a three-hundred-year-old colony world, was now nil. Only the water in him would someday return to the upper world to fall as rain on the lakes and rivers and as snow on the great northern glacier. Already, perhaps, he was dry and flaming in the awful heat forty miles below.

Or had he stopped falling, even yet?

Jesus Pietro, Head of Implementation, stepped back with an effort. The formless mist sometimes brought strange hallucinations and stranger thoughts—like that odd member of the Rorschach inkblot set, the one sheet of cardboard which is blank. Jesus Pietro had caught himself thinking that when his time came, if it ever came, this was the way he would like to go. And that was treason.

• • •

"So you're a miner now?"

"Right, and regretting it every waking hour. I rue the day Earth sent us those little snakes."

"It must be better than digging the holes yourself."

"Think so? Are you ready for a lecture?"

"Just a second." Hood drained his glass in a heroic gesture. "Ready."

"A mining worm is five inches long and a quarter inch in diameter, mutated from an earthworm. Its grinding orifice is rimmed with little diamond teeth. It ingests metal ores for pleasure, but for food it has to be supplied with blocks of synthetic stuff which is different for each breed of worm—and there's a breed for every metal. This makes things complicated. We've got six breeds out at the mine site, and I've got to see that each breed always has a food block within reach."

"It doesn't sound too complicated. Can't they find their own food?"

"In theory, sure. In practice, not always. But that's not all. What breaks down the ores is a bacterium in the worm's stomach. Then the worm drops metal grains around its food block, and we sweep them up. Now, that bacterium dies very easily. If the bacterium dies, so does the worm, because there's metal ore blocking his intestines. Then the other worms eat his body to recover the ore. Only, five times out of six it's the wrong ore."

"The worms can't tell each other apart?"

"Flaming right they can't. They eat the wrong metals, they eat the wrong worms, they eat the wrong food blocks; and when they do everything right, they still die in ten days. They were built that way because their teeth wear out so fast. They're supposed to breed like mad to compensate, but the plain truth is they don't have time when they're on the job. We have to keep going back to the crew for more."

"So they've got you by the gonads."

"Sure. They charge what they like."

"Could they be putting the wrong chemical cues in some of the food blocks?"

Matt looked up, startled. "I'll bet that's just what they're doing. Or too little of the right cues; that'd save them money at the same time. They won't let us grow our own, of course. The—" Matt swallowed the word. After all, he hadn't seen Hood in years. The crew didn't like being called names.

"Time for dinner," said Hood.

They finished the beer and went to the town's one restaurant. Hood wanted to know what had happened to his old school friends, or schoolmates; Hood had not made friends easily. Matt, who knew in many cases, obliged. They talked shop, both professions. Hood was teaching school on Delta. To Matt's surprise, the introverted boy had become an entertaining storyteller. He had kept his dry, precise tone, and it only made his jokes funnier. They were both fairly good at their jobs, and both making enough money to live on. There was no real poverty anywhere on the Plateau. It was not the colonists' money the crew wanted, as Hood pointed out over the meat course.

"I know where there's a party," Hood said over coffee.

"Are we invited?"

"Yes."

Matt had nothing planned for the night, but he wanted reassurance. "Party crashers welcome?"

"In your case, party crashers solicited. You'll like Harry Kane. He's the host."

"I'm sold."

The sun dipped below the edge of Gamma Plateau as they rode up. They left their bicycles in back of the house. As they walked around to the front, the sun showed again, a glowing red half-disk above the eternal sea of cloud beyond the void edge. Harry Kane's house was just forty yards from the edge. They stopped a moment to watch the sunset fade, then turned toward the house.

It was a great sprawling bungalow, laid out in a rough cross, with the bulging walls typical of architectural coral. No attempt had been made to disguise its origin. Matt had never before seen a house which was not painted, but he had to admire the effect. The remnants of the shaping balloon, which gave all architectural coral buildings their telltale bulge, had been carefully scraped away. The exposed walls had been polished to a shining pink sheen. Even after sunset the house glowed softly.

As if it were *proud* of its thoroughly colonist origin.

Architectural coral was another gift of the ramrobots. A genetic manipulation of ordinary sea coral, it was the cheapest building material known. The only real cost was in the plastic balloon that guided the growth of the coral and enclosed the coral's special airborne food. All colonists lived in buildings of coral. Not many would have built in stone or wood or brick even were it allowed. But most attempted to make their dwellings look somewhat like those on Alpha plateau. With paint, with wood and metal and false stone-sidings, with powered sandpaper disks to flatten the inevitable bulges, they tried to imitate the crew.

In daylight or darkness Harry Kane's house was flagrantly atypical.

The noise hit them as they opened the door. Matt stood still while his ears adjusted to the noise level—a survival trait his ancestors had developed when Earth's population numbered nineteen billion, even as it did that night, eleven point nine light-years away. During the last four centuries a man of Earth might as well have been stone deaf if he could not carry on a conversation with a thousand drunks bellowing in his ears. Matt's people had kept some of their habits too. The great living room was jammed, and the few chairs were largely being ignored.

The room *was* big, and the bar across from the entrance was enormous. Matt shouted, "Harry Kane must do a lot of entertaining."

"He does! Come with me; we'll meet him!"

Matt caught snatches of conversation as they pushed their way across the room. The party hadn't been going long, he gathered, and several people knew practically nobody; but they all had drinks. They were of all ages, all professions. Hood had spoken true. If a party crasher wasn't welcome, he'd never know it, because no one would recognize him as one.

The walls were like the outside, a glowing coral pink. The floor, covered with a hairy-looking wall-to-wall rug of mutated grass, was flat except at the walls; no doubt it had been sanded flat after the house was finished and the forming balloon removed.

• • •

A visit from a crew always upset Jesus Pietro's men.

At least Parlette had come to him. Once Parlette had summoned him to his own house, and that had been bad. Here, Jesus Pietro was in his element. His office was practically an extension of his personality. The desk had the shape of a boomerang, enclosing him in an obtuse angle for more available working space. He had three guests' chairs of varying degrees of comfort, for crew and Hospital personnel and colonist. The office was big and square, but there was a slight curve to the back wall. Where the other walls were cream colored, easy on the eye, the back wall was smoothly polished dark metal.

It was part of the outer hull of the *Planck*. Jesus Pietro's office was right up against the source of half the spiritual strength of Mount Lookitthat, and half the electrical power too: the ship that had brought men to this world. Sitting at his desk, Jesus Pietro felt the power at his back.

• • •

An officer had found the housecleaner nest, a niche in the south wall, near the floor. The man reached in and carefully removed two unconscious adult housecleaners and four pups, put them on the floor, reached in to remove the nest and the food dish. The niche would have to be searched.

Jesus Pietro's clothes dried slowly, in wrinkles. He sat with his eyes closed and his hands folded on his belly. Presently he opened his eyes, sighed, and frowned slightly.

—Jesus Pietro, this is a very strange house.

—Yes. Almost garishly colonist. (Overtones of disgust.)

Jesus Pietro looked at the pink coral walls, the flat-sanded floor which curved up at the edge of the rug to join the walls. Not a bad effect if a woman were living here. But Harry Kane was a bachelor.

—How much would you say a house like this cost?

—Oh, about a thousand stars, not including furnishings. Furnishings would cost twice that. Rugs, ninety stars if you bought one and let it spread. Two housecleaners, mated, fifty stars.

—And how much to put a basement under such a house?

—Mist Demons, what an idea! Basements have to be dug by hand, by human beings! It'd cost twenty thousand stars easily. You could build a school for that. Who would ever think of digging a basement under an architectural coral house?

—Who indeed?

Jesus Pietro stepped briskly to the door. "Major Jansen!"

• • •

Geologists (*don't* give me a hard time about that word) believed that Mount Lookitthat was geologically recent. A few hundreds of thousands of years ago, part of the planet's skin had turned molten. Possibly a convection current in the interior had carried more than ordinarily hot magma up to melt the surface; possibly an asteroid had died a violent, fiery death. A slow extrusion had followed, with viscous magma rising and cooling and rising and cooling until a plateau with fluted sides and an approximately flat top stood forty miles above the surface.

It had to be recent. Such a preposterous anomaly could not long resist the erosion of Mount Lookitthat's atmosphere.

And because it was recent, the surface was jagged. Generally the northern end was higher, high enough to hold a permanent sliding glacier, and too high and too cold for comfort. Generally rivers and streams ran south, to join either the Muddy or the Long Fall, both of which had carved deep canyons for themselves through the southland. Both canyons ended in spectacular waterfalls. the tallest in the known universe. Generally the rivers ran south; but there were exceptions, for the surface of Mount Lookitthat was striated, differentiated, a maze of plateaus divided by cliffs and chasms.

Some plateaus were flat; some of the cliffs were straight and vertical. Most of these were in the south. In the north the surface was all tilted blocks and strange lakes with deep, pointed bottoms, and the land would have been cruel to a mountain goat. Nonetheless these regions would be settled someday, just as the Rocky Mountains of Earth were now part of suburbia.

The slowboats had landed in the south, on the highest plateau around. The colonists had been forced to settle lower down. Though they were the more numerous, they covered less territory, for the crew had cars, and flying cars can make a distant mountain-home satisfactory where bicycles will not. Yet Alpha Plateau was Crew Plateau, and for many it was better to live elbow to elbow with one's peers than out in the boondocks in splendid isolation.

So Alpha Plateau was crowded.

What Matt saw below him were all houses. They varied enormously in size, in color, in style, in building material. To Matt, who had lived out his life in architectural coral, the dwellings looked like sheer havoc, like debris from the explosion of a time machine. There was even a clump of deserted, crumbling coral bungalows, each far bigger than a colonist's home. Two or three were as large as Matt's old grade school. When architectural coral first came to the Plateau, the crew had reserved it for their own use. Later it had gone permanently out of style.

None of the nearby buildings seemed to be more than two stories tall. Someday there would be skyscrapers if the crew kept breeding. But in the distance two squat towers rose from a shapeless construction in stone and metal. The Hospital, without a doubt. And straight ahead.

Matt was beginning to feel the strain of flying. He had to divide his attention between the dashboard, the ground, and the Hospital ahead. It was coming closer, and he was beginning to appreciate its size.

Each of the empty slowboats had been built to house six crew in adequate comfort and fifty colonists in stasis. Each slowboat also included a cargo hold, two water-fueled reaction motors and a water fuel tank. And all of this had to be fitted into a hollow double-walled cylinder the shape of a beer can from which the top and bottom have been removed with a can opener. The slowboats had been circular flying wings. In transit between worlds they had spun on their axes to provide centrifugal gravity; and the empty space inside the inner hull, now occupied only by two intersecting tailfins, had once held two throwaway hydrogen balloons.

They were big. Since Matt could not see the inner emptiness which the crew called the Attic, they looked far bigger. Yet they were swamped by the haphazard-looking stone construction of the Hospital. Most of it was two stories high, but there were towers which climbed halfway up the ships' hulls. Some would be power stations, others—he couldn't guess. Flat, barren rock surrounded the Hospital in a half-mile circle, rock as naked as the Plateau had been before the slowboats brought a carefully selected ecology.

• • •

"Matt!" Laney called over her shoulder. She was standing inches from the void.

"Get back from there!"

"No! Come here!"

Matt went. So did Mrs. Hancock. The three of them stood at the edge of the grass, looking down into their shadows.

The sun was at their backs, shining down at forty-five degrees. The water-vapor mist which had covered the southern end of the Plateau that morning now lay just beyond the void edge, almost at their feet. And they looked into their shadows—three shadows reaching down into infinity, three contoured black tunnels growing smaller and narrower as they bored through the lighted mist, until they reached their blurred vanishing points. But for each of the three it seemed that only his own shadow was surrounded by a small, vivid, perfectly circular rainbow.

A fourth shadow joined them, moving slowly and painfully. "Oh, for a camera," mourned Harry Kane.

"I never saw it like that before," said Matt.

"I did, once, a long time ago. It was like I'd had a vision. Myself, the representative of Man, standing at the edge of the world with a rainbow about his head. I joined the Sons of Earth that night."

● ● ●

• • •

> Orson popped open one of the cans, drank, and made a face at Snow Goose. "You brought me all the way to Hell for *sugar-free 7-Up?*"
>
> THE BARSOOM PROJECT, 1989

FOR A FOGGY NIGHT

This is the story Jerry Pournelle quotes to demonstrate why he writes with me. I'm the crazy one.

He comes to me with a map of a city-sized building; I put a high diving board at the edge of the roof. I put a surfer on a tidal wave in LUCIFER'S HAMMER; he moves the beach to where it would work. Jerry puts High Frontier weapons in the grip of the invading fithp, but mine is the vision of baby elephants in tennis shoes gliding out of the sky under paper airplanes.

And I wrote the story that demonstrates that fog is the visible sign of a merging of time tracks . . .

• •

The bar was selling a lot of Irish coffee that night. I'd bought two myself. It was warm inside, almost too warm, except when someone pushed through the door. Then a puff of chill, damp fog would roll in.

Beyond the window was grey chaos. The fog picked up all the various city lights: yellow light leaking from inside the bar, passing automobile headlights, white light from frosted street globes, and the rainbow colors of neon signs. The fog stirred all the lights together into a cold gray-white paste and leaked it back through the windows.

Bright spots drifted past at a pedestrian's pace. Cars. I felt sorry for the drivers. Rolling through a gray formless limbo, running from street globe to invisible street globe, alert for the abrupt, dangerous red dot of a traffic light: an intersection; you couldn't tell otherwise . . . I had friends in San Francisco; there were other places I could be. But it wasn't my city, and I was damned if I'd drive tonight.

A lost night. I'd finished my drink. One more, and I'd cross the street to my hotel.

''You'd best wait until the fog thins out,'' said the man next to me.

He was a stranger, medium all over; medium height and weight, regular features, manicured nails, feathery brown hair, no scars. The invisible man. I'd never have looked his way if he hadn't spoken. But he was smiling as if he knew me.

I said, "Sorry?"

"The point is, your hotel might not be there when you've crossed the street. Don't be surprised," he added. "I can read minds. We've learned the knack, where I come from."

There are easy ways to interrupt a conversation with a stranger. A blank stare will do it. But I was bored and alone, and a wacky conversation might be just what I needed.

I said, "Why shouldn't my hotel be exactly where I left it?"

He frowned into his scotch-and-soda, then took a swallow. "Do you know the theory of multiple world lines? It seems that whenever a decision is made, it's made both ways. The world becomes two or more worlds, one for each way the decision can go. Ah, I see you know of it. Well, sometimes the world lines merge again."

"But—"

"That's exactly right. The world must split on the order of a trillion times a second. What's so unbelievable about that? If you want a real laugh, ask a physicist about furcoated particles."

"But you're saying it's *real*. Every time I get a haircut—"

"One of you waits until tomorrow," said the brown-haired man. "One of you keeps the sideburns. One gets a manicure, one cuts his own nails. The size of the tip varies too. Each of you is as real as the next, and each belongs to a different world line. It wouldn't matter if the world lines didn't merge every so often."

"Uh huh." I grinned at him. "What about my hotel?"

"I'll show you. Look through that window. See the street lamp?"

"Vaguely."

"You bet, vaguely. San Francisco is a town with an active history. The world lines are constantly merging. What you're looking at is the probability of a street lamp being in a particular place. Looks like a big fuzzy ball, doesn't it? That's the locus of points where a bulb might be —or a gas flame. Greatest probability density is in the center, where it shows brightest."

"I don't get it."

"When the world lines merge, everything blurs. The further away something is, the more blurred it looks. I shouldn't say *looks*, because the blurring is real; it's no illusion. Can you see your hotel from here?"

I looked out the appropriate window, and I couldn't. Two hours ago I'd nearly lost my way just crossing the street. Tonight a man could lose himself in any city street, and wander blindly in circles in hopes of finding a curb . . .

"You see? Your hotel's too far away. In the chaos out there, the probability of your hotel being anywhere specific is too small to see. Vanishingly small. You'd never make it."

Something about the way he talked . . .

"I wondered when you'd notice that." He smiled as if we shared a secret.

"All this time," I said, "I've been thinking that you talk just like everyone else. But you don't. It's not just the trace of accent. Other people don't say *probability density* or *theorem* or *on the order of*."

"No, they don't."

"Then we must both be mathematicians!" I smiled back at him.

"No," he said.

"But then . . ." But I backed away from the problem, or from the answer. "My glass is empty. Could you use a refill?"

"Thanks, I could."

I fixed it with the bartender. "Funny thing," I told the brown-haired man. "I always thought the blurring effect of fog came from water droplets in the air."

"Bosh," he said. "Bosh and tish. The water's there, all right, whenever the fog rolls in. I can't explain it. The condensation must be a side effect from the blurring of the world lines. But that's not interfering with your vision. Water's transparent."

"Of course. How could I have forgotten that?"

"I forgot it myself, a long time ago." The scotch was beginning to reach him, I think. He had an accent, and it was growing stronger. "That's why I'm here. That's why I stopped you. Because you'd remember."

The bartender brought us our drinks. His big shoulders were hunched inward against the damp gray light that seeped in the windows.

I sipped at the burning hot glass. Irish whiskey and strong black coffee poured warmth through me, to counteract the cold beyond the walls. A customer departed, and the fog swirled around him and swallowed him.

"I walked into the fog one afternoon," said the brown-haired man. "The fog was thick, like tonight. A cubic mile of cotton, as we say. I was just going out for a pouch of snuff. When I reached the tobacconist's he tried to sell me a bundle of brown paper sticks with a Spanish trademark."

"Uh huh. What did you do?"

"Tried to get home, of course. Things changed oddly while I wandered in the fog. When it cleared and left me stranded, even my money was no good. The worst of it was that I couldn't even tell my story. Nobody could read my mind to see that I was sane. It was find another fog bank or try to make a life for myself."

"With no money?"

"Oh, I sold my ring and found a poker game."

"Oh. *Oh*!"

"That was a year ago. It's worked out well enough. I thought I might invent something, like the zipper, but that fell through. You're far ahead of us in the physical sciences. But money's no problem. Sometimes there's a fixed horse race. Sometimes I find a poker game, or a crooked crap game where they'll let me bet the right way."

"Sounds great." But not very honest, I thought.

"You disapprove?" My companion's voice had gone thin and cold.

"I didn't say that."

"I compensate for what I take," the brown-haired man said angrily. "I know how to untwist a sick man's mind. If a player sits down with emotional problems, I can help him. If he really needs the money, I can see that it comes to him."

"Why don't you become a psychiatrist?"

He shook his head. "It would take years, and then I'd never be able to hold a patient long enough to do myself any good. He'd get well too fast. Besides that, I *hate* certain people; I'd want to harm them instead of helping them. . . .

"Anyway, I don't go out in the fog anymore. I like it here. I stopped you because you're one of those who remember."

"You said that before. What exactly—?"

"After all, people are constantly walking into fogs. Why is it that we don't hear more about people wandering in from alternate world lines? It's because their memories adjust."

"Ah."

"I caught it happening once. A girl from somewhere else . . . I didn't catch the details; they faded too fast. I got her a job as a go-go dancer. I think she was a prize concubine in someone's harem before she ran into the fog.

"Their memories adjust. They forget their friends, their relatives, their husbands and wives in the old world line. They remember what man is king or president or chairman in the new. But not us. You and I are different. I can recognize the rare ones."

"Because you can read minds." Sarcastically. Part of me still disbelieved; yet . . . it fit too well. The brown-haired man talked like a mathematics professor because he was talking to me, and I was a mathematics professor, and he was reading my mind.

He looked thoughtfully into his glass. "It's funny, how many sense the truth. They won't walk or drive in the fog if they can help it. At the bottom of their minds, they know that they might return home to find a Romish camp, or a Druidic dancing ground, or the center of a city, or a sand dune. You knew it yourself. The top of your mind thinks I'm an entertaining liar. The deepest part of you knew it all before I spoke."

"I just don't like fog," I said. I looked out the window, toward my hotel, which was just across the street. I saw only wet gray chaos and a swirling motion.

"Wait until it clears."

"Maybe I will. Refill?"

"Thanks."

Somehow, I found myself doing most of the talking. The brown-haired man listened, nodded occasionally, asked questions from time to time.

We did not mention fog.

"I need an ordered universe," I said at one point. "Why else would I have studied math? There's never an ambiguity in mathematics."

"Whereas in interpersonal relationships . . ."

"Yes! Exactly!"

"But mathematics is a game. Abstract mathematics doesn't connect with the real universe except by coincidence or convenience. Like the imaginary number system: it's used in circuit design, but it certainly wasn't intended for that."

"No, of course not."

"So that's why you never got married?"

"Right," I said sadly. "Ordered universe. Hey, I never knew that. Did I?"

"No."

The fog cleared about one o'clock. My brown-haired friend accompanied me out.

"Mathematics doesn't fit reality," he was saying. "No more than a game of bridge. The real universe is chaotic."

"Like in-ter-personal re-lationships."

"Maybe you'll find them easier now."

"Like fog. Well, maybe I will. I know some new things about myself . . . Where's my hotel?"

There was no hotel across the street.

Suddenly I was cold sober, and cold scared.

"So," said my drinking partner. "You must have lost it earlier. Was it foggy when you crossed?"

"Thick as paste. Oh, brother. Now what do I do?"

"I think the fog's starting to roll in again. Why not wait? The bar won't close until four."

"They close at two in my world." *In my world*. When I admitted that, I made it real.

"Then maybe you should stay in this one. At least the bartender took your money. Which reminds me. Here." He handed me my wallet.

He must have picked my pocket earlier. "For services rendered," he said. "But it looks like you'll need the money."

I was too worried to be angry. "My money passes, but my checks won't. I've got half a term of teaching to finish at Berkeley . . . Tenure, dammit! I've got to get back."

"I'm going to run for it," said the brown-haired man. "Try the fog if you like. You might find your way home." And off he went, running to beat the fog. It was drifting in in gray tendrils as I went back into the bar.

An hour later the fog was a cubic mile of cotton, as they say. I walked into it.

I intended to circle the block where I had left my hotel. But there was no way to get my bearings, and the outlines of the block would not hold still. Sight was gone, sound was strangely altered and muffled. I walked blind and half-deaf, with my arms outstretched to protect my face, treading lightly for fear of being tripped.

One thing, at least, the brown-haired man had failed to warn me about. I walked up to a pedestrian-sized gray blur to ask directions, and when I reached it it wasn't human. It watched me dispassionately as I sidled off.

I might have drifted away from the area. The hotel varied from an ancient barrow to a hot springs (I smelled warm pungent steam) to a glass-sided skyscraper to a vertical slab of black basalt to an enormous pit with red-glowing rock at the bottom. It never became a hotel.

The mist was turning white with dawn. I heard something coming near: the putt-putt-putt of a motor scooter, but distorted. Distorted to the clop-clop-clop of a horse's hooves . . . and still approaching. It became a pad-pad-pad-pad, the sound of something heavy and catlike. I stood frozen. . . .

The fog blew clear, and the sound was two sets of footsteps, two oddly dressed men walking toward me. It was dawn, and the fog was gone, and I was stranded.

In eerie silence the men took me by the elbows, turned me about and walked me into the building which had been my hotel. It had become a kind of hospital.

At first it was very bad. The attendants spoke an artificial language, very simple and unambiguous, like deaf-mute sign language. Until I learned it, I thought I had been booked into a mental hospital.

It was a retraining center for people who can't read minds.

I was inside for a month, and then an outpatient for another six. Quick progress, they say; but then, I hadn't suffered organic brain damage. Most patients are there because of damage to the right parietal lobe.

It was no trouble to pay the hospital fees. I hold patents on the pressure spray can and the butane lighter. Now I'm trying to design a stapler.

And when the fog is a cubic mile of cotton, as we say, I stay put until it goes away.

• • •

• • •

Chintithpit-mang remembered the man's rib cage sagging under his foot. It thrashed and clawed and finally stopped moving ... It didn't know how to surrender. They didn't know how to surrender. *Bad.*

FOOTFALL, 1985

THE MEDDLER

"The Meddler" began as satire. The Mickey Spillane school of writing was still alive and well in those days. What I learned was that if I set out to satirize a school of writing, I must know how to use it too. "The Meddler" is detective fiction; I was forced to make it a fair puzzle.

• •

Someone was in my room.

It had to be one of Sinc's boys. He'd been stupid. I'd left the lights off. The yellow light now seeping under the door was all the warning I needed.

He hadn't used the door: the threads were still there. That left the fire escape outside the bedroom window.

I pulled my gun, moved back a little in the corridor to get elbow room. Then—I'd practiced it often enough to drive the management crazy—I kicked the door open and was into the room in one smooth motion.

He should have been behind the door, or crouching behind a table, or hidden in the closet with his eyes to the keyhole. Instead he was right out in the middle of the living room, facing the wrong way. He'd barely started to turn when I pumped four GyroJet slugs into him. I saw the impacts twitching his shirt. One over the heart.

He was finished.

So I didn't slow down to watch him fall. I crossed the living-room rug in a diving run and landed behind the couch. He couldn't be alone. There had to be others. If one had been behind the couch he might have gotten me, but there wasn't. I scanned the wall behind me, but there was nothing to hide under. So I froze, waiting, listening.

Where were they? The one I'd shot couldn't have come alone.

I was peeved at Sinc. As long as he'd sent goons to waylay me, he might have sent a few who knew what they were doing. The one I'd shot hadn't had time to know he was in a fight.

"Why did you do that?"

Impossibly, the voice came from the middle of the living room, where I'd left a falling corpse. I risked a quick look and brought my head down fast. The afterimage:

He hadn't moved. There was no blood on him. No gun visible, but I hadn't seen his right hand.

Bulletproof vest? Sinc's boys had no rep for that kind of thing, but that had to be it. I stood up suddenly and fired, aiming between the eyes.

The slug smashed his right eye, off by an inch, and I knew he'd shaken me. I dropped back and tried to cool off.

No noises. Still no sign that he wasn't alone.

"I said, 'Why did you do that?' "

Mild curiosity colored his high-pitched voice. He didn't move as I stood up, and there was no hole in either eye.

"Why did I do what?" I asked cleverly.

"Why did you make holes in me? My gratitude for the gift of metal, of course, but—" He stopped suddenly, like he'd said too much and knew it. But I had other worries.

"Anyone else here?"

"Only we two are present. I beg pardon for invasion of privacy, and will indemnify—" He stopped again, as suddenly, and started over. "Who were you expecting?"

"Sinc's boys. I guess they haven't caught on yet. Sinc's boys want to make holes in *me*."

"Why?"

Could he be that stupid? "To turn me off! To kill me!"

He looked surprised, then furious. He was so mad he gurgled. "I should have been informed! Someone has been unforgivably sloppy!"

"Yah. Me. I thought you must be with Sinc. I shouldn't have shot at you. Sorry."

"Nothing," he smiled, instantly calm again.

"But I ruined your suit . . ." I trailed off. Holes showed in his jacket and shirt, but no blood. "Just what *are* you?"

He stood about five feet four, a round little man in an old-fashioned brown one-button suit. There was not a hair on him, not even eyelashes. No warts, no wrinkles, no character lines. A nebbish, one of these guys whose edges are all round, like someone forgot to put in the fine details.

He spread smoothly manicured hands. "I am a man like yourself."

"Nuts."

"Well," he said angrily, "you would have thought so if the preliminary investigation team had done their work properly!"

"You're a—martian?"

"I am *not* a martian. I am—" He gurgled. "Also I am an anthropologist. Your word. I am here to study your species."

"You're from outer space?"

"Very. The direction and distance are secret, of course. My very existence should have been secret." He scowled deeply. Rubber face, I thought, not knowing the half of it yet.

"I won't talk," I reassured him. "But you came at a bad time. Any minute now, Sinc's going to figure out who it is that's on his tail. Then he'll be on mine, and this dump'll be ground zero. I hate to brush you. I've never met a . . . whatever."

"I too must terminate this interview, since you know me for what I am. But first, tell me of your quarrel. Why does Sinc want to make holes in you?"

"His name is Lester Dunhaven Sinclair the third. He runs every racket in this city. Look, we've got time for a drink—maybe. I've got scotch, bourbon—"

He shuddered. "No, I thank you."

"Just trying to set you at ease." I was a little miffed.

"Then perhaps I may adapt a more comfortable form, while you drink—whatever you choose. If you don't mind."

"Please yourself." I went to the rolling bar and poured bourbon and tap water, no ice. The apartment house was dead quiet. I wasn't surprised. I've lived here a couple of years now, and the other tenants have learned the routine. When guns go off, they hide under their beds and stay there.

"You won't be shocked?" My visitor seemed anxious. "If you are shocked, please say so at once."

And he melted. I stood there with the paper cup to my lip and watched him flow out of his one-button suit and take the compact shape of a half-deflated gray beach ball.

I downed the bourbon and poured more, no water. My hands stayed steady.

"I'm a private op," I told the martian. He'd extruded a convoluted something I decided was an ear. "When Sinc showed up about three years ago and started taking over the rackets, I stayed out of his way. He was the law's business, I figured. Then he bought the law, and that was okay too. I'm no crusader."

"Crusader?" His voice had changed. Now it was deep, and it sounded like something bubbling up from a tar pit.

"Never mind. I tried to stay clear of Sinc, but it didn't work. Sinc had a client of mine killed. Morrison, his name was. I was following Morrison's wife, getting evidence for a divorce. She was shacking up with a guy named Adler. I had all the evidence I needed when Morrison disappeared.

"Then I found out Adler was Sinc's right hand."

"Right hand? Nothing was said of hive cultures."

"Huh?"

"One more thing the prelim team will have to answer for. Continue talking. You fascinate me."

"I kept working on it. What could I do? Morrison was my client, and he was dead. I collected plenty of evidence against Adler, and I turned it over to the cops. Morrison's body never turned up, but I had good corpus delicti evidence. Anyway, Sinc's bodies never do turn up. They just disappear.

"I turned what I had over to the cops. The case was squashed. Somehow the evidence got lost. One night I got beat up."

"Beat up?"

"Almost any kind of impact," I told him, "can damage a human being."

"Really!" he gurgled. "All that water, I suppose."

"Maybe. In my line you have to heal fast. Well, that tore it. I started looking for evidence against Sinc himself. A week ago I sent Xeroxes off to the Feds. I let one of Sinc's boys find a couple of the copies. Bribery evidence, nothing exciting, but enough to hurt. I figured it wouldn't take Sinc long to figure out who made them. The Xerox machine I borrowed was in a building he owns."

"Fascinating. I think I will make holes in the Lady of Preliminary Investigation."

"Will that hurt?"

"She is not a—" gurgle. "She is a—" loud, shrill bird whistle.

"I get it. Anyway, you can see how busy I'm going to be. Much too busy to talk about, uh, anthropology. Any minute now I'll have Sinc's boys all over me, and the first one I kill I'll have the cops on me too. Maybe the cops'll come first. I dunno."

"May I watch? I promise not to get in your path."

"Why?"

He cocked his ear, if that was what it was. "An example. Your species has developed an extensive system of engineering using alternating current. We were surprised to find you transmitting electricity so far, and using it in so many ways. Some may even be worth imitating."

"That's nice. So?"

"Perhaps there are other things we can learn from you."

I shook my head. "Sorry, short stuff. This party's bound to get rough, and I don't want any bystanders getting hurt. *What* the hell am I talking about. Holes don't hurt you?"

"Very little hurts me. My ancestors once used genetic engineering to improve their design. My major weaknesses are susceptibility to certain organic poisons, and a voracious appetite."

"Okay, stay then. Maybe after it's all over you can tell me about Mars, or wherever you came from. I'd like that."

"Where I come from is classified. I can tell you about Mars."

"Sure, sure. How'd you like to raid the fridge while we wait? If you're so hungry all the time—Hold it."

Sliding footsteps.

They were out there. A handful of them, if they were trying to keep it a secret. And these had to be from Sinc, because all the neighbors were under their beds by now.

The martian heard it too. "What shall I do? I cannot reach human form fast enough."

I was already behind the easy chair. "Then try something else. Something easy."

A moment later I had two matching black leather footstools. They both matched the easy chair, but maybe nobody'd notice.

The door slammed wide open. I didn't pull the trigger, because nobody was there. Just the empty hallway.

The fire escape was outside my bedroom window, but that window was locked and bolted and rigged with alarms. They wouldn't get in that way. Unless—

I whispered, "Hey! How did you get in?"

"Under the door."

So that was all right. The window alarms were still working. "Did any of the tenants see you?"

"No."

"Good." I get enough complaints from the management without *that*.

More faint rustling from outside the door. Then a hand and gun appeared for an instant, fired at random, vanished. Another hole in my walls. He'd had time to see my head, to place me. I ran low for the couch. I was getting set again, both eyes on the door, when a voice behind me said, "Stand up slow."

You had to admire the guy. He'd got through the window alarms without a twitch, into the living room without a sound. He was tall, olive-skinned, with straight black hair and black eyes. His gun was centered on the bridge of my nose.

I dropped the GyroJet and stood up. Pushing it now would only get me killed.

He was very relaxed, very steady. "That's a GyroJet, isn't it? Why not use a regular heater?"

"I like this," I told him. Maybe he'd come too close, or take his eyes off me, or—anything. "It's light as a toy, with no recoil. The gun is just a launching chamber for the rocket slugs, and they pack the punch of a forty-five."

"But, man! The slugs cost a buck forty-five each!"

"I don't shoot that many people."

"At those prices, I believe it. Okay, turn around slow. Hands in the air." His eyes hadn't left me for a moment.

I turned my back. Next would be a sap—

Something metal brushed against my head, feather-light. I whirled, struck at his gun hand and his larynx. Pure habit. I'd moved the instant the touch told me he was in reach.

He was stumbling back with his hand to his throat. I put a fist in his belly and landed the other on his chin. He dropped, trying to curl up. And sure enough, he was holding a sap.

But why hadn't he hit me with it? From the feel of it, he'd laid it gently on top of my head, carefully, as if he thought the sap might shatter.

"All right, stand easy." The hand and gun came through the doorway, attached to six feet of clean living. I knew him as Handel. He looked like any blond brainless hero, but he wasn't brainless, and he was no hero.

He said, "You're going to hate yourself for doing that."

The footstool behind him began to change shape.

"Dammit," I said, "that's not fair."

Handel looked comically surprised, then smiled winningly. "Two to one?"

"I was talking to my footstool."

"Turn around. We've got orders to bring you to Sinc, if we can. You could still get out of this alive."

I turned around. "I'd like to apologize."

"Save it for Sinc."

"No, honest. It wasn't my idea to have someone else mix in this. Especially—" Again I felt something brush against the side of my head. The martian must be doing something to stop the impact.

I could have taken Handel then. I didn't move. It didn't seem right that I could break Handel's neck when he couldn't touch me. Two to one I don't mind, especially when the other guy's the one. Sometimes I'll even let some civic-minded bystander help, if there's some chance he'll live through it. But *this* . . .

"What's not fair?" asked a high, complaining voice.

Handel screamed like a woman. I turned to see him charge into the door jamb, back up a careful two feet, try for the door again and make it.

Then I saw the footstool.

He was already changing, softening in outline, but I got an idea of the shape Handel had seen. No wonder it had softened his mind. I felt it softening my bones, melting the marrow, and I closed my eyes and whispered, "Dammit, you were supposed to *watch*."

"You told me the impact would damage you."

"That's not the point. Detectives are *always* getting hit on the head. We *expect* it."

"But how can I learn anything from watching you if your little war ends so soon?"

"Well, what do you learn if you keep jumping in?"

"You may open your eyes."

I did. The martian was back to his nebbish form. He had fished a pair of orange shorts out of his pile of clothes. "I do not understand your objection," he said. "This Sinc will kill you if he can. Do you want that?"

"No, but—"

"Do you believe that your side is in the right?"

"Yes, but—"

"Then why should you not accept my help?"

I wasn't sure myself. It felt wrong. It was like sneaking a suitcase bomb into Sinc's mansion and blowing it up.

I thought about it while I checked the hall. Nobody there. I closed the door and braced a chair under the knob. The dark one was still with us: he was trying to sit up.

"Look," I told the martian. "Maybe I can explain, maybe I can't. But if I don't get your word to stay out of this, I'll leave town. I swear it. I'll just drop the whole thing. Understand?"

"No."

"Will you promise?"

"Yes."

The Spanish type was rubbing his throat and staring at the martian. I didn't blame him. Fully dressed, the martian could have passed for a man, but not in a pair of orange undershorts. No hair or nipples marked his chest, no navel pitted his belly. The hood turned a flashing white smile on me and asked, "Who's he?"

"I'll ask the questions. Who're you?"

"Don Domingo." His accent was soft and Spanish. If he was worried, it didn't show. "Hey, how come you didn't fall down when I hit you?"

"I said I'll ask the—"

"Your face is turning pink. Are you embarrassed about something?"

"Dammit, Domingo, where's Sinc? Where were you supposed to take me?"

"The place."

"What place? The Bel Air place?"

"That's the one. You know, you have the hardest head—"

"Never mind that!"

"Okay okay. What will you do now?"

I couldn't call the law in. "Tie you up, I guess. After this is over, I'll turn you in for assault."

"After this is over, you won't be doing much, I think. You will live as long as they shoot at your head, but when—"

"Now *drop* that!"

The martian came out of the kitchen. His hand was flowing around a tin of corned beef, engulfing it tin and all. Domingo's eyes went wide and round.

Then the bedroom exploded.

It was a fire bomb. Half the living room was in flames in an instant. I scooped up the GyroJet, stuck it in my pocket.

The second bomb exploded in the hall. A blast of flame blew the door inward, picked up the chair I'd used to brace the door and flung it across the room.

"No!" Domingo yelled. "Handel was supposed to wait! *Now* what?"

Now we roast, I thought, stumbling back with my arm raised against the flames. A calm tenor voice asked, "Are you suffering from excessive heat?"

"Yes! Dammit, yes!"

A huge rubber ball slammed into my back, hurling me at the wall. I braced my arms to take up some of the impact. It was still going to knock me silly. Just before I reached it, the wall disappeared. It was the outside wall. Completely off balance, I dashed through an eight-foot hole and out into the empty night, six floors above concrete.

I clenched my teeth on the scream. The ground came up—the ground came up—where the hell was the ground? I opened my eyes. Everything was happening in slow motion. A second stretched to eternity. I had time to see strollers turning to crane upward, and to spot Handel near a corner of the building, holding a handkerchief to his bleeding nose. Time to look over my shoulder as Domingo stood against a flaming background, poised in slow-motion in an eight-foot circle cut through the wall of my apartment.

Flame licked him. He jumped.

Slow motion?

He went past me like a falling safe. I saw him hit; I heard him hit. It's not a good sound. Living on Wall Street during November '68, I heard it night after night during the weeks following the election. I never got used to it.

Despite everything my belly and groin were telling me, I was not falling. I was sinking, like through water. By now half a dozen people were watching me settle. They all had their mouths open. Something poked me in the side, and I slapped at it and found myself clutching a .45 slug. I plucked another off my cheek. Handel was shooting at me.

I fired back, not aiming too well. If the martian hadn't been "helping" me I'd have blown his head off without a thought. As it was—anyway, Handel turned and ran.

I touched ground and walked away. A dozen hot, curious eyes bored into my back, but nobody tried to stop me.

There was no sign of the martian. Nothing else followed me either. I spent half an hour going through the usual contortions to shake a tail, but that was just habit. I wound up in a small, anonymous bar.

My eyebrows were gone, giving me a surprised look. I found myself studying my reflection in the bar mirror, looking for other signs that I'd been in a fight.

My face, never particularly handsome, has been dignified by scar tissue over the years, and my light brown hair never wants to stay in place. I had to move the part a year back to match a bullet crease in my scalp. The scars were all there, but I couldn't find any new cuts or bruises. My clothes weren't mussed. I didn't hurt anywhere. It was all unreal and vaguely dissatisfying.

But my next brush with Sinc would be for real.

I had my GyroJet and a sparse handful of rocket slugs in one pocket. Sinc's mansion was guarded like Fort Knox. And Sinc would be expecting me; he knew I wouldn't run.

We knew a lot about each other, considering we'd never met.

Sinc was a teetotaler. Not a fanatic; there was liquor on the premises of his mansion/fort. But it had to be kept out of Sinc's sight.

A woman usually shared his rooms. Sinc's taste was excellent. He changed his women frequently. They never left angry, and that's unusual. They never left poor, either.

I'd dated a couple of Sinc's exes, letting them talk about Sinc if they cared to. The consensus:

Sinc was an all-right guy, a spender, inventive and enthusiastic where it counted.

And neither particularly wanted to go back.

Sinc paid well and in full. He'd bail a man out of jail if the occasion arose. He never crossed anyone. Stranger yet, nobody ever crossed him. I'd had real trouble learning anything about Sinc. Nobody had wanted to talk.

But he'd crossed Domingo. That had caught us both by surprise.

Put it different. Someone had crossed Domingo. Domingo had been waiting for rescue, not bombs. So had I. It was Sinc's policy to pull his boys out if they got burned.

Either Domingo had been crossed against Sinc's orders, or Sinc was serious about wanting me dead.

I meet all kinds of people. I like it that way. By now I knew enough about Sinc to want to know more, much more. I wanted to meet him. And I was damn glad I'd shaken the martian, because . . .

Just what was it that bugged me about the martian?

It wasn't the strangeness. I meet all kinds. The way he shifted shape could throw a guy, but I don't bug easy.

Manners? He was almost too polite. And helpful.

Much too helpful.

That was part of it. The lines of battle had been drawn . . . and then something had stepped in from outer space. He was deus ex machina, the angel who descends on a string to set everything right, and incidentally to ruin the story. Me tackling Sinc with the martian's help was like a cop planting evidence. It was wrong. But more than that, it seemed to rob the thing of all its point, so that nothing mattered.

I shrugged angrily and had another drink. The bartender was trying to close. I drank up fast and walked out in a clump of tired drunks.

My car had tools I could use, but by now there'd be a bomb under the hood. I caught a cab and gave him an address on Bellagio, a couple of blocks from Sinc's place, if you can number anything in that area in "blocks." It's all hills, and the streets can drive you nuts. Sinc's home ground was a lumpy triangle with twisted sides, and big. It must have cost the Moon to landscape. One afternoon I'd walked past it, casing it. I couldn't see anything except through the gate. The fence was covered by thick climbing ivy. There were alarms in the ivy.

I waited till the taxi was gone, then loaded the GyroJet and started walking. That left one rocket slug still in my pocket.

In that neighborhood there was something to duck behind every time a car came by. Trees, hedges, gates with massive stone pillars. When I saw headlights I ducked, in case Sinc's boys were patrolling. A little walking took me to within sight of the ivy fence. Any closer and I'd be spotted.

So I ducked onto the property of one of Sinc's neighbors.

The place was an oddity: a rectangular pool with a dinky poolhouse at one end, a main house that was all right angles, and, between the two, a winding brook with a small bridge across it and trees hanging over the water. The brook must have been there before the house, and some of the trees too. It was a bit of primal wilderness that jarred strangely with all the right angles around it. I stuck with the brook, naturally.

This was the easy part. A burglary rap was the worst that could happen to me.

I found a fence. Beyond was asphalt, streetlamps, and then the ivy barrier to Sinc's domain.

Wire cutters? In the car. I'd be a sitting duck if I tried to go over. It could have been sticky, but I moved along the fence, found a rusty gate, and persuaded the padlock to open for me. Seconds later I was across the street and huddled against the ivy, just where I'd taken the trouble to hunt out a few of the alarms.

Ten minutes later I went over.

Sitting duck? Yes. I had a clear view of the house, huge and mostly dark. In the moment before I dropped, someone would have had a clear view of me, too, framed by lamplight at the top of the fence.

I dropped between inner and outer fence and took a moment to think. I hadn't expected an inner fence. It was four feet of solid brick topped by six feet of wiring; and the wiring had a look of high voltage.

Now what?

Maybe I could find something to short out the fence. But that would alert the house just as I was going over. Still, it might be the best chance.

Or I could go back over the ivy and try the gate defenses. Maybe I could even bluff my way through. Sinc must be as curious about me by now as I was about him. Everything I knew about Sinc was in the present tense. Of his past I knew only that there were no records of his past. But if Sinc had heard about my floating lightly down from a sixth-floor window, not unlike Mary Poppins . . . it might be worth a try. At least I'd live long enough to see what Sinc looked like.

Or—

"Hello. How does your war proceed?"

I sighed. He drifted down beside me, still man-shaped, dressed in a dark suit. I saw my mistake when he got closer. He'd altered his skin color to make a suit, shirt, and tie. At a distance it would pass. Even close up, he had nothing that needed hiding.

"I thought I'd got rid of you," I complained. "Are you bigger?" At a guess, his size had nearly doubled.

"Yes. I became hungry."

"You weren't kidding about your appetite."

"The war," he reminded me. "Are you planning to invade?"

"I was. I didn't know about this fence."

"Shall I—?"

"No! No, you shall not whatever you were thinking about. Just watch!"

"What am I to watch? You have done nothing for several minutes."

"I'll think of something."

"Of course."

"But whatever I do, I won't use your help, now or ever. If you want to watch, fine, be my guest. But don't help."

"I do not understand why not."

"It's like bugging a guy's telephone. Sinc has certain rights, even if he is a crook. He's immune from cruel and unusual punishment. The FBI can't bug his phone. You can't kill him unless you try him first, unless he's breaking a law at the time. And he shouldn't have to worry about armed attack by martians!"

"Surely if Sinc himself breaks the rules—"

"There are *rules* for dealing with lawbreakers!" I snapped.

The martian didn't answer. He stood beside me, seven feet tall and pudgy, a dark, manlike shape in the dim light from the house.

"Hey. How do you do all those things you do? Just a talent?"

"No. I carry implements." Something poked itself out of his baby-smooth chest, something hard that gleamed like metal. "This, for instance, damps momentum. Other portable artifacts lessen the pull of gravity, or reprocess the air in my lung."

"You keep them all inside you?"

"Why not? I can make fingers of all sizes inside me."

"Oh."

"You have said that there are rules for dealing with rule breakers. Surely you have already broken those rules. You have trespassed on private property. You have departed the scene of an accident, Don Domingo's death. You have—"

"All right."

"Then—"

"All right, I'll try again." I was wasting too much time. Getting over the fence was important. But so, somehow, was this. Because in a sense the martian was right. This had nothing to do with rules . . .

"It has nothing to do with rules," I told him. "At least, not exactly. What counts is power. Sinc has taken over this city, and he'll want others too, later. He's got too much power. That's why someone has to stop him.

"And you give me too much power. A—a man who has too much power loses his head. I don't trust myself with you on my side. I'm a detective. If I break a law I expect to be jailed for it unless I can explain why. It makes me careful. If I tackle a crook who can whip me, I get bruised. If I shoot someone who doesn't deserve it, I go to prison. It all tends to make me careful. But with you around—"

"You lose your caution," said the dark bulk beside me. He spoke almost musingly, with more of human expression than I'd heard before. "You may be tempted to take more power than is good for you. I had not expected your species to be so wise."

"You thought we were stupid?"

"Perhaps. I had expected you to be grateful and eager for any help I might give. Now I begin to understand your attitude. We, too, try to balance out the amount of power given to individuals. What is that noise?"

It was a rustling, a scampering, barely audible but not at all furtive.

"I don't know."

"Have you decided upon your next move?"

"Yes. I—damn! Those are dogs!"

"What are dogs?"

Suddenly they were there. In the dark I couldn't tell what breed, but they were big, and they didn't bark. In a rustling of claws scrabbling on cement, they rounded the curve of the brick wall, coming from both sides, terribly fast. I hefted the GyroJet and knew there were twice as many dogs as I had shots.

Lights came on, bright and sudden, all over the grounds. I fired, and a finger of flame reached out and touched one of the dogs. He fell, tumbling, lost in the pack.

All the lights went deep red, blood red. The dogs stopped. The noise stopped. One dog, the nearest, was completely off the ground, hovering in mid-leap, his lips skinned back from sharp ruby teeth.

"It seems I have cost you time," the martian murmured. "May I return it?"

"What did you do?"

"I have used the damper of inertia in a projected field. The effect is as if time has stopped for all but us. In view of the length of time I have kept you talking, it is the least I can do."

Dogs to the left and dogs to the right, and lights all the hell over the place. I found men with rifles placed like statues about the wide lawn.

"I don't know if you're right or wrong," I said. "I'll be dead if you turn off that time stopper. But this is the last time. Okay?"

"Okay. We will use only the inertia damper."

"I'll move around to the other side of the house. Then you turn off the gadget. It'll give me some time to find a tree."

We went. I stepped carefully among the statues of dogs. The martian floated behind like a gigantic, pudgy ghost.

The channel between inner and outer fence went all the way around to the gate of the front of the house. Near the gate the inner fence pinched against the outer, and ended. But before we reached that point I found a tree. It was big, and it was old, and one thick branch stretched above the fence to hover over our heads.

"Okay, turn off the gadget."

The deep red lights glared a sudden white.

I went up the ivy. Long arms and oversized hands are a big help to my famous monkey act. No point now in worrying about alarms. I had to balance standing on the outer fence to reach the branch with my fingers. When I put my weight on it it dipped three feet and started to creak. I moved along hand over hand, and swung up into the leaves before my feet could brush the inner fence. At a comfortable crotch I settled myself to take stock.

There were at least three riflemen on the front lawn. They were moving in a search pattern, but they didn't expect to find anything. All the action was supposed to be in back.

The martian floated into the air and moved across the fence.

He nicked the top going over. A blue spark snapped, and he dropped like a sack of wheat. He landed against the fence, grounded now, and electricity leaped and sizzled. Ozone and burnt meat mixed in the cold night air. I dropped out of the tree and ran to him. I didn't touch him. The current would have killed me.

It had certainly killed him.

And that was something I'd never thought of. Bullets didn't faze him. He could produce miracles on demand. How could he be killed by a simple electric fence? If he'd only mentioned that! But he'd been surprised even to find that we had electricity.

I'd let a bystander be killed. The one thing I'd sworn I would never do again . . .

Now he was nothing like human. Metal things poked gleaming from the dead mass that had been an anthropologist from the stars. The rustle of current had stopped seconds ago. I pulled one of the metal gadgets out of the mass, slid it in a pocket, and ran.

They spotted me right away. I took a zigzag course around a fenced tennis court, running for the front door. There were man-length windows on either side of the door. I ran up the steps, brought the GyroJet down in a hurried slashing blow that broke most of the panes in one window, and dove off the steps into a line of bushes.

When things happen that fast, your mind has to fill the gaps between what you saw and what you didn't. All three gunmen chased me frantically up the steps and through the front door, shouting at the tops of their lungs.

I moved along the side of the house, looking for a window.

Somebody must have decided I couldn't go through all that jagged glass. He must have outshouted the others, too, because I heard the hunt start again. I climbed a piece of wall, found a little ledge outside a darkened second-floor window. I got the window up without too much noise.

For the first time on this crazy night, I was beginning to think I knew what I was doing. That seemed odd, because I didn't know much about the layout of the house, and I hadn't the faintest idea where I was. But at least I knew the rules of the game. The variable, the martian, the deus ex machina, was out of the picture.

The rules were: whoever saw me would kill me if he could. No bystanders, no good guys would be here tonight. There would be no complex moral choices. I would not be offered supernatural help, in return for my soul or otherwise. All I had to do was try to stay alive.

(But a bystander had died.)

The bedroom was empty. Two doors led to a closet and a bathroom. Yellow light seeped under a third door. No choice here. I pulled the GyroJet and eased the third door open.

A face jerked up over the edge of a reading chair. I showed it the gun, kept it aimed as I walked around in front of the chair. Nobody else was in the room.

The face could have used a shave. It was beefy, middle-aged, but symmetrical enough except for an oversized nose. ''I know you,'' it said, calmly enough considering the circumstances.

"I know you too." It was Adler, the one who'd gotten me into this mess, first by cohabiting with Morrison's wife and then by killing Morrison.

"You're the guy Morrison hired," said Adler. "The tough private eye. Bruce Cheseborough. Why couldn't you let well enough alone?"

"I couldn't afford to."

"You couldn't afford not to. Have some coffee."

"Thanks. You know what'll happen if you yell or anything?"

"Sure." He picked up a water glass, dumped the water in the wastebasket. He picked up a silver thermos and poured coffee into his own coffee cup and into the water glass, moving slowly and evenly. He didn't want to make me nervous.

He himself was no more than mildly worried. That was reassuring, in a way, because he probably wouldn't do anything stupid. But . . . I'd seen this same calm in Don Domingo, and I knew the cause. Adler and Domingo and everyone else who worked for Sinc, they all had perfect faith in him. Whatever trouble they were in, Sinc would get them out.

I watched Adler take a healthy gulp of coffee before I touched the glass. The coffee was black and strong, heavily laced with good brandy. My first gulp tasted so good I damn near smiled at Adler.

Adler smiled back. His eyes were wide and fixed, as if he were afraid to look away from me. As if he expected me to explode. I tried to think of a way he could have dropped something in the coffee without drinking it himself. There wasn't any.

"You made a mistake," I told him, and gulped more coffee. "If my name had been Rip Hammer or Mike Hero, I might have dropped the whole thing when I found out you were with Sinc's boys. But when your name is Bruce Cheseborough, Junior, you can't afford to back out of a fight."

"You should have. You might have lived." He said it without concentrating on it. A puzzled frown tugged at the corners of his eyes and mouth. He was still waiting for something to happen.

"Tell you what. You write me out a confession, and I can leave here without killing anyone. Won't that be nice?"

"Sure. What should I confess to?"

"Killing Morrison."

"You don't expect me to do that."

"Not really."

"I'm going to surprise you." Adler got up, still slow, and went behind the desk. He kept his hands high until I was around behind him. "I'll write your damn confession. You know why? Because you'll never use it. Sinc'll see to that."

"If anyone comes through that door—"

"I know, I know." He started writing. While he was at it, I examined the tool I'd taken from the martian's corpse. It was white shiny metal, with a complex shape that was like nothing I'd ever seen. Like the plastic guts in a toy gun, half melted and then cooled, so that all the parts were merged and rounded. I had no idea what it did. Anyway, it was no good to me. I could see slots where buttons or triggers were buried, but they were too small for fingers. Tweezers might have reached them, or a hatpin.

Adler handed me the paper he'd been writing on. He'd made it short and pointed: motive, means, details of time. Most of it I already knew.

"You don't say what happened to the body."

"Same thing that happened to Domingo."

"Domingo?"

"Domingo, sure. When the cops came to pick him up in back of your place, he was gone. Even the bloodstains were gone. A miracle, right?" Adler smiled nastily. When I didn't react he looked puzzled.

"How?" I asked him.

Adler shrugged uncomfortably. "You already know, don't you? I won't write it down. It would bring Sinc in. You'll have to settle for what you've got."

"Okay. Now I tie you up and wend my way homeward."

Adler was startled. He couldn't have faked it. "Now?"

"Sure. You killed my client, not Sinc."

He grinned, not believing me. And he still thought something was about to happen.

I used the bathrobe sash for his arms and a handkerchief for a gag. There were other bathrobes in the closet to finish the job. He still didn't believe I was going to leave, and he was still waiting for something to happen. I left him on the bed, in the dark.

Now what?

I turned off the lights in the sitting room and went to the window. The lawn was alive with men and dogs and far too much light. That was the direct way out.

I had Adler's hide in my pocket. Adler, who had killed my client. Was I still chasing Sinc? Or should I try to get clear with that piece of paper?

Get clear, of course.

I stood by the window, picking out shadows. There was a lot of light, but the shadows of bushes and trees were jet black. I found a line of hedge, lighted on this side; but I could try the other. Or move along *that* side of the tennis court, then hop across to *that* odd-looking statue—

The door opened suddenly, and I whirled.

A man in dark slacks and a smoking jacket stood facing my gun. Unhurriedly, he stepped through the door and closed it behind him.

It was Sinc. Lester Dunhaven Sinclair III was a man in perfect condition, not a pound overweight or underweight, with gymnasium muscles. I guessed his age at thirty-four or so. Once before I'd seen him, in public, but never close enough to see what I saw now: that his thick blond hair was a wig.

He smiled at me. "Cheseborough, isn't it?"

"Yah."

"What did you do with my . . . lieutenant?" He looked me up and down. "I gather he's still with us."

"In the bedroom. Tied up." I moved around to lock the door to the hall.

I understood now why Sinc's men had made him into something like a feudal overlord. He measured up. He inspired confidence. His confidence in himself was total. Looking at him, I could almost believe that nothing could stand against him.

"I gather you were too intelligent to try the coffee. A pity," said Sinc. He seemed to be examining my gun, but with no trace of fear. I tried to think it was a bluff, but I couldn't. No man could put across such a bluff. His twitching muscles would give him away. I began to be afraid of Sinc.

"A pity," he repeated. "Every night for the past year Adler has gone to bed with a pot of coffee spiked with brandy. Handel too."

What was he talking about? The coffee hadn't affected me at all. "You've lost me," I said.

"Have I?" Smiling as if he'd won a victory, Sinc began to gurgle. It was eerily familiar, that gurgle. I felt the rules changing again, too fast to follow. Smiling, gurgling rhythmically, Sinc put a hand in his pants pocket and pulled out an automatic. He took his time about it.

It was not a big gun, but it was a gun; and the moment I knew that, I fired.

A GyroJet rocket slug burns its solid fuel in the first twenty-five feet, and moves from there on momentum. Sinc was twenty-five feet away. Flame reached out to tap him on the shoulder joint, and Sinc smiled indulgently. His gun was steady on the bridge of my nose.

I fired at his heart. No effect. The third shot perforated the space between his eyes. I saw the hole close, and I knew. Sinc was cheating too.

He fired.

I blinked. Cold fluid trickled down from my forehead, stung my eyes, dribbled across my lips. I tasted rubbing alcohol.

"You're a martian too," I said.

"No need for insult," Sinc said mildly. He fired again. The gun was a squirtgun, a plastic kid's toy shaped like an automatic. I wiped the alcohol out of my eyes and looked at him.

"Well," said Sinc. "Well." He reached up, peeled his hair off, and dropped it. He did the same with his eyebrows and eyelashes. ''Well, where is he?''

''He told me he was an . . . anthropologist. Was he lying?''

''Sure, Cheseborough. He was the Man. The Law. He's tracked me over distances you couldn't even write down.'' Sinc backed up against a wall. ''You wouldn't even understand what my people called my crime. And you've no reason to protect him. He used you. Every time he stopped a bullet for you, it was to make me think you were him. That's why he helped you put on a floating act. That's why he disposed of Domingo's body. You were his stalking-horse. I'm supposed to kill you while he's sneaking up on me. He'll sacrifice you without a qualm. Now *where is he*?''

''Dead. He didn't know about electric fences.''

A voice from the hall, Handel's voice, bellowed, ''Mr. Sinclair! Are you all right in there?''

''I have a guest,'' Sinc called out. ''He has a gun.''

''What do we do?''

''Don't do anything,'' Sinc called to him. And then he started to laugh. He was losing his human contours, ''relaxing'' because I already knew what he was.

''I wouldn't have believed it,'' he chuckled. ''He tracked me all that way to die on an electric fence!'' His chuckles cut off like a broken tape, making me wonder how real they were, how real his laughter could be with his no doubt weird breathing system. ''The current couldn't kill him, of course. It must have shorted his airmaker and blown the battery.''

''The spiked coffee was for him,'' I guessed. ''He said he could be killed by organic poisons. He meant alcohol.''

''Obviously. And all I did was give you a free drink,'' he chuckled.

''I've been pretty gullible. I believed what your women told me.''

''*They* didn't know.'' He did a pretty accurate double take. ''You thought . . . Cheseborough, have I made rude comments about your sex life?''

''No. Why?''

''Then you can leave mine alone.''

He had to be kidding. No he didn't; he could take any shape he liked. Wow, I thought. Sinc's really gone native. Maybe he *was* laughing, or thought he was.

Sinc moved slowly toward me. I backed away, holding the useless gun.

''You realize what happens now?''

I took a guess. ''Same thing that happened to Domingo's body. All your embarrassing bodies.''

''Exactly. Our species is known for its enormous appetite.'' He moved toward me, the squirt gun forgotten in his right hand. His muscles had sagged and smoothed. Now he was like the first step in making a clay model of a man. But his mouth was growing larger, and his teeth were two sharp-edged horseshoes.

I fired once more.

Something smashed heavily against the door. Sinc didn't hear it. Sinc was melting, losing all form as he tried to wrap himself around his agony. From the fragments of his shattered plastic squirt gun, rubbing alcohol poured over what had been his hand and dripped to the floor.

The door boomed again. Something splintered.

Sinc's hand was bubbling, boiling. Sinc, screaming, was flowing out of his slacks and smoking jacket. And I . . . I snapped out of whatever force was holding me rooted, and I picked up the silver thermos and poured hot spiked coffee over whatever it was that writhed on the floor.

Sinc bubbled all over. White metal machinery extruded itself from the mass and lay on the rug.

The door crackled and gave. By then I was against the wall, ready to shoot anything that looked my way. Handel burst into the room and stopped dead.

He stood there in the doorway, while the stars grew old and went out. Nothing, I felt, could have torn his eyes from that twitching, bubbling mass. Gradually the mass stopped moving . . . and Handel gulped, got his throat working, shrieked, and ran from the room.

I heard the meaty thud as he collided with a guard, and I heard him babbling, "Don't go in there! Don't . . . oh, don't . . ." and then a sob, and the sound of uneven running feet.

I went into the bedroom and out the window. The grounds still blazed with light, but I saw no motion. Anyway, there was nothing out there but dogs and men.

• • •

• • •

> The long lens gave a good view through the observation port. Rick saw: half a dozen large masses, many more small ones and a myriad of tiny glinting points, all enmeshed in pearly fog. He heard Baker's voice behind him. "Duck's-eye view of a shotgun blast."
>
> LUCIFER'S HAMMER, 1977

PASSERBY

This story was sparked by an insurance advertisement.

• •

It was noon of a hot blue day. The park was lively with raised voices and bright clothing, children and adults and the geriatrics generation, of which I have the honor to be a member. I had come early enough to claim a bench, and was old and feeble enough to hold it.

I had brought a sandwich lunch in a Baggy. I ate slowly, saving out an orange and a second sac of beer for later. The populace danced before me, never dreaming that I was watching.

The afternoon sun burned warm on my scalp. A lizardlike torpor stole over me, so that the sound of adult voices and children's screaming-for-the-hell-of-it dimmed and faded.

But I heard the footsteps. They jarred the earth.

I opened my eyes and saw the rammer.

He was six feet tall and massively built. He wore a scarf and a pair of blue balloon pants, not too far out of style, but they didn't match. What they exposed of his skin was loose on him, as if he had shrunk within it. Indeed, he looked like a giraffe wearing an elephant's skin.

He walked without springs. His feet slapped hard into the gravel with all his weight behind them. Small wonder I had heard him coming. By now everyone in sight was either looking at him, or turning to see what everyone was looking at. Except the children, who had already lost interest.

To me he was irresistible.

There are the casual peoplewatchers who watch their neighbors in restaurants or monorail stations when they have nothing else to do. They develop their own amateurish technique, and they don't know what to look for, and they usually get caught. But I'm not that kind of people-watcher.

There are the fanatics, the dedicated ones, who learn their technique in a closed-circuit 3V class. They hold lifetime subscriptions to *Face In The Crowd* and *Eyes Of The City*, the hobby magazines. They write letters to the editor telling how they spotted Secretary-General Haruman in a drug store and he looked unhappy.

That's me.

And here I was not twenty yards from a rammer, a man from the stars.

He had to be that. His taste in clothing was odd, and his carelessly draped skin was alien. His legs had not yet learned to cushion his weight against Earth's heavier gravity. He projected an indefinable combination of discomfort and self-consciousness and interest and surprise and pleasure, that silently shouted: *Tourist*!

His eyes, looking out from behind the ill-fitting mask of his face, were bright and blue and happy. Our staring rudeness was noticed, but did not affect his almost religious joy. Nor did his feet, though they must have hurt. His smile was dreamy and very strange. Lift the corners of a spaniel's mouth with your forefingers, and you'd see such a smile.

He drew in life from the sky and the grass and the voices and the growing things. I watched his face and tried to read it. Was he the priest of some new Earth-worshipping religion? No. Probably he was seeing Earth for the first time: tuning his bio-rhythms to Earth for the first time, feeling Earthweight settle over and into his bones, watching suns rise twenty-four hours apart, until his very genes told him he was home.

It made his day when he saw the boy.

The boy was around ten, a handsome child, naked and tanned all over. (When I was growing up, even the infants wore clothing in public.) I had not noticed him until now, and he in turn had not noticed the rammer. He knelt on the path that passed my bench, his back toward me. I could not see what he was doing; but he was very intent and serious about it.

By now most of the passerby had turned away, from disinterest or an overdose of good manners. I watched the rammer watching the boy. I watched through half-closed eyes, practicing my famous imitation of an old man asleep in the sun. The Heisenberg Principle implies that no peoplewatcher should allow himself to be caught at it.

The boy stooped suddenly, then rose with his hands cupped. Moving with exaggerated care, he turned from the gravel path and crossed the grass toward a dark old oak.

The rammer's eyes went big and round. All his pleasure gave way to horror, and then the horror drained away and left nothing. The star man's eyes turned up in his head, his slack face went even slacker, and his knees began to buckle.

Stiff as I am these days, I reached him. I slid an admittedly bony shoulder under his armpit before he could fall. All the mass of him came gratefully down on me.

I should have folded like an accordion. Somehow I got the rammer to the bench before I had to let go of him. To an astonished matron I wheezed, "Get a doctor!"

She nodded briskly and waddled away. I turned back to the rammer.

Sick eyes looked up at me from under straight black bangs. The rammer's face was oddly tanned: dark where the sun could reach, white as milk where folded skin cast shadows. His chest and arms were like that too. Where the skin was pale it had paled further with shock. "No need for doctor," he whispered. "Not sick. Something I saw."

"Sure. Put your head between your legs. It'll keep you from fainting." I opened my remaining beer sac.

"I will be all right in a moment," he said from between his knees. He spoke the tongue oddly, and his weakness slurred it further. "It was the shock of what I saw."

"Here?"

"Yes. No. Not completely. . . ." He stopped to shift mental gears, and I handed him the beer. He looked at it as if wondering which end to suck on, found the nipple, raised the sac and half-drained it in one desperate draught.

"What was it you saw?" I asked.

He had to finish swallowing. "I saw an alien spacecraft. Without the spacecraft it would have meant nothing."

"What kind of ship? Smithpeople? Monks?" These are the only known spacegoing races, aside from ourselves. I'd never seen one of their ships; but they sometimes docked in the Léshy worlds.

The rammer's eyes narrowed in his quilted face. "I see. You think I speak of some registered alien ship in a human spaceport." His voice was no longer slurred; he picked his words with apparent care. "I was halfway between the Horvendile and Koschei systems, shipwrecked at the edge of lightspeed, waiting to die. And I saw a golden giant walking among the stars."

"A humanoid? Not a ship?"

"I . . . thought it was a ship. I can't prove it."

"Mmm."

"Let me tell you. I was a year and a half out from Horvendile, bound for Koschei. It would have been my first trip home in thirty-one years. . . ."

Flying a ramship under sail is like flying a spiderweb.

Even with the web retracted, a ramship is a flimsy beast. Cargo holds, external cargo netting and hooks, pilot cabin and life support system, and the insystem fusion motor are all contained in a rigid pod just three hundred feet long. All else is balloons and webbing.

At takeoff the balloons are filled with hydrogen fuel for the insystem fusion motor. By the time the ship reaches ramscoop speed the fuel is half gone, replaced by low-pressure gas. The balloons are retained as meteor shielding.

The ramscoop web is superconducting wire, thin as spiderweb, tens of thousands of miles of it. Coiled for takeoff, it forms a roll no bigger than the main pod. Put a uniform negative charge on it and it spreads to form a hoop two hundred miles across. It ripples at first under the differentiating fields. . . .

Interstellar hydrogen, thin as nothing, enters the mouth of the ramscoop web. An atom to a cubic centimeter. Differentiating fields compress it along the axis, compress it until it undergoes fusion. It burns in a narrow blue flame, yellow-tinged at the edges. The electromagnetic fields in the fusion flame begin to support the ramscoop web. Mighty forces add, making web and flame and incoming hydrogen one interlocking whole.

A rigid pod, invisibly small, rides the flank of a wispy cylinder of webbing two hundred miles across. A tiny spider on an enormous web.

Time slows down, distances compress at the higher velocities. Hydrogen flows faster through the web; the ramscoop fields increase in power, the web becomes more rigid, more stable.

A ship should not need supervision as it approaches the midpoint turnover.

"I was halfway to Koschei," said the rammer, "carrying the usual cargo: genetically altered seeds, machine prototypes, spices, and three corpsicles: passengers frozen for storage. We carry anything that cannot be sent by message laser.

"I still don't know what went wrong. I was asleep. I had been asleep for months, with a current pulsing through my brain. Perhaps a piece of meteoric iron entered the ramscoop. Perhaps the hydrogen grew thin for an hour, then thickened too fast. Perhaps we entered a sharply bounded OH+ region. In any case, something twisted the ramscoop field, and the web collapsed.

"I was wakened too late. The web had roman-candled, and was trailing the ship like a parachute that will not open. Wires must have touched, for much of the web was vaporized.

"It was my death," said the rammer. "Without the ramscoop web I was falling helplessly. I would enter the system of Koschei months too early, moving at nearly lightspeed, a dangerous missile. For my honor I must inform Koschei by laser, that I might be shot down before I arrive."

"Take it easy," I soothed him. His jaw had clenched, and the muscles that tightened in his face patterned the skin like a jigsaw puzzle. "Relax. It's all over. Smell the grass; you're on Earth now."

"I wept helplessly at first, though we consider weeping unmanly . . ."

The rammer looked around him as if coming awake. ''You are right. If I took off my shoes, would the law take offense?''

''No.''

He took his shoes off and wiggled his toes in the grass. His feet were too small for him, and his toes were long and agile, almost prehensile.

No doctor had appeared yet. Probably the matronly woman had simply walked away to avoid being involved. In any case, the rammer's strength had returned.

He said, ''On Koschei we tend to large girth. Gravity pulls less heavily at the meat of us. To qualify as a rammer I sweated away half my body weight, so that the unneeded two hundred earthweight pounds of me could be replaced by payload cargo.''

''You must have wanted the stars badly.''

''Yes. I was simultaneously learning disciplines whose very names most people can neither pronounce nor spell.'' The rammer pulled at his chin. The quilted skin stretched incredibly, and did not snap back immediately when he let go. ''I cut my weight by half, yet my feet hurt when I walk the Earth. My skin has not yet shrunk to fit my smaller mass. Perhaps you noticed.''

''What did you do about Koschei?''

''I sent the message. It would precede me to Koschei by just two ship's-months.''

''Then?''

''I thought to wait it out, to use what time was left to me. My taped library was adequate . . . but even in the face of death, I grew bored.

''After all, I had seen the stars before. Ahead they were blue-white and thickly clustered. To the side they were orange and red and somewhat sparse. Behind was black space, empty but for a handful of dying embers. Doppler shift made my velocity more than obvious. But there was no sense of *motion*, of *going* somewhere.

''A month and a half of this, and I was ready to go back to sleep.

''When the collision alarm went off, I tried to ignore it. My death was already certain. But the noise bothered me, and I went to the control room to shut it off. I saw then that a respectable mass was approaching, aimed dangerously, from behind.

''From behind! It was moving faster than my own ship! I searched among the sparse crimson dots with my scope at top magnification. Presently I found a golden man walking toward me.

''My first thought was that I had gone mad. My second was that my God had come for me. Then, as the intruder grew in the scope screen, I saw that it was not quite human.

''Somehow that made it better. A golden man walking between the stars was impossible. A golden alien was a lesser impossibility. At least I could examine it sanely.

''I found the alien larger than I had thought, much larger than human.

''It was a biped, definitely humanoid, with two arms and legs and a well-defined head. Its skin glowed like molten gold, all over, for it was hairless and without scales. Between its legs was nothing but smooth skin. Its feet were strange, without toes, and the knee and elbow joints were bulbous and knobby—''

''Were you really thinking in big expansive words like that?''

''I really was. I wanted to forget that I was terrified.''

''Oh.''

''The intruder was nearing fast. Three times I lowered the magnification. Each time I saw him more clearly. His hands were three-fingered, with a long middle finger and two thumbs. The knees and elbows were too far down the limbs, but seemed quite flexible. The eyes—''

''Flexible? You saw them move?''

The rammer became agitated. He stuttered; he had to stop to gain control of himself. When he spoke again he seemed to force the words through his throat.

''I . . . decided that the intruder was not actually walking. But as it approached my ship, it seemed to be walking on empty space.''

''Like a robot?''

''Like a not-quite-man. Like a Monk, perhaps, if we could see beneath the garment worn by Monk ambassadors.''

''But—''

''Think of a man-sized humanoid.'' The rammer would not let me interrupt. ''Think of him as belonging to a civilization advanced beyond our own. If his civilization had the power, and if he had the power within his civilization, and if he were very egotistical, then perhaps,'' said the rammer, ''perhaps he might command that a spacecraft be built in his own image.

''That is the way I thought of the intruder, in the ten minutes it took the intruder to reach me. I could not believe that a humanoid with smooth, molten gold skin would evolve in vacuum, nor that he could walk on emptiness. The humanoid shape is for gravity, for planets.

''Where does engineering become art? Once our ground-bound automobiles looked like spacecraft. An advanced spacecraft might be made to look like a given man, and move like him, yet still have the capabilities of a spacecraft. The man himself would ride inside. If a king or millionaire could cause this to be done, why, then he would stride like a god across the stars.''

''I wonder if you don't think of yourself in just that way.''

The rammer was astonished. ''Me? Nonsense. I am a simple rammer. But I find man-shaped spacecraft easier to believe in than golden giants walking on emptiness.''

''More comforting, too.''

"Yes." The rammer shuddered. "It came up very fast, so that I must damp the magnification to keep him in view. His middle finger was two joints longer than ours, and the thumbs were of different sizes. His eyes were set freakishly far apart, and too low in the head. They glowed red with their own light. His mouth was a wide, lipless horizontal line.

"Not once did I think to avoid the intruder. We could not have reached a collision course by accident. I assumed that he had altered course to follow me, and would alter course again to protect us.

"He was on me before I knew it. I had flipped the magnification down another notch, and when I looked the setting was at zero. I looked up at the sparse red stars, and found a golden dot as it exploded into a golden man.

"I blinked, of course. When my eyes opened he was reaching for me."

"For you?"

The rammer nodded convulsively. "For the pod of my ship. He was much larger than the pod, or rather, his ship was."

"You still thought it was a ship?" I would not have asked; but he kept changing the pronoun.

"I was looking for windows in the forehead and the chest. I did not find them. He moved like a very large man."

"I hate to suggest it," I said, "not knowing your religion. Could there be gods?"

He jumped as if stung. "Nonsense."

"How about superior beings? If we've evolved beyond the chimpanzees, couldn't—"

"No. Absolutely not," said the rammer. "You don't understand modern xenology. Do you not know that we and the Monks and the Smithpeople are all of equal intelligence? The Smithpeople are not remotely humanoid in shape, yet it makes no difference. When a species begins to use tools, evolution stops."

"I've heard that argument, but—"

"When a species begins to use tools, environment no longer shapes that species. The species shapes its environment to suit itself. Beyond this the species does not develop. It even begins to take care of its feebleminded and its genetically deficient.

"No, he could have better tools than mine, this intruder, but he could not be my intellectual superior. He was certainly nothing to worship."

"You seem awfully sure of that," I snapped.

Instantly I regretted it; for the rammer shivered and wrapped his arms around his chest. The gesture was ludicrous and pitiful at the same time, for his arms swept up an armful of folded skin and hugged it to him. "I needed to be sure. The intruder had taken my main pod in his hand and pulled me toward—toward his ship.

"I was glad of my crash straps. Without them I'd have bounced about like a pea in a dryer. As it was, I blacked out for an instant. When I opened my eyes I faced a great red iris with a black pupil.

"He looked me over with care. I . . . forced myself to look back. He had no ears, no chin. A bony ridge divided his face where a nose might have been, but there were no nostrils. . . .

"He pulled back for a better view of the main pod. This time I was not jolted. He must have realized that the jolting could hurt me, and done something to prevent it. Perhaps he made his ship inertialess.

"I saw him lift his eyes momentarily to see over my pod.

"You must remember that I was facing back along my own wake, back toward Horvendile, to where most of the stars had been red-shifted to black." The rammer was picking his words with care and patience. They came so slowly that I wanted to squirm. "I was not looking at the stars. But . . . suddenly there were a million clustered stars, and they were all white and bright.

"I did not understand. I put side and forward views on the screen. The stars looked the same in all directions. Still I did not understand.

"Then I turned back to the intruder. He was walking away across the sky.

"You must understand that as he walked, he receded at much faster than walking speed. Accelerating. In a few seconds he was invisible. I looked for signs of an exhaust, but there was none.

"Then I understood." The rammer lifted his head. "Where is the boy?"

"Boy?"

The rammer looked about him, his blue eyes searching. Children and adults looked back curiously, for he was a weird sight. He said, "I do not see the boy. Could he have left?"

"Oh, *that* boy. Sure, why not?"

"There is something I must see." The rammer eased his weight forward onto his bare and battered feet. I followed him as he crossed the gravel path, followed him onto the grass. And the rammer resumed his tale.

"The intruder had examined me and my ship with care. He had made himself and my ship inertialess, or otherwise cushioned us against acceleration. Then he had cancelled our velocity relative to Koschei."

"But that wasn't enough," I objected. "You'd still die."

The rammer nodded. "Still I was glad to see him go, at first. He was terrifying. And his last mistake was almost a relief. It proved that he was—human is not the word I want. But he could make mistakes."

"Mortal," I said. "He was mortal."

"I do not understand. But never mind. Think of the power of him. In a year and a half, at point six gravities, I had accelerated to a velocity which the intruder cancelled in no more than a second. I preferred death to his dreadful company. At first.

"Then I became afraid. It seemed unjust. He had found me halfway between stars, stranded, waiting to die. He had half-saved me—and then left me to die, no better off than before!

"I searched for him with the scope. Perhaps I could signal him, if I knew where to aim my com laser. . . . But I could not find him.

"Then I became angry. I—" The rammer swallowed. "I screamed insults after him. I blasphemed in seven different religions. The more distant he was, the less I feared him. I was reaching my stride when—when he returned.

"His face was outside my main window, his red eyes looked into mine, his strange hand was reaching for my main pod. My collision alarm was just beginning to sound, it had happened so suddenly. I screamed out—I screamed . . ." He stopped.

"What did you scream?"

"Prayers. I begged for forgiveness."

"Oh."

"He took my ship in his hand. I saw the stars explode in front of me."

We had reached the shade of a dark oak, one so old and so spread out that its lower limbs needed the support of iron pipes. A family picnicking beneath the tree watched our approach.

"Explode?"

"That lacks accuracy," the rammer apologized. "What happened was this: the stars became very much brighter, at the same time converging toward a point. They flared horribly. I was blinded. The intruder must have shifted me to within a meter-per-second of lightspeed.

"I rubbed my hand hard across my eyes. With my eyes closed, I felt acceleration. It remained constant while I waited for my eyes to recover. Through experience I was able to estimate its force at ten meters per second squared."

"But that's—"

"One gravity. When I could see again, I found myself on a yellow plain beneath a glaring blue sky. My pod was red hot, and was already sagging around me."

"Where did he put you?"

"On Earth, in a refertilized part of North Africa. My pod was never built for such things. If Earth's gravity collapsed it, then re-entry should have torn it to pieces. But the intruder must have taken care of that too."

I am a peoplewatcher, an expert. I can crawl into a man's mind without letting him know I exist. I never lose at poker. And I knew the rammer was not lying.

We stood beside the dark oak. The lowermost limb grew almost parallel to the ground, and was supported by three iron pipes. Long as were the rammer's arms, he could not have wrapped them around that limb. Its bark was rough and gray and powdery, and it smelled of dust. The top of it was level with the rammer's chin.

"You're a very lucky man," I said.

"No doubt. What is that?"

Black and furry, an inch and a half long; one end wiggling in blind curiosity as it moved along the bark.

"A caterpillar. You know, there's no computing the odds you ran against being alive now. You don't seem very cheerful about it."

"I was . . . but think about it," said the rammer. "Think what the intruder must have reasoned out, to do what he did.

"He looked through the main window to examine me as well as he could. I was tied to a chair by crash straps, and his sensors had to see through thick impact quartz designed for transparency in the other direction. He could see me, but only from the front. He could examine the ship, but it was damaged, and he had to guess to what extent.

"First he must have reasoned that I could not slow my ship without the ramscoop web. But he must also have deduced the presence of reserve fuel to decelerate me to zero speed from the lowest speed at which my ramscoop can operate. It is apparent that I must have it. Thus he stopped me dead, or nearly so, and left me to go home the slow way, using only my re-entry reserve fuel.

"After he had left me, he must have realized that I would be dead of age before I ended such a trip. Imagine how thorough his examination of me must have been! So he came back for me.

"By projecting my line of flight he must have known where I was going. But could I live there with a damaged ship? He did not know.

"And so he looked me over more carefully, deduced the star and planet where I must have evolved, and he put me there."

"That's pretty farfetched," I said.

"Yes! The solar system was twelve light-years distant, yet he reached it in an instant! But that is not the point. . . ." The rammer let his voice trail off. He seemed oddly fascinated by the black caterpillar, which was now defying gravity as it explored a vertical wall of bark. "He placed me not only on Earth, but in North Africa. He deduced not only my planet of origin, but the region where I had evolved.

"I stayed in my pod for two hours before I was found. Your United Nations police took a record of my mind, but they do not believe what they found. A ramship pod cannot be towed to Earth without radar finding it. Further, my ramscoop web is all over the desert. Even the hydrogen balloons survived the reentry. They think that it must be a hoax, that I was brainwashed as part of that hoax."

"And you? What do you think?"

Again the rammer's face tightened into jigsaw-puzzle lines. "I had convinced myself that the intruder was no more than another spacecraft pilot—a passerby who stopped to help, as some persons will stop to help if your car battery fails far from a city. His power might be greater than mine. He might be wealthier, even within the context of his own culture. We were of different species. Yet he had stopped to help a member of the great brotherhood, for we were both spacemen."

"Because your modern xenology says he couldn't have been your superior."

He didn't answer.

"I can pick a few holes in that theory."

"Can you?"

I ignored his disinterest. "You claim that evolution stops when a species starts building tools. But suppose two tool-users evolved on the same world? Then evolution might go on until one race was dead. We might have had real problems if the dolphins had had hands."

"It may be." He was still watching the caterpillar: an inch and a half of black fur exploring the dark bark. My ear brushed the bark as I faced him, and I smelled the damp wood.

"Then again, not all human beings are alike. There are Einsteins and there are morons. Your passerby might have been of a race that varies more. Make him a super-Einstein—"

"I had not thought of that. I had assumed that his deductions were made with the aid of a computer. At first."

"Then, a species could evolve itself. If they once started fiddling with their genes, they might not stop until their children were mile-high giants with a space drive stuck up their spines. What the *hell* is so interesting about the caterpillar?"

"You did not see what the boy did?"

"Boy? Oh. No, I didn't."

"There was a . . . caterpillar moving along the gravel walk. People passed. None looked down. The boy came, and he stooped to watch."

"Oh!"

"Presently the boy picked up the caterpillar, looked about him, then came here and put the caterpillar safely on the limb."

"And you fainted."

"I should not have been so affected by what, after all, is no more than a comparison. I would have cracked my skull had you not caught me."

"A poor return for the golden one, if you had."

The rammer did not smile. "Tell me . . . if an adult had seen the caterpillar, instead of a boy—"

"Probably he'd have stepped on it."

"Yes, I thought so." The rammer put his tongue in his cheek, which stretched incredibly. "He is nearly upside down. I hope he will not fall off."

"It won't."

"Do you think he is safe there?"

"Sure. Don't worry about it."

● ● ●

• • •

Water droplets come in all sizes here. Clouds may hold everything from fine mist, to globules the size of a fist, to spheroids that house all manner of life. The biggest "pond" we've seen massed ten million metric tons or so; but the tide from Levoy's Star had pulled it into two lobes and the differential winds were tearing it apart.

The ecology of the ponds is one rather than many. Life is queer and wonderful, but in every pond we have examined it is the same life. Ponds are temporary; pond life must occasionally migrate. In the Smoke Ring even the fish can fly.

THE SMOKE RING, 1987

DOWN IN FLAMES

The following requires some explanation. At least!

On January fourteenth, 1968, Norman Spinrad and I were at a party thrown by Tom and Terry Pinckard. We were filling coffee cups when Spinny started this whole thing.

"You ought to drop the Known Space series," he said. "You'll get stale." (Quotes are not necessarily accurate.)

I told him I was writing stories other than "Known Space" stories, and that I would give up the series as soon as I ran out of things to say within that framework. Which would be soon.

"Then why don't you write a story that tears it to shreds? Don't just *abandon* 'known space.' Destroy it!"

"But how?" I never did ask why. Norman and I think alike in some ways.

"Start with the premise that the whole thing is a shuck. There never was a chain reaction of novae in the galactic core. There *aren't* any thrintun. It's all a gigantic hoax. Write it that way. Then," said Spinny, "if the fans write letters threatening to lynch you, you write back saying, 'It's only a story . . .' "

We found a corner, and during the next four hours we worked out the details. Some I rejected. Like, he wanted to make the tnuctipun into minions of the Devil. (Yes, the Devil.) Like, he wanted me to be inconsistent. Why? Maybe to demonstrate my contempt for the story.

The incredible thing is that when we finished, we did indeed have a consistent framework. It's as complex as watchwork, more complex perhaps than WORLD OF PTAVVS, which was probably overcomplex; but it is consistent.

The structure it turns upside down already amounts to about 250,000 words. It includes three books (WORLD OF PTAVVS, A GIFT FROM EARTH, and the eight stories in NEUTRON STAR), and several stories published in *Galaxy*, including "The Adults" (*Galaxy*, June 1967). If you haven't read these (with the exception of A GIFT FROM EARTH, which is optional; published as "Slowboat Cargo" in *If*) then what follows will not make much sense.

What follows is, first, a list of the basic ideas behind "Down in Flames": changes in the structure of the "Known Space" series; and second, a rough plot outline.

I never got further than that. Along about April, I ran into an idea called a Dyson sphere. It gripped my imagination, and I designed a compromise structure which is in some ways superior: the Niven ring. It is the basis for a story called RINGWORLD.

RINGWORLD makes "Down in Flames" obsolete. The assumptions behind RINGWORLD are different assumptions. So "Down in Flames" becomes part of the limbo of unwritten stories, and nobody would ever have known about it were it not for Tom Reamy and *Trumpet*. Have fun.

PRELIMINARY OUTLINE:

1) Beowulf Shaeffer never went to the galactic core.
2) The alleged Quantum II hyperdrive ship in "At the Core" was a hoax. For eight months that ship rested somewhere in the West End of Jinx, while Beowulf Shaeffer thought he was making a round trip of 30,000 light-years. The puppeteer-built machinery he thought was hyperdrive equipment was cover-up for the real machinery: 3D movie projectors, sensory mechanisms, artificial gravity, et cetera.
3) The core is not exploding.
4) The thrintun/Slaver species never existed.
5) The tnuctipun are real enough; but they did not exist a billion and a half years ago. They are contemporary.
6) The puppeteers are in their pay.
7) They accepted employment because they dared not refuse the tnuctipun, which species is even more mean and vicious than I thought. And I never really liked them.
8) Obviously the puppeteers are not fleeing the radiation wave from the Core explosion. They are fleeing the tnuctipun. Another reason they accepted employment: they needed the funds to flee.
9) Kzanol is neither robot nor android. He is, now get this, he is a product of tnuctipun biological engineering: a tailored species with only one member! His memories are heavily detailed science fiction.
10) Many of the stasis boxes, ostensibly left behind after the Slaver War

a billion and a half years ago, are false. Others are for real. The genetically tailored plants and animals are real.

The tnuctipun once used a few worlds in Known Space. Jinx, for instance. They left behind them (not long ago; certainly less than a million years) a few stasis boxes, and, of course, the stage trees and bandersnatchi and sunflowers and so forth.

The only hoax involved is the Slaver War. Certain stasis boxes were left floating through Known Space; and Kzanol was created, very artistically, and dropped on the continental shelf for the dolphins to find. Other real evidence of the tnuctipun will be worked into the structure of the hoax. Thus the presence of the tnuctipun, *now*, will never be suspected.

11) The truth is that the tnuctipun are all through Known Space. It will be seen how this is possible.
12) The whitefood/bandersnatchi were not designed to spy on the thrintun/Slavers. Their purpose was much simpler. Tnuctipun enjoy feeding on the meat of sentient beings, so they built one.
13) As part of the hoax, they recently settled some of their number on a world of Known Space, with false memories and a drastically reduced technology. Their technology was just great enough that they could slow the advance of the frontiers of human space, until the tnuctipun could plant all the evidence they needed to.

    Another purpose of this group was to make it possible for tnuctipun to move freely about in Known Space.

    The group knows nothing of the tnuctipun or their plan. Their ancestors were not volunteers. They call themselves kzinti. Note that a tnuctipun caught doing anything, moral or not, in Known Space will be taken for a kzin.
14) Note also, a psychological point. Female kzinti are dumb animals, no more. Thus the kzinti may be thought of as asexual. So it is with the tnuctipun. A kzin will understand perfectly the kick they get from eating sentient meat. There has to be *something* to replace the missing sex kick.
15) This is one of the motives behind the hoax.
16) The core of the hoax is the Core explosion. In twenty thousand years, the alleged Core explosion will make all of Known Space uninhabitable. Thus, during the next twenty thousand years, Known Space must be evacuated by every sentient species.

The hoax may extend much further than Known Space. Refugees will be showing up from further in.

Most species will plan to return after the wave of radiation passes; or at least, they will consider the possibility. They will make at least some attempt to mothball their artifacts.

All the worlds of Known Space, with their maintenance machinery more or less preserved, will be open to the tnuctipun. Further, up to a trillion beings (and perhaps many more, depending how far the hoax extends) are available in spacecraft moving at Quantum I hyperdrive. All flavors, these beings. All moving at the same velocity; match direction and you've matched course for boarding. In most cases, no weapons; the species would concentrate on the enormous task of moving billions of individuals clear out of the galaxy, and would in most cases move as soon as they had the capability.

Obviously this must be the last of the Known Space stories. (If only Blish had stopped with the second Okie novel! He ended the universe there; and then he had to go backward!) Above are the assumptions I am forced to make to get a coherent picture. Some minor questions arise, and some are answered:

1) Why wasn't the Quantum II hyperdrive sold to some entrepreneur in human space? It was advertised for sale; why didn't someone buy it?

   Answer: those who tried couldn't get in contact with the right puppeteers. They got the runaround until they gave up in disgust. There is no Quantum II hyperdrive.
2) The Grogs are not the mutated descendants of the Slavers. They never claimed to be. But the tnuctipun knew of Grogs, and designed Kzanol with the Grogs in mind. They slipped up there. They should have made him female.
3) Since they were planted the Kzinti have changed. They were given a technology which would ensure their being beaten over and over again by the ships of human space. Evolution doesn't always hold for sentient beings who tailor their own environment instead of adapting to it, but it holds here. The most serious warmongers among kzinti, and the ones with the least self-control, were those who died first. And the kzinti population has dropped by half in half a dozen wars. Those left are not peaceable, but they have developed some self-control, some ability to think first before jumping. Further, telepaths are their own development.

   And they've been done wrong. Assuredly they will join the minions of human space when the hoax becomes known.
4) Consider "The Soft Weapon."

   It had to be a shuck, part of the hoax. The handle of the stasis box did not fit a kzinti, i.e. a tnuctip, claw. But a weapon so powerful could not be allowed to fall into the hands of humans.

So the tnuctipun planted the box for the Papandreous to find; but they were there to take it away, making sure the humans saw it first. Only one of the kzinti on the Traitor's Claw was a tnuctip. It was Flyer.

5) What of the Outsiders?

They are in no danger from the tnuctipun, who seek only meat of proper chemical composition. If they maintain their neutrality, nobody should harm them. And they must have known of the tnuctip plot for some time.

They sell information. How well can we balance profit against fear? Can we use them?

Obviously I am thinking in terms of Armageddon. The end result of exposure of the tnuctip fraud will be a cataclysm to shake the stars. Fire and death, and from here it looks like the tnuctipun will probably win. They will have no allies, none at all; but their technology will be enormous.

What happens to ships that go too deep into a gravity well? Snatched by the tnuctipun! There is no relevant physical law, no mysterious singularity in hyperspace. Such is part of the fraud; for the necessity of moving into a system at sublight speeds is enough to slow the spread of humanity and keep it from regions where the fraudulence of the Slaver War would become apparent. Their ships will be faster until we learn this.

Note that the tools we have found in Slaver stasis boxes are largely planted. They throw this technology away! What more are they hiding?

Now you have the background. What of the story itself?

I know some of the characters I'll need. Oddly, the most necessary are the most familiar. I'll need either Kzanol or Larry Greenberg to expose one side of the Slaver War hoax. At some point, on some city pedwalk, he will point to a large orange kzin and shout, "Heavens preserve us! It's a tnuctip!"

I'll need Beowulf Shaeffer. He's the key man in the Core explosion hoax.

It would be convenient to ring in Richard Harvey Schultz-Mann, expert on Slaver relics, to show how the hoax must have been worked, and to guess what must be true and what false.

Probably Elephant's money and ships will be needed for backing, as the tracking of the truth becomes a major project.

In addition, three strangers: a mountaineer girl with Plateau eyes (Matt Keller's power), and a kzin for a central character, and a grog to read the mind of a true-tnuctip prisoner.

DETAIL: KOBOLD

Brennan knows certain things. He knows them because he's had plenty of time to think about them and has figured them out.

He knows the *kind* of place to find the puppeteer world. He knows they probably took it with them.

He knows why the Outsiders follow starseeds. (But does he tell Shaeffer?)

He lives in a place he designed himself, using antigravity as an art form. It's way the hell out in the cometary belt of Sol, beyond the hyperspace singularity, but it didn't grow there; he built it from asteroids, in the Belt. It's Kobold. In Kobold, streams flow two ways; you can swim on either side of a stream; the tongue of flat rock which extends out as a runway for spacecraft has service installations back to back. On that space-port tongue are tractors to draw the ships into the air. A huge version of the ''pressure curtain'' in ''Relic of Empire'' surrounds the whole setup, except for the spaceport tongue. There are rooms for sports never invented before, including many that could be enjoyed only by adult-stage humans. Detail:

The sphere covered with grass. It's five hundred meters through, and that's all there is: grass, one asymmetrically shaped pool, and a huge tree. You reach it by jumping from another point to the top branches of the tree, then climbing down. Note that the sphere touches no other part of Kobold.

A kind of museum, holding sculptures made of water. Fields hold the place and shape of each statue.

The Moebius miniature golf course.

The shadowed place: a life support system for Outsiders, with mooring facilities for any kind of ship. Brennan can talk to them through a pressure curtain, with him on one side under pressure, and the Outsider in low-gee and vacuum.

The ''Finagle bullet'' mounted somewhere, with lighted warning signs. It's a captured ten-foot sphere of neutronium, like others in Known Space. There are other such traps, suitably labeled; in an emergency Brennan can turn off the signs. Even the machinery which makes the signs will vanish without a trace. That's one reason Brennan rarely invites humans to Kobold.

One thing about Kobold: its wonders are *human* wonders. There is nothing like the peculiar floor construction in WRONG WAY STREET. The things Brennan does with his artificial gravity and his fusion plants and his high IQ are the things any human would do, given an impulse to play.

PLOT:

1

Beowulf Shaeffer is relaxing somewhere, probably in an anarchpark, when the Brennan-monster taps him on the shoulder. "I need you," he says, and produces credentials. Shaeffer suffers himself to be led away, knowing very little. But Brennan has mentioned the Core explosion and Shaeffer's trip.

2

At the spaceport, gunshots. (Weaponry, anyway.) In fact, the weapons being used are unfamiliar, but they eat holes in things quick as hell. (They will turn out to be an improvement on the disintegrator, with two parallel beams, one to suppress electron charge, one to suppress proton charge. Brennan suspects this from the start.)

The shots lash out around them, and Brennan takes them both in a mad run. Knowing that losing a major limb would kill Shaeffer, he takes a beam meant for Shaeffer and loses a leg, cauterizes it with his own X-ray laser, and off they go, Brennan hopping.

What being has been shooting? It turns out to be a species as agile as Phssthpok, but without much brain. One thing marks them at once: they are drones of some kind. Perhaps there is a sentient queen bee somewhere.

3

They reach Brennan's ship and take off. En route, the Brennan-monster explains something of what he is, and gets Bey to go over the tale of his Core trip.

4

At Kobold, Brennan puts Shaeffer under drugs and gets a transcript of the Core trip. He still hasn't said what he's after. Whatever it is, he doesn't get it. Yet he knows it's there, if only because he and Shaeffer were shot at.

He does his research on the corpse of their attacker—the one he saved for examination. He guides Shaeffer around Kobold. They talk . . . (Exposition here!)

And Shaeffer mentions the trip to *Swoosh*.

Brennan knows a good deal about the Outsiders, and shows it.

Shaeffer wonders about some of the questions he was asked on that interview.

When Shaeffer names one question—"What will you do now that you know the Core is exploding?"—Brennan hops up yelling, "That's it!" Right then, the attack begins.

5

The attack starts with a whistle of a set frequency. Brennan blurs into motion. A pressure suit hits Shaeffer, and he stands stupidly holding it. Brennan flips some switches, *one* motion of both hands, and is gone in a long jump across one of the gaps on Kobold's space.

The beam spears him in midair, vaporizes him, and blasts the gravity controls.

Kobold's air gathers itself to vanish into space. Shaeffer, in sudden free fall, can hear the whisper of it. He jumps for the only door in sight. In his own opinion, this is quicker than trying to don the pressure suit in time.

The door is not marked. But Brennan has turned off all the markings.

Shaeffer is inside, safe. He inhales once in relief, once in glorious disbelief, once to find out where the incredibly delicious smell is coming from. Then his mind is off, and he's tracking the tree-of-life root, down through the corridors of Kobold's heart.

6

Shaeffer's transition from a vegetable to a superman is instantaneous, or nearly so. In his next moment of self-awareness he is consciously giving up every plan he ever had. He will never be a father. His travels, if any, will not be with Sharrol. Chances are he will never see Elephant again. Et cetera.

That's his first moment. His next is a driving urge to kill every last Grog. These are the only beings he *knows* must be destroyed. Then it comes to him that Brennan did *not* exterminate the Grogs.

Why?

Review the Grog problem, with reference to the Slavers, etc.

Why didn't Brennan take care of this? Is the answer connected with the other problem, the one he solved when Shaeffer said what he said? And what the hell did the Outsiders have to do with anything, including the Core explosion, which is even more important (though less urgent) than the Grogs?

There is some unknown race trying to destroy him. It has already destroyed Brennan. Further, Shaeffer must reach civilization without standard transport. But the Grog problem is most clearly defined, most puzzling, therefore most urgent. Shaeffer puts it first on agenda.

7

Escape is his first action. There's no ship; there's not much left of Kobold. Presumably the attackers were nonsentient, the same species that attacked them earlier. They may have been searching for thinking minds with a detector. This would explain why Shaeffer lived.

There's no ship, and no drive per se. But there are the gravity generators. Shaeffer lines them up as a momentum tube and aims himself for the sun. Someone is bound to discover him before he gets there.

Somebody does. The nonsentient enemy makes one more attack, as Shaeffer's makeshift ship drops toward the solar system. Shaeffer uses the momentum tube to throw rocks at them, following with the Finagle's Bullet. They go into hyperspace to avoid the rocks, and the mass of the Bullet keeps them there—forever.

Then the Pluto Watch picks him up. Shortly he's in contact with the few humans who know of him.

8

Now he has a small human army. He does research.

Data on Grogs tells him very little. But he sees the major point. If the Grogs are degenerate but dangerous Slavers, how did the dominant sex switch from male to female?

He needs the advice of a Slaver expert.

9

Rich Mann is on Silvereyes. Shaeffer finds him, takes his corpses along. Arranges a safe way of reviving Kzanol and instantly killing him.

Mann quickly recognizes the corpse as a tnuctip artifact.

Kzanol is a fraud.

What else is a fraud? Shaeffer shows Mann the corpse of one of his attackers. That, too, is a product of tnuctip biological engineering.

The tnuctipun are alive and well. Now what?

Chains of hypothesis lead Shaeffer to assume that there was no Slaver War, or indeed, even a Slaver race. Kzanol was copied from the Grogs, but the tnuctipun, whose sentient members are male, made him male.

Shaeffer can only guess the purpose of the deception. Since there was plenty of evidence of the tnuctipun presence, the beasties contrived a fraud to make it look like they had been gone a billion and a half years. Whereas they were actually contemporary, and dangerous.

What are they planning?

10

They need a Grog. Shaeffer and Mann leave Silvereyes for Gummidgy.

They are in hyperdrive when Shaeffer figures it out. He asks himself, what could the Outsiders have answered? How could their answer be so important?

By now he has an accomplice. Mann has used just enough booster-spice to put him in the right age bracket. Shaeffer has fed him tree-of-life.

What answer?

We will die. No.

We will flee. No.

The radiation cannot harm us. No.

We have a protection. Maybe. If it will work on humans.

The radiation is not dangerous. Maybe. Not even to humans?

There was no Core explosion. Nonsense. I saw it. *The whole thing was a hoax*. To what purpose? Yet there is *already* a hoax involved, and the tnuctipun are involved. *The whole thing was a tnuctip hoax. They blackmailed the puppeteers. The puppeteers then fled, not the Core explosion, but the tnuctipun*. Great! but the Crosshatch species—

The Crosshatchers are tnuctipun.

And their purpose is obvious.

11

Also obvious: the tnuctipun/crosshatchers can enter a ship in hyperdrive. Shaeffer sets up defenses and waits.

The attack comes. Again it's the nonsentient warriors, and again they lose. Mann-monster and Shaeffer-monster reach Earth.

Suspicions confirmed.

12

Now dig Shaeffer's complex plan.

The ships which are already fleeing the Core explosion, have decided to go up along the galactic axis to get clear space, then cut out toward the rim.

There is *no* Quantum II hyperdrive. Shaeffer is restricted to a light-year per three days. But he can take a diagonal and catch the third of the human ships. First and second are beyond his reach.

He takes a #4 hull, and half the men who know what he is. He takes them off boosterspice. In about ten years, he intercepts the third ship. (During the ten years, he has figured out how the tnuctip interception technique works.) Destroys boosterspice reserves of the ship. Leaves some of his men in control, drops back to the next ship. Repeats. Goes to third ship alone.

He now has three ships. The third, he controls alone. The first two are in the hands of adults who know what is going on.

Twenty years later, the first two ships have a number of protectors aboard. In thirty years, all three ships are all protectors.

Shaeffer's hypothesis: the tnuctipun come not from the Core, but from the rim. Thus all ships will move right into their territory. But where exactly are they? They've already come five thousand light-years.

Ten years and 1200 light years later, comes the attack.

13

So it's war.

And after the tnuctipun are exterminated, what then? Maybe it can't be done. If it can, then starts the final war.

Protector against protector, until only one is left.

It'll be quite a war. The stars will fall in flames. And the novel will end just as it is getting started. (Maybe not. I never end a novel as I thought I would.)

• • •

• • •

"It is a star with a ring around it," said the puppeteer. "A ring of solid matter. An artifact."

RINGWORLD, 1970

From RINGWORLD

Today it may not be obvious, but when I wrote RINGWORLD it was an act of courage.

Designing the Ringworld wasn't the hardest part, though I still found surprises as I traveled. The difficult part was to describe it without losing the reader! This was an environment outside all common experience, yet I planned to give the reader puzzles to be solved as he traveled. (If I don't have a puzzle, I don't have a story. It's not just a quirk. I'm a compulsive teacher.)

Then there was Teela Brown. Psi powers were common in fiction then, and I was fed up. With Teela I set out to show the ultimate psychic power: Author Control. As soon as it's obvious what Teela's power *is*, she's moved offstage; but it's still a lot to ask of a reader, that he continue to suspend his disbelief.

I used high-school geometry. Mercator maps at one-to-one scale laid across the width (forty) and length (24,000). The shadows of night subtend the same angle all the way around. From a few miles off the edge, everything looks like straight lines converging. Don Davis did a wonderful painting of this, in the moment of Mount Fist-of-God's formation.

I wanted the reader braced, forewarned against the Ringworld. I gave him the puppeteers' Fleet of Worlds as an intermediate step, to build his imagination. I showed him pictures and gave him scale comparisons and analogies. I stayed with one viewpoint and few characters, to keep it simple where I could. I let the size of the structure, the nature of it ("the mask of a world"), come as a recurring surprise to the characters.

Today you could fill a long shelf with books about (in David Gerrold's phrase) "the Enormous Big Thing." Eighteen years ago, RINGWORLD was the first to be written since the days when *all* the science was imaginary . . . since, say, Simak's *The Cosmic Engineers*.

Risky. The publishers must have agreed. RINGWORLD appeared as a paperback. There was no serial. The first hardback version appeared seven years later.

I didn't know what the response would be. Would *you* see what I saw? The artistry of a near-infinite landscape carved to order, the mask of a world stretched over vacuum, the incredible energies, the room for mistakes and the room to leave consequences behind, the hints of God-level civilizations since collapsed . . . Maybe none of you would understand it at all. Maybe you would laugh at the Ringworld.

"Playgrounds for the mind," remember? The Ringworld is the best playground I ever built. People have been reading RINGWORLD and commenting on the assumptions, overt and hidden, and the mathematics and the ecology and the philosophical implications, precisely as if it were a proposed engineering project and they were being paid for their work.

From Washington, D.C., there came a full proofreading job on the first edition of RINGWORLD, with the title "The Niven-MacArthur Papers, Vol. I." Robert MacArthur was of enormous help to me. That first edition had some serious mistakes in it.

A Florida high-school class determined that all of the Ringworld's topsoil will end up in the oceans in a few thousand years.

From Cambridge came an estimate for the minimum tensile strength of scrith: of the order of magnitude of the force that holds an atomic nucleus together.

Freeman Dyson has no trouble believing in the Ringworld, but can't see why the engineers wouldn't have built a lot of little ones instead. Safer.

In Philadelphia a member of the audience pointed out that, mathematically, the Ringworld can be treated as a suspension bridge with no endpoints. Simple in concept; harder to build.

Neil Jones wrote "Investigation of an Artifact" (*Durfed* 2) to demonstrate that the Pierson's puppeteers built the Ringworld. (I disagree.)

At the 1970 World Science Fiction Convention, students in the halls were chanting, "The Ringworld is unstable! The Ringworld is unstable!" Yeah, it needs attitude jets. Ctein and Dan Alderson, computer wizards working independently, took several years to work out the *exact* instability. Ctein also worked out data on *moving* the Ringworld. (*Yes*, for fun. Isn't that how you have fun?)

A stranger redesigned the shadow squares for me, too. There's too much twilight in my version, too much of partial sunlight. His superior version (in a thick envelope that included sketches) involves five much longer shadow squares moving *retrograde* . . . but of course it was too late to redesign *that*.

Did you laugh at RINGWORLD? Damn right you did!

The weekly fan magazine *APA-L* printed, as back covers, a string of cartoons showing huge structures of peculiar shape, usually with a sun hovering somewhere near the center. There was Wringworld and Wrongworld and Rinkworld and Rungworld (a tremendous stepladder, terraformed landscapes on the steps), and sketches of the Ringworld with lettering along the underside: ONE RING TO RULE THEM ALL and OCCUPANCY BY MORE THAN 3×10^{16} PERSONS IS DANGEROUS AND UNLAWFUL.

One of the interchangeable Hollander brothers wrote a short story, "Cupworld," using "half a Dyson sphere, with spaceports along the handle." There's a play, "Stringworld," based on *The Wizard of Oz*. One Thomas J. Remington agreed: his article demonstrates that I used the plot line from *The Wizard of Oz*! Harry Harrison borrowed the Ringworld to make a point about population control, in *Star Smashers of the Galaxy*

Rangers. There's a song, "The Ringworld Engineers," and a verse in a filksong:

"Oh the Ringworld is unstable,
Oh the Ringworld is unstable!
Did the best that he was able,
And it's good enough for me!"

Dan Alderson, making proper use of playground equipment, designed a system with four Ringworlds. Three are in contact with each other, spinning orthogonally to each other on frictionless bearings. But the fourth was built by Mesklinites (see Hal Clement's *Mission of Gravity.*) It's the size of Jupiter's orbit (Mesklinites like it cold) and to maintain hundreds of times Earth's surface gravity, it spins at an appreciable fraction of lightspeed. (I asked Dan if spinning it closer to lightspeed would cause it to contract like a noose. **No.**)

Ringworld has won awards: the Hugo and Nebula, and Best Foreign awards from Japan and Australia. There have been paintings. The aliens, the kzinti and puppeteers, have appeared in sketches and sculpture.

I've found some text that allows all of the major characters to demonstrate who and what they are. A quote that fully describes the Ringworld is impossible.

• •

"You fight with light," said the man with the tattooed hand. "Surely this is forbidden."

"—!" the crowd shouted, and was as suddenly silent.

"We did not know it," said Louis. "We apologize."

"Did not know it? How could you not know it? Did you not raise the Arch in sign of the Covenant with Man?"

"What arch is that?"

The hairy man's face was hidden, but his astonishment was evident. "The Arch over the world, O Builder!"

Louis understood then. He started to laugh.

The hairy man punched him unskillfully in the nose.

The blow was light, for the hairy man was slight and his hands were fragile. But it hurt.

Louis was not used to pain. Most people of his century had never felt pain more severe than that of a stubbed toe. Anesthetics were too prevalent, medical help was too easily available. The pain of a skier's broken leg usually lasted seconds, not minutes, and the memory was often suppressed as an intolerable trauma. Knowledge of the fighting disciplines, karate, judo, ju-jitsu, and boxing, had been illegal since long before Louis Wu was born. Louis Wu was a lousy warrior. He could face death, but not pain.

The blow hurt. Louis screamed and dropped his flashlight-laser.

The audience converged. Two hundred infuriated hairy men became a thousand demons; and things weren't nearly as funny as they had been a minute ago.

The reed-thin spokesman had wrapped both arms around Louis Wu, pinioning him with hysterical strength. Louis, equally hysterical, broke free with one frantic lunge. He was on his 'cycle, his hand was on the lift lever, when reason prevailed.

The other 'cycles were slaved to his. If he took off, they would take off, with or without their passengers.

Louis looked about him.

Teela Brown was already in the air. From overhead she watched the fight, her eyebrows puckered in concern. She had not thought of trying to help.

Speaker was in furious motion. He'd already felled half a dozen enemies. As Louis watched, the kzin swung his flashlight-laser and smashed a man's skull.

The hairy men milled about him in an indecisive circle.

Long-fingered hands were trying to pull Louis from his seat. They were winning, though Louis gripped the saddle with hands and knees. Belatedly he thought to switch on the sonic fold.

The natives shrieked as they were snatched away.

Someone was still on Louis's back. Louis pulled him away, let him drop, flipped the sonic fold off and then on again to eject him. He scanned the ex-parking lot for Nessus.

Nessus was trying to reach his 'cycle. The natives seemed to fear his alien shape. Only one blocked his way; but that one was armed with a metal rod from some old machine.

As Louis located them, the man swung the rod at the puppeteer's head.

Nessus snatched his head back. He spun on his forelegs, putting his back to danger, but facing away from his flycycle.

The puppeteer's own flight reflex had killed him—unless Speaker or Louis could help him in time. Louis opened his mouth to shout, and the puppeteer completed his motion.

Louis closed his mouth.

The puppeteer turned to his 'cycle. Nobody tried to stop him. His hind hoof left bloody footprints across the hard-packed dirt.

Speaker's circle of admirers were still out of his reach. The kzin spat at their feet—not a kzinti gesture but a human one—turned and mounted his 'cycle. His flashlight-laser was gory up to the elbow of his left hand.

The native who had tried to stop Nessus lay where he had fallen. Blood pooled lavishly about him.

The others were in the air. Louis took off after them. From afar he saw what Speaker was doing, and he called, "Hold it! That's not necessary."

Speaker had drawn the modified digging tool. He said, "Does it have to be necessary?"

But he had stayed his hand. "Don't do it," Louis implored him. "It'd be murder. How can they hurt us now? Throw rocks at us?"

"They may use your flashlight-laser against us."

"They can't use it at all. There's a taboo."

"So said the spokesman. Do you believe him?"

"Yah."

Speaker put his weapon away. (Louis sighed in relief; he'd expected the kzin to level the city.) "How would such a taboo evolve? A war of energy weapons?"

"Or a bandit armed with the Ringworld's last laser cannon. Too bad there's nobody to ask."

"Your nose is bleeding."

Now that he came to think about it, Louis's nose stung painfully. He slaved his 'cycle to Speaker's and set about making medical repairs. Below, a churning, baffled lynch mob swarmed at the outskirts of Zignamuclickclick.

• • •

"They should have been kneeling," Louis complained. "That's what fooled me. And the translation kept saying 'builder' when it should have been saying 'god.' "

"God?"

"They've made gods of the Ringworld engineers. I should have noticed the silence. Tanjit, nobody but the priest was making a sound! They all acted like they were listening to some old litany. Except that I kept giving the wrong responses."

"A religion. How weird! But you shouldn't have laughed," Teela's intercom image said seriously. "Nobody laughs in church, not even tourists."

They flew beneath a fading silver of noon sun. The Ringworld showed above itself in glowing blue stripes, brighter every minute.

"It seemed funny at the time," said Louis. "It's still funny. They've forgotten they're living on a ring. They think it's an arch."

A rushing sound penetrated the sonic fold. For a moment it was a hurricane, then it cut off sharply. They had crossed the speed of sound.

Zignamuclickclick dwindled behind them. The city would never have its vengeance on the demons. Probably it would never see them again.

"It *looks* like an arch," said Teela.

"Right. I shouldn't have laughed. We're lucky, though. We can leave our mistakes behind us," said Louis. "All we have to do, any time, is get airborne. Nothing can catch us."

"Some mistakes we must carry with us," said Speaker-To-Animals.

"Funny you should say so." Louis scratched absently at his nose, which was as numb as a block of wood. It would be healed before the anaesthetic wore off.

He made up his mind. "Nessus?"

"Yes, Louis."

"I realized something, back there. You've been claiming that you're insane because you demonstrate courage. Right?"

"How tactful you are, Louis. Your delicacy of tongue—"

"Be serious. You and all the other puppeteers have been making the same wrong assumption. A puppeteer instinctively turns to run from danger. Right?"

"Yes, Louis."

"Wrong. A puppeteer instinctively turns *away* from danger. It's to free his hind leg for action. That hoof makes a deadly weapon, Nessus."

All in one motion, the puppeteer had spun on his forelegs and lashed out with his single hind leg. His heads were turned backwards and spread wide, Louis remembered, to triangulate on his target. Nessus had accurately kicked a man's heart out through his splintered spine.

"I could not run," he said. "I would have been leaving my vehicle. That would have been dangerous."

"But you didn't stop to think about it," said Louis. "It was instinctive. You automatically turn your back on an enemy. Turn, and kick. A sane puppeteer turns to fight, not to run. You're not crazy."

"You are wrong, Louis. Most puppeteers run from danger."

"But—"

"The majority is always sane, Louis."

Herd animal! Louis gave it up. He lifted his eyes to watch the last sliver of sun disappear.

Some mistakes we must carry with us . . .

But Speaker must have been thinking of something else when he said that. Thinking of what?

At the zenith swarmed a ring of black rectangles. The one that hid the sun was framed in a pearly coronal glow. The blue Ringworld formed a paraboloid arch over it all, framed against a star-dotted sky.

It looked like something done with a Build-A-City set, by a child too young to know what he was doing.

Nessus had been steering when they left Zignamuclickclick. Later he had turned the fleet over to Speaker. They had flown all night. Now, overhead, a brighter glow along one edge of the central shadow square showed that dawn was near.

Sometime during these past hours, Louis had found a way to visualize the scale of the Ringworld.

It involved a Mercator projection of the planet Earth—a common, rectangular, classroom wall map—but with the equator drawn to one-to-one scale. One could relief-sculpt such a map, so that standing near the equator would be exactly like standing on the real Earth. But one could draw forty such maps, edge to edge, across the width of the Ringworld.

Such a map would be greater in area than the Earth. But one could map it into the Ringworld's topography, and look away for a moment, and never be able to find it again.

One could play cuter tricks than that, given the tools that shaped the Ringworld. Those matching salt oceans, one on each side on the ring, had each been larger in area than any world in human space. Continents, after all, were only large islands. One could map the Earth on to such an ocean and still have room left over at the borders.

"I shouldn't have laughed," Louis told himself. *It took me long enough to grasp the scale of this . . . artifact. Why should I expect the natives to be more sophisticated?*

Nessus had seen it earlier. Night before last, when they had first seen the arch, Nessus had screamed and tried to hide.

"Oh, what the tanj . . ." It didn't matter. Not when all mistakes could be left behind at twelve hundred miles per hour.

• • •

• • •

Speaker-to-Animals said one thing more before he turned back to his table. "Louis Wu, I found your challenge verbose. In challenging a kzin, a simple scream of rage is sufficient. You scream and you leap."

RINGWORLD, 1970

THE FOURTH PROFESSION

The doorbell rang around noon on Wednesday.

I sat up in bed and—it was the oddest of hangovers. My head *didn't* spin. My sense of balance was quiveringly alert. At the same time my mind was clogged with the things I knew: facts that wouldn't relate, churning in my head.

It was like walking the high wire while simultaneously trying to solve an Agatha Christie mystery. Yet I was doing neither. I was just sitting up in bed, blinking.

I remembered the Monk, and the pills. How many pills?

The bell rang again.

Walking to the door was an eerie sensation. Most people pay no attention to their somesthetic senses. Mine were clamoring for attention, begging to be tested—by a backflip, for instance. I resisted. I don't have the muscles for doing backflips.

I couldn't remember taking any acrobatics pills.

The man outside my door was big and blond and blocky. He was holding an unfamiliar badge up to the lens of my spy-eye, in a wide hand with short, thick fingers. He had candid blue eyes, a square, honest face—a face I recognized. He'd been in the Long Spoon last night, at a single table in a corner.

Last night he had looked morose, introspective, like a man whose girl has left him for Mr. Wrong. A face guaranteed to get him left alone. I'd noticed him only because he wasn't drinking enough to match the face.

Today he looked patient, endlessly patient, with the patience of a dead man.

And he had a badge. I let him in.

"William Morris," he said, identifying himself. "Secret Service. Are you Edward Harley Frazer, owner of the Long Spoon Bar?"

"Part-owner."

"Yes, that's right. Sorry to bother you, Mr. Frazer. I see you keep bartender's hours." He was looking at the wrinkled pair of underpants I had on.

"Sit down," I said, waving at the chair. I badly needed to sit down myself. Standing, I couldn't think about anything but standing. My balance was all conscious. My heels would not rest solidly on the floor. They barely touched. My weight was all on my toes; my body insisted on standing that way.

So I dropped onto the edge of the bed, but it felt like I was giving a trampoline performance. The poise, the grace, the polished ease! Hell. "What do you want from me, Mr. Morris? Doesn't the Secret Service guard the President?"

His answer sounded like rote-memory. "Among other concerns, such as counterfeiting, we do guard the President and his immediate family and the President-elect, and the Vice President if he asks us to." He paused. "We used to guard foreign dignitaries too."

That connected. "You're here about the Monk."

"Right." Morris looked down at his hands. He should have had an air of professional self-assurance to go with the badge. It wasn't there. "This is an odd case, Frazer. We took it because it used to be our job to protect foreign visitors, and because nobody else would touch it."

"So last night you were in the Long Spoon guarding a visitor from outer space."

"Just so."

"Where were you night before last?"

"Was that when he first appeared?"

"Yah," I said, remembering. "Monday night . . ."

He came in an hour after opening time. He seemed to glide, with the hem of his robe just brushing the floor. By his gait he might have been moving on wheels. His shape was wrong, in a way that made your eyes want to twist around to straighten it out.

There is something queer about the garment that gives a Monk his name. The hood is open in front, as if eyes might hide within its shadow, and the front of the robe is open too. But the loose cloth hides more than it ought to. There is too much shadow.

Once I thought the robe parted as he walked toward me. But there seemed to be nothing inside.

In the Long Spoon was utter silence. Every eye was on the Monk as he took a stool at one end of the bar, and ordered.

He looked alien, and was. But he *seemed* supernatural.

He used the oddest of drinking systems. I keep my house brands on three long shelves, more or less in order of type. The Monk moved down the top row of bottles, right to left, ordering a shot from each bottle. He took his liquor straight, at room temperature. He drank quietly, steadily, and with what seemed to be total concentration.

He spoke only to order.

He showed nothing of himself but one hand. That hand looked like a chicken's foot, but bigger, with lumpy-looking, very flexible joints, and with five toes instead of four.

At closing time the Monk was four bottles from the end of the row. He paid me in one-dollar bills, and left, moving steadily, the hem of his robe just brushing the floor. I testify as an expert: he was sober. The alcohol had not affected him at all.

"Monday night," I said. "He shocked the hell out of us. Morris, what was a Monk doing in a bar in Hollywood? I thought all the Monks were in New York."

"So did we."

"Oh?"

"We didn't know he was on the West Coast until it hit the newspapers yesterday morning. That's why you didn't see more reporters yesterday. We kept them off your back. I came in last night to question you, Frazer. I changed my mind when I saw that the Monk was already here."

"Question *me*. Why? All I did was serve him drinks."

"Okay, let's start there. Weren't you afraid the alcohol might kill a Monk?"

"It occurred to me."

"Well?"

"I served him what he asked for. It's the Monks' own doing that nobody knows anything about Monks. We don't even know what shape they are, let alone how they're put together. If liquor does things to a Monk, it's his own look-out. Let *him* check the chemistry."

"Sounds reasonable."

"Thanks."

"It's also the reason I'm here," said Morris. "We know too little about the Monks. We didn't even know they existed until something over two years ago."

"Oh?" I'd only started reading about them a month ago.

"It wouldn't be that long, except that all the astronomers were looking in that direction already, studying a recent nova in Sagittarius. So they caught the Monk starship a little sooner; but it was already inside Pluto's orbit.

"They've been communicating with us for over a year. Two weeks ago they took up orbit around the Moon. There's only one Monk starship, and only one ground-to-orbit craft, as far as we know. The ground-to-orbit craft has been sitting in the ocean off Manhattan Island, convenient to the United Nations Building, for those same two weeks. Its crew are supposed to be all the Monks there are in the world.

"Mr. Frazer, we don't even know how your Monk got out here to the

West Coast! Almost anything you could tell us would help. Did you notice anything odd about him, these last two nights?''

''Odd?'' I grinned. ''About a Monk?''

It took him a moment to get it, and then his answering smile was wan. ''Odd for a Monk.''

''Yah,'' I said, and tried to concentrate. It was the wrong move. Bits of fact buzzed about my skull, trying to fit themselves together.

Morris was saying, ''Just talk, if you will. The Monk came back Tuesday night. About what time?''

''About four thirty. He had a case of—pills—RNA . . .''

It was no use. I knew too many things, all at once, all unrelated. I knew the name of the Garment to Wear Among Strangers, its principle and its purpose. I knew about Monks and alcohol. I knew the names of the five primary colors, so that for a moment I was blind with the memory of the colors themselves, colors no man would ever see.

Morris was standing over me, looking worried. ''What is it? What's wrong?''

''Ask me anything.'' My voice was high and strange and breathless with giddy laughter. ''Monks have four limbs, all hands, each with a callus heel behind the fingers. I know their names, Morris. Each hand, each finger. I know how many eyes a Monk has. One. And the whole skull is an ear. There's no word for *ear*, but medical terms for each of the—resonating cavities—between the lobes of the brain . . .''

''You look dizzy. You don't sample your own wares, do you, Frazer?''

''I'm the opposite of dizzy. There's a compass in my head. I've got absolute direction. Morris, it must have been the pills.''

''Pills?'' Morris had small, squarish ears that couldn't possibly have come to point. But I got that impression.

''He had a sample case full of—education pills . . .''

''Easy now.'' He put a steadying hand on my shoulder. ''Take it easy. Just start at the beginning, and talk. I'll make some coffee.''

''Good.'' Coffee sounded wonderful, suddenly. ''Pot's ready. Just plug it in. I fix it before I go to sleep.''

Morris disappeared around the partition that marks off the kitchen alcove from the bedroom/living room in my small apartment. His voice floated back. ''Start at the beginning. He came back Tuesday night.''

''He came back Tuesday night,'' I repeated.

''Hey, your coffee's already perked. You must have plugged it in in your sleep. Keep talking.''

''He started his drinking where he'd left off, four bottles from the end of the top row. I'd have sworn he was cold sober. His voice didn't give him away . . .''

• • •

His voice didn't give him away because it was only a whisper, too low to make out. His translator spoke like a computer, putting single words together from a man's recorded voice. It spoke slowly and with care. Why not? It was speaking an alien tongue.

The Monk had had five tonight. That put him through the ryes and the bourbons and the Irish whiskeys, and several of the liqueurs. Now he was tasting the vodkas.

At that point I worked up the courage to ask him what he was doing.

He explained at length. The Monk starship was a commercial venture, a trading mission following a daisy chain of stars. He was a sampler for the group. He was mightily pleased with some of the wares he had sampled here. Probably he would order great quantities of them, to be freeze-dried for easy storage. Add alcohol and water to reconstitute.

"Then you won't be wanting to test all the vodkas," I told him. "Vodka isn't much more than water and alcohol."

He thanked me.

"The same goes for most gins, except for flavorings." I lined up four gins in front of him. One was Tanqueray. One was a Dutch gin you have to keep chilled like some liqueurs. The others were fairly ordinary products. I left him with these while I served customers.

I had expected a mob tonight. Word should have spread. *Have a drink in the Long Spoon, you'll see a Thing from Outer Space*. But the place was half empty. Louise was handling them nicely.

I was proud of Louise. As with last night, tonight she behaved as if nothing out of the ordinary was happening. The mood was contagious. I could almost hear the customers thinking: *We like our privacy when we drink. A Thing from Outer Space is entitled to the same consideration.*

It was strange to compare her present insouciance with the way her eyes had bugged at her first sight of a Monk.

The Monk finished tasting the gins. "I am concerned for the volatile fractions," he said. "Some of your liquors will lose taste from condensation."

I told him he was probably right. And I asked, "How do you pay for your cargos?"

"With knowledge."

"That's fair. What kind of knowledge?"

The Monk reached under his robe and produced a flat sample case. He opened it. It was full of pills. There was a large glass bottle full of a couple of hundred identical pills; and these were small and pink and triangular. But most of the sample case was given over to big, round pills of all colors, individually wrapped and individually labelled in the wandering Monk script.

No two labels were alike. Some of the notations looked hellishly complex.

"These are knowledge," said the Monk.

"Ah," I said, and wondered if I was being put on. An alien can have a sense of humor, can't he? And there's no way to tell if he's lying.

"A certain complex organic molecule has much to do with memory," said the Monk. "Ribonucleic acid. It is present and active in the nervous systems of most organic beings. Wish you to learn my language?"

I nodded.

He pulled a pill loose and stripped it of its wrapping, which fluttered to the bar like a shred of cellophane. The Monk put the pill in my hand and said, "You must swallow it now, before the air ruins it, now that it is out of its wrapping."

The pill was marked like a target in red and green circles. It was big and bulky going down.

"You must be crazy," Bill Morris said wonderingly.

"It looks that way to me, too, now. But think about it. This was a Monk, an alien, an ambassador to the whole human race. He wouldn't have fed me anything dangerous, not without carefully considering all the possible consequences."

"He wouldn't, would he?"

"That's the way it seemed." I remembered about Monks and alcohol. It was a pill memory, surfacing as if I had known it all my life. It came too late . . .

"A language says things about the person who speaks it, about the way he thinks and the way he lives. Morris, the Monk language says a lot about Monks."

"Call me Bill," he said irritably.

"Okay. Take Monks and alcohol. Alcohol works on a Monk the way it works on a man, by starving his brain cells a little. But in a Monk it gets absorbed more slowly. A Monk can stay high for a week on a night's dedicated drinking.

"I knew he was sober when he left Monday night. By Tuesday night he must have been pretty high."

I sipped my coffee. Today it tasted different, and better, as if memories of some Monk staple foods had worked their way as overtones into my taste buds.

Morris said, "And you didn't know it."

"Know it? I was counting on his sense of responsibility!"

Morris shook his head in pity, except that he seemed to be grinning inside.

"We talked some more after that—and I took some more pills."

"Why?"

"I was high on the first one."

"It made you drunk?"

"Not drunk, but I couldn't think straight. My head was full of Monk words all trying to fit themselves to meanings. I was dizzy with nonhuman images and words I couldn't pronounce."

"Just how many pills did you take?"

"I don't remember."

"Swell."

An image surfaced. "I do remember saying, 'But how about something unusual? *Really* unusual.' "

Morris was no longer amused. "You're lucky you can still talk. The chances you took, you should be a drooling idiot this morning!"

"It seemed reasonable at the time."

"You don't remember how many pills you took?"

I shook my head. Maybe the motion jarred something loose. "That bottle of little triangular pills. I know what they were. Memory erasers."

"Good God! You didn't . . ."

"No, no, Morris. They don't erase your whole memory. They erase pill memories. The RNA in a Monk memory pill is tagged somehow, so that the eraser pill can pick it out and break it down."

Morris gaped. Presently he said, "That's incredible. The education pills are wild enough, but *that* . . . You see what they must do, don't you? They hang a radical on each and every RNA molecule in each and every education pill. The active principle in the eraser pill is an enzyme for just that radical."

He saw my expression and said, "Never mind, just take my word for it. They must have had the education pills for a hundred years before they worked out the eraser principle."

"Probably. The pills must be very old."

He pounced. "How do you know that?"

"The name for the pill has only one syllable, like *fork*. There are dozens of words for kinds of pill reflexes, for swallowing the wrong pill, for side effects depending on what species is taking the pill. There's a special word for an animal training pill, and another one for a slave training pill. Morris, I think my memory is beginning to settle down."

"Good!"

"Anyway, the Monks must have been peddling pills to aliens for thousands of years. I'd guess tens of thousands."

"Just how many kinds of pill were in that case?"

I tried to remember. My head felt congested . . .

"I don't know if there was more than one of each kind of pill. There were four stiff flaps like the leaves of a book, and each flap had rows of little pouches with a pill in each one. The flaps were maybe sixteen pouches long by eight across. Maybe. Morris, we ought to call Louise. She probably remembers better than I do, even if she noticed less at the time."

"You mean Louise Schu the barmaid? She might at that. Or she might jar something loose in your memory."

"Right."

"Call her. Tell her we'll meet her. Where's she live, Santa Monica?"

He'd done his homework, all right.

Her phone was still ringing when Morris said, "Wait a minute. Tell her we'll meet her at the Long Spoon. And tell her we'll pay her amply for her trouble."

Then Louise answered and told me I'd jarred her out of a sound sleep, and I told her she's be paid amply for her trouble, and she said what the hell kind of a crack was *that*?

After I hung up I asked, "Why the Long Spoon?"

"I've thought of something. I was one of the last customers out last night. I don't think you cleaned up."

"I was feeling peculiar. We cleaned up a little, I think."

"Did you empty the wastebaskets?"

"We don't usually. There's a guy who comes in in the morning and mops the floors and empties the wastebaskets and so forth. The trouble is, he's been home with the flu the last couple of days. Louise and I have been going early."

"Good. Get dressed, Frazer. We'll go down to the Long Spoon and count the pieces of Monk cellophane in the wastebaskets. They shouldn't be too hard to identify. They'll tell us how many pills you took."

I noticed it while I was dressing. Morris's attitude had changed subtly. He had become proprietary. He tended to stand closer to me, as if someone might try to steal me, or as if I might try to steal away.

Imagination, maybe. But I began to wish I didn't know so much about Monks.

I stopped to empty the percolator before leaving. Habit. Every afternoon I put the percolator in the dishwasher before I leave. When I come home at three A.M. it's ready to load.

I poured out the dead coffee, took the machine apart, and stared.

The grounds in the top were fresh coffee, barely damp from steam. They hadn't been used yet.

There was another Secret Service man outside my door, a tall Midwesterner with a toothy grin. His name was George Littleton. He spoke not a word after Bill Morris introduced us, probably because I looked like I'd bite him.

I would have. My balance nagged me like a sore tooth. I couldn't forget it for an instant.

Going down in the elevator, I could feel the universe shifting around me. There seemed to be a four-dimensional map in my head, with me in the center and the rest of the universe traveling around me at various changing velocities.

The car we used was a Lincoln Continental. George drove. My map became three times as active, recording every touch of brake and accelerator.

"We're putting you on salary," said Morris, "if that's agreeable. You know more about Monks than any living man. We'll class you as a consultant and pay you a thousand dollars a day to put down all you remember about Monks."

"I'd want the right to quit whenever I think I'm mined out."

"That seems all right," said Morris. He was lying. They would keep me just as long as they felt like it. But there wasn't a thing I could do about it at the moment.

I didn't even know what made me so sure.

So I asked, "What about Louise?"

"She spent most of her time waiting on tables, as I remember. She won't know much. We'll pay her a thousand a day for a couple of days. Anyway, for today, whether she knows anything or not."

"Okay," I said, and tried to settle back.

"You're the valuable one, Frazer. You've been fantastically lucky. That Monk language pill is going to give us a terrific advantage whenever we deal with Monks. They'll have to learn about us. We'll know about them already. Frazer, what does a Monk look like under the cowl and robe?"

"Not human," I said. "They only stand upright to make us feel at ease. And there's a swelling along one side that looks like equipment under the robe, but it isn't. It's part of the digestive system. And the head is as big as a basketball, but it's half hollow."

"They're natural quadrupeds?"

"Yah. Four-footed, but climbers. The animal they evolved from lives in forests of like giant dandelions. They can throw rocks with any foot. They're still around on Center; that's the home planet. You're not writing this down."

"There's a tape recorder going."

"Really?" I'd been kidding.

"You'd better believe it. We can use anything you happen to remember. We still don't even know how your Monk got out here to California."

My Monk, forsooth.

"They briefed me pretty quickly yesterday. Did I tell you? I was visiting my parents in Carmel when my supervisor called me yesterday morning. Ten hours later I knew just about everything anyone knows about Monks. Except you, Frazer.

"Up until yesterday we thought that every Monk on Earth was either in the United Nations Building or aboard the Monk ground-to-orbit ship.

"We've been in that ship, Frazer. Several men have been through it, all trained astronauts wearing lunar exploration suits. Six Monks landed on Earth—unless more were hiding somewhere aboard the ground-to-orbit ship. Can you think of any reason why they should do that?"

"No."

"Neither can anyone else. And there are six Monks accounted for this morning. All in New York. Your Monk went home last night."

That jarred me. "How?"

"We don't know. We're checking plane flights, silly as that sounds. Wouldn't you think a stewardess would notice a Monk on her flight? Wouldn't you think she'd go to the newspapers?"

"Sure."

"We're also checking flying saucer sightings."

I laughed. But by now that sounded logical.

"If that doesn't pan out, we'll be seriously considering teleportation. Would you . . ."

"That's it," I said without surprise. It had come the way a memory comes, from the back of my mind, as if it had always been there. "He gave me a teleportation pill. That's why I've got absolute direction. To teleport I've got to know where in the universe I am."

Morris got bug-eyed. "You can teleport?"

"Not from a speeding car," I said with reflexive fear. "That's death. I'd keep the velocity."

"Oh." He was edging away as if I had sprouted horns.

More memory floated up, and I said, "Humans can't teleport anyway. That pill was for another market."

Morris relaxed. "You might have said that right away."

"I only just remembered."

"Why did you take it, if it's for aliens?"

"Probably for the location talent. I don't remember. I used to get lost pretty easily. I never will again. Morris, I'd be safer on a high wire than you'd be crossing a street with the Walk sign."

"Could that have been your 'something unusual'?"

"Maybe," I said. At the same time I was somehow sure that it wasn't.

• • •

Louise was in the dirt parking lot next to the Long Spoon. She was getting out of her Mustang when we pulled up. She waved an arm like a semaphore and walked briskly toward us, already talking. "Alien creatures in the Long Spoon, forsooth!" I'd taught her that word. "Ed, I keep telling you the customers aren't human. Hello, are you Mr. Morris? I remember you. You were in last night. You had four drinks. All night."

Morris smiled. "Yes, but I tipped big. Call me Bill, okay?"

Louise Schu was a cheerful blonde, by choice, not birth. She'd been working in the Long Spoon for five years now. A few of my regulars knew my name; but they all knew hers.

Louise's deadliest enemy was the extra twenty pounds she carried as padding. She had been dieting for some decades. Two years back she had gotten serious about it and stopped cheating. She was *mean* for the next several months. But, clawing and scratching and half starved every second, she had worked her way down to one hundred and twenty-five pounds. She threw a terrific celebration that night and—to hear her tell it afterward—ate her way back to one-forty-five in a single night.

Padding or not, she'd have made someone a wonderful wife. I'd thought of marrying her myself. But my marriage had been too little fun, and was too recent, and the divorce had hurt too much. And the alimony. The alimony was why I was living in a cracker box, and I couldn't afford to get married again.

While Louise was opening up, Morris bought a paper from the coin rack.

The Long Spoon was a mess. Louise and I cleaned off the tables and collected the dirty glasses and emptied the ashtrays into waste bins. But the collected glasses were still dirty and the waste bins were still full.

Morris began spreading newspaper over an area of floor.

And I stopped with my hand in my pocket.

Littleton came out from behind the bar, hefting both of the waste bins. He spilled one out onto the newspaper, then the other. He and Morris began spreading the trash apart.

My fingertips were brushing a scrap of Monk cellophane.

I'd worn these pants last night, under the apron.

Some impulse kept me from yelling out. I brought my hand out of my pocket, empty. Louise had gone to help the others sift the trash with their fingers. I joined them.

Presently Morris said, "Four. I hope that's all. We'll search the bar too."

And I thought: Five.

And I thought: I learned five new professions last night. What were the odds that I'll want to hide at least one of them?

If my judgment was bad enough to make me take a teleport pill intended for something with too many eyes, what else might I have swallowed last night?

I might be an advertising man, or a superbly trained thief, or a Palace Executioner skilled in the ways of torture. Or I might have asked for something really unpleasant, like the profession followed by Hitler or Alexander the Great.

"Nothing here," Morris said from behind the bar. Louise shrugged agreement. Morris handed the four scraps to Littleton and said, "Run these out to Douglass. Call us from there.

"We'll put them through chemical analysis," he said to Louise and me. "One of them may be real cellophane off a piece of candy. Or we might have missed one or two. For the moment, let's assume there were four."

"All right," I said.

"Does it sound right, Frazer? Should it be three, or five?"

"I don't know." As far as memory went, I really didn't.

"Four, then. We've identified two. One was a course in teleportation for aliens. The other was a language course. Right?"

"It looks that way."

"What else did he give you?"

I could feel the memories floating back there, but all scrambled together. I shook my head.

Morris looked frustrated.

"Excuse me," said Louise. "Do you drink on duty?"

"Yes," Morris said without hesitation.

And Louise and I weren't on duty. Louise mixed us three gin-and-tonics and brought them to us at one of the padded booths.

Morris had opened a flattish briefcase that turned out to be part tape recorder. He said, "We won't lose anything now. Louise, let's talk about last night."

"I hope I can help."

"Just what happened in here after Ed took his first pill?"

"Mmm." Louise looked at me askance. "I don't know when he took that first pill. About one A.M. I noticed that he was acting strange. He was slow on orders. He got drinks wrong.

"I remembered that he had done that for awhile last fall, when he got his divorce . . ."

I felt my face go stiff. That was unexpected pain, that memory. I am far from being my own best customer; but there had been a long lost weekend about a year ago. Louise had talked me out of trying to drink and bartend too. So I had gone drinking. When it was out of my system I had gone back to tending bar.

She was saying, "Last night I thought it might be the same problem.

I covered for him, said the orders twice when I had to, watched him make the drinks so he'd get them right.

"He was spending most of his time talking to the Monk. But Ed was talking English, and the Monk was making whispery noises in his throat. Remember last week, when they put the Monk speech on television? It sounded like that.

"I saw Ed take a pill from the Monk and swallow it with a glass of water."

She turned to me, touched my arm. "I thought you were crazy. I tried to stop you."

"I don't remember."

"The place was practically empty by then. Well, you laughed at me and said that the pill would teach you not to get lost! I didn't believe it. But the Monk turned on his translator gadget and said the same thing."

"I wish you'd stopped me," I said.

She looked disturbed. "I wish you hadn't said that. I took a pill myself."

I started choking. She'd caught me with a mouthful of gin and tonic.

Louise pounded my back and saved my life, maybe. She said, "You don't remember that?"

"I don't remember much of anything coherent after I took the first pill."

"Really? You didn't seem loaded. Not after I'd watched you awhile."

Morris cut in. "Louise, the pill you took. What did the Monk say it would do?"

"He never did. We were talking about me." She stopped to think. Then, baffled and amused at herself, she said, "I don't know how it happened. All of a sudden I was telling the story of my young life. To a Monk. I had the idea he was sympathetic."

"The *Monk*?"

"Yes, the Monk. And at some point he picked out a pill and gave it to me. He said it would help me. I believed him. I don't know why, but I believed him, and I took it."

"Any symptoms? Have you learned anything new this morning?"

She shook her head, baffled and a little truculent now. Taking that pill must have seemed sheer insanity in the cold gray light of afternoon.

"All right," said Morris. "Frazer, you took three pills. We knew what two of them were. Louise, you took one, and we have no idea what it taught you." He closed his eyes a moment, then looked at me. "Frazer, if you can't remember what you took, can you remember rejecting anything? Did the Monk offer you anything . . ." He saw my face and cut it off.

Because that had jarred something . . .

The Monk had been speaking his own language, in that alien whisper that doesn't need to be more than a whisper because the basic sounds of the Monk language are so unambiguous, so easily distinguished, even to a human ear. *This teaches proper swimming technique. A ——— can reach speeds of sixteen to twenty-four ——— per ——— using these strokes. The course also teaches proper exercises . . .*

I said, "I turned down a swimming course for intelligent fish."

Louise giggled. Morris said, "You're kidding."

"I'm not. And there was something else." That swamped-in-data effect wasn't as bad as it had been at noon. Bits of data must be reaching cubbyholes in my head, linking up, finding their places.

"I was asking about the shapes of aliens. Not about Monks, because that's bad manners, especially from a race that hasn't yet proven its sentience. I wanted to know about other aliens. So the Monk offered me three courses in unarmed combat techniques. Each one involved extensive knowledge of basic anatomy."

"You didn't take them?"

"No. What for? Like, one was a pill to tell me how to kill an armed intelligent worm, but only if I was an unarmed intelligent worm. I wasn't *that* confused."

"Frazer, there are men who would give an arm and a leg for any of those pills you turned down."

"Sure. A couple of hours ago you were telling me I was crazy to swallow an alien's education pill."

"Sorry," said Morris.

"You were the one who said they should have driven me out of my mind. Maybe they did," I said, because my hypersensitive sense of balance was still bothering the hell out of me.

But Morris's reaction bothered me worse. *Frazer could start gibbering any minute. Better pump him for all he's worth while I've got the chance.*

No, his face showed none of that. Was I going paranoid?

"Tell me more about the pills," Morris said. "It sounds like there's a lot of delayed reaction involved. How long do we have to wait before we know we've got it all?"

"He did say something . . ." I groped for it, and presently it came.

It works like a memory, the Monk had said. He'd turned off his translator and was speaking his own language, now that I could understand him. The sound of his translator had been bothering him. That was why he'd given me the pill.

But the whisper of his voice was low, and the language was new, and I'd had to listen carefully to get it all. I remembered it clearly.

The information in the pills will become part of your memory. You will not know all that you have learned until you need it. Then it will surface. Memory works by association, he'd said.

And: *There are things that cannot be taught by teachers. Always there is the difference between knowledge from school and knowledge from doing the work itself.*

"Theory and practice," I told Morris. "I know just what he meant. There's not a bartending course in the country that will teach you to leave the sugar out of an Old Fashioned during rush hour."

"*What* did you say?"

"It depends on the bar, of course. No posh bar would let itself get that crowded. But in an ordinary bar, anyone who orders a complicated drink during rush hour deserves what he gets. He's slowing the bartender down when it's crucial, when every second is money. So you leave the sugar out of an Old Fashioned. It's too much money."

"The guy won't come back."

"So what? He's not one of your regulars. He'd have better sense if he were."

I had to grin. Morris was shocked and horrified. I'd shown him a brand new sin. I said, "It's something every bartender ought to know about. Mind you, a bartending school is a trade school. They're teaching you to survive as a bartender. But the recipe calls for sugar, so at school you put in the sugar or you get ticked off."

Morris shook his head, tight-lipped. He said, "Then the Monk was warning you that you were getting theory, not practice."

"Just the opposite. Look at it this way, Morris . . ."

"Bill."

"Listen, Bill. The teleport pill can't make a human nervous system capable of teleportation. Even my incredible balance, and it *is* incredible, won't give me the muscles to do ten quick backflips. But I do know what it *feels* like to teleport. That's what the Monk was warning me about. The pills give field training. What you have to watch out for are the reflexes. Because the pills don't change you physically."

"I hope you haven't become a trained assassin."

One must be wary of newly learned reflexes, the Monk had said.

Morris said, "Louise, we still don't know what kind of an education you got last night. Any ideas?"

"Maybe I repair time machines." She sipped her drink, eyed Morris demurely over the rim of the glass.

Morris smiled back. "I wouldn't be surprised."

The idiot. He meant it.

"If you really want to know what was in the pill," said Louise, "why not ask the Monk?" She gave Morris time to look startled, but no time to interrupt. "All we have to do is open up and wait. He didn't even get through the second shelf last night, did he, Ed?"

"No, by God, he didn't."

Louise swept an arm about her. "The place is a mess, of course. We'd never get it clean in time. Not without help. How about it, Bill? You're a government man. Could you get a team to work here in time to get this place cleaned up by five o'clock?"

"You know not what you ask. It's three-fifteen now!"

Truly, the Long Spoon was a disaster area. Bars are not meant to be seen by daylight. Just because our worlds had been turned upside down, and just because the Long Spoon was clearly unfit for human habitation, we had been thinking in terms of staying closed tonight. Now it was too late . . .

"Tip Top Cleaners," I remembered. "They send out a four-man team with its own mops. Fifteen bucks an hour. But we'd never get them here in time."

Morris stood up abruptly. "Are they in the phone book?"

"Sure."

Morris moved.

I waited until he was in the phone booth before I asked, "Any new thoughts on what you ate last night?"

Louise looked at me closely. "You mean the pill? Why so solemn?"

"We've got to find out before Morris does."

"Why?"

"If Morris has his way," I said, "they'll classify my head Top Secret. I know too much. I'm likely to be a political prisoner the rest of my life; and so are you, if you learned the wrong things last night."

What Louise did then, I found both flattering and comforting. She turned upon the phone booth where Morris was making his call, a look of such poisonous hatred that it should have withered the man where he stood.

She believed me. She needed no kind of proof, and she was utterly on my side.

Why was I so sure? I had spent too much of today guessing at other people's thoughts. Maybe it had something to do with my third and fourth professions . . .

I said, "We've got to find out what kind of pill you took. Otherwise Morris and the Secret Service will spend the rest of their lives following you around, just on the off chance that you know something useful. Like me. Only they *know* I know something useful. They'll be picking my brain until Hell freezes over."

Morris yelled from the phone booth. "They're coming! Forty bucks an hour, paid in advance when they get here!"

"Great!" I yelled.

"I want to call in. New York." He closed the folding door.

Louise leaned across the table. "Ed, what are we going to do?"

It was the way she said it. We were in it together, and there was a way out, and she was sure I'd find it—and she said it all in the sound of her voice, the way she leaned toward me, the pressure of her hand around my wrist. *We*. I felt power and confidence rising in me; and at the same time I thought: *She couldn't do that yesterday*.

I said, "We clean this place up so we can open for business. Meanwhile you try to remember what you learned last night. Maybe it was something harmless, like how to catch trilchies with a magnetic web."

"Tril . . . ?"

"Space butterflies, kind of."

"Oh. But suppose he taught me how to build a faster-than-light motor?"

"We'd bloody have to keep Morris from finding out. But you didn't. The English words for going faster than light—hyperdrive, space warp—they don't have Monk translations except in math. You can't even say 'faster than light' in Monk."

"Oh."

Morris came back grinning like an idiot. "You'll never guess what the Monks want from us now."

He looked from me to Louise to me, grinning, letting the suspense grow intolerable. He said, "A giant laser cannon."

Louise gasped "What?" and I asked, "You mean a launching laser?"

"Yes, a launching laser. They want us to build it on the Moon. They'd feed our engineers pills to give them the specs and to teach them how to build it. They'd pay off in more pills."

I needed to remember something about launching lasers. And how had I known what to call it?

"They put the proposition to the United Nations," Morris was saying. "In fact, they'll be doing all of their business through the UN, to avoid charges of favoritism, they say, and to spread the knowledge as far as possible."

"But there are countries that don't belong to the UN," Louise objected.

"The Monks know that. They asked if any of those nations had space travel. None of them do, of course. And the Monks lost interest in them."

"Of course," I said, remembering. "A species that can't develop spaceflight is no better than animals."

"Huh?"

"According to a Monk."

Louise said, "But what *for*? Why would the Monks want a laser cannon? And on our Moon!"

"That's a little complicated," said Morris. "Do you both remember when the Monk ship first appeared, two years ago?"

"No," we answered more or less together.

Morris was shaken. "You didn't notice? It was in all the papers. Noted Astronomer Says Alien Spacecraft Approaching Earth. No?"

"No."

"For Christ's sake! I was jumping up and down. It was like when the radio astronomers discovered pulsars, remember? I was just getting out of high school."

"Pulsars?"

"Excuse me," Morris said overpolitely. "My mistake. I tend to think that everybody I meet is a science fiction fan. Pulsars are stars that give off rhythmic pulses of radio energy. The radio astronomers thought at first that they were getting signals from outer space."

Louise said, "You're a science fiction fan?"

"Absolutely. My first gun was a GyroJet rocket pistol. I bought it because I read Buck Rogers."

I said, "Buck who?" But then I couldn't keep a straight face. Morris raised his eyes to Heaven. No doubt it was there that he found the strength to go on.

"The noted astronomer was Jerome Finney. Of course he hadn't said anything about Earth. Newspapers always get that kind of thing garbled. He'd said that an object of artificial, extraterrestrial origin had entered the solar system.

"What had happened was that several months earlier, Jodrell Bank had found a new star in Sagittarius. That's the direction of the galactic core. Yes, Frazer?"

We were back to last names because I wasn't a science fiction fan. I said, "That's right. The Monks came from the galactic hub." I remembered the blazing night sky of Center. My Monk customer couldn't possibly have seen it in his lifetime. He must have been shown the vision through an education pill, for patriotic reasons, like kids are taught what the Star Spangled Banner looks like.

"All right. The astronomers were studying a nearby nova, so they caught the intruder a little sooner. It showed a strange spectrum, radically different from a nova and much more constant. It got even stranger. The light was growing brighter at the same time the spectral lines were shifting toward the red.

"It was months before anyone identified the spectrum.

"Then one Jerome Finney finally caught wise. He showed that the spectrum was the light of our own sun, drastically blue-shifted. Some kind of mirror was coming at us, moving at a hell of a clip, but slowing as it came."

"Oh!" I got it then. "That would mean a light-sail!"

"Why the big deal, Frazer? I thought you already knew."

"No. This is the first I've heard of it. I don't read the Sunday supplements."

Morris was exasperated. "But you knew enough to call the laser cannon a launching laser!"

"I just now realized why it's called that."

Morris stared at me for several seconds. Then he said, "You got it out of the Monk language course."

"I guess so."

He got back to business. "The newspapers gave poor Finney a terrible time. You didn't see the political cartoons either? Too bad. But when the Monk ship got closer it started sending signals. It *was* an interstellar sailing ship, riding the sunlight on a reflecting sail, and it was coming here."

"Signals. With dots and dashes? You could do that just by tacking the sail."

"You *must* have read about it."

"Why? It's so obvious."

Morris looked unaccountably ruffled. Whatever his reasons, he let it pass. "The sail is a few molecules thick and nearly five hundred miles across when it's extended. On light pressure alone they can build up to interstellar velocities—but it takes them a long time. The acceleration isn't high.

"It took them two years to slow down to solar system velocities. They must have done a lot of braking before our telescopes found them, but even so they were going far too fast when they passed Earth's orbit. They had to go inside Mercury's orbit and come up the other side of the sun's gravity well, backing all the way, before they could get near Earth."

I said, "Sure. Interstellar speeds have to be above half the speed of light, or you can't trade competitively."

"What?"

"There are ways to get the extra edge. You don't have to depend on sunlight, not if you're launching from a civilized system. Every civilized system has a moon-based launching laser. By the time the sun is too far away to give the ship a decent push, the beam from the laser cannon is spreading just enough to give the sail a hefty acceleration without vaporizing anything."

"Naturally," said Morris, but he seemed confused.

"So that if you're heading for a strange system, you'd naturally spend most of the trip decelerating. You can't count on a strange system having a launching laser. If you know your destination is civilized, that's a different matter."

Morris nodded.

"The lovely thing about the laser cannon is that if anything goes wrong with it, there's a civilized world right there to fix it. You go sailing out to the stars with trade goods, but you leave your launching motor safely at home. Why is everybody looking at me funny?"

"Don't take it wrong," said Morris. "But how does a paunchy bartender come to know so much about flying an interstellar trading ship?"

"What?" I didn't understand him.

"Why did the Monk ship have to dive so deep into the solar system?"

"Oh, that. That's the solar wind. You get the same problem around any yellow sun. With a light-sail you can get push from the solar wind as well as from light pressure. The trouble is, the solar wind is just stripped hydrogen atoms. Light bounces from a light-sail, but the solar wind just hits the sail and sticks."

Morris nodded thoughtfully. Louise was blinking as if she had double vision.

"You can't tack against it. Tilting the sail does from nothing. To use the solar wind for braking you have to bore straight in, straight toward the sun," I explained.

Morris nodded. I saw that his eyes were as glassy as Louise's eyes.

"Oh," I said. "Damn, I must be stupid today. Morris, that was the third pill."

"Right," said Morris, still nodding, still glassy-eyed. "That must have been the unusual, *really* unusual profession you wanted. Crewman on an interstellar liner. Jesus."

And he should have sounded disgusted, but he sounded envious.

His elbows were on the table, his chin rested on his fists. It is a position that distorts the mouth, making one's expression unreadable. But I didn't like what I could read in Morris's eyes.

There was nothing left of the square and honest man I had let into my apartment at noon. Morris was a patriot now, and an altruist, and a fanatic. He must have the stars for his nation and for all mankind. Nothing must stand in his way. Least of all, me.

Reading minds again, Frazer? Maybe being captain of an interstellar liner involves having to read the minds of the crew, to be able to put down a mutiny before some idiot can take a heat point to the *mpff glip habbabub*, or however a Monk would say it; it has something to do with straining ketones out of the breathing-air.

My urge to acrobatics had probably come out of the same pill. Free fall training. There was a lot in that pill.

This was the profession I should have hidden. Not the Palace Torturer, who was useless to a government grown too subtle to need such techniques; but the captain of an interstellar liner, a prize too valuable to men who have not yet reached beyond the Moon.

And I had been the last to know it. Too late, Frazer.

"Captain," I said. "Not crew."

"Pity. A crewman would know more about how to put a ship together. Frazer, how big a crew are you equipped to rule?"

"Eight and five."

"Thirteen?"

"Yes."

"Then why did you say eight and five?"

The question caught me off balance. Hadn't I . . . ? Oh. "That's the Monk numbering system. Base eight. Actually, base two, but they group the digits in threes to get base eight."

"Base two. Computer numbers."

"Are they?"

"Yes. Frazer, they must have been using computers for a long time. Eons."

"All right." I noticed for the first time that Louise had collected our glasses and gone to make fresh drinks. Good, I could use one. She'd left her own, which was half full. Knowing she wouldn't mind, I took a swallow.

It was soda water.

With a lime in it. It looked just like our gin and tonics. She must be back on the diet. Except that when Louise resumed a diet, she generally announced it to all and sundry . . .

Morris was still on the subject. "You use a crew of thirteen. Are they Monk or human or something else?"

"Monk," I said without having to think.

"Too bad. Are there humans in space?"

"No. A lot of two-feet, but none of them are like any of the others, and none of them are quite like us."

Louise came back with our drinks, gave them to us, and sat down without a word.

"You said earlier that a species that can't develop space flight is no better than animals."

"According to the Monks," I reminded him.

"Right. It seems a little extreme even to me, but let it pass. What about a race that develops spaceflight and then loses it?"

"It happens. There are lots of ways a space-going species can revert to animal. Atomic war. Or they just can't live with the complexity. Or they breed themselves out of food, and the world famine wrecks everything. Or waste products from the new machinery ruins the ecology."

" 'Revert to animal.' All right. What about nations? Suppose you have two nations next door, same species, but one has space flight . . ."

"Right. Good point, too. Morris, there are just two countries on Earth that can deal with the Monks without dealing through the United Nations. Us, and Russia. If Zimbabwe or Brazil or France tried it, they'd be publicly humiliated."

"That could cause an international incident." Morris's jaw tightened heroically. "We've got ways of passing the warning along so that it won't happen."

Louise said, "There are some countries I wouldn't mind seeing it happen to."

Morris got a thoughtful look—and I wondered if everybody would get the warning.

The cleaning team arrived then. We'd used Tip Top Cleaners before, but these four dark women were not our usual team. We had to explain in detail just what we wanted done. Not their fault. They usually clean private homes, not bars.

Morris spent some time calling New York. He must have been using a credit card; he couldn't have that much change.

"That may have stopped a minor war," he said when he got back. And we returned to the padded booth. But Louise stayed to direct the cleaning team.

The four dark women moved about us with pails and spray bottles and dry rags, chattering in Spanish, leaving shiny surfaces wherever they went. And Morris resumed his inquisition.

"What powers the ground-to-orbit ship?"

"A slow H-bomb going off in a magnetic bottle."

"Fusion?"

"Yah. The attitude jets on the main starship use fusion power too. They all link to one magnetic bottle. I don't know just how it works. You get fuel from water or ice."

"Fusion. But don't you have to separate out the deuterium and tritium?"

"What for? You melt the ice, run a current through the water, and you've got hydrogen."

"Wow," Morris said softly. "Wow."

"The launching laser works the same way," I remembered. What else did I need to remember about launching lasers? Something dreadfully important.

"Wow. Frazer, if we could build the Monks their launching laser, we could use the same techniques to build other fusion plants. Couldn't we?"

"Sure." I was in dread. My mouth was dry, my heart was pounding. I almost knew why. "What do you mean, *if*?"

"And they'd pay us to do it! It's a damn shame. We just don't have the hardware."

"What do you mean? We've *got* to build the launching laser!"

Morris gaped. "Frazer, what's wrong with you?"

The terror had a name now. "My God! What have you told the Monks? Morris, listen to me. You've got to see to it that the Security Council promises to build the Monks' launching laser."

"Who do you think I am, the Secretary-General? We can't build it anyway, not with just Saturn launching configurations." Morris thought I'd gone mad at last. He wanted to back away through the wall of the booth.

"They'll do it when you tell them what's at stake. And we can build a launching laser, if the whole world goes in on it. Morris, look at the good it can do! Free power from seawater! And light-sails work *fine* within a system.''

''Sure, it's a lovely picture. We could sail out to the moons of Jupiter and Saturn. We could smelt the asteroids for their metal ores, using laser power . . .'' His eyes had momentarily taken on a vague, dreamy look. Now they snapped back to what Morris thought of as reality. ''It's the kind of thing I daydreamed about when I was a kid. Someday we'll do it. Today—we just aren't ready.''

''There are two sides to a coin,'' I said. ''Now, I know how this is going to sound. Just remember there are reasons. Good reasons.''

''Reasons? Reasons for what?''

''When a trading ship travels,'' I said, ''it travels only from one civilized system to another. There are ways to tell whether a system has a civilization that can build a launching laser. Radio is one. The Earth puts out as much radio flux as a small star.

''When the Monks find that much radio energy coming from a nearby star, they send a trade ship. By the time the ship gets there, the planet that's putting out all the energy is generally civilized. But not so civilized that it can't use the knowledge a Monk trades for.

''Do you see that they *need* the launching laser? That ship out there came from a Monk colony. This far from the axis of the galaxy, the stars are too far apart. Ships launch by starlight and laser, but they brake by starlight alone, because they can't count on the target star having a launching laser. If they had to launch by starlight too, they probably wouldn't make it. A plant-and-animal cycle as small as the life support system on a Monk starship can last only so long.''

''You said yourself that the Monks can't always count on the target star staying civilized.''

''No, of course not. Sometimes a civilization hits the level at which it can build a launching laser, stays there just long enough to send out a mass of radio waves, then reverts to animal. That's the point. If we tell them we can't build the laser, we'll be animals to the Monks.''

''Suppose we just refuse? Not *can't* but *won't*.''

''That would be stupid. There are too many advantages. Controlled fusion . . .''

''Frazer, think about the cost.'' Morris looked grim. He wanted the laser. He didn't think he could get it. ''Think about politicians thinking about the cost,'' he said. ''Think about politicians thinking about explaining the cost to the taxpayers.''

''Stupid,'' I repeated, ''and inhospitable. Hospitality counts high with the Monks. You see, we're cooked either way. Either we're dumb animals, or we're guilty of a criminal breach of hospitality. And the Monk ship *still* needs more light for its light-sail than the sun can put out.''

"So?"

"So the captain uses a gadget that makes the sun explode."

"The," said Morris, and "He," and "Explode?" He didn't know what to do. Then suddenly he burst out in great loud cheery guffaws, so that the women cleaning the Long Spoon turned with answering smiles. He'd decided not to believe me.

I reached across and gently pushed his drink into his lap.

It was two-thirds empty, but it cut his laughter off in an instant. Before he could start swearing, I said, "I am not playing games. The Monks will make our sun explode if we don't build them a launching laser. Now go call your boss and tell him so."

The women were staring at us in horror. Louise started toward us, then stopped, uncertain.

Morris sounded almost calm. "Why the drink in my lap?"

"Shock treatment. And I wanted your full attention. Are you going to call New York?"

"Not yet." Morris swallowed. He looked down once at the spreading stain on his pants, then somehow put it out of his mind. "Remember, I'd have to convince him. I don't believe it myself. Nobody and nothing would blow up a sun for a breach of hospitality!"

"No, no, Morris. They have to blow up the sun to get to the next system. It's a serious thing, refusing to build the launching laser! It could wreck the *ship*!"

"Screw the ship! What about a whole planet?"

"You're just not looking at it right . . ."

"Hold it. Your ship is a trading ship, isn't it? What kind of idiots would the Monks be, to exterminate one market just to get on to the next?"

"If we can't build a launching laser, we aren't a market."

"But we might be a market on the next circuit!"

"What next circuit? You don't seem to grasp the *size* of the Monks' marketplace. The communications gap between Center and the nearest Monk colony is about . . ." I stopped to transpose. ". . . sixty-four thousand years! By the time a ship finishes one circuit, most of the worlds she's visited have already forgotten her. And then what? The colony world that built her may have failed, or refitted the spaceport to service a different style of ship, or reverted to animal; even Monks do that. She'd have to go on to the next system for refitting.

"When you trade among the stars, *there is no repeat business*."

"Oh," said Morris.

Louise had gotten the women back to work. With a corner of my mind I heard their giggling discussion as to whether Morris would fight, whether he could whip me, etc.

Morris asked, "How does it work? How do you make a sun go nova?"

"There's a gadget the size of a locomotive fixed to the—main supporting strut, I guess you'd call it. It points straight astern, and it can swing sixteen degrees or so in any direction. You turn it on when you make departure orbit. The math man works out the intensity. You beam the sun for the first year or so, and when it blows, you're just far enough away to use the push without getting burned."

"But how does it work?"

"You just turn it on. The power comes from the fusion tube that feeds the attitude jet system . . . Oh, you want to know why does it make a sun explode. I don't know that. Why should I?"

"Big as a locomotive. And it makes suns explode." Morris sounded slightly hysterical. Poor bastard, he was beginning to believe me. The shock had hardly touched me, because truly I had known it since last night.

He said, "When we first saw the Monk light-sail, it was just to one side of a recent nova in Sagittarius. By any wild chance, was that star a market that didn't work out?"

"I haven't the vaguest idea."

That convinced him. If I'd been making it up, I'd have said yes. Morris stood up and walked away without a word. He stopped to pick up a bar towel on his way to the phone booth.

I went behind the bar to make a fresh drink. Cutty over ice, splash of soda; I wanted to taste the burning power of it.

Through the glass door I saw Louise getting out of her car with her arms full of packages. I poured soda over ice, squeezed a lime in it, and had it ready when she walked in.

She dumped the load on the bar top. "Irish coffee makings," she said. I held the glass out to her and she said, "No thanks, Ed. One's enough."

"Taste it."

She gave me a funny look, but she tasted what I handed her. "Soda water. Well, you caught me."

"Back on the diet?"

"Yes."

"You never said *yes* to that question in your life. Don't you want to tell me all the details?"

She sipped at her drink. "Details of someone else's diet are boring. I should have known that a long time ago. To work! You'll notice we've only got twenty minutes."

I opened one of her paper bags and fed the refrigerator with cartons of whipping cream. Another bag held perking coffee. The flat, square package had to be a pizza.

"Pizza. Some diet," I said.

She was setting out the percolators. "That's for you and Bill."

I tore open the paper and bit into a pie-shaped slice. It was a deluxe, covered with everything from anchovies to salami. It was crisp and hot, and I was starving.

I snatched bites as I worked.

There aren't many bars that will keep the makings for Irish coffee handy. It's too much trouble. You need massive quantities of whipping cream and ground coffee, a refrigerator, a blender, a supply of those glass figure-eight-shaped coffee perkers, a line of hot plates, and—most expensive of all—room behind the bar for all of that. You learn to keep a line of glasses ready, which means putting the sugar in them at spare moments to save time later. Those spare moments are your smoking time, so you give that up. You learn not to wave your arms around because there are hot things that can burn you. You learn to half-whip the cream, a mere spin of the blender, because you have to do it over and over again, and if you overdo it the cream turns to butter.

There aren't many bars that will go to all that trouble. That's why it pays off. Your average Irish coffee addict will drive an extra twenty minutes to reach the Long Spoon. He'll also down the drink in about five minutes, because otherwise it gets cold. He'd have spent half an hour over a Scotch and soda.

While we were getting the coffee ready, I found time to ask, "Have you remembered anything?"

"Yes," she said.

"Tell me."

"I don't mean I know what was in the pill. Just—I can do things I couldn't do before. I think my way of thinking has changed. Ed, I'm worried."

"Worried?"

She got the words out in a rush. "It feels like I've been falling in love with you for a very long time. But I haven't. Why should I feel that way so suddenly?"

The bottom dropped out of my stomach. I'd had thoughts like this—and put them out of my mind, and when they came back I did it again. I couldn't afford to fall in love. It would cost too much. It would hurt too much.

"It's been like this all day. It scares me, Ed. Suppose I feel like this about every man? What if the Monk thought I'd make a good call girl?"

I laughed much harder than I should have. Louise was getting really angry before I was able to stop.

"Wait a minute," I said. "Are you in love with Bill Morris too?"

"No, of course not!"

"Then forget the call girl bit. He's got more money than I do. A call girl would love him more, if she loved anyone, which she wouldn't, because call girls are generally frigid."

"How do you know?" she demanded.

"I read it in a magazine."

Louise began to relax. I began to see how tense she really had been. "All right," she said, "but that means I really am in love with you."

I pushed the crisis away from us. "Why didn't you ever get married?"

"Oh . . ." She was going to pass it off, but she changed her mind. "Every man I dated wanted to sleep with me. I thought that was wrong, so . . ."

She looked puzzled. "Why did I think that was wrong?"

"Way you were brought up."

"Yes, but . . ." She trailed off.

"How do you feel about it now?"

"Well, I wouldn't sleep with *any*one, but if a man was worth dating he might be worth marrying, and if he was worth marrying he'd certainly be worth sleeping with, wouldn't he? And I'd be crazy to marry someone I hadn't slept with, wouldn't I?"

"I did."

"And look how that turned out! Oh, Ed, I'm sorry. But you did bring it up."

"Yah," I said, breathing shallow.

"But I used to feel that way too. Something's changed."

We hadn't been talking fast. There had been pauses, gaps, and we had worked through them. I had had time to eat three slices of pizza. Louise had had time to wrestle with her conscience, lose, and eat one.

Only she hadn't done it. There was the pizza, staring at her, and she hadn't given it a look or a smell. For Louise, that was unusual.

Half-joking, I said, "Try this as a theory. Years ago you must have sublimated your sex urge into an urge for food. Either that or the rest of us sublimated our appetites into a sex urge, and you didn't."

"Then the pill un-sublimated me, hmm?" She looked thoughtfully at the pizza. Clearly its lure was gone. "That's what I mean. I didn't used to be able to outstare a pizza."

"Those olive eyes."

"Hypnotic, they were."

"A good call girl should be able to keep herself in shape." Immediately I regretted saying it. It wasn't funny. "Sorry," I said.

"It's all right." She picked up a tray of candles in red glass vases and moved away, depositing the candles on the small square tables. She moved with grace and beauty through the twilight of the Long Spoon, her hips swaying just enough to avoid the sharp corners of tables.

I'd hurt her. But she'd known me long enough; she must know I had foot-in-mouth disease . . .

I had seen Louise before and known that she was beautiful. But it seemed to me that she had never been beautiful with so little excuse.

She moved back by the same route, lighting the candles as she went.

Finally she put the tray down, leaned across the bar and said, "I'm sorry. I can't joke about it when I don't *know*."

"Stop worrying, will you? Whatever the Monk fed you, he was trying to help you."

"I love you."

"What?"

"I love you."

"Okay. I love you too." I use those words so seldom that they clog in my throat, as if I'm lying, even when it's the truth. "Listen, I want to marry you. Don't shake your head. I want to marry you."

Our voices had dropped to whispers. In a tormented whisper, then, she said, "Not until I find out what I *do*, what was in the *pill*. Ed, I can't trust myself until then!"

"Me too," I said with great reluctance. "But we can't wait. We don't have time."

"What?"

"That's right, you weren't in earshot. Sometime between three and ten years from now, the Monks may blow up our sun."

Louise said nothing. Her forehead wrinkled.

"It depends on how much time they spend trading. If we can't build them the launching laser, we can still con them into waiting for awhile. Monk expeditions have waited as long as . . ."

"Good Lord. You mean it. Is that what you and Bill were fighting over?"

"Yah."

Louise shuddered. Even in the dimness I saw how pale she had become. And she said a strange thing.

She said, "All right, I'll marry you."

"Good," I said. But I was suddenly shaking. Married. Again. Me. Louise stepped up and put her hands on my shoulders, and I kissed her.

I'd been wanting to do that for—five years? She fitted wonderfully into my arms. Her hands closed hard on the muscles of my shoulders, massaging. The tension went out of me, drained away somewhere. Married. Us. At least we could have three to ten years.

"Morris," I said.

She drew back a little. "He can't hold you. You haven't done anything. Oh, I *wish* I knew what was in that pill I took! Suppose I'm the trained assassin?"

"Suppose I am? We'll have to be careful of each other."

"Oh, we know all about you. You're a starship commander, an alien teleport and a translator for Monks."

"And one thing more. There was a fourth profession. I took four pills last night, not three."

"Oh? Why didn't you tell Bill?"

"Are you kidding? Dizzy as I was last night, I probably took a course in how to lead a successful revolution. God help me if Morris found *that* out."

She smiled. "Do you really think that was what it was?"

"No, of course not."

"Why did we do it? Why did we swallow those pills? We should have known better."

"Maybe the Monk took a pill himself. Maybe there's a pill that teaches a Monk how to look trustworthy to a generalized alien."

"I did trust him," said Louise. "I remember. He seemed so sympathetic. Would he really blow up our sun?"

"He really would."

"That fourth pill. Maybe it taught you a way to stop him."

"Let's see. We know I took a linguistics course, a course in teleportation for Martians, and a course in how to fly a light-sail ship. On that basis . . . I probably changed my mind and took a karate course for worms."

"It wouldn't hurt you, at least. Relax. . . . Ed, if you remember taking the pills, why don't you remember what was in them?"

"But I don't. I don't remember anything."

"How do you know you took four, then?"

"Here." I reached in my pocket and pulled out the scrap of Monk cellophane. And knew immediately that there was something in it. Something hard and round.

We were staring at it when Morris came back.

"I must have cleverly put it in my pocket," I told them. "Sometime last night, when I was feeling sneaky enough to steal from a Monk."

Morris turned the pill like a precious jewel in his fingers. Pale blue it was, marked on one side with a burnt orange triangle. "I don't know whether to get it analyzed or take it myself, now. We need a miracle. Maybe this will tell us—"

"Forget it. I wasn't clever enough to remember how fast a Monk pill deteriorates. The wrapping's torn. That pill has been bad for at least twelve hours."

Morris said a dirty thing.

"Analyze it," I said. "You'll find RNA, and you may even be able to tell what the Monks use as a matrix. Most of the memories are probably intact. But don't swallow the damn thing. It'll scramble your brains. All it takes is a few random changes in a tiny percentage of the RNA."

"We don't have time to send it to Douglass tonight. Can we put it in the freezer?"

"Good. Give it here."

I dropped the pill in a sandwich-size plastic Baggy, sucked the air out the top, tied the end, and dropped it in the freezer. Vacuum and cold would help preserve the thing. It was something I should have done last night.

"So much for miracles," Morris said bitterly. "Let's get down to business. We'll have several men outside the place tonight, and a few more in here. You won't know who they are, but go ahead and guess if you like. A lot of your customers will be turned away tonight. They'll be told to watch the newspapers if they want to know why. I hope it won't cost you too much business."

"It may make our fortune. We'll be famous. Were you maybe doing the same thing last night?"

"Yes. We didn't want the place too crowded. The Monks might not like autograph hounds."

"So that's why the place was half empty."

Morris looked at his watch. "Opening time. Are we ready?"

"Take a seat at the bar. And look nonchalant, dammit."

Louise went to turn on the lights.

Morris took a seat to one side of the middle. One big square hand was closed very tightly on the bar edge. "Another gin and tonic. Weak. After that one, leave out the gin."

"Right."

"Nonchalant. Why should I be nonchalant? Frazer, I had to tell the President of the United States of America that the end of the world is coming unless he does something. I had to talk to him myself!"

"Did he buy it?"

"I hope so. He was so goddam calm and reassuring, I wanted to scream at him. God, Frazer, what if we can't build the laser? What if we try and fail?"

I gave him a very old and classic answer. "Stupidity is always a capital crime."

He screamed in my face. "Damn you and your supercilious attitude and your murdering monsters too!" The next second he was ice-water calm. "Never mind, Frazer. You're thinking like a starship captain."

"I'm what?"

"A starship captain has to be able to make a sun go nova to save the ship. You can't help it. It was in the pill."

Damn, he was right. I could *feel* that he was right. The pill had warped my way of thinking. Blowing up the sun that warms another race *had* to be immoral. Didn't it?

I couldn't trust my own sense of right and wrong!

Four men came in and took one of the bigger tables. Morris's men? No. Real estate men, here to do business.

"Something's been bothering me," said Morris. He grimaced. "Among all the things that have been ruining my composure, such as the impending end of the world, there was one thing that kept nagging at me.''

I set his gin-and-tonic in front of him. He tasted it and said, ''Fine. And I finally realized what it was, waiting there in the phone booth for a chain of human snails to put the President on. Frazer, are you a college man?''

''No. Webster High.''

''See, you don't really talk like a bartender. You use big words.''

''I do?''

''Sometimes. And you talked about 'suns exploding,' but you knew what I meant when I said 'nova.' You talked about 'H-bomb power,' but you knew what fusion was.''

''Sure.''

''I got the possibly silly impression that you were learning the words the instant I said them. Parlez-vous français?''

''No. I don't speak any foreign languages.''

''None at all?''

''Nope. What do you think they teach at Webster High?''

''Je parle la langue un peu, Frazer. Et tu?''

''Merde de cochon! Morris, je vous dit—oops.''

He didn't give me a chance to think it over. He said, ''What's fanac?''

My head had that *clogged* feeling again. I said, ''Might be anything. Putting out a zine, writing to the lettercol, helping put on a Con—Morris, what *is* this?''

''That language course was more extensive than we thought.''

''Sure as hell, it was. I just remembered. Those women on the cleaning team were speaking Spanish, but I understood them.''

''Spanish, French, Monkish, technical languages, even fannish. What you got was a generalized course in how to understand languages the instant you hear them. I don't see how it could work without telepathy.''

''Reading minds? Maybe.'' Several times today, it had felt like I was guessing with too much certainty at somebody's private thoughts.

''Can you read *my* mind?''

''That's not quite it. I get the feel of *how* you think, not *what* you're thinking. Morris, I don't like the idea of being a political prisoner.''

''Well, we can talk that over later.'' *When my bargaining position is better*, Morris meant. *When I don't need the bartender's good will to con the Monk*. ''What's important is that you might be able to read a Monk's mind. That could be crucial.''

''And maybe he can read mine. And yours.''

I let Morris sweat over that one while I set drinks on Louise's tray. Already there were customers at four tables. The Long Spoon was filling rapidly; and only two of them were Secret Service.

Morris said, "Any ideas on what Louise Schu ate last night? We've got *your* professions pretty well pegged down. Finally."

"I've got an idea. It's kind of vague." I looked around. Louise was taking more orders. "Sheer guesswork, in fact. Will you keep it to yourself for awhile?"

"Don't tell Louise? Sure—for awhile."

I made four drinks and Louise took them away. I told Morris, "I have a profession in mind. It doesn't have a simple one or two word name, like teleport or starship captain or translator. There's no reason why it should, is there? We're dealing with aliens."

Morris sipped at his drink. Waiting.

"Being a woman," I said, "can be a profession, in a way that being a man can never be. The word is *housewife*, but it doesn't cover all of it. Not nearly."

"Housewife. You're putting me on."

"No. You wouldn't notice the change. You never saw her before last night."

"Just what kind of change have you got in mind? Aside from the fact that she's beautiful, which I did notice."

"Yes, she is, Morris. But last night she was twenty pounds overweight. Do you think she lost it all this morning?"

"She *was* too heavy. Pretty, but also pretty well padded." Morris turned to look over his shoulder, casually turned back. "Damn. She's still well padded. Why didn't I notice before?"

"There's another thing. By the way. Have some pizza."

"Thanks." He bit into a slice. "Good, it's still hot. Well?"

"She's been staring at that pizza for half an hour. She bought it. But she hasn't tasted it. She couldn't possibly have done that yesterday."

"She may have had a big breakfast."

"Yah." I knew she hadn't. She'd eaten diet food. For years she'd kept a growing collection of diet food, but she'd never actively tried to survive on it before. But how could I make such a claim to Morris? I'd never even been in Louise's apartment.

"Anything else?"

"She's gotten good at nonverbal communication. It's a very womanly skill. She can say things just by the tone of her voice or the way she leans on an elbow or . . ."

"But if mind reading is one of *your* new skills . . ."

"Damn. Well—it used to make Louise nervous if someone touched her. And she never touched anyone else." I felt myself flushing. I don't talk easily of personal things.

Morris radiated skepticism. "It all sounds very subjective. In fact, it sounds like you're making yourself believe it. Frazer, why would Louise Schu want such a capsule course? Because you haven't described a housewife at all. You've described a woman looking to persuade a man to marry her.'' He saw my face change. ''What's wrong?''

''Ten minutes ago we decided to get married.''

''Congratulations,'' Morris said, and waited.

''All right, you win. Until ten minutes ago we'd never even kissed. I'd never made a pass, or vice versa. No, damn it, I don't believe it! I *know* she loves me; I ought to!''

''I don't deny it,'' Morris said quietly. ''That would be why she took the pill. It must have been strong stuff, too, Frazer. We looked up some of your history. You're marriage shy.''

It was true enough. I said, ''If she loved me before, I never knew it. I wonder how a Monk could know.''

''How would he know about such a skill at all? Why would he have the pill on him? Come on, Frazer, you're the Monk expert!''

''He'd have to learn from human beings. Maybe by interviews, maybe by—well, the Monks can map an alien memory into a computer space, then interview that. They may have done that with some of your diplomats.''

''Oh, *great*.''

Louise appeared with an order. I made the drinks and set them on her tray. She winked and walked away, swaying deliciously, followed by many eyes.

''Morris. Most of your diplomats, the ones who deal with the Monks, they're men, aren't they?''

''Most of them. Why?''

''Just a thought.''

It was a difficult thought, hard to grasp. It was only that the changes in Louise had been all to the good from a man's point of view. The Monks must have interviewed many men. Well, why not? It would make her more valuable to the man she caught—or to the lucky man who caught her . . .

''Got it.''

Morris looked up quickly. ''Well?''

''Falling in love with me was part of her pill learning. A *set*. They made a guinea pig of her.''

''I wondered what she saw in you.'' Morris's grin faded. ''You're serious. Frazer, that still doesn't answer . . .''

''It's a slave indoctrination course. It makes a woman love the first man she sees, permanently, and it trains her to be valuable to him. The Monks were going to make them in quantity and sell them to men.''

Morris thought it over. Presently he said, ''That's awful. What'll we do?''

''Well, we can't tell her she's been made into a domestic slave! Morris, I'll try to get a memory eraser pill. If I can't—I'll marry her, I guess.

Don't look at me that way,'' I said, low and fierce. ''I didn't do it. And I can't desert her now!''

''I know. It's just—oh, put gin in the next one.''

''Don't look now,'' I said.

In the glass of the door there was darkness and motion. A hooded shape, shadow-on-shadow, supernatural, a human silhouette twisted out of true . . .

He came gliding in with the hem of his robe just brushing the floor. Nothing was to be seen of him but his flowing gray robe, the darkness in the hood and the shadow where his robe parted. The real estate men broke off their talk of land and stared, popeyed, and one of them reached for his heart attack pills.

The Monk drifted toward me like a vengeful ghost. He took the stool we had saved him at one end of the bar.

It wasn't the same Monk.

In all respects he matched the Monk who had been here the last two nights. Louise and Morris must have been fooled completely. But it wasn't the same Monk.

''Good evening,'' I said.

He gave an equivalent greeting in the whispered Monk language. His translator was half on, translating my words into a Monk whisper, but letting his own speech alone. He said, ''I believe we should begin with the Rock and Rye.''

I turned to pour. The small of my back itched with danger.

When I turned back with the shot glass in my hand, he was holding a fist-sized tool that must have come out of his robe. It looked like a flattened softball, grooved deeply for five Monk claws, with two parallel tubes poking out in my direction. Lenses glinted in the ends of the tubes.

''Do you know this tool? It is a . . .'' and he named it.

I knew the name. It was a beaming tool, a multi-frequency laser. One tube locked on the target; thereafter the aim was maintained by tiny flywheels in the body of the device.

Morris had seen it. He didn't recognize it, and he didn't know what to do about it, and I had no way to signal him.

''I know that tool,'' I confirmed.

''You must take two of these pills.'' The Monk had them ready in another hand. They were small and pink and triangular. He said, ''I must be convinced that you have taken them. Otherwise you must take more than two. An overdose may affect your natural memory. Come closer.''

I came closer. Every man and woman in the Long Spoon was staring at us, and each was afraid to move. Any kind of signal would have trained four guns on the Monk. And I'd be fried dead by a narrow beam of X-rays.

The Monk reached out with a third hand/foot/claw. He closed the fingers/toes around my throat, not hard enough to strangle me, but hard enough.

Morris was cursing silently, helplessly. I could feel the agony in his soul.

The Monk whispered, "You know of the trigger mechanism. If my hand should relax now, the device will fire. Its target is yourself. If you can prevent four government agents from attacking me, you should do so."

I made a palm-up gesture toward Morris. *Don't do anything*. He caught it and nodded very slightly without looking at me.

"You can read minds," I said.

"Yes," said the Monk—and I knew instantly what he was hiding. He could read everybody's mind, except mine.

So much for Morris's little games of deceit. But the Monk could not read my mind, and I could see into his own soul.

And, reading his alien soul, I saw that I would die if I did not swallow the pills.

I placed the pink pills on my tongue, one at a time, and swallowed them dry. They went down hard. Morris watched it happen and could do nothing. The Monk felt them going down my throat, little lumps moving past his finger.

And when the pills had passed across the Monk's finger, I worked a miracle.

"Your pill-induced memories and skills will be gone within two hours," said the Monk. He picked up the shot glass of Rock and Rye and moved it into his hood. When it reappeared it was half empty.

I asked, "Why have you robbed me of my knowledge?"

"You never paid for it."

"But it was freely given."

"It was given by one who had no right," said the Monk. He was thinking about leaving. I had to do something. I knew now, because I had reasoned it out with great care, that the Monk was involved in an evil enterprise. But he must stay to hear me or I could not convince him.

Even then, it wouldn't be easy. He was a Monk crewman. His ethical attitudes had entered his brain through an RNA pill, along with his professional skills.

"You have spoken of rights," I said. In Monk. "Let us discuss rights." The whispery words buzzed oddly in my throat; they tickled; but my ears told me they were coming out right.

The Monk was startled. "I was told that you had been taught our speech, but not that you could speak it."

"Were you told what pill I was given?"

"A language pill. I had not known that he carried one in his case."

"He did not finish his tasting of the alcohols of Earth. Will you have another drink?"

I felt him guess at my motives, and guess wrong. He thought I was taking advantage of his curiosity to sell him my wares for cash. And what had he to fear from me? Whatever mental powers I had learned from Monk pills, they would be gone in two hours.

I set a shot glass before him. I asked him, "How do you feel about launching lasers?"

The discussion became highly technical. "Let us take a special case," I remember saying. "Suppose a culture has been capable of starflight for some sixty-fours of years—or even for eights of times that long. Then an asteroid slams into a major ocean, precipitates an ice age . . ." It had happened once, and well he knew it. "A natural disaster can't spell the difference between sentience and non-sentience, can it? Not unless it affects brain tissue directly."

At first it was his curiosity that held him. Later it was me. He couldn't tear himself loose. He never thought of it. He was a sailship crewman, and he was cold sober, and he argued with the frenzy of an evangelist.

"Then take the general case," I remember saying. "A world that cannot build a launching laser is a world of animals, yes? And Monks themselves can revert to animal."

Yes, he knew that.

"Then build your own launching laser. If you cannot, then your ship is captained and crewed by animals."

At the end I was doing all the talking. All in the whispery Monk tongue, whose sounds are so easily distinguished that even I, warping a human throat to my will, need only whisper. It was a good thing. I seemed to have been eating used razor blades.

Morris guessed right. He did not interfere. I could tell him nothing, not if I had had the power, not by word or gesture or mental contact. The Monk would read Morris's mind. But Morris sat quietly drinking his tonic-and-tonics, waiting for something to happen, while I argued in whispers with the Monk.

"But the ship!" he whispered. "What of the ship?" His agony was mine; for the ship must be protected . . .

At one fifteen the Monk had progressed halfway across the bottom row of bottles. He slid from the stool, paid for his drinks in one-dollar bills, and drifted to the door and out.

All he needed was a scythe and hour glass, I thought, watching him go. And what I needed was a long morning's sleep. And I wasn't going to get it.

"Be sure nobody stops him," I told Morris.

"Nobody will. But he'll be followed."

"No point. The Garment to Wear Among Strangers is a lot of things. It's bracing; it helps the Monk hold human shape. It's a shield and an air filter. And it's a cloak of invisibility."

"Oh?"

"I'll tell you about it if I have time. That's how he got out here, probably. One of the crewmen divided, and then one stayed and one walked. He had two weeks."

Morris stood up and tore off his sport jacket. His shirt was wet through. He said, "What about a stomach pump for you?"

"No good. Most of the RNA-enzyme must be in my blood by now. You'll be better off if you spend your time getting down everything I can remember about Monks, while I can remember anything at all. It'll be nine or ten hours before everything goes." Which was a flat-out lie, of course.

"Okay. Let me get the dictaphone going again."

"It'll cost you money."

Morris suddenly had a hard look. "Oh? How much?"

I'd thought about that most carefully. "One hundred thousand dollars. And if you're thinking of arguing me down, remember whose time we're wasting."

"I wasn't." He was, but he'd changed his mind.

"Good. We'll transfer the money now, while I can still read your mind."

"All right."

He offered to make room for me in the booth, but I declined. The glass wouldn't stop me from reading Morris's soul.

He came out silent; for there was something he was afraid to know. Then: "What about the Monks? What about our sun?"

"I talked that one around. That's why I don't want him molested. He'll convince others."

"Talked him around? How?"

"It wasn't easy." And suddenly I would have given my soul to sleep. "The profession pill put it in his genes; he must protect the ship. It's in me too. I know how strong it is."

"Then . . ."

"Don't be an ass, Morris. The ship's perfectly safe where it is, in orbit around the Moon. A sailship's only in danger when it's between stars, far from help."

"Oh."

"Not that that convinced him. It only let him consider the ethics of the situation rationally."

"Suppose someone else unconvinces him?"

"It could happen. That's why we'd better build the launching laser."

The next twelve hours were rough.

In the first four hours I gave them everything I could remember about the Monk teleport system, Monk technology, Monk family life, Monk ethics, relations between Monks and aliens, details on aliens, directions of various inhabited and uninhabited worlds—everything. Morris and the Secret Service men who had been posing as customers sat around me like boys around a campfire, listening to stories. But Louise made us fresh coffee, then went to sleep in one of the booths.

Then I let myself slack off.

By nine in the morning I was flat on my back, staring at the ceiling, dictating a random useless bit of information every thirty seconds or so. By eleven there was a great black pool of lukewarm coffee inside me, my eyes ached marginally more than the rest of me, and I was producing nothing.

I was convincing, and I knew it.

But Morris wouldn't let it go at that. He believed me. I felt him believing me. But he was going through the routine anyway, because it couldn't hurt. If I was useless to him, if I knew nothing, there was no point in playing soft. What could he lose?

He accused me of making everything up. He accused me of faking the pills. He made me sit up, and damn near caught me that way. He used obscure words and phrases from mathematics and Latin and fan vocabulary. He got nowhere. There wasn't any way to trick me.

At two in the afternoon he had someone drive me home.

Every muscle in me ached; but I had to fight to maintain my exhausted slump. Else my hindbrain would have lifted me onto my toes and poised me against a possible shift in artificial gravity. The strain was double, and it hurt. It had hurt for hours, sitting with my shoulders hunched and my head hanging. But now—if Morris saw me walking like a trampoline performer . . .

Morris's man got me to my room and left me.

I woke in darkness and sensed someone in my room. Someone who meant me no harm. In fact, Louise. I went back to sleep.

I woke again at dawn. Louise was in my easy chair, her feet propped on a corner of the bed. Her eyes were open. She said, "Breakfast?"

I said, "Yah. There isn't much in the fridge."

"I brought things."

"All right." I closed my eyes.

Five minutes later I decided I was all slept out. I got up and went to see how she was doing.

There was bacon frying, there was bread already buttered for toasting in the Toast-R-Oven, there was a pan hot for eggs, and the eggs scrambled in a bowl. Louise was filling the percolator.

"Give that here a minute," I said. It only had water in it. I held the pot in my hands, closed my eyes and tried to remember . . .

Ah.

I knew I'd done it right even before the heat touched my hands. The pot held hot, fragrant coffee.

"We were wrong about the first pill," I told Louise. She was looking at me very curiously. "What happened that second night was this. The Monk had a translator gadget, but he wasn't too happy with it. It kept screaming in his ear. Screaming English, too loud, for my benefit.

"He could turn off the part that was shouting English at me, and it would still whisper a Monk translation of what *I* was saying. But first he had to teach me the Monk language. He didn't have a pill to do that. He didn't have a generalized language-learning course either, if there is one, which I doubt.

"He was pretty drunk, but he found something that would serve. The profession it taught me was an old one, and it doesn't have a one-or-two-word name. But if it did, the word would be *prophet*!"

"Prophet," said Louise. "Prophet?" She was doing a remarkable thing. She was listening with all her concentration, and scrambling eggs at the same time.

"Or disciple. Maybe *apostle* comes closer. Anyway, it included the Gift of Tongues, which was what the Monk was after. But it included other talents too."

"Like turning cold water into hot coffee?"

"Miracles, right. I used the same talent to make the little pink amnesia pills disappear before they hit my stomach. But an apostle's major talent is persuasion.

"Last night I convinced a Monk crewman that blowing up suns is an evil thing.

"Morris is afraid that someone might convert him back. I don't think that's possible. The mind-reading talent that goes with the prophet pill goes deeper than just reading minds. I read souls. The Monk is my apostle. Maybe he'll convince the whole crew that I'm right.

"Or he may just curse the *hachiroph shisp*, the little old nova maker. Which is what I intend to do."

"Curse it?"

"Do you think I'm kidding or something?"

"Oh, no." She poured our coffee. "Will that stop it working?"

"Yes."

"Good," said Louise. And I felt the power of her own faith, her faith in me. It gave her the serenity of an idealized nun.

When she turned back to serve the eggs, I dropped a pink triangular pill in her coffee.

She finished setting breakfast and we sat down. Louise said, "Then that's it. It's all over."

"All over." I swallowed some orange juice. Wonderful, what fourteen hours' sleep will do for a man's appetite. "All over. I can go back to my fourth profession, the only one that counts."

She looked up quickly.

"Bartender. First, last, and foremost, I'm a bartender. You're going to marry a bartender."

"Good," she said, relaxing.

In two hours or so the slave sets would be gone from her mind. She would be herself again: free, independent, unable to diet, and somewhat shy.

But the pink pill would not destroy real memories. Two hours from now, Louise would still know that I loved her; and perhaps she would marry me after all.

I said, "We'll have to hire an assistant. And raise our prices. They'll be fighting their way in when the story gets out."

Louise had pursued her own thoughts. "Bill Morris looked awful when I left. You ought to tell him he can stop worrying."

"Oh, no. I *want* him scared. Morris has got to talk the rest of the world into building a launching laser, instead of just throwing bombs at the Monk ship. And we *need* the launching laser."

"Mmm! That's good coffee. Why do we need a launching laser?"

"To get to the stars."

"That's Morris's bag. You're a bartender, remember? The fourth profession."

I shook my head. "You and Morris. You don't see how *big* the Monk marketplace is, or how thin the Monks are scattered. How many novas have you seen in your lifetime?

"Damn few," I said. "There are damn few trading ships in a godawful lot of sky. There are things out there besides Monks. Things the Monks are afraid of, and probably others they don't know about.

"Things so dangerous that the only protection is to be somewhere else, circling some other star, when it happens here! The Monk drive is our lifeline and our immortality. It would be cheap at any price . . ."

"Your eyes are glowing," she breathed. She looked half hypnotized, and utterly convinced. And I knew that for the rest of my life, I would have to keep a tight rein on my tendency to preach.

Usually I know the ending of a story before I write it. Sometimes I just start writing . . . and write a few pages, and throw it away. Sometimes I keep writing.

Through most of "The Fourth Profession" I didn't even know how many pills Frazer had taken! And when I understood the first pill, I knew an important truth: you can *always* rewrite the opening.

I want to thank Marilyn Hacker for pointing out an important aspect of that fourth pill. At her suggestion I did considerable rewriting.

• • •

• • •

A grendel head popped through the hole, inverted, looking at them with fixed, milky, dead eyes. Cadmann sank a baling hook into its neck and dragged it through the opening.

Rick said quietly, "You wouldn't want to do that to a live and curious grendel. Whack the tail with a stick first and see if it wiggles."

THE LEGACY OF HEOROT (with Jerry Pournelle and Steven Barnes), 1987

"SHALL WE INDULGE IN RISHATHRA?"

LETTER TO *SCIENCE FICTION REVIEW*, NOVEMBER 1978

Enclosed are five cartoons and a possibly cryptic list, and this letter. They all relate to the word "rishathra."

"Rishathra" is a word used extensively in THE RINGWORLD ENGINEERS, a sequel to RINGWORLD, now two-thirds finished. It is one of the few words common to all of the Ringworld languages.

The word means "Sex outside of one's species, but within the hominids." Sometimes rishathra applies to intelligent hominids only, and sometimes not, depending on who (and what) you're talking to. A given species' attitude toward rishathra, whether determined by custom or by biology, can be very important in trading, in treaties, in war.

Obviously, what Louis Wu was doing with Halrloprillalar was "rishathra."

I was having lunch with Bill Rotsler and Sharman DiVono a year ago, and I broached this subject. I had been jotting down a list of possible replies to the question, "Shall we do rishathra?" Bill looked it over. Then he started drawing cartoons. He's given me permission to send them to you for publication.

Some of what's on the list of replies will go into the book. Some are useless, of course. "You do not have sufficient openings" would surely not apply to the hominids!

• •

"SHALL WE INDULGE IN RISHATHRA?"

1) Sure.
2) You're too big/small.
3) If that's what it takes to make a trade deal . . .
4) It is not my season. Can you wait around, or come back in a *falen* or so?
5) Taboo!
6) Our species cannot. Please do not be angry/insulted.
7) Only during our menstrual period. Day after tomorrow?
8) Only with sentient beings. Would you mind taking a short intelligence test?

9) Only with nonsentient beings. It lets us avoid becoming involved.
10) Does your companion indulge? (This would require long explanation, given that Louis Wu's companion is a kzin.)
11) Yes. We will choose you a companion if you will state your sex.
12) May my family watch?
13) My family insists on watching.
14) We have certain practices to be used as a substitute . . .
15) We must eat together first.
16) Our form of foreplay may be dangerous to you.
17) Can you function underwater?
18) No! You have the odor of a meat eater.
19) May we watch you with your companion? We will reciprocate . . . (Sorry, Chmeee is male.)
20) You do not have sufficient openings.
21) Negotiate first! Then discuss rishathra.
22) No, but we like to talk about it.
23) We would like to make tape recordings for our communal archives.
24) Only during our fertile period, as a means of birth control.

YOU MENTIONED
SEX WITH
ALIEN RACES—?

THOSE RINGWORLD
ENGINEER CONVENTIONS—!
THEY'LL
RISHATHRA
WITH ANYTHING!

• • •

• • •

I could have taken a transfer booth straight to the hotel, I decided to walk a little first.

Everyone on Earth had made the same decision.

... No two looked alike. There were reds and blues and greens, yellows and oranges, plaids and stripes. I'm talking about hair, you understand, and skin.

"Flatlander," 1967

MAN OF STEEL, *WOMAN OF KLEENEX*

At the ripe old age of forty,* Kal-El (alias Superman, alias Clark Kent) is still unmarried. Almost certainly he is still a virgin. This is a serious matter. The species itself is in danger!

An unwed Superman is a mobile Superman. Thus it has been alleged that those who chronicle the Man of Steel's adventures are responsible for his condition. But the cartoonists are not to blame.

Nor is Superman handicapped by psychological problems.

Granted that the poor oaf is not entirely sane. How could he be? He is an orphan, a refugee, and an alien. His homeland no longer exists in any form, save for gigatons upon gigatons of dangerous, prettily colored rocks.

As a child and young adult, Kal-El must have been hard put to find an adequate father-figure. What human could control his anti-social behavior? What human would dare try to punish him? His actual, highly social behavior during this period indicates an inhuman self-restraint.

What wonder if Superman drifted gradually into schizophrenia? Torn between his human and kryptonian identities, he chose to be both, keeping his split personalities rigidly separate. A psychotic desperation is evident in his defense of his "secret identity."

But Superman's sex problems are strictly physiological, and quite real.

The purpose of this article is to point out some medical drawbacks to being a kryptonian among human beings, and to suggest possible solutions. The kryptonian humanoid must not be allowed to go the way of the pterodactyl and the passenger pigeon.

*Superman first appeared in *Action Comics*, June 1938.

I

What turns on a kryptonian?

Superman is an alien, an extraterrestrial. His humanoid frame is doubtless the result of parallel evolution, as the marsupials of Australia resemble their mammalian counterparts. A specific niche in the ecology calls for a certain shape, a certain size, certain capabilities, certain eating habits.

Be not deceived by appearances. Superman is no relative to homo sapiens.

What arouses Kal-El's mating urge? Did kryptonian women carry some subtle mating cue at appropriate times of the year? Whatever it is, Lois Lane probably doesn't have it. We may speculate that she smells wrong, less like a kryptonian woman than like a terrestrial monkey. A mating between Superman and Lois Lane would feel like sodomy—and would be, of course, by church and common law.

II

Assume a mating between Superman and a human woman, designated LL for convenience.

Either Superman has gone completely schizo and believes himself to be Clark Kent; or he knows what he's doing, but no longer gives a damn. Forty years is a long time. For Superman it has been even longer. He has X-ray vision; he knows just what he's missing.*

The problem is this. Electroencephalograms taken of men and women during sexual intercourse show that orgasm resembles "a kind of pleasurable epileptic attack." One loses control over one's muscles.

Superman has been known to leave his fingerprints in steel and in hardened concrete, accidentally. What would he do to the woman in his arms during what amounts to an epileptic fit?

III

Consider the driving urge between a man and a woman, the monomaniacal urge to achieve greater and greater penetration. Remember also that we are dealing with kryptonian muscles.

Superman would literally crush LL's body in his arms, while simul-

*One should not think of Superman as a Peeping Tom. A biological ability must be used. As a child Superman may never have known that things had surfaces, until he learned to suppress his X-ray vision.

If millions of people tend shamelessly to wear clothing with no lead in the weave, that is hardly Superman's fault.

taneously ripping her open from crotch to sternum, gutting her like a trout.

IV

Lastly, he'd blow off the top of her head.

Ejaculation of semen is entirely involuntary in the human male, and in all other forms of terrestrial life. It would be unreasonable to assume otherwise for a kryptonian. But with kryptonian muscles behind it, Kal-El's semen would emerge with the muzzle velocity of a machine gun bullet.*

In view of the foregoing, normal sex is impossible between LL and Superman.

Artificial insemination may give us better results.

V

First we must collect the semen. The globules will emerge at transsonic speeds. Superman must first ejaculate, then fly frantically after the stuff to catch it in a test tube. We assume that he is on the Moon, both for privacy and to prevent the semen from exploding into vapor on hitting air at such speeds.

He can catch the semen, of course, before it evaporates in vacuum. He's faster than a speeding bullet.

But can he keep it?

All known forms of kryptonian life have superpowers. The same must hold true of living kryptonian sperm. We may reasonably assume that kryptonian sperm are vulnerable only to starvation and to green kryptonite; that they can travel with equal ease through water, air, vacuum, glass, brick, boiling steel, solid steel, liquid helium, or the core of a star; and that they are capable of translight velocities.

What kind of a test tube will hold such beasties?

Kryptonian sperm and their unusual powers will give us further trouble. For the moment we will assume (because we must) that they tend to stay in the seminal fluid, which tends to stay in a simple glass tube. Thus Superman and LL can perform artificial insemination.

At least there will be another generation of kryptonians.

Or will there?

*One can imagine that the Kent home in Smallville was riddled with holes during Superboy's puberty. And why did Lana Lang never notice *that*?

VI

A ripened but unfertilized egg leaves LL's ovary, begins its voyage down her Fallopian tube.

Some time later, tens of millions of sperm, released from a test tube, begin their own voyage up LL's Fallopian tube.

The magic moment approaches . . .

Can human breed with Kryptonian? Do we even use the same genetic code? On the face of it, LL could more easily breed with an ear of corn than with Kal-El. But coincidence does happen. If the genes match . . .

One sperm arrives before the others. It penetrates the egg, forms a lump on its surface. The cell wall now thickens to prevent other sperm from entering. Within the now-fertilized egg, changes take place . . .

And ten million kryptonian sperm arrive slightly late.

Were they human sperm, they would be out of luck. But these tiny blind things are more powerful than a locomotive. A thickened cell wall won't stop them. They will *all* enter the egg, obliterating it entirely in an orgy of microscopic gang rape. So much for artificial insemination.

But LL's problems are just beginning.

VII

Within her body there are still tens of millions of frustrated kryptonian sperm. The single egg is now too diffuse to be a target. The sperm scatter.

They scatter without regard to what is in their path. They leave curved channels, microscopically small. Presently all will have found their way to the open air.

That leaves LL with several million microscopic perforations all leading deep into her abdomen. Most of the channels will intersect one or more loops of intestine.

Peritonitis is inevitable. LL becomes desperately ill.

Meanwhile, tens of millions of sperm swarm in the air over Metropolis.

VIII

This is more serious than it looks.

Consider: these sperm are virtually indestructible. Within days or weeks they will die for lack of nourishment. Meanwhile they cannot be affected by heat, cold, vacuum, toxins, or anything short of green kryptonite.*

*And other forms of kryptonite. For instance, there are chunks of red kryptonite that make giants of kryptonians. Imagine ten million earthworm-sized spermatozoa swarming over a Metropolis beach, diving to fertilize the beach balls . . . but I digress.

There they are, minuscule but dangerous; for each has supernormal powers.

Metropolis is shaken by tiny sonic booms. Worm-holes, charred by meteoric heat, sprout magically in all kinds of things: plate glass, masonry, antique ceramics, electric mixers, wood, household pets, and citizens. Some of the sperm will crack lightspeed. The Metropolis night comes alive with a network of narrow, eerie blue lines of Cherenkov radiation.

And women whom Superman has never met find themselves in a delicate condition.

Consider: LL won't get pregnant because there were too many of the blind mindless beasts. But whenever one sperm approaches an unfertilized human egg in its panic flight, it will attack.

How close is close enough? A few centimeters? Are sperm attracted by chemical cues? It seems likely. Metropolis had a population of millions; and a kryptonian sperm could travel a long and crooked path, billions of miles, before it gives up and dies.

Several thousand blessed events seem not unlikely.*

Several thousand lawsuits would follow. Not that Superman can't afford to pay. There's a trick where you squeeze a lump of coal into its allotropic diamond form . . .

IX

The above analysis gives us part of the answer. In our experiment in artificial insemination, we must use a single sperm. This presents no difficulty. Superman may use his microscopic vision and a pair of tiny tweezers to pluck a sperm from the swarm.

X

In its eagerness the single sperm may crash through LL's abdomen at transsonic speeds, wreaking havoc. Is there any way to slow it down?

There is. We can expose it to gold kryptonite.

Gold kryptonite, we remember, robs a kryptonian of all of his supernormal powers, permanently. Were we to expose Superman himself to gold kryptonite, we would solve all his sex problems, but he would be Clark Kent forever. We may regard this solution as somewhat drastic.

But we can expose the test tube of seminal fluid to gold kryptonite, then use standard techniques for artificial insemination.

*If the pubescent Superboy plays with himself, we have the same problem over Smallville.

By any of these methods we can get LL pregnant, without killing her. Are we out of the woods yet?

XI

Though exposed to gold kryptonite, the sperm still carries kryptonian genes. If these are recessive, then LL carries a developing human fetus. There will be no more Supermen; but at least we need not worry about the mother's health.

But if some or all of the kryptonian genes are dominant . . .

Can the infant use his X-ray vision before birth? After all, with such a power he can probably see through his own closed eyelids. That would leave LL sterile. If the kid starts using heat vision, things get even worse.

But when he starts to kick, it's all over. He will kick his way out into the open air, killing himself and his mother.

XII

Is there a solution?

There are several. Each has drawbacks.

We can make LL wear a kryptonite* belt around her waist. But too little kryptonite may allow the child to damage her, while too much may damage or kill the child. Intermediate amounts may do both! And there is no safe way to experiment.

A better solution is to find a host-mother.

We have not yet considered the existence of Supergirl.† She could carry the child without harm. But Supergirl has a secret identity, and her secret identity is no more married than Supergirl herself. If she turned up pregnant, she would probably be thrown out of school.

A better solution may be to implant the growing fetus in Superman himself. There are places in a man's abdomen where a foetus could draw adequate nourishment, growing as a parasite, and where it would not cause undue harm to surrounding organs. Presumably Clark Kent can take a leave of absence more easily than Supergirl's schoolgirl alter ego.

When the time comes, the child would be removed by Caesarian section. It would have to be removed early, but there would be no problem

*For our purposes, all forms of kryptonite are available in unlimited quantities. It has been estimated, from the startling tonnage of kryptonite fallen to Earth since the explosion of krypton, that the planet must have outweighed our entire solar system. Doubtless the 'planet' Krypton was a cooling black dwarf star, one of a binary pair, the other member being a red giant.

†She can't mate with Superman because she's his first cousin. And only a cad would suggest differently.

with incubators as long as it was fed. I leave the problem of cutting through Superman's invulnerable skin, as an exercise for the alert reader.

The mind boggles at the image of a pregnant Superman cruising the skies of Metropolis. Batman would refuse to be seen with him; strange new jokes would circulate the prisons . . . and the race of Krypton would be safe at last.

Surely every child who ever read a comic book has wondered about these matters? But my venture into xenofertility was only party conversation until Bjo Trimble made me type it up.

It's generated tremendous levels of feedback, and more damned *fun* . . .

There's a dramatization: an underground comic that looks very like a DC treatment except for being black and white. It begins as Superman drops and smashes the Kandor bottle, and ends as The Atom (the little one) implants a fertilized egg.

People read the article to their friends over the phone.

Kirk Alyn is a wedge-shaped old man, looks like you'd want to look at that age. He played Superman in the serials. He read "Man of Steel . . ." because a young lady recognized him on an airplane; she handed him a copy of ALL THE MYRIAD WAYS with the article marked. He says he's always wondered what she had in mind.

When the Superman movie was about to happen, a Brit videotaped some interviews at the Griffith Park Planetarium. At his behest I described, on videotape, the problems a Kryptonian would face living a normal life on Earth. He held his straight face until he had what he wanted, then cracked up. A real pro.

And Ben Bova bought reprint rights for *Omni* magazine. I altered and signed the contract, cashed the check, and waited. Nothing. At *Omni*'s first anniversary party at Griffith Observatory, I asked Ben, "When will you publish 'Man of Steel . . .'?"

He wouldn't.

Why not?

Well, the Superman movie people and the DC Comics people all know about "Man of Steel." They wouldn't let Ben *illustrate* the article, and *Omni* is such a visual magazine . . .

In June of '88 Superman's 50th birthday was celebrated with a convention in Cleveland, his true birthplace. They'd promised a statue; it never happened. A panel on crossbreeding of humans and aliens turned out to be just me! I managed to hold the audience by reading this article, then discussing Reed and Sue Richards, Mr. Spock, V-for-Visitors, rishathra . . . Sex with aliens seems to fascinate people.

• • •

• • •

Up from the Plateau on Mount Lookitthat came Douglas Hooker, rising like a star.

"The Ethics of Madness," 1967

INCONSTANT MOON

I

I was watching the news when the change came, like a flicker of motion at the corner of my eye. I turned toward the balcony window. Whatever it was, I was too late to catch it.

The moon was very bright tonight.

I saw that, and smiled, and turned back. Johnny Carson was just starting his monologue.

When the first commercials came on I got up to reheat some coffee. Commercials came in strings of three and four, going on midnight. I'd have time.

The moonlight caught me coming back. If it had been bright before, it was brighter now. Hypnotic. I opened the sliding glass door and stepped out onto the balcony.

The balcony wasn't much more than a railed ledge, with standing room for a man and a woman and a portable barbecue set. These past months the view had been lovely, especially around sunset. The Power and Light Company had been putting up a glass-slab style office building. So far it was only a steel framework of open girders. Shadow-blackened against a red sunset sky, it tended to look stark and surrealistic and hellishly impressive.

Tonight . . .

I had never seen the moon so bright, not even in the desert. *Bright enough to read by*, I thought, and immediately, *but that's an illusion*. The moon was never bigger (I had read somewhere) than a quarter held nine feet away. It couldn't possibly be bright enough to read by.

It was only three-quarters full!

But, glowing high over the San Diego Freeway to the west, the moon seemed to dim even the streaming automobile headlights. I blinked against its light, and thought of men walking on the moon, leaving corrugated footprints. Once, for the sake of an article I was writing, I had been allowed to pick up a bone-dry moon rock and hold it in my hand. . . .

I heard the show starting again, and I stepped inside. But, glancing once behind me, I caught the moon growing even brighter—as if it had come from behind a wisp of scudding cloud.

Now its light was brain-searing, lunatic.

The phone rang five times before she answered.

"Hi," I said. "Listen—"

"Hi," Leslie said sleepily, complainingly. Damn. I'd hoped she was watching television, like me.

I said, "Don't scream and shout, because I had a reason for calling. You're in bed, right? Get up and—can you get up?"

"What time is it?"

"Quarter of twelve."

"Oh, Lord."

"Go out on your balcony and look around."

"Okay."

The phone clunked. I waited. Leslie's balcony faced north and west, like mine, but it was ten stories higher, with a correspondingly better view.

Through my own window, the moon burned like a textured spotlight.

"Stan? You there?"

"Yah. What do you think of it?"

"It's gorgeous. I've never seen anything like it. What could make the moon light up like that?"

"I don't know, but isn't it gorgeous?"

"You're supposed to be the native." Leslie had only moved out here a year ago.

"Listen, I've *never* seen it like this. But there's an old legend," I said. "Once every hundred years the Los Angeles smog rolls away for a single night, leaving the air as clear as interstellar space. That way the gods can see if Los Angeles is still there. If it is, they roll the smog back so they won't have to look at it."

"I used to know all that stuff. Well, listen, I'm glad you woke me up to see it, but I've got to get to work tomorrow."

"Poor baby."

"That's life. 'Night."

"'Night."

Afterward I sat in the dark, trying to think of someone else to call. Call a girl at midnight, invite her to step outside and look at the moonlight . . . and she may think it's romantic or she may be furious, but she won't assume you called six others.

So I thought of some names. But the girls who belonged to them had all dropped away over the past year or so, after I started spending all my time with Leslie. One could hardly blame them. And now Joan was in Texas and Hildy was getting married, and if I called Louise I'd probably get Gordie too. The English girl? But I couldn't remember her number. Or her last name.

Besides, everyone I knew punched a time clock of one kind or another. Me, I worked for a living, but as a freelance writer I picked my hours. Anyone I woke up tonight, I'd be ruining her morning. Ah, well . . .

The Johnny Carson Show was a swirl of gray and a roar of static when I got back to the living room. I turned the set off and went back out on the balcony.

The moon was brighter than the flow of headlights on the freeway, brighter than Westwood Village off to the right. The Santa Monica Mountains had a magical pearly glow. There were no stars near the moon. Stars could not survive that glare.

I wrote science and how-to articles for a living. I ought to be able to figure out what was making the moon do that. Could the moon be suddenly larger?

. . . Inflating like a balloon? No. Closer, maybe. The moon, falling?

Tides! Waves fifty feet high . . . and earthquakes! San Andreas Fault splitting apart like the Grand Canyon! Jump in my car, head for the hills . . . no, too late already . . .

Nonsense. The moon was brighter, not bigger. I could see that. And what could possibly drop the moon on our heads like that?

I blinked, and the moon left an afterimage on my retinae. It was *that* bright.

A million people must be watching the moon right now, and wondering, like me. An article on the subject would sell big . . . if I wrote it before anyone else did . . .

There must be some simple, obvious explanation.

Well, how could the moon grow brighter? Moonlight was reflected sunlight. Could the sun have gotten brighter? It must have happened after sunset, then, or it would have been noticed. . . .

I didn't like that idea.

Besides, half the Earth was in direct sunlight. A thousand correspondents for *Life* and *Time* and *Newsweek* and Associated Press would all be calling in from Europe, Asia, Africa . . . unless they were all hiding in cellars. Or dead. Or voiceless, because the sun was blanketing everything with static, radio and phone systems and television . . . television. Oh my God.

I was just barely beginning to be afraid.

All right, start over. The moon had become very much brighter. Moonlight, well, moonlight was reflected sunlight; any idiot knew that. Then . . . something had happened to the sun.

II

"Hello?"

"Hi. Me," I said, and then my throat froze solid. Panic! What was I going to *tell* her?

"I've been watching the moon," she said dreamily. "It's wonderful. I even tried to use my telescope, but I couldn't see a thing; it was too bright. It lights up the whole city. The hills are all silver."

That's right, she kept a telescope on her balcony. I'd forgotten.

"I haven't tried to go back to sleep," she said. "Too much light."

I got my throat working again. "Listen, Leslie love, I started thinking about how I woke you up and how you probably couldn't get back to sleep, what with all this light. So let's go out for a midnight snack."

"Are you out of your mind?"

"No, I'm serious. I mean it. Tonight isn't a night for sleeping. We may never have a night like this again. To hell with your diet. Let's celebrate. Hot fudge sundaes, Irish Coffee—"

"That's different. I'll get dressed."

"I'll be right over."

Leslie lived on the fourteenth floor of Building C of the Barrington Plaza. I rapped for admission, and waited.

And waiting, I wondered without any sense of urgency: Why Leslie?

There must be other ways to spend my last night on Earth, than with one particular girl. I could have picked a different particular girl, or even several not too particular girls, except that that didn't really apply to me, did it? Or I could have called my brother, or either set of parents—

Well, but brother Mike would have wanted a good reason for being hauled out of bed at midnight. "But, Mike, the moon is so beautiful—" Hardly. Any of my parents would have reacted similarly. Well, I had a good reason, but would they believe me?

And if they did, what then? I would have arranged a kind of wake. Let 'em sleep through it. What I wanted was someone who would join my . . . farewell party without asking the wrong questions.

What I wanted was Leslie. I knocked again.

She opened the door just a crack for me. She was in her underwear. A stiff, misshapen girdle in one hand brushed my back as she came into my arms. "I was about to put this on."

"I came just in time, then." I took the girdle away from her and dropped it. I stooped to get my arms under her ribs, straightened up with effort, and walked us to the bedroom with her feet dangling against my ankles.

Her skin was cold. She must have been outside.

"So!" she demanded. "You think you can compete with a hot fudge sundae, do you?"

"Certainly. My pride demands it." We were both somewhat out of breath. Once in our lives I had tried to lift her cradled in my arms, in conventional movie style. I'd damn near broken my back. Leslie was a big girl, my height, and almost too heavy around the hips.

I dropped us on the bed, side by side. I reached around her from both sides to scratch her back, knowing it would leave her helpless to resist me, *ah* ha hahahaha. She made sounds of pleasure to tell me where to scratch. She pulled my shirt up around my shoulders and began scratching my back.

We pulled pieces of clothing from ourselves and each other, at random, dropping them over the edges of the bed. Leslie's skin was warm now, almost hot . . .

All right, now *that's* why I couldn't have picked another girl. I'd have to teach her how to scratch. And there just wasn't time.

Some nights I had a nervous tendency to hurry our lovemaking. Tonight we were performing a ritual, a rite of passage. I tried to slow it down, to make it last. I tried to make Leslie like it more. It paid off incredibly. I forgot the moon and the future when Leslie put her heels against the backs of my knees and we moved into the ancient rhythm.

But the image that came to me at the climax was vivid and frightening. We were in a ring of blue-hot fire that closed like a noose. If I moaned in terror and ecstasy, then she must have thought it was ecstasy alone.

We lay side by side, drowsy, torpid, clinging together. I was minded to go back to sleep then, renege on my promise, sleep and let Leslie sleep . . . but instead I whispered into her ear: "Hot fudge sundae." She smiled and stirred and presently rolled off the bed.

I wouldn't let her wear the girdle. "It's past midnight. Nobody's going to pick you up, because I'd thrash the blackguard, right? So why not be comfortable?" She laughed and gave in. We hugged each other once, hard, in the elevator. It felt much better without the girdle.

III

The gray-haired counter waitress was cheerful and excited. Her eyes glowed. She spoke as if confiding a secret. "Have you noticed the moonlight?"

Ships's was fairly crowded, this time of night and this close to UCLA. Half the customers were university students. Tonight they talked in hushed voices, turning to look out through the glass walls of the twenty-four-hour restaurant. The moon was low in the west, low enough to compete with the street globes.

"We noticed," I said. "We're celebrating. Get us two hot fudge sundaes, will you?" When she turned her back I slid a ten-dollar bill under the paper place mat. Not that she'd ever spend it, but at least she'd have the pleasure of finding it. I'd never spend it either.

I felt loose, casual. A lot of problems seemed suddenly to have solved themselves.

Who would have believed that peace could come to Vietnam and Cambodia in a single night?

This thing had started around eleven-thirty, here in California. That would have put the noon sun just over the Arabian Sea, with all but a few fringes of Asia, Europe, Africa, and Australia in direct sunlight.

Already Germany was reunited, the Wall melted or smashed by shock waves. Israelis and Arabs had laid down their arms. Apartheid was dead in Africa.

And I was free. For me there were no more consequences. Tonight I could satisfy all my dark urges, rob, kill, cheat on my income tax, throw bricks at plate glass windows, burn my credit cards. I could forget the article on explosive metal forming, due Thursday. Tonight I could substitute cinnamon candy for Leslie's Pills. Tonight—

"Think I'll have a cigarette."

Leslie looked at me oddly. "I thought you'd given that up."

"You remember. I told myself if I got any overpowering urges, I'd have a cigarette. I did that because I couldn't stand the thought of never smoking again."

"But it's been months!" she laughed.

"But they keep putting cigarette ads in my magazines!"

"It's a plot. All right, go have a cigarette."

I put coins in the machine, hesitated over the choice, finally picked a mild filter. It wasn't that I wanted a cigarette. But certain events call for champagne, and others for cigarettes. There is the traditional last cigarette before a firing squad . . .

I lit up. *Here's to lung cancer.*

It tasted just as good as I remembered; though there was a faint stale undertaste, like a mouthful of old cigarette butts. The third lungful hit me oddly. My eyes unfocused and everything went very calm. My heart pulsed loudly in my throat.

"How does it taste?"

"Strange. I'm buzzed," I said.

Buzzed! I hadn't even heard the word in fifteen years. In high school we'd smoked to get that buzz, that quasi-drunkenness produced by capillaries constricting in the brain. The buzz had stopped coming after the first few times, but we'd kept smoking, most of us . . .

I put it out. The waitress was picking up our sundaes.

Hot and cold, sweet and bitter: there is no taste quite like that of a hot fudge sundae. To die without tasting it again would have been a crying shame. But with Leslie it was a *thing*, a symbol of all rich living. Watching her eat was more fun than eating myself.

Besides . . . I'd killed the cigarette to taste the ice cream. Now, instead of savoring the ice cream, I was anticipating Irish coffee.

Too little time.

Leslie's dish was empty. She stage-whispered, "Aahh!" and patted herself over the navel.

A customer at one of the small tables began to go mad.

I'd noticed him coming in. A lean scholarly type wearing sideburns and steel-rimmed glasses, he had been continually twisting around to look out at the moon. Like others at other tables, he seemed high on a rare and lovely natural phenomenon.

Then he got it. I saw his face changing, showing suspicion, then disbelief, then horror, horror and helplessness.

"Let's go," I told Leslie. I dropped quarters on the counter and stood up.

"Don't you want to finish yours?"

"Nope. We've got things to do. How about some Irish coffee?"

"And a Pink Lady for me? Oh, look!" She turned full around.

The scholar was climbing up on a table. He balanced, spread wide his arms and bellowed, "Look out your windows!"

"You get down from there!" a waitress demanded, jerking emphatically at his pants leg.

"The world is coming to an end! Far away on the other side of the sea, death and hellfire—"

But we were out the door, laughing as we ran. Leslie panted, "We may have—escaped a religious—riot in there!"

I thought of the ten I'd left under my plate. Now it would please nobody. Inside, a prophet was shouting his message of doom to all who would hear. The gray-haired woman with the glowing eyes would find the money and think: They knew it too.

Buildings blocked the moon from the Red Barn's parking lot. The street lights and the indirect moonglare were pretty much the same color. The night only seemed a bit brighter than usual.

I didn't understand why Leslie stopped suddenly in the driveway. But I followed her gaze, straight up to where a star burned very brightly just south of the zenith.

"Pretty," I said.

She gave me a very odd look.

There were no windows in the Red Barn. Dim artificial lighting, far dimmer than the queer cold light outside, showed on dark wood and quietly cheerful customers. Nobody seemed aware that tonight was different from other nights.

The sparse Tuesday night crowd was gathered mostly around the piano bar. A customer had the mike. He was singing some half-familiar song in a wavering weak voice, while the black pianist grinned and played a schmaltzy background.

I ordered two Irish coffees and a Pink Lady. At Leslie's questioning look I only smiled mysteriously.

How ordinary the Red Barn felt. How relaxed; how happy. We held hands across the table, and I smiled and was afraid to speak. If I broke the spell, if I said the wrong thing . . .

The drinks arrived. I raised an Irish coffee glass by the stem. Sugar, Irish whiskey, and strong black coffee, with thick whipped cream floating on top. It coursed through me like a magical potion of strength, dark and hot and powerful.

The waitress waved back my money. ''See that man in the turtleneck, there at the end of the piano bar? He's buying,'' she said with relish. ''He came in two hours ago and handed the bartender a hundred-dollar bill.''

So that was where all the happiness was coming from. Free drinks! I looked over, wondering what the guy was celebrating.

A thick-necked, wide-shouldered man in a turtleneck and sports coat, he sat hunched over into himself, with a wide bar glass clutched tight in one hand. The pianist offered him the mike, and he waved it by, the gesture giving me a good look at his face. A square, strong face, now drunk and miserable and scared. He was ready to cry from fear.

So I knew what he was celebrating.

Leslie made a face. ''They didn't make the Pink Lady right.''

There's one bar in the world that makes a Pink Lady the way Leslie likes it, and it isn't in Los Angeles. I passed her the other Irish coffee, grinning an I-told-you-so grin. Forcing it. The other man's fear was contagious. She smiled back, lifted her glass and said, ''To the blue moonlight.''

I lifted my glass to her, and drank. But it wasn't the toast I would have chosen.

The man in the turtleneck slid down from his stool. He moved carefully toward the door, his course slow and straight as an ocean liner cruising into dock. He pulled the door wide, and turned around, holding it open, so that the weird blue-white light streamed past his broad black silhouette.

Bastard. He was waiting for someone to figure it out, to shout out the truth to the rest. *Fire and doom—*

''Shut the door!'' someone bellowed.

''Time to go,'' I said softly.

''What's the hurry?''

The hurry? He might *speak*! But I couldn't say that . . .

Leslie put her hand over mine. "I know. I *know*. But we can't run away from it, can we?"

A fist closed hard on my heart. She'd known, and I hadn't noticed?

The door closed, leaving the Red Barn in reddish dusk. The man who had been buying drinks was gone.

"Oh, God. When did you figure it out?"

"Before you came over," she said. "But when I tried to check it out, it didn't work."

"Check it out?"

"I went out on the balcony and turned the telescope on Jupiter. Mars is below the horizon these nights. If the sun's gone nova, all the planets ought to be lit up like the moon, right?"

"Right. Damn." I should have thought of that myself. But Leslie was the stargazer. I knew some astrophysics, but I couldn't have found Jupiter to save my life.

"But Jupiter wasn't any brighter than usual. So then I didn't know *what* to think."

"But then—" I felt hope dawning fiery hot. Then I remembered. "That star, just overhead. The one you stared at."

"Jupiter."

"All lit up like a fucking neon sign. Well, that tears it."

"Keep your voice down."

I *had* been keeping my voice down. But for a wild moment I wanted to stand up on a table and scream! *Fire and doom*—What right had they to be ignorant?

Leslie's hand closed tight on mine. The urge passed. It left me shuddering. "Let's get out of here. Let 'em think there's going to be a dawn."

"There is." Leslie laughed a bitter, barking laugh like nothing I'd ever heard from her. She walked out while I was reaching for my wallet—and remembering that there was no need.

Poor Leslie. Finding Jupiter its normal self must have looked like a reprieve—until the white spark flared to shining glory an hour and a half late. An hour and a half, for sunlight to reach Earth by way of Jupiter.

When I reached the door Leslie was half-running down Westwood toward Santa Monica. I cursed and ran to catch up, wondering if she'd suddenly gone crazy.

Then I noticed the shadows ahead of us. All along the other side of Santa Monica Boulevard: moon shadows, in horizontal patterns of dark and blue-white bands.

I caught her at the corner.

The moon was setting.

A setting moon always looks tremendous. Tonight it glared at us through the gap of sky beneath the freeway, terribly bright, casting an incredible complexity of lines and shadows. Even the unlighted crescent glowed pearly bright with earthshine.

Which told me all I wanted to know about what was happening on the lighted side of Earth.

And on the moon? The men of Apollo Nineteen must have died in the first few minutes of nova sunlight. Trapped out on a lunar plain, hiding perhaps behind a melting boulder . . . Or were they on the night side? I couldn't remember. Hell, they could outlive us all. I felt a stab of envy and hatred.

And pride. We'd put them there. We reached the moon before the nova came. A little longer, we'd have reached the stars.

The disc changed oddly as it set. A dome, a flying saucer, a lens, a line . . .

Gone.

Gone. Well, that was that. Now we could forget it; now we could walk around outside without being constantly reminded that something was *wrong*. Moonset had taken all the queer shadows out of the city.

But the clouds had an odd glow to them. As clouds glow after sunset, tonight the clouds shone livid white at their western edges. And they streamed too quickly across the sky. As if they tried to run . . .

When I turned to Leslie, there were big tears rolling down her cheeks.

"Oh, damn." I took her arm. "Now stop it. Stop it."

"I can't. You know I can't stop crying once I get started."

"This wasn't what I had in mind. I thought we'd do things we've been putting off, things we like. It's our last chance. Is this the way you want to die, crying on a street corner?"

"I don't want to die at all!"

"Tough shit!"

"Thanks a lot." Her face was all red and twisted. Leslie was crying as a baby cries, without regard for dignity or appearance. I felt awful. I felt guilty, and I *knew* the nova wasn't my fault, and it made me angry.

"I don't want to die either!" I snarled at her. "You show me a way out and I'll take it. Where would we go? The South Pole? It'd just take longer. The moon must be molten all across its day side. Mars? When this is over Mars will be part of the sun, like the Earth. Alpha Centauri? The acceleration we'd need, we'd be spread across a wall like peanut butter and jelly—"

"Oh, shut up."

"Right."

"Hawaii. Stan, we could get to the airport in twenty minutes. We'd get two hours extra, going west! Two hours more before sunrise!"

She had something there. Two hours was worth any price! But I'd worked this out before, staring at the moon from my balcony. "No. We'd die sooner. Listen, love, we saw the moon go bright about midnight. That means California was at the back of the Earth when the sun went nova."

"Yes, that's right."

"Then we must be furthest from the shock wave."

She blinked. "I don't understand."

"Look at it this way. First the sun explodes. That heats the air and the oceans, all in a flash, all across the day side. The steam and superheated air expand *fast*. A flaming shock wave comes roaring over into the night side. It's closing on us right now. Like a noose. But it'll reach Hawaii first. Hawaii is two hours closer to the sunset line."

"Then we won't see the dawn. We won't live even that long."

"No."

"You explain things so well," she said bitterly. "A flaming shock wave. So graphic."

"Sorry. I've been thinking about it too much. Wondering what it will be like."

"Well, stop it." She came to me and put her face in my shoulder. She cried quietly. I held her with one arm and used the other to rub her neck, and I watched the streaming clouds, and I didn't think about what it would be like.

Didn't think about the ring of fire closing on us.

It was the wrong picture anyway.

I thought of how the oceans had boiled on the day side, so that the shock wave had been mostly steam to start with. I thought of the millions of square miles of ocean it had to cross. It would be cooler and wetter when it reached us. And the Earth's rotation would spin it like the whirlpool in a bathtub.

Two counterrotating hurricanes of live steam, one north, one south. That was how it would come. We were lucky. California would be near the eye of the northern one.

A hurricane wind of live steam. It would pick a man up and cook him in the air, strip the steamed flesh from him and cast him aside. It was going to hurt like hell.

We would never see the sunrise. In a way that was a pity. It would be spectacular.

Thick parallel streamers of clouds were drifting across the stars, too fast, their bellies white by city light. Jupiter dimmed, then went out. Could it be starting already? Heat lightning jumped—

"Aurora," I said.

"What?"

"There's a shock wave from the sun, too. There should be an aurora like nothing anybody's ever seen before."

Leslie laughed suddenly, jarringly. "It seems so strange, standing on a street corner talking like this! Stan, are we dreaming it?"

"We could pretend—"

"No. Most of the human race must be dead already."

"Yah."

"And there's nowhere to go."

"Damn it, you figured that out long ago, all by yourself. Why bring it up now?"

"You could have let me sleep," she said bitterly. "I was dropping off to sleep when you whispered in my ear."

I didn't answer. It was true.

" 'Hot fudge sundae,' " she quoted. Then, "It wasn't a bad idea, actually. Breaking my diet."

I started to giggle.

"Stop that."

"We could go back to your place now. Or my place. To sleep."

"I suppose. But we couldn't sleep, could we? No, don't say it. We take sleeping pills, and five hours from now we wake up screaming. I'd rather stay awake. At least we'll know what's happening."

But if we took all the pills . . . but I didn't say it. I said, "Then how about a picnic?"

"Where?"

"The beach, maybe. Who cares? We can decide later."

IV

All the markets were closed. But the liquor store next to the Red Barn was one I'd been using for years. They sold us foie gras, crackers, a couple of bottles of chilled champagne, six kinds of cheese and a hell of a lot of nuts—I took one of everything—more crackers, a bag of ice, frozen rumaki hors d'oeuvres, a fifth of an ancient brandy that cost twenty-five bucks, a matching fifth of Cherry Heering for Leslie, six-packs of beer and Bitter Orange . . .

By the time we had piled all that into a dinky store cart, it was raining. Big fat drops spattered in flurries across the acre of plate glass that fronted the store. Wind howled around the corners.

The salesman was in a fey mood, bursting with energy. He'd been watching the moon all night. "And now this!" he exclaimed as he packed our loot into bags. He was a small, muscular old man with thick arms and shoulders. "It *never* rains like this in California. It comes down straight and heavy, when it comes at all. Takes days to build up."

"I know." I wrote him a check, feeling guilty about it. He'd known me long enough to trust me. But the check was good. There were funds to cover it. Before opening hours the check would be ash, and all the banks in the world would be bubbling in the heat of the sun. But that was hardly my fault.

He piled our bags in the cart, set himself at the door. "Now when the rain lets up, we'll run these out. Ready?" I got ready to open the door. The rain came like someone had thrown a bucket of water at the window. In a moment it had stopped, though water still streamed down the glass. "Now!" cried the salesman, and I threw the door open and we were off. We reached the car laughing like maniacs. The wind howled around us, sweeping up spray and hurling it at us.

"We picked a good break. You know what this weather reminds me of? Kansas," said the salesman. "During a tornado."

Then suddenly the sky was full of gravel! We yelped and ducked, and the car rang to a million tiny concussions, and I got the car door unlocked and pulled Leslie and the salesman in after me. We rubbed our bruised heads and looked out at white gravel bouncing everywhere.

The salesman picked a small white pebble out of his collar. He put it in Leslie's hand, and she gave a startled squeak and handed it to me, and it was cold.

"Hail," said the salesman. "Now I really don't get it."

Neither did I. I could only think that it had something to do with the nova. But what? How?

"I've got to get back," said the salesman. The hail had expended itself in one brief flurry. He braced himself, then went out of the car like a marine taking a hill. We never saw him again.

The clouds were churning up there, forming and disappearing, sliding past each other faster than I'd ever seen clouds move; their bellies glowing by city light.

"It must be the nova," Leslie said shivering.

"But how? If the shock wave were here already, we'd be *dead*—or at least deaf. Hail?"

"Who cares? Stan, we don't have *time*!"

I shook myself. "All right. What would you like to do most, right now?"

"Watch a baseball game."

"It's two in the morning," I pointed out.

"That lets out a lot of things, doesn't it?"

"Right. We've hopped our last bar. We've seen our last play, and our last clean movie. What's left?"

"Looking in jewelry store windows."

"Seriously? Your last night on Earth?"

She considered, then answered. "Yes."

By damn, she meant it. I couldn't think of anything duller. "Westwood or Beverly Hills?"

"Both."

"Now, *look*—"

"Beverly Hills, then."

We drove through another spatter of rain and hail—a capsule tempest. We parked half a block from the Tiffany salesroom.

The sidewalk was one continuous puddle. Second-hand rain dripped on us from various levels of the buildings overhead. Leslie said, "This is great. There must be half a dozen jewelry stores in walking distance."

"I was thinking of driving."

"No no no, you don't have the proper attitude. One must window shop on foot. It's in the rules."

"But the rain!"

"You won't die of pneumonia. You won't have time," she said, too grimly.

Tiffany's had a small branch office in Beverly Hills, but they didn't put expensive things in the windows at night. There were a few fascinating toys, that was all.

We turned up Rodeo Drive—and stuck it rich. Tibor showed an infinite selection of rings, ornate and modern, large and small, in all kinds of precious and semiprecious stones. Across the street, Van Cleef & Arpels showed brooches, men's wristwatches of elegant design, bracelets with tiny watches in them, and one window that was all diamonds.

"Oh, lovely," Leslie breathed, caught by the flashing diamonds. "What they must look like in daylight! . . . Wups—"

"No, that's a good thought. Imagine them at dawn, flaming with nova light, while the windows shatter to let the raw daylight in. Want one? The necklace?"

"Oh, *may* I? Hey, hey, I was kidding! Put that down, you idiot, there must be alarms in the glass."

"Look, nobody's going to be wearing any of that stuff between now and morning. Why shouldn't we get some good out of it?"

"We'd be caught!"

"Well, you *said* you wanted to window shop . . ."

"I don't want to spend my last hour in a cell. If you'd brought the car we'd have *some* chance—"

"—Of getting away. Right. I *wanted* to bring the car—" But at that point we both cracked up entirely, and had to stagger away holding onto each other for balance.

There were a good half dozen jewelry stores on Rodeo. But there was more. Toys, books, shirts and ties in odd and advanced styling. In Francis Orr, a huge plastic cube full of new pennies. A couple of damn strange clocks further on. There was an extra kick in window shopping, knowing that we could break a window and take anything we wanted badly enough.

We walked hand in hand, swinging our arms. The sidewalks were ours alone; all others had fled the mad weather. The clouds still churned overhead.

"I wish I'd known it was coming," Leslie said suddenly. "I spent the whole day fixing a mistake in a program. Now we'll never run it."

"What would you have done with the time? A baseball game?"

"Maybe. No. The standings don't matter now." She frowned at dresses in a store window. "What would you have done?"

"Gone to the Blue Sphere for cocktails," I said promptly. "It's a topless place. I used to go there all the time. I hear they've gone full nude now."

"I've never been to one of those. How late are they open?"

"Forget it. It's almost two-thirty."

Leslie mused, looking at giant stuffed animals in a toy store window. "Isn't there someone you would have murdered, if you'd had the time?"

"Now, you *know* my agent lives in New York."

"Why him?"

"My child, why would any writer want to murder his agent? For the manuscripts he loses under other manuscripts. For his ill-gotten ten percent, and the remaining ninety percent that he sends me grudgingly and late. For—"

Suddenly the wind roared and rose up against us. Leslie pointed, and we ran for a deep doorway that turned out to be Gucci's. We huddled against the glass.

The wind was suddenly choked with hail the size of marbles. Glass broke somewhere, and alarms lifted thin, frail voices into the wind. There was more than hail in the wind! There were rocks!

I caught the smell and taste of seawater.

We clung together in the expensively wasted space in front of Gucci's. I coined a short-lived phrase and screamed, "Nova weather! How the blazes did it—" But I couldn't hear myself, and Leslie didn't even know I was shouting.

Nova weather. How did it get here so fast? Coming over the pole, the nova shock wave would have to travel about four thousand miles—at least a five-hour trip.

No. The shock wave would travel in the stratosphere, where the speed of sound was higher, then propagate down. Three hours was plenty of time. Still, I thought, it should not have come as a rising wind. On the other side of the world, the exploding sun was tearing our atmosphere away and hurling it at the stars. The shock should have come as a single vast thunderclap.

For an instant the wind gentled, and I ran down the sidewalk pulling Leslie after me. We found another doorway as the wind picked up again. I thought I heard a siren coming to answer the alarm.

At the next break we splashed across Wilshire and reached the car. We sat there panting, waiting for the heater to warm up. My shoes felt squishy. The wet clothes struck to my skin.

Leslie shouted, "How much longer?"

"I don't know! We ought to have *some* time."

"We'll have to spend our picnic indoors!"

"Your place or mine? Yours," I decided, and pulled away from the curb.

V

Wilshire Boulevard was flooded to the hubcaps in spots. The spurt of hail and sleet had become a steady, pounding rain. Fog lay flat and waist-deep ahead of us, broke swirling over our hood, churned in a wake behind us. Weird weather.

Nova weather. The shock wave of scalding superheated steam hadn't happened. Instead, a mere hot wind roaring through the stratosphere, the turbulence eddying down to form strange storms at ground level.

We parked illegally on the upper parking level. My one glimpse of the lower level showed it to be flooded. I opened the trunk and lifted two heavy paper bags.

"We must have been crazy," Leslie said, shaking her head. "We'll never use all this."

"Let's take it up anyway."

She laughed at me. "But why?"

"Just a whim. Will you help me carry it?"

We took double armfuls up to the fourteenth floor. That still left a couple of bags in the trunk. "Never mind them," Leslie said. "We've got the rumaki and the bottles and the nuts. What more do we need?"

"The cheeses. The crackers. The foie gras."

"Forget 'em."

"No."

"You're out of your mind," she explained to me, slowly so that I would understand. "You could be steamed dead on the way down! We might not have more than a few minutes left, and you want food for a week! *Why?*"

"I'd rather not say."

"Go then!" She slammed the door with terrible force.

The elevator was an ordeal. I kept wondering if Leslie was right. The shrilling of the wind was muffled, here at the core of the building. Perhaps it was about to rip electrical cables somewhere, leave me stranded in a darkened box. But I made it down.

The upper level was knee-deep in water.

My second surprise was that it was lukewarm, like old bathwater, unpleasant to wade through. Steam curdled on the surface, then blew away on a wind that howled through the concrete echo chamber like the screaming of the damned.

Going up was another ordeal. If what I was thinking was wish fulfillment, if a roaring wind of live steam caught me now . . . I'd feel like such an idiot. . . . But the doors opened, and the lights hadn't even flickered.

Leslie wouldn't let me in.

"Go away!" She shouted through the locked door. "Go eat your cheese and crackers somewhere else!"

"You got another date?"

That was a mistake. I got no answer at all.

I could almost see her viewpoint. The extra trip for the extra bags was no big thing to fight about; but why did it have to be? How long was our love affair going to last, anyway? An hour, with luck. Why back down on a perfectly good argument, to preserve so ephemeral a thing?

"I wasn't going to bring this up," I shouted, hoping she could hear me through the door. The wind must be three times as loud on the other side. "We may need food for a week! And a place to hide!"

Silence. I began to wonder if I could kick the door down. Would I be better off waiting in the hall? Eventually she'd have to—

The door opened. Leslie was pale. "That was cruel," she said quietly.

"I can't promise anything. I wanted to wait, but you forced it. I've been wondering if the sun really has exploded."

"That's cruel. I was just getting used to the idea." She turned her face to the door jamb. Tired, she was tired. I'd kept her up too late. . . .

"Listen to me. It was all wrong," I said. "There should have been an aurora borealis to light up the night sky from pole to pole. A shock wave of particles exploding out of the sun, traveling at an inch short of the speed of light, would rip into the atmosphere like—why, we'd have seen blue fire over every building!

"Then, the storm came too slow," I screamed, to be heard above the thunder. "A nova would rip away the sky over half the planet. The shock wave would move around the night side with a sound to break all the glass in the world, all at once! And crack concrete and marble—and, Leslie love, it just hasn't happened. So I started wondering."

She said it in a mumble. "Then what is it?"

"A flare. The worst—"

She shouted it at me like an accusation. "A flare! A solar flare! You think the sun could light up like that—"

''Easy, now—''

''—could turn the moon and planets into so many torches, then fade out as if nothing had happened! Oh, you idiot—''

''May I come in?''

She looked surprised. She stepped aside, and I bent and picked up the bags and walked in.

The glass doors rattled as if giants were trying to beat their way in. Rain had squeezed through cracks to make dark puddles on the rug.

I set the bags on the kitchen counter. I found bread in the refrigerator, dropped two slices in the toaster. While they were toasting I opened the foie gras.

''My telescope's gone,'' she said. Sure enough, it was. The tripod was all by itself on the balcony, on its side.

I untwisted the wire on a champagne bottle. The toast popped up, and Leslie found a knife and spread both slices with foie gras. I held the bottle near her ear, figuring to trip conditioned reflexes.

She did smile fleetingly as the cork popped. She said, ''We should set up our picnic grounds here. Behind the counter. Sooner or later the wind is going to break those doors and shower glass all over everything.''

That was a good thought. I slid around the partition, swept all the pillows off the floor and the couch and came back with them. We set up a nest for ourselves.

It was kind of cozy. The kitchen counter was three and a half feet high, just over our heads, and the kitchen alcove itself was just wide enough to swing our elbows comfortably. Now the floor was all pillows. Leslie poured the champagne into brandy snifters, all the way to the lip.

I searched for a toast, but there were just too many possibilities, all depressing. We drank without toasting. And then carefully set the snifters down and slid forward into each other's arms. We could sit that way, face to face, leaning sideways against each other.

''We're going to die,'' she said.

''Maybe not.''

''Get used to the idea, I have,'' she said. ''Look at you, you're all nervous now. Afraid of dying. Hasn't it been a lovely night?''

''Unique. I wish I'd known in time to take you to dinner.''

Thunder came in a string of six explosions. Like bombs in an air raid. ''Me too,'' she said when we could hear again.

''I wish I'd known this afternoon.''

''Pecan pralines!''

''Farmer's Market. Double-roasted peanuts. Who would *you* have murdered, if you'd had the time?''

''There was a girl in my sorority—''

—and she was guilty of sibling rivalry, so Leslie claimed. I named an editor who kept changing his mind. Leslie named one of my old girl friends, I named her only old boy friend that I knew about, and it got to be kind of fun before we ran out. My brother Mike had forgotten my birthday once. The fiend.

The lights flickered, then came on again.

Too casually, Leslie asked, "Do you really think the sun might go back to normal?"

"It better *be* back to normal. Otherwise we're dead anyway. I wish we could see Jupiter."

"Dammit, answer me! Do you think it was a flare?"

"Yes."

"Why?"

"Yellow dwarf stars don't go nova."

"What if ours did?"

"The astronomers know a lot about novas," I said. "More than you'd guess. They can see them coming months ahead. Sol is a gee-naught yellow dwarf. They don't go nova at all. They have to wander off the main sequence first, and that takes millions of years."

She pounded a fist softly on my back. We were cheek to cheek; I couldn't see her face. "I don't want to believe it. I don't dare. Stan, nothing like this has ever happened before. How can you know?"

"Something did."

"What? I don't believe it. We'd remember."

"Do you remember the first moon landing? Aldrin and Armstrong?"

"Of course. We watched it at Earl's Lunar Landing Party."

"They landed on the biggest, flattest place they could find on the moon. They sent back several hours of jumpy home movies, took a lot of very clear pictures, left corrugated footprints all over the place. And they came home with a bunch of rocks.

"Remember? People said it was a long way to go for rocks. But the first thing anyone noticed about those rocks was that they were half melted.

"Sometime in the past, oh, say the past hundred thousand years; there's no way of marking it closer than that—the sun flared up. It didn't stay hot enough long enough to leave any marks on the Earth. But the moon doesn't have an atmosphere to protect it. All the rocks melted on one side."

The air was warm and damp. I took off my coat, which was heavy with rainwater. I fished the cigarettes and matches out, lit a cigarette and exhaled past Leslie's ear.

"We'd remember. It *couldn't* have been this bad."

"I'm not so sure. Suppose it happened over the Pacific? It wouldn't do *that* much damage. Or over the American continents. It would have sterilized some plants and animals and burned down a lot of forests, and who'd know? The sun is a four percent variable star. Maybe it gets a touch more variable than that, every so often."

Something shattered in the bedroom. A window? A wet wind touched us, and the shriek of the storm was louder.

"Then we could live through this," Leslie said hesitantly.

"I believe you've put your finger on the crux of the matter. Skol!" I found my champagne and drank deep. It was past three in the morning, with a hurricane beating at our doors.

"Then shouldn't we be doing something about it?"

"We are."

"Something like trying to get up into the hills! Stan, there're going to be floods!"

"You bet your ass there are, but they won't rise this high. Fourteen stories. Listen, I've thought this through. We're in a building that was designed to be earthquake proof. You told me so yourself. It'd take more than a hurricane to knock it over.

"As for heading for the hills, what hills? We won't get far tonight, not with the streets flooded already. Suppose we could get up into the Santa Monica Mountains; then what? Mudslides, that's what. That area won't stand up to what's coming. The flare must have boiled away enough water to make another ocean. It's going to rain for forty days and forty nights! Love, this is the safest place we could have reached tonight."

"Suppose the polar caps melt?"

"Yeah . . . well, we're pretty high, even for that. Hey, maybe that last flare was what started Noah's Flood. Maybe it's happening again. Sure as hell, there's not a place on Earth that isn't the middle of a hurricane. Those two great counterrotating hurricanes, by now they must have broken up into hundreds of little storms—"

The glass doors exploded inward. We ducked, and the wind howled about us and dropped rain and glass on us.

"At least we've got food!" I shouted. "If the floods maroon us here, we can last it out!"

"But if the power goes, we can't cook it! And the refrigerator—"

"We'll cook everything we can. Hardboil all the eggs—"

The wind rose about us. I stopped trying to talk.

Warm rain sprayed us horizontally and left us soaked. Try to cook in a hurricane? I'd been stupid; I'd waited too long. The wind would tip boiling water on us if we tried it. Or hot grease—

Leslie screamed, "We'll have to use the oven!"

Of course. The oven couldn't possibly fall on us.

We set it for 400° and put the eggs in, in a pot of water. We took all the meat out of the meat drawer and shoved it in on a broiling pan. Two artichokes in another pot. The other vegetables we could eat raw.

What else? I tried to think.

Water. If the electricity went, probably the water and telephone lines would too. I turned on the faucet over the sink and started filling things: pots with lids, Leslie's thirty-cup percolator that she used for parties, her wash bucket. She clearly thought I was crazy, but I didn't trust the rain as a water source; I couldn't control it.

The sound. Already we'd stopped trying to shout through it. Forty days and nights of this and we'd be stone deaf. Cotton? Too late to reach the bathroom. Paper towels! I tore and wadded and made four plugs for our ears.

Sanitary facilities? Another reason for picking Leslie's place over mine. When the plumbing stopped, there was always the balcony.

And if the flood rose higher than the fourteenth floor, there was the roof. Twenty stories up. If it went higher than that, there would be damn few people left when it was over.

And if it was a nova?

I held Leslie a bit more closely, and lit another cigarette one-handed. All the wasted planning, if it was a nova. But I'd have been doing it anyway. You don't stop planning just because there's no hope.

And when the hurricane turned to live steam, there was always the balcony. At a dead run, and over the railing, in preference to being boiled alive.

But now was not the time to mention it.

Anyway, she'd probably thought of it herself.

The lights went out about four. I turned off the oven, in case the power should come back. Give it an hour to cool down, then I'd put all the food in Baggies.

Leslie was asleep, sitting up in my arms. How could she sleep, not knowing? I piled pillows behind her and let her back easy.

For some time I lay on my back, smoking, watching the lightning make shadows on the ceiling. We had eaten all the foie gras and drunk one bottle of champagne. I thought of opening the brandy, but decided against it, with regret.

A long time passed. I'm not sure what I thought about. I didn't sleep, but certainly my mind was in idle. It only gradually came to me that the ceiling, between lightning flashes, had turned gray.

I rolled over, gingerly, soggily. Everything was wet.

My watch said it was nine-thirty.

I crawled around the partition into the living room. I'd been ignoring the storm sounds for so long that it took a faceful of warm whipping rain to remind me. There was a hurricane going on. But charcoal-gray light was filtering through the black clouds.

So. I was right to have saved the brandy. Floods, storms, intense radiation, fires lit by the flare—if the toll of destruction was as high as I expected, then money was about to become worthless. We would need trade goods.

I was hungry. I ate two eggs and some bacon—still warm—and started putting the rest of the food away. We had food for a week, maybe . . . but hardly a balanced diet. Maybe we could trade with other apartments. This was a big building. There must be empty apartments, too, that we could raid for canned soup and the like. And refugees from the lower floors to be taken care of, if the waters rose high enough . . .

Damn! I missed the nova. Life had been simplicity itself last night. Now . . . Did we have medicines? Were there doctors in the building? There would be dysentery and other plagues. And hunger. There was a supermarket near here; could we find a scuba rig in the building?

But I'd get some sleep first. Later we could start exploring the building. The day had become a lighter charcoal-gray. Things could be worse, far worse. I thought of the radiation that must have sleeted over the far side of the world, and wondered if our children would colonize Europe, or Asia, or Africa.

I'm extremely pleased with this tale. I've written too few love stories. This one was for Marilyn. The characters were our earlier selves, and the settings are in West Los Angeles, where we lived. I had written most of the story before we married.

But I couldn't finish it until I showed it to Jerry Pournelle. Jerry gave me the ending: he simply reminded me that I am an optimist. I do not normally write stories in which there is no hope.

From time to time someone tries to turn "Inconstant Moon" into a movie. I grant that it's a little short; we'd have to follow a few more characters. But the locations are easily available, and there aren't any of the fantastically expensive special effects one tends to find in my novels.

Then again, I remember having to explain what a "nova" is to a "producer." Maybe that's the real problem.

• • •

• • •

"Luke, if flatlanders need thought police to keep them alive, they shouldn't stay alive. You're trying to hold back evolution."

"We are not thought police! What we police is technology ..."

WORLD OF PTAVVS, 1966

WHAT CAN YOU SAY ABOUT CHOCOLATE COVERED MANHOLE COVERS?

It was the last party. Otherwise it was only one of many, so many that they merged in the memory. We all knew each other. George had invited around thirty of us, a heterogeneous group, aged from teen to retirement, in dress that varied from hippie to mod to jeans and sneakers to dark suits, and hair that varied from crew cut to shoulder-length.

It was a divorce party.

Granted that it's been done before, still it was done well. George and Dina had planned it a year earlier, to celebrate the night their Decree became Final. The cake was frosted in black, and was surmounted by the usual wax figures, but facing outward from opposite edges of the cake. Jack Keenan donned a minister's reversed collar to officiate. His makeshift sacrament included part of the funniest prayer in literature: the agnostic's prayer from Zelazny's *Creatures of Light and Darkness*. George and Dina kissed with obvious sincerity, for the last time, and everybody clapped like mad.

Afterward I got coffee and a piece of divorce cake and found a flat place to set them. Without a third hand to handle the plastic fork, I was as good as trapped there; and there it was that Tom Findlay found me.

Tom Findlay was all red hair and beard. The beard was full and thick, the hair long enough to tie in back with a rubber band. Once he had gone to a costume party with his hair combed forward over his eyes and the bridge of his nose, and a placard around his neck that read NOT A SHEEP DOG. He generally wore knee-length socks and leather shorts. His legs too were thickly covered with red hair. He spoke in a slow midwestern drawl, and grinned constantly, as if he were watching very funny pictures inside his head.

He was always part of these groups. Once a month he held a BYOB party of his own. He had a tendency to monopolize a conversation; but even those who avoided him on that account had to admit that he gave fair warning. He would walk up to any friend or stranger he found standing alone and open conversation with, "Hey. Would a Muslim vampire be terrified of a copy of the Koran?"

Or, "It seems to me that anarchy would be a very unstable form of government, don't you think?"

Or, "What about chocolate covered manhole covers?"

That one fell pretty flat, I remember. What can anyone say about chocolate covered manhole covers? Most of Findlay's ideas were at least worth discussing. Vampires, for instance. What significance has the vampire's religion? Or the victim's blood type? Could you hold off a vampire with a sunlamp, or kill him with a stake of grained plastic wood? If a bullet won't kill a vampire, what about a revolver loaded with a blank cartridge and a wooden pencil?

And one night someone had come running in to interrupt the poker game in the other room. "What do you think Findlay just came up with?" And it was a new form of ice skating. You strap blocks of ice to your feet, see, and you skate over a field of razor blades set on edge.

Wild? Consider the ramifications! Straps will be cut, unless you embed them in the ice itself. God help you if you take a spill, or let the ice melt too far. And the blades have to be lined up. So how can you change directions? The only answer to that one is to lay the blades in a loop, like a skating rink.

That night, the night of the divorce party, Findlay perched on the edge of the table I was using for my cup and plate, and said, "Hey. Suppose all the Adam and Eve legends were true?"

I could have gotten away, but it would have meant finding another flat spot. I said, "That story's been done to death. A rocket ship crashes on Earth, see, with two people aboard—"

"No, no, you don't take my meaning. Every big and little group in the world, past and present, has a creation myth." Findlay's Midwest accent did odd things to the two-dollar words he was fond of using. "They all involve one man and one woman. In every case all of humanity sprang from that one couple. Suppose they were *all* true?"

My wife moved up from behind me and slid one arm around my waist. "You mean five hundred different Edens? That wouldn't make sense." She nestled against me, unobtrusively, feeling warm and silky in a loose, flowing pant dress.

Findlay turned to her eagerly. "Carol, do you know anything about breeding horses? Or cattle?"

I said, "Dogs. My mother raises keeshonden."

We didn't see where he was going, but Findlay seemed to sense we were hooked. He settled himself more comfortably on the table. "There's a stock method of improving a breed. It always works, but it takes a long time. How long depends on what you're trying to improve, of course.

"Suppose you're working with horses, just for argument. You've got a hundred horses for base stock. What you do is, you fence them off into say twenty-five corrals of four horses each. A large number of small groups. You make them breed within the group.

"Pretty quick you get severe inbreeding. All the little deadly recessive traits start to come out, and combine. You lose a lot of each generation. You help it along by weeding out the traits you don't like, like blindness or early senility.

"You keep it up for as many generations as you've got time for. Then you run them all together. You know how hybrid vigor works?"

"It's a mathematical thing, really," someone muttered deprecatingly. I realized that we'd acquired an audience. Four or five male teens were standing around listening, attracted either by Findlay's carrying voice or by my wife, who is uncommonly pretty. They were looking puzzled but interested, except for the one who had spoken.

Hal Grant was a small, dark fifteen-year-old with an astonishing vocabulary. With his full black beard and collar-length hair he looked like a young baron out of the Middle Ages; but he talked like a college professor. People tended to see him as an adult, and to react with astonishment on the rare occasions when he acted like a fifteen-year-old.

When nobody tried to stop him, he went on. "Say you've got a strain of horses that has a dominant for weak eyes, and another that has weak hindquarters. You breed a stallion from one strain to a mare from the other strain until you get four colts. In general one colt won't have either of the bad traits, one will have the weak eyes, one will have weak hindquarters, and one will have both. That's straight Mendelian genetics. Where the hybrid vigor comes in is, the one with both of the bad traits can't compete. He dies. That leaves three colts, and one is an improvement over both his parents. The average quality goes up."

Findlay was nodding his approval. "Right. That's how it works. So you run all the horses together. A lot of the weak traits that didn't get killed off in the interbreeding phase, combine and kill their owners. You wind up with a superior strain of horses."

"It wouldn't work with dogs," said Carol. "Mongrels don't win dog shows."

"But in a fair fight they tend to kill the winners," Hal pointed out.

"The technique works on just about anything," said Findlay. "Horses, dogs, cattle, chinchillas. Split the base stock into small groups, make them interbreed for several generations, then run them all together. Now keep it in mind, and we'll make some assumptions.

"We assume an alien race, and we assume they've got a pet that's almost bright enough to make a good servant. Its hands can hold a serving tray. They could almost repair machinery—"

"Homo habilis," said somebody.

"Right. You have to assume the overlord race had a lot of time, and endless patience—"

"And cheap space travel."

"Wouldn't have to be faster than light, though. Not if they had all that endless patience." We could see where Findlay was going now, and everyone wanted to get there first. Hence the interruptions.

Findlay said, "So they pick out about a thousand of the brightest of their animals, and they split them up into pairs, male and female. They find an Earthlike world and set down five hundred couples in five hundred locations."

"Then the Noah legend—"

"Came first," I said. "And you get five hundred Edens. Beautiful."

"Right. Now look at how it works. Each of the little groups undergoes severe inbreeding. They're all cut off from each other by fences of one kind or another, mountains, rivers, deserts. The recessive traits come out, and some of the groups die off completely. Others spread out.

"Remember, it's the most successful ones that are spreading. They infringe on other groups. The genes start to mix. The quality of the mix goes up, partly because of hybrid vigor. If they're going to develop intelligence, this is where it starts."

"Hah! They'd start inventing ways around the fences," said an older kid. Short blond hair, pale fringe of mustache, knitted sailing cap surgically attached to his head; I forget his name. "Bridges across the rivers, canteens for the deserts—"

"And camels."

"Passes across the mountains. Ways to tell each other how to find them."

"Ships!"

"Right," said Findlay, his blue eyes glowing with pleasure. "Now notice that the most intelligent groups are the ones that spread their genes around the most, because they're the ones that do all the traveling. Also, the more inventions you get, the easier it is to mix; the more mixing you get, the higher the intelligence goes; and that makes for more inventions, like paved roads and better rigging for the ships and better breeds of horses. Eventually you get airplanes, buses, guided tours and printed language guides and international credit organizations."

"And tourist traps."

"And multilingual whores."

"Not to put a damper on any of this fun stuff," said Hal Grant, the dark youth with the very adult vocabulary, "but eventually they'll be coming back to see how we're doing."

"How would they know when we're ready?" someone wondered. "Just stop by for a look every thousand years?"

Hal said, "Not good enough. Look how far we've come in the last five hundred years. Give us another five hundred and we'll be competitors, not slaves."

"Or dead of pollution."

"But they wouldn't have to check. They just wait until—"

"Project Ozma!"

"But how could they be sure we'd signal *them*?"

"They must be in one of the nearby stellar systems. Alpha Centauri, Tau Ceti—"

"Or they left signal devices in all the likely systems—"

"Wouldn't it depend on how intelligent they want us? Maybe we're supposed to be repairmen for a starship motor. Then they—"

"They'd damn well wait for *us* to come to *them*, wouldn't they? To prove we can build a starship!"

Jack Keenan tapped me on the shoulder. He was still wearing his clerical collar. He spoke low, near my ear. "There's a place at the poker table. They sent me to tell you."

My cake was gone, and the conversation here was turning chaotic. I got up. Behind me Tom Findlay was saying, "But they'd have to *find* our starships some way. Maybe a large metallic mass moving faster than light would put out heavy Cherenkov radiation . . ."

I played for an hour and lost a dollar twenty. Presently Carol put her head around the corner, caught my eye, showed her teeth and snapped them at me several times in rapid succession. I nodded and cashed in.

It means, "I'm starving. Let's collect some people and go eat."

There was still a group around Tom Findlay. I caught bits and pieces of sentences. They were talking about the things you could do with neutronium, if you could get it in four-foot globs and had the technology to move it around. I broke in to ask if anyone was hungry, and got Hal Grant that way.

We looked up our host (our hostess had gone home with her date), thanked him for a great party, told him we might be back in an hour or so, and asked if he'd like to come along. The guests could take care of themselves, and he knew it, but he declined anyway.

Joy Benjamin was outside sitting on the wall, breathing. There was precious little oxygen left inside. She joined us too. We drove off to find a place we knew of, an all-night pizza place.

Sometimes they get forgotten instantly. Sometimes they go on and on. This latest of Findlay's brainstorms was one of Those. I came back from the counter carrying a tremendous deluxe pizza, and Hal Grant was saying, "See, that way you wouldn't need a Project Ozma, or an FTL spacecraft detector either." And both women were nodding, rapt.

Joy Benjamin was young and pretty and a bit pudgy, and her front teeth showed when she smiled. It all gave her a cuddly, innocent look that I had never found occasion to mention to my wife; but if she had been in the group around Findlay I would have noticed her. She must have gotten her details at second hand. She looked up as I set the pizza down, and said, "He's got a point. You know about Tom Findlay's Multiple Eden Hypothesis?"

"Yes."

"This planet puts out as much radio flux as a small star," she said seriously. "The overlords could put a detector on the Moon and then just wait for us to invent radios."

"That means they must be on their way here now," my wife put in.

Hal smiled sardonically, an effect he couldn't have managed without the beard. "Maybe they're already here. There were flying saucers all over the place when radio was *really* popular, before everybody had two television sets."

"It's been done, that bit about a detector on the Moon. In *2001*. Put it on Mars."

"Okay, it's on Mars. The point is, with the radio detector they can get here after we develop as much intelligence as we're going to, but before we can pollute ourselves to death or bomb ourselves to death. After all, they probably weren't trying to develop anything *supremely* intelligent. Just bright enough to take orders."

"How young you are, to be so cynical."

It took him a moment to decide I was kidding. He said, "Someday, Howards," and shook his head sorrowfully, contemplating awful carnage. He went to work on the pizza.

It was delicious. I wish I'd paid more attention, because it was the last time I ever tasted pizza. We ate on a wooden bench, and used up an inch-high stack of paper napkins. Off in one corner, a man with garters on his sleeves played a player piano.

"So we can expect them any minute." Joy made whirring noises and moved her hands expressively. "Big ships in the sky, coming down to ssscoop us up."

"Or little ships to take samples."

"If they were the flying saucers, they must have rejected us already," Hal put in. "They've been here too long. They'd have started major scooping operations long ago."

And if we'd dropped it there, we'd be home now.

There are tunes that go round and round in your head, driving you nuts, driving others nuts because you're humming under your breath. There are ideas you can't leave alone. You toy with them, or they toy with you . . . I got my fair share of the pizza and a bit more. While we were waiting for Carol to finish, I said, "Suppose they did reject us. Suppose we didn't meet their presumably exacting standards. What then?"

"They'd destroy the Earth," Joy said instantly.

"Typical bloodthirsty female."

Hal said, "Maybe they'd start us over. Give us IQ tests. Pick a thousand off the top. Settle us on a new planet."

"*Then* destroy the Earth."

"Maybe. Maybe even settle us back on Earth, after clearing it for us."

Grant's "us" had not escaped me. He would be one of the thousand, and so would his friends. I let it pass. Truth to tell, I was flattered.

The pizza was gone, and much of the cardboard disc beneath it. We piled in the car and started back to George's place.

Carol ended a reflective silence. "Does it seem to anyone that there are more written tests around than there used to be? Army IQ tests, motivational research, testing for jobs, even the forms for computer dating. Now—"

We started laughing. Hal said, "Are you still on that?"

"Well, they have to test us *some* way."

"It's a lovely idea, but I can't bring myself to trust those IQ tests. I know too much psychology. There's not a printed test that's good for anything, especially at the top of the scale."

"What, then?"

"There Are Aliens Among Us," Hal Grant intoned. "Or their agents. And they choose by intuition and superior judgment. You, and you—"

"Hey," I said, hit by a lovely idea. "Hey. You know who would make a great intelligence tester?"

"Who?"

"Tom Findlay! He's a walking, talking intelligence test. Remember what he was talking about just before we left? Blobs of neutron star matter—"

"That's lovely stuff, neutronium. It's unreasonably heavy. If you just let it sit, it's *got* to be a shiny sphere. The surface gravity would flatten any surface roughness, see? If you toss a glob of the stuff at an enemy spaceship, it'll just *drift* through the hull and leave a gaping hole and come out a fraction of an inch thicker. Spin it and you don't get an ellipsoid, you get like a flying saucer, a ball with a rim around it. It's all theoretical, of course."

"See what I mean?"

Behind me in the darkened car, Hal Grant said, "I guess so. Findlay makes you think. If you can't think, you go away. After awhile there's nobody left talking to Findlay except people who like playing with ideas. He's a filter. Then I suppose he tags the best of us and off we go, right?''

''Right. Well, nobody's disappeared yet.''

''Nobody that was noticed. How many of us do you know, away from these parties? Sometimes I run across Jack Keenan in the supermarket, but that's it. All we know for sure is, *we* haven't been picked yet.'' Grant laughed uneasily. ''Maybe we'd better not go back to George's.''

The feel of the car changed drastically. I hit the brake fast, but it was hardly necessary; we were only starting to move from a dead stop. A moment ago we'd been doing seventy.

I heard the sea before I saw it: breakers crunching ahead of us, flashing white in the headlights. If I'd kept the throttle down we'd have driven right into them. The freeway lighting had become a pale pink glow far across the sea; dawn or dusk, I couldn't tell. We were in soft dry sand. It might have been a California beach, and our car sitting mired in sand might have been a television commercial or a practical joke, except that it wasn't.

''S-s-sonofabitch took me at my word,'' said Hal Grant. Then, ''This can't be real. Can it?''

Joy was furious. ''He was *listening* to us! That—eavesdropper!''

I got out.

It felt like sand. It crunched beneath my feet, like sand. How could it be part of another world? But the sinking feeling in my belly felt like an elevator starting down. Terror? Or low gravity?

I threw back my head and screamed, ''Findlay!''

And he was there, grinning out of a metal cagework affair. ''Figured it out, did you?''

''Christ no, Findlay! What's going on here? We're terribly confused! One minute we were driving along the freeway, and the next we're here at Hermosa Beach!''

First he was flabbergasted. Then he burst out laughing. Well, it had been worth a try.

So was my next move. His head was thrown back and his beard was raised, and I stepped forward fast and hit him in the throat, putting all my weight behind it.

Not murder. Justice. And we needed that cage affair to get home.

It was like hitting a padded pillar. My head snapped forward, my teeth came together with a sharp click, and something gave agonizingly in my shoulder. Tom Findlay must have weighed over a ton.

He stopped laughing, gradually. ''Very good. Nobody's ever adjusted quite that fast. Let's say you pass with honors,'' he said. ''And here's your diploma.''

It appeared beside him in the cage: a black disc on edge, two feet high. He caught it before it could topple, and he sent it rolling out. I let it go past me.

Grant had come up behind me. In resignation he said, "Where are we?"

"A lot of use you'll get out of that! I'll tell you anyway. It's the second planet out from Alpha Centauri A. If you were hoping for double suns and wild new constellations, you can forget it. We used the closest available water world."

"Gonna be dull," said Hal. He'd given up.

So had I. I inhaled; the air smelled incredibly clean. A door slammed behind me. The women. God, don't let them beg. I said, "So they came and sampled us and found us wanting. So they're doing it over with another five hundred Edens. So where do you come in, Findlay? They aren't human, are they?"

"Not by a long way," said Findlay, with reverence. "Neither am I. I'm a robot. I'm also the ideal they're aiming for, in case you were wondering."

"I wasn't."

"Now, now."

"If you're just what they want, why do they need us?"

"I'm expensive. Robots don't breed. You can forget about genetic engineering, too. It's immoral. I don't know why. It's enough that they think so. Anything else?"

"We were doing seventy on the freeway," said Hal. "What happened to the momentum?"

"You were also doing about twenty miles per second with respect to this beach. We just took it all in one vector sum. What else? Oh, you won't be separated. This Eden will hold all four of you. We did it that way last time, too. The Eden story is only a myth."

"Are there any others?" Carol cried. "What direction are they."

But he was gone, and the metal frame around him. We were alone on a beach, four of us and a car, in the growing light of dawn.

"This thing is *sticky*," Hal said suddenly. He was holding the black disc that Findlay had rolled past me. He looked at his hand, then licked a finger. "Right. It's a memento, his signature, as it were. What can you say about chocolate covered manhole covers?"

"Don't get it sandy," my wife said briskly. "We can eat the chocolate. It's the only thing on this world that we know we can eat."

All characters were members of the Los Angeles Science Fantasy Society at the time of writing. All of the oddball ideas are derived from Tom Digby—"Digby-isms"—except the central one, the theory of multiple Edens, which is mine.

The LASFS liked the story to this extent at least: Jack Harness presented a parchment scroll to me at a banquet. It says: THE AMERICAN DENTAL ASSOCIATION SAYS THEY ARE BAD FOR CHILDREN'S TEETH. And somebody made up a miniature chocolate covered manhole cover. It appears as one of the gifts at the LASFS Christmas Gift Exchange, every year. From time to time the chocolate coating needs replacing.

• • •

• • •

"East takes you out. Out takes you west. West takes you in. In takes you east. North and south bring you back." The laws of motion within the Smoke Ring are also the rules of orbital mechanics.

THE GHOST SHIPS, unpublished

CLOAK OF ANARCHY

"Cloak of Anarchy" was written for Jerry Pournelle's *2020 vision*, to explain why I am not a Libertarian.

It's the only story John W. Campbell ever bought from me; and it may be the last story he bought.

It caused me to be involved in a duel.

"Cloak of Anarchy" required a character who was capable of knocking out all the monitoring devices in King's Free Park, turning a fake anarchy into a real anarchy, and would do it. What I needed was a combination of Russell Seitz (who lives on the East Coast, and who tends to carry advanced technological toys in his pockets) and Don Simpson (a West Coast fan who uses technology to create his own art forms). I combined them into "Ron Cole."

I must have done it right. All the East Coast fans recognized Russell. All the West Coast fans recognized Don.

Comes the Los Angeles World Science Fiction Convention. We were at a room party. I recognized Russell Seitz. "Hi, Russell!"

"You used me in a story."

"Yeah!"

"You, er, didn't ask permission."

I'm spoiled, maybe. I expect such a thing to be taken as flattery. I disengaged myself. A few minutes later I ran across Gordon Dickson.

"Hi, Gordy!"

"Russell Seitz has asked me to speak for him in an affair of honor."

Oooops! Through the humming in my ears I said, "I expect I should choose a second to speak for me."

Gordy agreed.

I looked around and there was Ben Bova. Ben had published "Cloak of Anarchy" in *Analog*. Choosing Ben meant that I would have to do less explaining.

Gordy explained that a venerable dueling law set a limit on the bore size of weapons. "We'll have to settle for magnums."

Champagne corks?

Ara Pashinian is a world traveler who shows occasionally at world conventions. He kindly offered us his roomy suite "to test-fire the propellants."

Gordy and Russell disappeared to get weaponry Russell had brought along. In Ara's suite Ben and I discussed strategy. "Don't argue about the weaponry," Ben said. "Remember, Russell Seitz is the world's sixth nuclear power!"

Oooops! It was true. As one of the Board of Trustees of a Boston museum, Russell had built a Titan II missile from parts he acquired from junkyards for under a thousand dollars.

"Not to worry," Ben said. "I know some Air Force people. I can promise instant massive retaliation the instant you're dead."

Marilyn is an admirer of Georgette Heyer's tales of the English Regency period. She knew what to do. She threw her arms around me crying, "Give up this madness! You'll be killed!"

But time was passing, and where were Russell and Gordy?

Here they came, bursting through the door in full 7th century Samurai armor! (Remember the Boston museum?) Ben cried, "No, no, no! No armor during the duel!"

"During the duel, no armor," Gordy said. "During the negotiations we take no chances."

Which raised a question. The badges at that convention were metal disks three inches across. Did they constitute armor? We decided they did not; they would be worn.

Our seconds test-fired the champagne bottles. It was decided that Russell and I would take two paces, turn and fire. And we drank the propellants.

By High Dawn (designated as 1:00 PM) I had bought replacement champagne. I went up to the swimming pool to fight for my honor. I didn't realize that I'd replaced cork corks with more dangerous plastic corks. I wore a bathing suit, thinking I might want a swim too.

I'd forgotten my big metal badge. Marilyn noticed and loaned me hers. I pinned it where it might do me some good. My genitalia were now labelled as the property of Marilyn Niven.

Russell appeared. He noticed the harder plastic corks, but said nothing. "Given the known propensities of my opponent—" he said, and pinned his badge between his shoulder blades.

We squared off, took two paces, faced each other—

I twisted the wire open. Worked it off. Peeled away the foil. Went to work on the cork with my thumbs. Easy does it, don't want to break the cork. . . . Looked up, and Russell was ready.

He fired past my shoulder.

I went back to work. Ease the cork loose. Russell was standing at attention, expressionless. The cork was easing out . . . faster than I thought. I fired through his hair.

And we drank the propellants.

• •

Square in the middle of what used to be the San Diego Freeway, I leaned back against a huge, twisted oak. The old bark was rough and powdery against my bare back. There was dark green shade shot with tight parallel beams of white gold. Long grass tickled my legs.

Forty yards away across a wide strip of lawn was a clump of elms, and a small grandmotherly woman sitting on a green towel. She looked like she'd grown there. A stalk of grass protruded between her teeth. I felt we were kindred spirits, and once when I caught her eye I wiggled a forefinger at her, and she waved back.

In a minute now I'd have to be getting up. Jill was meeting me at the Wilshire exits in half an hour. But I'd started walking at the Sunset Boulevard ramps, and I was tired. A minute more. . . .

It was a good place to watch the world rotate.

A good day for it, too. No clouds at all. On this hot blue summer afternoon, King's Free Park was as crowded as it ever gets.

Someone at police headquarters had expected that. Twice the usual number of copseyes floated overhead, waiting. Gold dots against blue, basketball-sized, twelve feet up. Each a television eye and a sonic stunner, each a hookup to police headquarters, they were there to enforce the law of the park.

No violence.

No hand to be raised against another—and no other laws whatever. Life was often entertaining in a Free Park.

North toward Sunset, a man carried a white rectangular sign, blank on both sides. He was parading back and forth in front of a square-jawed youth on a plastic box, who was trying to lecture him on the subject of fusion power and the heat pollution problem. Even this far away I could hear the conviction and the dedication in his voice.

South, a handful of yelling marksmen were throwing rocks at a copseye, directed by a gesticulating man with wild black hair. The golden basketball was dodging the rocks, but barely. Some cop was baiting them. I wondered where they had gotten the rocks. Rocks were scarce in King's Free Park.

The black-haired man looked familiar. I watched him and his horde chasing the copseye . . . then forgot them when a girl walked out of a clump of elms.

She was lovely. Long, perfect legs, deep red hair worn longer than shoulder length, the face of an arrogant angel, and a body so perfect that it seemed unreal, like an adolescent's daydream. Her walk showed training; possibly she was a model or dancer. Her only garment was a cloak of glowing blue velvet.

It was fifteen yards long, that cloak. It trailed back from two big gold discs that were stuck somehow to the skin of her shoulders. It trailed back and back, floating at a height of five feet all the way, twisting and turning to trace her path through the trees. She seemed like the illustration to a book of fairy tales, bearing in mind that the original fairy tales were not intended for children.

Neither was she. You could hear neck vertebrae popping all over the park. Even the rock throwers had stopped to watch.

She could sense the attention, or hear it in a whisper of sighs. It was what she was here for. She strolled along with a condescending angel's smile on her angel's face, not overdoing the walk, but letting it flow. She turned regardless of whether there were obstacles to avoid, so that fifteen yards of flowing cloak could follow the curve.

I smiled, watching her go. She was lovely from the back, with dimples.

The man who stepped up to her a little further on was the same who had led the rock throwers. Wild black hair and beard, hollow cheeks and deep-set eyes, a diffident smile and a diffident walk. . . . Ron Cole. Of course.

I didn't hear what he said to the girl in the cloak, but I saw the result. He flinched, then turned abruptly and walked away with his eyes on his feet.

I got up and moved to intercept him. "Don't take it personally," I said.

He looked up, startled. His voice, when it came, was bitter. "How should I take it?"

"She'd have turned any man off the same way. That lady has staples in her navel. She's to look, not to touch."

"You know her?"

"Never saw her before in my life."

"Then—?"

"Her cloak. Now you *must* have noticed her cloak."

The tail end of her cloak was just passing us, its folds rippling an improbably deep, rich blue. Ronald Cole smiled as if it hurt his face. "Yah."

"All right. Now suppose you made a pass, and suppose the lady liked your looks and took you up on it. What would she do next? Bearing in mind that she can't stop walking even for a second."

He thought it over first, then asked, "Why not?"

"If she stops walking she loses the whole effect. Her cloak just hangs there like some kind of tail. It's supposed to wave. If she lies down with you it's even worse. A cloak floating at five feet, then swooping into a clump of bushes and bobbing frantically—" Ron laughed helplessly in falsetto. I said, "See? Her audience would get the giggles. That's not what she's after."

He sobered. "But if she really wanted to, she wouldn't *care* about . . . oh. Right. She must have spent a fortune to get that effect."

"Sure. She wouldn't ruin it for Jacques Casanova himself." I thought unfriendly thoughts toward the girl in the cloak. There are polite ways to turn down a pass. Ronald Cole was easy to hurt.

I asked, "Where did you get the rocks?"

"Rocks? Oh, we found a place where the center divider shows through. We knocked off some chunks of concrete." Ron looked down the length of the park just as a kid bounced a missile off a golden ball. "They got one! Come on!"

The fastest commercial shipping that ever sailed was the clipper ship; yet the world stopped building them after just twenty-five years. Steam had come. Steam was faster, safer, more dependable, cheaper in time and men.

The freeways served America for almost fifty years. Then modern transportation systems cleaned the air and made traffic jams archaic and left the nation with an embarrassing problem. What to do with ten thousand miles of unsightly abandoned freeways?

King's Free Park had been part of the San Diego Freeway, the section between Sunset and the Santa Monica interchange. Decades ago the concrete had been covered with topsoil. The borders had been landscaped from the start. Now the Park was as thoroughly covered with green as the much older Griffith Free Park.

Within King's Free Park was an orderly approximation of anarchy. People were searched at the entrances. There were no weapons inside. The copseyes, floating overhead and out of reach, were the next best thing to no law at all.

There was only one law to enforce. All acts of attempted violence carried the same penalty for attacker and victim. Let anyone raise his hand against his neighbor, and one of the golden basketballs would stun them both. They would wake separately, with copseyes watching. It was usually enough.

Naturally people threw rocks at copseyes. It was a Free Park, wasn't it?

"They got one! Come on!" Ron tugged at my arm. The felled copseye was hidden, surrounded by those who had destroyed it. "I hope they don't kick it apart. I told them I need it intact, but that might not stop them."

"It's a Free Park. And they bagged it."

"With my missiles!"

"Who are they?"

"I don't know. They were playing baseball when I found them. I told them I needed a copseye. They said they'd get me one."

I remembered Ron quite well now. Ronald Cole was an artist and an inventor. It would have been two sources of income for another man, but Ron was different. He invented new art forms. With solder and wire and diffraction gratings and several makes of plastics kits, and an incredible collection of serendipitous junk, Ron Cole made things the like of which had never been seen on Earth.

The market for new art forms had always been low, but now and then he did make a sale. It was enough to keep him in raw materials, especially since many of his raw materials came from basements and attics. There was an occasional *big* sale, and then, briefly, he would be rich.

There was this about him: he knew who I was, but he hadn't remembered my name. Ron Cole had better things to think about than what name belonged with whom. A name was only a tag and a conversational gambit. "Russel! How are you?" A signal. Ron had developed a substitute.

Into a momentary gap in the conversation he would say, "Look at this," and hold out—miracles.

Once it had been a clear plastic sphere, golfball-sized, balanced on a polished silver concavity. When the ball rolled around on the curved mirror, the reflections were *fantastic*.

Once it had been a twisting sea serpent engraved on a Michelob beer bottle, the lovely vase-shaped bottle of the early 1960s that was too big for standard refrigerators.

And once it had been two strips of dull silvery metal, unexpectedly heavy. "What's this?"

I'd held them in the palm of my hand. They were heavier than lead. Platinum? But nobody carries that much platinum around. Joking, I'd asked, "U-235?"

"Are they warm?" he'd asked apprehensively. I'd fought off an urge to throw them as far as I could and dive behind a couch.

But they *had* been platinum. I never did learn why Ron was carrying them about. Something that didn't pan out.

Within a semicircle of spectators, the felled copseye lay on the grass. It was intact, possibly because two cheerful, conspicuously large men were standing over it, waving everyone back.

"Good," said Ron. He knelt above the golden sphere, turned it with his long artist's fingers. To me he said, "Help me get it open."

"What for? What are you after?"

"I'll tell you in a minute. Help me get—Never mind." The hemispherical cover came off. For the first time ever, I looked into a copseye.

It was impressively simple. I picked out the stunner by its parabolic reflector, the cameras, and a toroidal coil that had to be part of the floater device. No power source. I guessed that the shell itself was a power-beam antenna. With the cover cracked there would be no way for a damn fool to electrocute himself.

Ron knelt and studied the strange guts of the copseye. From his pocket he took something made of glass and metal. He suddenly remembered my existence and held it out to me, saying, "Look at this."

I took it, expecting a surprise, and I got it. It was an old hunting watch, a big wind-up watch on a chain, with a protective case. They were in common use a couple of hundred years ago. I looked at the face, said, "Fifteen minutes slow. You didn't repair the whole works, did you?"

"Oh, no." He clicked the back open for me.

The works looked modern. I guessed, "Battery and tuning fork?"

"That's what the guard thought. Of course that's what I made it from. But the hands don't move; I set them just before they searched me."

"Aha. What does it do?"

"If I work it right, I think it'll knock down every copseye in King's Free Park."

For a minute or so I was laughing too hard to speak. Ron watched me with his head on one side, clearly wondering if I thought he was joking.

I managed to say, "That ought to cause all *kinds* of excitement."

Ron nodded vigorously. "Of course it all depends on whether they use the kind of circuits I think they use. Look for yourself; the copseyes aren't supposed to be foolproof. They're supposed to be cheap. If one gets knocked down, the taxes don't go up much. The other way is to make them expensive and foolproof, and frustrate a lot of people. People aren't supposed to be frustrated in a Free Park."

"So?"

"Well, there's a cheap way to make the circuitry for the power system. If they did it that way, I can blow the whole thing. We'll see." Ron pulled thin copper wire from the cuffs of his shirt.

"How long will this take?"

"Oh, half an hour."

That decided me. "I've got to be going. I'm meeting Jill Hayes at the Wilshire exits. You've met her, a big blonde girl, my height—"

But he wasn't listening. "Okay, see you," he muttered. He began placing the copper wire inside the copseye, with tweezers. I left.

Crowds tend to draw crowds. A few minutes after leaving Ron, I joined a semicircle of the curious to see what they were watching.

A balding, lantern-jawed individual was putting something together: an archaic machine, with blades and a small gasoline motor. The T-shaped wooden handle was brand new and unpainted. The metal parts were dull with the look of ancient rust recently removed.

The crowd speculated in half whispers. What was it? Not part of a car; not an outboard motor, though it had blades; too small for a motor scooter; too big for a motor skateboard. . . .

"Lawn mower," said the white-haired lady next to me. She was one of those small, birdlike people who shrivel and grow weightless as they age, and live forever. Her words meant nothing to me. I was about to ask, when—

The lantern-jawed man finished his work, and twisted something, and the motor started with a roar. Black smoke puffed out. In triumph he gripped the handles. Outside, it was a prison offense to build a working internal combustion machine. Here—

With the fire of dedication burning in his eyes, he wheeled his infernal machine across the grass. He left a path as flat as a rug. It was a Free Park, wasn't it?

The smell hit everyone at once: a black dirt in the air, a stink of half-burned hydrocarbons attacking nose and eyes. I gasped and coughed. I'd never smelled anything like it.

The crescent of crowd roared and converged.

He squawked when they picked up his machine. Someone found a switch and stopped it. Two men confiscated the tool kit and went to work with screwdriver and hammer. The owner objected. He picked up a heavy pair of pliers and tried to commit murder.

A copseye zapped him and the man with the hammer, and they both hit the lawn without bouncing. The rest of them pulled the lawn mower apart and bent and broke the pieces.

"I'm half-sorry they did that," said the old woman. "Sometimes I miss the sound of lawn mowers. My dad used to mow the lawn on Sunday mornings."

I said, "It's a Free Park."

"Then why can't he build anything he pleases?"

"He can. He did. Anything he's free to build, we're free to kick apart." And my mind flashed, *Like Ron's rigged copseye*.

Ron was good with tools. It would not surprise me a bit if he knew enough about copseyes to knock out the whole system.

Maybe someone ought to stop him.

But knocking down copseyes wasn't illegal. It happened all the time. It was part of the freedom of the park. If Ron could knock them all down at once, well. . . .

Maybe someone ought to stop him.

I passed a flock of high school girls, all chittering like birds, all about sixteen. It might have been their first trip inside a Free Park. I looked back because they were so cute, and caught them staring in awe and wonder at the dragon on my back.

A few years and they'd be too blasé to notice. It had taken Jill almost half an hour to apply it this morning: a glorious red-and-gold dragon breathing flames across my shoulder, flames that seemed to glow by their own light. Lower down were a princess and a knight in golden armor, the princess tied to a stake, the knight fleeing for his life. I smiled back at the girls, and two of them waved.

Short blonde hair and golden skin, the tallest girl in sight, wearing not even a nudist's shoulder pouch: Jill Hayes stood squarely in front of the Wilshire entrance, visibly wondering where I was. It was five minutes after three.

There was this about living with a physical culture nut. Jill insisted on getting me into shape. The daily exercises were part of that, and so was this business of walking half the length of King's Free Park.

I'd balked at doing it briskly, though. Who walks briskly in a Free Park? There's too much to see. She'd given me an hour; I'd held out for three. It was a compromise, like the paper slacks I was wearing despite Jill's nudist beliefs.

Sooner or later she'd find someone with muscles, or I'd relapse into laziness, and we'd split. Meanwhile . . . we got along. It seemed only sensible to let her finish my training.

She spotted me, yelled, "Russel! Here!" in a voice that must have reached both ends of the park. In answer I lifted my arm semaphore-style, slowly over my head and back down.

And every copseye in King's Free Park fell out of the sky, dead.

Jill looked about her at all the startled faces and all the golden bubbles resting in bushes and on the grass. She approached me somewhat uncertainly. She asked, "Did you do that?"

I said, "Yah. If I wave my arms again they'll all go back up."

"I think you'd better do it," she said primly. Jill had a fine poker face. I waved my arm grandly over my head and down, but of course the copseyes stayed where they had fallen.

Jill said, "I wonder what happened to them?"

"It was Ron Cole. You remember him. He's the one who engraved some old Michelob beer bottles for Steuben—"

"Oh, yes. But *how*?"

We went off to ask him.

A brawny college man howled and charged past us at a dead run. We saw him kick a copseye like a soccer ball. The golden cover split, but the man howled again and hopped up and down hugging his foot.

We passed dented golden shells and broken resonators and bent parabolic reflectors. One woman looked flushed and proud; she was wearing several of the copper toroids as bracelets. A kid was collecting the cameras. Maybe he thought he could sell them outside.

I never saw an intact copseye after the first minute.

They weren't all busy kicking copseyes apart. Jill stared at the conservatively dressed group carrying POPULATION BY COPULATION signs, and wanted to know if they were serious. Their grim-faced leader handed us pamphlets that spoke of the evil and the blasphemy of man's attempts to alter himself through gene tampering and extra-uterine growth experiments. If it was a put-on, it was a good one.

We passed seven little men, each three to four feet high, traveling with a single tall, pretty brunette. They wore medieval garb. We both stared; but I was the one who noticed the makeup and the use of UnTan. African pigmies, probably part of a U.N.-sponsored tourist group; and the girl must be their guide.

Ron Cole was not where I had left him.

"He must have decided that discretion is the better part of cowardice. May be right, too," I surmised. "Nobody's ever knocked down *all* the copseyes before."

"It's not illegal, is it?"

"Not illegal, but excessive. They can bar him from the park, at the very least."

Jill stretched in the sun. She was all golden and big. Scaled down, she would have made a nice centershot for a men's videozine. She said, "I'm thirsty. Is there a fountain around?"

"Sure, unless someone's plugged it by now. It's a—"

"Free Park. Do you mean to tell me they don't even protect the *fountains*?"

"You make one exception, it's like a wedge. When someone ruins a fountain, they wait and fix it that night. That way if I see someone trying to wreck a fountain, I'll generally throw a punch at him. A lot of us do. After a guy's lost enough of his holiday to the copseye stunners, he'll get the idea, sooner or later."

The fountain was a solid cube of concrete with four spigots and a hand-sized metal button. It was hard to jam, hard to hurt. Ron Cole stood near it, looking lost.

He seemed glad to see me, but still lost. I introduced him. "You remember Jill Hayes." He said, "Certainly. Hello, Jill," and, having put her name to its intended purpose, promptly forgot it.

Jill said, "We thought you'd made a break for it."

"I did."

"Oh?"

"You know how complicated the exits are. They have to be, to keep anyone from getting in through an exit with like a shotgun." Ron ran both hands through his hair, without making it any more or less neat. "Well, all the exits have stopped working. They must be on the same circuits as the copseyes. I wasn't expecting that."

"Then we're locked in," I said. That was irritating. But underneath the irritation was a funny feeling in the pit of my stomach. "How long do you think—?"

"No telling. They'll have to get new copseyes in somehow. And repair the beamed power system, and figure out how I bollixed it, and fix it so it doesn't happen again. I suppose someone must have kicked my rigged copseye to pieces by now, but the police don't know that."

"Oh, they'll just send in some cops," said Jill.

"Look around you."

There were pieces of copseyes in all directions. Not one remained whole. A cop would have to be out of his mind to enter a Free Park.

Not to mention the damage to the spirit of the park.

"I wish I'd brought a bag lunch," said Ron.

I saw the cloak off to my right: a ribbon of glowing blue velvet hovering at five feet, like a carpeted path in the air. I didn't yell or point or anything. For Ron it might be pushing the wrong buttons.

Ron didn't see it. "Actually I'm kind of glad this happened," he said animatedly. "I've always thought that anarchy ought to be a viable form of society."

Jill made polite sounds of encouragement.

"After all, anarchy is only the last word in free enterprise. What can a government do for people that people can't do for themselves? Protection from other countries? If all the other countries are anarchies too, you don't need armies. Police, maybe; but what's wrong with privately owned police?"

"Fire departments used to work that way," Jill remembered. "They were hired by the insurance companies. They only protected houses that belonged to their own clients."

"Right! So you buy theft and murder insurance, and the insurance companies hire a police force. The client carries a credit card—"

"Suppose the robber steals the card too?"

"He can't use it. He doesn't have the right retina prints."

"But if the client doesn't have the credit card, he can't sic the cops on the thief."

"Oh." A noticeable pause. "Well—"

Half-listening, for I had heard it all before, I looked for the end points of the cloak. I found empty space at one end and a lovely red-haired girl at the other. She was talking to two men as outré as herself.

One can get the impression that a Free Park is one gigantic costume party. It isn't. Not one person in ten wears anything but street clothes, but the costumes are what get noticed.

These guys were part bird.

Their eyebrows and eyelashes were tiny feathers, green on one, golden on the other. Larger feathers covered their heads, blue and green and gold, and ran in a crest down their spines. They were bare to the waist, showing physiques Jill would find acceptable.

Ron was lecturing. "What does a government do for *anyone* except the people who run the government? Once there were private post offices, and they were cheaper than what we've got now. Anything the government takes over gets more expensive, *immediately*. There's no reason why private enterprise can't do anything a government—"

Jill gasped. She said, "Ooh! How lovely."

Ron turned to look.

As if on cue, the girl in the cloak slapped one of the feathered men hard across the mouth. She tried to hit the other one, but he caught her wrist. Then all three froze.

I said, "See? Nobody wins. She doesn't even like standing still. She—" And I realized why they weren't moving.

In a Free Park it's easy for a girl to turn down an offer. If the guy won't take no for an answer, he gets slapped. The stun beam gets him and the girl. When she wakes up, she walks away.

Simple.

The girl recovered first. She gasped and jerked her wrist loose and turned to run. One of the feathered men didn't bother to chase her; he simply took a double handful of the cloak.

This was getting serious.

The cloak jerked her sharply backward. She didn't hesitate. She reached for the big gold discs at her shoulders, ripped them loose and ran on. The feathered men chased her, laughing.

The redhead wasn't laughing. She was running all out. Two drops of blood ran down her shoulders. I thought of trying to stop the feathered men, decided in favor of it—but they were already past.

The cloak hung like a carpeted path in the air, empty at both ends.

Jill hugged herself uneasily. "Ron, just how does one go about hiring your private police force?"

"Well, you can't expect it to form spontaneously—"

"Let's try the entrances. Maybe we can get out."

It was slow to build. Everyone knew what a copseye did. Nobody thought it through. Two feathered men chasing a lovely nude? A pretty sight; and why interfere? If she didn't want to be chased, she need only—what? And nothing else had changed. The costumes, the people with causes, the people looking for causes, the peoplewatchers, the pranksters. . . .

Blank Sign had joined the POPULATION BY COPULATION faction. His grass-stained pink street tunic jarred strangely with their conservative suits, but he showed no sign of mockery; his face was as preternaturally solemn as theirs. Nonetheless they did not seem glad of his company.

It was crowded near the Wilshire entrance. I saw enough bewildered and frustrated faces to guess that it was closed. The little vestibule area was so packed that we didn't even try to find out what was wrong with the doors.

"I don't think we ought to stay here," Jill said uneasily.

I noticed the way she was hugging herself. "Are you cold?"

"No." She shivered. "But I wish I were dressed."

"How about a strip of that velvet cloak?"

"Good!"

We were too late. The cloak was gone.

It was a warm September day, near sunset. Clad only in paper slacks, I was not cold in the least. I said, "Take my slacks."

"No, hon, I'm the nudist." But Jill hugged herself with both arms.

"Here," said Ron, and handed her his sweater. She flashed him a grateful look, then, clearly embarrassed, she wrapped the sweater around her waist and knotted the sleeves.

Ron didn't get it at all. I asked him, "Do you know the difference between nude and naked?"

He shook his head.

"Nude is artistic. Naked is defenseless."

Nudity was popular in a Free Park. That night, nakedness was not. There must have been pieces of that cloak all over King's Free Park. I saw at least four that night: one worn as a kilt, two being used as crude sarongs, and one as a bandage.

On a normal day, the entrances to King's Free Park close at six. Those who want to stay, stay as long as they like. Usually they are not many, because there are no lights to be broken in a Free Park; but light does seep in from the city beyond. The copseyes float about, guided by infrared, but most of them are not manned.

Tonight would be different.

It was after sunset, but still light. A small and ancient lady came stumping toward us with a look of murder on her lined face. At first I thought it was meant for us, but that wasn't it. She was so mad she couldn't see straight.

She saw my feet and looked up. "Oh, it's you. The one who helped break the lawn mower," she said; which was unjust. "A Free Park, is it? A Free Park! Two men just took away my dinner!"

I spread my hands. "I'm sorry. I really am. If you still had it, we could try to talk you into sharing it."

She lost some of her mad, which brought her embarrassingly close to tears. "Then we're all hungry together. I brought it in a plastic bag. Next time I'll use something that isn't transparent, by d-damn!" She noticed Jill and her improvised sweater-skirt, and added, "I'm sorry, dear, I gave my towel to a girl who needed it even more."

"Thank you anyway."

"Please, may I stay with you people until the copseyes start working again? I don't feel safe, somehow. I'm Glenda Hawthorne."

We introduced ourselves. Glenda Hawthorne shook our hands. By now it was quite dark. We couldn't see the city beyond the high green hedges, but the change was startling when the lights of Westwood and Santa Monica flashed on.

The police were taking their own good time getting us some copseyes.

We reached the grassy field sometimes used by the Society for Creative Anachronism for their tournaments. They fight on foot with weighted and padded weapons designed to behave like swords, broadaxes, morningstars, etc. The weapons are bugged so that they won't fall into the wrong hands. The field is big and flat and bare of trees, sloping upward at the edges.

On one of the slopes, something moved.

I stopped. It didn't move again, but it showed clearly in light reflected down from the white clouds. I made out something man-shaped and faintly pink, and a pale rectangle nearby.

I spoke low. "Stay here."

Jill said, "Don't be silly. There's nothing for anyone to hide under. Come on."

The blank sign was bent and marked with shoe prints. The man who had been carrying it looked up at us with pain in his eyes. Drying blood ran from his nose. With effort he whispered, "I think they dislocated my shoulder."

"Let me look." Jill bent over him. She probed him a bit, then set herself and pulled hard and steadily on his arm. Blank Sign yelled in pain and despair.

"That'll do it." Jill sounded satisfied. "How does it feel?"

"It doesn't hurt as much." He smiled, almost.

"What happened?"

"They started pushing me and kicking me to make me go away. I was *doing* it, I was walking away. I *was*. Then one of the sons of bitches snatched away my sign—'' He stopped for a moment, then went off at a tangent. ''I wasn't hurting anyone with my sign. I'm a psych major. I'm writing a thesis on what people read into a blank sign. Like the blank sheets in the Rorschach tests.''

''What kind of reactions do you get?''

''Usually hostile. But nothing like *that*.'' Blank Sign sounded bewildered. ''Wouldn't you think a Free Park is the one place you'd find freedom of speech?''

Jill wiped at his face with a tissue from Glenda Hawthorne's purse. She said, ''Especially when you're not saying anything. Hey, Ron, tell us more about your government by anarchy.''

Ron cleared his throat. ''I hope you're not judging it by *this*. King's Free Park hasn't been an anarchy for more than a couple of hours. It needs time to develop.''

Glenda Hawthorne and Blank Sign must have wondered what the hell he was talking about. I wished him joy in explaining it to them, and wondered if he would explain who had knocked down the copseyes.

This field would be a good place to spend the night. It was open, with no cover and no shadows, no way for anyone to sneak up on us.

We lay on wet grass, sometimes dozing, sometimes talking. Two other groups no bigger than ours occupied the jousting field. They kept their distance; we kept ours. Now and then we heard voices, and knew that they were not asleep; not all at once, anyway.

Blank Sign dozed restlessly. His ribs were giving him trouble, though Jill said none of them were broken. Every so often he whimpered and tried to move and woke himself up. Then he had to hold himself still until he fell asleep again.

''Money,'' said Jill. ''It takes a government to print money.''

''But you could get I.O.U.'s printed. Standard denominations, printed for a fee and notarized. Backed by your good name.''

Jill laughed softly. ''Thought of everything, haven't you? You couldn't travel very far that way.''

''Credit cards, then.''

I had stopped believing in Ron's anarchy. I said, ''Ron, remember the girl in the long blue cloak?''

A little gap of silence. ''Yah?''

''Pretty, wasn't she? Fun to watch.''

''Granted.''

''If there weren't any laws to stop you from raping her, she'd be muffled to the ears in a long dress and carrying a tear gas pen. What fun would that be? I *like* the nude look. Look how fast it disappeared after the copseyes fell.''

''Mmm,'' said Ron.

The night was turning cold. Faraway voices, occasional distant shouts, came like thin gray threads in a black tapestry of silence. Mrs. Hawthorne spoke into that silence.

"What was that boy really saying with his blank sign?"

"He wasn't saying anything," said Jill.

"Now, just a minute, dear. I think he was, even if he didn't know it." Mrs. Hawthorne talked slowly, using the words to shape her thoughts. "Once there was an organization to protest the forced contraception bill. I was one of them. We carried signs for hours at a time. We printed leaflets. We stopped people passing so that we could talk to them. We gave up our time, we went to considerable trouble and expense, because we wanted to get our ideas across.

"Now, if a man had joined us with a blank sign, he would have been *saying* something. His sign says that he has no opinion. If he joins us he says that we have no opinion either. He's saying our opinions aren't worth anything."

I said, "Tell him when he wakes up. He can put it in his notebook."

"But his notebook is *wrong*. He wouldn't push his blank sign in among people he agreed with, would he?"

"Maybe not."

"I . . . suppose I don't like people with no opinions." Mrs. Hawthorne stood up. She had been sitting tailor-fashion for some hours. "Do you know if there's a pop machine nearby?"

There wasn't, of course. No private company would risk getting their machines smashed once or twice a day. But she had reminded the rest of us that we were thirsty. Eventually we all got up and trooped away in the direction of the fountain.

All but Blank Sign.

I'd *liked* that blank sign gag. How odd, how ominous, that so basic a right as freedom of speech could depend on so slight a thing as a floating copseye.

I was thirsty.

The park was bright by city light, crossed by sharp-edged shadows. In such light it seems that one can see much more than he really can. I could see into every shadow; but, though there were stirrings all around us, I could see nobody until he moved. We four, sitting under an oak with our backs to the tremendous trunk, must be invisible from any distance.

We talked little. The park was quiet except for occasional laughter from the fountain.

I couldn't forget my thirst. I could feel others being thirsty around me.

The fountain was right out there in the open, a solid block of concrete with five men around it.

They were dressed alike in paper shorts with big pockets. They looked alike: like first-string athletes. Maybe they belonged to the same order or frat or R.O.T.C. class.

They had taken over the fountain.

When someone came to get a drink, the tall ash-blond one would step forward with his arm held stiffly out, palm forward. He had a wide mouth and a grin that might otherwise have been infectious, and a deep, echoing voice. He would intone, "Go back. None may pass here but the immortal Cthulhu," or something equally silly.

Trouble was, they weren't kidding. Or: they were kidding, but they wouldn't let anyone have a drink.

When we arrived, a girl dressed in a towel had been trying to talk some sense into them. It hadn't worked. It might even have boosted their egos: a lovely half-naked girl begging them for water. Eventually she'd given up and gone away.

In that light her hair might have been red. I hoped it was the girl in the cloak. She'd sounded healthy . . . unhurt.

And a beefy man in a yellow business jumper had made the mistake of demanding his rights. It was not a night for rights. The blond kid had goaded him into screaming insults, a stream of unimaginative profanity, which ended when he tried to hit the blond kid. Then three of them had swarmed over him. The man had left crawling, moaning of police and lawsuits.

Why hadn't somebody done something?

I had watched it all from sitting position. I could list my own reasons. One: it was hard to face the fact that a copseye would not zap them both, any second now. Two: I didn't like the screaming fat man much. He talked dirty. Three: I'd been waiting for someone else to step in.

As with the girl in the cloak. Damn it.

Mrs. Hawthorne said, "Ronald, what time is it?"

Ron may have been the only man in King's Free Park who knew the time. People generally left their valuables in lockers at the entrances. But years ago, when Ron was flush with money from the sale of the engraved beer bottles, he'd bought an implant-watch. He told time by one red mark and two red lines glowing beneath the skin of his wrist.

We had put the women between us, but I saw the motion as he glanced at his wrist. "Quarter of twelve."

"Don't you think they'll get bored and go away? It's been twenty minutes since anyone tried to get a drink," Mrs. Hawthorne said plaintively.

Jill shifted against me in the dark. "They can't be any more bored than we are. I think they'll get bored and stay anyway. Besides—" She stopped.

I said, "Besides that, we're thirsty *now*."

"Right."

"Ron, have you seen any sign of those rock throwers you collected? Especially the one who knocked down the copseye."

"No."

I wasn't surprised. In this darkness? "Do you remember his—" And I didn't even finish.

"Yes!" Ron said suddenly.

"You're kidding."

"No. His name was Bugeyes. You don't forget a name like that."

"I take it he had big, bulging eyes?"

"I didn't notice."

Well, it was worth a try. I stood and cupped my hands for a megaphone and shouted, "*Bugeyes*!"

One of the Water Monopoly shouted, "Let's keep the noise down out there!"

"Bugeyes!"

A chorus of remarks from the Water Monopoly. "Strange habits these peasants." "Most of them are just thirsty. *This* character—"

From off to the side: "What do you want?"

"We want to talk to you! Stay where you are!" To Ron I said, "Come on." To Jill and Mrs. Hawthorne, "Stay here. Don't get involved."

We moved out into the open space between us and Bugeyes's voice.

Two of the five kids came immediately to intercept us. They must have been bored, all right, and looking for action.

We ran for it. We reached the shadows of the trees before those two reached us. They stopped, laughing like maniacs, and moved back to the fountain.

A fourteen-year-old kid spoke behind us. "Ron?"

Ron and I, we lay on our bellies in the shadows of low bushes. Across too much shadowless grass, four men in paper shorts stood at parade rest at the four corners of the fountain. The fifth man watched for a victim.

A boy walked out between us into the moonlight. His eyes were shining, big, expressive eyes, maybe a bit too prominent. His hands were big, too, with knobby knuckles. One hand was full of acorns.

He pitched them rapidly, one at a time, overhand. First one, then another of the Water Trust twitched and looked in our direction. Bugeyes kept throwing.

Quite suddenly, two of them started toward us at a run. Bugeyes kept throwing until they were almost on him; then he threw his acorns in a handful and dived into the shadows.

The two of them ran between us. We let the first go by: the wide-mouthed blond spokeman, his expression low and murderous now. The other was short and broad-shouldered, an intimidating silhouette seemingly all muscle. A tackle. I stood up in front of him, expecting him to stop in surprise; and he did, and I hit him in the mouth as hard as I could.

He stepped back in shock. Ron wrapped an arm around his throat.

He bucked. Instantly. Ron hung on. I did something I'd seen often enough on television: linked my fingers and brought both hands down on the back of his neck.

The blond spokesman should be back by now; and I turned, and he was. He was on me before I could get my hands up. We rolled on the ground, me with my arms pinned to my sides, him unable to use his hands without letting go. It was lousy planning for both of us. He was squeezing the breath out of me. Ron hovered over us, waiting for a chance to hit him.

Suddenly there were others, a lot of others. Three of them pulled the blond kid off me, and a beefy, bloody man in a yellow business jumper stepped forward and crowned him with a rock.

The blond kid went limp.

I was still trying to get my breath.

The man squared off and threw a straight left hook with the rock in his hand. The blond kid's head snapped back, fell forward.

I yelled, "Hey!" Jumped forward, got hold of the arm that held the rock.

Someone hit me solidly in the side of the neck.

I dropped. It felt like all my strings had been cut. Someone was helping me to my feet—Ron—voices babbling in whispers, one shouting, "Get him—"

I couldn't see the blond kid. The other one, the tackle, was up and staggering away. Shadows came from between the trees to play pileup on him. The woods were alive, and it was just a *little* patch of woods. Full of angry, thirsty people.

Bugeyes reappeared, grinning widely. "Now what? Go somewhere else and try it again?"

"Oh, no. It's getting very vicious out tonight. Ron, we've got to stop them. They'll kill him!"

"It's a Free Park. Can you stand now?"

"Ron, they'll *kill* him!"

The rest of the Water Trust was charging to the rescue. One of them had a tree branch with the leaves stripped off. Behind them, shadows converged on the fountain.

We fled.

I had to stop after a dozen paces. My head was trying to explode. Ron looked back anxiously, but I waved him on. Behind me the man with the branch broke through the trees and ran toward me to do murder.

Behind him, all the noise suddenly stopped.

I braced myself for the blow.

And fainted.

He was lying across my legs, with the branch still in his hand. Jill and Ron were pulling at my shoulders. A pair of golden moons floated overhead.

I wriggled loose. I felt my head. It seemed intact.

Ron said, "The copseyes zapped him before he got to you."

"What about the others? Did they kill them?"

"I don't know." Ron ran his hands through his hair. "I was wrong. Anarchy isn't stable. It comes apart too easily."

"Well, don't do any more experiments, okay?"

People were beginning to stand up. They streamed toward the exits, gathering momentum, beneath the yellow gaze of the copseyes.

• • •

• • •

I heard footsteps. They jarred the earth.
I opened my eyes and saw the rammer.
He was six feet tall and massively built. He wore a scarf and a pair of blue balloon pants, not too far out of style, but they didn't match. What they exposed of his skin was loose on him, as if he had shrunk within it. Indeed, he looked like a giraffe wearing an elephant's skin.

"Passerby," 1971

From PROTECTOR

Nick felt panic close around his throat. "You. You're Brennan?"

"Yah. And you're Nick Sohl. I saw you once in Confinement. But I don't recognize your friend."

"Lucas Garner." Luke had himself under control. "Your photographs don't do you justice, Brennan."

"I did something stupid," said the Brennan-monster. Its voice was no more human, its appearance no less intimidating. "I went to meet the Outsider. You were trying to do the same, weren't you?"

"Yes." There was a sardonic amusement in Luke's eyes and Luke's voice. Whether or not he believed the Brennan-monster, he was enjoying the situation. "Was there really an Outsider, Brennan?"

"Unless you want to quibble about definitions."

Sohl broke in. "For God's sake, Brennan! What *happened* to you?"

"That's a long story. Are we pressed for time? Of course not, you'd have started the motor. All right, I'd like to tell this my own way, so please maintain a respectful silence, remembering that if I hadn't gotten in the way you'd look just like this, and serve you right, too." He looked hard at the two men. "I'm wrong. You wouldn't. You're both past the age.

"Well, bear with me. There exists a race of bipeds that live near the edge of the globe of close-packed suns at the core of the galaxy . . .

"The most important thing about them is that they live in three stages of maturity. There is childhood, which is self-explanatory. There is the breeder stage, a biped just short of intelligence, whose purpose is to create more children. And there is the protector.

"At around age forty-two, our time, the breeder stage gets the urge to eat the root of a certain bush. Up to then he stayed away from it, because its smell was repugnant to him. Suddenly it smells delicious.

The bush grows all over the planet; there's no real chance that the root won't be available to any breeder who lives long enough to want it.

"The root initiates certain changes, both physiological and emotional. Before I go into detail, I'll let you in on the big secret. The race I speak of calls itself—" The Brennan-monster clicked its horny beak sharply together. *Pak.* "But we call it *Homo habilis.*"

"What?" Nick seemed forced into the position of straight man, and he didn't like it. But Luke sat hugging his useless legs to his chest, grinning with huge enjoyment.

"There was an expedition that landed on Earth some two and a half million years ago. The bush they brought wouldn't grow right, so there haven't been any protector stage Pak on Earth. I'll get to that.

"When a breeder eats the root, these changes take place. His or her gonads and obvious sexual characteristics disappear. His skull softens and his brain begins to grow, until it is comfortably larger and more complex than yours, gentlemen. The skull then hardens and develops a bony crest. The teeth fall out, whatever teeth are left; the gums and lips grow together and form a hard, almost flat beak. My face is *too* flat; it works better with *Homo habilis*. All hair disappears. Some joints swell enormously, to supply much greater leverage to the muscle. The moment arm increases, you follow? The skin hardens and wrinkles to form a kind of armor. Fingernails become claws, retractile, so that a protector's fingertips are actually more sensitive than before, and better toolmakers. A simple two-chamber heart forms where the two veins from the legs, whatever the hell they're called, join to approach the heart. Notice that my skin is thicker there? Well, there are less dramatic changes, but they all contribute to make the protector a powerful, intelligent fighting machine. Garner, you no longer seem amused."

"It all sounds awfully familiar."

"I wondered if you'd spot that . . . The emotional changes are drastic. A protector who has bred true feels no urge except the urge to protect those of his blood line. He recognizes them by smell. His increased intelligence does him no good here, because his hormones rule his motives. Nick, has it occurred to you that all of these changes are a kind of exaggeration of what happens to men and women as they get older? Garner saw it right away."

"Yes, but—"

"The extra heart," Luke broke in. "What about that?"

"Like the expanded brain, it doesn't form without tree-of-life. After fifty, without modern medical care, a normal human heart becomes inadequate. Eventually it stops."

"Ah."

"Do you two find this convincing?"

Luke was reserving judgment. "Why do you ask?"

"I'm really more interested in convincing Nick. My Belt citizenship depends on my convincing you I'm Brennan. Not to mention my bank account and my ship and cargo. Nick, I've got an abandoned fuel tank from the Mariner XX attached to my ship, which I last left falling across the solar system at high speed."

"It's still doing that," said Nick. "Likewise the Outsider ship. We ought to be doing something about recovering it."

"Finagle's eyes, *yes*! It's not that good a design, I could improve it blindfold, but you could buy Ceres with the monopoles!"

"First things first," Garner said mildly.

"That ship is receding, Garner. Oh, I see what you mean; you're afraid to put an alien monster near a working spacecraft." The Brennan-monster glanced back at the flare gun, flickeringly, then apparently abandoned the idea of hijacking the dustboat. "We'll stay out here until you're convinced. Is that a deal? Could you get a better deal anywhere?"

"Not from a Belter. Brennan, there is considerable evidence that man is related to the other primates of Earth."

"I don't doubt it. I've got some theories."

"Say on."

"About that lost colony. A big ship arrived here, and four landing craft went down with some thirty protectors and a lot of breeders. A year later the protectors knew they'd picked the wrong planet. The bush they needed grew wrong. They sent a message for help, by laser, and then they died. Starvation is a normal death for a protector, but it's usually voluntary. These starved against their will." There was no emotion in the Brennan-monster's voice or mask-like face.

"They died. The breeders were breeding without check. There was endless room, and the protectors must have wiped out any dangerous life forms. What happened next has to be speculation. The protectors were dead, but the breeders were used to their helping out, and they stayed around the ships."

"And?"

"And the piles got hot without the protectors to keep them balanced. They had to be fission piles, given the state of the art. Maybe they exploded. Maybe not. The radiation caused mutations resulting in everything from lemurs to apes and chimpanzees to ancient and modern man.

"That's one theory," said the Brennan-monster. "Another is that the protectors deliberately started breeding mutations, so that breeders would have a chance to survive in some form until help came. The results would be the same."

"I don't believe it," said Nick.

"You will. You should now. There's enough evidence, particularly in religions and folk tales. What percentage of humanity genuinely expects to live forever? Why do so many religions include a race of immortal beings who are constantly battling one another? What's the justification for ancestor worship? You know what happens to a man without modern geriatrics: as he ages his brain cells start to die. Yet people tend to respect him, to listen to him. Where do guardian angels come from?''

''Race memory?''

''Probably. It's hard to believe a tradition could survive that long.''

''South Africa,'' said Luke. ''They must have landed in South Africa, somewhere near Olduvai Gorge National Park. All the primates are there.''

''Not quite. Maybe one ship landed in Australia, for the metals. You know, the protectors may have just scattered radioactive dust around and left it at that. The breeders would breed like rabbits without natural enemies, and the radiation would help them change. With all the protectors dead, they'd have to develop new shticks. Some got strength, some got agility, some got intelligence. Most got dead, of course. Mutations do.''

''I seem to remember,'' said Luke, ''that the aging process in man can be compared to the program running out in a space probe. Once the probe has done its work it doesn't matter what happens to it. Similarly, once we pass the age at which we can have children—''

''—Evolution is through with you. You're moving on inertia only, following your course with no corrective mechanisms.'' The Brennan-monster nodded. ''Of course the root supplies the program for the third stage. Good comparison.''

Nick said, ''Any idea what went wrong with the root?''

''Oh, that's no mystery. Though it had the protectors of Pak going crazy for awhile. No wonder a small colony couldn't solve it. There's a virus that lives in the root. It carries the genes for the change from breeder to protector. It can't live outside the root, so a protector has to eat more root every so often. If there's no thallium in the soil, the root still grows, but it won't support the virus.''

''That sounds pretty complicated.''

''Ever work with a hydroponics garden? The relationships in a stable ecology can be complicated. There was no problem on the Pak world. Thallium is a rare earth, but it must be common enough among all those Population II stars. And the root grows everywhere.''

Nick said, ''Where does the Outsider come in?''

A hiss and snap of beak: *Phssth-pok*. ''Phssthpok found old records, including the call for help. He was the first protector in two and a half million years to realize that there was a way to find Sol, or at least to narrow the search. And he had no children, so he had to find a Cause quick, before the urge to eat left him. That's what happens to a protector when his blood line is dead. More lack of programming. Incidentally, you might note the heavy protection against mutation in the Pak species.

A mutation doesn't smell right. That could be important in the galactic core, where radiation is heavy."

"So he came barreling out here with a hold full of seeds?"

"And bags of thallium oxide. The oxide was easiest to carry. I wondered about the construction of his ship, but you can see why he trailed his cargo section behind his lifesystem. Radiation doesn't bother him, in small amounts. He can't have children."

"Where is he now?"

"I had to kill him."

"What?" Garner was shocked. "Did he attack you?"

"No."

"Then—I don't understand."

The Brennan-monster seemed to hesitate. It said, "Garner, Sohl, listen to me. Twelve miles from here, some fifty feet under the sand, is part of an alien spacecraft filled with roots and seeds and bags of thallium oxide. The roots I can grow from those seeds can make a man nearly immortal. Now what? What are we going to do with them?"

The two men looked at each other. Luke seemed about to speak, closed his mouth.

"That's a tough one, right? But you can guess what Phssthpok expected, can't you?"

Phssthpok dreamed.

He knew to within a day just how long it would take for Brennan to wake up. He could have been wrong, of course. But if he were, then Brennan's kind would have mutated too far from the Pak form.

Knowing how long he had, Phssthpok could time his dreaming. The martians were no threat now, though something would have to be done about them eventually. Dreaming was a fine art to a protector. He had about ten days. For a week he dreamed the past, up until the day he left the Pak planet. Sensory stimulation had been skimpy during the voyage. He moved on into the future.

Phssthpok dreamed . . .

It would begin when his captive woke. From the looks of him, the captive's brain would be larger than Phssthpok's; there was that frontal bulge, ruining the slope of the face. He would learn fast. Phssthpok would teach him how to be a protector, and what to do with the roots and seeds of tree-of-life.

Did the breeder have children? If so, he would take the secret for his own, using tree-of-life to make protectors of his own descendants. That was all right. If he had sense enough to spread his family around, avoiding inbreeding, his blood line should reach out to include most of this system's Pak race.

Probably he would kill Phssthpok to keep the secret. That was all right too.

There was a nightmare tinge to Phssthpok's dreaming. For the captive didn't look right. His fingernails were developing wrong. His head was certainly not the right shape. That frontal bulge . . . and his beak was as flat as his face had been. His back wasn't arched, his legs were wrong, his arms were too short. His kind had had too much time to mutate.

But he'd reacted correctly to the roots.

The future was uncertain . . . except for Phssthpok. Let the captive learn what he needed to know, if he could; let him carry on the work, if he could. There would come a day when Earth was a second Pak world. Phssthpok had done his best. He would teach, and die.

Brennan stirred. He unfolded his curled body, stretched wide and opened his eyes. He stared unwinking at Phssthpok, stared as if he were reading the protector's mind. All new protectors did that: orienting themselves through memories they were only now beginning to understand.

"I wonder if I can make you understand how fast it all was," said the Brennan-monster. He gazed at the two old men, one twice the age of the other but both past the transition age, and wondered that they should be his judges.

"In two days we learned each other's language. His is much faster than mine and fits my mouth better, so we used it. He told me his life story. We discussed the martians, working out the most efficient way to exterminate them—"

"What?"

"To exterminate them, Garner. Hell, they've killed thirteen men already! We talked practically nonstop, with Phssthpok doing most of the talking, and all the time we were hard at work: calisthenics to build me up, fins for Phssthpok's suit so he could swim the dust, widgets to get every atom of air and water out of the life support system and take it to the base. I've never seen the base; we had to extrapolate the design so we'd know how to re-inflate it and protect it.

"The third day he told me how to get a tree-of-life crop growing. He had the box open and was telling me how to unfreeze the seeds safely. He was giving me orders just as if I were a voice-box computer. I was about to ask, 'Don't I get any choices at all?' And I *didn't*."

"I don't follow," said Garner.

"I didn't get any choices. I was too intelligent. It's been that way ever since I woke up. I get answers before I can finish formulating the question. If I always see the best answer, then where's my choice? Where's my free will? You can't believe how fast this all was. I saw the whole chain of logic in one flash. I slammed Phssthpok's head hard against the edge of the freezer. It stunned him long enough so that I could break his throat against the edge. Then I jumped back in case he attacked. I figured I could hold him off until he strangled. But he didn't attack. He hadn't figured it out, not yet."

"It sounds like murder, Brennan. He didn't want to kill you?"

"Not yet. I was his shining hope. He couldn't even defend himself for fear of bruising me. He was older than me, and he knew how to fight. He could have killed me if he'd wanted to, but he couldn't want to. It took him thirty-two thousand years of real time to bring us those roots. I was supposed to finish the job.

"I think he died believing he'd succeeded. He half-expected me to kill him."

"Brennan. *Why?*"

The Brennan-monster shrugged cantaloupe shoulders. "He was wrong. I killed him because he would have tried to wipe out humanity when he learned the truth." He reached into the slit balloon that had brought him across twelve miles of fluid dust. He pulled out a jury-rigged something that hummed softly—his air renewal setup, made from parts of Phssthpok's control board—and dropped it in the boat. Next he pulled out half of a yellow root like a raw sweet potato. He held it under Garner's nose. "Smell."

Luke sniffed. "Pleasant enough. Like a liqueur."

"Sohl?"

"Nice. How's it taste?"

"If you knew it would turn you into something like me, would you take a bite of it? Garner?"

"This instant. I'd like to live forever, and I'm afraid of going senile."

"Sohl?"

"NO. I'm not ready to give up sex yet."

"How old are you?"

"Seventy-four. Birthday two months from now."

"You're already too old. You were too old at fifty; it would have killed you. Would you have volunteered at forty-five?"

Sohl laughed. "Not likely."

"Well, that's half the answer. From Phssthpok's point of view we're a failure. The other half is that no sane man would turn the root loose on Earth or Belt or anywhere else."

"I should hope not. But let's hear *your* reasons."

"War. The Pak world has never been free from war at any time in its history. Naturally not, with every protector acting to expand and protect his blood line at the expense of all the others. Knowledge keeps getting lost. The race can't cooperate for a minute beyond the point where one protector sees an advantage in betraying the others. They can't make any kind of progress because of that continual state of war.

"And I'm to turn that loose on Earth? Can you imagine a thousand protectors deciding their grandchildren need more room? Your eighteen billion flatlanders live too close to the edge already; you can't afford the resources.

"Besides which, we don't really need tree-of-life. Garner, when were you born? Nineteen forty or thereabouts?"

"'Thirty-nine."

"Geriatrics is getting so good so fast that my kids could live a thousand years. We'll get longevity without tree-of-life, without sacrificing anything at all.

"Now look at it from Phssthpok's viewpoint," the Brennan-monster continued. "We're a mutation. We've settled the solar system and started some interstellar colonies. We will and must refuse the root, and even when it's forced on us, the resulting mutated protectors are atypical. Phssthpok thought in terms of the long view. We're not Pak, we're no use to the Pak, and it's conceivable that someday we'll reach the core suns. The Pak will attack us the moment they see us, and we'll fight back." He shrugged. "And we'll win. The Pak don't unite effectively. We do. We'll have a better technology than theirs."

"We will?"

"I told you, they can't keep their technology. Whatever can't be used immediately, gets lost until someone files it in the Library. Military knowledge never gets filed; the families keep it a deep, dark secret. And the only ones to use the Library are childless protectors. There aren't many of them, and they aren't highly motivated."

"Couldn't you have tried to talk to him?"

"Garner, I'm not getting through to you. He'd have killed me the moment he figured it out! He was trained to fight protectors. I wouldn't have had a chance. Then he'd have tried to wipe out the human species. We'd have been much worse to him than hostile aliens. We're a corruption of the Pak form itself."

"But he couldn't do it. He was all alone."

"I've thought of half a dozen things he could have tried. None of them sure things, but I couldn't risk it."

"Name one."

"Plant tree-of-life all through Congo National Park. Organize the monkey and chimpanzee protectors."

My premise was a cute one: that every symptom of aging in man is an aborted version of something designed to make us stronger. In particular, we lose intelligence with age because we were supposed to grow more brain tissue, when the thymus gland dissolves around age 42–45.

Once I accepted that premise, I was in deep water.

The toughest challenge for a writer is a character brighter than the author. It's not impossible. Puzzles the writer needs months to solve, or to design, the character may solve in moments. But God help the writer if his abnormally bright character is *wrong*!

This was my first such attempt. I put heavy restraints on the Pak. *Homo habilis* is the breeding stage, but the adult is a neutered warrior with instincts hard-wired. The characteristic smell of his gene line goes straight to his motivation, without intermediate thought. Means are under his control; goals are not.

I should not have made a protector the author. It forced me to assume (as a protector would) an abnormally bright reader.

For my next attempt at superhuman intelligence, see A WORLD OUT OF TIME . . . but I expect to try again.

● ● ●

• • •

The most beautiful girl aboard turned out to have a husband with habits so solitary that I didn't know about him until the second week. He was about five feet four and middle-aged, but he wore a hellflare tattoo on his shoulder, which meant he'd been in Kzin during the war thirty years back, which meant he'd been trained to kill adult Kzinti with his bare hands, feet, elbows, knees, and whatnot. When we found out about each other, he very decently gave me a first warning, and broke my arm to prove he meant it.

The arm still ached a day later ...

"Flatlander," 1967

THE HOLE MAN

Out of five Hugo Awards, this is the only one that surprised me. I always think I earned it; I'm always half-sure I'll take it home; except this once. "The Hole Man" is a straightforward crime story rendered distinctive only by an unusual murder weapon.

• •

One day Mars will be gone.

Andrew Lear says that it will start with violent quakes, and end hours or days later, very suddenly. He ought to know. It's all his fault.

Lear also says that it won't happen for from years to centuries. So we stay, Lear and the rest of us. We study the alien base for what it can tell us, while the center of the world we stand on is slowly eaten away. It's enough to give a man nightmares.

It was Lear who found the alien base.

We had reached Mars: fourteen of us, in the cramped bulbous life-support system of the *Percival Lowell*. We were circling in orbit, taking our time, correcting our maps and looking for anything that thirty years of Mariner probes might have missed.

We were mapping mascons, among other things. Those mass concentrations under the lunar maria were almost certainly left by good-sized asteroids, mountains of rock falling silently out of the sky until they struck with the energies of thousands of fusion bombs. Mars has been cruising through the asteroid belt for four billion years. Mars would show bigger and better mascons. They would affect our orbits.

So Andrew Lear was hard at work, watching pens twitch on graph paper as we circled Mars. A bit of machinery fell alongside the *Percival Lowell*, rotating. Within its thin shell was a weighted double lever system, deceptively simple: a Forward Mass Detector. The pens mapped its twitchings.

Over Sirbonis Palus they began mapping strange curves.

Another man might have cursed and tried to fix it. Andrew Lear thought it out, then sent the signal that would stop the free-falling widget from rotating.

It had to be rotating to map a stationary mass.

But now it was mapping simple sine waves.

Lear went running to Captain Childrey.

Running? It was more like trapeze artistry. Lear pulled himself along by handholds, kicked off from walls, braked with a hard push of hands or feet. Moving in free fall is hard work when you're in a hurry, and Lear was a forty-year-old astrophysicist, not an athlete. He was blowing hard when he reached the control bubble.

Childrey—who *was* an athlete—waited with a patient, slightly contemptuous smile while Lear caught his breath.

He already thought Lear was crazy. Lear's words only confirmed it. "Gravity for sending signals? Dr. Lear, will you please quit bothering me with your weird ideas. I'm busy. We all are."

This was not entirely unfair. Some of Lear's enthusiasms were peculiar. Gravity generators. Black holes. He thought we should be searching for Dyson spheres: stars completely enclosed by an artificial shell. He believed that mass and inertia were two separate things: that it should be possible to suck the inertia out of a spacecraft, say, so that it could accelerate to near lightspeed in a few minutes. He was a wide-eyed dreamer, and when he was flustered he tended to wander from the point.

"You don't understand," he told Childrey. "Gravity radiation is harder to block than electromagnetic waves. Patterned gravity waves would be easy to detect. The advanced civilizations in the galaxy may all be communicating by gravity. Some of them may even be modulating pulsars—rotating neutron stars. That's where Project Ozma went wrong: they were only looking for signals in the electromagnetic spectrum."

Childrey laughed. "Sure. Your little friends are using neutron stars to send you messages. What's that got to do with us?"

"Well, look!" Lear held up the strip of flimsy, nearly weightless paper he'd torn from the machine. "I got this over Sirbonis Palus. I think we ought to land there."

"We're landing in Mare Cimmerium, as you perfectly well know. The lander is already deployed and ready to board. Dr. Lear, we've spent four days mapping this area. It's flat. It's in a green-brown area. When spring comes next month, we'll find out whether there's life there! And everybody wants it that way except you!''

Lear was still holding the graph paper before him like a shield. ''Please. Take one more circuit over Sirbonis Palus.''

Childrey opted for the extra orbit. Maybe the sine waves convinced him. Maybe not. He would have liked inconveniencing the rest of us in Lear's name, to show him for a fool.

But the next pass showed a tiny circular feature in Sirbonis Palus. And Lear's mass indicator was making sine waves again.

The aliens had gone. During our first few months we always expected them back any minute. The machinery in the base was running smoothly and perfectly, as if the owners had only just stepped out.

The base was an inverted pie plate two stories high, and windowless. The air inside was breathable, like Earth's air three miles up, but with a bit more oxygen. Mars' air is far thinner, and poisonous. Clearly they were not of Mars.

The walls were thick and deeply eroded. They leaned inward against the internal pressure. The roof was somewhat thinner, just heavy enough for the pressure to support it. Both walls and roof were of fused Martian dust.

The heating system still worked—and it was also the lighting system: grids in the ceiling glowing brick-red. The base was always ten degrees too warm. We didn't find the off switches for almost a week: they were behind locked panels. The air system blew gusty winds until we fiddled with it.

We could guess a lot about them from what they'd left behind. They must have come from a world smaller than Earth, circling a red dwarf star in close orbit. To be close enough to be warm enough, the planet would have to be locked in by tides, turning one face always to its star. The aliens must have evolved on the lighted side, in a permanent red day, with winds constantly howling over the border from the night side.

And they had no sense of privacy. The only doorways that had doors in them were air locks. The second floor was a hexagonal metal gridwork. It would not block you off from your friends on the floor below. The bunk room was an impressive expanse of mercury-filled water bed, wall to wall. The rooms were too small and cluttered, the furniture and machinery too close to the doorways, so that at first we were constantly bumping elbows and knees. The ceilings were an inch short of six feet high on both floors, so that we tended to walk stooped even if we were short enough to stand upright. Habit. But Lear was just tall enough to knock his head if he stood up fast, anywhere in the base.

We thought they must have been smaller than human. But their padded benches seemed human-designed in size and shape. Maybe it was their minds that were different: they didn't need psychic elbow room.

The ship had been bad enough. Now this. Within the base was instant claustrophobia. It put all of our tempers on hair triggers.

Two of us couldn't take it.

Lear and Childrey did not belong on the same planet.

With Childrey, neatness was a compulsion. He had enough for all of us. During those long months aboard *Percival Lowell*, it was Childrey who led us in calisthenics. He flatly would not let anyone skip an exercise period. We eventually gave up trying.

Well and good. The exercise kept us alive. We weren't getting the healthy daily exercise anyone gets walking around the living room in a one-gravity field.

But after a month on Mars, Childrey was the only man who still appeared fully dressed in the heat of the alien base. Some of us took it as a reproof, and maybe it was, because Lear had been the first to doff his shirt for keeps. In the mess Childrey would inspect his silverware for water spots, then line it up perfectly parallel.

On Earth, Andrew Lear's habits would have been no more than a character trait. In a hurry, he might choose mismatched socks. He might put off using the dishwasher for a day or two if he were involved in something interesting. He would prefer a house that looked "lived in." God help the maid who tried to clean up his study. He'd never be able to find anything afterward.

He was a brilliant but one-sided man. Backpacking or skin diving might have changed his habits—in such pursuits you learn not to forget any least trivial thing—but they would never have tempted him. An expedition to Mars was something he simply could not turn down. A pity, because neatness is worth your life in space.

You don't leave your fly open in a pressure suit.

A month after the landing, Childrey caught Lear doing just that.

The "fly" on a pressure suit is a soft rubber tube over your male member. It leads to a bladder, and there's a spring clamp on it. You open the clamp to use it. Then you close the clamp and open an outside spigot to evacuate the bladder into vacuum.

Similar designs for women involve a catheter, which is hideously uncomfortable. I presume the designers will keep trying. It seems wrong to bar half the human race from our ultimate destiny.

Lear was addicted to long walks. He loved the Martian desert scene: the hard violet sky and the soft blur of whirling orange dust, the sharp close horizon, the endless emptiness. More: he needed the room. He was spending all his working time on the alien communicator, with the ceiling too close over his head and everything else too close to his bony elbows.

He was coming back from a walk, and he met Childrey coming out. Childrey noticed that the waste spigot on Lear's suit was open, the spring broken. Lear had been out for hours. If he'd had to go, he might have bled to death through flesh ruptured by vacuum.

We never learned all that Childrey said to him out there. But Lear came in very red about the ears, muttering under his breath. He wouldn't talk to anyone.

The NASA psychologists should not have put them both on that small a planet. Hindsight is wonderful, right? But Lear and Childrey were each the best choice for competence coupled to the kind of health they would need to survive the trip. There were astrophysicists as competent and as famous as Lear, but they were decades older. And Childrey had a thousand spaceflight hours to his credit. He had been one of the last men on the Moon.

Individually, each of us was the best possible man. It was a damn shame.

The aliens had left the communicator going, like everything else in the base. It must have been hellishly massive, to judge by the thick support pillars slanting outward beneath it. It was a bulky tank of a thing, big enough that the roof had to bulge slightly to give it room. That gave Lear about a square meter of the only head room in the base.

Even Lear had no idea why they'd put it on the second floor. It would send through the first floor, or through the bulk of a planet. Lear learned that by trying it, once he knew enough. He beamed a dot-dash message through Mars itself to the Forward Mass Detector aboard *Lowell*.

Lear had set up a Mass Detector next to the communicator, on an extremely complex platform designed to protect it from vibration. The Detector produced waves so sharply pointed that some of us thought we could *feel* the gravity radiation coming from the communicator.

Lear was in love with the thing.

He skipped meals. When he ate he ate like a starved wolf. "There's a heavy point-mass in there," he told us, talking around a mouthful of food, two months after the landing. "The machine uses electromagnetic fields to vibrate it at high speed. Look—" He picked up a toothpaste tube of tuna spread and held it in front of him. He vibrated it rapidly. Heads turned to watch him around the zigzagged communal table in the alien mess. "I'm making gravity waves now. But they're too mushy because the tube's too big, and their amplitude is virtually zero. There's something very dense and massive in that machine, and it takes a hell of a lot of field strength to keep it there."

"What is it?" someone asked. "Neutronium? Like at the heart of a neutron star?"

Lear shook his head and took another mouthful. "That size, neutronium wouldn't be stable. I think it's a quantum black hole. I don't know how to measure its mass yet."

I said, "A *quantum* black hole?"

Lear nodded happily. "Luck for me. You know, I was against the Mars expedition. We could get a lot more for our money by exploring the asteroids. Among other things, we might have found if there are really quantum black holes out there. But this one's already captured!" He stood up, being careful of his head. He turned in his tray and went back to work.

I remember we stared at each other along the zigzag mess table. Then we drew lots . . . and I lost.

The day Lear left his waste spigot open, Childrey had put a restriction on him. Lear was not to leave the base without an escort.

Lear had treasured the aloneness of those walks. But it was worse than that. Childrey had given him a list of possible escorts: half a dozen men Childrey could trust to see to it that Lear did nothing dangerous to himself or others. Inevitably they were the men most thoroughly trained in space survival routines, most addicted to Childrey's own compulsive neatness, least likely to sympathize with Lear's way of living. Lear was as likely to ask Childrey himself to go walking with him.

He almost never went out anymore. I knew exactly where to find him.

I stood beneath him, looking up through the gridwork floor.

He'd almost finished dismantling the protective panels around the gravity wave communicator. What showed inside looked like parts of a computer in one spot, electromagnetic coils in most places, and a square array of pushbuttons that might have been the aliens' idea of a typewriter. Lear was using a magnetic induction sensor to try to trace wiring without actually tearing off the insulation.

I called, "How you making out?"

"No good," he said. "The insulation seems to be one hundred percent perfect. Now I'm afraid to open it up. No telling how much power is running through there, if it needs shielding that good." He smiled down at me. "Let me show you something."

"What?"

He flipped a toggle above a dull gray circular plate. "This thing is a microphone. It took me a while to find it. I am Andrew Lear, speaking to anyone who may be listening." He switched it off, then ripped paper from the Mass Indicator and showed me squiggles interrupting smooth sine waves. "There. The sound of my voice in gravity radiation. It won't disappear until it's reached the edges of the universe."

"Lear, you mentioned quantum black holes back there. What's a quantum black hole?"

"Um. You know what a black hole is."

"I ought to." Lear had educated us on the subject, at length, during the months aboard *Lowell*.

When a not-too-massive star has used up its nuclear fuel, it collapses into a white dwarf. A heavier star—say, 1.44 times the mass of the sun and larger—can burn out its fuel, then collapse into itself until it is ten kilometers across and composed solely of neutrons packed edge to edge: the densest matter in this universe.

But a big star goes further than that. When a really massive star runs its course . . . when the gas and radiation pressures within are no longer strong enough to hold the outer layers against the star's own ferocious gravity . . . then it can fall into itself entirely, until gravity is stronger than any other force, until it is compressed past the Swarzschild radius and effectively leaves the universe. What happens to it then is problematical. The Swarzschild radius is the boundary beyond which nothing can climb out of the gravity well, not even light.

The star is gone then, but the mass remains: a lightless hole in space, perhaps a hole into another universe.

"A collapsing star can leave a black hole," said Lear. "There may be bigger black holes, whole galaxies that have fallen into themselves. But there's no other way a black hole can form, *now*."

"So?"

"There was a time when black holes of all sizes could form. That was during the Big Bang, the explosion that started the expanding universe. The forces in that blast could have compressed little local vortices of matter past the Swarzschild radius. What that left behind—the smallest ones, anyway—we call quantum black holes."

I heard a distinctive laugh behind me as Captain Childrey walked into view. The bulk of the communicator would have hidden him from Lear, and I hadn't heard him come up. He called, "Just how big a thing are you talking about? Could I pick one up and throw it at you?"

"You'd disappear into one that size," Lear said seriously. "A black hole the mass of the Earth would only be a centimeter across. No, I'm talking about things from 10^{-5} grams on up. There could be one at the center of the Sun—"

"Eek!"

Lear was trying. He didn't like being kidded, but he didn't know how to stop it. Keeping it serious wasn't the way, but he didn't know that either. "Say, 10^{17} grams in mass and 10^{-11} centimeters across. It would be swallowing a few atoms a day."

"Well, at least you know where to find it," said Childrey. "Now all you have to do is go after it."

Lear nodded, still serious. "There could be quantum black holes in asteroids. A small asteroid could capture a quantum black hole easily enough, especially if it was charged; a black hole can hold a charge, you know—"

"Ri-ight."

"All we'd have to do is check out a small asteroid with the Mass Detector. If it masses more than it should, we push it aside and see if it leaves a black hole behind."

"You'd need little teeny eyes to see something that small. Anyway, what would you do with it?"

"You put a charge on it, if it hasn't got one already, and then you manipulate it with electromagnetic fields. You can vibrate it to make gravity radiation. I think I've got one in here," he said, patting the alien communicator.

"Ri-ight," said Childrey, and he went away laughing.

Within a week the whole base was referring to Lear as "the Hole Man," the man with the black hole between his ears.

It hadn't sounded funny when Lear was telling me about it. The rich variety of the universe . . . but when Childrey talked about the black hole in Lear's Anything Box, it sounded hilarious.

Please note: Childrey did not misunderstand anything Lear had said. Childrey wasn't stupid. He merely thought Lear was crazy. He could not have gotten away with making fun of Lear, not among educated men, without knowing exactly what he was doing.

Meanwhile the work went on.

There were pools of Marsdust, fascinating stuff, fine enough to behave like viscous oil, and knee deep. Wading through it wasn't dangerous, but it was very hard work, and we avoided it. One day Brace waded out into the nearest of the pools and started feeling around under the dust. Hunch, he said. He came up with some eroded plastic-like containers. The aliens had used the pool as a garbage dump.

We were having little luck with chemical analysis of the base materials. They were virtually indestructible. We learned more about the chemistry of the alien visitors themselves. They had left traces of themselves on the benches and on the communal waterbed. The traces had most of the chemical components of protoplasm, but Arsvey found no sign of DNA. Not surprising, he said. There must be other giant organic molecules suitable for genetic coding.

The aliens had left volumes of notes behind. The script was a mystery, of course, but we studied the photographs and diagrams. A lot of them were notes on anthropology!

The aliens had been studying Earth during the first Ice Age.

None of us were anthropologists, and that was a damn shame. We never learned if we'd found anything new. All we could do was photograph the stuff and beam it up to *Lowell*. One thing was sure: the aliens had left very long ago, and they had left the lighting and air systems running and the communicator sending a carrier wave.

For us? Who else?

The alternative was that the base had been switched off for some six hundred thousand years, then come back on when something detected *Lowell* approaching Mars. Lear didn't believe it. "If the power had been off in the communicator," he said, "the mass wouldn't be in there any more. The fields have to be going to hold it in place. It's smaller than an atom; it'd fall through anything solid."

So the base power system had been running for all that time. What the hell could it be? And where? We traced some cables and found that it was under the base, under several yards of Marsdust fused to lava. We didn't try to dig through that.

The source was probably geophysical: a hole deep into the core of the planet. The aliens might have wanted to dig such a hole to take core samples. Afterward they would have set up a generator to use the temperature difference between the core and the surface.

Meanwhile, Lear spent some time tracing down the power sources in the communicator. He found a way to shut off the carrier wave. Now the mass—if there was a mass—was at rest in there. It was strange to see the Forward Mass Detector pouring out straight lines instead of drastically peaked sine waves.

We were ill-equipped to take advantage of these riches. We had been fitted out to explore Mars, not a bit of civilization from another star. Lear was the exception. He was in his element, with but one thing to mar his happiness.

I don't know what the final argument was about. I was engaged on another project.

The Mars lander still had fuel in it. NASA had given us plenty of fuel to hover while we looked for a landing spot. After some heated discussion, we had agreed to take the vehicle up and hover it next to the nearby dust pool on low thrust.

It worked fine. The dust rose up in a great soft cloud and went away toward the horizon, leaving the pond bottom covered with other-worldly junk. And more! Arsvey started screaming at Brace to back off. Fortunately Brace kept his head. He tilted us over to one side and took us away on a gentle curve. The backblast never touched the skeletons.

We worked out there for hours, being very finicky indeed. Here was another skill none of us would own to, but we'd read about how careful an archaeologist has to be, and we did our best. Traces of water had had time to turn some of the dust to natural cement, so that some of the skeletons were fixed to the rock. But we got a couple free. We put them on stretchers and brought them back. One crumbled the instant the air came hissing into the lock. We left the other outside.

The aliens had not had the habit of taking baths. We'd set up a bathtub with very tall sides, in a room the aliens had reserved for some incomprehensible ritual. I had stripped off my pressure suit and was heading for the bathtub, very tired, hoping that nobody would be in it.

I heard the voices before I saw them.

Lear was shouting.

Childrey wasn't, but his voice was a carrying one. It carried mockery. He was standing between the supporting pillars. His hands were on his hips, his teeth gleamed white, his head was thrown back to look up at Lear.

He finished talking. For a time neither of them moved. Then Lear made a sound of disgust. He turned away and pushed one of the buttons on what might have been an alien typewriter keyboard.

Childrey looked startled. He slapped at his right thigh and brought the hand away bloody. He stared at it, then looked up at Lear. He started to ask a question.

He crumpled slowly in the low gravity. I got to him before he hit the ground. I cut his pants open and tied a handkerchief over the blood spot. It was a small puncture, but the flesh was puckered above it on a line with his groin.

Childrey tried to speak. His eyes were wide. He coughed, and there was blood in his mouth.

I guess I froze. How could I help if I couldn't tell what had happened? I saw a blood spot on his right shoulder, and I tore the shirt open and found another tiny puncture wound.

The doctor arrived.

It took Childrey an hour to die, but the doctor had given up much earlier. Between the wound in his shoulder and the wound in his thigh, Childrey's flesh had been ruptured in a narrow line that ran through one lung and his stomach and part of his intestinal tract. The autopsy showed a tiny, very neat hole drilled through the hipbones.

We looked for, and found, a hole in the floor beneath the communicator. It was the size of a pencil lead, and packed with dust.

"I made a mistake," Lear told the rest of us at the inquest. "I should never have touched that particular button. It must have switched off the fields that held the mass in place. It just dropped. Captain Childrey was underneath."

And it had gone straight through him, eating the mass of him as it went.

"No, not quite," said Lear. "I'd guess it massed about 10^{14} grams. That only makes it 10^{-6} Angstrom across, much smaller than an atom. It wouldn't have absorbed much. The damage was done to Childrey by tidal effects as it passed through him. You saw how it pulverized the material of the floor."

Not surprisingly, the subject of murder did come up.

Lear shrugged it off. "Murder with what? Childrey didn't believe there was a black hole in there at all. Neither did many of you." He smiled suddenly. "Can you imagine what the trial would be like? Imagine the prosecuting attorney trying to tell a jury what he thinks happened. First he's got to tell them what a black hole is. Then a quantum black hole. Then he's got to explain why he doesn't have the murder weapon, and where he left it, freely falling through Mars! And if he gets that far without being laughed out of court, he's still got to explain how a thing smaller than an atom could hurt anyone!"

But didn't Dr. Lear know the thing was dangerous? Could he not have guessed its enormous mass from the way it behaved?

Lear spread his hands. "Gentlemen, we're dealing with more variables than just mass. Field strength, for instance. I might have guessed its mass from the force it took to keep it there, but did any of us expect the aliens to calibrate their dials in the metric system?"

Surely there must have been safeties to keep the fields from being shut off accidentally. Lear must have bypassed them.

"Yes, I probably did, accidentally. I did quite a lot of fiddling to find out how things worked."

It got dropped there. Obviously there would be no trial. No ordinary judge or jury could be expected to understand what the attorneys would be talking about. A couple of things never did get mentioned.

For instance: Childrey's last words. I might or might not have repeated them if I'd been asked to. They were: "All right, show me! Show it to me or admit it isn't there!"

As the court was breaking up I spoke to Lear with my voice lowered. "That was probably the most unique murder weapon in history."

He whispered, "If you said that in company I could sue for slander."

"Yeah? Really? Are *you* going to explain to a jury what you think I implied happened?"

"No, I'll let you get away with it this time."

"Hell, you didn't get away scot-free yourself. What are you going to study now? The only known black hole in the universe, and you let it drop through your fingers."

Lear frowned. "You're right. Partly right, anyway. But I knew as much about it as I was going to, the way I was going. Now . . . I stopped it vibrating in there, then took the mass of the entire setup with the Forward Mass Sensor. Now the black hole isn't in there anymore. I can get the mass of the black hole by taking the mass of the communicator alone."

"Oh."

"And I can cut the machine open, see what's inside. How they controlled it. Damn it, I wish I were six years old."

"What? Why?"

"Well . . . I don't have the times straightened out. The math is chancy. Either a few years from now, or a few centuries, there's going to be a black hole between Earth and Jupiter. It'll be big enough to study. I think about forty years."

When I realized what he was implying, I didn't know whether to laugh or scream.

"Lear, you can't think that something that small could absorb Mars!"

"Well, remember that it absorbs everything it comes near. A nucleus here, an electron there . . . and it's not just waiting for atoms to fall into it. Its gravity is ferocious, and it's falling back and forth through the center of the planet, sweeping up matter. The more it eats, the bigger it gets, with its volume going up as the cube of the mass. Sooner or later, yes, it'll absorb Mars. By then it'll be just less than a millimeter across. Big enough to see."

"Could it happen within thirteen months?"

"Before we leave? Hm-m-m." Lear's eyes took on a faraway look. "I don't think so. I'll have to work it out. The math is chancy . . ."

● ● ●

• • •

... "meet Ftaxanthir and Hrofilliss and Chorrikst. Chorrikst tells me she's nearly two billion years old!"

... Chorrikst spoke slowly, in a throaty whisper, but her translator box was standard: voice a little flat, pronunciation perfect. "I have circled the galaxy numberless times, and taped the tales of my travels for funds to feed my wanderlust. Much of my life has been spent at the edge of lightspeed, under relativistic time-compression. So you see, I am not nearly so old as all that."

"The Green Marauder," 1980

NIGHT ON MISPEC MOOR

One night I sat down to write a swords-and-sorcery-style horror story. This is what came out.

• •

In predawn darkness the battle began to take shape. Helicopters circled, carrying newstapers and monitors. Below, the two armies jockeyed for position. They dared not meet before dawn. The monitors would declare a mistrial and fine both sides heavily.

In the red dawn the battle began. Scout groups probed each other's skills. The weapons were identical on both sides: heavy swords with big basket hilts. Only the men themselves differed in skill and strength.

By noon the battle had concentrated on a bare plain strewn with white boulders and a few tight circles of green Seredan vegetation. The warriors moved in little clumps. Where they met, the yellow dirt was stained red, and cameras in the helicopters caught it all for public viewing.

Days were short in Sereda. For some, today was not short enough.

As Sereda's orange dwarf sun dropped toward the horizon, the battle had become a massacre with the Grays at the wrong end. When Tomás Vatch could not longer hold a sword, he ran. Other Grays had fled, and Amber soldiers streamed after them, yelling. Vatch ran with blood flowing down his sword arm and dripping from his fingertips. He was falling behind, and the Ambers were coming close.

He turned sharp left and kept running. The swarm moved north, toward the edge of Mispec Moor, toward civilization. Alone, he had a chance. The Ambers would not concern themselves with a single fleeing man.

But one did. One golden-skinned red-haired man shouted something, waved his sword in a circle over his head, and followed.

An ancient glacier had dropped blocks of limestone and granite all over this flat, barren region. The biggest rock in sight was twice the height of a man and wider than it was tall. Vatch ran toward it. He had not yet begun to wonder how he would climb it.

He moved in a quick unbalanced stumble now, his sword and his medical kit bouncing awkwardly at either side. He had dropped the sword once already, when a blade had sliced into him just under the armpit. The heavy-shouldered warrior had paused to gloat, and Vatch had caught the falling sword in his left hand and jabbed upward. Now he cradled his right arm in his left to keep it from flopping loose.

He'd reached the rock.

It was split wide open down the middle.

The red-haired Amber came on like an exuberant child. Vatch had noticed him early in the battle. He'd fought that way too, laughing and slashing about him with playful enthusiasm. Vatch thought this attitude inappropriate to so serious a matter as war.

Vatch stepped into the mammoth crack, set his back to one side and his feet to the other, and began to work his way up. Recent wounds opened, and blood flowed down the rock. Vatch went on, concentrating on the placement of his feet, trying not to wonder what would happen if the Amber caught him halfway up.

The red-haired man arrived, blowing and laughing, and found Vatch high above him. He reached up with his sword. Vatch, braced awkwardly between two lips of granite, felt the sharp tip poking him in the small of the back. The Amber was standing on tiptoe; he could reach no further.

The top was flat. Vatch rolled over on his belly and rested. The world whirled around him. He had lost much blood.

And he couldn't afford this. He forced himself to sit up and look around. Where was the enemy?

A rock whizzed past his head. A voice bellowed, "Rammer! Give my regards to the nightwalkers!"

Vatch heard running footsteps, fading. He stood up.

Omicron 2 Eridani was a wide, distorted red blob on the flat horizon. Vatch could see far across Mispec Moor. He found his erstwhile enemy jogging north. Far ahead of him swarmed the army of the Ambers. Above them, the helicopters were bright motes.

Vatch smiled and dropped back to prone position. He was safe. No man, woman or child of Sereda would stay at night upon Mispec Moor.

On Sereda war is a heavily supervised institution. Battles are fought with agreed-upon weaponry. Strategy lies in getting the enemy to agree to the right weapons. This day the Grays had been out-strategied. The Ambers had the better swordsmen.

Seredan war set no limits to the use of medicine, provided that nothing in a medical kit could be used as a weapon, and provided that all medicines must be carried by fighting men. The convention was advantageous to an outworld mercenary.

Vatch fumbled the medical kit open, one-handed. He suspected that the gathering darkness was partly in his own eyes. But the Spectrum Cure was there: a soft plastic bottle, half-liter size, with a spray hypo and a pistol grip attached. Vatch pressure-injected himself, put the bottle carefully away and let himself roll over on his back.

The first effect was a tingling all through him.

Then his wounds stopped bleeding.

Then they closed.

His fatigue began to recede.

Vatch smiled up at the darkening sky. He'd be paid high for this day's work. His sword arm wasn't very good; he'd thought that Sereda's lower gravity would make a mighty warrior of him, but that hadn't worked out. But this Spectrum Cure was tremendous stuff! The biochemists of Miramon Lluagor had formulated it. It was ten years old there, and brand new on Sereda, and the other worlds of the Léshy circuit probably hadn't even heard of it yet. At the start of the battle he'd had enough to inject forty men, to heal them of any wound or disease, as long as their hearts still beat to distribute the stuff. The bottle was two-thirds empty now. He'd done a fair day's work, turning casualties back into fighting men while the battle raged about him.

The only adverse effect of Spectrum Cure began to show itself. Hunger. His belly was a yawning pit. Healing took metabolic energy. Tomás Vatch sat up convulsively and looked about him.

The damp air of Sereda was turning to mist around the foot of the rock.

He let himself over the lip, hung by his fingertips, and dropped. His belly was making grinding noises and sending signals of desperation. He had not eaten since early this morning. He set off at a brisk walk toward the nearest possible source of dinner: the battleground.

Twilight was fading rapidly. The mist crept over the ground like a soggy blanket. There were patches of grass-green on the yellow dirt, far apart, each several feet across and sharply bordered, each with a high yellow-tipped stalk springing from the center. The mist covered these too. Soon Vatch could see only a few blossoms like frilly yellow morels hovering at waist level, and shadowy white boulders looming like ghosts around him. His passage set up swirling currents.

Like most of the rammers, the men who travel the worlds of the Léshy circuit, Vatch had read the fantasies of James Branch Cabell. The early interstellar scout who discovered these worlds four hundred years ago had read Cabell. Toupan, Miramon Lluagor, Sereda, Horvendile, Koschei: the powerful though mortal Léshy of Cabell's fantasies had become five worlds circling five suns in a bent ring, with Earth and Sol making a sixth. Those who settled the Léshy worlds had followed tradition in the naming of names. A man who had read Cabell could guess the nature of a place from its name alone.

The Mispec Moor of Cabell's writings had been a place of supernatural mystery, a place where reality was vague and higher realities showed through.

Mispec Moor on Sereda had just that vague look, with darkness falling over waist-high mist and shadowy boulders looming above; and Vatch now remembered that this Mispec Moor had a complementary set of legends. Sereda's people did not call them vampires or ghouls, but the fearsome nightwalkers of Mispec Moor seemed a combination of the two legends: things that had been men, whose bite would turn living or dead alike into more nightwalkers. They could survive ordinary weapons, but a silver bullet would stop them, especially if it had been dumdummed by a cross cut into its nose.

Naturally Tomás Vatch carried no silver bullets and no gun. He was lucky to be carrying a flashlight. He had not expected to be out at night, but the flashlight was part of his kit. He had often needed light to perform his secondary battlefield duties.

As he neared the place of the fallen soldiers he thought he saw motion in the mist. He raised the flashlight high over his head and drew his sword.

Thin shapes scampered away from the light. Tomás jumped violently—and then he recognized lopers, the doglike scavengers of Sereda. He kept his sword in hand. The lopers kept their distance, and he let them be. They were here for the same reason he was, he thought with no amusement at all.

Some soldiers carried bread or rolls of hard candy into battle.

Some of these never ate their provisions.

It was a repugnant task, this searching of dead men. He found the body of Robroy Tanner, who had come with him to Sereda aboard a Lluagorian ramship; and he cried, out here where nobody could see him. But he continued to search. He was savagely hungry.

The lopers had been at some of the bodies. More than once he was tempted to end his whimsical truce. The lopers still moved at the periphery of his vision. They seemed shy of the light, but would that last? Certainly the legends pointed to something dangerous on Mispec Moor. Could the lopers themselves be subject to something like rabies?

He found hard candy, and he found two canteens, both nearly empty. He sucked the candy a roll at a time, his cheeks puffed out like a squirrel's.

Presently he found the slashed corpse of a man he had eaten breakfast with. *Jackpot*. He had watched Erwin Mudd take a block of stew from a freezer and double-wrap it in plastic bags, just before they entered the battlefield.

The stew was there. Vatch ate it as it was, cold, and was grateful for it.

Motion in the mist made him look up.

Two shadows were coming toward him. They were much bigger than lopers . . . and man-shaped.

Vatch stood up and called, "Hello?"

They came on, taking shape as they neared. A third blurred shadow congealed behind them. They had not answered. Annoyed, Vatch swung the flashlight beam toward them.

The light caught them full. Vatch held it steady, staring, not believing. Then, still not believing, he screamed and ran.

There is a way a healthy man can pace himself so that he can jog for hours across flat land, especially on a low-gravity world like Sereda. Tomás Vatch had that skill.

But now he ran like a mad sprinter, in sheer panic, his chest heaving, his legs burning. It was a minute or so before he thought to turn off the flashlight so that the things could not follow its glow. It was much longer before he could work up the courage to look back.

One of the things was following him.

He did not think to stand and fight. He had seen it too clearly. It was a corpse, weeks dead. He thought of turning toward the city, but the city was a good distance away; and now he remembered that they locked the gates at night. The first time he had seen them do that, he had asked why, and a native policeman had told him of the nightwalkers. He had had to hear the story from other sources before he knew that he was not being played for a gullible outworlder.

So he did not turn toward the city. He turned toward the rock that had been his refuge once before.

The thing followed. It moved at a fast walk; but, where Tomás Vatch had to stop and rest with his hands on his knees to catch his breath before he ran on, the nightwalker never stopped at all. It was a distant shadow when he reached the rock; but his haste was such that he skinned his shoulders working himself up the crack.

The top of the rock was still warm from daylight. Vatch lay on his back and felt the joy of breathing. The stars were clear and bright above him. There was no sound at all.

But when his breathing quieted he heard heavy, uneven footsteps.

He looked over the edge of the rock.

The nightwalker came wading through the mist in a wobbling shuffle. It walked like it would fall down at every step, and its feet fell joltingly hard. Yet it came fast. Its bulging eyes stared back into Vatch's flashlight.

Why should a nightwalker care if it sprained its ankles at every step? It was dead, dead and bloated. It still wore a soldier's kilt in green plaid, the sign of a commercial war now two weeks old. Above the broad belt a slashed belly wound gaped wide.

Vatch examined the corpse with self-conscious care. The only way he knew to quell his panic was to put his mind to work. He searched for evidence that this nightwalker was not what it seemed, that it was something else, a native life form, say, with a gift for mimickry.

It stood at the base of the rock, looking up with dull eyes and slack mouth. A walking dead man.

There was more motion in the mist . . . and two lopers came lurching up to stand near the nightwalker. When Vatch threw the light on them they stared back unblinking. Presently Vatch realized why. They, too, were dead.

The policeman had told him that too: that nightwalkers could take the form of lopers and other things.

He had believed very little of what he had heard . . . and now he was trying frantically to remember details. They were not dangerous in daytime; hadn't he heard that? Then if he could hold out here till morning, he would be safe. He could return to the city.

But three more man-shapes were coming to join the first.

And the first was clawing at the side of the rock, trying to find purchase for its fingers. It moved along the base, scraping at the rough side. It entered the crack . . .

Three shadows came out of the mist to join their brother. One wore the familiar plaid kilt from that two-week-old battle. One wore a businessman's tunic; its white hair had come away in patches, taking scalp with it. The third had been a small, slender woman, judging from her dress and her long yellow hair.

They clawed at the rock. They began to spread out along the base.

And Vatch backed away from the edge and sat down.

What the hell was this? Legends like this had been left behind on Earth! Dead men did not walk, not without help. Ordinarily they just *lay* there. What was different about Sereda? What kind of biology could fit—? Vatch shook his head violently. The question was nonsense. This was fantasy, and he was in it.

Yet his mind clutched for explanations:

Costumes? Suppose a group of Seredans had something to hide out here. (What?) A guard of four in dreadful costumes might hold off a whole city, once the legend of the nightwalker was established (But the legend was a century old. Never mind, the legend could have come first.) Anyone who came close enough to see the fraud could quietly disappear. (Costume and makeup? That gaping putrescent belly wound!)

Out of the crack in the rock came a fantasy arm, the bone showing through the forearm, the first joints missing on all the ragged fingers. Vatch froze. *(Costume?)* The other arm came up, and then a dead slack face. The smell reached him . . .

Vatch unfroze very suddenly, snatched up his sword and struck overhand. He split the skull to the chin.

The nightwalker was still trying to pull itself up.

Vatch struck at the arms. He severed one elbow, then the other, and the nightwalker dropped away without a cry.

Vatch began to shudder. He couldn't stop the spasms; he could only wait until they passed. He was beginning to understand how the fantasy would end. When the horror became too great, when he could stand it no longer, he would leap screaming to the ground and try to kill them all. And his sword would not be enough.

It was real! The dead forearms lay near his feet!

Fantasy!

Real!

Wait, wait. A fantasy was something that categorically could not happen. It was *always* a story, *always* something that originated in a man's mind. Could he be starring in somebody's fantasy?

This, a form of entertainment? Then it had holovision beat hands down. But Vatch knew of no world that had the technology to create such a total-experience entertainment, complete with what had to be ersatz memories! No world had that, let alone backward Sereda!

Wait. Was he really on Sereda? Was the date really 2731? Or was he living through some kind of Gothic historical?

Was he even Tomás Vatch the rammer? Rammer was a high-prestige career. Someone might well have paid for the illusion that he was a rammer . . . and if he had, someone had gotten more than he had bargained for. They'd pull him out of his total-environment cubical or theater in total catatonic withdrawal, if Tomás Vatch didn't get a grip on himself.

Wait. Was that motion in the mist, off toward the battlefield?

Or more of his runaway imagination? But no, the mist was a curdling, swirling line, aimed at his rock.

That almost did it. He almost leapt from the rock and ran. If the city gates were closed he'd run right up the walls . . . But he waited. In a minute he'd know for sure, one way or another.

Within the crack the one he had struck sat slumped with its head bowed, disconsolate or truly dead. The other three seemed to be accomplishing very little.

The dead men from the battlefield streamed toward Vatch's place of refuge. They wore kilts of gray and amber. Less than a hundred of them, casualties in a war between two medium-sized companies, a war which would not have been fought at all if the cost could not be partly defrayed by holovision rights. When they came close Vatch began to recognize individuals. There was Erwin Mudd, whose stew he had stolen. There was Roy Tanner the Lluagorian, the rammer, the medic. Death cancels all friendships. There—Enough. *Forget about costumes, Tomás.*

Enough, and too late. The nightwalkers swarmed around the rock and began trying to climb. Vatch stood above the crack, sword ready. The sword was all he had.

Hands came over the edge. He struck at them.

He looked around in time to see more hands coming up everywhere along the perimeter. He yelled and circled madly, striking, striking. They were not climbing the rock itself; they were climbing over each other to reach the top. And his sword, its edge dulled by repeated blows against rock and bone, was turning into a club . . .

Suddenly he stopped.

Fantasy? Real? What kind of biology . . . ?

He spilled his medical kit open and snatched at the bottle of Spectrum Cure. More than his life was at stake here. He was trying to save his sanity.

The pistol grip fitted his hand neatly. A nightwalker pulled itself over the edge and tottered toward him, and he sprayed Spectrum Cure between its eyes. An eroded face appeared near his feet; he sprayed Spectrum Cure into its mouth. Then he stepped back and watched.

The first one dropped like a sack. The second let go and disappeared from view.

Nightwalkers were coming up all around him. Vatch moved among them in calm haste, spraying life into them, and they stopped moving. In his mind he gloated. It should have worked, and it had.

For if anything in this experience was real, then it had to be caused by the biology of Sereda. So: something could infect the dead, to make them move. Bacterium? Fungus? Virus? Whatever it was, it had to have evolved by using dead lopers and other native life forms to spread itself.

It would walk the infected corpse until there was no sugar or oxygen left in the blood or muscle tissues of the host. That alone could carry the disease further than it could travel by itself. And if it found another host to infect along the way, well and good.

But the first step in infection would be to restart the heart. It *had* to be, or the bacterium couldn't spread throughout the host.

And if the heart was going . . .

The Spectrum Cure seemed to be healing them right up. He'd cured about eight of them. They lay at the base of the rock and did not move. Other nightwalkers clustered around them. For the moment they had given up on Vatch's rock.

Vatch watched some of them bend over the bodies of those he had injected. They might have been nibbling at the flesh above the hearts. A minute of that, and then they fell over and lay as dead as the ones they had been trying to rescue.

Good enough, thought Vatch. He flashed the light on his bottle to check the supply of Spectrum Cure.

It was just short of dead empty.

Vatch sighed. The horde of dead men had drawn away from the casualties—the *dead* dead ones—and gone back to trying to climb the rock. Some would make it. Vatch picked up his sword. An afterthought: he injected himself. Even if they got to him, they would not rouse him from death before morning.

The scrabbling of finger bones against rock became a cricket chorus.

Vatch stood looking down at them. Most of these had only been dead for hours. Their faces were intact, though slack. Vatch looked for Roy Tanner.

He circled the edge rapidly, striking occasionally at a reaching arm, but peering down anxiously. Where the blazes was Roy Tanner?

There, pulling himself over the lip of the crack.

In fact they were all swarming into the crack and climbing over each other. Their dead brains must be working to some extent. The smell of them was terrific. Vatch breathed through his mouth, closed his imagination tight shut, and waited.

The nightwalker remains of Roy Tanner pulled itself up on the rock. Vatch sprayed it in the face, turned the body over in haste, and found it: Roy Tanner's medical kit, still intact. He spilled out the contents and snatched up Roy's bottle of Spectrum Cure.

He sprayed it before him, and then into the crack, like an insecticide. He held his aim until they stopped moving . . . and then, finally, he could roll away from the choking smell. It was all right now. Roy had fallen early in the battle. His bottle had been nearly full.

For something like six hours they had watched each other: Tomás Vatch on the lip of the rock, seven nightwalkers below. They stood in a half circle, well out of range of Vatch's spray gun, and they stared unblinking into Vatch's flashlight.

Vatch was dreadfully tired. He had circled the rock several times, leaping the crack twice on each pass. "Cured" corpses surrounded the base and half filled the crack. He had seen none of them move. By now he was sure. There were only these seven left.

"I want to sleep," he told them. "Can't you understand? I won. You lost. Go away. I want to sleep." He had been telling them this for some time.

This time it seemed that they heard.

One by one they turned and stumbled off in different directions. Vatch watched, amazed, afraid to believe. Each nightwalker seemed to find a patch of level ground it liked. There it fell and did not move.

Vatch waited. The east was growing bright. It wasn't over yet, but it would be soon. With burning eyes he watched for the obvious dead to move again.

Red dawn touched the tops of glacier-spilled rocks. The orange dwarf sun made a cool light; he could almost look straight into it. He watched the shadows walk down the sides of the rocks to the ground.

When the light touched the seven bodies, they had become bright green patches, vaguely man-shaped.

Vatch watched until each patch had sprouted a bud of yellow in its center. Then he dropped to the ground and started walking north.

• • •

• • •

The landscape was marked by queer sharp lines. Here there was the green patchwork quilt of cultivated fields, there a lifeless landscape, almost lunar but for the softening of erosion. It was strange to see a broad river meandering unconcerned from cultivation to desert. There were no weeds. Nothing grew wild. The forest grove they were passing now had the same sharp borders and orderly arrangement as the broad strips of flower beds they had passed earlier.

THE MOTE IN GOD'S EYE, 1974

FLARE TIME

For the full story of how this tale came to be written, read *Medea: Harlan's World*. It's the definitive study of how a shared universe should be orchestrated, from its creation by invitation, to the generation of ideas on and around a stage at a university, to the stories themselves.

Medea will *not* tell you that Larry Niven was driven to the edge of insanity by delays in publication! This is one of the best stories I've ever written, and in seven years almost nobody had read it! It had appeared in two very small markets. I repossessed it from Harlan (the contract was long defunct) in order to get it into my own collection, LIMITS, then returned to him the right to publish it in *Medea*, all because I wasn't willing to beg again.

The other side of that coin is that *Medea* did indeed become a book.

Eight creative people once set forth to produce another shared universe. Good things emerged; but no book. In the case of THRAXISP we were eight creators all created equal.

You *must* have a dictator.

• •

If the starship's arrival had done nothing else for Bronze Legs, this was enough: he was seeing the sky again.

For this past week the rammers had roamed through Touchdown City. The fifty-year-old colony was still small; everybody knew everybody. It was hard to get used to, this influx of oddly-accented strangers stumbling about with vacuous smiles and eyes wide with surprise and pleasure. Even the Medean humans were catching the habit. In his thirty-four earthyears of life Calvin "Bronze Legs" Miller had explored fifteen thousand square miles of the infinite variety that was Medea. Strange, that it took people from another world to make him look up.

Here was a pretty picture: sunset over the wild lands north of the colony. Peaks to the south were limned in bluish-white from the farmlands beyond, from the lamps that kept terrestrial plants growing. Everything else was red, infinite shades of red. To heatward a level horizon cut the great disk of Argo in half. You could feel the heat on your cheek, and watch sullenly glowing storms move in bands across the face of the red-hot superjovian world. To coldward, Phrixus and Helle were two glaring pink dots following each other down to the ridge. The Jet Stream stretched straight across the blue sky, a pinkish-white band of cloud from horizon to horizon. Thirty or forty multicolored balloons, linked in a cluster, were settling to graze a scum-covered rain pool in the valley below him.

Blue-tinged shadows pooled in the valley, and three human shapes moved through the red and orange vegetation. Bronze Legs recognized Lightning Harness and Grace Carpenter even at this distance. The third had a slightly hunchbacked look, and a metal headdress gleamed in her straight black hair. That would be Rachel Subramaniam's memory recording equipment. Her head kept snapping left and right, ever eager for new sights.

Bronze Legs grinned. He tried to imagine how this must look to a rammer, an offworlder; he succeeded only in remembering himself as a child. All this strangeness; all this red.

He turned the howler and continued uphill.

At the crest of the ridge a fux waited for him, the pinkish-white suns behind her. She was a black silhouette, four thin legs and two thin arms, a pointed face and a narrow torso bent in an L: a lean, mean centaur-shape.

As he topped the ridge and let the howler settle on its air cushion, the fux backed away several meters. Bronze Legs wondered why, then guessed the answer. It wasn't the smell of him. Fuxes liked that. She was putting the ridge between herself and the white glare from Touchdown City's farming lamps. She said, "I am Long Nose."

"Bronze Legs. I meet you on purpose."

"I meet you on purpose. How goes your foray to heatward?"

"We start tomorrow at dawn."

"You postponed it once before." She was accusing him. The fuxes were compulsive about punctuality; an odd trait in a Bronze Age culture. Like certain traits in humans, it probably tied into their sex lives. Timing could be terribly important when a fux was giving birth.

"The ship from the stars came," he said. "We waited. We want to take one of the star people along, and the delay lets us recheck the vehicles."

Long Nose was black with dull dark-red markings. She bore a longbow over one shoulder and a quiver and shovel slung over her lower back. Her snout was sharply pointed, but not abnormally so, for a fux. She might be named for keen curiosity or a keen sense of smell. She said, "I learn that your purpose is more than exploration, but not even the post-males can tell what it is."

"Power," said Bronze Legs. "The harnessed lightning that makes our machines go comes as light from Argo. In the Hot End the clouds will never hide Argo from our sight. Our lightning makers can run without rest."

"Go north instead," said Long Nose. "You will find it safer and cooler too. Storms run constantly in the north; I have been there. Free lightning for your use."

If she'd been talking to Lightning Harness she would have suffered through an hour's lecture. How the heat exchangers ran on the flood of infrared light from Argo, focused by mirrors. How Argo stayed always in the same place in Medea's sky, so that mirrors could be mounted on a hillside facing to heatward, and never moved again. But the colony was growing, and Medea's constant storms constantly blocked the mirrors . . . Bronze Legs only grinned at her. "Why don't we just do it our way? Who-all is coming?"

"Only six of us. Dark Wind's children did not emerge in time. Deadeye will desert us early; she will give birth in a day and must stay to guard the . . . Is 'nest' the word you use?"

"Right." Of all the words that might describe the fuxes' way of giving birth, "nest" carried the least unpleasant connotations.

"So, she will be guarding her 'nest' when we return. She will be male then. Sniffer intends to become pregnant tonight; she will leave us further on, and be there to help us on our return, if we need help."

"Good."

"We take a post-male, Harvester, and another six-leg female, Broad Flanks, who can carry him some of the time. Gimpy wants to come. Will she slow us?"

Bronze Legs laughed. He knew Gimpy; a four-leg female as old as some post-males, who had lost her right foreleg to the viciously fast Medean monster humans called a B-70. Gimpy was fairly agile, considering. "She could crawl on her belly for all we care. It's the crawlers that'll slow us, and the power plant. We're moving a lot of machinery: the prefab power plant, housing for technicians, sensing tools, digging tools—"

"What tools should we take?"

"Go armed. You won't need water bags; we'll make our own water. We made you some parasols made from mirror-cloth. They'll help you stand the heat, for awhile. When it gets really hot you'll have to ride in the crawlers."

"We will meet you at the crawling machines, at dawn." Long Nose turned and moved downslope into a red-and-orange jungle, moving something like a cat in its final rush at a bird: legs bent, belly low.

They had been walking since early afternoon: twelve hours, with a long break for lunch. Lightning sighed with relief as he set down the farming lamp he'd been carrying on his shoulders. Grace helped him spread the tripod and extend the mount until the lamp stood six meters tall.

Rachel Subramaniam sat down in the orange grass and rubbed her feet. She was puffing.

Grace Carpenter, a Medean xenobiologist and in her early forties, was a large-boned woman, broad of silhouette and built like a farm wife. Lightning Harness was tall and lean and lantern-jawed, a twenty-four-year-old power plant engineer. Both were pale as ghosts beside Rachel. On Medea only the farmers were tanned.

Rachel was built light. Some of her memory recording equipment was embedded in padding along her back, giving her a slightly hunchbacked look. Her scalp implants were part of a polished silver cap, the badge of her profession. She had spent the past two years under the sunlights aboard a web ramship. Her skin was bronze. To Rachel, Medea's pale citizens had seemed frail, unathletic, until now. Now she was annoyed. There had been little opportunity for hikes aboard *Morven*; but she might have noticed the muscles and hard hands common to any recent colony.

Lightning pointed uphill. "Company."

Something spidery stood on the crest of the coldward ridge, black against the suns. Rachel asked, "What is it?"

"Fux. Female, somewhere between seven and eighteen years of age, and not a virgin. Beyond that I can't tell from here."

Rachel was astonished. "How can you know all that?"

"Count the legs. Grace, didn't you tell her about fuxes?"

Grace was chuckling. "Lightning's showing off. Dear, the fuxes go fertile around age seven. They generally have their first litter right away. They drop their first set of hindquarters with the eggs in them, and that gives them a half a lifetime to learn how to move as a quadruped. Then they wait till they're seventeen or eighteen to have their second litter, unless the tribe is underpopulated, which sometimes happens. Dropping the second set of hindquarters exposes the male organs."

"And she's got four legs. 'Not a virgin.' I thought you must have damn good eyes, Lightning."

"Not that good."

"What are they like?"

"Well," said Grace, "the post-males are the wise ones. Bright, talkative, and not nearly so . . . frenetic as the females. It's hard to get a female to stand still for long. The males . . . oh, for three years after the second litter they're kind of crazy. The tribe keeps them penned. The females only go near them when they want to get pregnant.''

Lightning had finished setting the lamp. ''Take a good look around before I turn this on. You know what you're about to see?''

Dutifully, Rachel looked about her, memorizing.

The farming lamps stood everywhere around Touchdown City; it was less a city than a village surrounded by farmlands. For more than a week Rachel had seen only the tiny part of Medea claimed by humans . . . until, in early afternoon of this long Medean day, she and Grace and Lightning had left the farmlands. The reddish light had bothered her for a time. But there was much to see; and after all, this was the *real* Medea.

Orange grass stood knee-high in slender leaves with sharp hard points. A score of flaccid multicolored balloons, linked by threads that resembled spiderweb, had settled on a stagnant pond. There was a grove of almost-trees, hairy rather than leafy, decked in all the colors of autumn. The biggest was white and bare and dead.

Clouds of bugs filled the air everywhere except around the humans. A pair of things glided into the swarms, scooping their dinner out of the air. They had five-meter wingspans, small batlike torsos, and huge heads that were all mouth, with gaping hair-filled slits behind the head, where gill slits would be on a fish. Their undersides were sky blue.

A six-legged creature the size of a sheep stood up against the dead almost-tree, gripped it with four limbs, and seemed to chew at it. Rachel wondered if it was eating the wood. Then she saw myriads of black dots spread across the white, and a long, sticky tongue slurping them up.

Grace tapped Rachel's arm and pointed into the grass. Rachel saw a warrior's copper shield painted with cryptic heraldics. It was a flattened turtle shell, and the yellow-eyed beaked face that looked back at her was not turtle-like at all. Something small struggled in its beak. Suddenly the mock turtle whipped around and *zzzz*ed away on eight churning legs. There was no bottom shell to hamper the legs.

The *real* Medea.

''Now,'' said Lightning. He turned on the farming lamp.

White light made the valley suddenly less alien. Rachel felt something within her relaxing . . . but things were happening all around her.

The flat turtle stopped abruptly. It swallowed hard, then pulled head and limbs under its shell. The flying bug-strainers whipped around and flew hard for the hairy trees. The clouds of bugs simply vanished. The long-tongued beast let go of its tree, turned and scratched at the ground and was gone in seconds.

''This is what happens when a sun flares,'' Lightning said. ''They're both flare suns. Flares don't usually last more than half an hour, and most Medean animals just dig in till it's over. A lot of plants go to seed. Like this grass—''

Yes, the slender leaves were turning puffy, cottony. But the hairy trees reacted differently; they were suddenly very slender, the foliage pulled tight against the trunks. The balloons weren't reacting at all.

Lightning said, ''That's why we don't worry much about Medean life attacking the crops. The lamps keep them away. But not all of them—''

''On Medea every rule has exceptions,'' Grace said.

''Yeah. Here, look under the grass.'' Lightning pushed cotton-covered leaves aside with his hands, and the air was suddenly full of white fluff. Rachel saw millions of black specks covering the lower stalks. ''We call them locusts. They swarm in flare time and eat everything in sight. Terran plants poison them, of course, but they wreck the crops first.'' He let the leaves close. By now there was white fluff everywhere, like a low-lying fog patch moving east on the wind. ''What else can I show you? Keep your eyes on the balloons. And are there cameras in that thing?''

Rachel laughed and touched the metal helmet. Sometimes she could forget she was wearing it; but her neck was thicker, more muscular than the average woman's. ''Cameras? In a sense. My eyes are cameras for the memory tape.''

The balloons rested just where they had been. The artificial flare hadn't affected them . . . wait, they weren't flaccid any more. They were swollen, taut, straining at the rootlets that held them to the bottom of the pond. Suddenly they rose, all at once, still linked by spiderweb. Beautiful.

''They use the UV for energy to make hydrogen,'' said Grace. ''UV wouldn't bother them anyway; they have to take more of it at high altitude.''

''I've been told . . . are they intelligent?''

''Balloons? No!'' Grace actually snorted. ''They're no brighter than so much seaweed . . . but they own the planet. We've sent probes to the Hot End, you know. We saw balloons all the way. And we've seen them as far coldward . . . west, you'd say . . . as far west as the Icy Sea. We haven't gone beyond the rim of ice yet.''

''But you've been on Medea fifty years?''

''And just getting started,'' Lightning said. He turned off the farming lamp.

The world was plunged into red darkness.

The fluffy white grass was gone, leaving bare soil aswarm with black specks. Gradually the hairy trees loosened, fluffed out. Soil churned near the dead tree and released the tree feeder.

Grace picked up a few of the ''locusts.'' They were no bigger than termites. Held close to the eye they each showed a translucent bubble on its back. ''They can't swarm,'' Grace said with satisfaction. ''Our flare didn't last long enough. They couldn't make enough hydrogen.''

"Some did," Lightning said. There were black specks on the wind; not many.

"Always something new," said Grace.

Tractor probe Junior was moving into the Hot End. Ahead was the vast desert, hotter than boiling water, where Argo stood always at noon. Already the strange dry plants were losing their grip, leaving bare rock and dust. At the final shore of the Ring Sea the waves were sudsy with salt in solution, and the shore was glittering white. The hot steamy wind blew inland, to heatward, and then upward, carrying a freight of balloons.

The air was full of multicolored dots, all going up into the stratosphere. At the upper reach of the probe's vision some of the frailer balloons were popping, but the thin membranous corpses still fluttered toward heaven.

Rachel shifted carefully in her chair. She caught Bronze Legs Miller watching her from a nearby table. Her answering grin was rueful.

She had not finished the hike. Grace and Lightning had been setting up camp when Bronze Legs Miller came riding down the hill. Rachel had grasped that golden opportunity. She had returned to Touchdown City riding behind Bronze Legs on the howler's saddle. After a night of sleep she still ached in every muscle.

"Isn't it a gorgeous sight?" Mayor Curly Jackson wasn't eating. He watched avidly, with his furry chin in his hands and his elbows on the great oaken table—the dignitaries' table the Medeans were so proud of; it had taken forty years to grow the tree.

Medea had changed its people. Even the insides of buildings were different from those of other worlds. The communal dining hall was a great dome lit by a single lamp at its zenith. It was bright, and it cast sharp shadows. As if the early colonists, daunted by the continual light show—the flare suns, the bluish farming lamps, the red-hot storms moving across Argo—had given themselves a single sun indoors. But it was a wider, cooler sun, giving yellower light than a rammer was used to.

One great curve of the wall was a holograph projection screen. The tractor probe was tracing the path the expedition would follow and broadcasting what it saw. Now it moved over hills of white sea salt. The picture staggered and lurched with the probe's motion, and wavered with rising air currents.

Captain Janice Borg, staring avidly with a forkful of curry halfway to her mouth, jumped as Mayor Curly lightly punched her shoulder. The Mayor was blue eyes and a lump of nose poking through a carefully tended wealth of blond hair and beard. He was darkened by farming lamps. Not only did he supervise the farms; he farmed. "See it, Captain? That's why the Ring Sea is mostly fresh water."

Captain Borg's hair was auburn going gray. She was handsome rather than pretty. Her voice of command had the force of a bullwhip; one obeyed by reflex. Her off-duty voice was a soft, dreamy contralto. "Right. Right. The seawater moves always to the Hot End. It starts as glaciers, doesn't it? They break off in the Icy Sea and float heatward. Any salt goes that way too. In the Hot End the water boils away . . . and you get some tides, don't you? Argo wobbles a little?"

"Well, it's Medea that wobbles a little, but—"

"Right, so the seawater spills off into the salt flats at high tide and boils away there. And the vapor goes back to the glaciers along the Jet Stream." She turned suddenly to Rachel and barked, "You getting all this?"

Rachel nodded, hiding a smile. More than two hundred years had passed on the settled worlds while Captain Borg cruised the trade circuit. She didn't really understand memory tapes. They were too recent.

Rachel looked about the communal dining hall and was conscious as always of the vast unseen audience looking through her eyes, listening through her ears, feeling the dwindling aches of a stiff hike, tasting blazing hot Medean curry through her mouth. It was all going into the memory tape, with no effort on her part.

Curly said, "We picked a good site for the power plant before the first probe broke down. Heatward slope of a hillside. We'll be coming up on it in a few hours. Is this the kind of thing you want, or am I boring you?"

"I want it all. Did you try that tape?"

The Mayor shook his head, his eyes suddenly evasive.

"Why not?"

"Well," the Mayor said slowly, "I'm a little leery of what I might remember. It's all filtered through your brain, isn't it, Rachel?"

"Of course."

"I don't think I'd like remembering being a girl."

Rachel was mildly surprised. Role-changing was part of the kick. Male or female, an epicurean or a superbly muscled physical culture addict or an intellectual daydreamer, a child again or an old woman . . . well, some didn't like it. "I could give you a man's tape, Curly. There's McAuliffe's balloon trip into the big gas giant in Sol system."

Captain Borg cut in sharply. "What about the Charles Baker Sontag tape? He did a year's tour in Miramon Lluagor system, Curly. The Lluagorians use balloons for everything. You'd love it."

Curly was confused. "Just what kind of balloons—"

"Not living things, Curly. Fabric filled with gas. Lluagor has a red dwarf sun. No radiation storms and not much ultraviolet. They have to put their farms in orbit, and they do most of their living in orbit, and it's all inflated balloons, even the spacecraft. The planet they use mainly for mining and factories, but it's pretty, too, so they've got cities slung under hundreds of gasbags.''

The tractor probe lurched across mile after mile of dim-lit pink salt hills. Rachel remembered a memory tape in *Morven*'s library: a critical reading of the Elder and Younger Eddas by a teacher of history and poetry. Would Medeans like that? Here you had the Land of the Frost Giants and the Land of the Fire Giants, with Midgard between . . . and the Ring Sea to stand in for the Midgard Serpent . . . and no dearth of epic monsters, from what she'd heard.

Captain Borg spoke with an edge in her voice. ''Nobody's going to force you to use a new and decadent entertainment medium from the stars, Curly—''

''Oh, now, I didn't—''

''But there's a point you might consider. Distance.''

''Distance?''

''There's the trade circuit. Earth, Toupan, Lluagor, Sereda, Horvendile, Koschei, Earth again. Six planets circling six stars a few light-years apart. The web ramships go round and round, and everyone on the ring gets news, entertainment, seeds and eggs, new inventions. There's the trade circuit, and there's Medea. You're too far from Horvendile, Curly.''

''Oddly enough, we're aware of that, Captain Borg.''

''No need to get huffy. I'm trying to make a point.''

''Why did *you* come?''

''Variety. Curiosity. The grass-is-always-greener syndrome. The same thing that made us rammers in the first place.'' Captain Borg did not add altruism, the urge to keep the worlds civilized. ''But will we keep coming? Curly, Medea is the strangest place that ever had a breathable atmosphere. You've got a potential tourist trap here. You could have ramships dropping by every twenty years!''

''We need that.''

''Yes, you do. So remember that rammers don't build starships. It's taxpayers that build starships. What do they get out of it?''

''Memory tapes?''

''Yes. It used to be holos. Times change. Holos aren't as involving as memory tapes, and they take too long to watch. So it's memory tapes.''

''Does that mean we have to use them?''

''No,'' said Captain Borg.

''Then I'll try your tourist's view of Lluagor system, when I get time.'' Curly stood. ''And I better get going. Twenty-five hours to dawn.''

''It only takes ten minutes,'' Rachel said.

''How long to recover? How long to assimilate a whole earthyear of someone else's memories? I better wait.''

After he was gone, Rachel asked, "What was wrong with giving him the Jupiter tape?"

"I remembered McAuliffe was a homosexual."

"So what? He was all alone in that capsule."

"It might matter to someone like Curly. I don't say it would, I say it might. Every world is different."

"You ought to know." The rumor mill said that Mayor Curly and Captain Borg had shared a bed. Though he hadn't shown it . . .

Too lightly, Captain Borg said, "I should but I don't."

"Oh?"

"He's . . . closed. It's the usual problem, I think. He sees me coming back in sixty or seventy years, and me ten years older. Doesn't want to get too involved."

"Janice?"

"Dammit, if they're so afraid of change, how could their parents have busted their asses to settle a whole new world? Change is the one thing . . . yeah? What is it?"

"Did you ask him, or did he ask you?"

Captain Borg frowned. "He asked me. Why?"

"Nobody's asked me," said Rachel.

"Oh . . . Well, ask someone. Customs differ."

"But he asked you."

"I dazzled him with sex appeal. Or maybe not. Rachel, shall I ask Curly about it? There might be something we don't know. Maybe you wear your hair wrong."

Rachel shook her head. "No."

"But . . . okay. The rest of the crew don't seem to be having problems."

Nearly dawn. The sky was thick with dark clouds, but the heatward horizon was clear, with Argo almost fully risen. The dull red disk would never rise completely, not here. Already it must be sinking back.

It was earthnight now; the farming lamps were off. Crops and livestock kept terrestrial time. Rows of green plants stretched away to the south, looking almost black in this light. In the boundary of bare soil between the wilds and the croplands, half a dozen fuxes practiced spear casts. That was okay with Bronze Legs. Humans didn't spend much time in that border region. They plowed the contents of their toilets into it, to sterilize it of Medean microorganisms and fertilize it for next year's crops. The fuxes didn't seem to mind the smell.

Bronze Legs waited patiently beside his howler. He wished Windstorm would do the same.

The two house-sized crawlers were of a pattern familiar to many worlds: long, bulbous pressure hulls mounted on ground-effect platforms. They were decades old, but they had been tended with loving care. Hydrogen fuel cells powered them. One of the crawlers now carried, welded to its roof, a sender capable of reaching *Morven* in its present equatorial orbit: another good reason for waiting for the web ramship's arrival.

The third and largest vehicle was the power plant itself, fully assembled and tested, mounted on the ground-effect systems from two crawlers and with a crawler's control cabin welded on in front. It trailed a raft: yet another ground effect system covered by a padded platform with handrails. The fuxes would be riding that.

All vehicles were loaded and boarded well ahead of time. Windstorm Wolheim moved among them, ticking off lists in her head and checking them against what she could see. The tall, leggy redhead was a chronic worrier.

Phrixus (or maybe Helle) was suddenly there, a hot pink point near Argo. The fuxes picked up their spears and trotted off northward. Bronze Legs lifted his howler on its air cushion and followed. Behind him the three bigger vehicles whispered into action, and Windstorm ran for her howler.

Rachel was in the passenger seat of the lead crawler, looking out through the great bubble windscreen. In the Hot End the crawlers would house the power plant engineers. Now they were packed with equipment. Square kilometers of thin silvered plastic sheet, and knock-down frames to hold it all, would become solar mirrors. Black plastic and more frames would become the radiator fins, mounted on the back of that hill in the Hot End. There were spools of superconducting cable and flywheels for power storage. Rachel kept bumping her elbow on the corner of a crate.

The pinkish daylight was dimming, graying, as the Jet Stream spread to engulf the sky. The fuxes were far ahead, keeping no obvious formation. In this light they seemed a convocation of mythical monsters: centaurs, eight-limbed dragons, a misshapen dwarf. The dwarf was oddest of all. Rachel had seen him close: A nasty caricature of a man, with a foxy face, huge buttocks, exaggerated male organs, and (the anomaly) a tail longer than he was tall. Yet Harvester was solemn and slow-moving, and he seemed to have the respect of fuxes and humans both.

The vehicles whispered along at thirty kilometers an hour, uphill through orange grass, swerving around hairy trees. A fine drizzle began. Lightning Harness turned on the wipers.

Rachel asked, ''Isn't this where we were a few days back?''

''Medean yesterday. That's right,'' said Grace.

''Hard to tell. We're going north, aren't we? Why not straight east?''

"It's partly for our benefit, dear. We'll be in the habitable domains longer. We'll see more variety; we'll both learn more. When we swing around to heatward we'll be nearer the north pole. It won't get hot so fast."

"Good."

Bronze Legs and a woman Rachel didn't know flanked them on the one-seater ground-effect vehicles, the howlers. Bronze Legs wore shorts, and in fact his legs were bronze. Black by race, he'd paled to Rachel's color during years of Medean sunlight. Rachel asked, half to herself, "Why not just Bronze?"

Grace understood. "They didn't mean his skin."

"What?"

"The fuxes named him for the time his howler broke down and stranded him forty miles from civilization. He walked home. He was carrying some heavy stuff, but a troop of fuxes joined him and they couldn't keep up. They've got lots of energy but no stamina. So they named him Bronze Legs. Bronze is the hardest metal they knew, till we came."

The rain had closed in. A beast like yesterday's flying bug strainers took to the air almost under the treads. For a moment it was face to face with Rachel, its large eyes and tremendous mouth all widened in horror. A wing ticked the windshield as it dodged.

Lightning cursed and turned on the headlights. As if by previous agreement, lights sprang to life on the howlers and the vehicles behind. "We don't like to do that," said Lightning.

"Do what?"

"Use headlights. Every domain is different. You never know what the local life will do when a flare comes, not till you've watched it happen. Here it's okay. Nothing worse than locusts."

Even the headlights had a yellowish tinge, Rachel thought.

The gray cliffs ahead ran hundreds of kilometers to heatward and coldward. They were no more than a few hundred feet high, but they were fresh and new. Medea wobbled a little in its course around Argo, and the tides could raise savage quakes. All the rocks had sharp angles; wind and life had not had a chance to wear them down.

The pass was new too, as if God had cleft the spine of the new mountains with a battle-ax. The floor of it was filled with rubble. The vehicles glided above the broken rock, riding high, with fans on maximum.

Now the land sloped gently down, and the expedition followed. Through the drizzle Bronze Legs glimpsed a grove of trees, hairy trees like those near Touchdown City, but different. They grew like spoons standing on end, with the cup of the spoon facing Argo. The ground was covered with tightly curled black filaments, a plant the color and texture of Bronze Legs' own hair.

They had changed domain. Bronze Legs hadn't been in this territory, but he remembered that Windstorm had. He called, "Anything unexpected around here?"

"B-70s."

"They do get around, don't they? Anything else?"

"It's an easy slope down to the shore," Windstorm called, "but then there's a kind of parasitic fungus floating on the ocean. Won't hurt us, but it can kill a Medean animal in an hour. I told Harvester. He'll make the others wait for us."

"Good."

They rode in silence for a bit. Drizzle made it hard to see much. Bronze Legs wasn't worried. The B-70s would stay clear of their headlights. This was explored territory; and even after they left it, the probes had mapped their route.

"That professional tourist," Windstorm called suddenly. "Did you get to know her?"

"Not really. What about her? Mayor Curly said to be polite."

"When was I ever not polite? But I didn't grow up with her, Bronze Legs. Nobody did. We know more about fuxes than we do about rammers, and this one's peculiar for a rammer! How could a woman give up all her privacy like that?"

"You tell me."

"I wish I knew what she'd do in a church."

"At least she wouldn't close her eyes. She's a dedicated tourist. Can you picture that? But she might not get involved either." Bronze Legs thought hard before he added, "I tried one of those memory tapes."

"What? You?"

"History of the Fission Period in Eurasia, 1945-2010, from *Morven*'s library. Education, not entertainment."

"Why that?"

"Whim."

"Well, what's it like?"

"It's . . . it's like I did a lot of research, and formed conclusions and checked them out and sometimes changed my mind, and it gave me a lot of satisfaction. There are still some open questions, like how the Soviets actually got the fission bomb, and the Vietnam War, and the Arab Takeover. But I know who's working on that, and . . . It's like that, but it doesn't connect to anything. It sits in my head in a clump. But it's kind of fun, Windstorm, and I got it all in ten minutes. You want to hear a libelous song about President Peanut?"

"No."

Through the drizzle they could see the restless stirring of the Ring

Ocean. A band of fuxes waited on the sand. Windstorm turned her howler in a graceful curve, back toward the blur of the crawlers' headlights, to lead them. Bronze Legs dowsed his lights and glided toward the fuxes.

They had chosen a good resting place, far from the dangerous shore, in a broad stretch of "black man's hair" that any marauder would have to cross. Most of the fuxes were lying down. The four-legged female had been impregnated six Medean days ago. Her time must be near. She scratched with sharp claws at her itching hindquarters.

Harvester came to meet Bronze Legs. The post-male biped was slow with age, but not clumsy. That tremendous length of black tail was good for his balance. It was tipped with a bronze spearhead. Harvester asked, "Will we follow the shoreline? If we may choose, we will keep your vessels between us and the shore."

"We plan to go straight across," Bronze Legs told him. "You'll ride the raft behind the bigger vessel."

"In the water are things dangerous to us," said Harvester. He glanced shoreward and added, "Things small, things large. A large one comes."

Bronze Legs took one look and reached for his intercom. "Lightning, Hairy, Jill! Turn your searchlights on that thing, fast!"

The fuxes were up and reaching for their spears.

"So it's the fuxes who give you your nicknames," Rachel said. "Why did they call you Lightning?"

"I tend the machines that make lightning and move it through metal wires. At least, that's how we explained it to the fuxes. And Windstorm—you saw the big redhead girl on the other howler? She was on guard one earthnight when a troop of fuxes took a short cut through the wheat crop. She really gave them hell. Half of Touchdown City must have heard her."

"And you? Grace."

"They named me when I was a lot younger." Grace glared at Lightning, who was very busy driving and clearly not listening, and by no means was he smiling. "But they didn't call me Grace. The way we have children, the fuxes think that's hilarious."

Rachel didn't ask.

"They called me Boobs."

Rachel felt the need for a change of subject. "Lightning, are you getting tired? Would you like me to take over?"

"I'm okay. Can you drive a crawler?"

"Actually, I've never done it. I can run a howler, though. In any terrain."

"Maybe we'll give you one after—"

Then Bronze Legs' voice bellowed from the intercom.

Something came out of the ocean: a great swollen myriapod with tiny jointed arms moving around a funnel-shaped mouth. Teeth churned in the gullet.

The fuxes cast their spears and fled. Bronze Legs tucked Harvester under one arm and sped shoreward; the howler listed to port. Deadeye fell behind; two fuxes turned back and took her arms and pulled her along.

The monster flowed up the beach, faster than any of them, ignoring the spears stuck in its flesh.

One, two, three searchlights flashed from the vehicles and played over the myriapod. The beams were bluish, unlike the headlights. Flare sunlight.

The myriapod stopped. Turned, clumsily, and began to retreat down the beach. It had nearly reached the water when it lost coordination. The legs thrashed frantically and without effect. As Rachel watched in horrible fascination, things were born from the beast.

They crawled from its back and sides. Hundreds of them. They were dark red and dog-sized. They did not leave the myriapod; they stayed on it, feeding. Its legs were quiet now.

Three of the fuxes darted down the beach, snatched up their fallen spears and retreated just as fast. The myriapod was little more than a skeleton now, and the dog-sized feeders were beginning to spread across the sand.

The fuxes climbed aboard the air-cushioned raft that trailed behind the mobile power plant. They arranged their packs and settled themselves. The paired vehicles lifted and glided toward the water. Lightning lifted the crawler and followed.

Rachel said, "But—"

"We'll be okay," Lightning assured her. "We'll stay high and cross fast, and there are always the searchlights."

"Grace, tell him! There are animals that like the searchlights!"

Grace patted her hand. The expedition set off across the water.

The colony around Touchdown City occupied part of a fat peninsula projecting deep into the Ring Sea. It took the expedition twelve hours to cross a bay just smaller than the Gulf of Mexico.

Vermilion scum patches covered the water. Schools of flying non-fish veered and dived at sight of the wrong-colored headlights. The fuxes stayed flat on their platform . . . but the water was smooth, the ride was smooth, and nothing attacked them.

The rain stopped, and left Phrixus and Helle far up the morning sky. The cloud-highway of the Jet Stream showed through a broken cloud deck. Lightning and the other drivers left their headlights on, since the sea life seemed to avoid them.

Somewhere in there, Rachel reclined her chair and went to sleep.

She woke when the crawler settled and tilted under her. Her brain was muzzy . . . and she had slept with the recorder on. That disturbed her. Usually she switched it off to sleep. Dreams were private.

The crawler's door had dropped to form a stairway, and the crawler was empty. Rachel went out.

The crawlers, howlers, raft and mobile power plant were parked in a circle, and tents had been set up inside. There was no living human being in sight. Rachel shrugged; she stepped between a howler and the raft, and stopped.

This was nothing like the Medea she'd seen up to now.

Rolling hills were covered with chrome yellow bushes. They stood waist high, and so densely packed that no ground was visible anywhere. Clouds of insects swarmed, and sticky filaments shot up from the bushes to stab into the swarms.

The fuxes had cut themselves a clearing. They tended one who was restless, twitching. Bronze Legs Miller hailed her from their midst.

Rachel waded through the bushes. They resisted her like thick tar. The insects scattered away from her.

"Deadeye's near her time," Bronze Legs said. "Poor baby. We won't move on until she's dropped her 'nest.' "

The fux showed no swelling of pregnancy. Rachel remembered what she had been told of the fux manner of bearing children. Suddenly she didn't want to see it. Yet how could she leave? She would be omitting a major part of the experience of Medea.

She compromised. She whispered earnestly to Bronze Legs, "Should we be here? Won't they object?"

He laughed. "We're here because we make good insect repellents."

"No. We like humans." Deadeye's voice was slurred. Now Rachel saw that the left eye was pink, with no pupil. "Are you the one who has been among the stars?"

"Yes."

The feverish fux reached up to take Rachel's hand. "So much strangeness in the world. When we know all of the world, it may be we will go among the stars too. You have great courage." Her fingers were slender and hard, like bones. She let go to claw at the hairless red rash between her front and back legs. Her tail thrashed suddenly, and Bronze Legs dodged.

The fux was quiet for a time. A six-legged fux sponged her back with water; the sponge seemed to be a Medean plant. Deadeye said, "I learned from humans that 'deadeye' meant 'accurate of aim.' I set out to be the best spear-caster in . . .'' She trailed off into a language of barking and yelping. The odd-looking biped held conversation with her. Perhaps he was soothing her.

Deadeye howled—and fell apart. She crawled forward, pulling against the ground with hands and forefeet, and her hindquarters were left behind. The hindquarters were red and dripping at the juncture, and the tail slid through them: more than a meter of thick black tail, stained with red, and as long as Harvester's now. The other fuxes came forward, some to tend Deadeye, some to examine the hindquarters . . . in which muscles were still twitching.

Ten minutes later Deadeye stood up. He made it look easy; given his tail and his low center of mass, perhaps it was. He spoke in his own language, and the fuxes filed away into the yellow bushes. In the human tongue Deadeye said, ''I must guard my nest. Alone. Travel safely.''

''See you soon,'' Bronze Legs said. He led Rachel after the fuxes. ''He won't want company now. He'll guard the 'nest' till the little ones eat most of it and come out. Then he'll go sex-crazy, but by that time we'll be back. How are you feeling?''

''A little woozy,'' Rachel said. ''Too much blood.''

''Take my arm.''

The color of their arms matched perfectly.

''Is she safe here? I mean he. Deadeye.''

''He'll learn to walk faster than you think, and he's got his spear. We haven't seen anything dangerous around. Rachel, they don't have a safety hangup.''

''I don't understand.''

''Sometimes they get killed. Okay, they get killed. Deadeye has his reasons for being here. If his children live, they'll own this place. Some of the adults'll stay to help them along. That's how they get new territory.''

Confusing. ''You mean they have to be born here?''

''Right. Fuxes visit. They don't conquer. After awhile they have to go home. Grace is still trying to figure if that's physiology or just a social quirk. But sometimes they visit to give birth, and that's how they get new homes. I don't think fuxes'll ever be space travelers.''

''We have it easier.''

''That we do.''

''Bronze Legs, I want to make love to you.''

He missed a step. He didn't look at her. ''No. Sorry.''

''Then,'' she said a little desperately, ''will you at least tell me what's wrong? Did I leave out a ritual, or take too many baths or something?''

Bronze Legs said, ''Stage fright.''

He sighed when he saw that she didn't understand. ''Look, ordinarily I'd be looking for some privacy for us . . . which wouldn't be easy, because taking your clothes off in an unfamiliar domain . . . never mind. When I make love with a woman I don't want a billion strangers criticizing my technique."

"The memory tapes."

"Right. Rachel, I don't know *where* you find men who want that kind of publicity. Windstorm and I, we let a post-male watch us once . . . but after all, they aren't *human*."

"I could turn off the tape."

"It records memories, right? Unless you forgot about me completely, which I choose to consider impossible, you'd be remembering me for the record. Wouldn't you?"

She nodded. And went back to the crawler to sleep. Others would be sleeping in the tents; she didn't want the company.

The howler's motor was half old, half new. The new parts had a handmade look: bulky, with file marks. One of the fans was newer, cruder, heavier than the other. Rachel could only hope the Medeans were good with machinery.

The tough-looking redhead asked, "Are you sure you want to go through with this?"

"I took a howler across most of Koschei," Rachel told her. She straightened, then swung up onto the saddle. Its original soft plastic seat must have disintegrated; what replaced it looked and felt like tanned skin. "Top speed, a hundred and forty kilometers an hour. Override—this switch—boosts the fans so I can fly. Ten minutes of flight, then the batteries block up and I've got to come down. Six slots in the ground-effect skirt so I can go in any direction. The main thing is to keep my balance. Especially when I'm flying."

Windstrom did not seem reassured. "You won't get that kind of performance out of a fifty-year-old machine. Treat it tender. And don't fly if you're in a hurry, because you'll be using most of the power just to keep you up. Two more things—" She reached out to put Rachel's hands on a switch and a knob. Her own hands were large and strong, with prominent veins. "Searchlight. This knob swings it around, and *this* raises and lowers it. It's your best weapon. If it doesn't work, flee. Second thing is your goggles. Sling them around your neck."

"Where are they?"

Windstorm dug goggles from the howler's saddlebag: a flexible strap and two large hemispheres of red glass. A similar set swung from her own neck. "You should never have to ask that question again on Medea. Here."

The other vehicles were ready to go. Windstorm jogged to her own howler, leaving Rachel with the feeling that she had failed a test.

It was past noon of the Medean day. Harvester was riding Giggles, the six-legged virgin. The rest of the fuxes rode the ground-effect raft. The vehicles rode high, above the forest of chrome yellow bushes.

Windstorm spoke from the intercom. "We stay ahead of the crawlers and to both sides. We're looking for anything dangerous. If you see something you're afraid of, sing out. Don't wait."

Rachel eased into position. The feel of the howler was coming back to her. It weighed half a kiloton, but you still did some of your steering by shifting weight. . . . "Windstorm, aren't you tired?"

"I got some sleep while Deadeye was dropping her hindquarters."

Maybe Windstorm didn't trust anyone else to supervise the rammer. Rachel was actually relieved. It struck her that most Medeans had lost too many of their "safety hangups."

The bushes ended sharply, at the shore of a fast-flowing river carrying broad patches of scarlet scum. Some of the patches bloomed with flowers of startling green. Harvester boarded the raft to cross.

There was wheatfield beyond, but the yellow plants were feathery and four meters high. Hemispheres of white rock appeared with suspicious regularity. The expedition had swung around to north-and-heatward. Argo stood above the peaks of a rounded mountain range. Many-limbed birds rode the air above them.

Rachel looked up to see one dropping toward her face.

She could see the hooked beak and great claws aiming at her eyes. Her blind fingers sought the searchlight controls. She switched on the searchlight and swung the beam around and up. Like a laser cannon: *first* fire, *then* aim. Calmly, now.

The beam found the bird and illuminated it in blue fire: a fearsome sight. Wings like oiled leather, curved meat-ripping beak, muscular forelegs with long talons: and the hind legs were long, slender, and tipped each with a single sword blade. They weren't for walking at all, nor for anything but weaponry.

The bird howled, shut its eyes tight, and tried to turn in the air. Its body curled in a ball; its wings folded around it. Rachel dropped the beam to keep it pinned until it smacked hard into the wheatfield.

The intercom said, "Nice."

"Thank you." Rachel sounded deceptively calm.

"Grace wants to call a halt," Windstorm said. "Up by that next boulder."

"Fine."

The boulders were all roughly the same size: fairly regular hemispheres one and a half meters across.

Grace and Bronze Legs came out of the crawler lugging instruments on a dolly. They unloaded a box on one side of the boulder, and Grace went to work on it. Bronze Legs moved the dolly around to the other side and unfurled a silver screen. When Rachel tried to speak, Grace shushed her. She fiddled a bit with various dials, then turned on the machine.

A shadow-show formed on the screen: a circle of shadow, and darker shapes within. Grace cursed and touched dials, feather-lightly. The blurred shadows took on detail.

Shadows of bones, lighter shadows of flesh. There were four oversized heads, mostly jaws, overlapping near the center; and four tails near the rim, and a maze of legs and spines between. Four creatures all wrapped intimately around each other to just fill the shell.

"I knew it!" Grace cried. "They were too regular. They had to be eggs or nests or plants or *something* like that. Windstorm, dear, if we pile this junk back on the dolly, can you tow it to the next rock?"

They did that. The next rock was very like the first: an almost perfect hemisphere with a surface like white plaster. Rachel rapped it with her knuckles. It felt like stone. But the deep-radar shadow showed three big-headed foetuses just filling their enviroment, plus a tiny one that had failed to grow.

"Well. They all seem to be at the same stage of development," Grace observed. "I wonder if it's a seasonal thing?"

Rachel shook her head. "It's different every time you turn around. Lord! You learn a place, you walk a couple of kilometers, you have to start all over again. Grace, don't you ever get frustrated? You can't run fast enough to stay in one place!"

"I love it. And it's worse than you think, dear." Grace folded the screen and stacked it on the dolly. "The domains don't stay the same. We have spillovers from other domains, from high winds and tidal slosh and migration. I'd say a Medean ecology is ruined every ten years. Then I have to learn it all over again. Windstorm, dear, I'd like to look at one more of these rock eggs. Will you tow—"

The windstorm was sudden and violent. "Damn it, Grace, this isn't the way we planned it! We do our biological research on the way back! *After* we set up the power system, *then* we can give the local monsters a chance to wreck us."

Grace's voice chilled. "Dear, it seems to me that this bit of research is quite harmless."

"It uses up time and supplies. We'll do it on the way back, when we know we've *got* the spare time. We've been through this. Pack up the deep-radar and let's move."

• • •

Now the rolling hills of feather-wheat sloped gently up toward an eroded mountain range whose peaks seemed topped with pink cotton. The three-legged female, Gimpy, trotted alongside Rachel, talking of star travel. Her gait was strange, rolling, but she kept up as long as Rachel held her howler to the power plant's twenty KPH.

She could not grasp interstellar distances. Rachel didn't push. She spoke of wonders instead: of the rings of Saturn, and the bubble cities of Lluagor, and the Smithpeople, and the settling of whale and dolphin colonies in strange oceans. She spoke of time compression: of gifting Sereda with designs for crude steam engines and myriads of wafer-sized computer brains, and returning to find steam robots everywhere: farmland, city streets, wilderness, households, disneylands; of fads that could explode across a planet and vanish without a trace, like tobacco pipes on Koschei, op-art garments on Earth, weight lifting on low-gravity Horvendile.

It was long before she got Gimpy talking about herself.

"I was of my parent's second litter, within a group that moved here to study your kind," Gimpy said. "They taught us bow and arrow, and a better design of shovel, and other things. We might have died without them."

"The way you said that: second litter. Is there a difference?"

"Yes. One has the first litter when one can. The second litter comes to one who proves her capability by living that long. The third litter, the male's litter, comes only with the approval of one's clan. Else the male is not allowed to breed."

"That's good genetics." Rachel saw Gimpy's puzzlement. "I mean that your custom makes better fuxes."

"It does. I will never see my second litter," Gimpy said. "I was young when I made my mistake, but it was foolish. The breed improves. I will not be a one-legged male."

They moved into a rift in the eroded mountain range, and the incredible became obvious. The mountains were topped with pink cotton candy. It must have been sticky like cotton candy, too. Rachel could see animals trapped in it. Gimpy wanted no part of that. She dropped back and boarded the raft.

They crossed the cotton candy with fans blasting at maximum. The big vehicles blew pink froth in all directions. Something down there wasn't trapped at all. A ton of drastically flattened pink snail, with a perfect snail shell perched jauntily on its back, cruised over the cotton candy leaving a slime trail that bubbled and expanded to become more pink froth. It made for the still corpse of a many-limbed bird, flowed over it, and stopped to digest it.

The strangeness was getting to Rachel; and that was a strange thing for her. She was a rammer. Strangeness was the one constant in her life. Born aboard a ramship, not *Morven*, she had already gone once around the trade circuit. Even a rammer who returned to a world he knew must expect to find it completely changed; and Rachel *knew* that. But the strangeness of Medea came faster than she could swallow it or spit it out.

She fiddled with the intercom until she got Grace.

"Yes, dear, I'm driving. What is it?"

"It's confusion. Grace, why aren't all planets like Medea? They've all got domains, don't they? Deserts, rain forests, mountains, poles and equators . . . you see what I mean?"

She heard the xenobiologist's chuckle. "Dear, the Cold Pole is covered with frozen carbon dioxide. Where we're going it's hotter than boiling water. What is there on the trade circuit worlds that splits up the domains? Mountain ranges? An ocean for a heat sink? Temperature, altitude, rainfall? Medea has all of that, plus the one-way winds and the one-way ocean currents. The salinity goes from pure water to pure brine. The glaciers carry veins of dry ice heatward, so there are sudden jumps in the partial pressure of carbon dioxide. Some places there are no tides. Other places, Argo wobbles enough to make a terrific tidal slosh. Then again, everything has to adapt to the flares. Some animals have shells. Some sea beasts can dive deep. Some plants seed, others grow a big leaf for an umbrella."

Beyond the pass the mountains dropped more steeply, down to an arm of the Ring Sea. Rachel had no problem controlling the howler, but the mobile power plant was laboring hard, with its front vents wide open to hold it back and little pressure left for steering. There should be no real danger. Two probes had mapped this course.

"Everything is *more* different, huh?"

"Excuse me, dear . . . that's got it. Sonofabitch, we could live without that sonofabitching tail wind. Okay. Do you remember the mock turtle we showed you yesterday evening? We've traced it six thousand kilometers to coldward. In the Icy Sea it's seagoing and much larger. Follow it heatward and it gets smaller and more active. We think it's the food supply. Glaciers stir up the bottom, and the sea life loves that. To heatward a bigger beast starves . . . sometimes. But we could be wrong. Maybe it has to conserve heat in the colder climates. I'd like to try some experiments someday."

The white boulders that turned out to be giant eggs were thicker here on the heatward slopes. And on the lower slopes—But this was *strange*.

The mountainsides were gay with pennants. Thousands of long, flapping flags, orange or chrome yellow. Rachel tried to make it out. Grace was still talking; Rachel began to feel she'd opened a Pandora's Box.

"The closer you look to the Hot Pole, the more competition you find among the sea life. New things flow in from coldward, constantly. All the six-limbed and eight-limbed forms, we think they were forced onto the land, kicked out of the ocean by something bigger or meaner. They left the ocean before they could adopt the usual fish shape, which is four fins and a tail."

"Grace, wait a minute, now. Are you saying . . . we . . . ?"

"Yes, dear." The smile Rachel couldn't see had to be a smirk. "Four limbs and a tail. We dropped the tail, but the human form is perfectly designed for a fish."

Rachel switched her off.

The hillside trees had extensive root systems that gripped rock like a strong man's fist, and low, almost conical trunks. On each tree the tip of the trunk sprouted a single huge leaf, a flapping flag, orange or chrome yellow and ragged at the end. All pennants and no armies. Some of the flags were being torn apart by the air blast from the ground-effect vehicles. Perhaps that was how they spread their seeds, Rachel thought. Like tapeworms. Ask Grace? She'd had enough of Grace, and she'd probably have to start with an apology. . . .

The day brightened as if clouds had passed from before the sun.

The slopes were easing off into foothills now. Gusts of wind turned some of the flapping pennants into clouds of confetti. It was easier to go through the papery storms than to steer around. Rachel used one hand as a visor; the day had turned quite bright. Was she carrying dark glasses? Of course, the goggles—

It was a flare!

She kept her eyes resolutely lowered until she'd pulled the red cups over her eyes and adjusted them. Then she turned to look. The suns were behind her left shoulder, and one was nearly lost in the white glare of the other.

Bronze Legs was asleep in a reclined passenger chair in the trailing crawler. It was like sleeping aboard a boat at anchor . . . but the sudden glare woke him instantly.

Going downhill, the mobile power plant rode between the two crawlers, for greater safety. The angle of descent hadn't seriously hampered the ponderous makeshift vehicle. But all bets were off now. *Flare!*

The fuxes were still on the raft. They could be hurt if they tumbled off at this speed, but their every instinct must be telling them to get off and *dig*. Bronze Legs flattened his nose against the windscreen. Charles "Hairy" McBundy, fighting to slow the power plant and raft, wouldn't have attention to spare; and there *had* to be a place to stop. Someplace close, someplace flat, dirt rather than rock, and damn quick! There, to the left? Not quite flat, and it ended short, in a cliff. Tough. Bronze Legs hit the intercom button and screamed, "Hard left, Hairy, and when you stop, stop fast!"

Hairy was ahead of him. Vents had already opened in the air cushion skirts of raft and power plant. Robbed of thrust through the forward vents, the vehicles surged left and forward. Bronze Legs' teeth ground against each other. One silver parasol had opened on the raft, probably Harvester's, and five sharp fux faces were under it. Their tails thrashed with their agitation.

Grace brought the crawler around to follow. Left and forward, too fast, like the power plant. Hairy was on the ledge now. He cut his air cushion all at once. The power plant dropped. Its skirt screamed against rock, then dirt, then, at the edge of the drop, quit. The fuxes boiled off the raft, raised parasols, and began digging.

The crawler vibrated sickeningly as Grace cut the air cushion.

She was wearing her ruby goggles. So was Bronze Legs; he must have donned them without help from his conscious mind. He glanced again at the fuxes and saw only silver disks and a fog of brown dirt. The other crawler had stopped on the slant.

Windstorm's howler sat tilted, but not rolling. Windstorm herself was sprinting uphill. Good enough. She should be inside, in one of the crawlers. Strange things could emerge in flare time. Where was the other howler pilot?

Far downslope and losing ground. Too far to climb back in any reasonable time. That was Rachel, the rammer, wasn't it? With a little skill she could turn the howler and use the larger rear vents to bring her back; but she wasn't showing that skill. She seemed to be trying to back up. Not good at all.

"Grace? Can we take the crawler down to her?"

"We may have to try. Try the intercom first, dear. See if you can talk her back up."

Bronze Legs tried. "Her intercom's off."

"Off? Really? The little idiot—"

"And she's not about to notice the little light. Wait, here she comes." Rachel's howler lifted on emergency power, hovered, then started uphill.

Grace said, "She may have trouble landing."

Then Bronze Legs saw what was happening around them.

To Rachel it seemed that everyone was in panic. Far above her, both crawlers and the power plant had come to a screeching halt. Tough, competent Windstorm had abandoned her own vehicle and was fleeing in terror from nothing visible. The fuxes, the native Medeans, were nowhere in sight. Could they *all* know something Rachel didn't?

She was having her own problems. The damned obsolete sluggish howler refused to back up; it coasted slowly, frictionlessly downhill, further and further from safety. To hell with that. She flipped the override.

The howler went up. Rachel leaned far back, and the howler tilted with her, staying low, following the upward curve of terrain. If the power quit early she wanted some chance to land. But the howler purred nicely uphill, faster now, while Rachel concentrated on her balance. She was marginally aware that the gay orange pennants had all turned to dead black crepe, and that certain round white boulders were cracking, crumbling.

But when things emerged from the boulders, she screamed.

All in an instant the mountains were acrawl with a thousand monsters. Their skins were shiny white. Their eyes were mere slits in heads that were mostly teeth. As Rachel rose toward the precarious safety of the crawlers, the creatures chose their target and converged. They ran with bodies low, tails high, legs an invisible blur. In seconds that meager flat place where the crawlers rested was covered with rock demons.

No safety there.

She flew over the crawlers, glimpsed peering faces behind the windscreens, and kept going. The boulders had been rare near the crest, and the rock demons weren't there yet. Neither was Rachel, of course. She'd get as far as possible before the howler quit. And then what?

She flipped on the headlights and the searchlight too. The rock demons throve in flare time, but even they might fear too much flare sunlight. It was worth a try.

The mountain's rock face grew steeper and steeper. No place to land, unless she could reach the crest. The fans howled.

Here was the ridge, coming level. Rachel cursed venomously. The crest was carpeted in pink, sticky cotton candy. Its proprietors had withdrawn into huge snail shells.

The howl of the fans dropped from contralto toward bass.

Pale six-legged monsters, searching for meat on bare rock, turned big heads to squint as Rachel sank low. They blurred into motion.

The crawler coasted just above the pink froth, riding the ground effect now, not really flying. Strange corpses and strange skeletons were marooned in that sea. The wind from the fans was full of pink froth.

Then she had crossed and was coasting downhill, and it was already too late to land. The howler rode centimeters above the rock, too fast and gaining speed. Here the slope was shallower, and she was still in the pass chosen weeks ago by Medeans monitoring a tractor probe. But the howler rode too low. If she opened a slot to brake, the skirt would scrape rock, the howler would flip over. Find a level spot—

A quick glance back told her she didn't want to stop anyway. A dozen of the rock demons had crossed the cotton candy. Probably used their siblings for stepping stones after *they* got stuck! Rachel held hard to her sanity and concentrated on staying right side up. The things were holding their own in the race. Maybe they were even catching up.

Bronze Legs squeezed between the crates and the roof to reach the crawler's observation bubble. It was big enough for his head and shoulders. He found one of the rock demons with its forelegs wrapped around the bubble, blocking part of his view while it gnawed at the glass.

Rock demons swarmed on the ground. The fuxes couldn't be seen, but a few rock demons lay unnaturally quiet where the fuxholes were, and Bronze Legs saw a spear thrust through the melee. He called down, "Try the searchlights."

"Won't work," Grace answered. She tried it anyway. Other searchlights joined hers, and the thrashing rock demons blazed painfully bright even through goggles. They turned, squinted at the situation, then came all in a quick rush. The bronze spearhead on Harvester's tail stabbed deep into a straggler. The rock demon's blood jetted an incredible distance. It died almost instantly.

If there were live fuxes under the somewhat tattered silver parasols, they were safe now. All the rock demons were swarming round the vehicle's searchlights. They *liked* the light.

Grace chortled. "Tell me you expected *that*!"

"I wouldn't dare. I feel a lot safer now." The monsters weren't tearing at the lights; they fought each other for a place in the glare. "What do they think they're doing?"

"We've seen this kind of reaction before," Grace answered. "Medean life either loves flares or hates them. All the flare-loving forms act like they're programmed to stay out of shadows during flares. Like, in the shadow of a mountain they'd be in just the conditions they aren't designed for. Most of 'em have high blood pressure, too, and terrific reserves of energy. They have to accomplish a lot in the little time a flare lasts. Be born, eat, grow, mate, give birth—"

"Grace, get on the intercom and find out if everyone's still alive. And see if anyone knows which sun flared."

"Why? What possible difference could it make?"

"Phrixus flares last up to three quarters of an hour. Helle flares don't last as long. We're going to have to wait it out. And see if Rachel called anyone."

"Right."

Bronze Legs half-listened to the intercom conversation. Along the heatward slopes of the mountains the black flags flew in triumph, growing longer almost as Bronze Legs watched, making sugar while the sun flared. The rock demons milling in the searchlight beams were now hungry enough to be attacking each other in earnest. A vastly larger number of rock demons had deserted the mountainsides entirely, had swarmed straight down to the shoreline. The waves were awash with sea monsters of all sizes; the rock demons were wading out to get them.

Grace called up to him. "Rachel didn't call anyone. Lightning says she made it over the crest."

"Good."

"What do you think she'll do?"

"Nobody knows her very well. Hmm . . . She won't land in the cotton candy. She probably could, because those snails are probably hiding in their shells. Right?"

"But she won't. It's be too messy. She'll stop on the coldward slope, or beyond, anywhere it's safe to wait it out. If there is anywhere. Do you think she'll find anywhere safe?"

"She won't know what's safe. She won't find anyplace that isn't swarming with *something*, not this far to heatward. The further you look to heatward, the more ferocious the competition gets."

"Then she'll keep going. If she doesn't wreck herself, she'll go straight back to Touchdown City. Let's see, *Morven*'s on the other side of the planet now. Say it'll be up in an hour, and we'll let them know what's happening. That way we'll know she's safe almost as soon as she does. Grace, you don't think she'd try to rejoin us?"

"She can't get lost, and she can't stop, and Touchdown's visible from fifty miles away. She'll just head home. Okay . . ." There was a funny edge of doubt in Grace's voice. She stabbed at an intercom button. "Lightning? Me. You watched Rachel go over the crest, right? Did she have her headlights on?"

Bronze Legs was wondering just how teed off the rammers would be if Rachel was dead. It took him a moment to see the implications of what Grace was saying.

"The searchlight too? All right, Lightning. The long range sender is on your roof. I want it ready to send a message to *Morven* by the time *Morven* rises, which will be to south of coldward in about an hour. . . . No, don't go out yet. The way the beasts are running around they should die of heatstroke pretty quick. When they fall off the roof, you go."

The rock demons followed Rachel twelve kilometers downslope before anything distracted them.

The howler was riding higher now, but Rachel wasn't out of trouble. The emergency override locked the vents closed. If she turned it off the power would drop, and so would the howler. She was steering with her weight alone. Her speed would last as long as she was going down. She had almost run out of mountain. The slope leveled off as it approached the river.

The vicious pegasus-type birds had disappeared. The rolling mountainsides covered with feathery wheat were now covered with stubble, stubble with a hint of motion in it, dark flecks that showed and were gone. Millions of mice, maybe?

Whatever: they were meat. The demons scattered in twelve directions across the stubble, their big heads snapping, snapping. Rachel leaned forward across her windscreen to get more speed. Behind her, three rock demons converged on a golden Roman shield . . . on a mock turtle that had been hidden by feather-wheat and was now quite visible and helpless. The demons turned it over and ripped it apart and ate and moved on.

The howler slid across the shore and onto flowing water.

Each patch of scarlet scum had sprouted a great green blossom. Rachel steered between the stalks by body english. She was losing speed, but the shore was well behind her now.

And all twelve rock demons zipped downhill across the stubble and into the water. Rachel held her breath. Could they *swim*? They were under water, drinking or dispersing heat or both. Now they arched upward to reach the air.

The howler coasted to a stop in midstream.

Rachel nerved herself to switch off the override. The howler dropped, and hovered in a dimple of water, churning a fine mist that rapidly left Rachel dripping wet. She waited. Come what may, at least the batteries were recharging. Give her time and she'd have a howler that could steer and fly.

The heatward shore was black with a million mouse-sized beasties. They'd cleaned the field of feather-wheat; but what did they think they were doing now? Watching Rachel? The rock demons noticed. They waded clumsily out of the water and, once on land, blurred into motion. The shore churned with six-legged white marauders and tiny black prey.

It seemed the fates had given Rachel a break. The water seemed quite empty but for the scarlet scum and its huge blossoms. No telling what might be hugging the bottom while the flare passed. Rachel could wait too. The coldward shore looked safe enough . . . though it had changed. Before the flare, it had been one continuous carpet of chrome yellow bushes. The bushes were still there, but topped now with a continuous sheet of silver blossoms. The clouds of insects swarmed still, though they might be different insects.

Upstream, something was walking toward her on stilts. It came at its own good time, stopping frequently. Rachel kept her eye on it while she tried the intercom.

She got static on all bands. Mountains blocked her from the expedition; other mountains blocked her from Touchdown City. The one sender that could reach *Morven* in orbit was on a crawler. Dammit. She never noticed the glowing pinpoint that meant Bronze Legs had called. It was too dim.

Onshore, two of the rock demons were mating head-to-tail.

The thing upstream seemed to be a great silver daddy longlegs. Its legs were slender and almost long enough to bridge the river; its torso proportionately tiny. It paused every so often to reach deep into the water with the thumbless hands on its front legs. The hands were stubby, armored in chitin, startlingly quick. They dipped, they rose at once with something that struggled, they conveyed the prey to its mouth. Its head was wide and flat, like a clam with bulging eyes. It stepped delicately downstream, with all the time in the world . . . and it was bigger than Rachel had realized, and *faster*.

So much for her rest break. She opened the rear vent. The howler slid across the river and onto shore, and stopped, nudging the bushes.

The daddy longlegs was following her. Ten of the dozen rock demons were wading across. As the bottom dipped the six-legged beasts rose to balance on four legs, then two. As bipeds they were impressively stable. Maybe their tails trailed in the mud bottom to serve as anchors. And the mice were coming too. Thousands of them, swimming in a black carpet among the patches of scum.

Rachel used the override for fifteen seconds. It was enough to put her above the silver-topped bushes. The lily-pad-shaped silver blossoms bowed beneath the air blast, but the ground effect held her. She wasn't making any great speed. Bugs swarmed around her. Sticky filaments shot from between the wide silver lily pads, and sometimes found bugs, and sometimes struck the fans or the ground effect skirt.

She looked for the place that had been cleared for a fux encampment. Deadeye would be there, a feisty male biped guarding his nest, if Deadeye still lived. She couldn't find the gap in the bushes. It struck her that that was good luck for Deadeye, considering what was following her.

But she was lonely, and scared.

The daddy longlegs stepped delicately among the bushes. Bushes rustled to show where ten rock demons streaked after her, veering to snatch a meal from whatever was under the blossoms, then resuming course. Of the plant-eating not-mice there was no sign, except that here and there a bush had collapsed behind her.

But they were all falling behind as the fuel cells poured power into the howler's batteries.

Rachel oriented herself by Argo and the Jet Stream and headed south and coldward. She was very tired. The land was darkening, reddening . . . and it came to her that the flare was dying.

• • •

The flare was dying. The goggles let Bronze Legs look directly at the suns, now, to see the red arc enclosing the bright point of Helle. A bubble of hellfire was rising, cooling, expanding into the vacuum above the lesser hell of a red dwarf star.

There were six-legged rock demons all around them, and a few on the roofs. All were dead, from heatstroke or dehydration. A far larger number were gathering all along the Ring Sea shore. Now they swarmed uphill in a wave of silver. They paired off as they came, and stopped by twos in the rocks to mate.

The diminished wave swept around the expedition and petered out. Now the mountains were covered with writhing forms: an impressive sight. "They make the beast with twelve legs," Bronze Legs said. "Look at the size of those bellies! Hey, Grace, aren't the beasts themselves bigger than they were?"

"They have to be. They've got to form those eggs. Dammit, don't distract me."

The intercom lit. Grace wasn't about to notice anything so mundane. The paired rock demons were growing quiet, but they were still linked head to tail. Bronze Legs opened the intercom.

Lightning's voice said, "I've got Duty Officer Toffler aboard *Morven*."

"Okay. Toffler, this is Miller. We've got an emergency."

"Sorry to hear it." The male voice sounded sleepy. "What can we do about it?"

"You'll have to call Touchdown City. Can you patch me through, or shall I record a message?"

"Let's check . . ." The voice went away. Bronze Legs watched a nearby pair of rock demons crawling away from each other. The thick torsos seemed different. A belly swelling that had extended the length of the torso was now a prominent swelling between the middle and hind legs. It was happening fast. The beasts seemed gaunt, all bone and skin, except for the great spherical swelling. With fore and middle legs they scratched at the earth, digging, digging.

"Miller, you'd better record. By the time we got their attention they'd be over the horizon. We'll have them in another hour."

"Good—"

"But I don't see how they can help either. Listen, Miller, is there something we can do with an interstellar message laser? At this range we can melt a mountain or boil a lake, and be accurate to—"

"Dammit, Toffler, *we're* not in trouble! Touchdown City's in trouble, and they don't know it yet!"

"Oh? Okay, set to record."

"To Mayor Curly Jackson, Touchdown City. We've weathered the flare. We don't know if the fuxes survived yet. The rammer, Rachel Subramaniam, is on the way to you on a howler. She has no reason to think she's dangerous, but she is. By the time you spot her you'd be too late to stop her. If you don't move damn quick, the human colony on Medea could be dead within the year. You'll need every vehicle you can get your hands on . . ."

The expedition had crossed a great bay of the Ring Sea in twelve hours. Rachel could cross it in three; but she'd be rid of what followed her moments after she left shore. She had heard Lightning mention the parasitic fungus that floated on this arm of the Ring Sea, that was deadly to fuxes and any Medean life . . . unless the flare had burned it away.

The flare was long over. She rode through the usual red-lit landscape, in a circle of the white light from headlights, taillights, searchlight. She hungered and thirsted for the light of farming lamps, the color of Sol, of ship's sunlights; the sign that she had come at last to Touchdown City.

But she hungered more for the fungus that would kill the rock demons and the daddy longlegs. She hated them for their persistence, their monstrous shapes, their lust for her flesh. She hated them for being themselves! Let them rot, slow or quick. Then three hours to cross the bay, half an hour more to find and navigate that rubble-strewn pass, and downhill toward the blue-white light.

That was the shoreline ahead.

Ominously blood-colored beasts milled there. One by one they turned toward the howler.

Rachel cursed horribly and without imagination. She had seen these things before. The expedition's searchlights had pinned a tremendous thousand-legged worm, and these things had been born from its flesh. They were dog-sized, tailless quadrupeds. Flare time must have caught a lot of the great myriapods, brought vast populations of parasites to life, for this many to be still active this long after the flare.

More than active. They leapt like fleas . . . toward Rachel. She turned to heatward. Weak as she felt now, *one* could knock her out of the saddle.

Her entourage turned with her. Two more rock demons had dropped out. Eight followed, and the great spider, and a loyal population of proto-mice, exposed now that the bushes had ended. And hordes of insects. Rachel's reason told her that she was taking this all too personally. But what did they *see* in her? She wasn't that much meat, and the spider wasn't that hungry. It reached down now and then to pluck a proto-mouse, and once it plucked up a rock demon, with equal nonchalance. The demon raved and snapped and died within the spider's clamshell mouth, but it clawed out an eye, too.

And the demons had the proto-mice for food, but they had to streak down to the water every so often to cool off, and fight their way back through the blood-red quadrupeds, eating what they killed. The mice had fed well on the yellow bushes, and who knew about the tiny might-be-insects? *What did they all want with Rachel?*

After a couple of hours the shore curved south, and now it was white tinged with other colors: a continuous crust of salt. Rachel's climate suit worked well, but her face and hands were hot. The wind was hot with Argo-heat and the heat of a recent flare. The daddy longlegs had solved its heat problem. It waded offshore, out of reach of the red parasites, pacing her.

It was five hours before the shore turned sharply to coldward. Rachel turned with it, staying well back from shore, where blood-colored quadrupeds still prowled. She worried now about whether she could find the pass. There would be black, tightly curled ground cover, and trees foliated in gray hair with a spoon-shaped silhouette; and sharp-edged young mountains to the south. But she felt stupid with fatigue, and she had never adjusted to the light and never would: dull red from Argo, pink from two red dwarf suns nearing sunset.

More hours passed. She saw fewer of the red parasites. Once she caught the daddy longlegs with another rock demon in its clamshell jaws. The hexapod's own teeth tore at the side of the spider's face . . . the side that was already blind. Flare-loving forms used themselves up fast. Those trees . . .

Rachel swung her searchlight around. The ground cover, the "black man's hair," was gone. A black fog of insects swarmed over bare dirt. But the trees were hairy, with a spoon-shaped silhouette. How far had those trees spread on Medea? She could be in the wrong place. . . .

She turned left, uphill.

There were low mountains ahead, young mountains, all sharp edges. A kilometer short, Rachel turned to parallel them. The pass had been so narrow. She could go right past it. She slowed down, then, impatient, speeded up again. Narrow it had been, but straight. Perhaps she would see farming lamps shining through it. She noticed clouds forming, and began cursing to drive away thoughts of rain.

When the light came it was more than a glimmer.

She saw a sun, a white sun, a *real* sun, shining against the mountains. As if flare time had come again! But Phrixus and Helle were pink dots sinking in the west. She swerved toward the glare. The rising ground slowed her, and she remembered the spider plodding patiently behind her; she didn't turn to look.

The glare grew terribly bright. She slowed further, puzzled and frightened. She pulled the goggles up over her eyes. That was better; but still she saw nothing but that almighty glare at the end of a bare rock pass.

She rode into the pass, into the glare, into a grounded sun.

Her eyes adjusted. . . .

The rock walls were lined with vehicles: flyers, tractor probes, trucks, crawlers converted to firefighting and ambulance work, anything that could move on its own was there, and each was piled with farming lamps and batteries, and all the farming lamps were on. An aisle had been left between them. Rachel coasted down the aisle. She thought she could make out man-shaped shadows in the red darkness beyond.

They were human. By the pale mane around his head she recognized Mayor Curly Jackson.

Finally, finally, she slowed the howler, let it sink to the ground, and stepped off. Human shapes came toward her. One was Mayor Curly. He took her arm, and his grip drove pain even through the fog of fatigue. "You vicious little idiot," he said.

She blinked.

He snarled and dropped her arm and turned to face the pass. Half the population of Touchdown City stood looking down the aisle of light, ignoring Rachel . . . pointedly. She didn't try to shoulder between them. She climbed into the howler's saddle to see.

They were there: half a dozen rock demons grouped beneath the long legs of the spider; a black carpet of proto-mice; all embedded in a cloud of bright motes, insects. The monsters strolled up the aisle of light, and the watching men backed away. It wasn't necessary. Where the light stopped, Rachel's entourage stopped too.

Mayor Curly turned. "Did it *once* occur to you that something might be following your lights? Your *flare-colored* lights? You went through half a dozen domains, and every one had its own predators and its own plant eaters, and you brought them all *here*, you gutless moron! How many kinds of insects are there in that swarm? How many of them would eat our crops down to the ground before it poisoned them? Those little black things on the ground, they're plant-eaters too, aren't they? All flare-loving forms, and you brought them all here to *breed*! The next time a flare goes off would have been the last time any Medean human being had anything to eat! *You'd* be safe, of course. All you'd have to do is fly on to another star . . ."

The only way a human being can turn off her ears is to turn off her mind. Rachel didn't know whether she fainted or not. Probably she was led away rather than carried. Her next memory began some time later, beneath the light of home, with the sounds and the smells of home around her, strapped down in free-fall aboard the web ramship *Morven*.

On the curve of the wall the mobile power plant and one of the crawlers had finally left the realms of crusted salt. They ran over baked dirt now. The howler was moored in the center of the ground-effect raft, surrounded by piles of crates. It would be used again only by someone willing to wear a spacesuit. The four remaining fuxes were in the crawlers. Argo was out of camera range, nearly overhead. The view shifted and dipped with the motion of the trailing crawler.

"No, the beasts didn't actually do any harm. We did more damage to ourselves," Mayor Curly said. He wasn't looking at Captain Borg. He was watching the holo wall. A cup of coffee cooled in his hand. "We moved every single farming lamp out of the croplands and set them all going in the pass, right? And the flare-loving life forms just stayed there till they died. They aren't really built to take more than a couple of hours of flare time, what they'd get if both suns flared at once, and they aren't built to walk away from flarelight either. Maybe some of the insects bred. Maybe the big forms were carrying seeds and insect eggs in their hair. We know the six-legged types tried to breed as soon as we turned off the lamps, but they weren't in shape for it by then. It doesn't matter now. I suppose I should . . ."

He turned and looked at her. "In fact, I do thank you most sincerely for melting that pass down to lava. There can't be anything living in it now."

"So you came out of it with no damage."

"Not really. The locusts hurt us. We moved the farming lamps in a hurry, but we took our own good time getting them back in place. That was a mistake. Some flare-hating bugs were just waiting to taste our corn."

"Too bad."

"And a nest of B-70s killed two children in the oak grove."

Captain Borg's mind must have been elsewhere. "You really reamed Rachel out."

"I did," Curly said, without satisfaction and without apology.

"She was almost catatonic. We had to take her back up to *Morven* before she'd talk to anyone. Curly, is there any way to convince her she didn't make a prize idiot of herself?"

"At a guess I'd say no. Why would anyone want to?"

Captain Borg was using her voice of command now. "I dislike sounding childish, especially to you, Curly, but baby talk may be my best option. The problem is that Rachel didn't have any fun on Medea."

"You're breaking my heart."

"She won't even talk about coming down. She didn't like Medea. She didn't like the light, or the animals, or the way the fuxes bred. Too bloody. She went through thirty-odd hours of hell with your power plant expedition, and came back tired to death and being chased by things out of a nightmare, and when she finally got to safety you called her a dangerous incompetent idiot and made her believe it. She didn't even get laid on Medea—"

"What?"

"Never mind, it's trivial. Or maybe it's absolutely crucial, but *skip* it. Curly, I have sampled the official memory tape of Medea, the one we would have tried to peddle when we got back into the trade circuit—''

Curly's eyes got big. ''O-o-oh shit!''

''It comes to you, does it? That tape was an ugly experience. It's unpleasant, and uncomfortable, and humiliating, and exhausting, and scary, and there's no sex. That's Rachel's view of Medea, and there *isn't* any other, and *nobody*'s going to enjoy it.''

Curly had paled. ''What do we do? Put Rachel's equipment on somebody else?''

''I wouldn't wear it. No rammer is really manic about her privacy, but there are limits. What about a Medean?''

''Who?''

''Don't you have any compulsive exhibitionists?''

Curly shook his head. ''I'll ask around, but . . . no, maybe I won't. Doesn't it tell you something, that she couldn't get screwed? What man could go with a woman, knowing she'll be peddling the memory of it to millions of strangers? Yuk.''

The crawlers had stopped. Human shapes stepped outside, wearing skintight pressure suits and big transparent bubbles over their heads. They moved around to the ground-effect raft and began opening crates.

''It's no good. Curly, it's not easy to find people to make memory tapes. For a skill tape you need a genuine expert with twenty or thirty years experience behind him, plus a sharp-edged imagination and a one track mind and no sense of privacy. And Rachel's a tourist. She's got all of that, and she can learn new skills at the drop of a hat. She's very reactive, very emotive.''

''And she very nearly wiped us out.''

''She'll be making tapes till she dies. And every time something reminds her of Medea, her entire audience is going to know just what she thinks of the planet.''

''What'll happen to us?''

''Oh . . . we could be worried over nothing. I've seen fads before. This whole memory tape thing could be ancient history by the time we get back to civilization.''

Civilization? As opposed to what? Curly knew the answer to that one. He went back to watching the wall.

''And even if it's not . . . I'll be back. I'll bring another walking memory like Rachel, but more flexible. Okay?''

''How long?''

''One circuit, then back to Medea.''

Sixty to seventy earthyears. ''Good,'' said Curly, because there was certainly no way to talk her into any shorter journey. He watched men in silver suits setting up the frames for the solar mirrors. There was not even wind in the Hot End, and apparently no life at all. They had worried about that. But Curly saw nothing that could threaten Touchdown City's power supply for hundreds of years to come.

If Medea was to become a backwash of civilization, a land of peasants, then it was good that the farmlands were safe. Curly turned to Janice Borg to say so. But the rammer's eyes were seeing nothing on Medea, and her mind was already approaching Horvendile.

● ● ●

• • •

"... Take a biped that's man-shaped, enough so to use a tool, but without intelligence. Plant him on a world and watch him grow. Say he's adaptable; say he eventually spread over most of the fertile land masses of the planet. Now what?

"Now an actual physical change takes place. The brain expands ..."

"The Locusts" (with Steven Barnes), 1979

THE LOCUSTS (with STEVEN BARNES)

There are no men on Tau Ceti IV.

Near the equator on the ridged ribbon of continent which reaches north and south to cover both poles, the evidence of Man still shows. There is the landing craft, a great thick saucer with a rounded edge, gaping doors and vast empty space inside. Ragged clumps of grass and scrub vegetation surround its base, now. There is the small town where they lived, grew old, and died: tall stone houses, a main street of rock fused with atomic fire, a good deal of machinery whose metal is still bright. There is the land itself, overgrown but still showing the traces of a square arrangement that once marked it as farmland.

And there is the forest, reaching north and south along the sprawling ribbon of continent, spreading even to the innumerable islands which form two-thirds of Ridgeback's land mass. Where forest cannot grow, because of insufficient water or because the carefully bred bacteria have not yet built a sufficient depth of topsoil, there is grass, an exceptionally hardy hybrid of Buffalo and Cord with an abnormal number of branching roots, developing a dense and fertile sod.

There are flocks of moas, resurrected from a lost New Zealand valley. The great flightless birds roam freely, sharing their grazing land with expanding herds of wild cattle and buffalo.

There are things in the forest. They prefer it there, but will occasionally shamble out into the grasslands and sometimes even into the town. They themselves do not understand why they go: there is no food, and they do not need building materials or other things which may be there for the scavenging. They always leave the town before nightfall arrives.

When men came the land was as barren as a tabletop.

Doc and Elise were among the last to leave the ship. He took his wife's hand and walked down the ramp, eager to feel alien loam between his toes. He kept his shoes on. They'd have to make the loam first.

The other colonists were exceptionally silent, as if each were afraid to speak. Not surprising, Doc thought. The first words spoken on Ridgeback would become history.

The robot probes had found five habitable worlds besides Ridgeback in Earth's neighborhood. Two held life in more or less primitive stages, but Ridgeback was perfect. There was one-celled life in Ridgeback's seas, enough to give the planet an oxygenating atmosphere; and no life at all on land. They would start with a clean slate.

So the biologists had chosen what they believed was a representative and balanced ecology. A world's life was stored in the cargo hold now, in frozen fertilized eggs and stored seeds and bacterial cultures, ready to go to work.

Doc looked out over his new home, the faint seabreeze stinging his eyes. He had known Ridgeback would be barren, but he had not expected the *feel* of a barren world to move him.

The sky was bright blue, clouds shrouding Tau Ceti, a sun wider and softer than the sun of Earth. The ocean was a deeper blue, flat and calm. There was no dirt. There was dust and sand and rock, but nothing a farming man would call dirt. There were no birds, no insects. The only sound was that of sand and small dust-devils dancing in the wind, a low moan almost below the threshold of human hearing.

Doc remembered his college geology class's fieldtrip to the Moon. Ridgeback wasn't dead as Luna was dead. It was more like his uncle's face, after the embalmers got through with him. It looked alive, but it wasn't.

Jase, the eldest of them and the colony leader, raised his hand and waited. When all eyes were on him he crinkled his eyes happily, saving his biggest smile for his sister Cynnie, who was training a holotape camera on him. "We're here, people," his voice boomed in the dead world's silence. "It's good, and it's ours. Let's make the most of it."

There was a ragged cheer and the colonists surged toward the cargo door of the landing craft. The lander was a flattish dome now, its heat shield burned almost through, its Dumbo-style atomic motor buried in dust. It had served its purpose and would never move again. The great door dropped and became a ramp. Crates and machinery began to emerge on little flatbed robot trucks.

Elise put her arm around her husband's waist and hugged him. She murmured, "It's so empty."

"So far." Doc unrolled a package of birth control pills, and felt her flinch.

"Two years before we can have children."

Did she mean it as a question? "Right," he said. They had talked it through too often, in couples and in groups, in training and aboard ship. "At least until Jill gets the ecology going."

"Uh huh." An impatient noise.

Doc wondered if she believed it. At twenty-four, tall and wiry and with seven years of intensive training behind him, he felt competent to handle most emergencies. But children, and babies in particular, were a problem he could postpone.

He had interned for a year at Detroit Memorial, but most of his schooling related directly to General Colonization. His medical experience was no better than Elise's, his knowledge not far superior to that of a 20th century GP. Like his shipmates, Doc was primarily a trained crewman and colonist. His courses in world settling—"funny chemistry," water purification, basic mine engineering, exotic factor recognition, etc.—were largely guesswork. There were no interstellar colonies, not yet.

And bearing children would be an act of faith, a taking possession of the land. Some had fought the delay bitterly. The starship would have been smelling of babies shortly after takeoff if they'd had their way.

He offered Elise a pill. "Bacteria and earthworms come first. Men last," he said. "We're too high on the chain. We can't overload the ecology—"

"Uh huh."

"—before we've even got one. And look—"

She took a six-month birth control pill and swallowed it.

So Doc didn't say: suppose it doesn't work out? Suppose we have to go home? He passed out the pills and watched the women take them, crossing names off a list in his head.

The little robot trucks were all over the place now. Their flat beds were endless belts, and they followed a limited repertoire of voiced orders. They had the lander half unloaded already. When Doc had finished his pill pushing he went to work beside Elise, unloading crates. His thirty patients, including himself, were sickeningly healthy. As an unemployed doctor he'd have to do honest work until someone got ill.

He was wrong, of course. Doc had plenty of employment. His patients were doing manual labor in 1.07 gravities. They'd gained an average of ten pounds the moment the landing craft touched down. It threw their coordination and balance off, causing them to strain muscles and gash themselves.

One of the robot trucks ran over Chris's foot. Chris didn't wince or curse as Doc manipulated the bones, but his teeth ground silently together.

"All done here, Chris." Doc smiled. The meteorologist looked at him bleakly from behind wire-rimmed glasses, eyes blinking without emotion.

"Hey, you're a better man than I am. If I had a wound like that, I'd scream my head off—"

Something only vaguely like a smile crossed Chris's lips. "Thanks, Doc," he said, and limped out.

Remarkable control, Doc mused. But then again, that's Chris.

A week after landing, Ridgeback's nineteen-hour day caught up with them. Disrupted body rhythms are no joke; adding poor sleep to the weight adjustment led to chronic fatigue. Doc recognized the signs quickly.

"I'm surprised that it took this long," he said to Elise as she tossed, sleepless.

"Why couldn't we have done our adjusting on ship?" she mumbled, opening a bleary eye.

"There's more to it than just periods of light and darkness. Every planet has its own peculiarities. You just have to get used to them before your sleep cycles adjust."

"Well what am I supposed to do? Jesus, hand me the sleeping pills, wouldja please? I just want to sleep."

"Nope. Don't want anyone hooked on sleeping pills. We've got the 'russian sleep' sets. You'll have one tomorrow." The "russian sleep" headsets were much preferred over chemical sedatives. They produced unconsciousness with a tiny trickle of current through the brain.

"Good," Elise yawned. "Sunset and dawn, they both seem to come too soon."

The colony went up fast. It was all prefabs, makeshift and temporary, the streets cluttered with the tools, machinery and electric cables which nobody had put away because there was no place for them. Gradually places were made. Hydroponic tanks were assembled and stocked, and presently the colonists were back on fresh food.

Much more gradually, the stone houses began to appear.

They blasted their own rock from nearby cliffs with guncotton from the prefab chemical factory. They hauled the fractured stone on the robot trucks, and made concrete to stick it together. There was technology to spare, and endless power from the atomic motor in the landing craft. They took their time with the houses. Prefabs would weather the frequent warm rains for long enough. The stone houses were intended to last much longer. The colonists built thick walls, and left large spaces so that the houses could be expanded when later generations saw fit.

Doc squinted into the mirror, brushing his teeth with his usual precise vertical movements. He jumped when he felt a splash of hot water hit his back. "Cut that out, Elise," he laughed.

She settled back in her bathtub, wrinkling her nose at him. Three years of meager showers on the ship had left her dying for a real bathtub, where she could waste gallons of water without guilt.

"Spoilsport," she teased. "If you were any kind of fun, you'd come over here and . . ."

"And what?" he asked, interested.

"And rub my back."

"And that's supposed to be fun?"

"I was thinking that we could rub it with you." She grinned, seeing Doc's eyes light up. "And then maybe we could rub you with me . . ."

Later, they toweled each other off, still tingling. "Look!" Doc said, pulling her in front of the mirror. He studied her, marveling. Had Elise become prettier, or was he seeing her with new eyes? He knew she laughed louder and more often than when they had met years ago in school, she the child of a wealthy family and he a scholarship student who dreamt of the stars. He knew that her body was more firm and alive than it had been in her teens. The same sun that had burnt her body nut-brown had lightened her reddish hair to strawberry blond. She grinned at him from the mirror and asked, "Do you propose to take all the credit?"

He nodded happily. He'd always been fit, but his muscles had been stringy, the kind that didn't show. Now they bulged, handsome curves filling out chest and shoulders, legs strong from lifting and moving rock. His skin had darkened under the probing of a warm, friendly sun. He was sleeping well, and so was she.

All of the colonists were darker, more muscular, with thicker calluses on hands and feet. Under open sky or high ceilings they walked straighter than the men and women of Earth's cities. They talked more boldly and seemed to fill more space. In the cities of Earth, the ultimate luxury had been building space. It was beyond the means of all but the wealthiest. Here, there was land for the taking, and twelve-foot ceilings could be built. The house Doc was building for Elise—almost finished now—would be as fine as any her father could have built for her. One that would be passed on to their children, and then to their grandchildren . . .

She seemed to echo his thought. "One last step. I want a bulge, right here," and she patted her flat abdomen. "Your department."

"And Jill's. We're up to mammals already, and we're adjusting. I've got half the 'russian sleep' sets back in the infirmary already."

The Orion spacecraft was a big, obtrusive object, mace-shaped, cruising constantly across the sky. What had been a fifth of a mile of deuterium snowball, the fuel supply for the starship's battery of laser-fusion motors, was now a thin, shiny skin, still inflated by the residue of deuterium gas.

It was the head of the mace. The life support system, ending in motors and shock absorbers, formed the handle.

Roy had taken the ground-to-orbit craft up and was aboard the Orion now, monitoring the relay as Cynnie beamed her holotape up. It was lonely. Once there had been too little room; now there was too much. The ship still smelled of too many people crowded too close for too long. Roy adjusted the viewscreen and grinned back at Cynnie's toothy smile.

"This is Year Day on Ridgeback," she said in her smooth announcer's voice. "It was a barren world when we came. Now, slowly, life is spreading across the land. The farming teams have spent this last year dredging mulch from the sea bed and boiling it to kill the native life. Now it grows the tame bacteria that will make our soil." The screen showed a sequence of action scenes: tractors plowing furrows in the harsh dirt; colonists glistening with sweat as they pulled boulders from the ground; and Jill supervising the spreading of the starter soil. Grass seed and earthworms were sown into the trenches, and men and machines worked together to fold them into the earth.

Cynnie had mounted a camera on one of the small flyers for an aerial view. "The soil is being spread along a ten-mile strip," she said, "and grains are being planted. Later we'll have fruit trees and shade trees, bamboo and animal feed."

It was good, Roy thought, watching. It was smooth. Getting it all had been rough enough. Before they were finished the colonists had become damn sick of Roy and Cynnie poking their cameras into their every activity. That sign above the auditorium toilet: Smile! Roy Is Watching!

He'd tried to tell them. "Don't you know who it is that builds starships? It's taxpayers, that's who! And they've got to get something for their money. Sure we're putting on a show for them. If we don't, when election time comes around they may ask for a refund."

Oh, they probably believed him. But the sign was still up.

Roy watched Cynnie interview Jase and Brew in the fields; watched Angie and Chris constructing the animal pens. Jill thawed some of the fertilized goat eggs and a tape was shown of the wriggling embryos.

"At first," Cynnie reminisced, "Ridgeback was daunting. There was no sound: no crickets, no birdsongs, but no roar of traffic either. By day, the sky is Earthlike enough, but by night the constellations are brighter. It's impossible to forget how far from home we are—we can't even see Sol, invisible somewhere in the northern hemisphere. It's hard to forget that no help of any kind could come in much less than twenty-five years. It would take five years just to refuel the ship. It takes fourteen years to make the trip, although thanks to relativity it was only three years 'ship time.'

"Yes, we are alone." The image of Cynnie's sober face segued to the town hall, a geodesic dome of metal tubing sprayed with plastic. "But it is heartening that we have found, in each other, the makings of a community. We come together for midday meal, discussions, songfests and group worship services."

Cynnie's face was calm now, comforting. "We have no crime, and no unemployment. We're much too busy for marital squabbles or political infighting." She grinned, and the sparkle of her personality brought pleasure to Roy's analytical mind. "In fact, I have work to do myself. So, until next year, this is Cynnie Mitchell on Ridgeback, signing off."

A year and a half after landing, a number of animals were out of incubation with a loss of less than two percent. The mammals drank synthetic milk now, but soon they would be milling in their pens, eating Ridgeback grass and adding their own rich wastes to the cooking compost heaps.

Friday night was community night at the town hall.

From the inside the ribs of the dome were still visible through the sprayed plastic walls, and some of the decorations were less than stylish, but it was a warm place, a friendly, relaxing place where the common bond between the Ridgebackers was strengthened.

Jill, especially, seemed to love the stage, and took every opportunity to mount it, almost vibrating with her infectious energy.

"Everything's right on schedule," she said happily. "The fruit flies are breeding like mad." (Booo!) "And if I hear that again I'm gonna break out the mosquitoes. Gang, there are things we can live without, but we don't know what they are yet. Chances are we'll be raising the sharks sooner or later. We've been lucky so far. Really lucky." She cleared her throat dramatically. "And speaking of luck, we have Chris with some good news for the farmers, and bad news for the sunbathers. Chris?"

There was scattered applause, most vigorously from Chris's tiny wife Angie. He walked to the lectern and adjusted the microphone before speaking.

"We, uh," he took off his glasses, polishing them on his shirt, then replaced them, smiling nervously. "We've been having good weather, people, but there's a storm front moving over the mountains. I think Greg can postpone the irrigation canals for a week, we're going to get plenty wet."

He coughed, and moved the microphone close to his mouth. "June and I are working to program the atmospheric model into the computer. Until we do, weather changes will keep catching us unaware. We have to break down a fairly complex set of thermo and barometric dynamics into something that can be dealt with systematically—wind speed, humidity, vertical motion, friction, pressure gradients, and a lot of other factors still have to be fed in, but we're making progress. Maybe next year we'll be able to tell you how to dress for the tenth anniversary of Landing Day."

There were derisive snorts and laughter, and Chris was applauded back into his seat.

Jase bounded onto the stage and grabbed the mike. "Any more announcements? No? All right, then, we all voted on tonight's movie, so no groans, please. Lights?"

The auditorium dimmed. He slipped from the stage and the twin beams of the holo projector flickered onto the screen.

It was a war movie, shot in flatfilm but optically reconstructed to simulate depth. Doc found it boring. He slipped out during a barrage of cannon fire. He headed to the lab and found Jill there already, using one of the small microscopes.

"Hi hon," he called out, flipping on his desk light. "Working late?"

"Well, I'm maybe just a wee bit more bugged than I let on. Just a little."

"About what?"

"I keep thinking that one day we'll find out that we left something out of our tame ecology. It's just a feeling, but it won't go away."

"Like going on vacation," Doc said, deliberately flippant. "You know you forgot something. You'd just rather it was your toothbrush and not your passport."

She smeared a cover glass over a drop of fluid on a slide and set it to dry. "Yes, it feels like that."

"Do you really have mosquitoes in storage?"

She twinkled and nodded. "Yep. Hornets too."

"Just how good is it going? You know how impatient everyone is."

"No real problems. There sure as hell might have been, but thanks to my superior planning—" She stuck out her tongue at Doc's grimace. "We'll have food for ourselves and all the children we can raise. I've been getting a little impatient myself, you know? As if there's a part of me that isn't functioning at full efficiency."

Doc laughed. "Then I think you'd better tell Greg."

"I'll do better. I'll announce it tonight and let all the fathers-to-be catch the tidings in one shot."

"Oh boy."

"What?"

"No, it has to be done that way. I know it. I'm just thinking about nine months from now. Oh boy."

So it was announced that evening. As Doc might have expected, someone had already cheated. Somehow Nat, the midwestern earthmother blond, had taken a contraceptive pill and, even with Doc watching, had avoided swallowing it. Doc was fairly sure that her husband Brew knew nothing of it, although she was already more than four months along when she confessed.

Nat had jumped the gun, and there wasn't a woman on Ridgeback who didn't envy her. A year and eleven months after Landing Day, Doc delivered Ridgeback's first baby.

Sleepy, exhausted by her hours of labor, Nat looked at her baby with a pride that was only half maternal. Her face was flushed, yellow hair tangled in mats with perspiration and fatigue. She held her baby, swaddled in blankets, at her side. "I can hear them outside. What do they want?" she asked drowsily, fighting to keep her eyelids open.

Doc breathed deeply. Ridiculous, but the scentless air of Ridgeback seemed a little sweeter. "They're waiting for a glimpse of the little crown princess."

"Well, she's staying here. Tell them she's beautiful," Ridgeback's first mother whispered, and dropped off to sleep.

Doc washed his hands and dried them on a towel. He stood above the slumbering pair, considering. Then he gently pried the baby from her mother's grip and took her in his arms. Half-conscious mother's wish or no, the infant must be shown to the colony before they could rest. Especially Brew. He could see the Swede's great broad hands knotting into nervous fists as he waited outside. And the rest of them in a half-crescent around the door; and the inevitable Cynnie and Roy with their holotape cameras.

"It's a girl," he told them. "Nat's resting comfortably." The baby was red as a tomato and looked as fragile as Venetian glass. She and Doc posed for the camera, then Doc left her with Brew to make a short speech.

Elise and Greg, Jill's husband, had both had paramedic training. Doc set up a rotating eight-hour schedule for the three of them, starting with Elise. The group outside was breaking up as he left, but he managed to catch Jase.

"I'd like to be taken off work duties for a while," he told the colony leader, when the two were alone.

Jase gripped his arm. "Something's wrong with the baby?" There was a volume of concern in the question.

"I doubt it, but she is the first, and I want to watch her and Nat. Most of the women are pregnant now. I want to keep an eye on them, too."

"You're not worried about anything specific?"

"No."

When Elise left her shift at the maternity ward, she found him staring at the stone ceiling. She asked, "Insomnia again? Shall I get a 'russian sleep' set?"

"No."

She studied his face. "The baby?"

She'd seen it too, then. "You just left the baby. She's fine, isn't she?"

"They're both fine. Sleeping. Harry?" She was the only one who called him that. "What is it?"

"No, nothing's bothering me. You know everything *I* know. It's just that . . ."

"Well?"

"It's just that I want to do everything right. This is so important. So I keep checking back on myself, because there's no one I can call in to check my work. Can you understand what I'm getting at?"

She pursed her lips. Then said, "I know that the only baby in the world could get a lot more attention than she needs. There shouldn't be too many people around her, and they should all be smiling. That's important to a baby."

Doc watched as she took off her clothes and got into bed. The slight swell of her pregnancy was just beginning to show. Within six months there would be nine more children on Ridgeback, and one would be theirs.

Predictably, Brew's and Nat's daughter became Eve.

It seemed nobody but Doc had noticed anything odd about Eve. Even laymen know better than to expect a newborn child to be pretty. A baby doesn't begin to look like a baby until it is weeks old. The cherubs of the Renaissance paintings of Foucquet or Conegliano were taken from two-year-olds. Naturally Eve looked odd, and most of the colony, who had never seen newborn children, took it in their stride. . . .

But Doc worried.

The ship's library was a world's library. It was more comprehensive, and held more microfilm and holographically encoded information than any single library on Earth. Doc spent weeks running through medical tapes, and got no satisfaction thereby.

Eve wasn't sick. She was a "good baby"; she gave no more trouble than usual, and no less. Nat had no difficulty nursing her, which was good, as there were no adult cows available on Ridgeback.

Doc pulled a microfiche chip out of the viewer and yawned irritably. The last few weeks had cost him his adjustment to Ridgeback time, and gained him . . . well, a kind of general education in pediatrics. There was nothing specific to look for, no *handle* on the problem.

Bluntly put, Eve was an ugly baby.

There was nothing more to say, and nothing to do but wait.

Roy and Cynnie showed their tapes for the year. Cynnie had a good eye for detail. Until he watched the camera view trucking from the landing craft past the line of houses on Main Street, to Brew, to a closeup of Brew's house, Doc had never noticed how Brew's house reflected Brew himself. It was designed like the others: tall and squarish, with a sloped roof and small window. But the stones in Brew's house were twice the size of those in Doc's house. Brew was proud of his strength.

Roy was in orbit on Year Day, but Cynnie stayed to cover the festivities, such as they were. Earth's hypothetical eager audience still hadn't seen Year Day One. Jase spoke for the camera, comparing the celebration with the first Thanksgiving Day in New England. He was right: it was a feast, a display of the variety of foods Ridgeback was now producing, and not much more than that.

His wife June sang a nondenominational hymn, and they all followed along, each in his own key. Nat fed Eve a bit of corncake and fruit juice, and the colonists applauded Eve's gurgling smile.

The folks back on Earth might not have thought it very exciting, but to the Ridgebackers it meant everything. This was food they had grown themselves. All of them had bruises or blisters or calluses from weeding or harvesting. They were more than a community now, they were a world, and the fresh fruit and vegetables, and the hot breads, tasted better than anything they could have imagined.

Six months after the birth of Eve, Doc was sure. There was a problem.

The children of Ridgeback totaled seven. Two of the women had miscarried, fewer than he might have feared, and without complications. Jill was still carrying hers, and Doc was beginning to wonder, but it wasn't serious yet. Jill was big and strong with wide hips and a deep bust. Even now Greg was hard put to keep her from commandeering one of the little flyers and jouncing off to the coastline to check the soil, or inland to supervise the fresh water fish preserve. Give her another week . . .

The night Elise had delivered their child, it had been special. She had had a dry birth, with the water sack rupturing too early, and Doc had had to use a lubrication device. Elise was conscious during the entire delivery, eschewing painkillers for the total experience of her first birth. She delivered safely, for which Doc had given silent thanks. His nerves were scraped to supersensitivity, and he found himself just sitting and holding her hand, whispering affection and encouragement to her, while Greg did much of the work. With Elise's approval he named their son Gerald, shortened to Jerry. Jerry was three weeks old now, healthy and squalling, with a ferocious grip in his tiny hands.

But even a father's pride could not entirely hide the squarish jawline, the eyes, the . . .

All the children had it, all the six recent ones. And Eve hadn't lost it. Doc continued his research in the microlibrary, switching from pediatrics to genetics. He had a microscope and an electron microscope, worth their hundreds of thousands of dollars in transportation costs; he had scrapings of his own flesh and Eve's and Jerry's. What he lacked was a Nobel Prize geneticist to stand behind his shoulder and point out what were significant deviations as opposed to his own poor slide preparation techniques.

He caught Brew looking at him at mealtimes, as though trying to raise the nerve to speak. Soon the big man would break through his inhibitions, Doc could see it coming. Or perhaps Nat would broach the question. Her eldest brother had been retarded, and Doc knew she was sensitive about it. How long could it be before that pain rose to the surface?

And what would he say to them then?

It was not a mutation. One could hardly expect the same mutation to hit all of seven couples in the same way.

It was no disease. The children were phenomenally healthy.

So Doc worked late into the night, sometimes wearing a black scowl as he retraced dead ends. He needed advice, and advice was 11.9 light years away. Was he seeing banshees? Nobody else had noticed anything. Naturally not; the children all looked normal, for they all looked alike. Only Brew seemed disturbed. Hell, it was probably Doc that was worrying Brew, just as it was Doc that worried Elise. He ought to spend more time with Elise and Jerry.

Jill lost her baby. It was stillborn, pitiful in its frailty. Jill turned to Greg as the dirt showered down on the cloth that covered her child, biting her lip savagely, trying to stop the tears. She and her husband held each other for a long moment, then, with the rest of the colonists, they walked back to the dwellings.

The colonists had voted early, and unanimously, to give up coffins on Ridgeback. Humans who died here would give their bodies to the conquest of the planet. Doc wondered if a coffin would have made this ceremony easier, more comforting in its tradition. Probably not, he thought. Dead is dead.

Doc went home with Elise. He'd been spending more time there lately, and less time with the microscopes. Jerry was crawling now, and he crawled everywhere; you had to watch him like a hawk. He could pick his parents unerringly out of a crowd of adults, and he would scamper across the floor, cooing, his eyes alight . . . his deepset brown eyes.

It was a week later that Jase came to him. After eight hours of labor June had finally released her burden. For a newborn infant the body was big and strong, though in any normal context he was a fragile, precious thing. As father, Jase was entitled to see him first. He looked down at his son and said, "He's just like the others." His eyes and his voice were hollow, and at that moment Doc could no longer see the jovial colony leader who called squaredances at the weekly hoedown.

"Of course he is."

"Look, don't con me, Doc. I was eight when Cynnie was born. She didn't look like any of them. And she never looked like Eve."

"Don't you think that's for me to say?"

"Yes. And damned quick!"

Doc rubbed his jaw, considering. If he was honest with himself he had to admit he ached to talk to somebody. "Let's make it tomorrow. In the ship's library."

Jase's strong hand gripped his arm. "Now."

"Tomorrow, Jase. I've got a lot to say, and there are things in the library you ought to see."

"Here," he said, dialing swiftly. A page appeared on the screen, three-quarters illustration, and one-quarter print to explain it. "Notice the head? And the hands. Eve's fingers are longer than that. Her forehead slopes more. But look at these." He conjured up a series of growth states paired with silhouettes of bone structure.

"So?"

"She's maturing much faster than normal."

"Oh."

"At first I didn't think anything about the head. Any infant's head is distorted during passage from the uterus. It goes back to normal if the birth wasn't difficult. And you can't tell much from the features; all babies look pretty much alike. But the hands and arms bothered me."

"And now?"

"See for yourself. Her face is too big and her skull is too small and too flat. And I don't like the jaw, or the thin lips." Doc rubbed his eyes wearily. "And there's the hair. That much hair isn't unheard of at that age, but taken with everything else . . . you can see why I was worried."

"And all the kids look just like her. Even Jase Junior."

"Even Jerry. And Jill's stillbirth."

In the ship's library there was a silence as of mourning.

Jase said, "We'll have to tell Earth. The colony is a failure."

Doc shook his head. "We'd better see how it develops first."

"We can't have normal children, Doc."

"I'm not ready to give up, Jase. And if it's true, we can't go back to Earth, either."

"What? Why?"

"This thing isn't a mutation. Not in us, it can't be. What it could be is a virus replacing some of the genes. A virus is a lot like a free-floating chromosome anyway. If we've got a disease that keeps us from having normal children—''

''That's stupid. A virus here, waiting for us, where there's nothing for it to live on but plankton? You—''

''No, no, no. It had to come with us. Something like the common cold could have mutated aboard ship. There was enough radiation outside the shielding. Someone sneezes in the airlock before he puts his helmet on. A year later someone else inhales the mutant.''

Jase thought it through. ''We can't take it back to Earth.''

''Right. So what's the hurry? It'd be twenty-four years before they could answer a cry for help. Let's take our time and find out what we've really got.''

''Doc, in God's name, what can we tell the others?''

''Nothing yet. When the time comes I'll tell them.''

Those few months were a busy time for Ridgeback's doctor. Then they were over. The children were growing, and most of the women were pregnant, including Angie and Jill, who had both had miscarriages. Never again would all the women of Ridgeback be having children in one ear-shattering population explosion.

Now there was little work for Doc. He spoke to Jase, who put him on the labor routines. Most of the work was agricultural, with the heavy jobs handled by machines. Robot trucks, trailing plows, scored rectangular patterns across the land.

The fenced bay was rich in Earthborn plankton, and now there were larger forms to eat the plankton. Occasionally Greg opened the filter to let discolored water spread out into the world, contaminating the ocean.

At night the colonists watched news from Earth, 11.9 years in transit, and up to a year older before Roy boarded the starship to beam it down. They strung the program out over the year in hour segments to make it last longer. There were no wars in progress, to speak of; the Procyon colony project had been abandoned; Macrostructures Inc. was still trying to build an interstellar ramjet. It all seemed very distant.

Jase came whistling into Doc's lab, but backed out swiftly when he saw that he had interrupted a counseling session with Cynnie and Roy. Doc was the closest thing the colony had to a marriage therapist. Jase waited outside until the pair had left, then trotted in.

''Rough day?''

''Yeah. Jase, Roy and Cynnie don't fight, do they?''

"They never did. They're like twins. Married people do get to be like each other, but those two overdo it sometimes."

"I knew it. There's something wrong, but it's not between them." Doc rubbed his eyes on his sleeve. "They were sounding me out, trying to get me talking about the children without admitting they're scared. Anyway . . . what's up?"

Jase brought his hands from behind his back. He had two bamboo poles rigged for fishing. "What say we exercise our manly prerogatives?"

"Ye gods! In our private spawning ground?"

"Why not? It's big enough. There are enough fish. And we can't let the surplus go; they'd starve. It's a big ocean."

By now the cultivated strip of topsoil led tens of miles north and south along the continent. Jill claimed that life would spread faster that way, outward from the edges of the strip. The colony was raising its own chicken eggs and fruit and vegetables. On Landing Day they'd been the first in generations to taste moa meat, whose rich flavor had come *that* close to making the New Zealand bird extinct. Why shouldn't they catch their own fish?

They made a full weekend of it. They hauled a prefab with them on the flyer and set it up on the barren shore. For three days they fished with the springy bamboo poles. The fish were eager and trusting. They ate some of their catch, and stored the rest for later.

On the last day Jase said, "I kept waiting to see you lose some of that uptight look. You finally have, a little, I think."

"Yeah. I'm glad this happened, Jase."

"Okay. What about the children?"

He didn't need to elaborate. Doc said, "They'll never be normal."

"Then what are they?"

"I dunno. How do you tell people who came twelve light-years to build a world that their heirs will be . . ." he groped for words. "Whatever. Changed. Animals."

"Christ. What a mess."

"Give me time to tell Elise . . . if she hasn't guessed by now. Maybe she has."

"How long?"

"A week, maybe. Give us time to be off with Jerry. Might make it easier if we're with him."

"Or harder."

"Yeah, there's that." He cast his line out again. "Anyway, she'll keep the secret, and she'd never forgive me if I didn't tell her first. And you'd better tell June the night before I make the big announcement." The words seemed to catch in his throat and he hung his head, miserable.

Tentatively Jase said, "It's absolutely nobody's fault."

"Oh, sure. I was just thinking about the last really big announcement

I helped to make. Years ago. Seems funny now, doesn't it? 'It's safe, people. You can start dreaming now. Go ahead and have those babies, folks. It's all right . . .' " His voice trailed off and he looked to Jase in guilty confusion. "What could I do, Jase? It's like thalidomide. In the beginning, it all looked so wonderful."

Jase was silent, listening to the sound of water lapping against the boat. "I just hate to tell Earth, that's all," he finally said in a low voice. "It'll be like giving up. Even if we solve this thing, they'd never risk sending another ship."

"But we've got to warn them."

"Doc, what's *happening* to us?"

"I don't know."

"How hard have you—no, never mind." Jase pulled his line in, baited it and sent it whipping out again. Long silences are in order when men talk and fish.

"Jase, I'd give anything I have to know the answer. Some of the genes look different in the electron microscope. Maybe. Hell, it's all really too fuzzy to tell, and I don't really know what it means anyway. None of my training anticipated anything like *this*. *You* try to think of something."

"Alien invasion."

Pause. "Oh, really?"

Jase's line jumped. He wrestled in a deep sea bass and freed the hook. He said, "It's the safest, most painless kind of invasion. They find a world they want, but there's an intelligent species in control. So they design a virus that will keep us from bearing intelligent children. After we're gone they move in at their leisure. If they like they can use a countervirus, so the children can bear human beings again for slaves."

The bamboo pole seemed dead in Doc's hands. He said, "That's uglier than anything I've thought of."

"Well?"

"Could be. Insufficient data. If it's true, it's all the more reason to warn Earth. But Ridgeback is doomed."

Jerry had his mother's hair, sunbleached auburn. He had too much of it. On his narrow forehead it merged with his brows . . . his shelf of brow, and the brown eyes watching from way back. He hardly needed the shorts he was wearing; the hair would have been almost enough. He was nearly three.

He seemed to sense something wrong between his parents. He would spend some minutes scampering through the grove of sapling fruit trees, agile as a child twice his age; then suddenly return to take their hands and try to tug them both into action.

Doc thought of the frozen fertilized eggs of dogs in storage. Jerry with a dog . . . the thought was repulsive. Why? Shouldn't a child have a dog?

"Well, of course I guessed *something*," Elise said bitterly. "You were always in the library. When you were home, the way that you looked at Jerry . . . and me, come to think of it. I see now why you haven't taken me to bed much lately." She'd been avoiding his eyes, but now she looked full at him. "I *do* see. But, Harry, couldn't you have asked me for help? I have some medical knowledge, and, I'm your wife, and Jerry's mother, damn it, Harry!"

"Would you believe I didn't want you worrying?"

"Oh, really? How did it work?"

Her sarcasm cut deep. Bleeding, he said, "Nothing worked."

Jerry came out of the trees at a tottering run. Doc stood up, caught him, swung him around, chased him through the trees . . . came back puffing, smiling, holding his hand. He almost lost the smile, but Elise was smiling back, with some effort. She hugged Jerry, then pulled fried chicken from the picnic basket and offered it around.

She said, "That alien invasion idea is stupid."

"Granted. It'd be easy to think someone has 'done' it to us."

"Haven't you found anything? Isn't there anything I can help with?"

"I've found a lot. All the kids have a lower body temperature, two point seven degrees. They're healthy as horses, but hell, who would they catch measles from? Their brain capacity is too small, and not much of it is frontal lobe. They're hard to toilet train and they should have started babbling, at least, long ago. What counts is the brain, of course."

Elise took one of Jerry's small hands. Jerry crawled into her lap and she rocked him. "His hands are okay. Human. His eyes . . . are brown, like yours. His cheekbones are like yours, too. High and a little rounded."

Doc tried to smile. "His eyes look a little strange. They're not really slanted enough to suspect mongolism, but I'll bet there's a gene change. But where do I go from there? I can see differences, and they're even consistent, but there's no precedent for the analysis equipment to extrapolate from." Doc looked disgusted. Elise touched his cheek, understanding.

"Can you teach me to use an electron microscope?"

Doc sat at the computer console, watching over Jill's shoulder as she brought out the Orion vehicle's image of Ridgeback. The interstellar spacecraft doubled as a weather eye, and the picture, once drab with browns and grays, now showed strips of green beneath the fragmented cloud cover. If Ridgeback was dead, it certainly didn't show on the screen.

"Well, we've done a fair old job." Jill grinned and took off her headset. Her puffy natural had collected dust and seeds and vegetable fluff until she gave up and shaved it off. The tightly curled mat just covered her scalp now, framing her chocolate cameo features. "The cultivated strip has spread like weeds. All along the continent now I get CO_2-oxygen exchange. It jumped the ridges last year, and now I get readings on the western side."

"Are you happy?"

"No," she said slowly. "I've done my job. Is it too much to want a child too? I wouldn't care about the . . . problem. I just want . . ."

"It's nobody's fault," Doc said helplessly.

"I know, I know. But two miscarriages. Couldn't they have known back on Earth? Wasn't there any way to be sure? Why did I have to come all this way . . ." She caught herself and smiled thinly. "I guess I should count my blessings. I'm better off than poor Angie."

"Poor Angie," Doc echoed sadly. How could they have known about Chris? The night Doc announced his conclusions about the children, there had been tears and harsh words, but no violence. But then there was Chris.

Chris, who had wanted a child more than any of them could have known. Who had suffered silently through Angie's first miscarriage, who hoped and prayed for the safe delivery of their second effort.

It had been an easy birth.

And the morning after Doc's speech, the three of them, Chris, Angie and the baby, were found in the quiet of their stone house, the life still ebbing from Chris's eyes and the gaps in his wrists.

"I'm sorry," he said over and over, shaking his head as if he were cold, his watery brown eyes dulling. "I just couldn't take it. I just . . . I just . . ." and he died. The three of them were buried in the cemetery outside of town, without coffins.

The town was different after the deaths, a stifling quiet hanging in the streets. Few colonists ate at the communal meals, choosing to take their suppers at home.

In an effort to bring everyone together, Jase encouraged them to come to town hall for Movie Night.

The film was *The Sound of Music*. The screen erupted with sound and color, dazzling green Alps and snow-crested mountains, happy song and the smiling faces of normal, healthy children.

Half the colonists walked out.

Most of the women took contraceptives now, except those who chose not to tamper with their estrogen balance. For these, Doc performed painless menstrual extractions bimonthly.

Nat and Elise insisted on having more children. Maybe the problem only affected the firstborn, they argued. Doc fought the idea at first. He found himself combating Brew's sullen withdrawal, Nat's frantic insistence, and a core of hot anger in his own wife.

Earth could find a cure. It was possible. Then their grandchildren would be normal again, the heirs to a world.

He gave in.

But all the children were the same. In the end, Nat alone had not given up. She had borne five children, and was carrying her sixth.

The message of failure was halfway to Earth, but any reply was still nineteen years away. Doc had adapted the habit of talking things over with Jase, hoping that he would catch some glimpse of a solution.

"I still think it's a disease," he told Jase, who had heard that before, but didn't mention it. The bay was quiet and their lines were still. They talked only during fishing trips. They didn't want the rest of the colony brooding any more than they already were. "A mutant virus. But I've been wondering, could the changes have screwed us up? A shorter day, a longer year, a little heavier gravity. Different air mixture. No common cold, no mosquito bites; even that could be the key."

On a night like this, in air this clear, you could even see starglades casting streaks across the water. A fish jumped far across the bay, and phosphorescence lit that patch of water for a moment. The Orion vehicle, mace-shaped, rose out of the west, past the blaze of the Pleiades. Roy would be rendezvousing with it now, preparing for tomorrow's Year Day celebration.

Jase seemed to need these trips even more than Doc. After the murders the life seemed to have gone out of him, only flashes of his personality coming through at tranquil times like these. He asked, "Are you going to have Jill breed mosquitoes?"

". . . Yes."

"I think you're reaching. Weren't you looking at the genes in the cytoplasm?"

"Yeah. Elise's idea, and it was a good one. I'd forgotten there were genes outside the cell nucleus. They control the big things, you know: not the shape of your fingers, but how many you get, and where. But they're hard to find, Jase. And maybe we found some differences between our genes and the children's, but even the computer doesn't know what the difference *means*."

"Mosquitoes." Jase shook his head. "We know there's a fish down that way. Shall we go after him?"

"We've got enough. Have to be home by morning. Year Day."

"What exactly are we celebrating *this* time?"

"Hell, you're the mayor. You think of something." Doc sulked, watching the water ripple around his float. "Jase, we can't give up—"

Jase's face was slack with horror, eyes cast up to the sky. Doc followed his gaze, to where a flaring light blossomed behind the Orion spacecraft.

"Oh my God," Jase rasped, "Roy's up there."

Throwing his bamboo pole in the water, Jase started the engine and raced for shore.

Doc studied the readouts carefully. "Mother of God," he whispered. "How many engines did he fire?"

"Six." Jill's eyes were glued to the screen, her voice flat. "If he was aboard, he . . . well, there isn't much chance he survived the acceleration. Most of the equipment up there must be junk now."

"But what if he *did* survive? Is there a chance?"

"I don't know. Roy was getting set to beam the messages down, but said that he had an alarm to handle first. He went away for a while, and . . ." she seemed to search for words. She whispered, "Boom."

"If he was outside the ship, in one of the little rocket sleds, he could get to the shuttle vehicle."

Jase walked heavily into the lab.

"What about Cynnie? What did she say?" Doc asked quickly.

Jase's face was blank of emotion. "She talked to him before the . . . accident."

"And?"

"It's all she would say. I'm afraid she took it pretty bad. This was sort of the final straw." His eyes were hollow as he reminisced. "She was always a brave kid, you know? Anything I could do, she'd be right behind me, measuring up to big brother. There's just a limit, that's all. There's just a limit."

Doc's voice was firm, only a slight edge of unease breaking through his control. "I think we had better face it. Roy is dead. The Orion's ruined, and the shuttle-craft is gone anyway."

"He could be alive . . ." Jill ventured.

Doc tried to take the sting out of his voice, and was not entirely successful. "Where? On the ship, crushed to a paste? Not on the shuttle. It's tumbling further from the Orion every second. There's no one on it. In one of the rocket sleds?" His face softened, and they could see that he was afraid to have hope. "Yes. Maybe that. Maybe on one of the sleds."

They nodded to each other, and they and the other colonists spent long hours on the telescope hoping, and praying.

But there was nothing alive up there now. Ridgeback was entirely alone.

. . .

Cynnie never recovered. She would talk only to her brother, refusing even to see her child. She was morose and ate little, spending most of her time watching the sky with something like terrified awe in her eyes.

And one day, seven months after the accident, she walked into the woods and never returned.

Doc hadn't seen Jerry for three weeks.

The children lived in a community complex which had some of the aspects of a boarding school. The colonists took turns at nursing duty. Jill spent most of her time there since she and Greg were on the outs. Lately, Elise had taken up the habit too. Not that he blamed her; he couldn't have been very good company the last few months.

Parents took their children out to the T-shaped complex whenever they felt like it, so that some of the children had more freedom than others. But by and large they all were expected to live there eventually.

Brew was coming out of the woods with a group of six children when Doc stumbled out into the sunlight and saw Jerry.

He wore a rough pair of coveralls that fit him well enough, but he would have looked ludicrous if there had been anything to laugh about. Soft brown fur covered every inch of him. As Doc appeared he turned his head with a bird-quick movement, saw his father, and scampered over. Jerry bounced into him, wrapped long arms tight about his rib cage and said, eagerly, "Daddy."

There was a slight pause.

"Hello, Jerry." Doc slowly bent to the ground, looking into his son's eyes.

"Daddy Doc, Daddy Doc," he chattered, smiling up at his father. His vocabulary was about fifteen words. Jerry was six years old and much too big for his age. His fingers were very long and strong, but his thumbs were small and short and inconsequential. Doc had seen him handle silverware without much trouble. His nose pugged, jaw massive with a receding chin. There were white markings in the fur around his eyes, accentuating the heavy supraorbital ridges, making the poor child look like—

The poor child. Doc snorted with self-contempt. *Listen to me. Why not my child?*

Because I'm ashamed. Because we lock our children away to ease the pain. Because they look like—

Doc gently disengaged Jerry's fingers from his shirt, turned and half-ran back to the ship. Shivering, he curled up on one of the cots and cursed himself to sleep.

Hours later he roused himself and, woozy with fatigue, he went looking for Jase. He found him on a work detail in the north fields, picking fruit.

"I'm not sure," he told Jase. "They're not old enough for me to be sure. But I want your opinion."

"Show me," said Jase, and followed him to the library.

The picture on the tape was an artist's rendering of Pithecanthropus erectus. He stood on a grassy knoll looking warily out at the viewer, his long-fingered hand clutching a sharp-edged throwing rock.

"I'll smack your head," said Jase.

"I'm wrong, then?"

"You're calling them apes!"

"I'm not. Read the copy. Pithecanthropus was a small-brained Pleistocene primate, thought to be a transitional stage between ape and man. You got that? Pith is also called Java Man."

Jase glared at the reader. "The markings are different. And there is the fur—"

"Forget 'em. They're nothing but guesswork. All the artist had to go on were crumbling bones and some broken rocks."

"Broken rocks?"

"Pith used to break rocks in half to get an edged weapon. It was about the extent of his tool-making ability. All we know about what he looked like comes from fossilized bones—very much like the skeleton of a stoop-shouldered man with foot trouble, topped with the skull of an ape with hydrocephalus."

"Very nice. Will Eve's children be fish?"

"I don't know, dammit. I don't know anything at all. Look, Pith isn't the only candidate for missing link. Homo Habilis looked a lot more like us and lived about two million years ago. Kenyapithicus Africanus resembled us less, but lived eighteen million years earlier. So I can't say what we've got here. God only knows what the next generation will be like. That depends on whether the children are moving backwards or maybe sideways. I don't know, Jase, I just don't *know*!" The last words were shrill, and Doc punctuated them by slamming his fist against a wire window screen. Then, because he could think of nothing more to say, he did it again. And again. And—

Jase caught his arm. Three knuckles were torn and bleeding. "Get some sleep," he said, eyes sad. "I'll have them send Earth a description of Eve the way she is now. She's oldest, and best developed. We'll send them all we have on her. It's all we can do."

Momentum and the thoroughness of their training had kept them going for eight years. Now the work of making a world slowed and stopped.

It didn't matter. The crops and the meat animals had no natural enemies on Ridgeback. Life spread along the continent like a green plague. Already it had touched some of the islands.

Doc was gathering fruit in the groves. It was a shady place, cool, quiet, and it made for a tranquil day's work. There was no set quota. You took home approximately a third of what you gathered. Sometimes he worked there, and sometimes he helped with the cattle, examining for health and pregnancy, or herding the animals with the nonlethal sonic stunners.

He wished that Elise were here with him, so they could laugh together, but that was growing infrequent now. She was growing more involved with the nursery, and he spent little of his time there.

Jill's voice hailed him from the bottom of the ladder. "Hey up there, Doc. How about a break?"

He grinned and climbed down, hauling a sack of oranges.

"Tired of spending the day reading, I guess," she said lightly. She offered him an apple. He polished it on his shirt and took a bite. "Just needed to talk to somebody."

"Kinda depressed?"

"Oh, I don't know. I guess it's just getting hard to cope with some of the problems."

"I guess there have been a few."

Jill gave a derisive chuckle. "I sure don't know Greg anymore. Ever since he set up the brewery and the distillery, he doesn't really want to see me at all."

"Don't take it so hard," Doc comforted. "The strain is showing on all of us. Half the town does little more than read or play tapes or drink. Personally, I'd like to know who smuggled the hemp seeds on board."

Jill laughed, which he was glad for, then her face grew serious again. "You know, there'd probably be more trouble if we didn't need someone to look after the kids." She paused, looking up at Doc. "I spend a lot of my time there," she said unnecessarily.

"Why?" It was the first time he'd asked. They had left the groves and were heading back into town along the gravel road that Greg and Brew and the others had built in better days.

"We . . . I came here for a reason. To continue the human race, to cross a new frontier, one that my children could have a part in. Now, now that we know that the colony is doomed, there's just no motive to anything. No reason. I'm surprised that there isn't more drinking, more carousing and foursomes and divorces and everything else. Nothing seems to matter a whole lot. Nothing at all."

Doc took her by the shoulders and held her. Go on and cry, he silently said to her. God, I'm tired.

. . .

The children grew fast. At nine Eve reached puberty and seemed to shoot skyward. She grew more hair. She learned more words, but not many more. She spent much of her time in the trees in the children's complex. The older girls grew almost as fast as she did, and the boys.

Every Saturday Brew and Nat took some of the children walking. Sometimes they climbed the foothills at the base of the continental range; sometimes they wandered through the woods, spending most of their efforts keeping the kids from disappearing into the trees.

One Saturday they returned early, their faces frozen in anger. Eve and Jerry were missing. At first they refused to discuss it, but when Jase began organizing a search party, they talked.

They'd been ready to turn for home when Eve suddenly scampered into the trees. Jerry gave a whoop and followed her. Nat had left the others with Brew while she followed after the refugees.

It proved easy to find them, and easier still to determine what they were doing with each other when she came upon them.

Eve looked up at Nat, innocent eyes glazed with pleasure. Nat trembled for a moment, horrified, then drove them both away with a stick, screaming filth at them.

Over Nat's vehement objections and Brew's stony refusal to join, Jase got his search party together and set off. They met the children coming home. By that time Nat had talked to the other mothers and fathers at the children's complex.

Jase called a meeting. There was no way to avoid it now, feelings were running too deep.

"We may as well decide now," he told them that night. "There's no question of the children marrying. We could train them to mouth the words of any of our religions, but we couldn't expect them to understand what they were saying. So the question is, shall we let the children reproduce?"

He faced an embarrassed silence.

"There's no question of their being too young. In biological terms they aren't, or you could all go home. In our terms, they'll never be old enough. Anyone have anything to say?"

"Let's have Doc's opinion," a hoarse voice called. There was a trickle of supportive applause.

Doc rose, feeling very heavy. "Fellow colonists . . ." The smile he was trying on for size didn't fit his face. He let it drop. There was a desperate compassion in his voice. "This world will never be habitable to mankind until we find out what went wrong here. I say let our children breed. Someday someone on Earth may find out how to cure what we've caught. Maybe he'll know how to let our descendants breed men again.

Maybe this problem will only last a generation or two, then we'll get human babies again. If not, well, what have we lost? Who else is there to inherit Ridgeback?"

"No!" The sound was a tortured meld of hatred and venom. That was Nat, sunhaired loving mother of six, with her face a strained mask of frustration. "I didn't risk my life and leave my family and, and train for years and bleed and sweat and toil so my labor could fall to . . . to . . . a bunch of goddamned *monkeys*!"

Brew pulled her back to her seat, but by now the crowd was muttering and arguing to itself. The noise grew louder. There was shouting. The yelling, too, grew in intensity.

Jase shouted over the throng. "Let's talk this out peacefully!"

Brew was standing, screaming at the people who disagreed with him and Natalie. Now it was becoming a shoving match, and Brew was getting more furious.

Doc pushed his way into the crowd, hoping to reach Brew and calm him. The room was beginning to break down into tangled knots of angry, emotionally charged people.

He grabbed the big man's arm and tried to speak, but the Swede turned bright baleful eyes on him and swung a heavy fist.

Doc felt pain explode in his jaw and tasted blood. He fell to the ground and was helped up again, Brew standing over him challengingly. "Stay out of our lives, *Doctor*," he sneered, openly now. "You've never helped anything before. Don't try to start now."

He tried to speak but felt the pain, and knew his jaw was fractured. A soft hand took his arm and he turned to see Elise, big green eyes luminous with pity and fear. Without struggling, he allowed her to take him to the ship infirmary.

As they left the auditorium he could hear the shouting and struggling, Jase on the microphone trying to calm them, and the coldly murderous voices that screamed for "no monkey grandchildren."

He tried to turn his head towards the distant sound of argument as Elise set the bone and injected quick-healing serums. She took his face and kissed him softly, with more affection than she had shown in months, and said, "They're afraid, Harry." Then kissed him again, and led him home.

Doc raged inwardly at his jaw that week. Its pain prevented him from joining in the debate which now flared in every corner of the colony.

Light images swam across his closed eyes as the sound of fists pounding against wood roused him from dreamless sleep. Doc threw on a robe and padded barefoot across the cool stone floor of his house, peering at the front door with distaste before opening it. Jase was there, and some of the others, somber and implacable in the morning's cool light.

"We've decided, Doc," Jase said at last. Doc sensed what was coming.

"The children are not to breed. I'm sorry, I know how you feel—" Doc grunted. How could Jase know how he felt when he wasn't sure himself? "We're going to have to ask you to perform the sterilizations . . ." Doc's hearing faded down to a low fuzz, and he barely heard the words. This is the way the world ends. . . .

Jase looked at his friend, feeling the distaste between them grow. "All right. We'll give you a week to change your mind. If not, Elise or Greg will have to do it." Without saying anything more they left.

Doc moped around that morning, even though Elise swore to him that she'd never do it. She fussed over him as they fixed breakfast in the kitchen. The gas stove burned methane reclaimed from waste products, the flame giving more heat control than the microwaves some of the others had. Normally Doc enjoyed scrambling eggs and wok-ing fresh slivered vegetables into crisp perfection, but nothing she said or did seemed to lift him out of his mood.

He ate lightly, then got dressed and left the house. Although she was concerned, Elise did not follow him.

He went out to the distillery, where Greg spent much of his time under the sun, drunk and playing at being happy. "Would you?" The pain still muffled Doc's words. "Would you sterilize them?"

Greg looked at him blearily, still hung over from the previous evening's alcoholic orgy. "You don't understand, man." There was a stirring sound from the sheltered bedroom behind the distillery, and a woman's waking groan. Doc knew it wasn't Jill. "You just don't understand."

Doc sat down, wishing he had the nerve to ask for a drink. "Maybe I don't. Do you?"

"No. No, I don't. So I'll follow the herd. I'm a builder. I build roads, and I build houses. I'll leave the moralizing to you big brains."

Doc tried to say something and found that no words would come. He needed something. He needed . . .

"Here, Doc. You know you want it." Greg handed him a canister with a straw in it. "Best damn vodka in the world." He paused, and the slur dropped from his voice. "And this is the world, Doc. For us. For the rest of our lives. You've just got to learn to roll with it." He smiled again and mixed himself an evil-looking drink.

Greg's guest had evidently roused herself and dressed. Doc could hear her now, singing a snatch of song as she left. He didn't want to recognize the voice.

"Got any orange juice?" Doc mumbled, after sipping the vodka.

Greg tossed him an orange. "A real man works for his pleasures."

Doc laughed and took another sip of the burning fluid. "Good lord. What *is* that mess you're drinking?"

"It's a Black Samurai. Sake and soy sauce."

Doc choked. "How can you drink that?"

"Variety, my friend. The stimulation of the bizarre."

Doc was silent for a long time. Senses swimming, he watched the sun climb, feeling the warmth as morning melted into afternoon. He downed a slug of his third screwdriver and said irritably, "You can't do it, Greg. If you sterilize the children, it's over."

"So what? It's over anyway. If they wanna let a drunk slit the pee pees of their . . . shall we say atavistic progeny? Yeah, that sounds nice. Well, if they want me to do it, I guess I'll have to do it." He looked at Doc very carefully. "I do have my sense of civic duty. How about you, Doc?"

"I tried." He mumbled, feeling the liquor burning his throat, feeling the light-headedness exert its pull. "I tried. And I've failed."

"You've failed so far. What were your goals?"

"To keep—" he took a drink. Damn, that felt good. "To keep the colony healthy. That's what. It's a disaster. We're at each other's throats. We kill our babies—"

Doc lowered his head, unable to continue.

They were both silent, then Greg said, "If I've gotta do it, I will, Doc. If it's not me, it'll be someone else who reads a couple of medical texts and wants to play doctor. I'm sorry."

Doc sat, thinking. His hands were shaking. "I can't do that." He couldn't even feel the pain anymore.

"Then do what you gotta do, man," and Greg's voice was dead sober.

"Will you . . . can you help me?" Doc bit his lip. "This is *my* civic duty, you know?"

"Yea, I know." He shook his head. "I'm sorry. I wish I could help."

A few minutes passed, then Doc said drunkenly, "There's got to be a way. There just has to be."

"Wish I could help, Doc."

"I wish you could too," Doc said sincerely, then rose and staggered back to his house.

It rained the night he made his decision, one of the quick, hot rains that swept from the coast to the mountains in a thunderclap of fury. It would make a perfect cover.

He gathered his medical texts, a Bible and a few other books, regretting that most of the information available to him was electronically encoded. Doc took one of the silent stunners from the armory. The nonlethal weapons had only been used as livestock controllers. There had never been another need, until now. From the infirmary he took a portable medical kit, stocking it with extra bandages and medicine, then took it all to the big cargo flyer.

It was collapsible, with a fabric fuselage held rigid by highly compressed air in fabric structural tubing. He put it in one of the soundless electric trucks and inflated it behind the children's complex.

There was plenty of room inside the fence for building and for a huge playground with fruit trees and all the immemorial toys of the very young. After the children had learned to operate a latch, Brew had made a lock for the gate and given everyone a key. Doc clicked it open and moved in.

He stayed in the shadows, creeping close to the main desk where Elise worked.

You can't follow where I must go, he thought regretfully. *You and I are the only fully trained medical personnel. You must stay with the others. I'm sorry, darling.*

And he stunned her to sleep silently, moving up to catch her head as it slumped to the table. For the last time, he gently kissed her mouth and her closed eyes.

The children were in the left wing—one room for each sex, with floors all mattress and no covers, because they could not be taught to use a bed. He sprayed the sound waves up and down the sleeping forms. The parabolic reflector leaked a little, so that his arm was numb to the elbow when he was finished. He shook his hand, trying to get some feeling back into it, then gave up and settled into the hard work of carrying the children to the flyer.

He hustled them through the warm rain, bending under their weight but still working swiftly. Doc arranged them on the fabric floor in positions that looked comfortable—the positions of sleeping men rather than sleeping animals. For some time he stood looking down at Jerry his son and at Lori his daughter, thinking things he could not afterwards remember.

He flew north. The flyer was slow and not soundless; it must have awakened people, but he'd have some time before anyone realized what had happened.

Where the forest had almost petered out he hovered down and landed gently enough that only a slumbering moan rose from the children. Good. He took half of them, including Jerry and Lori, and spread them out under the trees. After he had made sure that they had cover from the air he took the other packages, the books and the medical kit, and hid them under a bush a few yards away from the children.

He stole one last look at them, his heirs, small and defenseless, asleep. He could see Elise in them, in the color of their hair, as Elise could see him in their eyes and cheeks.

Kneading his shoulder, he hurried back to the ship. There was more for him to do.

Skipping the ship off again, he cruised thirty miles west, near the stark ridge of mountains, their somber gray still broken only sparsely by patches of green. There he left the other seven children. Let the two groups develop separately, he thought. They wouldn't starve, and they wouldn't die of exposure, not with the pelts they had grown. Many would remain alive, and free. He hoped Jerry and Lori would be among them.

Doc lifted the flyer off and swept it out to the ocean. Only a quarter mile offshore were the first of the islands, lush now with primitive foliage. They spun beneath him, floating brownish-green upon a still blue sea.

Now he could feel his heartbeat, taste his fear. But there was resolve, too, more certain and calm than any he had known in his life.

He cut speed and locked the controls, setting the craft on a gradual decline. Shivering already, he pulled on his life jacket and walked to the emergency hatch, screwing it open quickly.

The wind whipped his face, the cutting edge of salt narrowing his eyes. Peering against the wall of air pressure he was able to see the island coming up on him now, looming close. The water was only a hundred feet below him, now eighty, sixty . . .

The rumbling of the shadow breakers joined with the tearing wind, and, fighting his fear, he waited until the last possible moment before hurling himself from the doorway.

He remembered falling.

He remembered hitting the water at awful speed, the spray ripping into him, the physical impact like the blow of a great hand. When his head broke surface Doc wheezed for air, swallowed salty liquid and thrashed for balance.

In the distance, he saw the flash of light, and a moment later heard the shattering roar as the flyer spent itself on the rocky shore.

Jase was tired. He was often tired lately, although he still managed to get his work done.

The fields had only recently become unkempt, as Marlow and Billie and Jill and the others grew more and more inclined to pick their vegetables from their backyard gardens.

So just he and a few more still rode out to the fields on the tractors, still kept close watch on the herds, still did the hand-pruning so necessary to keep the fruit trees healthy.

The children were of some help. Ten years ago a few of them had been captured around the foothill area. They had been sterilized, of course, and taught to weed, and carry firewood, and a few other simple tasks.

Jase leaned on his staff and watched the shaggy figures moving along the street, sweeping and cleaning.

He had grown old on this world, their Ridgeback. He regretted much that had happened here, especially that night thirty-some years before when Doc had taken the children.

Taken them—where? Some argued for the islands, some for the West side of the mountain range. Some believed that the children had died in the crash of the flyer. Jase had believed that, until the adult Piths were captured. Now, it was hard to say what happened.

It was growing chill now, the streetlights winking on to brighten the long shadows a setting Tau Ceti cast upon the ground. He drew his coat tighter across his shoulders and walked back to his house. It was a lonelier place to be since June had died, but it was still home.

Fumbling with the latch, he pushed the door open and reached around for the light switch. As it flicked on, he froze.

My God.

"Hello, Jase." The figure was tall and spare, clothes ragged, but graying hair and beard cut squarely. Three of the children were with him.

After all this time . . .

"Doc . . ." Jase said, still unbelieving. "It is you, isn't it?"

The bearded man smiled uncertainly, showing teeth that were white but chipped. "It's been a long time, Jase. A very long time."

The three Piths were quiet and alert, sniffing the air of this strange place.

"Are these—?"

"Yes. Jerry and Lori. And Eve. And a small addition." One of the three—God, could it be Eve?—sniffed up to Jase. The soft golden fur on her face was tinged with gray, but she carried a young child at her breast.

Jerry stood tall for a preman, eyeing Jase warily. He carried a sharpened stick in one knobby hand.

Jase sat down, speechless. He looked up into the burning eyes of the man he had known thirty years before. "You're still officially under a death sentence, you know."

Doc nodded his head. "For kidnapping?"

"Murder. No one was sure what had happened to you, whether you or any of the children had survived."

Doc, too, sat down. For the first time the light in his eyes dimmed. "Yes. We survived. I swam to shore after crashing the flyer, and found the place where I had left the children." He thought for a moment, then asked quietly. "How is Elise? And all the others?"

Jase was unable to raise his eyes from the floor. "She died three years ago, Doc. She was never the same after you left. She thought you were dead. That the children were dead. Couldn't you have at least told her about your plan? Or gotten her a message?"

Doc's fingers played absently with his beard as he shook his head. "I couldn't involve her. I couldn't. Could you . . . show me where she's buried, Jase?"

"Of course."

"What about the others?"

"Well, none of the people were the same after the children left. Some just seemed to lose purpose. Brew's dead. Greg drank himself under. Four of the others have died." Jase paused, thinking. "Do any of the others know you're here?"

"No. I slipped in just at dusk. I wasn't sure what kind of a reception I'd get."

"I'm still not sure." Jase hesitated. "Why did you do it?"

The room was quiet, save for a scratching sound as Jerry fingered an ear. Fleas? Absurd. Jill had never uncrated them.

"I had to know, Jase," he said. There was no uncertainty in his voice. In fact, there was an imperious quality he had never had in the old days. "The question was: Would they breed true? Was the Pith effect only temporary?"

"Was it?"

"No. It persisted. I had to know if they were regressing or evolving, and they remained the same in subsequent generations, save for natural selection, and there isn't much of that."

Jase watched Lori, her stubby fingers untangling mats in her fur. Her huge brown eyes were alive and vital. She was a lovely creature, he decided. "Doc, what are the children?"

"What do you think?"

"You know what I think. An alien species wants our worlds. In a hundred years they'll land and take them. What they'll do with the children is anybody's guess. I—" He couldn't bring himself to look at Eve. "I wish you'd sterilized them, Doc."

"Maybe you do, Jase. But, you see, I don't believe in your aliens."

Jase's breath froze in his throat.

"They might want our world," said Doc, "but why would they want our life forms? Everything but Man is spreading like a plague of locusts. If someone wants Ridgeback, why haven't they done something about it? By the time they land, terrestrial life will have an unstoppable foothold. Look at all the thousands of years we've been trying to stamp out just one life form, the influenza viruses.

"No, I've got another idea. Do you know what a locust is?"

"I know what they are. I've never seen one."

"As individuals they're something like a short grasshopper. As individuals, they hide or sleep in the daytime and come out at night. In open country you can hear them chirping after dusk, but otherwise nobody notices them. But they're out there, eating and breeding and breeding and eating, getting more numerous over a period of years, until one day there are too many for the environment to produce enough food.

"Then comes the change. On Earth it hasn't happened in a long time because they aren't allowed to get that numerous. But it used to be that when there were enough of them, they'd grow bigger and darker and more aggressive. They'd come out in the daytime. They'd eat everything in sight, and when all the food was gone, and when there were enough of them, they'd suddenly take off all at once.

"That's when you'd get your plague of locusts. They'd drop from the air in a cloud thick enough and broad enough to darken the sky, and when they landed in a farmer's field he could kiss his crops goodbye. They'd raze it to the soil, then take off again, leaving nothing."

Jase took off his glasses and wiped them. "I don't see what it is you're getting at."

"Why do they do it? Why were locusts built that way?"

"Evolution, I guess. After the big flight they'd be spread over a lot of territory. I'd say they'd have a much bigger potential food supply."

"Right. Now consider this. Take a biped that's man-shaped, enough so to use a tool, but without intelligence. Plant him on a world and watch him grow. Say he's adaptable; say he eventually spreads over most of the fertile land masses of the planet. Now what?

"Now an actual physical change takes place. The brain expands. The body hair drops away. Evolution had adapted him to his climate, but that was when he had hair. Now he's got to use his intelligence to keep from freezing to death. He'll discover fire. He'll move out into areas he couldn't live in before. Eventually he'll cover the whole planet, and he'll build spacecraft and head for the stars."

Jase shook his head. "*But why would they change back*, Doc?"

"Something in the genes, maybe. Something that didn't mutate."

"Not *how*, Doc. We know it's possible. *Why?*"

"We're going back to being grasshoppers. Maybe we've reached our evolutionary peak. Natural selection stops when we start protecting the weak ones, instead of allowing those with defective genes to die a natural death."

He paused, smiling. "I mean, look at us, Jase. You walk with a cane now. I haven't been able to read for five years, my eyes have weakened so. And we were the best Earth had to offer; the best minds, the finest bodies. Chris only squeaked by with his glasses because he was such a damn good meteorologist."

Jase's face held a flash of long-forgotten pain. "And I guess they still didn't choose carefully enough."

"No," Doc agreed soberly. "They didn't. On Earth we protected the sick, allowed them to breed, instead of letting them die . . . with pacemakers, with insulin, artificial kidneys and plastic hip joints and trusses. The mentally ill and retarded fought in the courts for the right to reproduce. Okay, it's humane. Nature isn't humane. The infirm will do their job by dying, and no morality or humane court rulings or medical advances will change the natural course of things for a long, long time."

"How long?"

"I don't know how stable they are. It could be millions of years, or . . . ?" Doc shrugged. "We've changed the course of our own development. Perhaps a simpler creature is needed to colonize a world. Something that has no choice but to change or die. Jase, remember the Cold War?"

"I read about it."

"And the Belt Embargo? Remember diseromide, and smog, and the spray-can thing, and the day the fusion seawater distillery at San Francisco went up and took the Bay area with it, and four states had to have their water flown in for a month?"

"So?"

"A dozen times we could have wiped out all life on Earth. As soon as we've used our intelligence to build spacecraft and seed another world, intelligence becomes a liability. Some old anthropologist even had a theory that a species needs abstract intelligence before it can prey on its own kind. The development of fire gave Man time to sit back and dream up ways to take things he hadn't earned. You know how gentle the children are, and you can remember how the carefully chosen citizens of Ridgeback acted the night we voted on the children's right to reproduce."

"So you gave that to them, Doc. They are reproducing. And when we're gone they'll spread all over the world. But are they *human*?"

Doc pondered, wondering what to say. For many years he had talked only to the children. The children never interrupted, never disagreed . . . "I had to know that too. Yes. They're human."

Jase looked closely at the man he had called friend so many years ago. Doc was so sure. He didn't discuss; he lectured. Jase felt an alienness in him that was deeper than the mere passage of time.

"Are you going to stay here now?"

"I don't know. The children don't need me any more, though they've treated me like a god. I can't pass anything on to them. I think our culture has to die before theirs can grow."

Jase fidgeted, uncomfortable. "Doc. Something I've got to tell you. I haven't told anyone. It's thirty years now, and nobody knows but me."

Doc frowned. "Go on."

"Remember the day Roy died? Something in the Orion blew all the motors at once? Well, he talked to Cynnie first. And she talked to me, before *she* disappeared. Doc, he got a laser message from Earth, and he knew he couldn't ever send it down. It would have destroyed us. So he blew the motors."

Doc waited, listening intently.

"It seems that every child being born on Earth nowadays bears an uncanny resemblance to Pithecanthropus erectus. They were begging us to make the Ridgeback colony work. Because Earth is doomed."

"I'm glad nobody knew that."

Jase nodded. "If intelligence is bad for us, it's bad for Earth. They've fired their starships. Now they're ready for another cycle."

"Most of them'll die. They're too crowded."

"Some will survive. If not there, then, thanks to you, here." He smiled. A touch of the old Jase in his eyes. "They'll *have* to become men, you know."

"Why do you put it like that?"

"Because Jill uncrated the wolves, to help thin out the herds."

"They'll cull the children, too," Doc nodded. "I couldn't help them become men, but I think that will do it. They will have to band together, and find tools, and fire." His voice took on a dreamy quality. "Eventually, the wolves will come out of the darkness to join them at their campfires, and Man will have dogs again." He smiled. "I hope they don't overbreed them like we did on Earth. I doubt if chihuahuas have ever forgotten what we did to them."

"Doc," Jase said, urgently, "will you trust me? Will you wait for a minute while I leave? I . . . I want to try something. If you decide to go there may never be another chance."

Doc looked at him, mystified. "All right, I'll wait."

Jase limped out of the door. Doc sat, watching his charges, proud of their alertness and flexibility, their potential for growth in the new land.

There was a creaking as the door swung open.

The woman's hair had been blond, once. Now it was white, heavy wrinkles around her eyes and mouth, years of hardship and disappointment souring what had once been beauty.

She blinked, at first seeing only Doc.

"Hello, Nat," he said to her.

She frowned. "What . . . ?" Then she saw Eve.

Their eyes locked, and Nat would have drawn back save for Jase's insistent hand at her back.

Eve drew close, peering into her mother's face as if trying to remember her.

The old woman stuttered, then said, "Eve?" The Pith cocked her head and came closer, touching her mother's hand. Nat pulled it back, eyes wide.

Eve cooed, smiling, holding her baby out to Nat.

At first she flinched, then looked at the child, so much like Eve had been, so much . . . and slowly, without words or visible emotion, she took the child from Eve and cradled it, held it, and began to tremble. Her hand stretched out helplessly, and Eve came closer, took her mother's hand and the three of them, mother, child and grandchild, children of different worlds, held each other. Nat cried for the pain that had driven them apart, the love that had brought them together.

Doc stood at the edge of the woods, looking back at the colonists who waved to them, asking for a swift return.

Perhaps so. Perhaps they could, now. Enough time had passed that understanding was a thing to be sought rather than avoided. And he missed the company of his own kind.

No, he corrected himself, the children *were* his kind. As he had told Jase, without explaining, he knew that they were human. He had tested it the only way he could, by the only means available.

Eve walked beside him, her hand seeking his. ''Doc,'' she cooed, her birdlike singsong voice loving. He gently took their child from her arms, kissing it.

At over sixty years of age, it felt odd to be a new father, but if his lover had her way, as she usually did, his strange family might grow larger still.

Together, the five of them headed into the forest, and home.

This was an early story, and I broke my heart over it. The idea is a good one, but not a happy one. I didn't know how to handle it. Presently I tossed it in my file cabinet to die.

Ten years later I met Steven Barnes at a LASFS meeting. It struck me that he might be able to do something with "The Locusts."

Take a lesson: this is the only easy way to collaborate. The effort *you* put into the story is already lost. The other writer has invested no effort, and need not. "Can you do something with this?" "No."

Steve said, "Yes."

• • •

• • •

All of them had craters. At least one crater. Three long, narrow asteroids in succession ... and each had a deep crater at one end. One rock twisted almost into a cashew shape; and the crater was at the inside of the curve. Each asteroid in the sequence had a big deep crater in it; and always a line through the center would have gone through the rock's center of mass.

Bury felt fear and laughter rising in him. "Yes, I see. You found that every one of those asteroids had been moved into place artificially. Therefore you lost interest."

THE MOTE IN GOD'S EYE, 1974

From THE MOTE IN GOD'S EYE (with JERRY POURNELLE)

Jerry Pournelle suggested that we try a collaboration. Working with David Gerrold on *The Flying Sorcerors* had been fun, so . . .

Jerry wouldn't work in Known Space because he couldn't believe in the politics or the history. (He must have changed his mind. "The Children's Hour," by Jerry Pournelle and S. M. Stirling, is a wonderful tale of the Man-Kzin Wars.) Instead, he offered a thousand years of a future history that uses the faster-than-light drive designed by our mutual friend Dan Alderson.

I looked it over. Peculiar. A thousand inhabited planets and no intelligent beings save humans? (This *is* the way to bet, but it seemed odd then.) And I realized that the laws of the Alderson Drive allow me to insert an undiscovered alien civilization right in the middle.

That did it: there was going to be a novel. I had abandoned a novella two-thirds written; I dug it out and resurected the alien. We spent a wild night extrapolating from the Motie Engineer form, to a dozen varieties of Motie, to a million years of history and three planet-busting wars. We swore we would write the novel we wanted to read when we were twelve.

Every time we thought we were finished, we found we weren't.

Jerry sent our "finished" manuscript to a friend: Robert Heinlein. Robert told us that he could put one terrific blurb on the cover *if* we made some changes. The first hundred pages had to go . . .

And we did that, and re-introduced characters and moved background data from the lost prologue to a later scene set on New Scotland, and did more chopping throughout. "There's a scene I've *never* liked," I told Jerry, and our whole relationship changed. This was when we learned not to be too polite to a collaborator; it hurts the book.

And we sent it back to Robert, *who did a complete line-editing job.*

I know of a man who offered Robert Heinlein a reading fee! The results were quite horrid. But in the case of MOTE, Robert hadn't expected us to take his advice. Nobody ever had before (he told us). But if "Possibly the finest science fiction novel I have ever read" were to appear on the cover above Robert Heinlein's name, then the book had to *be* that.

It took us forever to write. We won the LASFS's "Sticky" Award for "Best Unpublished Novel" two years running. It was worth every minute.

• •

Horace Bury had gone to his cabin after the coffee demonstration. He liked to work late at night and sleep after lunch, and although there wasn't anything to work on at the moment, he'd kept the habit.

The ship's alarms woke him. Somebody was ordering the Marines into combat uniform. He waited, but nothing else happened for a long time. Then came the stench. It choked him horribly, and there was nothing like it in any of his memories. Distilled quintessence of machines and body odor—and it was growing stronger.

More alarms sounded. "PREPARE FOR HARD VACUUM. ALL PERSONNEL WILL DON PRESSURE SUITS. ALL MILITARY PERSONNEL WILL DON BATTLE ARMOR. PREPARE FOR HARD VACUUM."

Nabil was crying in panic. "Fool! Your suit!" Bury screamed, and ran for his own. Only after he was breathing normal ship's air did he listen for the alarms again.

The voices didn't sound right. They weren't coming through the intercom, they were—shouted through the corridors. "CIVILIANS WILL ABANDON SHIP. ALL CIVILIAN PERSONNEL, PREPARE TO ABANDON SHIP."

Really. Bury almost smiled. This was a first time—was it a drill? There were more sounds of confusion. A squad of Marines in battle armor, weapons clutched at the ready, tramped past. The smile slipped and Bury looked about to guess what possessions he might save.

There was more shouting. An officer appeared in the corridor outside and began shouting in an unnecessarily loud voice. Civilians would be leaving *MacArthur* on a line. They could take one bag each, but would require one hand free.

Beard of the Prophet! What could cause this? Had they saved the golden asteroid metal, the superconductor of heat? Certainly they would not save the precious self-cleaning percolator. What should he try to save?

The ship's gravity lessened noticeably. Flywheels inside her were rotating to take off her spin. Bury worked quickly to throw together items needed by any traveler without regard to their price. Luxuries he could buy again, but—

The miniatures. He'd have to get that air tank from D air lock. Suppose he were assigned to a different air lock?

He packed in frenzy. Two suitcases, one for Nabil to carry. Nabil moved fast enough now that he had orders. There was more confused shouting outside, and several times squads of Navy men and Marines floated past the stateroom door. They all carried weapons and wore armor.

His suit began to inflate. The ship was losing pressure, and all thought of drill or exercise left him. Some of the scientific equipment couldn't stand hard vacuum—and nobody had once come into the cabin to check his pressure suit. The Navy wouldn't risk civilian lives in drills.

An officer moved into the corridor. Bury heard the harsh voice speaking in deadly calm tones. Nabil stood uncertainly and Bury motioned to him to turn on his suit communications.

"ALL CIVILIAN PERSONNEL, GO TO YOUR NEAREST AIR LOCKS ON THE PORT FLANK," the unemotional voice said. The Navy always spoke that way when there was a real crisis. It convinced Bury utterly. "CIVILIAN EVACUATION WILL BE THROUGH PORT-SIDE LOCKS ONLY. IF YOU ARE UNSURE OF YOUR DIRECTION ASK ANY OFFICER OR RATING. PLEASE PROCEED SLOWLY. THERE IS TIME TO EVACUATE ALL PERSONNEL." The officer floated past and turned into another corridor.

Port side? Good. Intelligently, Nabil had hidden the dummy tank in the *nearest* air lock. Praise to the Glory of Allah that had been on the port side. He motioned to his servant and began to pull himself from hand hold to hand hold along the wall. Nabil moved gracefully; he had had plenty of practice since they had been confined.

There was a confused crowd in the corridor. Behind him Bury saw a squad of Marines turn into the corridor. They faced away and fired in the direction they'd come. There was answering fire and bright blood spurted to form ever-diminishing globules as it drifted through the steel ship. The lights flickered overhead.

A petty officer floated down the corridor and fell in behind them. "Keep moving, keep moving," he muttered. "God bless the joeys."

"What are they shooting at?" Bury asked.

"Miniatures," the petty officer growled. "If they take this corridor, move out fast, Mr. Bury. The little bastards have weapons."

"Brownies?" Bury asked incredulously. "Brownies?"

"Yes, sir, the ship's got a plague o' the little sons of bitches. They changed the air plants to suit themselves . . . Get movin', sir. Please. Them joeys can't hold long."

Bury tugged at a hand hold and sailed to the end of the corridor, where he was deftly caught by an able spacer and passed around the turn. Brownies? But, they'd been cleared out of the ship . . .

There was a crowd bunched at the air lock. More civilians were coming, and now noncombatant Navy people began to add to the press. Bury pushed and clawed his way toward the air-bottle locker. Ah. It was still there. He seized the dummy and handed it to Nabil, who fastened it to Bury's suit.

"That won't be necessary, sir," an officer said. Bury realized he was hearing him through atmosphere. There was pressure here—but they hadn't come through any pressure-tight doors! The Brownies! They'd made the invisible pressure barrier that the miner had on her survey ship! He had to have it! "One never knows," Bury muttered to the officer. The man shrugged and motioned another pair into the cycling mechanism. Then it was Bury's turn. The Marine officer waved them forward.

The lock cycled. Bury touched Nabil on the shoulder and pointed. Nabil went, pulling himself along the line into the blackness outside. Blackness ahead, no stars, nothing. What was out there? Bury found himself holding his breath. Praise be to Allah, I witness that Allah is One— *No*! The dummy bottle was on his shoulders, and inside it two miniatures in suspended animation. Wealth untold! Technology beyond anything even the First Empire ever had! An endless stream of new inventions and design improvements. Only . . . just what kind of djinn bottle had he opened?

They were through the tightly controlled hole in *MacArthur*'s Field. Outside was only the blackness of space—and a darker black shape ahead. Other lines led to it from other holes in *MacArthur*'s Field, and minuscule spiders darted along them. Behind Bury was another space-suited figure, and behind that, another. Nabil and the others ahead of him, and . . . His eyes were adjusting rapidly now. He could see the deep red hues of the Coal Sack, and the blot ahead must be *Lenin*'s Field. Would he have to crawl through *that*? But no, there were boats outside it, and the space spiders crawled into them.

The boat was drawing near. Bury turned for a last look at *MacArthur*. In his long lifetime he had said good-by to countless temporary homes; *MacArthur* had not been the best of them. He thought of the technology that was being destroyed. The Brownie-improved machinery, the magical coffeepot. There was a twinge of regret. *MacArthur*'s crew was genuinely grateful for his help with the coffee, and his demonstration to the officers had been popular. It had gone well. Perhaps in *Lenin* . . .

The air lock was tiny now. A string of refugees followed him along the line. He could not see the cutter, where his Motie would be. Would he ever see him again?

He was looking directly at the space-suited figure behind him. It had no baggage, and it was overtaking Bury because it had both hands free.

The light from *Lenin* was shining on its faceplate. As Bury watched, the figure's head shifted slightly and the light shone right into the faceplate.

Bury saw at least three pairs of eyes staring back at him. He glimpsed the tiny faces.

It seemed to Bury, later, that he had never thought so fast in his life. For a heartbeat he stared at the thing coming up on him while his mind raced, and then— But the men who heard his scream said that it was the shriek of a madman, or a man being flayed alive.

Then Bury flung his suitcase at it.

He put words into his next scream. "They're in the suit! They're inside it!" He was wrenching at his back now, ripping the air tank loose. He poised the cylinder over his head, in both hands, and pitched it.

The pressure suit dodged his suitcase, clumsily. A pair of miniatures in the arms, trying to maneuver the fingers . . . it lost its hand hold, tried to pull itself back. The metal cylinder took it straight in the faceplate and shattered it.

Then space was filled with tiny struggling figures, flailing six limbs as a ghostly puff of air carried them away. Something else went with them, something football shaped, something Bury had the knowledge to recognize. That was how they had fooled the officer at the air locks. A severed human head.

Bury discovered he was floating three meters from the line. He took a deep, shuddering breath. Good: he'd thrown the right air tank. Allah was merciful.

He waited until a man-shaped thing came out of *Lenin's* boat on back-pack jets and took him in tow. The touch made him flinch. Perhaps the man wondered why Bury peered so intently into his faceplate. Perhaps not.

BUILDING THE MOTE IN GOD'S EYE (with JERRY POURNELLE)

Collaborations are unnatural. The writer is a jealous god. He builds his universe without interference. He resents the carping of mentally deficient critics and the editor's capricious demands for revisions. Let two writers try to make one universe, and their defenses get in the way.

But. Our fields of expertise matched each the other's blind spots, unnaturally well. There were books neither of us could write alone. We had to try it.

At first we were too polite, too reluctant to criticize each other's work. That may have saved us from killing each other early on, but it left flaws that had to be torn out of the book later.

We had to build the worlds. From Motie physiognomy we had to build Motie technology and history and life styles. Niven had to be coached in the basic history of Pournelle's thousand-year-old interstellar culture.

It took us three years. At the end we had a novel of 245,000 words . . . which was too long. We cut it to 170,000, to the reader's great benefit. We cut 50,000 words off the beginning, including in one lump our first couple of months of work: a prologue, a battle between space-going warcraft, and a prison camp scene. All of the crucial information had to be embedded in later sections.

We give that prologue here. When the Moties and the Empire and the star systems and their technologies and philosophies had become one interrelated whole, this is how it looked from New Caledonia system. We called it

MOTELIGHT

Last night at this time he had gone out to look at the stars. Instead a glare of white light like an exploding sun had met him at the door, and when he could see again a flaming mushroom was rising from the cornfields at the edge of the black hemisphere roofing the University. Then had come sound, rumbling, rolling across the fields to shake the house.

Alice had run out in terror, desperate to have her worst fears confirmed, crying, "What are you learning that's worth getting us all killed?"

He'd dismissed her question as typical of an astronomer's wife, but in fact he was learning nothing. The main telescope controls were erratic, and nothing could be done, for the telescope itself was on New Scotland's tiny moon. These nights interplanetary space rippled with the strange lights of war, and the atmosphere glowed with ionization from shock waves, beamed radiation, fusion explosions . . . He had gone back inside without answering.

Now, late in the evening of New Scotland's 27-hour day, Thaddeus Potter, Ph.D., strolled out into the night air.

It was a good night for seeing. Interplanetary war could play hell with the seeing; but tonight the bombardment from New Ireland had ceased. The Imperial Navy had won a victory.

Potter had paid no attention to the newscasts; still, he appreciated the victory's effects. Perhaps tonight the war wouldn't interfere with his work. He walked thirty paces forward and turned just where the roof of his house wouldn't block the Coal Sack. It was a sight he never tired of.

The Coal Sack was a nebular mass of gas and dust, small as such things go—eight to ten parsecs thick—but dense, and close enough to New Caledonia to block a quarter of the sky. Earth lay somewhere on the other side of it, and so did the Imperial Capital, Sparta, both forever invisible. The Coal Sack hid most of the Empire, but it made a fine velvet backdrop for two close, brilliant stars.

And one of them had changed drastically.

Potter's face changed too. His eyes bugged. His lantern jaw hung loose on its hinges. Stupidly he stared at the sky as if seeing it for the first time.

Then, abruptly, he ran into the house.

Alice came into the bedroom as he was phoning Edwards. "What's happened?" she cried. "Have they pierced the shield?"

"No," Potter snapped over his shoulder. Then, grudgingly, "Something's happened to the Mote."

"Oh for God's sake!" She was genuinely angry, Potter saw. *All that fuss about a star, with civilization falling around our ears!* But Alice had no love of the stars.

Edwards answered. On the screen he showed naked from the waist up, his long curly hair a tangled bird's nest. "Who the hell—? Thad. I might have known. Thad, do you know what time it is?"

"Yes. Go outside," Potter ordered. "Have a look at the Mote."

"The Mote? *The Mote?*"

"Yes. It's gone nova!" Potter shouted. Edwards growled, then sudden comprehension struck. He left the screen without hanging up. Potter reached out to dial the bedroom window transparent. And it was still there.

Even without the Coal Sack for backdrop Murcheson's Eye would be the brightest object in the sky. At its rising the Coal Sack resembled the silhouette of a hooded man, head and shoulders; and the off-centered red supergiant became a watchful, malevolent eye. The University itself had begun as an observatory funded to study the supergiant.

This eye had a mote: a yellow dwarf companion, smaller and dimmer, and uninteresting. The Universe held plenty of yellow dwarfs.

But tonight the Mote was a brilliant blue-green point. It was almost as bright as Murcheson's Eye itself, and it burned with a purer light. Murcheson's Eye was white with a strong red tinge; but the Mote was blue-green with no compromise, impossibly green.

Edwards came back to the phone.

"Thad, that's no nova. It's like nothing ever recorded. Thad, we've got to get to the observatory!"

"I know. I'll meet you there."

"I want to do spectroscopy on it."

"All right."

"God, I hope the seeing holds! Do you think we'll be able to get through today?"

"If you hang up, we'll find out sooner."

"What? Och, aye." Edwards hung up.

The bombardment started as Potter was boarding his bike. There was a hot streak of light like a *very* large shooting star; and it didn't burn out, but reached all the way to the horizon. Stratospheric clouds formed and vanished, outlining the shock wave. Light glared on the horizon, then faded gradually.

"Damn," muttered Potter, with feeling. He started the motor. The war was no concern of his, except that he no longer had New Irish students. He even missed some of them. There was one chap from Cohane who . . .

A cluster of stars streaked down in exploding fireworks. Something burned like a new star overhead. The falling stars winked out, but the other light went on and on, changing colors rapidly, even while the shock wave clouds dissipated. Then the night became clear, and Potter saw that it was on the moon.

What could New Ireland be shooting at on New Scotland's moon?

Potter understood then. "You bastards!" he screamed at the sky. "You lousy *traitor* bastards!"

The single light reddened.

He stormed around the side of Edwards's house shouting, "The traitors bombed the main telescope! Did you see it? All our work —oh."

He had forgotten Edwards's backyard telescope.

It had cost him plenty, and it was very good, although it weighed only four kilograms. It was portable—"Especially," Edwards used to say, "when compared with the main telescope."

He had bought it because the fourth attempt at grinding his own mirror produced another cracked disk and an ultimatium from his now dead wife about Number 200 Carbo grains tracked onto her New-Life carpets . . .

Now Edwards moved away from the eyepiece saying, "Nothing much to see there." He was right. There were no features. Potter saw only a uniform aquamarine field.

"But have a look at this," said Edwards. "Move back a bit . . ." He set beneath the eyepiece a large sheet of white paper, then a wedge of clear quartz.

The prism spread a fan-shaped rainbow across the paper. But the rainbow was almost too dim to see, vanishing beside a single line of aquamarine; and that line *blazed*.

"One line," said Potter. "Monochromatic?"

"I told you yon was no nova."

"Too right it wasn't. But what is it? Laser light? It has to be artificial! Lord, what a technology they've built!"

"Och, come now." Edwards interrupted the monologue. "I doubt yon's artificial at all. Too intense." His voice was cheerful. "We're seeing something new. Somehow yon Mote is generating coherent light."

"I don't believe it."

Edwards looked annoyed. After all, it was *his* telescope. "What think you, then? Some booby calling for help? If they were that powerful, they would send a ship. A ship would come thirty-five years sooner!"

"But there's no tramline from the Mote to New Caledonia! Not even theoretically possible. Only link to the Mote has to start inside the Eye. Murcheson looked for it, you know, but he never found it. The Mote's alone out there."

"Och, then how could there be a colony?" Edwards demanded in triumph. "Be reasonable, Thad! We hae a new natural phenomenon, something new in stellar process."

"But if someone *is* calling—"

"Let's hope not. We could no help them. We couldn't reach them, even if we knew the links! There's no starship in the New Cal system, and there's no likely to be until the war's over." Edwards looked up at the sky. The moon was a small, irregular half-disk; and a circular crater still burned red in the dark half.

A brilliant violet streak flamed high overhead. The violet light grew more intense and flared white, then vanished. A warship had died out there.

"Ah, well," Edwards said. His voice softened. "If someone's calling he picked a hell of a time for it. But at least we can search for modulations. If the beam is no modulated, you'll admit there's nobody there, will you not?"

"Of course," said Potter.

In 2862 there were no starships behind the Coal Sack. On the other side, around Crucis and the Capital, a tiny fleet still rode the force paths between stars to the worlds Sparta controlled. There were fewer loyal ships and worlds each year.

The summer of 2862 was lean for New Scotland. Day after day a few men crept outside the black dome that defended the city; but they always returned at night. Few saw the rising of the Coal Sack.

It climbed weirdly, its resemblance to a shrouded human silhouette marred by the festive two-colored eye. The Mote burned as brightly as Murcheson's Eye now. But who would listen to Potter and Edwards and their crazy tales about the Mote? The night sky was a battlefield, dangerous to look upon.

The war was not really fought for the Empire now. In the New Caledonia system the war continued because it would not end. Loyalist and Rebel were meaningless terms; but it hardly mattered while bombs and wrecked ships fell from the skies.

Henry Morrissey was still head of the University Astronomy Department. He tried to talk Potter and Edwards into returning to the protection of the Langston Field. His only success was that Potter sent his wife and two sons back with Morrissey. Edwards had no living dependents, and both refused to budge.

Morrissey was willing to believe that something had happened to the Mote, but not that it was visible to the naked eye. Potter was known for his monomaniacal enthusiasms.

The Department could supply them with equipment. It was makeshift, but it should have done the job. There was laser light coming from the Mote. It came with terrific force, and must have required terrific power, and enormous sophistication to build that power. No one would build such a thing except to send a message.

And there was no message. The beam was not modulated. It did not change color, or blink off and on, or change in intensity. It was a steady, beautifully pure, terribly intense beam of coherent light.

Potter watched to see if it might change silhouette, staring for hours into the telescope. Edwards was no help at all. He alternated between polite gloating at having proved his point, and impolite words muttered as he tried to investigate the new "stellar process" with inadequate equipment. The only thing they agreed on was the need to publish their observations, and the impossibility of doing so.

One night a missile exploded against the edge of the black dome. The Langston Field protecting University City could only absorb so much energy before radiating inward, vaporizing the town, and it took time to dissipate the hellish fury poured into it. Frantic engineers worked to radiate away the shield energy before the generators melted to slag.

They succeeded, but there was a burn-through: a generator left yellow-hot and runny. A relay snapped open, and New Caledonia stood undefended against a hostile sky. Before the Navy could restore the Field a million people had watched the rising of the Coal Sack.

"I came to apologize," Morrissey told Potter the next morning. "Something damned strange *has* happened to the Mote. What have you got?"

He listened to Potter and Edwards, and he stopped their fight. Now that they had an audience they almost came to blows. Morrissey promised them more equipment and retreated under the restored shield. He had been an astronomer in his time. Somehow he got them what they needed.

Weeks became months. The war continued, wearing New Scotland down, exhausting her resources. Potter and Edwards worked on, learning nothing, fighting with each other and screaming curses at the New Irish traitors.

They might as well have stayed under the shield. The Mote produced coherent light of amazing purity. Four months after it began, the light jumped in intensity and stayed that way. Five months later it jumped again.

It jumped once more, four months later, but Potter and Edwards didn't see it. That was the night a ship from New Ireland fell from the sky, its shield blazing violet with friction. It was low when the shield overloaded and collapsed, releasing stored energy in one ferocious blast.

Gammas and photons washed across the plains beyond the city, and Potter and Edwards were carried into the University hospital by worried students. Potter died three days later. Edwards walked for the rest of his life with a backpack attached to his shoulders: a portable life support system.

It was 2870 on every world where clocks still ran when the miracle came to New Scotland.

An interstellar trading ship, long converted for war and recently damaged, fell into the system with her Langston Field intact and her hold filled with torpedoes. She was killed in the final battle, but the insurrection on New Ireland died as well. Now all the New Caledonia system was loyal to the Empire; and the Empire no longer existed.

The University came out from under the shield. Some had forgotten that the Mote had once been a small yellow-white point.

Most didn't care. There was a world to be tamed, and that world had been bare rock terraformed in the first place. The fragile imported biosphere was nearly destroyed, and it took all their ingenuity and work to keep New Scotland inhabitable.

They succeeded because they had to. There were no ships to take survivors anywhere else. The Yards had been destroyed in the war, and there would be no more interstellar craft. They were alone behind the Coal Sack.

The Mote continued to grow brighter as the years passed. Soon it was more brilliant than the Eye, but there were no astronomers on New Scotland to care. In 2891 the Coal Sack was a black silhouette of a hooded man. It had one terribly bright blue-green eye, with a red fleck in it.

One night at the rising of the Coal Sack, a farmer named Howard Grote Littlemead was struck with inspiration. It came to him that the Coal Sack was God, and that he ought to tell someone.

Tradition had it that the Face of God could be seen from New Caledonia; and Littlemead had a powerful voice. Despite the opposition of the Imperial Orthodox Church, despite the protests of the Viceroy and the scorn of the University staff, the Church of Him spread until it was a power of New Scotland.

It was never large, but its members were fanatics; and they had the miracle of the Mote, which no scientist could explain. By 2895 the Church of Him was a power among New Scot farmers, but not in the cities. Still, half the population worked in the fields. The converter kitchens had all broken down.

By 2900 New Scotland had two working interplanetary spacecraft, one of which could not land. Its Langston Field had died. The term was appropriate. When a piece of Empire technology stopped working, it was dead. It could not be repaired. New Scotland was becoming primitive.

For forty years the Mote had grown. Children refused to believe that it had once been called the Mote. Adults knew it was true, but couldn't remember why. They called the twin stars Murcheson's Eye, and believed that the red supergiant had no special name.

The records might have showed differently, but the University records were suspect. The Library had been scrambled by electromagnetic pulses during the years of siege. It had large areas of amnesia.

In 2902 the Mote went out.

Its green light dimmed to nothing over a period of several hours; but that happened on the other side of the world. When the Coal Sack rose above University City that night, it rose as a blinded man.

All but a few remnants of the Church of Him died that year. With the aid of a handful of sleeping pills Howard Grote Littlemead hastened to meet his God . . . possibly to demand an explanation.

Astronomy also died. There were few enough astronomers and fewer tools; and when nobody could explain the vanishing of the Mote . . . and when telescopes turned on the Mote's remnant showed only a yellow dwarf star, with nothing remarkable about it at all . . .

People stopped considering the stars. They had a world to save.

The Mote was a G-2 yellow dwarf, thirty-five light-years distant: a white point at the edge of Murcheson's Eye. So it was for more than a century, while the Second Empire rose from Sparta and came again to New Caledonia.

Then astronomers read old and incomplete records, and resumed their study of the red supergiant known as Murcheson's Eye; but they hardly noticed the Mote.

And the Mote did nothing unusual for one hundred and fifteen years.

Thirty-five light years away, the aliens of Mote Prime had launched a light-sail spacecraft, using batteries of laser cannon powerful enough to outshine a neighboring red supergiant.

As for why they did it that way, and why it looked like that, and what the bejeesus is going on . . . explanations follow.

Most hard science fiction writers follow standard rules for building worlds. We have formulae and tables for getting the orbits right, selecting suns of proper brightness, determining temperatures and climates, building a plausible ecology. Building worlds requires imagination, but a lot of the work is mechanical. Once the mechanical work is done the world may suggest a story, or it may even design its own inhabitants. Larry Niven's "Known Space" stories include worlds which have strongly affected their colonists.

Or the exceptions to the rules may form stories. Why does Mote Prime, a nominally Earthlike world, remind so many people of the planet Mars? What strangeness in its evolution made the atmosphere so helium-rich? This goes beyond mechanics.

In THE MOTE IN GOD'S EYE (Simon and Schuster, 1974) we built not only worlds, but cultures.

From the start MOTE was to be a novel of first contact. After our initial story conference we had larger ambitions: MOTE would be, if we could write it, the *epitome* of first contact novels. We intended to explore every important problem arising from first contact with aliens—and to look at those problems from both human and alien viewpoints.

That meant creating cultures in far more detail than is needed for most novels. It's easy, when a novel is heavy with detail, for the details to get out of hand, creating glaring inconsistencies. (If civilization uses hydrogen fusion power at such a rate that world sea level has dropped by two feet, you will not have people sleeping in abandoned movie houses.) To avoid such inconsistencies we worked a great deal harder developing the basic technologies of both the Motie (alien) and the human civilizations.

In fact, when we finished the book we had nearly as much unpublished material as ended up in the book. There are many pages of data on Motie biology and evolutionary history; details on Empire science and technology; descriptions of space battles, how worlds are terraformed, how light-sails are constructed; and although these background details affected the novel and dictated what we would actually write, most of them never appear in the book.

We made several boundary decisions. One was to employ the Second Empire period of Pournelle's future history. That Empire existed as a series of sketches with a loose outline of its history, most of it previously published. MOTE had to be consistent with the published material.

Another parameter was the physical description of the aliens. Incredibly, that's all we began with: a detailed description of what became the prototype Motie, the Engineer: an attempt to build a nonsymmetrical alien, left over from a Niven story that never quite jelled. The history, biology, evolution, sociology, and culture of the Moties were extrapolated from that being's shape during endless coffee-and-brandy sessions.

That was our second forced choice. The Moties lived within the heart of the Empire, but had never been discovered. A simple explanation might have been to make the aliens a young civilization just discovering space travel, but that assumption contradicted Motie history as extrapolated from their appearance. We found another explanation in the nature of the Alderson drive, discussed later.

EMPIRE TECHNOLOGY

The most important technological features of the Empire were previously published in other stories: the Alderson Drive and Langston Field.

Both were invented to Jerry Pournelle's specifications by Dan Alderson, a resident genius at Cal Tech's Jet Propulsion Laboratories. It had always been obvious that the Drive and Field would affect the cultures that used them, but until we got to work on MOTE it wasn't obvious just how profound the effects would be.

THE ALDERSON DRIVE

Every sf writer eventually must face the problem of interstellar transportation. There are a number of approaches. One is to deny faster-than-light travel. This in practice forbids organized interstellar civilizations.

A second approach is to ignore General and Special Relativity. Readers usually won't accept this. It's a cop-out, and except in the kind of story that's more allegory than science fiction, it's not appropriate.

Another method is to retreat into doubletalk about hyperspace. Doubletalk drives are common enough. The problem is that when everything is permitted, nothing is forbidden. Good stories are made when there are difficulties to overcome, and if there are no limits to "hyperspace travel" there are no real limits to what the heroes and villains can do. In a single work the "difficulties" can be planned as the story goes along, and the drive then redesigned in rewrite; but we couldn't do that here.

Our method was to work out the Drive in detail and live with the resulting limitations. As it happens, the limits on the Drive influenced the final outcome of the story; but they were not invented for that purpose.

The Alderson Drive is consistent with everything presently known about physics. It merely assumes that additional discoveries will be made in about thirty years, at Cal Tech (as a tip o' the hat to Dan Alderson). The key event is the detection of a "fifth force."

There are four known forces in modern physics: two sub-nuclear forces responsible respectively for alpha and beta decay; electromagnetism, which includes light; and gravity. The Alderson force, then, is the fifth, and it is generated by thermonuclear reactions.

The force has little effect in our universe; in fact, it is barely detectable. Simultaneously with the discovery of the fifth force, however, we postulate the discovery of a second universe in point-to-point congruence with our own. The "continuum universe" differs from the one we're used to in that there are no known quantum effects there.

Within that universe particles may travel as fast as they can be accelerated; and the fifth force exists to accelerate them.

There's a lot more, including a page or so of differential equations, but that's the general idea.

You can get from one universe to another. For every construct in our universe there can be created a "correspondence particle" in the continuum universe. In order for your construct to go into and emerge from the continuum universe without change you must have some complex machinery to hold everything together and prevent your ship—and crew—from being disorganized into elementary particles.

Correspondence particles can be boosted to speeds faster than light: in fact, to speeds nearly infinite as we measure them. Of course they cannot emerge into our universe at such speeds: they have to lose their energy to emerge at all. More on that in a moment.

There are severe conditions to entering and leaving the continuum universe. To emerge from the continuum universe you must exit with precisely the same potential energy (measured in terms of the fifth force, not gravity) as you entered. You must also have zero kinetic energy relative to a complex set of coordinates that we won't discuss here.

The fifth force is created by thermonuclear reactions: generally, that is, in stars. You may travel by using it, but only along precisely defined lines of equipotential flux: tramways or tramlines.

Imagine the universe as a thin rubber sheet, very flat. Now drop heavy rocks of different weights onto it. The rocks will distort the sheet, making little cone-shaped (more or less) dimples. Now put two rocks reasonably close together: the dimples will intersect in a valley. The intersection will have a "pass," a region higher than the low points where the rocks (stars) lie, but lower than the general level of the rubber sheet.

The route from one star to another through that "pass" is the tramline. Possible tramlines lie between each two stars, but they don't always exist, because when you add third and fourth stars to the system they may interfere, so there is no unique gradient line. If this seems confusing, don't spend a lot of time worrying about it; we'll get to the effects of all this in a moment.

You may also imagine stars to be like hills; move another star close and the hills will intersect. Again, from summit to summit there will be one and only one line that preserves the maximum potential energy for that level. Release a marble on one hill and it will roll down, across the saddle, and up the side of the other. That too is a tramline effect. It's generally easier to think of the system as valleys rather than hills, because to travel from star to star you have to get over that "hump" between the two. The fifth force provides the energy for that.

You enter from the quantum universe. When you travel in the continuum universe you continually lose kinetic energy; it "leaks." This can be detected in our universe as photons. The effect can be important during a space battle. We cut such a space battle from MOTE, but it still exists, and we may yet publish it as a novella.

To get from the quantum to the continuum universe you must supply power, and this is available only in quantum terms. When you do this you turn yourself into a correspondence particle; go across the tramline; and come out at the point on the other side where your potential energy is equal to what you entered with, plus zero kinetic energy (in terms of the fifth force and complex reference axes).

For those bored by the last few paragraphs, take heart: we'll leave the technical details and get on with what it all means.

. . .

Travel by Alderson Drive consists of getting to the proper Alderson Point and turning on the Drive. Energy is used. You vanish, to reappear in an immeasurably short time at the Alderson Point in another star system some several light-years away. If you haven't done everything right, or aren't at the Alderson Point, you turn on your drive and a lot of energy vanishes. You don't move. (In fact you do move, but you instantaneously reappear in the spot where you started.)

That's all there is to the Drive, but it dictates the structure of an interstellar civilization.

To begin with, the Drive works only from point to point across interstellar distances. Once in a star system you must rely on reaction drives to get around. There's no magic way from, say, Saturn to Earth: you've got to slog across.

Thus space battles are possible, and you can't escape battle by vanishing into hyperspace, as you could in future history series such as Beam Piper's and Gordon Dickson's. To reach a given planet you must travel across its stellar system, and you must enter that system at one of the Alderson Points. There won't be more than five or six possible points of entry, and there may only be one.

Star systems and planets can be thought of as continents and islands, then, and Alderson Points as narrow sea gates such as Suez, Gibraltar, Panama, Malay Straits, etc. To carry the analogy further, there's telegraph but no radio: the fastest message between star systems is one carried by a ship, but within star systems messages go much faster than the ships . . .

Hmm. This sounds a bit like the early days of steam. *Not* sail; the ships require fuel and sophisticated repair facilities. They won't pull into some deserted star system and rebuild themselves unless they've carried the spare parts along. However, if you think of naval actions in the period between the Crimean War and World War One, you'll have a fair picture of conditions as implied by the Alderson Drive.

The Drive's limits mean that uninteresting stellar systems won't be explored. There are too many of them. They may be used as crossing-points if the stars are conveniently placed, but stars not along a travel route may never be visited.

Reaching the Mote, or leaving it, would be damned inconvenient. Its only tramline reaches to a star only a third of a light-year away—Murcheson's Eye, the red supergiant—and ends deep inside the red-hot outer envelope. The aliens' only access to the Empire is across thirty-five light-years of interstellar space—which no Empire ship would ever see. The gaps between the stars are as mysterious to the Empire as they are to you.

LANGSTON FIELD

Our second key technological building block was the Langston Field, which absorbs and stores energy in proportion to the fourth power of incoming particle energy: that is, a slow-moving object can penetrate it, but the faster it's moving (or hotter it is) the more readily it is absorbed.

(In fact it's not a simple fourth-power equation; but our readers surely don't need third-order differential equations for amusement.)

The Field can be used for protection against lasers, thermonuclear weapons, and nearly anything else. It isn't a perfect defense, however. The natural shape of the Field is a solid. Thus it wants to collapse and vaporize everything inside it. It takes energy to maintain a hole inside the Field, and more energy to open a control in it so that you can cause it selectively to radiate away stored energy. You don't get something for nothing.

This means that if a Field is overloaded, the ship inside vanishes into vapor. In addition, *parts* of the Field can be momentarily overloaded: a sufficiently high energy impacting a small enough area will cause a temporary Field collapse, and a burst of energy penetrates to the inside. This can damage a ship without destroying it.

COSMOGRAPHY

We've got to invent a term. What is a good word to mean the equivalent of "geography" as projected into interstellar space? True, planetologists have now adopted "geology" to mean geophysical sciences applied to any planet, not merely Earth; and one might reasonably expect "geography" to be applied to the study of physical features of other planets—but we're concerned here with the relationship of star systems to each other.

We suggest cosmography, but perhaps that's too broad? Should that term be used for relationships of *galaxies*, and mere star system patterns be studied as "astrography"? After all, "astrogator" is a widely used term meaning "navigator" for interstellar flight.

Some of the astrography of MOTE was given because it had been previously published. In particular, the New Caledonia system, and the red supergiant known as Murcheson's Eye, had already been worked out. There were also published references to the history of New Caledonia.

We needed a red supergiant in the Empire. There's only one logical place for that, and previously published stories had placed one there: Murcheson's Eye, behind the Coal Sack. It *has* to be behind the Coal Sack: if there were a supergiant that close anywhere else, we'd see it now.

Since we had to use Murcheson's Eye, we had to use New Caledonia. Not that this was any great imposition: New Scotland and New Ireland are interesting places, terraformed planets, with interesting features and interesting cultures.

There was one problem, though: New Scotland is inhabited by New Scots, a people who have preserved their subculture for a long time and defend it proudly. Thus, since much of the action takes place on New Scotland, some of the characters, including at least one major character, *had* to be New Scot. For structural reasons we had only two choices: the First Officer or the Chief Engineer.

We chose the Chief Engineer, largely because in the contemporary world it is a fact that a vastly disproportionate number of ship's engineers are Scots, and that seemed a reasonable thing to project into the future.

Alas, some critics have resented that, and a few have accused us of stealing Mr. Sinclair from *Star Trek*. We didn't. Mr. Sinclair is what he is for perfectly sound astrographical reasons.

The astrography eventually dictated the title of the book. Since most of the action takes place very near the Coal Sack, we needed to know how the Coal Sack would look close up from the back side. Eventually we put swirls of interplanetary dust in it, and evolving proto-stars, and all manner of marvels; but those came after we got *very* close. The first problem was the Coal Sack seen from ten parsecs.

Larry Niven hit on the happy image of a hooded man, with the supergiant where one eye might be. The supergiant has a small companion, a yellow dwarf not very different from our Sun. If the supergiant is an eye—Murcheson's Eye—then the dwarf is, of course, a mote in that eye.

But if the Hooded Man is seen by backward and superstitious peoples as the Face of God . . . then the name for the Mote becomes inevitable . . . and once suggested, "The Mote In God's Eye" is a near irresistible title. (Although in fact Larry Niven did resist it, and wanted "The Mote In Murcheson's Eye" up to the moment when the publisher argued strongly for the present title.)

THE SHIPS

Long ago we acquired a commercial model called "The Explorer Ship Leif Ericsson," a plastic spaceship of intriguing design. It is shaped something like a flattened pint whiskey bottle with a long neck. The "Leif Ericsson," alas, was killed by general lack of interest in spacecraft by model buyers; a ghost of it is still marketed in hideous glow-in-the-dark color as some kind of flying saucer.

It's often easier to take a detailed construct and work within its limits than it is to have too much flexibility. For fun we tried to make the Leif Ericsson work as a model for an Empire naval vessel. The exercise proved instructive.

First, the model is of a *big* ship, and is of the wrong shape ever to be carried aboard another vessel. Second, it had fins, only useful for atmosphere flight: what purpose would be served in having atmosphere capabilities on a large ship?

This dictated the class of ship: it must be a cruiser or battlecruiser. Battleships and dreadnaughts wouldn't ever land, and would be cylindrical or spherical to reduce surface area. Our ship was too large to be a destroyer (an expendable ship almost never employed on missions except as part of a flotilla). Cruisers and battlecruisers can be sent on independent missions.

MacArthur, a General Class Battlecruiser, began to emerge. She can enter atmosphere, but rarely does so, except when long independent assignments force her to seek fuel on her own. She can do this in either of two ways: go to a supply source, or fly into the hydrogen-rich atmosphere of a gas giant and scoop. There were scoops on the model, as it happens.

She has a large pair of doors in her hull, and a spacious compartment inside: obviously a hangar deck for carrying auxiliary craft. Hangar deck is also the only large compartment in her, and therefore would be the normal place of assembly for the crew when she isn't under battle conditions.

The tower on the model looked useless, and was almost ignored, until it occurred to us that on long missions not under acceleration it would be useful to have a high-gravity area. The ship is a bit thin to have much gravity in the "neck" without spinning her far more rapidly than you'd like; but with the tower, the forward area gets normal gravity without excessive spin rates.

And on, and so forth. In the novel, *Lenin* was designed from scratch; and of course we did have to make some modifications in Leif Ericsson before she could become INSS *MacArthur*; but it's surprising just how much detail you can work up through having to live with the limits of a model.

SOCIOLOGY

The Alderson Drive and the Langston Field determine what kinds of interstellar organizations will be possible. There will be alternatives, but they have to fit into the limits these technologies impose.

In THE MOTE IN GOD'S EYE we chose Imperial Aristocracy as the main form of human government. We've been praised for this: Dick

Brass in a *New York Post* review concludes that we couldn't have chosen anything else, and other critics have applauded us for showing what such a society might be like.

Fortunately there are no Sacred Cows in science fiction. Maybe we should have stuck to incest? Because other critics have been horrified! Do we, they ask, really *believe* in imperial government? and *monarchy*?

That depends on what they mean by "believe in." Do we think it's desirable? We don't have to say. Inevitable? Of course not. Do we think it's *possible*? Damn straight.

The political science in MOTE is taken from C. Northcote Parkinson's *Evolution of Political Thought*. Parkinson himself echoes Aristotle.

It is fashionable to view history as a linear progression: things get better, never worse, and of course we'll never go back to the bad old days of (for instance) personal government. Oddly enough, even critics who have complained about the aristocratic pyramid in MOTE—and thus rejected our Empire as absurd—have been heard to complain about "Imperial Presidency" in the USA. How many readers would bet long odds against John-John Kennedy becoming President within our lifetimes?

Any pretended "science" of history is the bunk. That's the problem with Marxism. Yet Marx wrote a reasonable economic view of history up to his time, and some of his principles may be valid.

Military history is another valid way to view the last several thousand years—but no one in his right mind would pretend that a history of battles and strategies is the whole of the human story. You may write history in terms of medical science, in terms of rats, lice, and plagues, in terms of agricultural development, in terms of strong leadership personalities, and each view will hold some truth.

There are many ways to view history, and Aristotle's cycles as brought up to date by Parkinson make one of the better ones. For those who don't accept that proposition, we urge you at least to read Parkinson before making up your minds and closing the door.

The human society in MOTE is colored by technology and historical evolution. In MOTE's future history the United States and the Soviet Union form an alliance and together dominate the world during the last decades of the 20th Century. The alliance doesn't end their rivalry, and doesn't make the rulers or people of either nation love their partners.

The CoDominium Alliance needs a military force. Military people need something or someone they can give loyalty; few men ever risked their lives for a "standard of living" and there's little that's more stupid than dying for one's standard of living—unless it's dying for someone else's standard of living.

Do the attitudes of contemporary police and soldiers lead us to suppose that "democracy" or "the people" inspire loyalty? The proposition is at least open to question. In the future that leads to MOTE, a Russian

Admiral named Lermontov becomes leader of CoDominium forces. Although he is not himself interested in founding a dynasty, he transfers the loyalty of the Fleet to leaders who are.

He brings with him the military people at a time of great crisis. Crises have often produced strong loyalties to single leaders: Churchill, Roosevelt, George Washington, John F. Kennedy during the Cuban Crisis, etc. (A year after Kennedy's death Senator Pastore could address a national convention and get standing ovations with the words "There stood John Kennedy, TEN FEET TALL!!!")

Thus develops the Empire.

Look at another trend: personal dictatorship. There are as many people ruled by tyrants as by "democracy" in nineteen seventy-five, and even in the democracies charges of tyranny are not lacking. Dictatorships may not be the wave of the future—but is it unreasonable to suppose they might be?

Dictatorship is often tried in times of severe crisis, energy crisis, pollution crisis, agricultural crisis—surely we do not lack for crises? The trouble with dictatorship is that it generates a succession crisis when the old man bows out. Portugal seems to be going through such at this moment. Chile, Uganda, Brazil, name your own examples: anyone want to bet that some of these won't turn to a new Caudillo with relief?

How to avoid succession crisis? One traditional method is to turn Bonapartist: give the job to a relative or descendant of the dictator. He may not do the job very well, but after enough crises people are often uninterested in whether the land is governed well. They just want things *settled* so they can get on with everyday life.

Suppose the dictator's son does govern well? A new dynasty is founded, and the trappings of legitimacy are thrust onto the new royal family. To be sure, the title of "King" may be abandoned. Napoleon chose to be "Emperor of the French," Cromwell chose "Lord Protector," and we suppose the US will be ruled by Presidents for a long time—but the nature of the Presidency, and the way one gets the office, may change.

See, for example, Niven's use of "Secretary-General" in the tales of Svetz the time-traveler.

We had a choice in MOTE: to keep the titles as well as the structure of aristocratic empire, or abandon the titles and retain the structure only. We could have abolished "Emperor" in favor of "President," or "Chairperson," or "Leader," or "Admiral," or "Posnitch." The latter, by the way, is the name of a particularly important President honored for all time by having his name adopted as the title for Leader . . .

We might have employed titles other than Duke (originally meant "leader" anyway) and Count (Companion to the king) and Marquis (Count of the frontier marches). Perhaps we should have. But any titles used would have been *translations* of whatever was current in the time of the novel, and the traditional titles had the effect of letting the reader know quickly the approximate status and some of the duties of the characters.

There are hints all through MOTE that the structure of government is not a mere carbon copy of the British Empire or Rome or England in the time of William III. On the other hand there are similarities, which are forced onto the Empire by the technology we assumed.

Imperial government is not inevitable. It is possible.

The alternate proposition is that we of nineteen seventy-five are so advanced that we will never go back to the bad old days. Yet we can show you essays "proving" exactly that proposition—and written thousands of years ago. There's a flurry of them every few centuries.

We aren't the first people to think we've "gone beyond" personal government, personal loyalties, and a state of religion. Maybe we won't be the last.

Anyway, MOTE is supposed to be entertainment, not an essay on the influence of science on social organization. (You're getting *that* here.)

The Empire is what it is largely because of the Alderson Drive and Langston Field. Without the Drive an Empire could not form. Certainly an interstellar Empire would look very different if it had to depend on lightspeed messages to send directives and receive reports. Punitive expeditions would be nearly impossible, hideously expensive, and probably futile: you'd be punishing the grandchildren of a generation that seceded from the Empire, or even a planet that put down the traitors after the message went out.

Even a rescue expedition might never reach a colony in trouble. A coalition of bureaucrats could always collect the funds for such an expedition, sign papers certifying that the ships are on the way, and pocket the money . . . in sixty years someone might realize what had happened, or not.

The Langston Field is crucial to the Empire, too. The Navy can survive partial destruction and keep fighting. Ships carry black boxes—plug-in sets of spare parts—and large crews who have little to do unless half of them get killed. That's much like the navies of fifty years ago.

A merchant ship might have a crew of forty. A warship of similar size carries a crew ten times as large. Most have little to do for most of the life of the ship. It's only in battles that the large number of self-programming computers become important. *Then* the outcome of the battle may depend on having the largest and best-trained crew—and there aren't many prizes for second place in battle.

Big crews with little to do demand an organization geared to that kind of activity. Navies have been doing that for a long time, and have evolved a structure that they tenaciously hold onto.

Without the Field as defense against lasers and nuclear weapons, battles would become no more than offensive contests. They'd last microseconds, not hours. Ships would be destroyed or not, but hardly ever wounded. Crews would tend to be small, ships would be different, including something like the present-day aircraft carriers. Thus technology dictates Naval organization.

It dictates politics, too. If you can't get the populace, or a large part of it, under a city-sized Field, then any given planet lies naked to space.

If the Drive allowed ships to sneak up on planets, materializing without warning out of hyperspace, there could be no Empire even with the Field. There'd be no Empire because belonging to an Empire wouldn't protect you. Instead there might be populations of planet-bound serfs ruled at random by successive hordes of space pirates. Upward mobility in society would consist of getting your own ship and turning pirate.

Given Drive and Field, though, Empires are possible. What's more likely? A representative confederacy? It would hardly inspire the loyalty of the military forces, whatever else it might do. (In the War Between the States, the Confederacy's main problem was that the troops were loyal to their own State, not the central government.)

Each stellar system independent? That's reasonable, but is it stable? Surely there might be pressures toward unification of at least parts of interstellar space.

How has unification been achieved in the past? Nearly always by conquest or colonization or both. How have they been held together? Nearly always by loyalty to a leader, an Emperor, or a dynasty, generally buttressed by the trappings of religion and piety. Even Freethinkers of the last century weren't ashamed to profess loyalty to the Widow of Windsor . . .

Government over large areas needs emotional ties. It also needs *stability*. Government by 50%-plus-one hasn't enjoyed particularly stable politics—and it lasts only so long as the 50%-minus-one minority is willing to submit. Is heredity a rational way to choose leaders? It has this in its favor: the leader is known from an early age to be destined to rule, and can be educated to the job. Is that preferable to education based on how to *get* the job? Are elected officials better at governing, or at winning elections?

Well, at least the counter-case can be made. That's all we intended to do. We chose a stage of Empire in which the aristocracy was young and growing and dynamic, rather than static and decadent; when the aristocrats are more concerned with duty than with privilege; and we made no hint that we thought that stage would last forever.

• • •

RANDOM DETAILS

Robert Heinlein once wrote that the best way to give the flavor of the future is to drop in, without warning, some strange detail. He gives as an example, "The door dilated."

We have a number of such details in MOTE. We won't spoil the book by dragging them all out in a row. One of the most obvious we use is the personal computer, which not only does computations, but also puts the owner in contact with any nearby data bank; in effect it will give the answer to any question whose answer is known and that you think to ask.

Thus no idiot block gimmicks in MOTE. Our characters may fail to guess something, or not put information together in the right way, but they won't *forget* anything important. The closest that comes to happening is when Sally Fowler can't quite remember where she filed the tape of a conversation, and she doesn't take long to find it then.

On the other hand, people can be swamped with too much information, and that does happen.

There were many other details, all needed to keep the story moving. A rational kind of space suit, certainly different from the clumsy things used now. Personal weapons. The crystal used in a banquet aboard *MacArthur*: crystal strong as steel, cut from the windshield of a wrecked First Empire reentry vehicle, indicating the higher technology lost in that particular war. Clothing and fashion; the status of women; myriads of details of everyday life.

Not that *all* of these differ from the present. Some of the things we kept the same probably will change in a thousand years. Others . . . well, the customs associated with wines and hard liquors are old and stable. If we'd changed everything, and made an attempt to portray every detail of our thousand-year-advanced future, the story would have gotten bogged down in details.

MOTE is probably the only novel ever to have a planet's orbit changed to save a line.

New Chicago, as it appeared in the opening scenes of the first draft of MOTE, was a cold place, orbiting far from its star. It was never a very important point, and Larry Niven didn't even notice it.

Thus when he introduced Lady Sandra Liddell Leonovna Bright Fowler, he used as viewpoint character a Marine guard sweating in hot sunlight. The Marine thinks, "She doesn't sweat. She was carved from ice by the finest sculptor that ever lived."

Now that's a good line. Unfortunately it implies a hot planet. If the line must be kept, the planet must be moved.

So Jerry Pournelle moved it. New Chicago became a world much closer to a cooler sun. Its year changed, its climate changed, its whole history had to be changed . . .

Worth it, though. Sometimes it's easier to build new worlds than think up good lines.

• • •

• • •

A bandersnatch is twice the size of a brontosaur. Its skeleton is flexible but has no joints; the only breaks in its smooth white skin are the tufts of sensory bristles on either side of its tapering blank head. It moves on a rippling belly foot. Bandersnatchi live in the lowlands of Jinx, browsing off the gray yeast along the shorelines. You'd think they were the most helpless things in known space ... until you saw one bearing down on you like a charging mountain. Once I saw an ancient armored car crushed flat across a lowlands rock, straddled by the broken bones of the beast that ran it down.

"The Handicapped," 1968

BRENDA

2656 AD, MARCH (FIREBEE CLOCK TIME)

Human-settled worlds all look alike from high orbit. Terry thought that the CoDominium explorers must have had it easy.

Alderson jump. ZZZTT! One white pinpoint among myriads has become a flood of white light. Nerve networks throughout ship and crew are strummed in four dimensions. Wait for the blur to go away. You had a hangover this bad, once. It lasted longer.

Now search the ecliptic a decent distance from the sun. Look for shadows in the neudar screen: planets. Big enough? Small enough? Colors: blue with a white froth of clouds, if men are to breathe the air. Is there enough land? How big are the icecaps? Three or four months to move close, and look.

Nuliajuk's icecaps had covered half the surface. If they ever melted, Nuliajuk would be all water. A cold world. Nobody else would settle, but what about Eskimos? So Terry Kakumee's ancestors had found a home, four centuries ago.

Tanith had no icecaps at all, and almost no axial tilt. Half land, but plenty of rainfall: the equatorial oceans boiled where they were shallow enough. Salt deserts around the equator. Swamps across both poles. Transportees had settled the north pole.

Terry Kakumee floated against the big window at *Firebee*'s nose. It was sixteen years since he'd seen Tanith.

Tanith was a growing crescent, blue with white graffiti, and a blazing highlight across the northern pole. Summer. One serious mountain, The Warden, stood six kilometers tall. It had been white-tipped in winter. Dagon City would be in the foothills, south.

The clouds were sparse. The city itself didn't show, but he found a glare-point that had to be the old spaceport.

Brenda's farm would be south of that.

Sharon Hayes drifted up behind him. "I've been talking to the Dagon Port Authority. One George Callahan, no rank given, tells me they don't have much in the way of repair facilities, but we're intensely welcome. I've got a dinner date."

"Good." On a world this far from what civilization was left near Sparta, the population would feel cut off. Ships would be welcome. "What about fuel?"

"They can make liquid hydrogen. There's a tanker. Callahan gave me a course down. Four hours from now, and we'll have to lower *Firebee*'s orbit. Time to move, troops. Are we all going down?"

She meant that for Charley. Charley Laine (cargo and purser) was almost covered in burn scars. His face was a smooth mask. There was an unmarred patch along his jaw that he had to shave, and good skin in strips along his back and the backs of his arms and legs, and just enough unburned scalp to grow a decent queue. Sometimes he didn't want to face strangers. He said, "Somebody'd better stay on duty, Captain Sharon. Did you ask about outies?"

"They haven't been raided since the Battle. They do have a couple of high-thrust mining ships. Charley, I think *Firebee*'s safe enough."

Charley let out a breath. "I'll come. I can't be the only war vet on Tanith. There was— I wonder—"

"Brenda," Terry said.

"Yeah. I wonder about Brenda sometimes."

"I wonder too."

2640A, NOVEMBER (TANITH LOCAL TIME)

Lieutenant Kakumee had been Second Engineer aboard the recon ship *Firebee* during the destruction of the Sauron Second Fleet. The enemy's gene-tailored warriors were dead or fled, but they had left their mark. Damaged ships were limping in from everywhere in Tanith system. *Firebee* would orbit Tanith until she could be refitted or rifled for parts.

Firebee's midsection was a blob of metal bubbles where the Langston Field generator had vaporized itself and half melted the hull around it. It was the only hit *Firebee* had taken. Charley Laine had been caught in the flare.

They'd taken him to St. Agnes Hospital in Dagon City.

"The sky's full of ruined ships," Terry told him. "Most of them have damaged Langston Field generators. First thing that goes in a battle. We'll never get replacements."

Charley didn't answer. He might have heard; he might have felt the touch of Terry's hand. He looked like a tremendous pillow stuck with tubes in various places.

"Without a Langston Field we don't have a ship. I'd give *Firebee* a decent burial if I could get her down. You'll be healed a long time before any part of her flies again," Terry said. He believed that Charley would heal. He might never look quite human again, and if he walked he'd never run; but his central nervous system wasn't damaged, and his heart beat, and his lungs sucked air through the hole at one end of the pillow, while regeneration went on inside.

Terry heard urgent voices through the door. Patients healthy enough for curiosity stirred restlessly.

"Something's going on." Terry patted the padded hand. "I'll come back and tell you about it."

At first glance she wasn't that badly hurt.

She was slumped in an armchair in the lobby. Half a dozen people swarmed about her: a doctor, two nurses, two MPs and a thick-necked Marine in a full leg cast who was trying to stay out of the way and see too. She was wearing a bantar cloth coverall. It was a mess: sky-blue with a green-and-scarlet landscape on the back, barely visible under several pounds of mud and swamp mold.

Bantar cloth had been restricted to Navy use up to eighty years ago. It was nearly indestructible. It wasn't high style, but farmers and others in high-risk jobs wore bantar cloth at half the price of a tractor. Whatever had happened to the woman, it would have been worse without that.

She had black ancestry with some white (skin like good milk chocolate, but weathered by fatigue and the elements) and oriental (the tilt of the eyes). Thick, tightly coiled black hair formed a cushion around her head. It carried its own share of mud. A nasty gash cut through the hair. It ran from above her left eye back to the crown of her head. A nurse had cleaned it with alcohol; it was bleeding.

She drained a paper cup of water. A doctor—Charley's doctor, Lex Hartner—handed her another, and she drained that too. "No more," Hartner said. "We'll get you some broth."

She nodded and said, "Uh." Her lip curled way up on the left. She tried to say something else. Stroke? Nonsense, she couldn't be past thirty. The head wound—

Poor woman.

Hartner said, "We'll get that soup into you before we look you over. How long were you out there?"

"Wumble." Her lip curled up; then half her face wrinkled in frustration. The other half remained slack. She held up one finger, then lifted another.

"A week or two?"

She nodded vigorously. Her eyes met Terry's. He smiled and turned away, feeling like an intruder. He went back to talk to Charley.

2656, JUNE (TANITH LOCAL TIME)

The wrecked ships that had haloed the planet after the Battle of Tanith were long gone. Shuttle #1 descended through a sky that seemed curiously empty.

What had been the Tanith spaceport still glared like a polished steel dish. Seen from low angle the crater became a glowing eye with a bright pupil.

The big Langston Field dome had protected Dagon City during the battle. The smaller dome at the spaceport had absorbed a stream of guided meteors, then given all of the energy back as the field collapsed.

A new port had grown around the crater's eastern rim. Terry and Charley, riding as passengers while Sharon flew, picked out a dozen big aircraft, then a horde of lighter craft. The crater must make a convenient airfield. The gleaming center was a small lake. Have to avoid that.

Both of *Firebee*'s shuttles had lost their hover capability. They'd been looking for repair facilities for six years now. Shuttle #1 came in a little fast because of the way the crater dipped, coasted across and braked to a stop at the rim.

Tanith was hot and humid, with a smell of alien vegetation. The sun was low. Big autumn-colored flutterbys formed a cloud around them as they emerged. These were new to Terry. He'd never seen a Tanith summer.

They had drawn a crowd of twenty-odd, still growing. Terry noticed how good they looked: shorter than average, but all well muscled, none obtrusively fat. A year in Tanith's 1.14 gravity made anyone look good. The early strokes and heart attacks didn't show.

Terry was a round man; he felt rounder by contrast. Sharon Hayes fit right in. She was past fifty, and it showed in the deep wrinkle patterns around eyes and mouth; but regular exercise and a childhood in Tanith gravity had kept her body tight and muscular.

. . .

The airport bar was cool and dry, and crowded now.

George Callahan was a burly man in his forties, red hair going gray, red fur along his thick arms. He and Sharon seemed to like each other on sight. They settled at a smaller table, and there they dealt with entry forms on Callahan's pocket computer. (Cargo: a Langston Field generator big enough to shield a small city. Purpose of entry: trade.)

Terry and Charley drank at the crowd's expense and tried to describe sixteen years of interstellar trading.

Terry let Charley do most of the talking. Let him forget the fright mask he wore. "*Yes* we are heroes, by damn! We saved Phoenix from famine two years ago." He'd tried to hold his breath when *Firebee*'s Langston Field generator blew up, but his voice still had a gravelly texture. "We'd just come from Hitchhiker's Rest. They've got a gene-tailored crop called kudzu grain. We went back and filled Firebee with kudzu grain, we were *living* in the stuff all the way back, and we strewed it across the Phoenix croplands. It came up before twenty-two million people quite ran out of stores. Then it died off, of course, because it isn't designed for Phoenix conditions, but by then they had their crops growing again. I never felt that good before or since."

The barmaids were setting out a free lunch, and someone brought them plates. Fresh food! Charley had his mouth full, so Terry said, "It's Hitchhiker's Rest that's in trouble. That kudzu grain is taking over everything. It really is wonderful stuff, but it eats the houses."

He bit into a sandwich: cheese and mystery meat and tomatoes and chili leaf between thick slices of bread. Sharon was working on another. She'd have little room for dinner . . . or was this lunch? The sun had looked like late afternoon. He asked somebody, "What time is it local?"

"Ten. Just short of noon." The woman grinned. "And nights are four hours long."

He'd forgotten: Dagon City was seven hundred kilometers short of the north pole. "Okay. I need to use a phone."

"I'll show you." She was a small brunette, wide at hips and shoulders. When she took Terry's arm she was about his height.

Charley was saying, "We don't expect to get rich. There aren't any rich worlds. The war hurt everybody, and some are a long time recovering. We don't try to stop outies. We just go away, and I guess everyone else does too. That means a lot of worlds are cut off."

The brunette led him down a hall to a bank of computer screens. He asked, "How do I get Information?"

"You don't have a card? No, of course not. Here." She pushed plastic into a slot. The screen lit with data, and Terry noticed her name: Maria Montez. She tapped QQQ.

The operator had the look of bony Spartan aristocracy: pale skin, high cheekbones and a small, pursed mouth. "What region?"

"I don't know the region. Brenda Curtis."

The small mouth pursed in irritation. (Not a recording?) Terry said, "Try south-south. Then west." Brenda had inherited the farm. She might have returned there, or she might still be working at the hospital.

"South-south, Brenda Curtis." The operator tapped at her own keyboard. "Six-two-one-one-six-eight. Do you have that?"

She was alive! "Yes. Thank you." He jotted it on his pocket computer.

Maria was still there . . . Naturally she'd want her card back. Did he care what she heard? He took his courage in both hands and tapped out the number.

A girl answered: ten years old, very curly blond hair, cute, with a serious look. "Brenda's."

"Can I talk to Brenda Curtis?"

"She's on the roof."

"Will you get her, please?"

"No, we don't bother her when she's on the roof."

"Oh. Okay. Tell her I called. Terry Kakumee. When should I call back?"

"After dinner. About eighteen."

"Thanks." Something about the girl . . . "Is Brenda your mother?"

"Yes. I'm Reseda Anderssen." The girl hung up.

Maria was looking at him. "You know Brenda Curtis?"

"I used to. How do you know her?"

"She runs the orphanage. I know one of her boys. Not hers, I mean, but one of the boys she raised."

"Tell me about her."

Maria shrug-sniffed. Maybe talking about another woman wasn't what she'd had in mind. "She moved to a swamp farm after the Battle of Tanith. The City paid her money to keep orphans, and I guess there were a lot of them. Not so many now. Lots of teenagers. They've got their own skewball team, and they've had the pennant two years running."

"She was in bad shape when I knew her. Head wound. Does her lip pull up on one side when she talks?"

"Not that I noticed."

"Well," he said, "I'm glad she's doing okay."

Thinking of her as a patient might have put a different light on things. Maria took his arm again. They made an interesting match, Terry thought. Same height, both rounded in the body, and almost the same shade of hair and skin. She asked, "Was she in the Navy? Like Mr. Laine—"

"No."

"How did she get hurt?"

"Maria, I'm not sure that's been declassified. She wasn't in the Navy, but she got involved with the Sauron thing anyway." And he wouldn't tell her any more.

2640A, NOVEMBER (TANITH LOCAL TIME)

He'd taken Dr. Hartner to dinner partly because he felt sorry for him, partly to get him talking.

Lex Hartner was thin all over, with a long, narrow face and wispy blond hair. Terry would always remember him as tired . . . but that was unfair. Every doctor on Tanith lived at the edge of exhaustion after the battle of Tanith.

"Your friend'll heal," he told Terry. "He was lucky. One of the first patients in after the battle. We still had eyes in stock, and we had a regeneration sleeve. His real problem is, we'll have to take it off him as soon as he can live without it."

"Scars be damned?"

"Oh, he'll scar. They wouldn't be as bad if we left the sleeve on him longer. But *Napoleon*'s coming in with burn cases—"

"Yeah. I wouldn't want your job."

"This is the hardest part."

It was clear to Terry: there was no way to talk Lex into leaving Charley in the sleeve for a little longer. So he changed the subject. "That woman in the hall this morning—"

Lex didn't ask who he meant. "We don't have a name yet. She appeared at a swamp farm south of here. Mrs. Maddox called the hospital. We sent an ambulance. She must have come out of the swamps. From the look of her, she was there for some time."

"She didn't look good."

"She's malnourished. There's fungus all over her. Bantar cloth doesn't let air through. You have to wear net underwear, and hers was rotted to shreds. That head wound gouged her skull almost through the bone. Beyond that I just can't tell, Terry. I don't have the instruments."

Terry nodded; he didn't have to ask about that.

There had been one massive burn-through during the Battle of Tanith. Raw plasma had washed across several city blocks for three or four seconds. A hotel had been slagged, and shops and houses, and a stream of flame had rolled up the dome and hovered at the apex while it died. The hospital had lost most of its windows . . . and every piece of equipment that could be ruined by an electromagnetic pulse.

"There's just no way to look inside her head. I don't want to open her up. She's coming along nicely, she can say a few words, and she can draw and use sign language. And she tries so hard.''

All of which Terry told to Charley the next day. They'd told him Charley wasn't conscious most of the time; but Terry pictured him going nuts from boredom inside that pillow.

2656, JUNE (TANITH LOCAL TIME)

The bar had turned noisy. At the big table you could still hear Charley. ''Boredom. You spend months getting to and from the Jump points. We've played every game program in ship's memory half to death. I think any one of us could beat anyone on Tanith at Rollerball, Chance, the Mirror Game—''

''We've got a Mirror Game,'' someone said. ''It's in the Library.''

''Great!''

Someone pushed two chairs into the pattern for Maria and Terry. Charley was saying, ''We did find something interesting this trip. There's a Sauron ship in orbit around EST 1310. We knew it was there, we could hear it every time we used the jump points, but EST 1310 is a flare star. We didn't dare go after it. But this trip we're carrying a mucking great Langston Field generator in the cargo hold . . .''

Captain Sharon looked dubious. Charley was talking a lot. They'd pulled valuable data from the Sauron wreck, salable data. But so what? Tanith couldn't reach the ship, and maybe they should be considered customers. And Brenda might hear. Let him talk.

''It was *Morningstar*, a Sauron hornet ship. The Saurons must have gutted it for anything they could use on other ships, then turned it into a signaling beacon. They'd left the computer. They had to have that to work the message sender. We disarmed some booby traps and managed to get into the programming . . .''

People drifted away, presumably to run the airport. Others came in. The party was shaping up as a long one. Terry was minded to stay. He'd maintained a pleasant buzz, and Brenda had waited for sixteen years. She'd wait longer.

At seven he spoke into Maria's ear. ''I'd be pleased to take you to dinner, if you can guide me to a restaurant.''

She said, ''Good! But don't you like parties?''

''Oh, hell yes. Stick with the crowd?''

''Good. Till later.''

''I still have to make that phone call.''

She nodded vigorously and fished her card out of a pocket. He got up and went back to the public phones.

2640A, NOVEMBER (TANITH LOCAL TIME)

When *Firebee*'s Shuttle #2 came down, there had been no repair facilities left on Tanith. There was little for a Second Engineer to do.

Napoleon changed that. *Napoleon* was an old Spartan troopship arriving in the wake of the Battle of Tanith. Word had it that it was loaded with repair equipment. Now *Napoleon*'s shuttles were bringing stuff down, and *Napoleon*'s purser was hearing requests from other ships in need of repairs.

Captain Shu and the others would be cutting their own deals in orbit. Terry and Charley were the only ones on the ground. Terry spent four days going through Shuttle #2, listing everything the little GO craft would need. When he went begging to *Napoleon*'s Spartan officers, he wanted to know exactly what to ask for. He made three lists: maximum repairs if he could get them, the minimum he could settle for, and a third list no other plaintiff would have made. He hoped.

He hadn't visited Charley in four days.

The tall dark woman in the corridor caught his attention. He would have remembered her. She was eight inches taller than Terry, in a dressing gown too short for her and a puffy shower cap. She was more striking than beautiful: square-jawed and lean enough to show ribs and hip bones where the cloth pulled taut.

She caught him looking and smiled with one side of her face. ''He'o! I member you!'' Her lip tugged way up on the left.

''Oh, it's you,'' Terry said. Six days ago: the head wound case. ''Hey, you can talk! That's good. I'm Terry Kakumee.''

''Benda Curris.''

It was an odd name. ''Benda?''

''Br, renda. Cur, tiss.''

''Brenda. Sorry. What were you doing out there in the swamps?'' He instantly added, ''Does it tire you to talk?''

She spoke slowly and carefully. ''Yes. I told my story to the Marines and Navy officers and Doctor Hartner. I don't like it. You wo-wouldn't like it. They smiled a lot when we all knew I wasn't pregnant.'' She didn't seem to see Terry's bewilderment. ''You're Charley's friend. He's out of the re-gener-ation sleeve.''

''Can he have visitors?''

''Ssure. I'll take you.''

Charley wasn't a pillow any more. He didn't look good, either. Wasted. Burned. He didn't move much on the water bed. His lips weren't quite mobile enough; he sounded a bit like Brenda. ''There are four regeneration sleeves on Tanith, and one tank to make the goo, and when they wear out there's nothing. My sleeve is on a Marine from Tabletop. Burn patient, like me. I asked. I see you've met Brenda?"

"Yeah."

"She went through a hell of an experience. We don't talk about it. So how's the work coming?"

"I'll go to the purser tomorrow. I want all my ducks in a row, but I don't want everyone getting their requests in ahead of me either. I made a list of things we could give up to other ships. That might help."

"Good idea. Very Eskimo."

"Charley, it isn't really. The old traditions have us giving a stranger what he needs whether we need it or not."

He noticed Brenda staring at him. She said, "How strange."

He laughed a little uncomfortably. "I suppose a stranger wouldn't ask for what the village had to have. Anyway, those days are almost gone."

Brenda listened while they talked about the ship. She wouldn't understand much of it, though both men tried to explain from time to time. "The Langston Field is your reentry shield and your weapons shield and your true hull. We'll never get it repaired, but *Firebee* could still function in the outer system. I'm trying to get the shuttles rebuilt. Maybe we can make her a trader. She sure isn't part of a Navy anymore."

Charley said, "The Tanith asteroids aren't mined out."

"So?"

"Asteroids. Metal. Build a metal shell around *Firebee* for a hull."

"Charley, you'd double her mass!"

"We could still run her around the inner system. If we could get a tank from some wrecked ship, a detachable fuel tank, we'd be interstellar again." His eyes flicked to Brenda and he said, "With more fuel we could still get to the Jump points and back. Everything'd be slower, we couldn't outrun anything . . . have to stay away from bandits . . ."

"You're onto something. Charley, we don't really want to be asteroid miners for five years. But if we could find *two* good tanks—"

"Ahhh! One for a hull. Big. Off a battleship, say."

"Yeah."

"Terry, I'm tired," Charley said suddenly, plaintively. "Take Brenda to dinner? They let her out."

"Brenda? I'd be honored."

She smiled one-sided.

November was twelve days long on Tanith, and there wasn't any December. Every so often they put the same number on two consecutive years, to stay even with Spartan time.

In November Dagon City was dark eighteen hours out of twenty-one-plus. The street lighting was back, but snatchers were still a problem. Maybe Terry's uniform protected him; and he went armed, of course.

He took her to a place that was still passable despite the shortages.

He did most of the talking. She'd never heard of the Nuliajuk migration. He told her how the CoDominium had moved twenty thousand Eskimos, tribes all mixed together, to a world too cold for the comfort of other peoples.

They'd settled the equator, where the edges of the icecaps almost met. They'd named the world for a myth-figure common to all the tribes, though names differed: the old woman at the bottom of the sea who brought game or withheld it. There was native sea life, and the imported seals and walruses and bears throve too. Various tribes taught each other their secrets. Some had never seen a seal, some had never built an igloo.

The colony throve; but the men studied fusion and Langston Field engineering, and many wound up on Navy and merchant ships. Eskimos don't really like to freeze. The engine room of a Navy ship is a better place, and Eskimos of all tribes have a knack with tools.

Nuliajuk was near Sol and Sparta. It might still be part of the shrinking Empire, but Terry had never seen it. He was a half-breed, born in a Libertarian merchant ship. What he knew of Nuliajuk came from his father.

And Brenda had lived all her life on a Tanith farm. "I took my education from a TV wall. No hands-on, but I learned enough to fix our machines. We had a fusion plant and some Gaineses and Tofflers. Those are special tractors. Maybe the Saurons left them alone."

"Saurons?"

"Sorry." Her grimace twisted her whole face around. "I spent the last four days talking about nothing else. I own that farm now. I don't own anything else." She studied him thoughtfully. Her face in repose was symmetrical enough, square-jawed, strong even by Tanith standards. "Would you like to see it?"

"What?"

"Would you like to see my farm? Can you borrow a plane?"

They set it up for two days hence.

2656, JUNE (TANITH LOCAL TIME)

Brenda's face lit when she saw him. "Terry! Have you gotten rich? Have you saved civilization? Have you had fun?"

"No, yes, yes. How are you?"

"You can see, can't you? It's all over, Terry. No more nightmares." He'd never seen her bubble like this. There was no slur in her voice . . .

but he could see the twitch at the left side of her mouth. Her face was animated on the right, calmer on the left. Her hair bloomed around her head like a great black dandelion, teased, nearly a foot across. The scar must have healed completely. She'd gained some weight.

He remembered that he had loved her. (But he didn't remember her having nightmares.)

"They tell me you opened an orphanage."

"Yeah, I had twenty kids in one schlumph," she said. "The city gave me financing to put the farm back on its legs, and there were plenty of workmen to hire, but I thought I'd go nuts taking care of the children and the farm both. It's easier now. The older kids are my farmers, and they learn to take care of the younger ones. Two of them got married and went off to start their own farm. Three are in college, and the oldest boy's in the Navy. I'm back down to twenty kids."

"How many of your own? I met Reseda."

"Four. She's the youngest. And one who died."

"I guess I'm surprised you moved back to the farm."

She shook her head. "I did it right. The children took the curse off the memories. So how are you? You must have stories to tell. What are you doing now?"

"There's a party at the spaceport, and we're the stars. Want to join us?"

"No. Busy."

"Can I come out there? Like tomorrow, noon or thereabouts?"

He was watching for hesitation, but it was too quick to be sure. "Good. Come. Noon is fine. You remember how to get here? And noon is just past eleven?"

"And midnight is twenty-two twenty."

"Right. See you then."

He hung up. Now: summon the Library function on the computer? He wondered how much of the Sauron story was still classified. But a party was running, and a spaceman learned to differentiate: there was a time for urgency and a time to hang loose.

When he pushed back into the crowd, Maria grabbed his arm and shouted in his ear. "Mayor Anderssen!" She pointed.

The Mayor nodded and smiled. He was tall, in his late thirties, with pale skin and ash-blond hair and a wispy beard. Terry reached across the table to offer his hand. The Mayor put something in it. "Card," he shouted. "Temporary."

"Thanks."

The Mayor circled the table and pulled up a chair next to him. "You're the city's guest while you're down. Restaurants, hotels, taxis, rentals."

"Very generous. How can we repay you?"

"Your Captain has already agreed to some interviews. Will you do the same? We're starved for news. I talked Purser Laine into speaking on radio.''

''Fine by me. I'm busy tomorrow, though.''

''I got a call from a friend of mine, a Brenda Curtis. She says she used to know you—''

''I just called her a minute ago. Hey, one of her kids—''

''Reseda. My daughter. Brenda isn't married, but she's had four children, and she's got something going with a neighbor, Bob Maddox. Anyway, she called to find out if I was getting you cards, which I already was.''

Terry's memory told him that nuclear families were the rule on Tanith. ''An unusual life-style,'' he said.

''Not so unusual. We've got more men than women. Four hundred ships wrecked in the Battle. Lots of rescue action. Some of the crews reached Tanith and never went any further. We tend to be generous with child support, and there are specialized marriage contracts. Can you picture the crime rate if every woman thought she had to get married?''

Tanith had changed.

Maria handed Terry a drink, something with fruit and rum. He sipped, and wondered.

Brenda must have called the Mayor as soon as the little girl told her about his first call. He remembered an injured woman trying to put her life back together. She'd been in no position to do spur-of-the-moment favors for others. Brenda had changed too.

2640A, NOVEMBER (TANITH LOCAL TIME)

''We're trying to save civilization,'' *Napoleon*'s Purser lectured Terry. ''Not individual ships. If Tanith doesn't have *some* working spacecraft, it won't survive until the Empire gets things straightened out. So. We're giving you . . . *Firebee*?—if you want it. The terms say that you have to run it as a merchant ship or lose it. That's if we decide it's worth repairing. Otherwise . . . Well. We'll have to give any working parts to someone else.''

Arrogant, harassed, defensive. He was dispensing other people's property as charity. The way he used the word *give*—

They discussed details. Terry's third list surprised him. He studied it. ''Your drives are intact? Alderson and fusion both?''

''Running like new. They are new, almost.'' Terry knew the danger here. *Firebee* was alive if her drives were alive . . . and some other ship might want those drives.

''Well. I don't know anyone who needs these spares, offhand, except . . . we'll record these diagnostic programs. Very bright of you to list these. Some of our ships lost most of their data to EMPs. Can I copy this list?''

''Yessir.''

''I can give you a rebuilt fusion zap. You'd never leave orbit without that, would you? We can re-core the hover motors on your #2 boat. Spinner for the air plant if you can mount it. *Don't* tell me you can if you can't. Someone else might need it. You could ruin it trying to make it fit.''

''I can fit it.''

''I dare say. Nuliajuk?''

''Half-breed. Libertarian mother.''

''Look, our engineers aren't Esks *or* Scots, but they've been with us for years. So we can't hire you ourselves, but some other ship—''

''I'd rather make *Firebee* fly again.''

''Good luck. I can't give you any more.''

From the temporary port he went directly to the hospital. Lex Hartner was in surgery. Terry visited with Charley until Lex came out.

''Brenda Curtis invited me to visit her farm with her. Anything I should know? What's likely to upset her?''

Lex stared at him in astonishment. He said, ''Take a gun. A big gun.''

''For what?''

''Man, you missed some excitement here. Brenda said something to a nurse a couple of days after she got here. You know what happened to her?''

''She doesn't want to talk about it.''

''She sure doesn't, and I don't blame her, but the more she said the more the Navy wanted. She'd have died of exhaustion if I hadn't dragged her away a couple of times. She was kidnapped by two Saurons! They killed the whole family.''

''On Tanith itself?''

''Yeah, a landing craft got down. More like a two-seater escape pod, I guess. I haven't seen pictures. It came down near an outback farm, way south. The Saurons killed off her family from ambush. They stayed on the farm for a month. She . . . belonged to one of them.'' Lex was wringing his hands. Likely he didn't know it. ''We looked her over to see if she was pregnant.''

''I should think you bloody would! Can they still breed with human beings?'' Rumor had it that some of the Sauron genes had been borrowed from animals.

''We won't find out from Brenda. She's had a child, though. It probably died at the farm. She won't talk about that either.''

''Lord. How did she get away?''

''One went off by himself. Maybe they fought over Brenda. The other one stayed. One day a Weem's beast came out of the water and attacked them in the rice paddy. It clawed her; that's how she got the head wound. When she got the blood out of her eyes the Sauron was dead and so was the Weem's beast. So she started walking. She had to live for two weeks in the swamps, with that wound. Hell of a woman.''

''Yeah. You're telling me there's a Sauron loose on Tanith.''

''Yup. They're hunting for him. She took the Marines to the farm, and they found the escape pod and the corpse. I've been doing the autopsy. You can see where they got the traits—''

''Animal?''

''No, that's just a rumor. It's all human, but the way it's put together . . . think of Frankenstein's monster. A bit here, a bit there, the shape changes a little. Maybe add an extra Y gene to turn it mean. I'm guessing there. The high-power microscope's down.''

''The other one?''

''Could be anywhere. He's had almost a month.''

''Not likely he'd stick around. Okay, I'll take a big gun. Anything else I should know?''

''I don't know how she'll react. Terry, I'll give you a trank spray. Put her out if she gets hysterical and get her back here fast. Other than that . . . watch her. See if you think she can live on that farm. Bad memories there. I think she should sell the place.''

2656, JUNE (TANITH LOCAL TIME)

Dinner expeditions formed and went off in three directions. The cluster that took Terry along still crowded the restaurant. A blackboard offered a single meal of several courses, Spartan cooking strangely mutated by local ingredients.

The time change caught up with him as desserts arrived. ''I'm running out of steam,'' he told Maria Montez.

''Okay.'' She led him out and waved at a taxi. The gray-haired driver recognized him for what he was. She kept him talking all the way to Maria's apartment house. She wasn't interested in planets; it was the space between that held her imagination.

On the doorstep Maria carefully explained that Terry couldn't possibly presume on an acquaintanceship of one afternoon (though he hadn't asked yet). She kissed him quickly and went inside.

Terry started down the steps, grinning. Customs differ. Now where the hell was he, and where was a taxi likely to be hiding?

So Brenda was alive and doing well. Friend of the Mayor. Running an orphanage. Four children. Well, well.

Maria came out running. "I forgot, you don't have a place to stay! Terry, you can come in and sleep on the couch if you promise to behave yourself."

"I can't really do that, Maria, but if you'll call me a taxi?"

She was affronted. "Why not?"

He went back up the steps. "I haven't set foot on a world for four months. I haven't held a woman in my arms in longer than that. Now, we heroes have infinite self-control—"

"But—"

"I could probably leave you alone all night. But I wouldn't sleep and I'd wake up depressed and frustrated. So what I want is a hotel."

She thought it over. "Come in. Have some coffee."

"Were you listening?"

"Come in."

They entered. The place was low-tech but roomy. He asked, "Was I supposed to lie?"

"It's not a lie, exactly. It just, just leaves things open. Like I could be telling you we could have some coffee and then get you a taxi, and we could wind up sniffing some borloi, and . . . You could be persuasive?"

"Nuliajuks lie. It's called tact. My mother made sure I knew how to keep a promise. She wasn't just a Libertarian. She was a Randist."

Maria smiled at him, much amused. "Four months, hey? But you should learn to play the game, Terry."

He shook his head. "There's a different game on every world, almost in every city. I can't sniff borloi with you either. I tried it once. That stuff could hook me fast. I just have to depend on charisma."

She had found a small bottle. "Take a couple of these. Vitamins, hangover formula. Take lots of water. Does wonders for the charisma."

Maria made scrambled eggs with sausage and fungus, wrapped in chili leaves. It woke him up fast and made him forget his hangover. He'd been looking forward to Tanith cooking.

There were calls registered on his pocket computer. He used Maria's phone. Nobody answered at Polar Datafile or Other Worlds. When he looked at his watch it was just seven o'clock.

No wonder Maria was yawning. She'd woken when he did, and that must have been about six. "Hey, I'm sorry. It's the time change."

"No sweat, Terry. I'll sleep after you leave. Want to go back to bed?"

He tried again later. Polar Datafile wanted him tomorrow, five o'clock news. An interviewer for Other Worlds wanted all three astronauts for two days, maybe more. Good payment, half in gold, for exclusive rights. How exclusive? he asked. She reassured him: radio and TV spots would be considered as publicity. What she wanted was depth, and no other vidtapes competing. He set it up.

He called Information. "I need to rent a plane."

Maria watched him with big dark eyes. "Brenda Curtis?"

"Right." The number answered, and he dealt with it. A hoverplane would pick him up at the door. He was expected to return the pilot to the airport and then go about his business. How far did he expect to fly? About forty miles round trip.

Maria asked, "Were you in love with her?"

"For about two months."

"Are you going to tell her about us?"

That might put both women in danger. "No. In fact, I'm going to get a hotel room—"

"Damn your eyes, Terry Kakumee!"

"I'll be back tonight, Maria. I've got my reasons. No, I can't tell you what they are."

"All right. Are they honest?"

"I . . . Dammit. They're right on the edge."

She studied his face. "Can you tell me after it's over?"

". . . No." Either way, he wouldn't be able to do that.

"Okay. Come back tonight." She wasn't happy. He didn't blame her.

The land had more color than he remembered. Fields of strange flowers bloomed in the swampland. Huge dark purple petals crowned plants the size of trees. A field of sunlovers, silver ahead of him, turned green in his rear-view camera.

Farms were sparse pale patches in all that color. In the wake of the Battle of Tanith they had had a scruffy look. They were neater now, with more rice and fewer orange plots of borloi. The outworld market for the drug had disintegrated, of course.

He should be getting close. He took the plane higher. Farms all looked alike, but the crater wouldn't have disappeared.

It was there, several miles south, a perfect circle of lake . . .

2640B, JANUARY (TANITH LOCAL TIME)

. . . A perfect circle of lake surrounded by blasted trees lying radially outward. "A big ship made a big bang when it fell," Brenda said. She was wearing dark glasses, slacks and a chamois shirt. Her diction was as precise as she could make it, but he still had to listen hard. A Tanith farm girl's accent probably slurred it further. "We were on the roof. We wanted to watch the battle."

"Sauron or Empire ship?"

"We never knew. It was only a light. Bright enough to fry the eyeballs. It gave us enough warning. We threw ourselves flat. We would have been blown off the roof."

They turned east. Presently he asked, "Is that your farm?"

"No. There, beyond."

Four miles east of the fresh crater, a wide stretch of rice paddies. The other farm was miles closer. The Saurons must have gone around it. Why?

They'd passed other farms. Here the paddies seemed to be going back to the wild. The house nestled on a rise of ground. The roof was flat, furnished with tables and chairs and a swimming pool in the shape of a blobby eagle. The walls sloped inward.

"You don't like windows?"

"No. It rains. When it doesn't, we work outside. On a good day we all went up on the roof."

The door showed signs of damage. It might have been blasted from its hinges, then rehung.

Lights came on as they entered. Terry trailed Brenda as she moved through the house.

Pantry shelves were in neat array, but depleted. The fridge was empty. The freezer was working, but it stank. He told her, "There've been power failures. You'll have to throw all this out." She sniffed; half her face wrinkled.

He found few obvious signs of damage. Missing furniture had left its marks on the living room floor, and the walls had been freshly painted.

There were muddy footprints everywhere. "The Marines did that," Brenda said.

"Did they find anything?"

"Not here. Not even dried blood. Horatius made me clean up. They found the escape pod three miles away."

Beds in the master bedroom were neatly made. Brenda turned on the TV wall and got Dagon City's single station, and a picture of Boat #1 floating gracefully toward the landing field. "This works too."

Terry shook his head. "What did these Saurons look like?"

"Randus was bizarre. Horatius was more human—"

"It looks like he was ready to stay here. To pass himself off as a man, an ordinary farmer."

She paused. "He could have done that. It may be why he left. We never saw a Sauron on Tanith. He was muscular. His bones were heavy. He looked . . . Round shoulders. His eyes had an epicanthic fold, and the pupils were black, jet black." Pause. "He made sex like an attack."

The smiling faces of *Firebee*'s crew flashed and died. The lights died too. Terry said, "Foo."

"Never mind." Brenda took his arm and led him two steps backward through the dark. The bed touched his knees and he sat.

"What did Randus look like?"

"A monster. I hated Horatius, but I wanted him to protect me from Randus."

Could he pass as a farmer? He'd have to hide Randus the monster and Brenda the prisoner, or kill them. But he hadn't. Honor among Saurons?

Or . . . leave the monster to guard his woman. Find or carve a safe house. Come back later, see if it worked. The risk would not be to Horatius. So. "Did Horatius think you were pregnant?"

"Maybe. Terry, I would like to take the taste of Horatius out of my mind."

"Time will do that."

"Sex will do that."

He tried to look at her. He saw nothing. They were sitting on a water bed in darkness like a womb.

"I haven't been with a woman in over a year. Brenda, are you sure you're ready for this?" He hadn't thought to ask Lex about *this*!

She pulled him to his feet, hands on his upper arms. Strong! "You're a good man, Terry. I've watched you. I couldn't do better. Do you maybe think I'm too tall for you?" She pulled him against her, and his cheek was against her breasts. "You can't do this with a short woman."

"Not standing up." His arms went around her, but how could he help that?

"Is it my face? We're in the dark." He could hear her amusement.

"Brenda, I'm not exactly fighting. It's just, I still think of you as a patient."

"So be patient."

She didn't need his patience. She had none herself. He'd expected the aftereffects of the head wound to make her clumsy. She was, a little. She came on as if she would swallow him up and go looking for dessert. He was appalled, then delighted, then . . . exhausted, but she wouldn't let him go . . .

He woke in darkness. He wasn't tempted to move. The water bed was kind to his gravity-abused muscles. He felt the warmth of the woman in his arms, and presently knew that she was awake.

No warning: she attacked.

She disappeared into the dark like a vampire leaving her victim. She draped his clothes over him and dropped the heavy flechette gun on his belly. He giggled, and presently dressed.

She led him stumbling through a black maze and out into the dusk of a winter morning. "There. After all, I know the house."

"This is the trouble with not having windows," he groused.

"Weem's beasts like windows too. In rain they can come this far."

The graveyard was eight stone markers cut with a vari-saw, letters and numbers cut with a laser. "The names and dates are wrong, except these old ones," she said. "Horatius hoped it would look like they all died many years ago. I'll get a chisel or a laser to fix it."

There was no *small* grave. "Lex told me you had a child."

"Miranda. He took her with him."

"God." He took her in his arms. "Did you tell the Marines?"

"No. I . . . try not to think about Miranda."

There was nothing more to see. She told him that the Navy men had found Randus' skeleton and taken that, and sent out a big copter for the rescue pod. When the lights came on around noon, Terry helped Brenda clean up the mudstains and empty the freezer and fridge.

"I need money to run the farm," Brenda said. "Maybe someone will hire me for work in Dagon."

"Why not sell the place?"

"It was ours for too long. It won't be bad. You can see for yourself, the Saurons left no trace. No trace at all."

2656, JUNE (TANITH LOCAL TIME)

Four miles east of the crater. He should be near. He was crossing extensive fields of rice. A dozen men and women worked knee-deep in water that glinted through the stalks like fragments of a shattered mirror. A man stood by with a gun. Terry swooped low, lowered his flaps, hovered. Several figures waved.

They were all children.

He set the plane down. The gun-carrier broke off work and came toward him. Terry waded to meet him; what the hell. "Brenda Curtis's?"

The boy had an oriental look despite the black, kinky hair. He grinned and said, "Where else would you find all these kids? I'm Tarzan Kakumee."

"Terry Kakumee. I'm visiting. You'd be about sixteen?"

The boy's jaw dropped. "Seventeen, but that's Tanith time. Kakumee? Astronaut? You'd be my father!"

"Yeah. Can I stare a little?"

They examined each other. Tarzan was an inch or two taller than Terry, narrower in the hips and face and chest, and his square jaw was definitely Brenda's. Black eyes with an oriental slant: Terry and Brenda both had that. The foolish grins felt identical.

"I'm on duty," Tarzan said. "I'll see you later?"

"Can't you come with me? I'm due for lunch."

"No, I've got my orders. There are Weem's beasts and other things around here. I once shot a tax collector the size of my arm. It had its suckers in Gerard's leg and Gerard was screaming bloody murder." Tarzan grinned. "I blew it right off him."

Smaller fields of different colors surrounded a sprawling structure. If that was the farmhouse it had doubled in size . . . right. He could make out the original farmhouse in the center. The additions had windows.

Fields of melons, breadfruit, and sugar cane surrounded the house. Three children in a mango grove broke off work to watch him land.

Brenda came through the door with a man beside her.

He knew her at once. (But was it her?) She waved both arms and ran to meet him. (She'd changed.) "Terry, I'm so glad to see you! The way you went off—my fault, of course, but I kept wondering what had happened to you out there and why you didn't come back!" Her dress looked like current Tanith style, cut above the knee and high at the neck. Her grip on his arm was farmhand-strong. "You wouldn't have had to see me, it just would have been good to know—Well, it *is* good to know you're alive and doing all right! Bob, this is Terry Kakumee the astronaut. Terry, Bob Maddox is my neighbor three miles southeast."

"Pleased to meet you." Bob Maddox was a brown-haired white man, freckled and tanned. He was large all over, and his hand was huge, big-knuckled and rough with work. "Brenda's told me about you. How's your ship?"

"Truth? *Firebee* is gradually and gracefully disintegrating. There's a double hull instead of a Langston Field, and we have to patch it every so often. We got Boat #1 repaired on Phoenix. Maybe we can hold it all together till the Empire gets back out here. You interested in space-flight?"

Maddox hesitated. "Not really. I mean, it's surprising more of us don't want to build rocket ships, considering. We weren't all transportees, our ancestors."

Brenda turned at the door. She clapped her hands twice and jerked her thumb. The children who had been climbing over Terry's rental plane dropped off and scampered happily back toward the mangoes.

They went in. Reseda Anderssen, busy at a samovar, smiled at them and went out through another door. There was new furniture, couches and small tables and piles of pillows, enough to leave the living room quite cluttered. Brenda saw him looking and said, "Some of the kids sleep in here."

It didn't look it. "You keep them neat." He noticed noises coming from what he remembered as the kitchen.

"I've got a real knack for teaching. Have some tea?"

"Borloi tea? I'd better not."

"I made Earl Grey." She poured three cups. She'd always had grace, even with the head injury to scramble the signals. He could see just a trace of her lip pulling up on the left when she spoke. She settled him and Bob on a couch and faced them. "Now talk. Where've you been?"

"Phoenix. Gafia. Hitchhiker's Rest. Medea. Uhura. We commute. We tried Lenin, but three outie ships came after us. We ran and didn't come back, and that cuts us off from the planets beyond. And we found a Sauron ship at EST 1310."

It was Maddox who stared. "Well, go on! What's left of it? Were there Saurons?"

"Bob, we were clever. We knew there was a ship there because we caught the signal every time we used the jump points to get to Medea. We couldn't get down there because the star's a flare star and we don't have a Langston Field.

"Only, this time we do. Phoenix sold us—actually, they *gave* us a mucking great Langston Field generator. We left it on. We moved in and matched orbit with the signal ship, and we expanded the field to put both ships inside."

"Clever, right. Terry, we Taniths are a little twitchy about Saurons—"

"Just one. Dead. They rifled it and left it for a message beacon. They left a Sauron on duty. Maybe a flare got him." The corpse had been a skewed man-shape, a bogey man. Like Randus? "I managed to get into the programming. Now we're thinking of going on to Sparta. We learned some things they might want to know."

"Let me just check on lunch," Brenda said, and she went.

It left Terry feeling awkward. Maddox said, "So there are still Sauron supermen out there?"

"Just maybe. The beacon was set to direct Saurons to a Jump point in that system. Maybe nobody ever got the message. If they did, I don't know where they went. I ran the record into *Firebee*'s memory and ran a translation program on it, but I didn't look at the result. I'd have to go back to *Firebee*, then come back here."

Maddox grimaced. "We don't have ships to do anything about it. Sparta might. I'd be inclined to leave them the hell alone."

"Did they ever catch—?"

"Nope. Lot of excitement. Every so often some nut comes screaming that he saw a Sauron in the marshes. The Mayor's got descriptions of a Sauron officer, and he says they don't check out. How the hell could that thing still be hiding?"

"Those two must have gone right past your place to get here."

"Yeah. Brenda had to backtrack to get to my place. Weeks in the wild, fungus and tax collectors, polluted water, God knows what she ate . . . Well, yeah, I've wondered. Maybe they saw we had guns."

"That's not it."

Bob hesitated. "Okay, why?"

He'd spoken without thinking. "You'd think I'm crazy. Anyway, I could be wrong."

"Kakumee, everyone knows more about Saurons than the guy he's talking to. It's like skewball scores. What I want to know about is, I never saw Brenda's lip curl up like that when she talks."

"Old head injury."

"I haven't seen her face do that since the day she staggered through my gate. I wonder if meeting you again might be upsetting her."

Bob Maddox was coming on like a protective husband.

Terry asked, "Have you thought of marriage?"

"That's none of your business, Kakumee—"

"Brenda's—"

"—But I've asked, and she won't." His voice was still low and reasonably calm. "She'd rather live alone, and I don't know why. Ventura's mine."

"I haven't met her."

"I guess I don't mind you worrying over Brenda. Have you met any of the kids?"

"Yeah—"

Brenda was back. "We can serve any time you get hungry. Terry, can you stay for dinner? You could meet the rest of the children. They'll be coming in around five."

"I'd like that. Bob, feel like lunchtime?"

"Yeah."

The men hung back for a moment. "I'll leave after dinner," Terry said. "I tell you, though, I don't think anything's bothering Brenda. She's tougher than that."

Bob nodded. "Tough lady. Kakumee, I think she's working on how to tell you one of the kids is yours."

2640B, JANUARY TO MARCH (TANITH LOCAL TIME)

Their idyll lasted two months.

They made an odd couple. Tall and lean; short and round. He could see it in the mirror, he could see the amusement in strangers and friends too.

Terry's rented room was large enough for both. Brenda began buying clothes and other things after she had a job, but she never crowded the closets. Brenda cleaned. Terry did all the cooking. It was the only task he'd ever seen her fail at.

He was busy much of the time. In a week the work on Boat #2 was finished. There were parts for Boat #1, and he carried them to orbit to work. Boat #1 still wouldn't be able to make a reentry.

He talked *Napoleon*'s purser out of a ruined battleship's hydrogen tank. Over a period of three weeks (with two two-day leaves in Dagon) Terry and the rest of the crew moved *Firebee* into it. Had Charley been thinking in terms of a regeneration sleeve for the ship?

Firebee was now the silliest-looking ship since the original Space Shuttle, and too massive for interstellar capability. Without an auxiliary tank she couldn't even use a Jump point with any hope of reaching a planet on the far side.

Captain Shu had done something about that. *Firebee* now owned a small H_2 tank aboard *Armadillo*, but they'd have to wait for it to arrive. Terry went back down to Dagon City.

Brenda was still attending the clinic every two days. She was working there too, and trying to arrange something with the local government. She wouldn't talk about that; she wasn't sure it would work.

He made her a different offer. "Four of our crew want to stay. Cropland doesn't cost much on Tanith. But you've got a knack for machines. Let me teach you how to make repairs on *Firebee*. Come as my apprentice."

"Terry—"

"And wife."

"I get motion sickness."

"Damn." There had never been a lover like Brenda. She could play his nervous system like a violin. She knew his moods. She maintained civilization around him. The thought of leaving her made him queasy.

Armadillo had won an expensive victory in the outer Tanith system. The hulk was just capable of thrust, and it didn't reach Tanith until months after the battle. Then crews from other ships swarmed over it and took it apart. *Firebee*'s crew came back with an intact tank and fuel-feed system. Terry had to tear that apart and put it together different, in vacuum. It would ride outside the second hull.

Firebee was fragile now, fit to be a trader, but never a warship or a miner.

Charley was in decent shape by then and working out in a local gym. He came up to help weld the fuel tank. He seemed fit for space. "Captain Shu wants to go home, but we've got you and me and Sharon Hayes and that kid off *Napoleon*, Murray Weiss. I say we go interstellar."

"I know you do, but think about it, Charley. No defenses. We can haul cargo back and forth between the mining asteroids, and if outies ever come to take over we'd have someplace to run to."

"And you could see Brenda every couple of months."

The argument terminated when Terry returned to Dagon.

Brenda was gone. Brenda's clothes were gone. There was a phone message from Lex Hartner; he looked grim and embarrassed.

Phoning him felt almost superfluous, but Terry did it.

"We've been seeing each other," Lex said. "I think she's carrying my child. Terry, I want to marry her."

"Good luck to you." The days in which an Ihalmiut hunter might gather up a band of friends and hunt down a bride were long ago, far away. He considered it anyway. And went to the stars instead.

2656, JUNE (TANITH LOCAL TIME)

Reseda and three younger children served lunch, then joined them at the table. Three more came in from the fields. There was considerable chatter. Terry found he was doing a lot of the talking.

Dessert was mangoes still hot from the sun.

Brenda went away and came back wearing a bantar-cloth coverall. It was the garment she'd worn the day she reached the hospital, like as not, but much cleaner. The three adults spend the afternoon pulling weeds in the sugar cane. Brenda and Bob Maddox instructed him by turns.

Terry had never done field work. He found he was enjoying himself, sweating in the sun.

The sun arced around the horizon, dropping gradually. Other children came flocking from the rice fields shortly after five. The adults pulled weeds for a little longer, then joined the children in the courtyard. He could smell his own sweat, and Bob's, different by race or by diet.

Twenty children all grinned at some shared joke. Brenda must have briefed them. When?

"Brenda, I can sort them out," Terry said.

"Go ahead."

"The Mayor already told me Reseda was his. The freckled girl must be Ventura Maddox. Hello, Ventura!" She was big for twelve, tanned dark despite the freckles, and round in the face, like Bob himself. A tall girl, older, had Brenda's tightly kinked black hair, pale skin and a pointed chin. "I don't know her name, but she's . . . Lex's?" Lex's face, but it would still be a remarkable thing.

"Yes, that's Sepulveda."

"Hello, Sepulveda. And the boy—" Tarzan grinned at him but didn't wave. Tactful: he didn't know whether they were supposed to have met. "—is mine."

"Right again. Terry, meet Tarzan."

"Hello, Tarzan. Brenda, I set down in the rice field before I got here."

She laughed. "Dammit, Terry! I had it all planned."

"And they're named for suburbs of some city on Earth."

"I never thought you'd see *that*."

A different crew served dinner. Bob and Brenda took one end of the table. Terry and Tarzan talked as if nobody else was present, but every so often he noticed how the other children were listening.

But tracks in his mind ran beneath what he was saying. *They look good together. He's spent time with these children, probably watched them grow up. She should marry him.*

She can't! Unless I'm all wrong from beginning to end.

Wouldn't that be nice? "We've been carrying kudzu grain in the cargo ever since. Someday we'll find another famine—"

She must have been carrying Tarzan when she took up with Lex. She held his attention while she carried Tarzan to term, and she held him after Lex knew Tarzan wasn't his, and then she had Sepulveda. She could have held him if she'd married him, but she didn't. Held him anyway.

Quite a woman. And then she gave him up. Why?

Terry took the car up into the orange sunset glow and headed north. En route he used his card and the car phone to get a hotel room. By nine he had checked into the Arco-Elsewhere and was calling Maria.

"Want to see the best hotel on the planet? Or shall I get a cab and come to you?"

"I guess I'll come there. Hey, why not? It's close to work."

He used an operator to track down Charley and Sharon, and wasn't surprised to find they had rooms in the same hotel. "Call me for breakfast," Sharon said groggily. "I'm not on Dagon time yet."

Charley seemed alert. "Terry! How's Brenda?"

"Brenda's running the planet, or at least twenty kids' worth of planet. One of the boys is mine. She looks wonderful. Got a burly protector, likable guy, wants to be her fiancé but isn't."

"You've got a kid! What's he like?"

Terry had to sort out his impressions. "She raised 'em all well. He's self-confident, delighted to see me, taller than me . . . If he saves civilization I'll take half the credit."

"That good, huh?"

"Easily."

"I've been working. We've sold the big Langston Field generator. Farmer, lots of land, he may be thinking about becoming a suburb for the wealthy. I got a good price, Terry. He thought he could beat me at the Mirror Game—"

"He bet you?"

"He did. And I've signed up for eight tons of borloi, but I'll have to see how much bulk that is before—"

"Borloi!"

"Sure, Terry, borloi had medical uses too. We'll deal with a government at our next stop, give it plenty of publicity too. That way it'll be used right.''

''I'm glad to see you've put some brain sweat into this. What occurs to me is—''

The door went *bingbong*.

''Company.'' Terry went to open the door. Maria was in daytime dress, with a large handbag. ''Come on in. Check out the bathroom, it's really sybaritic. I'm on the phone.'' He returned. ''Borloi, right? It's not worth stealing on the way out, but after we jump we tell the whole population of Gaea about it? Shrewd. We'll be a target for any thief who wants to *sell* eight tons of borloi on the black market.''

''Good point. What do you think?''

''Oh, I think we raise the subject with Sharon, and then I think we'll do it anyway.''

''Let's meet for breakfast. Eight? Someone I want you to meet.''

''Good.'' He hung up. He called, ''I can offer you three astronauts for breakfast.''

Maria came out to the sound of bathwater running. ''Sounds delicious. It has to be early, Terry. Tomorrow's a working day.''

''Oh, it'll be early. Early to bed?'' He'd wanted to use the city computer files, but he was tired too. It wasn't the time change; the shorter days would have caught him up by now. It was stoop labor in high G.

Maria said, ''I want to try that spa. Come with me? You look like you need it. And tell me about your day.''

They all met for breakfast in Charley's suite.

Charley had a groupie. Andrea Soucek was a university student, stunningly beautiful, given to clichés. She was goshwowed-out by the presence of *three* star-travelers. Sharon had George Callahan. Terry had Maria.

The conversation stayed general for awhile. Then George had to leave, and so did Maria. Over coffee it degenerated into shop talk, while Andrea Soucek listened in half-comprehending awe.

Eight tons of dry borloi (they'd freeze-dry it by opening the airlock) would fill more than half the cargo hold. Not much mass, though. The rest of the cargo space could go to heavy machinery. Their next stop, Gaea, had a small population unlikely to produce much for export, unlikely to buy much of the borloi. Most of it would be with them on two legs of their route.

Sharon asked, ''Tanith doesn't manufacture much heavy machinery, do they?''

''I haven't found any I can buy. I'm working on it,'' Charley said.

Terry had an idea. ''We want to freeze-dry the borloi anyway. We could pack it between the hull and the sleeve. Plenty of room for light stuff in the cargo hold.''

''Hmm. Yeah! Any drug-running raider attacks us, his first shot would blow the borloi all across the sky! No addicts on our conscience.''

''Rape the addicts. Evolution in action,'' Sharon said. ''What kind of idiot would hook himself on borloi when the source is light-years away? Get 'em out of the gene pool.''

Andrea began to give her an argument. All humans were worthwhile, all could be saved. And borloi was a harmless vice—

Terry returned to his room carrying a mug of coffee.

The aristocratic phone operator recognized him by now. ''Mr. Kakumee! Who may I track down for you?''

''Lex Hartner, M.D., surgeon. Lived in Dagon City, Dryland sector, fifteen years ago.''

''Fifteen years? Thanks a lot.'' But she'd stopped showing irritation. ''Mmm. Not Dryland . . . He doesn't appear to be anywhere in Dagon.''

''Try some other cities, please. He won't be outside a city.''

Almost a minute crawled by. ''I have a Lex Hartner in Coral Beach.''

It was Lex. He was older, grayer; his cheeks sagged in Tanith gravity. ''Terry Kakumee?''

''Hello. I met your daughter yesterday.''

The sagging disappeared. ''How is she?''

''She's wonderful. All of Brenda's kids are wonderful. Are you wondering whether to tell me I've got a boy?''

''Yeah.''

''He's wonderful too.''

''Of course he is.'' Lex smiled at last. ''How's Brenda?''

''She's wonderful. I asked her to marry me too, Lex. I mean sixteen years ago.''

''Who else has she turned down?''

''Brawny farmer type named Maddox. Lex, I don't think she needs a man.''

''How are you?''

''I'm fine. Would you believe Charley Laine is fine too? He looks like you'd expect, but his groupie is prettier than mine, if not as smart.''

''I did a good job there, didn't I?''

''That's what I'm telling you.''

''Is it too late to say I'm sorry?''

''No, forget that. She didn't need me. Lex, you did an autopsy on the corpse of a Sauron superman. Remember?''

''A man isn't likely to forget that. They rot fast in the swamps. It was pretty well chewed, too.''

''Was there enough left for a gene analysis?''

"Some. Not enough to make me famous. It matched what the Navy already knew. I didn't find anything inhuman, anything borrowed from animals."

"Yeah. Anything startling?"

"Nope. It's all in the records."

"A Sauron and a Weem's beast, you don't expect them to go to a photo finish."

"It must have been something to see. From a distance, that is. Brenda never wanted to talk about it, but that was a long time ago. Maybe she'd talk now."

"Okay, thanks. Lex, I still think of you as a friend. I won't be on Tanith very long. Everything I do is on the city account for awhile—"

"Maybe I'll come into town."

"Call me when and if, and everything goes on the card. I'm at the Arco-Elsewhere."

Next he linked into the Dagon City computer files.

Matters relating to Saurons had been declassified. Navy ships had transferred much of their data to city computers on Tanith and other worlds. Terry found a picture he'd seen before: a Sauron, no visible wounds, gassed in an attack on Medea. It rotated before him, a monster out of nightmare. Randus?

An XYY, the text said. All of the Sauron soldiers, any who had left enough meat to be analyzed, had had freaky gene patterns—males with an extra Y gene, where XY was male and XX was female—until the Battle of Tanith. There they'd found some officers.

Those pictures were of slides and electron-microscope photographs. No officer's corpse had survived unshredded. Their gene patterns included the XY pair, but otherwise resembled those of the XYY berserkers.

Results of that gene pattern were known. Eyes that saw deep into the infrared; the altered eye structure could be recognized. Blood that clotted fast to block a wound. Rapid production of endorphins to block pain. Stronger bones. Bigger adrenal glands. Powerful muscles. Skin that changed color fast, from near-white (to make vitamin D in cold, cloudy conditions, where a soldier had to cover most of his skin or die) to near-black (to prevent lethal sunburn in field conditions under a hotter sun). Officers would have those traits too.

Nothing new yet.

Ah, here was Lex Hartner's autopsy report on Randus himself. XYY genes. Six-times-lethal damage from a Weem's beast's teeth, and one wound . . . one narrow wound up through the base of the skull into the cerebellum, that must have paralyzed or killed him at once.

A Sauron superman working in a rice paddy might not expect something to come at him out of the water.

Terry studied some detail pictures of a Weem's beast. It was something like a squat crocodile, with huge pads for front paws, claws inward-pointing to hold prey, a single dagger of a front tooth . . . That might have made the brain puncture if the thing was biting Randus's head. Wouldn't the lower teeth have left other marks on, say, the forehead?

So.

And a stranger, human-looking but with big bones and funny eyes, had run loose on Tanith for sixteen years. Had a man with a small daughter appeared somewhere, set up a business, married perhaps? By now he would have an identity and perhaps a position of power.

Saurons were popularly supposed to have been exterminated. Terry had never found any record of an attack on whatever world had bred the monsters, and he didn't now, though it must have happened. No mention of further attempts to track down fleets that might have fled across the sky. The Navy had left some stuff classified.

Early files on the Curtis family had been scrambled. He found a blurred family picture: a dark man, a darker woman, five children; he picked out a gawky eleven-year-old (the file said) who might have grown to be Brenda. The file on the Maddoxes was bigger, with several photographs. The men all looked like Bob Maddox, all muscle and confidence and freckled tans. The women were not much smaller and tended to be freckled and burly.

So.

An XY officer, a male, might have wanted children. Might have had children. They were gene-tailored, but the doctors had used mostly human genes; maybe all-human, despite the tales. They weren't a different species, after all. What would such children look like? How would they grow up?

The Polar Datafile interview was fun. The Other Worlds interview the next day felt more like work. Charley's voice gave out, so they called it off for a few days.

The borloi arrived in several planeloads. Terry didn't notice any special attempts at security. On many worlds there would have been a police raid followed by worldwide publicity. Memo: call all possible listeners in Gaea system *immediately* after jump. Sell to government only. Run if anything looks funny.

They flew half the borloi to orbit and packed it into *Firebee*'s outer hull, with no objection from Sharon. The work went fast. The next step was taken slowly, carefully.

The Langston Field generator from Phoenix system was too big for either boat.

Sharon put *Firebee* in an orbit that would intersect the atmosphere. With an hour to play with, they moved the beast out of the cargo hold with an armchair-type pusher frame and let it get a good distance away. They all watched as Terry beamed the signal that turned it on.

The generator became a black sphere five hundred meters across.

Charley and Terry boarded Shuttle #1. Sharon set *Firebee* accelerating back to orbit.

When the black sphere intersected the atmosphere there was little in the way of reentry flame. Despite the massive machine at the center, the huge sphere was a near-vacuum. It slowed rapidly and drifted like a balloon. Boat #1 overshot, then circled back.

Air seeped through the black forcefield to fill the vacuum inside. It ceased to be a balloon.

It touched down in the marshes south and east of Dagon City, more or less as planned. No signal would penetrate the field. Terry and Charley had to go into the Field with a big inflatable cargo raft, mount it beneath the generator and turn it off.

At that point it became the owner's problem. He'd arranged for two heavy-lift aircraft. *Firebee*'s crew waited until the planes had landed, then took Boat #1 back to Dagon.

They were back at the hotel thirty-six hours after they'd left. Maria found the door open and Terry lolling in the spa. "I think I'm almost dissolved," he told her.

Lex didn't call. Brenda didn't call.

They ferried the rest of the borloi up a day later. Some went into the outer hull. The rest they packed around the cargo hold, leaving racks open in the center. Dried borloi for padding, to shield whatever else Charley found to carry.

It was morning when they landed, with time for sightseeing. Andrea and Charley opted to rent equipment and do some semiserious mountain climbing in the foothills of The Warden. Terry called Maria, but she couldn't get off work, and couldn't see him tonight either. That made mountain climbing less attractive. Terry hiked around Dagon City for a while, looked through the major shopping mall, then went back to the hotel.

He was half asleep with his shoes off when the phone chimed.

The face was Brenda's. Terry rubbed his palms together and tapped the answer pad.

"Hi, Terry. I'm in the lobby. Can I come up?"

"Sure, Brenda. Can I order you a drink? Lunch?"

"Get me a rum collins."

Terry rang off, then ordered from room service. His palms were sweating.

I ran the record into Firebee's *memory and ran a translation program on it, but I didn't look at the result. I'd have to go back to* Firebee, *then come back here. Has Bob Maddox told her? Probably not.*

She walked in like she owned the hotel, smiling as if nobody was supposed to know. Her dress was vivid orange; it went well with her color. The drink trolley followed her in. When it had rolled out she asked, "How long are you going to be on Tanith?"

"Two weeks, give or take a week. Charley has to find us something to sell. Besides borloi, that is."

"Have you tried bantar cloth? It's just about the only hi-tech stuff we make enough of. Don't take clothing. Styles change. Get bolts, and be sure you've got the tools to shape it."

"Yeah . . . Brenda, is there anything you can't do?"

"Cook. And I'm not the marrying type."

"I know that now."

"But I have children. Do you like Tarzan?"

He smiled and relaxed a little. "Good job there. I'm glad I met him."

"Let's do it again."

His drink slopped. Somehow he hadn't expected this. "Hold it, Brenda. I'm with another woman this trip."

"Maria? Terry, Maria's with Fritz Marsden tonight and all tomorrow. Fritz is one of mine. He works at the fusion plant at Randall's Point, and he only gets into town every couple of weeks. Maria isn't going to give *him* up for a, well, a transient."

He sipped at his drink to give himself time to think. When he took the glass from his lips, she pulled it out of his hand without spilling it and set it down. She pulled him to his feet with a fist in his belt. "I'm not asking for very much, am I?"

"Ah, no. Child support? We'll be leaving funds behind us anyway. Are you young enough?" Was she *serious*?

"I don't know. What's the worst that can happen?" She had unzipped his shirt and was pulling it loose. And with wild hope he thought, *It could be*!

She stripped him naked, then stepped back to examine him. "I don't think you've gained or lost an ounce. Same muscle tone too. You people don't even wrinkle."

"We wrinkle all at once. You've changed incredibly."

"I wanted to. I needed to. Terry, am I coming on too strong? You're tense. Let me show you something else I learned. Face down on the bed—" She helped him irresistibly. "I'll keep my dress on. Okay? And if you've got anything like massage oil around, tell me now."

"I've never had a massage of any kind."

The next hour was a revelation. She kept telling him to relax, and somehow he did that, while she tenderized muscles he'd strained moving borloi bags in free-fall. He wondered if he'd been wrong; he wondered if he was going to die; he wondered why he'd never tried this before.

"I took massage training after you left. I used it at the hospital. I never had to work through a Nuliajuk's fat padding before . . . No sweat, I can reach the muscle underneath."

"Hell, you could reach through the ribs!"

"Is this too hard? Were you having trouble in orbit?"

"Nope. Everything went fine."

"Then why the tension? Turn over." She rolled him over and resumed work on his legs, then his arms and shoulders. "You didn't used to be shy with me."

"Am I shy now?"

"You keep tensing up." Her skirt was hiked up and she straddled his hips to work on his belly. "Good muscle here. Ease up—Well."

He had a respectable erection.

She caressed him. "I was afraid you'd changed." She slid forward and, hell, she didn't have panties.

"I kept my promise," she gloated.

"True," he croaked. "Take it off."

She pulled her dress over her head. There was still a brassiere; no woman would go without one in Tanith gravity. She took that off too.

She was smoothly dark, with no pale areas anywhere. His hands remembered her breasts as smaller. Four kids—and it had been too long, far too long. He cried out, and it might have been ecstasy or grief or both.

She rolled away, then slid up along the length of him. "And that was a massage."

"Well, I've been missing something."

"I did you wrong all those years ago. Did you hate me? Is that why you're so tense?"

"That wasn't it." He felt good: relaxed, uncaring. She'd come here only to seduce him, to mend fences, to revive memories. Or she already knew, and he might as well learn. "There's a Sauron message sender, galactic south of the Coal Sack. It was there to send Sauron ships to a certain Jump point."

"So?"

"Would you like to know where they were supposed to go? I could find out."

"No."

"Flat-out no? Suppose they come back?"

"Cut the crap, Terry. Hints and secrets. You never did *that* to me before."

"I'm sorry, love—"

"Why did two Saurons go around the Maddox farm and straight to us? You told Bob you knew."

"Because they're white."

Brenda's face went uncannily blank. Then she laughed. "Poor Bob! He'd think you were absolutely loony."

"He sure would. I didn't *want* to know this, Brenda. Why don't you want to find the Saurons?"

"What would I want with them? I want to see my children safe—"

"Send them."

"Not likely! Terry, how much have you figured out?"

"I think I've got it all. I keep testing it, Brenda, and it fits every time."

She waited, her nose four centimeters from his, her breath on his face. The scent of her was very faint.

He said, "You saw to it that three of your own children were out in the rice paddy, including Tarzan. The girl you kept at the house was Reseda, the blond, the girl with the least obvious of Sauron genes. You invited Bob over. Maybe he'd get rid of me before the kids came back."

"Just my luck. He likes you."

"They took away your scent. No enemy could smell you out. They gave you an epicanthic fold to protect your eyes. The flat, wide nose is less vulnerable and pulls in more air." He pushed his fingers into her hair. Spongy, resilient, thick. She didn't flinch; she smiled in pleasure. "And this kind of hair to protect your skulls. It'd take an impact. You grow your own skewball helmets!"

"How gracefully you put it."

"But it looks like a black woman's hair, so you want black skin. So you spend an hour on the roof every afternoon. Naked?" There were no white areas.

"Sure."

"There was a burn-through over Dagon City, and the EMP destroyed most of the records, but maybe not all. Whatever was left had to say that the Curtis family was mostly black."

"Whereas the Maddoxes are white," she said.

"That burn-through was important. You had to be sure. I'm betting you caused it yourself. It didn't have any serious military importance, did it? The pulse wiped out hospital equipment too, so they couldn't look inside you. Couldn't see that you aren't built—"

"If you say, 'Not quite like a woman,' I'll turn you upside down." She reached down to grip his ankle.

"You came down in a two-man escape pod. One XYY Sauron, and you. There wasn't any Horatius loose for fifteen years. No Miranda either."

"Only an XX," she said. Oh, she felt good lying alongside him. The

Saurons weren't a different species. Gene-tailored, but human, quite human.

He said, "But you didn't speak Anglic. Here you were on Tanith with some chance of passing for a . . . citizen. But you couldn't speak a word, and you were with a Sauron berserker—"

"We say soldier. Soldiers and officers. We don't say Sauron."

"Okay."

"We killed a family and took over the house. It was still war, Terry. We cleaned up as best we could. Hid one body, a girl about my size, and buried the rest. I painted our bantar cloth armor. Turned on the TV wall and left it on. It didn't tell me what they were talking about, but I got the accents. Worked naked in the fields, but that didn't help. It left my feet white up to the knees!"

"The soldier couldn't hide, so you had to kill him. Lex found the knife wound. He wouldn't tell me about it, Brenda."

"Lex knows. He delivered Van, our second. Van was a soldier."

He couldn't think of anything to say. Brenda said, "I killed Randus. I found a Weem's beast and gave him to it. We don't think much of the soldiers, Terry. I cut a claw off the Weem's beast and made the wound—"

"Almost through your skull."

"It had to be done in one stroke. And kept septic. And in the jungle I had to climb a tree when I had daylight and take off all my clothes to keep the tan. I waved at a plane once. Too late to hide. If the pilot saw me he must have thought he was hallucinating."

"What'd you eat out there?"

"Everything! What good is a soldier who gets food poisoning? Anything a De Lap's Ghoul can eat, I can eat."

"*That's* not in the records."

"That's why I can't cook. I can't tell when it tastes wrong, I can't tell when meat's rotten. I used recipes till I could teach some of the kids to cook."

"You couldn't talk, but you could fake the symptoms of a stroke. That's the part I just couldn't believe— God damn!"

The left side of her face had gone slack as a rubber mask. She grinned with the other side. "Benda Curris," she said.

"Don't do that."

She reached across him and finished the collins in two swallows. "How long have you known?"

"Maybe fifteen years, but I didn't *know*, Brenda. I was still angry. There's a lot of time to think between the stars. I made up this *tale*. And worked on the kinks, and then I started thinking I must be crazy, because I couldn't pick a hole in it. You told the Marines about the Saurons to make them talk to you. They wouldn't notice how fast your speech improved. They were hanging on every word, trying to get a line on the escaped Sauron, and chattering away to each other. They taught you Anglic.

"I used to wonder what you saw in me. I'm an outworlder. I couldn't recognise a Tanith accent. You made love to me in the dark because you'd lost too much of your tan in the hospital—"

He stopped because her hand had closed hard on his arm. "I wanted your child! I wanted children, and Tarzan would *look* like he was half outworlder. I didn't plan the power failure, Terry. Hell, it probably tipped you off."

"Yeah, you moved like you could almost see in the dark. And wore dark glasses in daylight. The Tanith sun doesn't get that bright, love."

"Bright enough."

"Tanith must have been perfect for you. The sun never gets high. In this gravity *everybody's* got muscles."

"True, but I didn't pick Tanith. Tanith was where the ships went. What else did you notice?"

"Nothing you could have covered up. I talked marriage at you so you switched to Lex. While you were carrying my child."

"But I *can't* get married. In winter the tan goes away. I have to use tanning lotion and do everything by phone."

"What was it like for . . . you? Before?"

Brenda sat up. "For Sauron women? All right. I'm second generation. Test-tube children, all of us. Women are kept in . . . It's like a laboratory and a harem both. The first generation didn't work out. The women didn't like being brood mares, so to speak, and one day they killed half the doctors and ran loose."

"Good."

"There's nothing good about any of this. They were hunted down and shot, and I got all of this by rumor. Maybe it's true and maybe it isn't."

"They made you a brood mare too, didn't they?"

"Oh, sure. The second generation Sauron women, we like having children. I don't know if they fiddled with our genes or if they just kept the survivors for . . . for breeding after the revolt. They gave us a TV wall and let us learn. I think the first group was suffering from sensory deprivation. Most of the children were bottled, but we tended them, and every so often they'd let us carry a child to term, after they were sure it'd survive. I had two. One was Miranda."

"Survive?" He was sitting up now too, with the remains of his collins.

"Mating two Saurons is a bad idea. The doctors don't give a shit about side effects. Out of ten children you get a couple of soldiers and an officer and a couple of girls. They're the heterozygotes. The homozygotes die. Paired genes for infrared eyes give blindness. Paired genes for fast blood clotting gets you strokes and heart attacks in your teens. You get albinos. You get freaks who die of shock just because the adrenal glands got too big."

"Yuk."

"Can you see why I don't want to find the Saurons? But these are good genes—" Her hands moved down her body, inviting him to witness: good genes, yes. "As long as you don't backbreed. My children are an asset to the human race, Terry."

"I—"

"Six of us escaped. We killed some doctors on the way. Once we reached the barracks it was easy. The XYYs will do anything for us. They smuggled us into four of the troop ships. I don't know what happened to the others. I got aboard *Deimos* as a soldier. None of the officers ever saw me. We were part of the attack on Tanith. When I saw we had a good burn-through in the Dagon City shield, the whole plan just popped into my mind. I grabbed a soldier and we took an escape pod and ran it from there."

"You're incredible." He pulled back to look at her. Not quite a woman . . . not quite *his* woman, ever.

"Terry, did you wonder if I might kill you?"

"Yeah. I thought you'd want to know where the Saurons went first."

"You bet your life on that?"

"I bet on you."

"Fool."

"I'm not dead yet," he pointed out.

"Bad bet, love. When I knew you knew, I assumed you'd made a record somewhere, somehow, that would spill it all if you died. I couldn't find it in the city records. But suppose I decided to wipe out everyone who might know? Everyone you might have talked to. Charley, Sharon, Maria—"

Oh my God.

"—Lex, Bob because you might have talked to him, George Callahan in case Sharon talked, maybe a random lawyer; do you think I can't trace your phone calls? Okay, calm down now." Hands where his neck joined his shoulders, fingers behind the shoulder blades, rubbing smooth and hard. The effort distorted her voice. "We Saurons . . . we have to decide . . . *not* to kill. I've decided. But you've got a . . . real blind spot there, Terry. You put some people in danger."

"I guess I just don't think that way. I had to know whether you'd kill me, before I told you anything useful. I had to know what you are."

"What am I?" she asked.

"I'm not dead. Nobody's dead since you reached the hospital."

"Except Van."

"Yeah. Van. But if any of this got out, you'd be dead and Tarzan would be dead and, hell, they'd probably kill every kid who ever lived with you, just in case you trained them somehow. So."

"So," she said. "Now what?"

2656 AD, APRIL (FIREBEE CLOCK TIME)

Firebee approached the Alderson jump point with a load of borloi and bantar cloth.

Tanith's sun had turned small. Terry searched the sky near that hurtingly bright point for some sign of Tanith itself. But stars don't waver outside an atmosphere, and he couldn't find the one point among many.

"We made some good memories there," Sharon said. "Another two minutes . . . Troops, are we really going to try to reach Sparta?"

Charley called from aft. "Sparta's a long way away. See what they buy on Gaea first."

Terry said, "I'm against it. Sparta's got six Alderson points. If they're not at war they'll be the center of all local trade. This beloved wreck won't be worth two kroner against that competition. We might have to join a guild too, if they let us."

"Isn't there a chance the Emperor would buy the data we got from *Morningstar*?"

"I'll run through those records, Captain, but my guess is we've got nothing to sell. There won't be anything Sparta doesn't have."

She nodded. "Okay. Jumping *now*."

And *Firebee* was gone.

Jerry Pournelle says I invented the Sauron supermen for THE MOTE IN GOD'S EYE. I don't remember. I did not (then!) have any mental portrait of these super-soldiers. It was just words.

A year ago he told me he was putting together an anthology of stories of the Sauron supermen. Would I like to get in on that?

I try not to make a promise until I know I can keep it. So we started downstairs for coffee . . . and I was beginning to describe a story before we hit bottom.

My pleasure in my own stories does not always depend on character development; but I am well satisfied with Brenda.

• • •

• • •

He had miscalculated, the blithering toad—a moon is too big a thing for one man's revenge! Its weight would destroy a world for one man's pride!

And then it was drifting down, down like a monstrous soap bubble—Shoogar *hadn't* miscalculated—down to where Purple capered on the black-scarred hill.

THE FLYING SORCERERS (with David Gerrold), 1971

THE RETURN OF WILLIAM PROXMIRE

Through the peephole in Andrew's front door the man made a startling sight.

He looked to be in his eighties. He was breathing hard and streaming sweat. He seemed slightly more real than most men: photogenic as hell, tall and lean, with stringy muscles and no potbelly, running shoes and a day pack and a blue windbreaker, and an open smile. The face was familiar, but from where?

Andrew opened the front door but left the screen door locked. "Hello?"

"Doctor Andrew Minsky?"

"Yes." Memory clicked. "William Proxmire, big as life."

The ex-Senator smiled acknowledgment. "I've only just finished reading about you in the *Tribune*, Dr. Minsky. May I come in?"

It had never been Andrew Minsky's ambition to invite William Proxmire into his home. Still—"Sure. Come in, sit down, have some coffee. Or do your stretches." Andrew was a runner himself when he could find the time.

"Thank you."

Andrew left him on the rug with one knee pulled against his chest. From the kitchen he called, "I never in my life expected to meet you face to face. You must have seen the article on me and Tipler and Penrose?"

"Yes. I'm prepared to learn that the media got it all wrong."

"I bet you are. Any politician would. Well, the *Tribune* implied that what we've got is a time machine. Of course we don't. We've got a schematic based on a theory. Then again, it's the new improved version. It doesn't involve an infinitely long cylinder that you'd have to make out of neutronium—"

"Good. What would it cost?"

Andrew Minsky sighed. Had the politician even recognized the reference? He said, "Oh . . . hard to say." He picked up two cups and the coffee pot and went back in. "Is that it? You came looking for a time machine?"

The old man was sitting on the yellow rug with his legs spread wide apart and his fingers grasping his right foot. He released, folded his legs heel to heel, touched forehead to toes, held, then stood up with a sound like popcorn popping. He said, "Close enough. How much would it cost?"

"Depends on what you're after. If you—"

"I can't get you a grant if you can't name a figure."

Andrew set his cup down very carefully. He said, "No, of course not."

"I'm retired now, but people still owe me favors. I want a ride. One trip. What would it cost?"

Andrew hadn't had enough coffee yet. He didn't feel fully awake. "I have to think out loud a little. Okay? Mass isn't a problem. You can go as far back as you like if . . . mmm. Let's say under sixty years. Cost might be twelve, thirteen million if you could also get us access to the proton-antiproton accelerator at Washburn University, or maybe CERN in Switzerland. Otherwise we'd have to build that too. By the way, you're not expecting to get younger, are you?"

"I hadn't thought about it."

"Good. The theory depends on maneuverings between event points. You don't ever go backward. Where and when, Senator?"

William Proxmire leaned forward with his hands clasped. "Picture this. A Navy officer walks the deck of a ship, coughing, late at night in the 1930s. Suddenly an arm snakes around his neck, a needle plunges into his buttocks—"

"The deck of a ship at sea?"

Proxmire nodded, grinning.

"You're just having fun, aren't you? Something to do while jogging, now that you've retired."

"Put it this way," Proxmire said. "I read the article. It linked up with an old daydream of mine. I looked up your address. You were within easy running distance. I hope you don't mind?"

Oddly enough, Andrew found he didn't. Anything that happened before his morning coffee was recreation.

So dream a little. "Deck of a moving ship. I was going to say it's ridiculous, but it isn't. We'll have to deal with much higher velocities. Any point on the Earth's surface is spinning at up to half a mile per second and circling the sun at eighteen miles per. In principle I think we could solve all of it with one stroke. We could scan one patch of deck, say, over a period of a few seconds, then integrate the record into the program. Same coming home."

"You can do it?"

"Well, if we can't solve that one we can't do anything else either. You'd be on a tight schedule, though. Senator, what's the purpose of the visit?"

"Have you ever had daydreams about a time machine and a scope-sighted rifle?"

Andrew's eyebrows went up. "Sure, what little boy hasn't? Hitler, I suppose? For me it was always Lyndon Johnson. Senator, I do not commit murder under any circumstances."

"A time machine and a scope-sighted rifle, and me," William Proxmire said dreamily. "I get more anonymous letters than you'd believe, even now. They tell me that every space advocate daydreams about me and a time machine and a scope-sighted rifle. Well, I started daydreaming too, but my fantasy involves a time machine and a hypodermic full of antibiotics."

Andrew laughed. "You're plotting to do someone good behind his back?"

"Right."

"Who?"

"Robert Anson Heinlein."

All laughter dropped away. "Why?"

"It's a good deed, isn't it?"

"Sure. Why?"

"You know the name? Over the past forty years or so I've talked to a great many people in science and in the space program. I kept hearing the name Robert Heinlein. They were seduced into science because they read Heinlein at age twelve. These were the people I found hard to deal with. No grasp of reality. Fanatics."

Andrew suspected that the Senator had met more of these than he realized. Heinlein spun off ideas at a terrific rate. Other writers picked them up . . . along with a distrust for arrogance combined with stupidity or ignorance, particularly in politicians.

"Well, Heinlein's literary career began after he left the Navy because of lung disease."

"You're trying to destroy the space program."

"Will you help?"

Andrew was about to tell him to go to hell. He didn't. "I'm still talking. Why do you want to destroy the space program?"

"I didn't, at first. I was opposed to waste," Proxmire said. "My colleagues, they'll spend money on any pet project, as if there was a money tree out there somewhere—"

"Milk price supports," Andrew said gently. For several decades now, the great state of Wisconsin had taken tax money from the other states so that the price they paid for milk would stay *up*.

Proxmire's lips twitched. "Without milk price supports, there would be places where families with children can't buy milk."

"Why?"

The old man shook his head hard. "I've just remembered that I don't have to answer that question anymore. My point is that the government has spent far more taking rocks from the Moon and photographs from Saturn. Our economy would be far healthier if that money had been spent elsewhere."

"I'd rather shoot Lyndon. Eliminate welfare. Save a *lot* more money that way."

"A minute ago you were opposed to murder."

The old man did have a way with words. "Point taken. Could you get us funding? It'd be a guaranteed Nobel Prize. I like the fact that you don't need a scope-sighted rifle. A hypo full of sulfa drugs doesn't have to be kept secret. What antibiotic?"

"I don't know what cures consumption. I don't know which year or what ship. I've got people to look those things up, if I decide I want to know. I came straight here as soon as I read the morning paper. Why not? I run every day, any direction I like. But I haven't heard you say it's impossible, Andrew, and I haven't heard you say you won't do it."

"More coffee?"

"Yes, thank you."

Proxmire left him alone in the kitchen, and for that Andrew was grateful. He'd have made no progress at all if he'd had to guard his expression. There was simply too much to think about.

He preferred not to consider the honors. Assume he had changed the past; how would he prove it before a board of his peers? "How would I prove it *now*? What would I have to show them?" he muttered under his breath, while the coffee water was heating. "Books? Books that didn't get written? Newspapers? There are places that'll print any newspaper headline I ask for. 'Waffen SS to Build Work Camp in Death Valley.' I can mint Robert Kennedy half-dollars for a lot less than thirteen million bucks. Hmm . . ." But the Nobel Prize wasn't the point.

Keeping Robert Heinlein alive a few years longer: was *that* the point? It shouldn't be. Heinlein wouldn't have thought so.

Would the science fiction field really have collapsed without the Menace From Earth? Tradition within the science fiction field would have named Campbell, not Heinlein. But think: was it magazines that had sucked Andrew Minsky into taking advanced physics classes? Or . . . *Double Star, Red Planet*, Anderson's *Tau Zero*, Vance's *Tschai* series. Then the newsstand magazines, then the subscriptions, then (of course) he'd dropped it all to pursue a career. If Proxmire's staff investigated his past (as they must, if he was at all serious), they would find that Andrew Minsky, Ph.D., hadn't read a science fiction magazine in fifteen years.

Proxmire's voice came from the other room. "Of course it would be a major chunk of funding. But wouldn't my old friends be surprised to find me backing a scientific project! How's the coffee coming?"

"Done." Andrew carried the pot in. "I'll do it," he said. "That is, I and my associates will build a time machine. We'll need funding and we'll need active assistance using the Washburn accelerator. We should be ready for a man-rated experiment in three years, I'd think. *We* won't fail."

He sat. He looked Proxmire in the eye. "Let's keep thinking, though. A Navy officer walks the tilting deck of what would now be an antique Navy ship. An arm circles his throat. He grips the skinny wrist and elbow, bends the wrist downward and throws the intruder into the sea. They train Navy men to fight, you know, and he was young and you are old."

"I keep in shape," Proxmire said coldly. "A medical man who performs autopsies once told me about men and women like me. We run two to five miles a day. We die in our eighties and nineties and hundreds. A fall kills us, or a car accident. Cut into us and you find veins and arteries you could run a toy train through."

He was serious. "I was afraid you were thinking of taking along a blackjack or a trank gun or a Kalashnikov—"

"No."

"I'll say it anyway. Don't hurt him."

Proxmire smiled. "That would be missing the point."

And if that part worked out, Andrew would take his chances with the rest.

He had been reaching for a beer while he thought about revising the time machine paper he'd done with Tipler and Penrose four years ago. Somewhere he'd shifted over into daydreams, and that had sent him off on a weird track indeed.

It was like double vision in his head. The time machine (never built) had put William Proxmire (the ex-Senator!) on the moving deck of the *USS Roper* on a gray midmorning in December, 1933. Andrew never daydreamed this vividly. He slapped his flat belly, and wondered why, and remembered: he was ten pounds heavier in the daydream, because he'd been too busy to run.

So much detail! Maybe he was remembering a sweaty razor-sharp nightmare from last night, the kind in which you know you're doing something bizarrely stupid, but you can't figure out how to stop.

He'd reached for a Henry Weinhart's (Budweiser) from the refrigerator in his kitchen (in the office at Washburn, where the Weinhart's always ran out first) while the project team watched their monitors (while the KCET funding drive whined in his living room). In his head there were double vision, double memories, double sensations. The world of quantum physics was blurred in spots. But this was his kitchen and he could hear KCET begging for money a room away.

Andrew walked into his living room and found William Proxmire dripping on his yellow rug.

No, wait. That's the other—

The photogenic old man tossed the spray hypo on Andrew's couch. He stripped off his hooded raincoat, inverted it and dropped it on top. He was trying to smile, but the fear showed through. "Andrew? What I am doing *here*?"

Andrew said, "My head feels like two flavors of cotton. Give me a moment. I'm trying to remember two histories at once."

"I should have had more time. And then it should have been the Washburn accelerator! You said!"

"Yeah, well, I did and I didn't. Welcome to the wonderful world of Schrödinger's Cat. How did it go? You found a young Lieutenant Junior Grade gunnery officer alone on deck—" The raincoat was soaking his cushions. "In the rain—"

"Losing his breakfast overside in the rain. Pulmonary tuberculosis, consumption. Good riddance to an ugly disease."

"You wrestled him to the deck—"

"Heh heh heh. No. I told him I was from the future. I showed him a spray hypo. He'd never seen one. I was dressed as a civilian on a Navy ship. That got his attention. I told him if he was Robert Heinlein I had a cure for his cough."

" 'Cure for his cough'?"

"I didn't say it would kill him otherwise. I didn't say it wouldn't, and he didn't ask, but he may have assumed I wouldn't have come for anything trivial. I knew his name. This was Heinlein, not some Wisconsin dairy farmer. He *wanted* to believe I was a time traveler. He *did* believe. I gave him his shot. Andrew, I feel cheated."

"Me too. Get used to it." But it was Andrew who was beginning to smile.

The older man hardly heard; his ears must be still ringing with that long-dead storm. "You know, I would have liked to talk to him. I was supposed to have twenty-two minutes more. I gave him his shot and the whole scene popped like a soap bubble. *Why* did I come back *here*?"

"Because we never got funding for research into time travel."

"Ah . . . hah. There *have* been changes. What changes?"

It wasn't just remembering; it was a matter of selecting pairs of memories that were mutually exclusive, then judging between them. It was maddening . . . but it could be done. Andrew said, "The Washburn accelerator goes with the time machine goes with the funding. My apartment goes with *no* time machine goes with *no* funding goes with . . . Bill, let's go outside. It should be dark by now."

Proxmire didn't ask why. He looked badly worried.

The sun had set, but the sky wasn't exactly black. In a line across a smaller, dimmer full moon, four rectangles blazed like windows into the sun. Andrew sighed with relief. Collapse of the wave function: *this* was reality.

William Proxmire said, "Don't make me guess."

"Solar power satellites. Looking Glass Three through Six."

"What happened to your time machine?"

"Apollo Eleven landed on the Moon on July 20, 1969, just like clockwork. Apollo Thirteen left a month or two early, but something still exploded in the service module, so I guess it wasn't a meteor. They . . . shit."

"Eh?"

"They didn't get back. They died. We murdered them."

"Then?"

Could he put it back? Should he put it back? It was still coming together in his head. "Let's see, NASA tried to cancel Apollo Eighteen, but there was a hell of a write-in campaign—"

"Why? From whom?"

"The spec-fic community went absolutely apeshit. Okay, Bill, I've got it now."

"Well?"

"You were right, the whole science fiction magazine business just faded out in the fifties, last remnants of the pulp era. Campbell alone couldn't save it. Then in the sixties the literary crowd rediscovered the idea. There must have been an empty ecological niche and the lit-crits moved in.

"Speculative fiction, spec-fic, the literature of the possible. *The New Yorker* ran spec-fic short stories and critical reviews of novels. They thought *Planet of the Apes* was wonderful, and *Selig's Complaint*, which was Robert Silverberg's study of a telepath. Tom Wolfe started appearing in *Esquire* with his bizarre alien cultures. I can't remember an issue of *The Saturday Evening Post* that didn't have *some* spec-fic in it. Anderson, Vance, MacDonald . . . John D. MacDonald turns out novels set on a ring the size of Earth's orbit.

"The new writers were good enough that some of the early ones couldn't keep up, but a few did it by talking to hard science teachers. Benford and Forward did it in reverse. Jim Benford's a plasma physicist but he writes like he swallowed a college English teacher. Robert Forward wrote a novel called *Neutron Star*, but he built the Forward Mass Detector too.''

''Wonderful.''

''There's a lot of spec-fic fans in the military. When Apollo Twenty-one burned up during reentry, they raised so much hell that Congress took the manned space program away from NASA and gave it to the Navy.''

William Proxmire glared and Andrew Minsky grinned. ''Now, you left office in the '60s because of the Cheese Boycott. When you tried to chop the funding for the Shuttle, the spec-fic community took offense. They stopped eating Wisconsin cheese. The San Francisco Locus called you the Cheese Man. Most of your supporters must have eaten nothing but their own cheese for about eight months, and then Goldwater chopped the milk price supports. 'Golden Fleece,' he called it. So you were out, and now there's no time machine.''

''We could build one,'' Proxmire said.

Rescue Apollo Thirteen? The possibility had to be considered . . . Andrew remembered the twenty years that followed the Apollo flights. In one set of memories, lost goals, pointlessness and depression, political faddishness leading nowhere. In the other, half a dozen space stations, government and military and civilian; Moonbase and Moonbase Polar; *Life* photographs of the Mars Project half-finished on the lunar plain, sitting on a hemispherical Orion-style shield made from lunar aluminum and fused lunar dust.

I do not commit murder under any circumstances.

''I don't think so, Bill. We don't have the political support. We don't have the incentive. Where would a Nobel Prize *come* from? We can't prove there was ever a time line different from this one. Besides, this isn't just a more interesting world, it's safer too. Admiral Heinlein doesn't let the Soviets build spacecraft.''

Proxmire stopped breathing for an instant. Then, ''I suppose he wouldn't.''

''Nope. He's taking six of their people on the Mars expedition, though. They paid their share of the cost in fusion bombs for propulsion.''

May 12, 1988—

Greg Benford called me a couple of months ago. He wants new stories about alternate time tracks for an anthology. I told him that the only sideways-in-time story in my head was totally unsalable. It's just recreation, daydreaming, goofing off. It's about how William Proxmire uses a time machine and a hypodermic full of sulfa drugs to wipe out the space program.

Greg made me write it.

I called Robert to get dates and other data, and asked if I could use his name. I had so much fun with this story! I made lots of copies and sent them to friends. I sent one to Robert, of course. That was only a few weeks ago.

And now I'm thinking that sometimes I really luck out. Robert's death feels bad enough, but it would be one notch worse if I didn't know he'd read this story.

• • •

• • •

Lovely, one of the guards was thinking. *But no expression. You'd think she'd be happy to be out of that stinking prison camp, but she doesn't look it.* Perspiration dripped steadily down his ribs, and he thought, *She doesn't sweat. She was carved from ice by the finest sculptor that ever lived.*

THE MOTE IN GOD'S EYE, 1974

THE TALE OF THE JINNI AND THE SISTERS

"The Tale of the Jinni and the Sisters" happened because Susan Shwartz wanted sequels to *The Arabian Nights.*

I found her suggestion irresistible. My shelves held two versions of *The Thousand and One Nights.* Almost immediately I saw that the clever Scheherezade had missed crucial clues . . .

Publishers Weekly compared me to Boccaccio for this story!

• •

Scheherezade said, "Tell me a story."

In the dark of the tent she could see the glint of his open eyes, but the King didn't stir. She would have felt that. King Shahryar said, "You do that better than I."

Four years they'd been married; seven years she had been his mate; three boys and a girl she had given him. Scheherezade was coming to believe that the bad times were over. But Shahryar was still a dangerous man, and he'd been wire-tight these past two days. Something had frightened him. Something he couldn't talk about.

Sometimes the danger of him excited her. Not tonight. She moved against him anyway and said, "What other diversion have we, awake in the night, with all of our entertainers left behind?"

He declined the hint. "Hah. This traveling-bed and the lumpy ground beneath—"

"—Are the reason we cannot sleep. Tomorrow night will bring us rooms in King Zaman's palace."

"Yes. Well, we left the scribes too."

"Then tell me a story you will not want studied by tomorrow's scholars."

He was quiet for a time. Did he sleep? But something burned in his mind. He'd tried to speak and then turned away, a dozen times in these two days of travel.

He said, "We never speak of the time before we met."

"My father, your Wazir, he warned me of your . . . trouble. I came to you anyway."

"Sometimes I think I might forgive myself for the women, and then forget. But who can forget a tale without an ending? You who know so many tales, what do you really know of the Jinni?"

"Whimsical. Powerful. Prone to extravagance. Dangerous, the ones who fought the Prophet's law. Why?"

"Ten years ago, my brother Zaman told me how he had caught his wife in adultery with a slave cook, and killed them. Then he told me he'd seen my own wife betray me. I could have killed him. I followed him instead, and watched, and still couldn't believe. The Wazir must have told you this much."

"Yes."

"Then we swore that we would depart our palaces and never return until we knew that someone, somewhere, had suffered a greater misfortune. Do you know how long we traveled?"

"Father didn't tell me that."

"He never knew. Two hours."

She laughed before she could stop herself.

"We traveled fast. Sometimes we ran to burn off our rage and sorrow. We were seven or eight leagues from my palace and into a meadow, with no dwellings in sight, and exactly one tree.

"Then a black whirlwind appeared and began to draw into itself. No monkey could have climbed faster than I, yet Zaman beat me into the tree."

She swallowed her laughter. His muscles were rigid and his arms were too tight around her.

"We were hidden before the Jinni became solid. That tree was the only shade anywhere. The Jinni set a crystal coffer down in the shade. There was a woman in it."

"Holes in the casket?" An experienced storyteller would have mentioned those.

"Holes? No, it was sealed like a treasure chest, with seven separate locks, but I could see her through the sides. The Jinni got it open and she came out."

"What was she like?"

"Not a girl. Twenty-two or -three years old, and lovely. Foreign. Yellow like the moon near setting. Straight black hair. Something about her eyes. I'd need a scribe's help to describe her."

"You're doing well."

"The Jinni went in unto her. I . . . wondered what I would see of foreign practices, but she only submitted. Then the Jinni slept. We were going to be there a long time. I tried to shift my weight, and the tree shook, and the woman looked up and saw us.

"She made us come down."

"How?"

"She swore she would wake the Afrit. We came down. She led us away from the tree, and ordered us to go in unto her." Shahryar laughed; he made himself laugh, and Scheherezade dared not. "We are kings, Zaman and I. When we desired a woman, we brought her to our beds and we took her. We are not *summoned*. We had a hard time of it—" He laughed again, painfully. "A soft time of it. We'd moved far from the tree, there was no shade, and we were desperately afraid of making noise. But Zaman succeeded in giving her what she willed, and watching them excited me . . . Should I be telling it the other way around?"

"Was she good?"

"She wrung us dry. We had trouble walking away . . . running when we could. But why not? She claimed five hundred and seventy lovers taken under the nose of the Afrit!"

"Incredible." How could he not feel her tension?

"A disgraceful episode. It put the seal on my opinion of women. If even a Jinni's precautions weren't enough to keep her for himself . . ."

Scheherezade's mind was racing. She had not thought so fast in many years; and what she chose to say was nothing.

"I was a long time losing that hatred. The Koran warns against women; I cannot blame myself too much. But sometimes I wonder. She told us that the Jinni had snatched her on her wedding night, while she was still a virgin. He keeps her beneath the sea, where no man can reach. How can he have been careless five hundred and seventy times?"

"Did you ask her age? She may have been older than she looked, by the magic of her Jinni lover."

"My clever love. I never thought of that."

"Or perhaps the Jinni set down near a caravan one night."

Shahryar laughed long and loud. And presently he slept; but the night was already turning gray.

Four years ago Zaman had left Samarkand to live in his brother's kingdom in the Banu Sasan. He had married Scheherezade's sister, Dunyazad. Now they took their turns on the throne.

Now the old Wazir, Scheherezade's and Dunyazad's father, ruled Samarkand; but every two years Zaman returned to see how the kingdom progressed.

Zaman had been gone for nearly a month.

Dunyazad had been told of their coming. She arrived with a retinue almost before they had broken camp. Her manner was reserved and overly formal. Cosmetics failed to hide dark shadows beneath her eyes.

By noon they had reached the palace. Dunyazad handled practical matters well, showing her sister and brother-in-law to a suite of rooms, adding her own servants to their sparse retinue. There was fruit and spiced meat, a pitcher of sherbet, water for washing, and enough bedding to hold a small party.

When the servants were gone, Shahryar told his wife, "We must go out tonight."

"Yes, my lord," said Scheherezade. "Where? Why?"

"I did not know how much to tell you."

"You have told me only that it was time to visit your brother's house, to see that all is in order. Well, all seems in order."

"But all is not. An accusation has been made. I must see for myself. I want you with me."

An accusation. If she had been standing she would have fallen, for the blood draining from her head. "I hear and obey."

"Then sleep now."

Dunyazad's dinner conversation was brittle-bright chatter interspersed with silences. Scheherezade and Shahryar retired early, pleading sleeplessness on the trip. And softly dressed themselves, and departed on bare feet.

"We need to enter the harem garden," Shahryar told her. "Can you lead me in?"

"Not all harems are alike. I can enter. You would be killed, and I might be held as a harem concubine, if we were discovered. Your rank would not save you."

"I know that, and it is just, but we must do this." Shahryar's scimitar was in his hand. "If I must kill a eunuch or two . . . well."

Scheherezade led.

The entrance was guarded by two eunuchs. Scheherezade engaged them, asking questions about the doings of the harem, until Shahryar had crept past them. Then she alleged a desire to see inside.

She found a wide corridor with a fountain in the middle. The splashing water would cover minor noises. Someone may have seen them around a corner, and recognized the king, and decided not to meddle in politics; or not. Beyond the large, ornate fountain were wide doors leading to a darkened garden, guarded by a pair of armed eunuchs. To left and right were narrower corridors which must lead into the main body of the harem.

She stood pensively beside the fountain. Shahryar was crouched below its rim. She asked, "Must we enter?"

Shahryar mulled it. "Perhaps not, but we must see. Do you hear footsteps?"

"Left, the corridor."

He sprinted. She strolled the long way around the fountain, to distract the guards. But the guards were watching the garden.

Shahryar had snuffed the torch. From the dark they watched Dunyazad pass through the doors. The guards' eyes were on her.

Shahryar had found a window.

"I never wanted to spy on my sister," Scheherezade whispered. "Must we do this?"

The garden was small. Dunyazad was in plain sight, walking as if she slept. Scheherezade noticed three low bushes; she jumped when one of them moved. A small sheep, or rather a lamb, got creakily to its feet and came to investigate the faces at the window. Scheherezade fondled its ears and peeked around it.

Dunyazad stopped beneath a wide tree and called softly. "Sa'ad al-Din Saood."

A man dropped from the tree. He was big, muscular, black in the moonlight. He landed easily, softly, and took Dunyazad in his arms.

Scheherezade continued to look. The interloper was seated on the grass; Dunyazad was in his lap; they were locked in sexual congress. The sounds she made seemed wrung from her. The man made no sound at all, until Scheherezade heard him chuckle, once. His teeth gleamed, white and regular.

Shahryar turned away. He slid slowly down the wall until he huddled at its base. He wrapped his face in his arms and sobbed.

A quick glance down the hall: the guards were facing away, standing rigidly with their scimitars before them. Their faces were immobile, but sweat set them gleaming. They could hardly avoid hearing.

Dunyazad and the interloper separated. The man chuckled again. They talked; Dunyazad seemed to be pleading. Then the man swarmed up the tree, very quickly and silently. Dunyazad sat huddled for a time. Then she stood, adjusted her clothing, and walked back inside.

"We must be out of here," Scheherezade whispered.

Shahryar nodded. He stood slowly. She had been afraid he would not move at all.

He reached the fountain in a silent sprint, and crawled backward behind its cover. Perhaps that was unneeded. The guards were looking out at the garden, now that Dunyazad couldn't see them, and they spoke in furious whispers. This must be agony for them, Sheherezade thought. They knew too much. How could their tale end but with a headsman's ax?

Shahryar sat limp on the pillows. His face was ashen. "It's like a recurring nightmare. How could this happen to us again? Has Allah decreed this as punishment for me and Zaman? Because once we behaved like rabid hyenas after our wives betrayed us—"

"What will you do?"

"I will not kill Dunyazad. I will not kill a woman ever again. Enough is enough!" He looked at her at last. "A woman came to me, one of your sister's harem retinue. She got past the guards somehow, came to me in the roof garden. She said that Dunyazad was betraying my brother. I should have been enraged. I wasn't. I was afraid."

Scheherezade only nodded.

"I *knew* I should kill the old woman. Lying or not, her mouth must be shut. You agree?"

"I—"

"But I've killed too many women! So I put her in a cell and we set out for Zaman's palace. But Zaman would kill Dunyazad, I think. And the children, because they might not be legitimate. How *could* she? She must *know* what a risk she takes."

Scheherezade said, "Allah is not your enemy."

"Do I have any enemy besides my own fate?"

"I think so." For her life, Scheherezade had learned how to be tactful; but this was not a time for tact. "You must have been thinking of betrayal last night, when you told me the tale of the Jinni and the crystal casket. Well, the woman was a Jinni too."

He stared at her. "The *woman* was a Jinni?"

"She was."

"But how can you know?"

"There were no holes in the casket. A woman would have suffocated. And, really, my lord! Five hundred and seventy lovers? And Jinni fly, don't they? Yours must have seen you and Zaman from leagues away, yet he came straight to you."

"May Allah take my soul. Now."

"Not yet, my lord. We have work before us."

"But this is terrible! I've killed more than fifty women!"

"Far more. I can count, my lord. Three years, one each night—"

"No! I tried to live without a woman. I could not. Your father can count them, for he procured them for me. Each night I took a woman's virginity, and each morning I slew her. But not one each night!

"The first half dozen, it felt like vengeance on all the breed of women. After the sixth I would have stopped. But she was not a virgin, and the tenth and eleventh weren't either, and—I was mad, of course."

"You were made mad."

"Scheherezade, I took my revenge on women for three years, for the wrong our wives did to us and the wrong that woman did to her Jinni husband despite all of his extravagant precautions. But that was a *lie*, and she wasn't even a woman!—You knew?"

"It was obvious. I knew you'd suffer if I told you, but it's gone beyond that. *Now* what?"

For Shahryar had gone rigid. He said, "I *thought* I knew those grotesque syllables. My wife's lover called out his name when . . . when. 'Sa'ad al-Din Saood.' It's him. The same Jinni. Not a man. Again."

"It would seem," said Scheherezade, "that a pair of Jinni have chosen our family as exceptionally entertaining playthings. See how it fits. Zaman discovered his wife in adultery and slew both. A pair of Jinni saw. They wondered if you would do the same. One seduced your wife, which I grant must have been easy enough; the orgies sounded . . . well, practiced. Afterward they heard you and Zaman swear your oath. Everybody likes a good story, my heart. Everyone wants to improve it a little."

"But *why is Dunyazad*—"

"We'll have to ask."

"He threatened me," she said.

Scheherezade wondered what Shahryar would say now. *You chose dishonor over death?* But her husband only sipped his coffee.

"I was in my garden the evening after Zaman departed. I heard a laugh from all around me. A whirlwind snatched me into the air, flew after the caravan, circled high over my husband's tent! Then came to earth leagues ahead of the encampment. I was rigid with fear. I kept thinking, *What would my sister do*?"

"Scream."

"I screamed, I begged, I pissed myself, I vomited into the wind. When I reached the ground I ran. The whirlwind became a man twenty feet tall. He ambled alongside me with a big crystal casket under his arm, until I fell over with black spots before my eyes. Then he set the casket down, and unlocked it, and a woman came out."

"By Allah, it really is him, and I am not mad!" Shahryar exclaimed. "Was she slant-eyed, with yellow—"

"She was me! Do you know how many mirrors there are in this palace? I've been avoiding them ever since, but I can't avoid *him*. He has my image, my *self*!"

"I think I see," said Scheherezade. "Calm down, Dunyazad. Have some coffee. Try to think of it as a tale."

"They took their pleasure in every position Zaman and I have ever tried, and one that I don't think any human shapes could take. Nauseating. They didn't stop till morning. The woman grinned at me and said that they would . . . perform, she said. Perform in my harem, and then in the palace itself, and then in the public square, until all the land knew that Dunyazad is a whore. Or the . . . the male might take his pleasure with me for one night."

"He lied, of course," Scheherezade said.

"Of course he lied. Every night for eight nights now. I—" She stopped. Suddenly her fingernails were digging runnels down her cheeks. Scheherezade quickly snatched her hands away, and held them.

"Why do they do this?" Shahryar wondered. "My love, in all the tales about Jinni, have they ever gotten a woman with child?"

She thought. "No. Never."

"Good." He might be thinking that at least the succession was safe. "It's not for that, then. But why?"

"Power. Dunyazad, my sister, how does it feel?"

Dunyazad looked at the king.

"No secrets now!" Scheherezade snapped. "We need to know everything, to fight this thing—"

"We can't fight Jinni!"

"The fisherman did. Aladdin had to fight too. So. How does it feel?"

"He makes me—He makes my body—" She couldn't go on.

"Better than a human lover?"

She nodded.

"He makes your body betray you. My husband, he drove you and your brother to a madness never seen before. Do you remember the tales of Caliph Haroun al-Rashid? The woman in the trunk?"

"Yes. The Caliph found a man who had strangled his wife, then chopped her to pieces. She was innocent, but he believed the words of a malicious slave he had never seen before or since. The Caliph freed the man, and found him a wife from among his own courtiers! That bothered me, Scheherezade. I would never have done that. And he freed the slave, and two women who tried to murder their sister and killed her betrothed—"

"He did it to be admired for his mercy, to feel his power of life and death. So it is with the Jinni. He feels his power over all of us. Even women play games of power in their harems."

"What can we do?"

"We must learn as much as we can. Dunyazad, what do the sheep in the garden have to do with the Jinni?"

"What? Nothing. They're Persian lambs. A trader brought them as a gift. Four of them. One disappeared night before last. The Jinni ate it, hooves and wool and bones and all."

"He's getting bored," Scheherezade said. "He gave you one more thing you'll have to lie about. We'll have to do something soon."

Dunyazad poured more coffee. Her hands shook but nothing spilled. "Magic rings, lamps, bottles. Sister, have you ever seen one? Are you carrying one?"

"Not I. But Jinni can be made drunk, and slain while drunk. Can you procure wine?"

"Wine!" Dunyazad laughed. "No, there's no wine in this palace. Once Zaman allowed wine to be brought for foreign visitors. Once in four years, and after the Sheik departed we poured the rest of it out. Sister, it's hopeless!"

"It's not. The Afrits don't know that *I* know what they are. Perhaps we can tell them a tale."

"*What?*"

"Tell them a story. What else have I to fight with? Dunyazad, you must show me through every part of the harem. My husband, you may not come. We shall return in a few hours."

The harem was small by the standards of the day. Zaman's peers might have mocked if they knew how empty it was.

They met a dozen servants, women and eunuchs, including a lean eunuch doctor named Saburin. There were two concubines, virgins, kept ready for visitors. "Zaman had a bad time of it," Dunyazad said. "He still doesn't trust any woman except me and possibly you. It means I must do all the supervising myself."

"Shahryar's the same way."

She found a large room, windowless, with only one doorway, and a curtain to cover it. There were benches and tables and a small bed. Scheherezade nodded. "What is it used for?"

"If one of the women becomes ill, we put her here. The night air can be blocked off. One can fill it with poppy fumes or whatever smokes Saburin calls for. It's apart from the other quarters, in case she has something contagious."

"Good! Perfect. Now, does the Afrit spend all of his time in the tree?"

"In daylight I see no sign of him, and the guards saw nothing when the lamb disappeared. I must come to him after dark."

"How soon after dark? Always at the same time?"

Dunyazad sighed. "I wait until I feel safe. But I've been careless, my sister. It isn't only his threats. It's . . . I'm coming to like it."

"Ah."

"He knows me inside and out! How can I—"

"Concentrate, sister. He doesn't know when you will come? Have you ever come as early as sunset?"

"No, never that early. Only after pitch dark. These last two days I came early, to get it *over* with!"

"Or as late as morning?"

"No. Wait. The second night I couldn't make myself move. I came very late. We were still together when I saw colors in my robe. I ran."

"Well, we must take a risk. Now, quickly, get me workmen and paint and a brazier and a great pot of wax, and wood to make a door! He's never been in the harem itself?"

"No, never."

"I need the bedclothes from your chamber. Unwashed, I hope. Curtains hung here and here. And I need something else, but I'll see to that myself."

"I've thought of something else."

Scheherezade listened, then nodded. "You have a gift. See to it they they don't use too much perfume or too little poppy smoke!"

She found her husband pacing their quarters. He smelled of exertion. "I practiced swordplay with one of the men who instruct Zaman's sons. He had children by three of his concubines, you know, before the curse fell on us. But time passed and you were still gone—"

"Yes. I have a plan." She talked rapidly.

He listened, and mulled it after she had finished, and presently said, "There are *two* Jinni. You plan to attack two Jinni, without me?"

"You can't enter a king's harem, my lord."

"And if everything goes exactly right, you might trap *one*?"

"We'll ransom him. The female will have to agree. All we want is to be left alone, after all."

"They're known liars, Scheherezade!"

"Then you think of something!"

It was as if he held his rage wriggling in both fists. "Allah has not made me clever enough!"

"Then help! I need a seal of Solomon, with certain inscriptions. I've drawn a picture. I hope I remembered it right. Find a jeweler. Find the best! Have it for me by sunset."

"You don't understand money. I'll send servants to hire *six* jewelers. We'll use the best seal."

"I will be very glad when this is over."

The garden wasn't large, but it was a wonderful place, full of color and fragrances, the colors dimming with the dusk. Sounds of traffic came over the high wall: the last merchants going home. Eunuchs moved about lighting torches, while Dunyazad showed her sister around.

The lambs were curious and friendly. "In Persia they use the wool from the lambs, not the sheep. Hazad treats them like pets." She named them. She was trying to seem bright and cheerful, but her voice was brittle.

She seemed to be avoiding the big tree in the center.

Scheherezade led her to it nonetheless. It was huge and strong; it dominated the enclosure. When Scheherezade peered up into it she saw only textured darkness.

And when she turned to her sister, Dunyazad was gaping, her hands at her throat. She wasn't breathing.

"Sister?"

Dunyazad crumpled gracefully.

"Guards! Help!"

The two eunuchs came running. There was foam at the corners of Dunyazad's mouth, and her eyes were rolled up nearly out of sight. Scheherezade wrung her hands. "Is there a place for the sick? Well inside, away from the night air?"

"Yes, O queen."

"Take her there. Then get me cold perfumed water and the doctor." Doctor Saburin was already running toward them. "Maybe she only needs rest. Oh, she's looked so tired lately!"

She kept Saburin until midnight, then repeated her final instructions and sent him to his bed.

The shape under the bedclothes was quite covered up, with only black hair showing. The covers moved shallowly and rapidly; the occupant was panting.

Scheherezade sipped a sugar sherbet. Presently she set the empty goblet down and went to sit on the bed. Her hand beneath the blanket felt the heat of neck and shoulder. She said, "I haven't been so frightened in four years."

There was only the panting, and a twitch of the quilts.

"Dunyazad is seen to be taken ill. She is carried inside. Guards describe the room. One who finds the room will find Scheherezade nursing the poor creature. I wish you could understand. Never tell a story when you can show it!"

The curtains moved back. A eunuch guard stood in the doorway. She'd seen him before: a pudgy fellow, not too bright. Scheherezade snapped, "What do you want?"

The guard grinned. Leered. "Both of you."

"What? Oh, Allah preserve me!" He was changing shape.

He was taller, leaner. His clothing distorted itself to fit. His skin darkened, his lips and nose filled out. "Your sister is mine already," he said. "I want you too."

Scheherezade's knife was in her fist, the point at her heart. "You may have me dead."

"You know what I am?"

"A Jinni. Of course. Did you cause my sister's sickness?"

"We'll let her rest." He brushed past her. "We'll move her from the bed and—"

"Leave her alone!"

"You do not give me orders, Queen Scheherezade. Let me tell you what will happen if you use that knife. First, your corpse will disappear into the desert. But none will know that, because you will be seen to leave this room. Then you will be seen to do dreadful things."

"Nonsense." Scorn and disbelief.

The Jinni was still changing. Now it was like looking into a mirror, even to the clothing. "You slight the Jinni if you doubt me," said Scheherezade's voice. "Your husband will find his wife taking her pleasure with some slave in the market at high noon."

"No slave would dare."

"The slave would be my companion."

It was one of the skills of the storyteller: Scheherezade's face showed withering contempt. "Companion! You're really not very convincing. Did you cozen my poor sister with this tale?"

"I can make my threats real, but let us have done with threats." Scheherezade moved close; she put her hands on Scheherezade's arms. Scheherezade screamed at once, and Scheherezade released her with a frown of distaste. "Don't be foolish. I've put them all to sleep." But she glanced down and saw blood on the tip of Scheherezade's knife.

Scheherezade had known the risk.

"I can be of any shape you like," the Jinni said. "Man, woman, old or young, human or slightly different or wildly different. Only name your desire."

"To see you gone. Companion? The Jinni don't have companions. How could even you tolerate the company of a Jinni?" Her arms were getting tired; she still held the knife poised above her heart.

"You are a highly opinionated fool." The woman considered. "Very well. Wait here."

The Jinni had been gone for more than a minute before Scheherezade gave vent to a shuddering sigh. And drew breath as if there were no air anywhere. And hiccoughed painfully when the curtain was thrown back.

Two Scheherezades entered, identical in every respect. "Show, don't tell. Isn't that what you were saying, storyteller? So, this is what the whole city will see tomorrow unless you grant my will," one said. "But you shall be first."

That one changed. It became the man she had seen with Dunyazad; and then it was Shahryar. Shahryar and the Scheherezade-shape moved to each other. Their hands moved beneath each other's clothing, then clothing began to fall away. Scheherezade watched as if mesmerized. The blade sagged in her hands.

Robes and undergarments and slippers faded into air as they fell away.

Both Jinni seemed to have forgotten her until, just once, the woman turned to smile at her. "We take turns," she said. "Oh!" as the man entered her.

The sounds were those of Scheherezade's wedding night. Had they watched? She covered her eyes; she turned her back; she staggered from the room, retching. She heard a chuckle behind her. They need hardly fear that she would call guards to see *this*!

Now she moved in frantic haste. The new door was wide open, flat against the wall, behind a second curtain. She'd counted on help for the heavy door; now she saw guards sprawled everywhere, snoring. But Dunyazad came running down the hall, struck the door and wrestled it like an enemy.

It slammed shut. The seal of Solomon was painted across it in bright scarlet. A third curtain concealed the pot of wax on its brazier. Dunyazad picked it up in both arms. She poured wax down each side of the door, while Scheherezade stamped the best of four seals (two jewelers had been late) along the congealing wax. The sounds from inside had stopped.

They both lifted the pot and poured along the top of the door, knelt and poured along the bottom. Scheherezade stamped carefully, making each mark perfect. Without turning she asked, "Are you all right?"

"When they don't come through that door, then I'm all right! Here, I've got the nails—"

A voice spoke through the door. "Open this door at once, or suffer the agonies of the damned!"

Scheherezade ignored that. The door shuddered, and some large animal squealed in pain. Another thump, another incredulous yelp. Her belly unfolded like a tight fist relaxing.

"They can't touch the door. It burns them," Dunyazad realized. "It worked. I can't believe it worked!"

"Why not? It's just a big bottle like the one the fisherman found. Putting Arrow in the bed was brilliant. I was going to just cover up some pillows. He didn't smell at all—"

"We washed him half to death."

"He panted like you were really sick, and he kicked just enough."

"Oh, I wish I could get him out of there."

"The poppy will kill him, sister. Two Jinni and a dead lamb in there forever."

"She's still sleeping," Scheherezade told her husband. "I won't disturb her. She earned it."

"So did you, my warrior."

"I can't sleep. I'm still shaking."

"The harem doctor might have something."

Scheherezade seemed not to hear. "We've warned everybody. We've posted warnings on the door. Now they're building another wall outside it. Brick. The seal on each brick. Better not forget to brick the roof up too. Oh, Allah, what can we tell Zaman?"

"I've thought about that." Shahryar sampled a sweetmeat, at leisure. "My brother is a bit in awe of you. We'll tell him part of the truth. You tricked a pair of Jinni in there and walled them up. You had your sister's help, but you never told her any more than what to do. The workmen won't know any different. I'll talk to the eunuchs who watch the garden. When Zaman comes home you'll have some tale to tell him. Something to sear the hair off his ears."

"I cherish your faith in me, my love. So it's not over yet, is it?"

"It will never be over. Zaman will build a new harem, now that there have been Jinni in it, but we can't keep everyone away forever. Suppose those *things* make promises through the door? One day they'll get loose, whatever we do . . ."

"It may not happen until we're all dead." Scheherezade was beginning to relax, finally. "A pity I can't ever tell the tale."

"Living through it was something Allah might have spared us. All of us. All these ten years."

"Some stories are like that."

"I wouldn't have minded hearing it sometime," the King said. "As something that happened to some half-forgotten people, long ago, far away."

• • •

• • •

Toward dawn the frantic sky became even more frantic. There was a bright spot in there. If it was the head, it was hard to see, looking down through the luminous tunnel of the tail. Cold light and shifting shadows, faint color splashes of aurora even in daytime. Then the light was afire with dawn, but the light was still funny. Elfin. Gordie shivered.

LUCIFER'S HAMMER, 1977

MADNESS HAS ITS PLACE

Sometimes an idea suggests a story, and then has to be discarded. And every writer learns this; but then he must learn *when*.

I was following Fred Pohl's suggestion: writing about the odd pockets of the universe. (Truly, I've never stopped.) I looked at a painting of the galaxy seen along its axis, and pictured two ships departing at the edge of light-speed, the first fleeing the other, the second being flown by a computer program and a dead man . . .

"The Ethics of Madness" evolved into a very different story. I started with the ending, but I should have thrown that away. It no longer applied; it wasn't what I was trying to say. The *theme* got lost.

This time I think I got it right.

"Madness Has Its Place" came about because Jim Baen suggested throwing the Man-Kzin Wars period of Known Space open to selected authors. I'm not good at war stories—I've never been in any armed forces—and this scheme lets me read Known Space stories without writing them first.

When I first started, I was trying to write like Poul Anderson. Jerry Pournelle, when we first began collaborating, told me that he wouldn't work in Known Space. He couldn't buy the sociology. But both writers have been at play within THE MAN-KZIN WARS.

I was hoping the new stories would inspire me, as the "Warlock's World" stories did. It's worked. "Madness Has Its Place" is the first Known Space story since THE RINGWORLD ENGINEERS.

I

• •

A lucky few of us know the good days before they're gone.

I remember my eighties. My job kept me in shape, and gave me enough variety to keep my mind occupied. My love life was imperfect but interesting. Modern medicine makes the old fairy tales look insipid; I almost never worried about my health.

Those were the good days, and I knew them. I could remember worse.

I can remember when my memory was better too. That's what this file is for. I keep it updated for that reason, and also to maintain my sense of purpose.

The Monobloc had been a singles bar since the 2320s.

In the '30s I'd been a regular. I'd found Charlotte there. We held our wedding reception at the Monobloc, then dropped out for twenty-eight years. My first marriage, hers too, both in our forties. After the children grew up and moved away, after Charlotte left me too, I came back.

The place was much changed.

I remembered a couple of hundred bottles in the hologram bar display. Now the display was twice as large and seemed more realistic—better equipment, maybe—but only a score of bottles in the middle were liquors. The rest were flavored or carbonated water, high-energy drinks, electrolytes, a thousand kinds of tea; food to match, raw vegetables and fruits kept fresh by high-tech means, arrayed with low-cholesterol dips; bran in every conceivable form short of injections.

The Monobloc had swallowed its neighbors. It was bigger, with curtained alcoves, and a small gym upstairs for working out or for dating.

Herbert and Tina Schroeder still owned the place. Their marriage had been open in the '30s. They'd aged since. So had their clientele. Some of us had married or drifted away or died of alcoholism; but word of mouth and the Velvet Net had maintained a continuous tradition. Twenty-eight years later they looked better than ever . . . wrinkled, of course, but lean and muscular, both ready for the Gray Olympics. Tina let me know before I could ask: she and Herb were lockstepped now.

To me it was like coming home.

For the next twelve years the Monobloc was an intermittent part of my life.

I would find a lady, or she would find me, and we'd drop out. Or we'd visit the Monobloc and sometimes trade partners; and one evening we'd go together and leave separately. I was not evading marriage. Every woman I found worth knowing, ultimately seemed to want to know someone else.

I was nearly bald even then. Thick white hair covered my arms and legs and torso, as if my head hairs had migrated. Twelve years of running construction robots had turned me burly. From time to time some muscular lady would look me over and claim me. I had no trouble finding company.

But company never stayed. Had I become dull? The notion struck me as funny.

I had settled myself alone at a table for two, early on a Thursday evening in 2375. The Monobloc was half empty. The earlies were all keeping one eye on the door when Anton Brillov came in.

Anton was shorter than me, and much narrower, with a face like an axe. I hadn't seen him in thirteen years. Still, I'd mentioned the Monobloc; he must have remembered.

I semaphored my arms. Anton squinted, then came over, exaggeratedly cautious until he saw who it was.

"Jack Strather!"

"Hi, Anton. So you decided to try the place?"

"Yah." He sat. "You look good." He looked a moment longer and said, "Relaxed. Placid. How's Charlotte?"

"Left me after I retired. Just under a year after. There was too much of me around and I . . . maybe I was too placid? Anyway. How are you?"

"Fine."

Twitchy. Anton looked twitchy. I was amused. "Still with the Holy Office?"

"Only citizens call it that, Jack."

"I'm a citizen now. Still gives me a kick. How's your chemistry?"

Anton knew what I meant and didn't pretend otherwise. "I'm okay. I'm down."

"Kid, you're looking over both shoulders at once."

Anton managed a credible laugh. "I'm not the kid any more. I'm a weekly."

The ARM had made me a weekly at forty-eight. They couldn't turn me loose at the end of the day anymore, because my body chemistry couldn't shift fast enough. So they kept me in the ARM building Monday through Thursday, and gave me all of Thursday afternoon to shed the schitz madness. Another twenty years of that and I was even less flexible, so they retired me.

I said, "You do have to remember. When you're in the ARM building, you're a paranoid schizophrenic. You have to be able to file that when you're outside."

"*Hah*. How can anyone—"

"You get used to the schitz. After I quit, the difference was *amazing*. No fears, no tension, no ambition."

"No Charlotte?"

"Well . . . I turned boring. And what are you doing here?"

Anton looked around him. "Much the same thing you are, I guess. Jack, am I the youngest one here?"

"Maybe." I looked around, double-checking. A woman was distracting me, though I could see only her back and a flash of a laughing profile. Her back was slender and strong, and a thick white braid ran down her spine, two and a half feet of clean, thick white hair. She was in animated conversation with a blond companion of Anton's age plus a few.

But they were at a table for two: they weren't inviting company. I forced my attention back. "We're gray singles, Anton. The young ones tend to get the message quick. We're slower than we used to be. We *date*. You want to order?"

Alcohol wasn't popular here. Anton must have noticed, but he ordered guava juice and vodka and drank as if he needed it. This looked worse than Thursday jitters. I let him half finish, then said, "Assuming you can tell me—"

"I don't know anything."

"I know the feeling. What *should* you know?"

A tension eased behind Anton's eyes. "There was a message from the *Angel's Pencil*."

"*Pencil* . . . oh." My mental reflexes had slowed down. The *Angel's Pencil* had departed twenty years ago for . . . was it Epsilon Eridani? "Come on, kid, it'll be in the boob cubes before you have quite finished speaking. Anything from deep space is public property."

"*Hah*! No. It's restricted. I haven't seen it myself. Only a reference, and it must be more than ten years old."

That was peculiar. And if the Belt stations hadn't spread the news through the solar system, *that* was peculiar. No wonder Anton was antsy. ARMs react that way to puzzles.

Anton seemed to jerk himself back to here and now, back to the gray singles regime. "Am I cramping your style?"

"No problem. Nobody hurries in the Monobloc. If you see someone you like—" My fingers danced over lighted symbols on the rim of the table. "This gets you a map. Locate where she's sitting, put the cursor on it. That gets you a display . . . hmm."

I'd set the cursor on the white-haired lady. I liked the readout. "Phoebe Garrison, seventy-nine, eleven or twelve years older than you. Straight. Won a Second in the Gray Jumps last year . . . That's the Americas Skiing Matches for seventy and over. She could kick your tail if you don't watch your manners. It says she's smarter than we are, too.

"Point is, she can check you out the same way. Or me. And she probably found this place through the Velvet Net, which is the computer network for unlocked lifestyles."

"So. Two males sitting together—"

"Anyone who thinks we're bent can check if she cares enough. Bends don't come to the Monobloc anyway. But if we want company, we should move to a bigger table."

We did that. I caught Phoebe Garrison's companion's eye. They played with their table controls, discussed, and presently wandered over.

Dinner turned into a carouse. Alcohol was involved, but we'd left the Monobloc by then. When we split up, Anton was with Michiko. I went home with Phoebe.

Phoebe had fine legs, as I'd anticipated, though both knees were teflon and plastic. Her face was lovely even in morning sunlight. Wrinkled, of course. She was two weeks short of eighty and wincing in anticipation. She ate breakfast with a cross-country skier's appetite. We told of our lives as we ate.

She'd come to Santa Maria to visit her oldest grandson. In her youth she'd done critical work in nanoengineering. The Board had allowed her four children. (I'd known I was outclassed.) All were married, scattered across the Earth, and so were the grandkids.

My two sons had emigrated to the Belt while still in their twenties. I'd visited them once during an investigation, trip paid for by the United Nations—

"You were an ARM? Really? How interesting! Tell me a story . . . if you can."

"That's the problem, all right."

The interesting tales were all classified. The ARM suppresses dangerous technology. What the ARM buries is supposed to stay buried. I remembered a kind of time compressor, and a field that would catalyze combustion, both centuries old. Both were first used for murder. If turned loose or rediscovered, either would generate more interesting tales yet.

I said, "I don't know anything current. They bounced me out when I got too old. Now I run construction robots at various spaceports."

"Interesting?"

"Mostly placid." She wanted a story? Okay. The ARM enforced more than the killer-tech laws, and some of those tales I could tell.

"We don't get many mother hunts these days. This one was wished on us by the Belt—" And I told her of a lunie who'd sired two clones. One he'd raised on the Moon and one he'd left in the Saturn Conserve. He'd moved to Earth, where one clone is any normal citizen's entire birthright. When we found him he was arranging to culture a third clone . . .

• • •

I dreamed a bloody dream.

It was one of those: I was able to take control, to defeat what had attacked me. In the black of an early Sunday morning the shreds of the dream dissolved before I could touch them; but the sensations remained. I felt strong, balanced, powerful, victorious.

It took me a few minutes to become suspicious of this particular flavor of wonderful, but I'd had practice. I eased out from under Phoebe's arm and leg and out of bed. I lurched into the medical alcove, linked myself up and fell asleep on the table.

Phoebe found me there in the morning. She asked, "Couldn't that wait till after breakfast?"

"I've got four years on you and I'm going for infinity. So I'm careful," I told her. It wasn't quite a lie . . . and she didn't quite believe me either.

On Monday Phoebe went off to let her eldest grandson show her the local museums. I went back to work.

In Death Valley a semicircle of twenty lasers points at an axial array of mirrors. Tracks run across the desert to a platform that looks like strands of spun caramel. Every hour or so a spacecraft trundles along the tracks, poses above the mirrors, and rises into the sky on a blinding, searing pillar of light.

Here was where I and three companions and twenty-eight robots worked between emergencies. Emergencies were common enough. From time to time Glenn and Skii and ten or twenty machines had to be shipped off to Outback Field or Baikonur, while I held the fort at Death Valley Field.

All of the equipment was old. The original mirrors had all been slaved to one system, and those had been replaced again and again. Newer mirrors were independently mounted and had their own computers, but even these were up to fifty years old and losing their flexibility. The lasers had to be replaced somewhat more often. Nothing was ready to fall apart, quite.

But the mirrors have to adjust their shapes to match distorting air currents all the way up to vacuum; because the distortions themselves must focus the drive beam. A laser at 99.3% efficiency is keeping too much energy, getting too hot. At 99.1% something would melt, lost power would blow the laser into shrapnel, and a cargo would not reach orbit.

My team had been replacing mirrors and lasers long before I came on the scene. This circuit was nearly complete. We had already reconfigured some robots to begin replacing track.

The robots worked alone while we entertained ourselves in the monitor room. If the robots ran into anything unfamiliar, they stopped and beeped. Then a story or songfest or poker game would stop just as abruptly.

Usually the beep meant that the robot had found an acute angle, an uneven surface, a surface not strong enough to bear a loaded robot, a bend in a pipe, a pipe where it shouldn't be . . . a geometrical problem. The robot couldn't navigate just anywhere. Sometimes we'd have to unload it and move the load to a cart, by hand. Sometimes we had to pick it up with a crane and move it or turn it. Lots of it was muscle work.

Phoebe joined me for dinner Thursday evening.

She'd whipped her grandson at laser tag. They'd gone through the museum at Edwards AFB. They's skied . . . He needed to get serious about that, and maybe get some surgery too . . .

I listened and smiled and presently tried to tell her about my work. She nodded; her eyes glazed. I tried to tell her how good it was, how restful, after all those years in the ARM.

The ARM: that got her interest back. *Stet.* I told her about the Henry Program.

I'd been saving that. It was an embezzling system good enough to ruin the economy. It made Zachariah Henry rich. He might have stayed rich if he'd quit in time . . . and if the system hadn't been so good, so dangerous, he might have ended in prison. Instead . . . well, let his tongue whisper secrets to the ears in the organ banks.

I could speak of it because they'd changed the system. I didn't say that it had happened twenty years before I joined the ARM. But I was still running out of declassified stories. I told her, "If a lot of people know something can be done, somebody'll do it. We can suppress it and suppress it again—"

She pounced. "Like what?"

"Like . . . well, the usual example is the first cold fusion system. They did it with palladium and platinum, but half a dozen other metals work. And organic superconductors: the patents listed a wrong ingredient. Various grad students tried it wrong and still got it. If there's a way to do it, there's probably a lot of ways."

"That was before there was an ARM. Would you have suppressed superconductors?"

"No. What for?"

"Or cold fusion?"

"No."

"Cold fusion releases neutrons," she said. "Sheath the generator with spent uranium, what do you get?"

"Plutonium, I think. So?"

"They used to make bombs out of plutonium."

"Bothers you?"

"Jack, the fission bomb was *it* in the mass murder department. Like the crossbow. Like the Ayatollah's Asteroid." Phoebe's eyes held mine. Her voice had dropped; we didn't want to broadcast this all over the restaurant. "Don't you ever wonder just how *much* of human knowledge is lost in that . . . black limbo inside the ARM building? Things that could solve problems. Warm the Earth again. Ease us through the light-speed wall."

"We don't suppress inventions unless they're dangerous," I said.

I could have backed out of the argument; but that too would have disappointed Phoebe. Phoebe liked a good argument. My problem was that what I gave her wasn't good enough. Maybe I couldn't get angry enough . . . Maybe my most forceful arguments were classified . . .

Monday morning, Phoebe left for Dallas and a granddaughter. There had been no war, no ultimatum, but it felt final.

Thursday evening I was back in the Monobloc.

So was Anton. "I've played it," he said. "Can't talk about it, of course."

He looked mildly bored. His hands looked like they were trying to break chunks off the edge of the table.

I nodded placidly.

Anton shouldn't have told me about the broadcast from *Angel's Pencil*. But he *had*; and if the ARM had noticed, they'd better hear him mention it again.

Company joined us, sampled and departed. Anton and I spoke to a pair of ladies who turned out to have other tastes. (Some bends like to bug the straights.) A younger woman joined us for a time. She couldn't have been over thirty, and was lovely in the modern style . . . but hard, sharply defined muscle isn't my sole standard of beauty . . .

I remarked to Anton, "Sometimes the vibes just aren't right."

"Yeah. Look, Jack, I have carefully concealed a prehistoric Calvados in my apt at Maya. There isn't really enough for four—"

"Sounds nice. Eat first?"

"Stet. There's *sixteen* restaurants in Maya."

A score of blazing rectangles meandered across the night, washing out the stars. The eye could still find a handful of other space artifacts, particularly around the moon.

Anton flashed the beeper that would summon a taxi. I said, "So you viewed the call. So why so tense?"

Security devices no bigger than a basketball rode the glowing sky, but the casual eye would not find those. One must assume they were there. Patterns in their monitor chips would match vision and sound patterns of a mugging, a rape, an injury, a cry for help. Those chips had gigabytes to spare for words and word patterns the ARM might find of interest.

So: no key words.

Anton said, "Jack, they tell a hell of a story. A . . . foreign vehicle pulled alongside Angela at four-fifths of legal max. It tried to cook them."

I stared. *A spacecraft matched course with the* Angel's Pencil *at eighty percent of lightspeed? Nothing man-built could do that. And warlike*? Maybe I'd misinterpreted everything. That can happen when you make up your code as you go along.

But how could the Pencil *have escaped*? "How did Angela manage to phone home?"

A taxi dropped. Anton said, "She sliced the bread with the, you know, motor. I said it's a hell of a story."

Anton's apartment was most of the way up the slope of Maya, the pyramidal arcology north of Santa Maria. Old wealth.

Anton led me through great doors, into an elevator, down corridors. He played tour guide: "The Fertility Board was just getting some real power about the time this place went up. It was built to house a million people. It's never been fully occupied."

"So?"

"So we're en route to the east face. Four restaurants, a dozen little bars. And here we stop—"

"This your apt?"

"No. It's empty, it's always been empty. I sweep it for bugs, but the authorities . . . I *think* they've never noticed."

"Is that your mattress?"

"No. Kids. They've got a club that's two generations old. My son tipped me off to this."

"Could we be interrupted?"

"No. *I'm* monitoring *them*. I've got the security system set to let them in, but only when I'm not here. Now I'll set it to recognize you. Don't forget the number: Apt 23309."

"What is the ARM going to think we're doing?"

"Eating. We went to one of the restaurants, then came back and drank Calvados . . . which we will do, later. I can fix the records at Buffalo Bill. Just don't argue about the credit charge, stet?"

"But—Yah, stet." Hope you won't be noticed, that's the real defense. I was thinking of bailing out . . . but curiosity is part of what gets you into the ARM. "Tell your story. You said she 'sliced the bread with the, you know, motor'?"

"Maybe you don't remember. *Angel's Pencil* isn't your ordinary Bussard ramjet. The field scoops up interstellar hydrogen to feed a fusion-pumped laser. The idea was to use it for communications too. Blast a message half across the galaxy with that. A Belter crewman used it to cut the alien ship in half."

"*There's* a communication you can live without. Anton . . . What they taught us in school. A sapient species doesn't reach space unless the members learn to cooperate. They'll wreck the environment, one way or another, war or straight libertarianism or overbreeding . . . remember?"

"Sure."

"So do you believe all this?"

"I think so." He smiled painfully. "Director Bernhardt didn't. He classified the message and attached a memo too. Six years of flight aboard a ship of limited size, terminal boredom coupled with high intelligence and too much time, elaborate practical jokes, yadda yadda. Director Harms *left* it classified . . . with the cooperation of the Belt. Interesting?"

"But he *had* to have *that*."

"But they had to agree. There's been more since. *Angel's Pencil* sent us hundreds of detailed photos of the alien ship. It's unlikely they could be faked. There are corpses. Big sort-of cats, orange, two-and-a-half meters tall, big feet and elaborate hands with thumbs. We're in mucking great trouble if we have to face those."

"Anton, we've had three hundred and fifty years of peace. We must be doing something right. The odds say we can negotiate."

"You haven't seen them."

It was almost funny. Jack was trying to make me nervous. Twenty years ago the terror would have been fizzing in my blood. Better living through chemistry! This was all frightening enough; but my fear was a cerebral thing, and I was its master.

I wasn't nervous enough for Anton. "Jack, this isn't just vaporware. A lot of those photos show what's maybe a graviton generator, maybe not. Director Harms set up a lab on the Moon to build one for us."

"Funded?"

"Heavy funding. *Somebody* believes in this. But they're getting results! It *works*!"

I mulled it. "Alien contact. As a species we don't seem to handle that too well."

"Maybe this one can't be handled at all."

"What else is being done?"

"Nothing, or damn close. Silly suggestions, career-oriented crap designed to make a bureau bigger . . . Nobody wants to use the magic word. *War*."

"War. Three hundred and fifty years out of practice, we are. Maybe C. Cretemaster will save us." I smiled at Anton's bewilderment. "Look it up in the ARM records. There's supposed to be an alien of sorts living in the cometary halo. He's the force that's been keeping us at peace this past three and a half centuries."

"Very funny."

"Mmm. Well, Anton, this is a lot more real for you than me. *I* haven't yet seen anything upsetting."

I hadn't called him a liar. I'd only made him aware that I knew nothing to the contrary. For Anton there might be elaborate proofs; but I'd seen nothing, and heard only a scary tale.

Anton reacted gracefully. "Of course. Well, there's still that bottle."

Anton's Calvados was as special as he'd claimed, decades old and quite unique. He produced cheese and bread. Good thing: I was ready to eat his arm off. We managed to stick to harmless topics, and parted friends.

The big catlike aliens had taken up residence in my soul.

Aliens aren't implausible. Once upon a time, maybe. But an ancient ETI in a stasis field had been in the Smithsonian since the opening of the twenty-second century, and a quite different creature—C. Cretemaster's real-life analog—had crashed on Mars before the century ended.

Two spacecraft matching course at near lightspeed, *that* was just short of ridiculous. Kinetic energy considerations . . . why, two such ships colliding might as well be made of antimatter! Nothing short of a gravity generator could make it work. But Anton was *claiming* a gravity generator.

His story was plausible in another sense. Faced with warrior aliens, the ARM would do only what they could not avoid. They would build a gravity generator because the ARM must control such a thing. Any further move was a step toward the unthinkable. The ARM took sole credit (and other branches of the United Nations also took sole credit) for the fact that Man had left war behind. I shuddered to think what force it would take to turn the ARM toward war.

I would continue to demand proof of Anton's story. Looking for proof was one way to learn more, and I resist seeing myself as stupid. But I believed him already.

On Thursday we returned to suite 23309.

"I had to dig deep to find out, but they're not just sitting on their thumbs," he said. "There's a game going in Aristarchus Crater, Belt against flatlander. They're playing peace games."

"Huh?"

"They're making formats for contact and negotiation with hypothetical aliens. The models all have the look of those alien corpses, cats with bald tails, but they all think differently—"

"Good." Here was my proof. I could check this claim.

"Good. Sure. Peace games." Anton was brooding. Twitchy. "What about war games?"

"How would you run one? Half your soldiers would be dead at the end . . . unless you're thinking of rifles with paint bullets. War gets more violent than that."

Anton laughed. "Picture every building in Chicago covered with scarlet paint on one side. A nuclear war game."

"Now what? I mean for us."

"Yah. Jack, the ARM isn't *doing* anything to put the human race back on a war footing."

"Maybe they've done something they haven't told you about."

"Jack, I don't think so."

"They haven't let you read all their files, Anton. Two weeks ago you didn't know about peace games in Aristarchus. But okay. What *should* they be doing?"

"I don't *know*."

"How's your chemistry?"

Anton grimaced. "How's yours? Forget I said that. Maybe I'm back to normal and maybe I'm not."

"Yah, but you haven't thought of anything. How about weapons? Can't have a war without weapons, and the ARM's been suppressing weapons. We should dip into their files and make up a list. It would save some time, when and if. I know of an experiment that might have been turned into an inertialess drive if it hadn't been suppressed."

"Date?"

"Early twenty-second. And there was a field projector that would make things burn, late twenty-third."

"I'll find 'em." Anton's eyes took on a faraway look. "There's the archives. I don't mean just the stuff that was built and then destroyed. The archives reach all the way back to the early twentieth. Stuff that was proposed, tanks, orbital beam weapons, kinetic energy weapons, biologicals—"

"We don't want biologicals."

I thought he hadn't heard. "Picture crowbars six feet long. A short burn takes them out of orbit, and they steer themselves down to anything with the silhouette you want . . . a tank or a submarine or a limousine, say. Primitive stuff now, but at least it would *do* something." He was really getting into this. The technical terms he was tossing off were masks for horror. He stopped suddenly, then, "Why not biologicals?"

"Nasty bacteria tailored for *us* might not work on warcats. We want *their* biological weapons, and we don't want them to have ours."

". . . Stet. Now here's one for you. How would you adjust a 'doc to make a normal person into a soldier?"

My head snapped up. I saw the guilt spread across his face. He said, "I had to look up your dossier. *Had* to, Jack."

"Sure. All right, I'll see what I can find." I stood up. "The easiest way is to pick schitzies and train *them* as soldiers. We'd start with the same citizens the ARM has been training since . . . date classified, three hundred years or so. People who need the 'doc to keep their metabolism straight, or else they'll ram a car into a crowd, or strangle—"

"We wouldn't find enough of them. When you need soldiers, you need thousands. Maybe millions."

"True. It's a rare condition. Well, good night, Anton."

I fell asleep on the 'doc table again.

Dawn poked under my eyelids and I got up and moved toward the holophone. Caught a glimpse of myself in a mirror. Rethought. If David saw me looking like this, he'd be booking tickets to attend the funeral.

So I took a shower and a cup of coffee first.

My eldest son looked like I had: decidedly rumpled. "Dad, can't you read a clock?"

"I'm sorry. Really." These calls are so expensive that there's no point in hanging up. "How are things in Aristarchus?"

"Clavius. We've been moved out. We've got half the space we used to, and we'd need twice the space to hold everything we own. Ah, the time change isn't your fault, Dad, we're all in Clavius now, all but Jennifer. She—" David vanished. A mechanically soothing voice said, "You have impinged on ARM police business. The cost of your call will be refunded."

I looked at the empty space where David's face had been. I *was* ARM . . . but maybe I'd already heard enough.

My granddaughter Jennifer is a medic. The censor program had reacted to her name in connection with David. David said she wasn't with him. The whole family had been moved out but for Jennifer.

If she'd stayed on in Aristarchus . . . or been kept on . . .

Human medics are needed when something unusual has happened to a human body or brain. Then they study what's going on, with an eye to writing more programs for the 'docs. The bulk of these problems are psychological.

Anton's "peace games" must be stressful as hell.

II

Anton wasn't at the Monobloc Thursday. That gave me another week to rethink and recheck the programs I'd put on a dime disk; but I didn't need it.

I came back the next Thursday. Anton Brillov and Phoebe Garrison were holding a table for four.

I paused—backlit in the doorway, knowing my expression was hidden—then moved on in. "When did you get back?"

"Saturday before last," Phoebe said gravely.

It felt awkward. Anton felt it too; but then, he would. I began to wish I didn't ever have to see him on a Thursday night.

I tried tact. "Shall we see if we can conscript a fourth?"

"It's not like that," Phoebe said. "Anton and I, we're *together*. We had to tell you."

But I'd never thought . . . I'd never *claimed* Phoebe. Dreams are private. This was coming from some wild direction. "Together as in?"

Anton said, "Well, not married, not yet, but thinking about it. And we wanted to talk privately."

"Like over dinner?"

"A good suggestion."

"I like Buffalo Bill. Let's go there."

Twenty-odd habitués of the Monobloc must have heard the exchange and watched us leave. *Those three long-timers seem friendly enough, but too serious . . . and three's an odd number . . .*

We didn't talk until we'd reached Suite 23309.

Anton closed the door before he spoke. "She's in, Jack. Everything."

I said, "It's really love, then."

Phoebe smiled. "Jack, don't be offended. Choosing is what humans do."

Trite, I thought, and *Skip it*. "That bit there in the Monobloc seemed overdone. I felt excessively foolish."

"That was for *them*. My idea," Phoebe said. "After tonight, one of us may have to go away. This way we've got an all-purpose excuse. You leave because your best friend and favored lady closed you out. Or Phoebe leaves because she can't bear to ruin a friendship. Or big, burly Jack drives Anton away. See?"

She wasn't just in, she was taking over. Ah, well. "Phoebe, love, do you believe in murderous cats eight feet tall?"

"Do you have doubts, Jack?"

"Not any more. I called my son. Something secretive is happening in Aristarchus, something that requires a medic."

She only nodded. "What have you got for us?"

I showed them my dime disk. "Took me less than a week. Run it in an autodoc. Ten personality choices. The chemical differences aren't big, but . . . infantry, which means killing on foot and doesn't have anything to do with children . . . Where was I? Yah. Infantry isn't at all like logistics, and neither is like espionage, and Navy is different yet. We may have lost some of the military vocations over the centuries. We'll have to reinvent them. This is just a first cut. I wish we had a way to try it out."

Anton set a dime disk next to mine, and a small projector. "Mine's nearly full. The ARM's stored an incredible range of dangerous devices. We need to think hard about where to store this. I even wondered if one of us should be emigrating, which is why—"

"To the Belt? Further?"

"Jack, if this all adds up, we won't have *time* to reach another star."

We watched stills and flat motion pictures of weapons and tools in action. Much of it was quite primitive, copied out of deep archives. We watched rock and landscape being torn, aircraft exploding, machines destroying other machines . . . and imagined flesh shredding.

"I could get more, but I thought I'd better show you this first," Anton said.

I said, "Don't bother."

"What? Jack?"

"It only took us a week! Why risk our necks to do work that can be duplicated that fast?"

Anton looked lost. "We need to do *something*!"

"Well, maybe we don't. Maybe the ARM is doing it all for us."

Phoebe gripped Anton's wrist hard, and he swallowed some bitter retort. She said, "Maybe we're missing something. Maybe we're not looking at it right."

"What's on your mind?"

"Let's *find* a way to look at it differently." She was looking straight at me.

I said, "Stoned? Drunk? Fizzed? Wired?"

Phoebe shook her head. "We need the schitz view."

"Dangerous, love. Also, the chemicals you're talking about are massively illegal. *I* can't get them, and Anton would be caught for sure—" I saw the way she was smiling at me. "Anton, I'll break your scrawny neck."

"Huh? Jack?"

"No, no, he didn't tell me," Phoebe said hastily, "though frankly I'd think either of you might have trusted me that much, Jack! I remembered you in the 'doc that morning, and Anton coming down from that twitchy state on a Thursday night, and it all clicked."

"Okay."

"You're a schitz, Jack. But it's been a long time, hasn't it?"

"Thirteen years of peace," I said. "They pick us for it, you know. Paranoid schizophrenics, born with our chemistry screwed up, hair-trigger temper and a skewed view of the universe. Most schitzies never have to feel that. We use the 'docs more regularly than you do and that's that. But some of us go into the ARM . . . Phoebe, your suggestion is still off. Anton's crazy four days out of the week, just like I used to be. Anton's all you need."

"Phoebe, he's right."

"No. The ARM used to be *all* schitzies, right? The genes have thinned out over three hundred years."

Anton nodded. "They tell us in training. The ones who could be Hitler or Napoleon or Castro, they're the ones the ARM wants. They're the ones you can send on a mother hunt, the ones with no social sense . . . but the Fertility Board doesn't let them breed either, unless they've got something special. Jack, you were special, high intelligence or something—"

"Perfect teeth, and I don't get sick in free-fall, and Charlotte's people never develop back problems. That helped. Yah . . . but every century there are less of us. So they hire some Antons too, and *make* you crazy—"

"But carefully," Phoebe said. "Anton's not evolved for paranoia, Jack. You are. When they juice Anton up they don't make him too crazy, just enough to get the viewpoint they want. I bet they leave the top management boringly sane. But *you*, Jack—"

"I *see* it." Centuries of ARM tradition were squarely on her side.

"*You* can go as crazy as you like. It's all natural, and medics have known how to handle it since Only One Earth. We need the schitz viewpoint, and we don't have to steal the chemicals."

"Stet. When do we start?"

Anton looked at Phoebe. Phoebe said, "Now?"

We played Anton's tape all the way through, to a running theme of graveyard humor.

"I took only what I thought we could use," Anton said. "You should have seen some of the rest. Agent Orange. Napalm. Murder stuff."

Phoebe said, "Isn't this murder?"

That remark might have been unfair. We were watching this bizarre chunky rotary-blade flyer. Fire leaped from underneath it, once and again . . . weapons of some kind.

Anton said, "Aircraft design isn't the same when you use it for murder. It changes when you expect to be shot at. Here—" The picture had changed. "That's another weapons platform. It's not just fast, it's supposed to hide in the sky. Jack, are you all right?"

"I'm scared green. I haven't felt any effect yet."

Phoebe said, "You need to relax. Anton delivers a terrific massage. I never learned."

She wasn't kidding. Anton didn't have my muscle, but he had big strangler's hands. I relaxed into it, talking as he worked, liking the way my voice wavered as his hands pounded my back.

"It hasn't been that long since a guy like me let his 'doc run out of beta-dammasomething. An indicator light ran out and he didn't notice. He tried to kill his business partner by bombing his partner's house, and got some family members instead."

"We're on watch," Phoebe said. "If you go berserk we can handle it. Do you want to see more of this?"

"We've missed something. Children, I'm a *registered* schitz. If I don't use my 'doc for three days, they'll be trying to find me before I remember I'm the Marsport Strangler."

Anton said, "He's right, love. Jack, give me your door codes. If I can get into your apt, I can fix the records."

"Keep talking. Finish the massage, at least. We might have other problems. Do we want fruit juice? Munchies? Foodlike substances?"

When Anton came back with groceries, Phoebe and I barely noticed.

Were the warcats real? Could we fight them with present tech? How long did Sol system have? And the other systems, the more sparsely settled colony worlds? Was it enough to make tapes and blueprints of the old murder machines, or must we set to building clandestine factories? Phoebe and I were spilling ideas past each other as fast as they came, and I had quite forgotten that I was doing something dangerous.

I noticed myself noticing that I was thinking much faster than thoughts could spill from my lips. I remembered knowing that Phoebe was brighter than I was, and that didn't matter either. But Anton was losing his Thursday edge.

We slept. The old airbed was a big one. We woke to fruit and bread and dived back in.

We re-invented the Navy using only what Anton had recorded of seagoing navies. We had to. There had never been space navies; the long peace had fallen first.

I'm not sure when I slid into schitz mode. I'd spent four days out of seven without the 'doc, every week for forty-one years excluding vacations. You'd think I'd remember the feel of my brain chemistry changing. Sometimes I do; but it's the central *me* that changes, and there's no way to control that.

Anton's machines were long out of date, and none had been developed even for interplanetary war. Mankind had found peace too soon. Pity. But if the warcats' gravity generators could be copied before the warcats arrived, that alone could save us!

Then again, whatever the cats had for weapons, kinetic energy was likely to be the ultimate weapon, *however* the mass was moved. Energy considerations don't lie . . . I stopped trying to anticipate individual war machines; what I needed was an overview.

Anton was saying very little.

I realized that I had been wasting my time making medical programs. Chemical enhancement was the most trivial of what we'd need to remake an army. Extensive testing would be needed, and then we might not get soldiers at all unless they retained *some* civil rights, or unless officers killed enough of them to impress the rest. Our limited pool of schitzies had better be trained as our officers. For that matter, we'd better start by taking over the ARM. They had all the brightest schitzies.

As for Anton's work in the ARM archives, the most powerful weapons had been entirely ignored. They were too obvious.

I saw how Phoebe was staring at me, and Anton too, both gape-jawed.

I tried to explain that our task was nothing less than the reorganization of humanity. Large numbers might have to die before the rest saw the wisdom in following our lead. The warcats would teach that lesson . . . but if we waited for them, we'd be too late. Time was breathing hot on our necks.

Anton didn't understand. Phoebe was following me, though not well, but Anton's body language was pulling him back and closing him up while his face stayed blank. He feared me worse than he feared warcats.

I began to understand that I might have to kill Anton. I hated him for that.

We did not sleep Friday at all. By Saturday noon we should have been exhausted. I'd caught catnaps from time to time, we all had, but I was still blazing with ideas. In my mind the pattern of an interstellar invasion was shaping itself like a vast three-dimensional map.

Earlier I might have killed Anton, because he knew too much or too little, because he would steal Phoebe from me. Now I saw that that was foolish. Phoebe wouldn't follow him. He simply didn't have the . . . the internal power. As for knowledge, he was our only access to the ARM!

Saturday evening we ran out of food . . . and Anton and Phoebe saw the final flaw in their plan.

I found it hugely amusing. My 'doc was halfway across Santa Maria. They had to get me there. Me, a schitz.

We talked it around. Anton and Phoebe wanted to check my conclusions. Fine: we'd give them the schitz treatment. But for that we needed my disk (in my pocket) and my 'doc (at the apt). So we had to go to my apt.

With that in mind, we shaped plans for a farewell bacchanal.

Anton ordered supplies. Phoebe got me into a taxi. When I thought of other destinations she was persuasive. And the party was waiting . . .

We were a long time reaching the 'doc. There was beer to be dealt with, and a pizza the size of Arthur's Round Table. We sang, though Phoebe couldn't hold a tune. We took ourselves to bed. It had been years since my urge to rut ran so high, so deep, backed by a sadness that ran deeper yet and wouldn't go away.

When I was too relaxed to lift a finger, we staggered singing to the 'doc with me hanging limp between them. I produced my dime disk, but Anton took it away. What was this? They moved me onto the table and set it working. I tried to explain: they had to lie down, put the disk here . . . But the circuitry found my blood loaded with fatigue poisons, and put me to sleep.

Sunday noon:

Anton and Phoebe seemed embarrassed in my presence. My own memories were bizarre, embarrassing. I'd been guilty of egotism, arrogance, self-centered lack of consideration. Three dark blue dots on Phoebe's shoulder told me that I'd brushed the edge of violence. But the worst memory was of thinking like some red-handed conqueror, and out loud.

They'd never love me again.

But they could have brought me into the apt and straight to the 'doc. Why didn't they?

While Anton was out of the room I caught Phoebe's smile in the corner of my eye, and saw it fade as I turned. An old suspicion surfaced and has never faded since.

Suppose that the women I love are all attracted to Mad Jack. Somehow they recognize my schitz potential, though they find my sane state dull. There must have been a place for madness throughout most of human history. So men and women still seek in each other the capacity for madness . . .

And so what? Schitzies kill. The real Jack Strather is too dangerous to be let loose.

And yet . . . it had been worth doing. From that strange fifty-hour session I remembered one real insight. We spent the rest of Sunday discussing it, making plans, while my central nervous system returned to its accustomed, unnatural state. Sane Jack.

• • •

Anton Brillov and Phoebe Garrison held their wedding reception in the Monobloc. I stood as best man, bravely cheerful, running over with congratulations, staying carefully sober.

A week later I was among the asteroids. At the Monobloc they said that Jack Strather had fled Earth after his favored lady deserted him for his best friend.

III

Things ran smoother for me because John Junior had made a place for himself in Ceres.

Even so, they had to train me. Twenty years ago I'd spent a week in the Belt. It wasn't enough. Training and a Belt citizen's equipment used up most of my savings and two months of my time.

Time brought me to Mercury, and the lasers, eight years ago.

Light-sails are rare in the inner solar system. Between Venus and Mercury there are still lightsail races, an expensive, uncomfortable, and dangerous sport. Cargo craft once sailed throughout the asteroid belt, until fusion motors became cheaper and more dependable.

The last refuge of the light-sail is a huge, empty region: the cometary halo, Pluto and beyond. The light-sails are all cargo craft. So far from Sol, their thrust must be augmented by lasers, the same Mercury lasers that sometimes hurl an unmanned probe into interstellar space.

These were different from the launch lasers I was familiar with. They were enormously larger. In Mercury's lower gravity, in Mercury's windless environment, they looked like crystals caught in spiderwebs. When the lasers fired, the fragile support structures wavered like spiderweb in a wind.

Each stood in a wide black pool of solar collector, as if tar paper had been scattered at random. A collector sheet that lost fifty percent of power was not removed. We would add another sheet, but continue to use all the available power.

Their power output was dangerous to the point of fantasy. For safety's sake the Mercury lasers must be continually linked to the rest of the solar system across a lightspeed delay of several hours. The newer solar collectors also picked up broadcasts from space, or from the control center in Challenger Crater. Mercury's lasers must never lose contact. A beam that strayed where it wasn't supposed to could do untold damage.

They were spaced all along the planet's equator. They were hundreds of years apart in design, size, technology. They fired while the sun was up and feeding their square miles of collectors, with a few fusion generators for backup. They flicked from target to target as the horizon moved. When the sun set, it set for thirty-odd Earth days, and that was plenty of time to make repairs—

"In general, that is." Kathry Perritt watched my eyes to be sure I was paying attention. I felt like a schoolboy again. "In general we can repair and update each laser station in turn and *still* keep ahead of the dawn. But come a quake, we work in broad daylight and like it."

"Scary," I said, too cheerfully.

She looked at me. "You feel nice and cool? That's a million tons of soil, old man, and a layer cake of mirror sheeting on top of that, and these old heat exchangers are still the most powerful ever built. Daylight doesn't scare you? You'll get over that."

Kathry was a sixth-generation Belter from Mercury, taller than me by seven inches, not very strong, but extremely dextrous. She was my boss. I'd be sharing a room with her . . . and yes, she rapidly let me know that she expected us to be bedmates.

I was all for that. Two months in Ceres had showed me that Belters respond to social signals I don't know. I had no idea how to seduce anyone.

Sylvia and Myron had been born on Mars in an enclave of areologists digging out the cities beneath the deserts. Companions from birth, they'd married at puberty. They were addicted to news broadcasts. News could get them arguing. Otherwise they behaved as if they could read each other's mind; they hardly talked to each other or to anyone else.

We'd sit around the duty room and wait, and polish our skills as storytellers. Then one of the lasers would go quiet, and a tractor the size of some old Chicago skyscraper would roll.

Rarely was there much of a hurry. One laser would fill in for another until the Monster Bug arrived. Then the robots, riding the Monster Bug like one of Anton's aircraft carriers, would scatter ahead of us and set to work.

Two years after my arrival, my first quake shook down six lasers in four different locations, and ripped a few more loose from the sunlight collectors. Landscape had been shaken into new shapes. The robots had some trouble. Sometimes Kathry could reprogram. Otherwise her team had to muscle them through, with Kathry to shout orders and me to supply most of the muscle.

Of the six lasers, five survived. They seemed built to survive almost anything. The robots were equipped to spin new support structure and to lift the things into place, with a separate program for each design.

Maybe John Junior *hadn't* used influence in my behalf. Flatlander muscles were useful, when the robots couldn't get over the dust pools or through the broken rock. For that matter, maybe it wasn't some Belt tradition that made Kathry claim me on sight. Sylvia and Myron weren't sharing; and I might have been female, or bend. Maybe she thought she was lucky.

After we'd remounted the lasers that survived, Kathry said, "They're all obsolete anyway. They're not being replaced."

"That's not good," I said.

"Well, good and bad. Light-sail cargoes are slow. If the light wasn't almost free, why bother? The interstellar probes haven't sent much back yet, and we might as well wait. At least the Belt Speakers think so."

"Do I gather I've fallen into a kind of a blind alley?"

She glared at me. "You're an immigrant flatlander. Were you expecting to be First Speaker for the Belt? You thinking of moving on?"

"Not really. But if the job's about to fold—"

"Another twenty years, maybe. Jack, I'd miss you. Those two—"

"It's all right, Kathry. I'm not going." I waved both arms at the blazing dead landscape and said, "I like it here," and smiled into her bellow of laughter.

I beamed a tape to Anton when I got the chance.

"If I was ever angry, I got over it, as I hope you've forgotten anything I said or did while I was, let's say, running on automatic. I've found another life in deep space, not much different from what I was doing on Earth . . . though that may not last. These light-sail pusher lasers are a blast from the past. Time gets them, the quakes get them, and they're not being replaced. Kathry says twenty years.

"You said Phoebe left Earth too. Working with an asteroid mining setup? If you're still trading tapes, tell her I'm all right and I hope she is too. Her career choice was better than mine, I expect . . ."

I couldn't think of anything else to do.

Three years after I expected it, Kathry asked. "Why did you come out here? It's none of my business, of course—"

Customs differ: it took her three years in my bed to work up to this. I said, "Time for a change," and "I've got children and grandchildren on the Moon and Ceres and Floating Jupiter."

"Do you miss them?"

I had to say *yes*. The result was that I took half a year off to bounce around the solar system.

After I visited my kids and grandkids, I stayed three weeks with Phoebe. She's second in command of a mining setup on a two-kilometer asteroid orbitting beyond Jupiter. They've been refining the metal ores and shaping them into scores of kilometers of electromagnetic mass driver, then running the slag down the mass driver: a rocket with real rocks in it and an arbitrarily high exhaust velocity, limited only by the length of the mass driver. The asteroid will reach Ceres as mostly refined metal.

I think she was bored; she was seriously glad to see me. Still, I came back early. My being away made us both antsy.

Kathry asked again a year later. I said, "What I did on Earth was a lot like this. The difference is, on Earth I'm dull. Here—am I dull?"

"You're fascinating. You won't talk about the ARM, so you're fascinating and mysterious. I can't believe you'd be dull just because of where you are. Why did you leave, really?"

So I said, "There was a woman."

"What was she like?"

"She was smarter than me. I was a little dull for her. So she left, and that would have been okay. But she came back to my best friend." I shifted uncomfortably and said, "Not that they drove me off Earth."

"No?"

"No. I've got everything I once had herding construction robots on Earth, plus one thing I wasn't bright enough to miss. I lost my sense of purpose when I left the ARM."

I noticed that Myron was listening. Sylvia was watching the holo walls, the three that showed the face of Mercury: rocks blazing like coals in the fading twilight, with only the robots and the lasers to give the illusion of life. The fourth we kept changing. Just then it showed a view up the trunk into the waving branches of the tremendous redwood they've been growing for three hundred years, in Hovestraydt City on the Moon.

"These are the good times," I said. "You have to notice, or they'll go right past. We're holding the stars together. Notice how much dancing we do? I'd be too old and creaky for that— Sylvia, *what*?"

Sylvia was shaking my shoulder. I heard it as soon as I stopped talking: "*Tombaugh Station relayed this picture, the last broadcast from the* Fantasy Prince. *Once again, the* Fantasy Prince *has apparently been—*"

Starscape glowed within the fourth holo wall. Something came out of nowhere, moving hellishly fast, and stopped so quickly that it might have been a toy. It was egg-shaped, studded with what I remembered as weapons.

Phoebe won't have made her move yet. The warcats will have to be deep in the solar system before her asteroid mining setup can be any deterrent. Then one or another warcat ship will find streams of slag sprayed across its path, impacting at comet speeds.

By now Anton must know whether the ARM actually has plans to repel an interstellar invasion.

Me, I've already done my part. I worked on the computer shortly after I first arrived. Nobody's tampered with it since. The dime disk is in place.

We kept the program relatively simple. Until and unless the warcats destroy something that's being pushed by a laser from Mercury, nothing will happen. The warcats must condemn themselves. Then the affected laser will lock onto the warcat ship . . . and so will every Mercury laser that's getting sunlight. Twenty seconds, then the system goes back to normal until another target disappears.

If the warcats can be persuaded that Sol system is defended, maybe they'll give us time to build defenses.

Asteroid miners dig deep for fear of solar storms and meteors. Phoebe might survive. We might survive here too, with shielding built to block the hellish sun, and laser cannon to battle incoming ships. But that's not the way to bet.

We might get one ship.

It might be worth doing.

• • •

• • •

The President was still laughing. "Somebody told me once that I'm not fit to mold the future because I'm only allowed to think up to the next election. Who is it that plans for the future of the human race?"

"Speaking."

FOOTFALL, 1985

NIVEN'S LAWS

From time to time I publish this list; from time to time I update it. I don't think it's possible to track its publishing history. The most recent appearance was in NIVEN'S LAWS from Owlswick Press. In this version I've amplified a little.

• •

To the best I've been able to tell in fifty years of observation, this is how the universe works. I hope I didn't leave anything out.

1a) **Never throw shit at an armed man.**

1b) **Never stand next to someone who is throwing shit at an armed man.**
You wouldn't think anyone would need to be told this. Does anyone remember the Democratic National Convention of 1968?

2) **Never fire a laser at a mirror.**

3) **Mother Nature doesn't care if you're having fun.**

You will not be stopped! There are things you can't do because you burn sugar with oxygen, or your bones aren't strong enough, or you're a mammal, or human. Funny chemicals may kill you slow or quick, or ruin your brain . . . or prolong your life. You can't fly like an eagle, nor yet like Daedalus, but you can fly. You're the only earthly life form that can even begin to deal with jet lag.

You can cheat. Nature doesn't care, but don't get caught.

4) **F × S = k.** The product of Freedom and Security is a constant. To gain more freedom of thought and/or action, you must give up some security, and vice versa.

These remarks apply to individuals, nations, and civilizations. Notice that the constant **k** is different for every civilization and different for every individual.

5) **Psi and/or magical powers, if real, are nearly useless.** Over the lifetime of the human species we would otherwise have done something with them.
6) **It is easier to destroy than to create.** If human beings didn't have a strong preference for creation, nothing would get built.
7) **Any damn fool can predict the past.** Military men are notorious for this, and certain writers too.
8) **History never repeats itself.**
9) **Ethics changes with technology.**
10) **Anarchy is the least stable of social structures. It falls apart at a touch.**
11) **There is a time and a place for tact.** (And there are times when tact is entirely misplaced.)
12) **The ways of being human are bounded but infinite.**
13) **The world's dullest subjects, in order:**
    A) **Somebody else's diet.**
    B) **How to make money for a worthy cause.**
    C) **Special Interest Liberation.**
14) The only universal message in science fiction: **There exist minds that think as well as you do, but differently.**
    Niven's corollary: **The gene-tampered turkey you're talking to isn't necessarily one of them.**
15) Fuzzy Pink Niven's Law: **Never waste calories.**

    Potato chips, candy, whipped cream, or hot fudge sundae consumption may involve you, your dietician, your wardrobe, and other factors. But Fuzzy Pink's Law implies:

    Don't eat soggy potato chips, or cheap candy, or fake whipped cream, or an inferior hot fudge sundae.
16) **There is no cause so right that one cannot find a fool following it.**

    This one's worth noticing.

    At the first High Frontier Convention the minds assembled were among the best in the world, and I couldn't find a conversation that didn't teach me something. But the only newspersons I ran across were interviewing the only handicapped person among us.

    To prove a point one may seek out a foolish Communist, 13th century Liberal, Scientologist, High Frontier advocate, Mensa member, science fiction fan, Jim Bakker acolyte, Christian, or fanatical devotee of Special Interest Lib; but that doesn't really reflect on the cause itself. *Ad hominem* argument saves time, but it's still a fallacy.
17) **No technique works if it isn't used.** If that sounds simplistic, look at some specifics:

Telling friends about your diet won't make you thin. Buying a diet cookbook won't either. Even reading the recipes doesn't help.

Knowing about Alcoholics Anonymous, looking up the phone number, even jotting it on real paper, won't make you sober.

Buying weights doesn't give you muscles. Signing a piece of paper won't make Soviet missiles disappear, even if you make lots of copies and tell every anchorperson on Earth. Endlessly studying designs for spacecraft won't put anything into orbit.

18) **Not responsible for advice not taken.**
19) Think before you make the coward's choice. **Old age is not for sissies.**

NIVEN'S LAWS FOR WRITERS

1) **Writers who write for other writers should write letters.**
2) **Never be embarrassed or ashamed by anything you choose to write.** (Think of this *before* you send it to a market.)
3) **Stories to end all stories on a given topic, don't.**
4) **It is a sin to waste the reader's time.**
5) **If you've nothing to say, say it any way you like.** Stylistic innovations, contorted story lines or none, exotic or genderless pronouns, internal inconsistencies, the recipe for preparing your lover as a cannibal banquet: feel free. **If what you have to say is important and/or difficult to follow, use the simplest language possible.** If the reader doesn't get it then, let it not be your fault.
6) **Everybody talks first draft.**

STAYING RICH

The average citizen of planet Earth is wealthier today than he has been throughout human history. From time to time we need to remember how much we've got to lose.

After all, you don't *feel* rich.

Do you understand how it can be that more people *feel* poor today than ever before? I give you a hint. It isn't smog, and it isn't too few negative ions in the air. It's the same effect that robbed the Vietnam War of any shadow of glory. It's one aspect of the rising crime rate. It's the reason everyone seems to be shouting in your ear. It's the reason most of us wouldn't consider powering our cars with liquid hydrogen.

It's communications. Faster and better and more realistic every decade.

Remember the Hindenburg disaster? Giant dirigible that burst into flame as it pulled up to a mooring tower. Two-thirds of the passengers survived, did you know that? That doesn't happen when a DC-10 crashes! But the Hindenburg disaster was the first such to be reported live on radio. The radio audience of the time had no defense against that vision of passengers writhing in a storm of flaming hydrogen. Later generations have learned not to respond so emotionally, not even when there are pictures and gory special effects to increase the impact.

We have learned, yes. Cast your memory back to Kitty Genovese, who was knifed to death in New York over a period of several hours. Witnesses watched from scores of windows in surrounding apartment buildings. None of them so much as phoned the police.

And everyone wondered why, but the answer is simple. They had been trained not to help . . . even as you and I have learned not to interfere with the horrors *we* see happening . . . on our television sets. From adult Westerns to *Alien* to *The Exorcist* to live coverage of the Vietnam War, we watch people bleeding and we remain seated.

Jon Sheen is an aspiring writer stationed in Germany. In 1984 he wrote to me as follows:

"I just witnessed a murder. Don't worry about me; I'm in no danger: the killer was caught immediately. In fact, you probably witnessed the same murder, and in the same way: on television. I'm sure you know the case I'm talking about: Gary Plauche murdered the man who kidnapped his son Jody: one Jeffrey Doucet. You've seen the same tape, I'm sure, and my God, it is astounding! If you were directing a suspense film, you couldn't ask for a more dramatic scene, right down to the way the victim's head eclipses the gun just as the shot is fired. This is the third such piece of astounding newsfilm I've seen since the beginning of February. . . .

"It's affected me strongly. *How*, precisely, I don't know, but watching that and, earlier, watching two grown men in Rhode Island walking to a car in a comical embrace (rendered entirely unamusing by the fact that one of the men was a cop, and the other a hunted criminal holding a gun to his head) and seeing the car shot to pieces by half-a-dozen cops, wounding the captive officer and killing the fugitive; and watching a Lebanese man in a light blue shirt writhing in pain, denying that his factory held armaments, his right arm broken and mangled and twisted within the sleeve—and then, watching the films taken moments later, of his corpse being carried away. . . . All these will stay with me for a long time, and I don't know how I'm going to judge this new capacity to eyewitness mayhem, but when I finally do decide how to react, it will be strongly.

"I know what I'll have to weigh against it, though: I've seen the Shuttle launch, and land, live. I've seen astronauts floating along through the void, untethered—live. I've seen the Earth, so huge and blue and beautiful—even on a 25″ RCA—that it made my throat close up. And I was one of the first human beings to gaze across the sands of Mars; at the same time as Sagan, Hibbs, and the whole gang at JPL, I looked at the *place* that is Mars, watched sliver after sliver of Viking's-eye-view of another planet—live.

"Electronic Global Village, the man said.

"Yeah."

You don't feel rich. Right? But you're very aware of the taxes you pay. In California some years ago, it reached the point of a taxpayer revolt. We set a legal limit on our property taxes.

But a taxpayers' revolt used to mean tax collectors hanging from trees! partly because society could not yet afford lampposts. Taxes are enormously higher now than they were during the Whiskey Rebellion in Vermont. Why aren't there tax collectors hanging from lampposts?

Because even after the tax collector gets through with you, you've still got too much to protect. Because you're rich.

And if *you* don't feel rich, the little old lady on a fixed income must feel still worse as she watches her dollar dwindle to its intrinsic value—high-quality paper. What is it that's doing this to you?

It's communications. Advertisements! An endless stream of advertisements interspersed with every kind of inducement to keep you watching. And while you learn of the wonders you can't afford, you're also learning not to believe what you hear; because after all, these products can't *all* be best. What were you thinking while you watched the Presidential candidates on your television sets?

The world is rich, and the easy resources that won the wealth are nearly gone. Outcroppings of copper and iron ore. Surface seepages of crude oil. A place to dump the pollution. Don't think that wasn't a form of wealth! Even coal can't be mined without technology; the first steam engines were built to pump water out of British coal mines. Once mined, the coal has to be moved to where it's needed, somehow.

If civilization collapsed today, it may be that no future civilization could be built on our bones.

We have a great deal to lose.

We expect starvation to be rare.

We expect paved streets. Sidewalks. Sidewalks with ramps for wheelchairs. Freeways. Lighted streets at night, all night. Universal schooling.

We used to expect cheap gasoline. Remember?

We expect that the streets will be empty of dead bodies in the morning. Every morning. All of this is fairly recent. Consider Welfare: for the failure, total failure has a bottom limit. Some can crawl back up from there. In *The Way the Future Was*, Frederik Pohl tells of being a boy in the Depression. It was ugly, before Welfare.

We expect help in time of disaster. Communications and easy transportation will mitigate the effects of famine and flood. Somebody will know it's happening; somebody will come with what we need.

We expect the freedom to go our own way, without the compulsion to be like our neighbors. But being unlike your neighbors has *always* been a crime. Your present freedom of lifestyle depends utterly on your freedom to move away from your neighbors, to find a place where you needn't conform, or even to find people who think like you do.

You are *not* a representative sampling of the population. Your freedom to assemble here, now, together, depends utterly on easy communications and easy transportation.

We can lose all of that. We can lose more. We can lose the vote.

Collecting and tabulating votes is terribly expensive. Many nations can't afford it. We could be one of them, if we continue shipping our money to the Arabs while we shut down power plants. Tyranny is cheaper than democracy. Only one nation in all of Africa offers its citizens the vote. Can you name it? It's the rich one. It's South Africa.

We are richer than other nations. If starvation among our neighbors didn't bother us, we wouldn't be human—and *all* nations are our neighbors on this single planet. But the wealthy nations are vulnerable to more than guilt. The have-not nations outnumber us. Modern communications, including advertisements, have told them what they're missing, and who's got it.

We could share the wealth equally—and make the whole world poor. You've heard that before, but you may not have grasped what it means.

As long as there have been cities, corpses in city streets have posed a continual health problem.

The police force paid by taxes is a recent invention.

Murder is a recent invention—as distinctly opposed to killing a man who has armed relatives. That has always been dangerous. But killing a tramp used to be quite safe.

Throughout human history, women have been property. In general women are less muscular than men, more vulnerable to enslavement.

Slavery in general was the result of better farming techniques. It allowed civilized peoples to take prisoners instead of killing them, because now they could *feed* prisoners. The horse collar was a first step in freeing slaves; it meant that the horse could do about three times as much work as a man, without strangling. But if civilization collapsed *now*, could we afford horses? And grasslands to feed them, instead of farms to feed us? I think we'd go back to slavery.

In the name of "protecting the environment"—surely a laudable aim in itself—there are those who would oppose *all* forms of industrial power. I believe that they have forgotten what the environment is like before men shape it. They have forgotten tigers and tsetse flies and rabies. It would cost us dearly to lose our present level of civilization.

We also can't stay where we are.

The easy resources are running out, yes, but there's more to it than that. *No* civilization has *ever* been able to stay in one place.

We have to deal, somehow, with the information explosion. The proliferation of laws and rules and regulations is part of that. Perhaps we can be educated to tolerate the flow, assimilate it. Perhaps we need information-free vacations—"anarchy parks," places with no news-flow and no rules at all, as in "Cloak of Anarchy"—for our sanity's sake.

Cars and freeways and airlines give us the freedom to be ourselves, but easy transportation carries its own penalties. Almost every state in the Union has too few state hospitals for the criminally insane. Every time a judge sends a patient to a California mental institution, some doctor has to decide not *whether* to put a patient back on the street, but *whom*. Now the patient is out here with me.

Why can't we build more psychiatric hospitals, and schools, and prisons? Because voting citizens are not trapped where they are. Some won't vote their money to improve their neighborhood because it's easier to move.

We can't stay the way we are. We have to go up—or down.

Today we have the power to make the whole world as wealthy as we are right now. It would take thirty to fifty years, if we start now . . . and we *have* to start now. If we wait, we may wait too long.

I'm pushing space travel. The resources are all up there, and the first resource we need is solar power.

We have several choices as to how to use it. Most people favor picking up the sunlight with collectors several miles across—which doesn't mean they're particularly heavy; the Echo satellite was both huge and flimsy. The collectors would convert the power into microwaves, or laser beams, and beam it down to collectors on Earth.

Or try this. Big, flimsy solar mirrors. Beam the sunlight down directly, all to one tiny patch of desert. Nobody would live there, of course. The collectors would run at around 350 degrees F.

Again we face choices. We can carefully intercept only the sunlight that would have reached Earth anyway. No heat pollution. Or we can pick up light that was on its way to interstellar space.

Do we want heat pollution? Ocean thermal difference plants (OTEC, using the temperature difference between the top and bottom of an ocean) produce none. Nuclear plants produce just as much heat pollution per kilowatt as coal plants do. But maybe heat pollution is what we want! We've got fair evidence that the next Ice Age is starting now. Right now.

We may have been holding off the next Ice Age for the last couple of hundred years, just by burning so much of our fossil fuels, polluting the troposphere, producing a greenhouse effect. The fuels are running out. If we build nuclear plants and put them on line as fast as we can, it may be enough; though we'd have to be producing *more* power, because there's no particulate pollution. But these mirrors would do the job for us too.

There's a second choice, and if you like protecting the environment, you'll love this. Besides beaming power down to the factories from orbit, we can move the factories into orbit, and beyond.

The resources of the Moon include metals and oxygen-bearing rock. An astronaut who has worked on Earth, in free-fall, and on the Moon prefers the Moon for working conditions. Something has been leached from Earthly soil over billions of years; mix lunar dust into it and the plants fall in love.

A nickel-iron asteroid a mile across would hold five years' worth of the Earth's total production of metals, in metal deposits richer than any now to be found on Earth. If you like iridium, you'll love the asteroids; it was that which gave Alvarez his clue to the extermination of the dinosaurs. We'll probably find water ice; certainly we'll find water loosely bound in compounds.

Behind the problem you just solved you will find another problem, always. There are social implications to making the whole world rich. "The poor are always with us"—up to now. Somebody's going to face a hell of a servant problem.

Well, we'll burn that bridge when we come to it.

• • •

• • •

His eyes shifted . . . and the sky had opened a mouth.

The shock only lasted a moment. A great empty mouth closed and opened again. It was rotating slowly. An eye bulged above one jaw; something like a skeletal hand was folded below the other. It was a klomter away and *still* big.

THE INTEGRAL TREES, 1983

THE KITEMAN

BLOWING SMOKE

We had come to Jet Propulsion Laboratory, northwest of Pasadena, to watch the pictures Voyager 1 would send back as it passed Saturn.

We were science fiction writers from everywhere in the United States. Over the years Jerry Pournelle had managed to establish a place for us at JPL: the SFWA members were a special case of "Press." Some of us had been here to watch the first pictures from the surface of Mars, and the featureless first close-up photos of Venus before JPL started playing with them, and the stunning pictures of Jupiter's moons, and Jupiter itself . . . as if God had taken a tremendous spray-painter and had Himself a wonderful time . . .

In the opening scenes of FOOTFALL Jerry and I captured some of the flavor of those wonderful few days. The probe fell past Saturn, past various moons, through the ring. We waited for some iceflake to smash it, but it never happened. The F Ring was twisted. ("Haven't you ever seen three earthworms in love?") The panel of experts hadn't figured out why ("We're sure Saturn is doing everything right . . ."). Perhaps the exhaust from a passing interstellar spacecraft had roiled it? Europa had a huge crater ("Well, we've found the Death Star.")

There was an orientation film for the Press. General laughter was heard when the narrator said, "We expect to find at least six rings." He hadn't seen the pictures. We had. Thousands of rings!

In the Press Kit was a lecture about the atmosphere of Titan. Astronomers have long known that Titan has a cloudy atmosphere. They can also demonstrate that Titan isn't massive enough to hold an atmosphere. What's it doing there?

They call it the gas torus effect, and it works like this—

Titan isn't massive enough, so molecules of atmosphere leak away. (It's happening to Earth's air, too, but much more slowly.) But the gas molecules are still bound by a strong gravitational field: Saturn's. They remain in orbit around Saturn.

The gas torus is of low density, and is shaped like an overinflated inner tube—or a smoke ring, if a smoke ring were spinning, with the inner part going somewhat faster than the outer. Some of the trapped gas escapes anyway. Most of it will end up back in Titan's atmosphere, and leak away again, and return . . .

Wow!

I made notes all over my press kit, and presently transferred them to my computer. Those notes include an intermediate case. It's up for grabs: you can easily beat me into print.

We'll put a Mars-size moon in orbit about a Jupiter-size body, and move it to halfway between Mars and Earth.

The Jovian primary will radiate some heat. If we want Earthlike temperature we must put the system farther from the sun than Earth is. It'll still be warmer than Saturn's moon Titan, so the warmer gas will escape faster unless we make the body more massive than Titan. Almost certainly it will be tidally locked, with one face turned toward the Jovian at all times; so days will be long. With all of that in mind . . . we now have a world with an Earthlike atmosphere and four-tenths of Earth's gravity.

Man-powered flight becomes easy. You need no more than bicycle gears and a propeller and a lot of wing . . . say a hang glider or a short-winged Gossamer Albatross . . . or even bird-wings, for a flyer with an injured leg. Notice that if I bring the moon closer to the Jovian (and move the Jovian farther from the sun, and make the sun a little bluer so it will put out more UV for plants, and so forth; don't forget that the moon will become gradually more egg-shaped) I can shrink the moon and thus the gravitational pull, until your arthritic Aunt Tanya can fly.

But I became fascinated by an extreme case.

Forget the dinky little Jovian. Let's put a neutron star at the center! That gives us a *ferocious* gravity gradient. We'll put a gas giant planet in close orbit around it . . . not necessarily something as big as Jupiter, but a world more like Neptune. The planet won't be habitable, not by a damn sight. But the gas torus itself should have enough pressure to support life. If we give it enough time, if we let life develop, and green plants . . .

We'll get a breathable Earthlike atmosphere in a doughnut-shape larger than a world, where everything is in free-fall except for tidal effects; where gravity is found only at the endpoint tufts of what I then called "spoke trees," that look like a tree with two tops and no bottom; where everything that lives can fly, except men.

Time must pass, not only for green life to produce raw oxygen, but for the neutron star to spin down. Remember, that's the ashes of a supernova explosion. It carried the magnetic field of a murdered star into itself when it collapsed. A star like that, spinning within a nebula-cloud that used to be the outer layer of that same murdered star, generates a signal powerful enough to shower Sol system with X-rays from hundreds of light-years away. That's why it's called a *pulsar.* We're describing enough radiation to fry any human.

So give it time to spin down. A billion years may be enough. Two would be better . . . except that the Smoke Ring is not really very stable. It might be gone by the time we arrive.

This is the point at which I began to need hard numbers.

Dr. Robert Forward worked at Hughes Research in Malibu, California. His interests were and are wide-ranging. When I first met him he had a prototype mass detector on display; I described it in "The Hole Man." And he was about to publish a paper demonstrating that gravity-wave storms can result if mass spirals down into a black hole . . . when Jerry Pournelle's "He Fell Into a Dark Hole" appeared in *Analog.*

So Forward located this Jerry Pournelle's phone number and called him to acknowledge that Jerry had beaten him into print. And Jerry wangled an interview. And invited me to go along.

Forward talked about everything under the sun. He described a new concept, Hawking's *quantum black holes,* black holes of all sizes formed in the extreme conditions of the Big Bang. They're a natural for stories, and I told Jerry I'd beat him into print. (And did.)

Forward must have liked science fiction writers. He became one himself with *Dragon's Egg,* which involves natives of a neutron star as described by the astronomer Frank Drake.

So I had access to an expert on neutron stars and hypergravity.

Please understand: I had a two-lobed novel in mind, two intimately related stories taking place twenty years apart. One story would speak of simple survival; one would speak of the founding of civilization. I wrote a fairly detailed outline (calling it THE SPOKE TREES) to nail down what I was after.

Then I sent it to Robert Forward and asked for help.

He gave it.

The numbers weren't too startling (to *me*). I'd get about one-twentieth of a gravity in a big tree. Bob did have some surprises for me.

First, I'd messed up some technical terms. *Gas torus, plasma torus, flux tube* are not interchangeable!

Second . . . I had not realized that the winds at the endpoints of the trees would be even more powerful than the tide! And so my spoke trees—pointing through the neutron star, like spokes in a wagon wheel—were shaped by the wind into long S-shapes, integral signs, *integral trees,* and gained a good deal more detail.

Details are where the fun is.

I had already decided to maroon a handful of human beings in the Smoke Ring, leave them alone for five hundred years, then see what they were up to. I needed oxygen, and therefore green plants. I needed normal sunlight, so I made the neutron star (Levoy's Star, or Voy) part of a binary. That implied oxygen; oxygen implied green plants. What else did I know about life-forms in free-fall and breathable atmosphere?

Well—

Water drops would come in all sizes, from fine mist through raindrops the size of your fist or your head up to blobs so big that the tide would pull them apart. (Call them *ponds.*) Whatever their size, they could not be considered stable. Whatever lives in a pond (call it a *fish*) might have to cross to another pond fairly frequently.

So they'll have lungs.

And they'll fly. In fact, any Smoke Ring life form will find some way of getting about. Wings are the most obvious way, and most life forms will have wings . . . . but they won't necessarily look like Earth's birds.

After all, there's no gravity. In the Smoke Ring a bird with a broken wing can still fly! There's no unique *down*; no need for bilateral symmetry. What's required is thrust, not lift. I gave most of the Smoke Ring's life forms trilateral symmetry, with plenty of room for evolution to fiddle around.

The birds look like fish and the fish act like birds.

The integral trees are more mobile than I at first realized. When a tree comes apart, *both* segments will eventually return to the median (the region where the air is thickest.) They do it by sailing: the tree is accelerated by the wind in its remaining tuft. (And when it reaches the median, where the fertilizer is adequate, it will not survive unless it can grow another tuft *fast.*)

There are other sailing plants, and plants that spray seeds, and seeds that spray compressed air. There are plants like rubber-band helicopters. Everything moves.

And how will humans adjust?

I'm dealing with savages here. (My choice.) They're environmentalists when they have to be: they keep their own region clean. Otherwise their philosophy may allow them to use their environment as they please.

Thanks to Bob Forward and the winds, my trees gained a way of gathering fertilizer: branchlets migrate forward along the branch, into the treemouth, carrying whatever they've sieved from the wind. And the treemouth is the key to a lot of things.

The treemouth is the tribe's toilet, and its funeral parlor, and its garbage pit. "Feed the tree" is a truly comprehensive insult.

I called the vegetation of the branch "the tuft." I made the foliage edible. The tribe will dig tunnels through it in the normal course of events. I left the branchlets springy enough to be woven into wickerwork "huts."

I had to design laundry and cooking techniques . . . and techniques of hunting and making war . . . and social hierarchies, different for every environment, including table manners and eating tools . . . and language.

The details are where the fun is. I talked with friends about the Smoke Ring. Several got in a contest to suggest weapons; I took the footbow from that. Later, someone suggested making wings; I used Isaac Asimov's suggestion as to what they would look like.

The cover for THE INTEGRAL TREES, by Michael Whelan, was the best I'd ever had. It should have been, for the effort he put into it! He read through the manuscript twice, then braced me at a world science fiction convention and held me prisoner for an hour while he asked questions.

The SMOKE RING cover was just as good.

Authors can be nearly psychotic as regards the accuracy of a cover.

A stranger in a bookstore once looked at that cover and said, "Oh, a fantasy!" Nope. It's hard science fiction in a peculiar place.

Bob Gleason and Tom Doherty were my guests for a few days in May. They came partly to give me some help with the book you're reading now.

I'd already chosen excerpts from various of my novels. I couldn't decide what to take from THE INTEGRAL TREES and THE SMOKE RING. The books were relatively new; Tom and Bob had read them; let them give me some help.

They spent most of a Friday rereading the books. Bob blames me for a blinding headache; Tom worked off the tension swimming back and forth in my pool, back and forth, like a damn machine. Their conclusion: there was nothing they could tear out of either book without it bleeding all over their hands.

Heh heh heh. Jerry and I did that to Bob Gleason once before. We turned over to him a quarter-million words of LUCIFER'S HAMMER: too big a book to sell well, he thought. "I have this nightmare in which we sell millions of copies of LUCIFER'S HAMMER and lose a nickel on every book!" Bob sat down to cut it to size . . . and there wasn't one damn word he could live without.

Serve him right. He's the man who taught us how to cut.

But Niven doesn't write excerpts; Niven writes novels!

On the other hand . . . they couldn't find an excerpt that would stand by itself. So they're demanding that I write a short story instead!

That's work.

Oh, well. I want to get back into the Smoke Ring universe anyway. There's a novel I want to write . . . involving really peculiar creatures who may have been shaped in the supernova explosion that began the Smoke Ring. And I want to bring them home.

• •

CHAPTER ONE

YEAR 419 DAY 110

The light filtering through the foliage had an ominous tinge: white with no blue in it, white like dry bone.

Alin crawled eastward through corridors that paralleled the branch. Slender branchlets grew airy, sweet stuff like green cotton candy, easy to brush aside. He ate the occasional handful of foliage without slowing. If nobody did that, the corridor would close completely.

Already it was uncomfortably narrow. The in tuft had been deserted these past two years.

Four boys crawled in Alin's wake. Their rolled-up kites caught in the foliage, slowing them. Alin knew how to keep his bundle pointed straight ahead through the branchlets.

The foliage thinned out, then ended in bare bark.

There was no sky. Brighton Tree was embedded in fog: one eighty-three-klomter tree fading into an empty white universe.

The boys caught up. Stevn trailed, looking down into the bone-white sky. Stevn was Alin's oldest son, though the long, straight brown hair and the exaggerated frown were exactly his uncle David's.

Alin laughed at their disappointment. If Gilly or Stevn were relieved, Alin chose not to see that. He said, "Get out on the branch. This'll be gone by the time we're set up."

They crawled out along the bark, fingers and toes clinging. Mist streamed past them, blowing hard. In the point-oh-three tidal force of Brighton Tree, it was amazing how much water a tunic could hold.

Halfway to nothing, Alin called a halt. "No wings, citizens. Today it's kites. Frame them."

Each boy unwrapped what he had brought: two sheets of fabric, four brace poles almost as tall as himself, and fifty meters of lines. Bertam was the quickest. He had the bound kite strapped to his back at the waist, and the free kite assembled in his hands, while Gilly was still wrestling with fabric.

Alin had not touched his own kites yet. Today his students would do without their teacher's example.

The fog shredded and streamed away, and suddenly there was sky.

What had been fog could now be seen as a two-hundred-klomter river of cloud streaming east and away through a universe of blue sky. The forward fringe of it roiled as it dipped into the chaotic currents of the Clump.

The Clump was an eternal sluggish storm a thousand klomters across. Matter tended to gather in the tidal anomaly sixty degrees ahead of Goldblatt's World in its orbit around Levoy's Star. From here the Clump covered almost half the sky, lit from behind by a rising Sun: flame-colored, darkening toward the axis.

Other trees floated around Brighton Tree, all on a level, dark against the bright Clump. Their trunks were vertical lines bent into near-horizontal branches at the in and out ends.

A Navy spinner ship puffed toward the grove, too distant for detail, leaving a white thread of smoke.

The boys were ready. Alin looked them over and said, "Good. Bertam, jump."

Bertam rolled forward and dropped into the violet-white glare of Voy. Alin wondered if he had closed his eyes. The wind gripped the kite on his back, the bound kite, and pulled him east.

"Stevn, go. Marlo. Gilly, go. Go!"

Gilly clutched the branch in terror.

They were calling Alin Newbry "Kitemaster" because he could fly with kites. "Kitemaster" instead of "Liftmaster's Apprentice"; but this was his first group of students. It had yet to be demonstrated that the Kitemaster could teach.

Every child took flying lessons with wings or jet pods, when he or she was old enough. Some were frightened. Some were reckless. Some were clumsy. Alin had watched, then chosen six, drilled them with their equipment for seven sleeps, taken them out onto the bare branch and drilled them there—and lost two more to their fear—

And he was about to lose another, on their first real flight.

"Jump or don't jump, Gilly, but you know the choices." Alin assembled his kites rapidly. "Don't let me beat you into the sky."

Gilly jumped with no grace, like a rag doll flung into the wind. A moment later the boy was using everything Alin had taught him. Left arm and leg reached out to turn him, then in again. Now he faced east, free kite clutched against his chest; the kite on his back blocked it from the wind. Now his hands and feet reached cautiously out, holding the running lines with fingers and toes. The free kite wafted east, and caught the wind.

Alin rolled into the sky.

Almost he felt Gilly's fear. Why would anyone jump out of a perfectly good tree? *Wings* had been new to Brighton Tree when Alin was a baby, but *kites*, now . . . Alin Newbry was Brighton Tree's expert with kites. He'd seen his first pair of kites less than a year ago, and possessed them immediately thereafter.

The wind pulled him east. Voy blazed violet-white below him. The bound kite framed him, two spokes at right angles. Kites were more awkward than a good pair of wings bound to one's ankles; but kites didn't have to be flapped or pedaled. They pulled themselves.

Bertam was nicely under sail. His free kite (banded red and white) deployed east-and-inward, pulling him away from Brighton Tree. His arms bowed to the pull. Bertam hadn't grown to his full strength yet.

Marlo was under sail too (yellow with a broad scarlet stripe). He seemed to be trying to join Bertam. Not a good idea. Collisions! But Bertram was laughing at Marlo, sailing away, racing.

Stevn (orange swordbird on black) was all tangled up.

Gilly was slow. Alin thought he could see the boy's tongue between his teeth. Slow, but he wasn't making any mistakes. His free kite (black stars on scarlet) flapped and eased east, then east-and-in. Gilly moved after the others, sailing, flying without effort, wearing a wide white smile.

The laws of motion throughout the Smoke Ring were: *East takes you out, out takes you west, west takes you in, in takes you east; north and south bring you back*. Today's goal was to sail outward, then return to Brighton Tree's midpoint. Still, Alin wouldn't be too disappointed if a boy wound up somewhere else.

The East Grove was nineteen trees positioned far enough from the Clump to get decent tide. Any tree would send wingmen to rescue a lost boy. A mistake need not be dangerous. Capability Tree was an obvious target, east and a little in . . .

And Natlee was hardly speaking to him, because he was trying to teach their oldest son to fly.

Alin was now moving almost with the wind's velocity. He deployed his free kite (a moby seen face-on, yellow on a scarlet background), but kept it on a short line. Was he going to have to rescue Stevn? Stevn was working more carefully now, getting himself untangled, glancing at Alin every few seconds while he tried to separate his running lines.

Stevn would overreact if his teacher-father began shouting instructions. Alin did too much of that anyway. Give him another few breaths.

One of the trees was getting longer.

Alin blinked. Capability Tree was separating into two halves.

There was no warning. There was only the numbing sight of a tree ripped in half at the midpoint, pulling ponderously apart, leaving a smoky trail of debris. One end fell into white Voylight, one toward the never-seen stars.

There were fifty to sixty people in Capability Tree, not counting children.

The Admiralty ship was still no more than a dot at the end of a vapor trail running through hazy blue-white. Alin watched the white curve as he worked his line.

Stevn had his line out now, east-and-in, as he'd been taught. He'd begun to accelerate.

Alin let his lines out gradually. The free kite pulled east-and-in, but he wrestled it horizontal. It went almost slack. Alin didn't stand a chance of catching any of the boys already in flight, not even Gilly. He'd have to catch Stevn.

The white curve of the Navy ship's path remained almost straight. They hadn't seen.

Alin passed out from Stevn; he let his free kite swing drastically inward, to pull him in earshot.

"Stevn!"

"It's all right, Kitemaster. I've got it."

"Look at Capability Tree!"

Stevn needed a moment to orient himself, and another to wonder if he had the right direction, and then—"What on Earth?"

"They need help. Now—"

"Dad, Dad, the whole tree's torn apart!"

"Don't lose it, boy. They need help. Do you think you can reach that Navy ship? Look straight east!"

The boy looked. "I'm not sure, Dad."

Frightened. "It has to be done. The haze may be blocking their view. Get their attention. We need Navy for rescue work. You don't have to get aboard. We'll come for you . . ." Stevn was drifting out of earshot. "Get their attention and tell them about Capability Tree!"

His kite was pulling him strongly now. He'd pass in from the debris cloud if he weren't careful.

The halves of the tree were already widely separated, in toward Voy and out into the sky. Alin manipulated the free kite out . . . out . . . waited until he felt no strain on the lines, then tilted the kite and let it continue moving. It was east of him now, blown toward him on a slack line. He tilted his body to adjust the bound kite, gathered as much of the line as he could, and was ready when it pulled taut.

By then he was deep inside a cloud of shredded bark, and a hundred million bark-dwelling insects were getting lost in his nose and mouth and ears. He spit and snorted and blinked and looked around for citizens needing rescue.

None yet. The free kite pulled westward, slowing him . . . and now he was among big cylindrical blocks of mud. He tilted both kites edge-on to the wind, and was at rest.

The stench struck him like a blow.

Over a dozen human lifetimes an integral tree swallows immense quantities of . . . stuff.

Foliage at both tufts spreads wide to sieve birds and lesser plants out of the wind. A pond impacts somewhere on the trunk; tide slides the water and the mud core down into the nearer tuft. Branchlets gradually migrate forward along the branch, through the tuft and into the treemouth, carrying foliage and everything embedded in it: mud and water, plants, dead animals, even old huts that men have woven from the living branchlets. Humans use the great conical pit as a toilet and garbage service and mortuary. Everything disappears into the treemouth, to feed the tree.

A tree has a mouth at both ends, and no anus. Tide pulls hard on an integral tree. The accumulating mud weakens its structure. The time comes when it must be rid of its mud core.

It pulls apart at the midpoint, and starts over as twins.

The core of Capability Tree had broken into cylindrical segments. The stench was horrid. Alin resisted breathing, for fear of inhaling foul dust. But the dust seemed to be all bark dust.

There was music in the wind, nonsense-words sung in a high, sweet contralto.

"We located the Titanic two miles deep in the Atlantic,
And we didn't know quite where that ship went down!"

Alin knew that voice. Where was she? "Harp!"

"Well, we photographed the wreck even down below her decks,
But those monsters in the lakes just can't be found."

North-and-out: human shapes clung to a black cylinder of mud. Alin shouted, "Hello!"

The singer stopped. A man's voice shouted from the mud-log. "Hello?"

"Do you have line?"

"Yes!"

The unseen bard sang again:

"Twenty-six miles by one short mile
and a hundred fathoms deep.
Jagged rock at the bottom of the Loch
And the water's thick with peat—"

A man cast loose from the mud log, kicking hard, trailing line. Wide fan-shaped wings were bound to his shins. As he kicked toward Alin, four more citizens let themselves be pulled loose. One, a six-year-old girl, was wailing in fear.

"The creature's shy and shuns the sky,
And that's why we must confess—
We can't find
We can't find
We can't find

We can't find
We can't find the creature in Loch Ness!"

Alin had his hands full keeping the kites tilted. They would pull him out of reach if he let them catch the wind. The winged man veered toward another mud block. The tow line trailed across it and picked up two more citizens, an older woman and a young man pulling a child by her ankle. Moments later an adolescent girl flew out of nowhere, out of the chaos of bark-dust fog and mud cylinders, with a baby in her arms and a larger boy clinging to her back. She caught the line with her toes.

Good enough. Alin tilted his kites and brought himself across their two line. It slid along his own main line, and Alin had it. He tied it to his kite-belt before it could go taut.

Now he let the free kite tilt. Lines grew taut and he felt himself pulled west. But where was Harp?

"We have sent a craft to Mars,
We have looked beyond the stars,
And a billion light-years don't stand in our way—"

The winged man called into the sky, urgently. "Harp? Can you catch us?"

A voice came back. "I think not, Captain, but there's other rescue coming." For the first time Alin saw the singer, clinging with her toes to a sheet of bark.

He called, "Hello, Harp! Remember me? Alin Newbry, Brighton!"

"Suuure! Liftmaster's Apprentice?"

"Kitemaster now. Are you really all right? I'd have trouble coming back for you."

"Fine. I saw another kiteman."

"I sent a Navy ship!"

"Fiiine!" She waved her windpipe in farewell, then resumed playing.

"We've sent rockets out to Saturn
and described its weather pattern,
But we still can't find that beast in Loch Linné."

The man pulled himself toward Alin until he was close enough to talk normally. Deep-set brown eyes, a curved sharp-edged nose, wide thin mouth, long gray hair bound by a ceramic ring: he looked like a man born to command. "I'm Captain Shan Ling, Capability Tree."

"Kitemaster Alin Newbry, Brighton. Will she be all right?"

"Harp? Yeah. She called *you* to us, didn't she? She'll call that Navy ship too when it gets close enough. Kitemaster, can you move us all?"

"Not fast." The kite was accelerating them nicely, pulling west. Maneuvering was going to be awkward. He must keep tension in the line; else his refugees would drift together.

There was no way he could wait for Capability's Harp. He would have liked to see her again . . . just see her.

Alin adjusted his lines and moved away from the debris cloud. Eight passengers formed a tail behind him.

Captain Blinda Murphy and three of her crew scampered over the ship like so many spiders. The flame-haired Captain was pregnant. The bulge barely showed on her two-point-two meters of jungle-giant height. She was trying to move more slowly, to let her crew do the work, but she just didn't have the habit.

Curtz didn't try to duck aside. They treated Curtz as a familiar obstacle, and went around.

Curtz was not a navvy. He was a Navy Guardian.

His chief claim to rank was that he could wear the ancient armor of the starmen. His dwarfish size and the encumbrance of the silver suit decreased his agility. He could fight; he was invulnerable in battle; but he could not dart about the surface of a spinner ship trying to keep lines in order.

Renho and Dunninger and Rabin were long, spindly citizens up to two and a half meters tall, compared to Maxell's one point eight, if you let him point his toes. Sometimes he wondered what they thought of him. The Captain might flay any navvy who insulted a Guardian. Blinda Murphy's mother had been a dwarf. She'd have been a Silver Man herself if the armor had fit.

There in the mist: a pair of kites.

One kiteman? Half a dozen wouldn't have been odd. Packs of Admiralty kitemen might fly out to the East Grove or farther yet, out to escort some incoming logger. But one? Could a party have got into trouble? The mist was too thin to hide more.

Guardian Maxell Curtz watched the kites coming . . . orange swordbird on a black field, intricately painted, very high quality compared to Admiralty work . . . coming almost straight at *Flutterby*.

Renho and Dunninger were pointing. Rabin scampered forward. The kiteman swept past by less than thirty meters. For a bare instant the Guardian saw him clearly: a boy, a ten-year-old climber frightened clean out of his mind.

Curtz jumped into the sky. A burst of his boot jets kicked him clear of *Flutterby*.

The prop blades were slowing, stopping. Rabin must have turned the motor off.

A rescue would look good on *Flutterby*'s record. Curtz's too. Might help the Admiralty's image. Climbers had been growing unhappy with Admiralty policies . . . All hindsight. Curtz had jumped by reflex.

The boy had tilted his kites flat to the wind. Curtz wouldn't have to use his jets again. Good! Only one tribe of climbers in the whole sky could recharge boot jets, and they charged high.

Curtz fixed wings to his ankles and flapped toward the boy.

The boy was methodically reeling in his free kite, dismounting it, rolling it around the brace sticks. Thin, two meters tall or less, with a broad flat nose and straight brown hair: he was older than Curtz had guessed. Twelve, maybe. People raised in a tide were shorter than Admiralty citizens.

Closer . . . The boy twisted like a ribbon bird, reached far out and snatched Curtz's wrist with panic strength. He was still frightened. Curtz wondered what the ancient pressure suit must look like to this savage. But he feared the sky more.

Curtz said, "I'm a Guardian, a Silver Man. That's *Flutterby*. We'll take you home."

"No, no, you have to save them. Capability Tree's come apart! Ripped in half!"

"What?"

The boy pointed. Curtz followed the line of his arm, west of out, following a dark wavering arc to a distant fisher-jungle . . . wait, it was farther away than that, bigger and . . . darksoil, was that a *tree*? Curtz looked in and east and found the other half.

"Your tree?"

"No, I'm from Brighton. That's Capability Tree. Dad sent me to alert you. They need help."

Flutterby wasn't large. The ship had once carried thirty troops into a riot; but they'd been clinging to the hull. Two could work in the tiny cabin; four or five could huddle there while the ship was battered by triunes or swarming drillbits or a major storm.

The climber boy was in the way, of course, but what choice did they have? He braced himself in a corner, gripping handgrips with all his fingers and toes, and he couldn't seem to stop shivering. Yet he spoke lucidly enough. He was Stevn Newbry, son of Kitemaster Newbry. He'd had a good flight, no surprises . . . other than the tree, of course . . .

Maxell left the cabin. The boy made *him* nervous.

Flutterby was in the debris cloud. Less than a day had passed, but both ends of the tree had vanished into the murky sky. The sun had nearly reached nadir: double sunlight made long single shadows through the dust. The sky was dark with wood dust and dirt and tree-dwelling insects, and mud.

A brave act for a climber, kiting across naked sky toward a moving target, and not even for his own people. A climber spent his life tunneling through green darkness. No Admiralty citizen would have been so shaken by a day or two of falling.

Guardsman Maxell Curtz gripped rope railings with hands and toes and let the sky turn past him.

Tremendous cylinders of black mud tumbled in the chaos. Maxell had heard that such things could happen, but he'd never tried to imagine a disaster on this scale. He wondered how the mud held together so well . . . and then he saw. The tree had wrapped the mud like a package, had lined its fertilizer core with wood fibers so that it would slide loose easily.

Fisher-jungles were already drifting into the debris cloud. Long tendrils stretched toward mud blocks tumbling in the chaos. In the roar of *Flutterby*'s motor could be heard an irregular ticking as bits of bark impacted the blades.

Flutterby's hull was all ledges, toeholds and fingerholds, and rope: rope in coils, guardrail ropes, rope to tie boxes and bails to the ledges, lines to set the vanes at the tail.

Flutterby pulled itself through the air by the long, long blades turning at her nose. Tilted vanes aft kept the whole ship from spinning the other way round . . . but Captain Murphy generally modified the tilt so that the sky slowly turned to show all possible views.

A wind beat down on Maxell's head, stinking of half-burned wood alcohol—which Maxell was used to—and eons-buried mud.

Captain Murphy poked her head into the doorway and bellowed, "Rabin? Cut to idle. How on Earth am I supposed to hear anything?"

The noise and the wind dropped almost to nothing. Maxell listened for the wailing of climbers lost in the sky. He heard the buzz of confused insects, and—

"We have set out traps to catch her
And sent dolphins down to fetch her,
And a million tourists watch from shore and ship—"

Somewhere a woman was singing some old nonsense-song as if she had never a care in the world.

The climber-kiteman's head poked through the cabin door. He shouted, "That's Capability's Harp!"

"But we still wind up embarrassed,
For this creature won't be harassed,
She just glides away and gives us all the slip."

Curtz said, "I thought you were from—"

"Harp sang in Brighton Tree once," the boy said. "She's wonderful. Can we get to her?"

Captain Murphy bellowed aft. "Rabin, I've reversed the prop. Start her up, but watch your tethers."

"Aye-firmative."

"You all hear? Watch your tethers!"

"Ambitious dreams of our research teams
Are touted by the press
But we can't find
We can't find
We can't find
We can't find
We can't find the creature in Loch Ness!"

Curtz tested his own tether as the prop spun up and the ship eased backward. Admiralty fitters had mounted the blades aft, like the motors on a rocket, on the first few spinner ships they built. They'd stopped that after a crewman lost his grip and fell into the blades. A navvy could still manage that while a spinner ship was backing up.

The songbird was standing upright as if in tide, clinging with her toes to a plug of black mud. Short golden hair haloed a pale triangular face. A musical instrument, nearly two meters of wooden tube with holes along its length, was strapped across her back. She watched *Flutterby*'s approach without sign of fear.

"Cut it!" called the Captain. The woman waited until the blades spun to a stop, then jumped toward *Flutterby*.

Renho and Dunninger were already in the sky, tethers trailing as they leapt to catch her. Across the sky it was difficult to tell navvies apart. They weren't identical. Renho was strong, but Dunninger had been a kiteman. His hands and wrists, feet and ankles were sinewy, laced with blood vessels, actually stronger than a dwarf's. But they were skeletally tall, their hair was cut identically short, and their identical red uniforms were only distinguished by big black number-letter designations on chest and back.

Graceful as hell, they tugged their lines to stop just alongside the songbird. She offered a hand to each, smiling her thanks.

They looked like giants next to her.

Against the wind and the *whupwhupwhup* of the motor Maxell Curtz could hear his heart pounding in his ears. *She was tiny.*

Her voice came to him, clear and musical. "—pulled a bunch of us off toward Brighton. I saw another kiteman coming too. Most of us must have been rescued by now."

"I'll tell the Captain," Renho said.

"But the citizens who didn't get out of the tufts are still in trouble. Can you get word to other Navy ships?"

They caught themselves against the hull, caught their breath, then pulled themselves aft toward the cabin. Capability's Harp looked him over as they passed. Her eyes were an intense and vivid blue. She was definitely interested. Curtz smiled back, admiring. A moment later she was gone.

Interest in *him*? Chances were that she'd never seen a silver suit.

Voices from the cabin: Harp was trying to describe Capability Tree's situation and calm the climber boy from Brighton, simultaneously.

The blades spun. The ship moved forward. Vanes tacked and backed as the ship wove a path among half-hidden bark sheets and masses of ancient mud. Suddenly there were insects everywhere, in Curtz's ears and hair and mouth. He slammed his helmet down and turned on the internal air, and breathed his first clean air in hours.

While he was at it . . .

He tongued a switch.

Colors went all wonky. He let the sky turn past him. Big crimson blotch: he switched the display off (and saw a huge gape-mouthed fish, a bug eater) and on. Three smaller brighter dots: switch off (a triune family swimming hard after *Flutterby*) and on. A cloud of tiny dots would be birds; he didn't bother to look. The big crimson blotch would be the bug eater again. A smaller glare (off) was the triune family, now joined for cursorial hunting, not that they'd ever catch *Flutterby*.

. . . and a crimson glare in his peripheral vision. He switched the display off and turned.

She was there beside him on the twenty-ce'meter-wide ledge.

She wasn't a dwarf. She was short and stocky, but longer than Maxell Curtz by ten or twelve ce'meters. As Curtz realized that, she smiled enchantingly, and dropped to one knee on the ledge. It brought them face to face.

"Thank you for my life," she said. "I'm Harp."

He opened his helmet and tilted it back. "Guardian Maxell Curtz. I've been looking for refugees with heat vision. All I'm finding is scavengers. How are you doing?"

"I'm all right. I'm worried about my people in the tufts."

"Are they really in trouble?"

"Well, they're not in *good* shape. They've got two short trees, each with one tuft, falling out of the median in opposite directions. The median's where everything is, air and water and food. The out tuft has the steam rocket, but the others could all die before they're blown back."

Harp's chin was pointed and her mouth was small, with a curve like a recurved bow. It would always look pursed for kissing. Curtz was having trouble concentrating. He said, "We'll send them ships."

"Thank you."

Guardian Curtz smiled back. "Trust the Navy, and be glad you live this close to the Admiralty. Rescue is what we do best."

The crew were in motion now, scampering over the hull, unrolling many square meters of silvered cloth onto a wire frame. Curtz said, "There, now, we're out of that goop," as if he were running the show. "Now we can send a mirror message to Headquarters. Four or five days, we'll have ships at both tufts."

"At what price, Guardian?"

Maxell was a bit jolted. Climbers didn't know about bargains and money, did they? He would have preferred to talk in terms of gallantry and rescue and the benefits of belonging to a mighty empire, and . . . "Your credit's good. Were you thinking of buying elsewhere?"

Her smile had faded. "It isn't as if we could do without. My father saw a half-tree once, before we moved into the Grove. The tree was fine, very green and thriving, already growing another out tuft. It must have taken its own sweet time floating back into the Smoke Ring. Some of the tribe must have jumped. The rest looked like they'd suffocated. All dead."

"Two ships can evacuate a whole tuft if there's not enough air for them."

"Your motor needs air, doesn't it?"

Oops.

Captain Murphy was near the nose, dictating to Renho as he shifted the mirror. Curtz jumped along the hull, stopped himself with a jerk at his line. Behind him there was music. Harp had begun playing, using the wind from the propeller.

> *"It's a matter now of pride!*
> *We are after Nessie's hide—"*

"Captain?"

"Guardian. How's our songbird?"

"Cool as a snow cloud. She must do this every day. In fact she's got a suggestion."

Murphy stared. "She's just a climber, stet?"

"I want to tell Headquarters to send *rockets* to the half-trees. Spinner ships are air-breathing. The motor could run out of air."

"Actually . . . good point, Guardian. Renho, you heard?"

Renho was already wobbling the mirror back and forth. The beam pulsed against the faint haze, pointing back into the Admiralty.

CHAPTER TWO

YEAR 419 DAY 115

Triunes were hunting birds, ubiquitous throughout the Smoke Ring. The tribemark for London Tree had been triunes mated for distance flying, male and female and child all locked belly-to-belly into a three-lobed torpedo, seen nose-on.

Brighton Tree was a colony of London Tree. Brighton's tribemark was a triune family just separating to hunt. Alin's kites bore the same mark.

The tribemark glowed at the tree's midpoint, scarlet and yellow dye on a black char background, nine meters across. Lift lines rose toward it from both tufts, and a pair of huts bracketed it. The dye was fading and half overgrown with bark. To Alin Newbry it was the sight of home, the certain knowledge that he was not lost in the sky.

Alin was decelerating, the free kite pulling in-and-east. His passengers led him westward toward the triune symbol. They had grown weary of terror during four days of flying. Now they only clung in silence. Alin had grown to hate their shifting, uneasy weight.

Somebody was waiting next to one of the huts.

Alin brought his passengers to a stop a few tens of meters short of the trunk. Better than smashing them against the bark. Tired men make mistakes. Alin started to bring the free kite around . . . almost no wind, and tricky too, distorted by the two-klomter thickness of the trunk . . . He gave up and stowed the kites instead, because Capability's Captain Ling was kick-kick-kicking at the end of the line, towing them all toward the tree.

The man on the bark came flapping out to help. Alin recognized his younger brother David. David and Ling flew the line back to the trunk and began pulling in the rest.

One by one the refugees spread themselves across the bark, men and women and children, facedown, clawing and twitching as if trying to mate with the tree. Alin was the last to be reeled in. He tethered himself and let it go at that, for his dignity's sake.

"You didn't say you'd gone hunting," David said.

"I'd gladly have shared the catch," Alin answered. His mind was fuzzy with exhaustion.

"Captain Burns says they can have the in tuft."

The in tuft had been empty for just over two years. Shortly after the tree arrived in the East Grove, most of the crops had died quite suddenly and for unknown reasons. Alin said, "Good. You can tell Captain Ling—*him*—but give him some time first."

"I'd say he needs it! Are *you* all right?"

"Tired."

"Bertam and Gilly got back without you. The others are still out."

"There was a Navy ship. I sent Stevn there to get help."

"Did you. What about Marlo?"

"He was flying nicely, last I saw him. He's the oldest, he did fine on the tests . . ." Two boys missing out of four.

Ling and two others had recovered a little. They were examining the lift arrangements, tactfully out of earshot.

David was studying his face. "You and Natlee are having trouble, stet?"

Alin shrugged. "Nothing special."

"She doesn't smile anymore, and the kids don't talk to each other. Now, what is it? She's carried guests before."

"Sure, David, and she turns mean as a snake. You never noticed?"

"No. Three children and, what, a dozen lost ones? She'd be used to it. Other women don't have trouble carrying guests."

"Nobody but Natlee. David, I'm too tired for this."

"I *would* have noticed. This is something else, Alin. When Bertam and Gilly came down, and no Stevn, I saw Natlee's face. Have you ever taken her flying?"

"Hah! I got her as far as the lift line. As soon as we . . . yeah."

"Yeah, what?"

"Natlee is afraid of falling. There's just no *reasoning* with that kind of fear."

"She doesn't want Stevn flying either. Stet?"

"As soon as the line lifted us clear of the foliage, as soon as she saw open sky, Natlee freaked. *No*, she doesn't want Stevn flying. She doesn't want *me* flying, and I'm the Kitemaster!"

"Look, if . . ." If Stevn doesn't come back. "If you need help, come to me."

"David, she'll be all right as soon as our guest is born. And Stevn, he's . . ." Had training? It was their first time in the sky. The boys had flown kites from the branch, they'd climbed to the midpoint and watched Alin flying. *That* wasn't training. First time out, and he'd lost two students including his own son.

First things first. "Captain Ling, you can leave the children with me. Take whoever can travel and go down on the lift line. There'll be a lift cage along for the children."

Ling said, "I'll wait for my people, Kitemaster."

"Stet." He was their Captain. "David, go home."

"Alin, have you noticed?" David pointed east.

A rectangular fleck . . . a pair of yellow flecks. Marlo?

"That's good. Now go down to your dinner." Alin would not be stared at while he waited.

"Will you and Marlo join us? Shall I tell—"

"I'll send Marlo down. The Navy ship— If Stevn—" And if it didn't come, he'd still sleep better on the trunk. If he went down without Stevn, Natlee would make him fight before she'd let him rest.

David seemed to read his thoughts. He moved away to speak to Captain Ling, who was stringing refugees on the line to the in tuft. "Captain Burns begs you to make free of our unoccupied in tuft . . ."

Alin tuned him out. The kites did seem to be coming here. Yellow? He didn't notice when David left.

Ling didn't try to rush his people. Many needed more time to huddle against the bark. He asked, "Who's running the treadwheel, Kitemaster?"

"No treadwheel, Captain. We've got a windmill moving the lift line."

Ling nodded and changed the subject. "And you don't seem to have a rocket. How on Earth did you get to the East Grove?"

"Classified, sir. You can examine the windmill, though." Ling clearly hadn't recognized the word.

The pair of kites was closer now. Yellow with a broad scarlet stripe. Alin felt the knot of his intestines sliding loose.

Ling was counting his citizens. Twenty citizens and eleven children: a big jump in Brighton Tree's population. No wonder Burns wanted them in the empty tuft. But Ling must be counting the ones who were missing. He didn't look happy . . . Hell, he looked as tired as they did, finally. He put them on the line and watched it carry them in. Adults only: a child might lose his grip.

The cage came up. Alin used a ratchet to disconnect it from the line. He helped Ling load the children in. While Captain Ling spoke to the children, Alin wandered away to wait for Marlo and his passengers.

Marlo was close now. His mouth was slack with exhaustion. His arms and legs moved in jerks. Two frightened older women clung to his tow line and each other.

An exhausted rage was trying to boil up inside Alin. He should be proud; perhaps he was . . . but it hurt his mind to watch his student trying to maneuver. His own musculature kept trying to help.

When Marlo thumped against the trunk, Ling and Alin were there to catch his line. They towed the women in. The old women wrapped themselves around Captain Ling. He made soothing noises and presently helped them into the lift cage.

"You were to come straight back to the midpoint," Alin said.

"Kitemaster, I saved lives!"

"You saved them. Good. But I might have had to go looking for you. Do I look as tired as I feel?" Marlo didn't answer. "I could go back and search through that cloud of bark and bugs. But you didn't have orders to be there. Maybe you lost your kites. Maybe I should be looking east and in—''

''Stet, Kitemaster, *stet.*'' I'm sorry. The boy was as tired as Alin.

''Look, when you get down, my wife will have questions. Tell her *I* didn't send you do to rescue work. You're a hero. It was all your own idea.''

That surprised Marlo through his fog of fatigue. ''You're not coming down?''

''No. I'll sleep better falling. Tell the out-Captain . . . tell everyone I'll be down for breakfast.''

Marlo took the out line and was carried away.

What he had taken for distant birds, and dismissed, weren't. Four more refugees, winged, definitely headed for Brighton if exhaustion and exposure didn't kill them first.

Ling hadn't reconnected the lift cage yet. He called, ''Kitemaster? Is *that* your Navy ship?''

Alin peered toward the darkened Clump.

''No, no, *down*!''

It still didn't register. Various tribes used *up* and *down* in various ways, often obscene . . . but Ling was pointing along the trunk, in toward Voy.

A Navy spinner ship was landing in the tuft.

Alin said, ''Hell, I thought they'd come to the midpoint. Captain, I think I'll join you.''

YEAR 419 DAY 116

Flutterby moved into place and hovered above the in tuft of Brighton Tree. The dark trunk seemed a pure mathematical entity, a cylinder rising to a vanishing point. The foliage looked like a soft, billowy green cloud.

Captain Murphy chopped air with her hand. Dunninger turned off the fuel feed. The propeller blades unblurred, slowed, stopped.

The tide eased to nothing under Maxell's feet: reassuring, until he realized . . .

Stevn Newbry, braced in the cabin doorway, said, ''Hey . . .'' and bit off further comment.

Capability's Harp tightened her grip on the lines. ''We'll fall.''

''I've done this before,'' Captain Murphy said briskly. ''Can't land on the bare branch. It's only a meter wide.''

Harp's voice went just a bit ragged. ''Can't you dock at the midpoint?''

''Oh, sure. And then ride forty klomters down to the tuft, hanging on to a line strung by somebody else? No, thank you.''

But *Flutterby* was definitely falling, and Maxell Curtz's knuckles were white. Surely Captain Murphy wouldn't risk the propeller. Of course not. And her smile was purely malicious.

The green billows caught them and buoyed them. A propeller blade bent, and recoiled. Murphy said, "All out. Renho, we'll have refugees coming down at us pretty quick. How many did you see?"

"Hard to tell, Captain. Two kitemen pulling . . . somewhere around twenty, thirty?"

"They'll need help. Renho, Dunninger, escort the climbers. Rabin, we'll stay with the ship. Hey, boy . . . Stevn? Show us a way in."

The young kiteman crawled out of the cabin and paused in the sunlight. Curtz had watched his fear dwindle as they approached the tree. Had seen his face light when they spotted one, then another pair of kites in flight. Now he watched him stretched like a growing plant as he savored the tide.

Curtz was feeling natural tide for the first time. It was weird but tolerable. He knew intellectually that he was under thrust, as in a ship's cabin. Tension in the trunk was pulling the tuft outward against the inward pull of Levoy's Star.

Stevn Newbry bounded across the greenery in shallow arcs. Against the constant whistle of the wind Renho called, "Hey!"

The boy called back, "Citizen Renho, the corridors are all choked off. Our whole tribe moved out of here two years ago. I've got to . . . here, maybe . . . find an opening. Here!"

Renho jumped in a shallow arc toward Stevn. Harp followed. That decided Maxell Curtz. He braced against a submerged spine branch and jumped after her.

Too high. A touch of boot jets put him almost behind Harp. Stevn waited until they were close, then disappeared: *poof* and a puff of pollen, gone.

Harp landed, looked about her, than dived into the green billows.

Maxell found a dimple in the foliage. He pushed through—and was blind.

The Sun at nadir is only dimmer and more blurred than the Sun at zenith. Voy's light never changes: it's always at nadir. Darkness can be found inside a storm. The Dark is the sunless core of the Clump, a sluggish storm of matter squeezed close until it is almost solid . . . yet darkness is rare in the Smoke Ring.

Curtz might have guessed that it would be dim in the in tuft of Brighton Tree, too. But it was black!

Curtz moved by feel and by Harp's rustling. Rustling behind him told him that Renho and Dunninger had found their way in. All the corridors had closed to the width of a child. Luxuriant foliage clogged everything, leaving no room for man. Man formed no part of an integral tree's intent.

Ahead of him, the climber boy said, "It turns here. Everyone all right?" Voices answered him.

Maxell reached what must be the turn: lower pressure *this* way . . .

Behind him Renho asked, "You all right, Guardian?"

"I feel claustrophobic . . . and blind, of course."

"Hungry?"

"That too. We'll have to make a chance to hunt."

Renho chuckled. Dunninger snickered. Stevn barked incredulous laughter, then tried to choke it back.

Renho had set him up. He should have remembered: he was buried in food! He stripped a branchlet of the fluffy stuff that covered it and brought it to his mouth. He licked it.

Renho was blind too. "Try some foliage, then, Silver Man."

"Mmmm!"

Harp called back, "That's the best thing about tree living. Eat all you want. It keeps the corridors open."

"Mmmm! Twuss me. I ne'wer— 'Ff thiss— Nemmine."

"I think he likes it," Renho chortled.

The corridors twisted like wormholes through an apple. The Sun circled unseen. How far had they traveled, for how long? Impossible to tell . . . but Maxell's knees recoiled from springy solidity. He reached down to touch interlaced spine branches.

Then the corridor opened out.

He'd grown used to the dark. The sudden light was painful. He had to guess some of what he was seeing:

All the outlines were soft and rounded, overgrown. Stevn Newbry bounded through the open space toward a westward-facing conical pit . . . the treemouth, no doubt, as this must have been the Commons. The smell was earthy, faintly unpleasant. Yellow-white Sunlight glared through sparser foliage in radial beams.

Stevn said, "Wow. I grew up here. It's like there were never people here at all."

A whirring, a steady mechanical sound from overhead. Maxell asked, "What's that?"

"Let's go see," Harp said instantly.

They followed the sound up toward the light.

Above the foliage, the trunk seemed to rise forever. Water collected all along its length and thundered down the east face into the tuft. And here on the north side, a bigger version of *Flutterby*'s motor spun round and round in the ceaseless west wind.

"Clever," Maxell said.

Harp examined the structure with some care. A line ran round a wheel that turned on the propeller's axis, then straight out along the trunk. She said, "I was here two years ago. They wouldn't let any of us see the lift mechanisms. They wanted to trade their secrets for ours. We don't have any."

"What, none?"

She smiled at him. "Whatever you want to know, just ask. We used a treadwheel and a line with loops along it. Cages are for effetes."

Stevn popped up nearby. He said, "In about two days we'll have a thousand refugees coming down at us. Misters Renho and Dunninger have gone hunting. We'll want to feed them."

Harp said, "Good. Did you have a garden?"

"Yah. The bad news is, you're in it."

Harp looked around her. "Hah! Well, we can search. Guardian, would you rather hunt? Mister Dunninger says he's hunted trees . . ."

"I'll help you look for crop plants." The silver suit made him too clumsy to hunt anything more agile than a carrot, and he wasn't about to take it off among strangers. "Let's see, branchlets migrate along the branch into the treemouth, so if the garden used to be here—"

Stevn was climbing. He called back, "Actually it was on top and forty meters east. Earthlife needs sunlight. We'd let it drift for a year and then replant. But the way the branchlets move, any plant that lived through the famine is going to be all over the top of the tuft. Like . . . here!" He dropped something the size of Maxell's head. "Most of the crops died, but there should be *something*."

The object drifted down; Maxell jumped and caught it halfway. A big mushroom.

They searched, burrowing through the greenery like worms in an apple, while the sun arced from west to east. There were runner beans, and little red beans, and oats. Harp found a corn plant, but nothing was growing on it. The find of the day was a string of small trees, the roots twined intimately with the foliage, bearing tiny red apples.

Harp looked tired, drained . . . hardly surprising, given what she'd been through. Her voice still set Maxell's nerves singing. "They'll want food and warmth and a bath and rest. Even if the hunters get nothing, we've got food. Let's do something about warmth."

Harp and Stevn burrowed back down into the wicker-floored open space, the Commons. They searched, half-burrowing. Stevn began tearing at foliage, throwing it behind him. Maxell joined him, for lack of a better idea. Suddenly his knuckles brushed stone.

Big stones formed a ring three meters across, buried beneath the foliage.

"Rock must be hard to find in a tree," Maxell said.

"They were pried out of the trunk," Stevn said. "After we moved to the out tuft, we kids had to find more. There weren't enough, so Captain Rennick took some wingmen out to a dried-up pond. But you've got to have *something*, because you sure don't want a fire getting loose in a tree tuft!''

Harp and Stevn had run out of strength. They settled into the foliage while Maxell continued to expose the stone ring. ''What do we burn here?'' he asked.

Stevn laughed. ''What have we got plenty of?''

Burning branchlets threw an orange light through the Commons, a light kinder than the daylight pouring in from above. Maxell let it warm his hands. ''Take a break,'' he called to Harp, who had wandered away and was searching through foliage.

A head popped through the Commons floor. Dunninger looked around him and said, ''Ah! A fire!'' His hand rose too. ''There are angel moles everywhere! I got these in a few minutes of just following the rustling.''

Maxell took the bundle: five narrow short-furred bodies. ''Where's Renho?''

''Underside. He still thinks he can catch a turkey or something.''

''That'd be good. Otherwise we could use a few more angel moles.''

Harp called, ''Come back in half a day, we'll have a bath.''

''Oh, lady-bard, that would go nicely!''

Maxell asked, ''Won't they want food and sleep first?''

Stevn said, ''If we're going to cook anything, we may want to dig out the bath and use it as a vat.''

Harp objected. ''No, Stevn, the bath is important! It binds us together. For that matter, *we* should be clean before the refugees get down. Tree-fodder, where did they put it? Stevn?''

''Maybe they didn't have one,'' Maxell suggested. ''Not all climber cultures are alike.''

''Oh, we had a bath,'' Stevn said. He jumped high, clutched foliage and began crawling down. Maxell realized that he was following the waterfall. ''Here,'' he said suddenly.

Again they tore away foliage. The work was getting to Maxell's back. He took it for granted that he was doing most of the work. Dwarves were stronger than normal men. He continued uprooting foliage until they had exposed a hemispherical ceramic bowl.

''Big enough to boil a dozen citizens at once,'' he said.

''Right. Help me move this.'' Harp had found a massive wooden wall, hinged at one end. The foliage that half-hid it impeded its swing. They pushed it across the waterfall, and were soaked before they finished.

The diverted waterfall began to fill the bowl.

''And we still don't have a cookpot,'' Maxell said.

"Nope." It didn't bother Harp. She seemed half-asleep, watching the bowl fill.

Would they expect him to take off the pressure suit? He couldn't do that; but it looked like he'd better have a damn good excuse. The silver suit was his uniform and his defenses and the measure of his value.

Renho and Dunninger returned. Dunninger had another cluster of angel moles. Renho pulled a respectable mass up through the foliage: a half-grown triune a bit smaller than he was. They moved away to butcher their catch.

On no visible signal, Harp and Stevn began taking off their clothes.

She was wonderful. Maxell tried to keep his jaw closed, his eyes half-lowered; he certainly couldn't keep them off Harp. Normal women had always seemed fragile to him, too long and narrow; and while they might admire his muscle, they chose taller men.

Renho and Dunninger noticed what was going on. They began to strip too. They all set their bundled clothes handy and entered the pool.

Harp grinned at him. "Doesn't it come off?"

"Classified," the Silver Man said automatically. But anyone who might steal a silver suit was here within his sight. Right? And a Navy-trained dwarf was the equal of any four citizens, right? And any fool could see that if he didn't get into that bath he'd be ostracizing himself, very bad vibes for the Admiralty, and he certainly couldn't do it with the suit on, because water might damage something inside—

He stepped into the foliage to get it off. The means were certainly classified.

If he'd had his life to live over again, he'd have been first into the bath. The way he'd hesitated, everyone watched him swim out of the foliage and enter the water. It was cold. He masked a grimace and submerged himself. He asked, "Is body heat supposed to make this warmer?"

Harp laughed. Stevn said, "Sitzen Tree is supposed to have their fireplace next to the bath, so one side gets hot."

"The whole grove thinks *they're* effetes," Harp said.

She didn't know about Admiralty practices. Renho and Dunninger were grinning, avoiding his eye and each other's. Maxell said, "What do we use for soap?"

"Soak a bit, then we rub each other clean. I'll show you."

Maxell didn't swallow his grin, because the rest were grinning too. Harp was going to be sparkingly clean.

"Guardian," she said, "How do you like tree life?"

"It's all new to me. Has its attractions, though. How are you feeling? It must have been a nightmare, your tree coming apart."

"Oh, yes." She took his hand underwater. Maxell was surprised, then pleased.

"Did you get any warning?"

She was silent for a few breaths. Then, "The whole tree was lurching around. The floor of the Commons twisted and ripped apart under us. We could hear a kind of bass scream, the sound of tearing wood, I guess. So we had some time, some warning, but what were we going to do with it? We tied the children in the loops and ran the treadmill to get them up quick, and then rode the line ourselves. Some of us snatched wings before it all ripped loose. I grabbed my windpipe instead.

"Some of us didn't want to come, and some of the children hid when we tried to gather them up. We weren't going to force them. We didn't have room. They're still in the tuft, I guess."

Stevn left the water to pluck spine branches. These he distributed with ritual precision. The ritual continued: the five fed each other foliage until the branches were bare, then began scraping each others' backs with the springy branchlets. Backs and shoulders, and then they scraped themselves.

Maxell, last to scrape Harp's back, took it easy. The skin was already pink. And while he was close enough, he half-whispered, "When I was surrounded by foliage and starving—"

"Yes?" Her head turned; her lips were very close.

"Thank you for not laughing."

"I've visited half the trees in the grove, you know. They're all different. I don't laugh at anyone."

"I try not to."

"Guardian, would you like to find some privacy with me?"

Though they were both naked and whispering, this seemed very sudden. Maxell felt a stutter coming on. He made himself say, "Yes. Absolutely. Can I take my suit?"

She was surprised, but she didn't laugh. "Something inventive?"

"No, I have to guard it. Standing orders."

"Oh."

CHAPTER THREE

YEAR 419 DAY 118

Sounds trickled through his sleeping mind: snores, voices, complaints, crying children; wind, growing gradually louder; "Kitemaster? Kitemaster?" all faintly irritating, all "Kitemaster?"

"Yuh." He was standing half-upright in a wobbly lift cage. Everything hurt. He felt beaten half to death . . . but not sleepy. Alert. His eyes were crusted and the Sun was too bright, west and a little in. The Sun had been west and a little out when the cage began to fall.

Between waking and waking was generally about four and a half days . . . standard days: orbits of Goldblatt's World. Nearer Levoy's Star the days ran shorter. Farther out, they ran longer. A sleep was a day and a half to two days; but a voyage from the midpoint to the in tuft took longer than that. He must have slept for two days and a little, because the tuft was coming up fast—

"Kitemaster, what do we do?"

"Brake. There's a brake. Ling, it's hardwood, eyeball height in one corner. I think it's behind those two white-haired—" Ling dove into the crowd; they made way. "Found it? Two flat pieces of wood. Squeeze them together." The lift cage jerked and surged, and everyone still sleeping woke. "Not so hard, Captain, you'll break it! Just gently, with both hands . . . a little harder. Remember, you're not just braking a cageful of citizens, you're braking the whole system. Spit on it if it smokes."

The cage slowed.

Below was a Navy spinner ship, deeply nested, the first Alin had seen so close. For a made thing, it was *big*. A windmill turning on an oddly curved box, a tank, an octagonal hut, all decorated unimaginatively in letters and numbers, like Admiralty wings; all festooned with rope. Green billows rose up to hide it.

The channel for the cage and lift lines had grown closed. No, there it was, just a pucker, and next to it the windmill spinning merrily, its blades almost cutting foliage. He'd seen it this way a hundred times . . .

When Alin was eight years old, the Scientist caused a windmill to be built and hooked to the treadwheel that ran the lift lines. After that the lift lines were simply left running. They only called the kids to the treadwheel for extra power to lift a loaded cage.

Alin had liked the treadwheel, the companionship, the chance to show off muscle. Maybe that was why he'd become the Liftmaster's Apprentice.

He was twenty when the crops failed. The tribe had migrated to the out tuft, traveling naked for fear of bringing contamination. Those had been frantically busy days. Lift lines had to be run to the out tuft, and a windmill built, and eventually a treadwheel and more lift cages; foraging parties on the trunk needed transportation, and so did any food they found; and everything needed to be lifted to the midpoint and then out . . .

He'd been Liftmaster's Apprentice when ten Admiralty kitemen came sailing out of the sky to touch down at Brighton's midpoint. He'd known his destiny in that instant.

He'd asked for a pair of kites.

They'd laughed. It must have seemed funny to these tourists, a *climber thing*, this unspoken understanding that a gift would be repaid, eventually, somehow. But the kiteman Chet Bussjak had offered a trade.

It was all arranged in advance, carefully spelled out. For Bussjak's set of kites, plus several sleeps spent teaching Alin how to make and bind more kites, Bussjak would take the kites they made together (proof that the making was taught well!) plus Alin's wings.

It was easy to see why Bussjak wanted those. The wings bound to the kitemen's backs were crude things, unpainted, ugly.

So Liftmaster Kent had taken another apprentice—

"Brake!" Alin shouted. He'd never descended the tree with such a load. The cage plunged into the foliage, into darkness and a roar of shattering branchlets loud enough to drown out the yelling, and slapped down hard. With his head ringing, Alin leapt to disconnect the cage before the lift line could pull it back out.

"Sorry," he said.

Ling bellowed, "I can't see a damn thing! Kitemaster, you've really . . . All right, so you've been gone for two years, but this place is *really* . . . What's next?"

Alin's sight was coming back. Parallel beams of sunlight flared from out. From in, from below . . . the red glow of a fire?

There were five shadows perched around the orange-white light of a rock firepit. Then one was flying toward him, backlighted by the glow. Stevn.

Alin caught him in the air. They drifted backward, and settled into green cloud.

"Boy, are you all right?"

"Sure. Well, I hurt."

"Where?"

"Everywhere. My hands. Wrists."

The cage had emptied. The chatter of Linnet's people faded as they all streamed toward the fire.

"Me too, but we did good. Everyone came back. What's going on here? Who's the—" In his concern for Stevn, Alin had only glimpsed the others at the fire. "Who's the gleaming . . . silver man? It's a Guardian!"

Stevn tugged at his arm. "Come on, I'll introduce you."

"No, hold a breath. I should know a little more. The Guardian?"

"He flew out to get me when I got close enough. They hadn't seen the tree. When I pointed it out they went right in, but all we found was Harp."

"Did you have any trouble with the kites?"

"No, Dad, it was just a straight shot, just set the kites and wait. I was afraid the fog would thicken up, but it didn't. Riding back in a Navy ship was a kick. Noisy, though. When the windmill spins it's like a thousand little men pounding with hammers."

"There's supposed to be little explosions going off in that box." Alin was watching while he listened. Captain Ling and his men and women and children had only paused at the fire. There was a flurry of activity back . . . "Isn't that where we had the bath?"

"Yes. We ripped out the foliage and filled it. Harp thinks it's important, 'important bonding ritual,' and maybe she had another reason too."

"Capability's Harp?"

"Right. Dad, there's food at the fire."

At the rock firepit the overgrowth of foliage had been torn away to prevent the fire's spreading, and used to feed the fire itself. There were angel moles and apples broiled on spine branches. The horde hadn't left much.

Stevn said, "Not all the earthlife died. We've got oats and two kinds of beans, but we couldn't figure how to cook them."

"Not to mention enough foliage to strangle us all if we don't eat fast enough. I'd say the tuft's ready for occupancy. What else don't I know?"

"This tuft's infested with angel moles. We should take some back. And we got the bath going."

"Who did you bring? Who *didn't* you bring?"

"Captain Murphy and one of the crew stayed with *Flutterby*. We've got two crew and Guardian Curtz and Harp."

From the blurred activity in the dark beyond the fire, one separated and climbed toward sunlight. Alin's dark vision must have been improving. He saw Capability's Harp with fire in her hair, vivid as his memory, where every other human shape had been a blur. She perched herself above the bath: a creature of magic, backlit by yellow-white sunlight, playing a windpipe in the low breeze. Half-heard music wafted toward them.

Stevn said, "She went off into the bushes with the Guardian. Right out of the bath, naked, hauling that silver suit after them."

Alin suppressed a guffaw.

"But she got the bath set up first. The silver suit has a smell to it that must be four hundred years old. Yug! Getting the suit off him was like pulling teeth, and getting the smell off took awhile, and now he's back in the suit."

"He did save her life . . . yours too."

"Sorry."

Harp recognized Alin, or maybe Stevn, and waved. They both waved back. Alin asked, "Did anyone ever tell you about bards?"

"What about bards?"

"Bards don't marry. It seems to be that way in every tree. There's always a bard, and bards belong to everyone. Nobody gets mad if his wife rubs up against a bard, and of course they're usually men. Harp is the only woman bard I know about."

"Have you rubbed up against Capability's Harp?"

Alin nodded.

"Does Mom know?"

"Yes."

"She doesn't care?"

"It makes Natlee furious every time she thinks about it. But it's not supposed to. Stevn—"

"We don't mention her."

"She'll ask. She'll know what tree came apart. Stick with me, stet? Harp will never speak a word to me without you right beside me."

"Stet."

"I wonder why the dwarf? They *all* saved her life. Did she—"

"Just the dwarf."

The little man was a power in the Admiralty. And he was short.

They worked their way down a slope of foliage half-shaped into ledges. Stevn and the rest had uncovered just the rim of the hemispherical bowl. It was very crowded. Above the sloshing and murmuring Alin called, "Captain Ling?"

"Who asks?"

"Your companion in flight."

"Kitemaster! Join us by all means!" Ling lolled in a soup of bodies. "I must say, it's startling to find such luxury beneath the mask of overgrown foliage. The seats above the treemouth, for instance. And the firepit. Elegant." Something in his tone suggested that Captain Ling did not quite approve.

Alin stripped and entered the water. It wasn't jarringly cold. Thirty-odd bodies must have warmed it.

He must have been in body contact with half that many. He let his eyelids fall and savored sensations. His head lolled on someone's shoulder, somebody's child wiggled under his arm, a near-infant stood on his knee and studied him. Ripples marched as someone scrubbed someone's back. A foot caressed his calf and a woman smiled. Sleepy eyes were all about him, the sloshing and the faintly heard music and the quiet.

And the Silver Man settling himself on a ledge above the bath. "Captain Ling, what's going to happen to the rest of your tribe? Just how much rescue are they going to need? Harp tried to tell me a little—"

"Yes. Well, splitting is how integral trees breed." Ling showed no anger at being confronted in his bath. "They fall apart. Now, the half that's falling *in*, it's got only the in tuft, stet? The other end was the midpoint; it's just broken wood.

"So the wind is blowing just on the in tuft, so it blows the whole tree east, the way the Smoke Ring turns. You push the tree east, it wants a wider orbit. East takes you out. Likewise the other half-tree, which is falling *out*—"

"So they're both being pushed back to the median."

"Exactly. The wind blows it west, against its motion, so it wants a narrower orbit. Then again, the out half-tree had the rocket motor. It can get back by itself."

"So now you've got two Capability Trees?"

"Maybe. Maybe inhabited by corpses. We'll be very glad of your rescue maneuvers."

A man began scrubbing Alin's upper back; a woman started on his lower back. Then they traded. Body language and blooming romance across Alin's back. It would have been fun without the treefeeding Silver Man . . . who . . .

He said, "Guardian, thank you for your courtesy to my son." Fair's fair.

Maxell Curtz was glad that he had bathed earlier. Older citizens often said that the Clump had grown crowded; but they never got as close together as this! His inclination was to loll in the foliage somewhere and remember Harp while he listened to Harp's voice. Instead, with Renho and Dunninger, he perched on the rim of the bowl and tried to make conversation.

To Alin Newbry he said, "Not at all. Stevn guided us to where we could do some real good." The so-called Kitemaster was in his thirties, short (but not dwarfed) and muscular, like any climber, but with a kiteman's startling muscular development in his wrists and forearms. Maxell asked, "Your people used to live here?"

"Up to a couple of years ago. A little after we joined the Grove, most of the crops died. We had to move out. Sitzen and Research and Capability Trees gave us seeds, but we still had to get to the Admiralty and buy more. It's the only time any of us have gone to the Admiralty."

"Good thing you were already in reach," Maxell said. *Give*. *Buy*. For sixty people in a tree, it was easy to keep obligations straight. For eleven trees in a Grove, not so easy. A tree might move, or come apart. For two thousand people in a region that changed shape faster than any artist could draw a map . . .

Money was less fragile than memory; money lost shape less easily than an obligation.

Admiralty ships had contacted a good many trees over past centuries. Some moved into the East Grove, for access to the Admiralty and the benefits of civilization. Too many did not. For that matter— "How did you get into the Grove, Kitemaster? We looked for a steam rocket."

"Guardian, that's classified."

The man was within his rights. Maxell changed the subject. "Captain Ling, we are gathering civilization. Why is it that any tree doesn't come to us right away?"

Harp's music had faded: she was listening.

"Our ships go out through the Smoke Ring to find the places of Man. We talk. We leave word how to find the Admiralty. We leave plans for steam rockets. You need a way to move your tree *anyway*, because any passage past Gold can hurl you out into the gas torus where you'll suffocate."

"We built our rocket without help," Ling said. Alin Newbry said nothing.

A tree couldn't just *drift* into the Grove, could it? Sure it could. It wasn't likely, but it could happen . . . and a treeful of climbers might well enjoy bewildering the all-powerful Admiralty.

"The Admiralty is the center of knowledge throughout the Smoke Ring. Why would any tribe hesitate?"

Harp was quietly settling between Curtz and Stevn.

Ling said, "I wouldn't want to offend our rescuers."

"I seriously want to know, Captain."

Captain Ling said, "Well, your Admiralty isn't *all* good."

"How so?"

"The air's thick with garbage."

"There are garbage *collectors*."

"They don't collect it all."

Ling had hit a nerve. The garbage problem had increased with the population, even in Maxell's brief lifespan.

Ling said, "We don't visit the Clump that often, but word does pass among the trees, Guardian. We're told about the garbage, the crime rate . . . theft . . . violence . . . fringe addiction."

"Don't you have these things in a tree?"

"Not really. We know each other, don't you see? You can't use what you steal. It'll be recognized. If you're a bully, six of us other bullies will give you flying lessons, and if it keeps up, you'll do it without wings. Fringe . . . well, fringe is fun, but it messes up your head. But nobody robs somebody for fringe. He finds it on the trunk. If he gets too fond of the stuff, we'll still take care of him. He'll be keeping the cookpot clean instead of hunting."

He was getting reasonable answers. Joy! Maxell asked, "Couldn't you be robbed by another tree?"

"They'd face hunting tools. Knives, harpoons, bows. But your Navy doesn't like it when climbers carry those things in the Clump, so we can be robbed there."

"Rescue?"

Harp spoke just beside him. "We hear stories about that too. We're in debt now, aren't we?"

Again? "Well, yes and no, Harp. The Admiralty thinks that charity works best if it pays for itself."

"If I don't understand that right away, it's because Capability Tree never heard about money until we reached the Grove. So how are we expected to pay?"

"Labor, and there's no hurry. You'll pay some of the debt in mud."

"Mud?"

"You have property rights in the mud that was the core of your tree. That stuff makes fine fertilizer."

Harp laughed.

Dunninger said, "I hauled mud myself before I joined the Navy."

Alin Newbry asked, "Can that be done with kites?"

"That's how we did it." Dunninger lifted his arms. "See?"

"Kiteman?"

"Right."

"If Brighton had had money, we could have just *bought* kites from a passing citizen. And kite-making instructions. And flying lessons. I don't mind how hard I had to work for my kites," Newbry said, "but what are we missing that we never thought of? We should have gone to the Clump long before. Then again . . . mud. We'd be competing with Admiralty kitemen. And you've been at it a lot longer than we have."

"Yup. And we've got ships to haul the bigger blocks. Too bad," said Dunninger.

Renho said, "You're closer, though."

"About ten times closer." Newbry was suffering badly from indecision.

"You could be in there now," Dunninger said. "Can't deal with the Admiralty unless you tree has money. The Vivarium pays money for mud. Half goes to the hauler. And if you're in there pulling mud around, you might run across a last refugee, the one who's injured and can't yell for help."

Curtz was wishing he'd planned this. He thought he knew what would end Newbry's hesitation. "The Admiralty merchants won't even be in the easterly fringes for twenty or thirty days. Take some time to rest, you'd still make it."

"Maybe." Newbry pulled himself out of the water. "Time we were going. Come on, Stevn."

YEAR 419 DAY 121

Where the lift lines turned at the midpoint, Alin and Stevn let go and kept coasting along the bark. Their kites were furled in their hands.

"You're going," Stevn said.

"I think so. Tow some of the mud from Capability Tree to the Vivarium. You want to come along?"

"Do I have a choice?"

Alin heard bitterness and didn't like it. "This isn't lives at stake, and the other boys have had time to rest. So?"

No answer.

"Bertam and Gilly and Marlow must have had five days' sleep already. I'm dead tired, but I'm the Kitemaster, and Hell can freeze over before I let the Admiralty take *all* our mud. You're dead tired too. So stay in the tuft."

Stevn said, "I was scared all the time."

"Ah."

"I got the sails set, and I was never sure they were right. At first I was going *way* wide of the Navy ship, but I got myself turned, and then I still wasn't sure. How far in can I go before the tree's too far behind me to ever get back? What if the fog thickens up and I get lost? The sky goes on forever. What if the navvies never see me? The Scientist says if I get too far from the air I'll pass out. Then what?"

"Yeah."

"I didn't want to say so."

The other pulley was near. Alin snatched at an edge of bark sheet with one hand, got Stevn's ankle with the other, and stopped their flight. "Here's your ride down."

Stevn didn't move.

"I thought I was going to die, my first solo flight," Alin said. "Everything I did took me farther from the tree. A triune family looked me over and never even bothered to separate."

Stevn laughed.

"The only reason I was out there was, I didn't want to be Liftmaster's Apprentice the rest of my life. It looked like Liftmaster Kent was going to live forever. Still does.

"So you go on. Tell the Captain what's going on, and ask him to send the other boys up. Tell your mother I'm going to make Brighton rich—"

"Dad, why don't you tell them yourself?"

"No, I'll stay on the trunk. I need the rest."

"The Silver Man says you've got twenty or thirty days to rest! Talk things over with the Captain. See what we want from the Clump. You might even talk Mom into something."

"Hah."

Stevn's face closed down. He reached for the lift line.

Alin said, "Hold it. I see a lob. Let's geta meal before we go down."

"Where?"

"He's poking an eye over the bark, just there. That must be where his burrow is. Got your harpoon?"

"Yeah."

"I just don't like arguing," Alin said. "I'd rather fly away, and I damn sure know some places nobody can follow me. I know I have to talk sometime, but it's . . . it's just . . . But if I can't talk to your *mother*, my children's *mother*, then I can't talk to anyone, can I? Even you."

"You're coming down?"

"Yeah. But first I'll show you how to boil a lob in zero tide."

• • •

• • •

In the aft and side views, all detail had become tiny: integral trees were toothpicks, ponds were drops of glitter, everything seemed embedded in fog. Gold had become a bulge within a larger lens of cloud patterns that trailed off to east and west: a storm pattern that spread across the Smoke Ring. The hidden planet seemed indecently close.

THE INTEGRAL TREES, 1983

THE ALIEN IN OUR MINDS

I

The only universal message in science fiction reads as follows: There are minds that think as well as we do, or better, but differently.

The appropriate questions are, why do you care? Why should *they* care? And, where are they?

I want to call your attention to humankind's ancient fascination with aliens. There's evolution at work here.

1) Meeting aliens has been a normal thing for humankind. For most of human history, successful tribes have numbered about a hundred. Hunter-gatherer economies need lots of territory, and they have to move frequently.

   A hundred thousand years ago, or a million, all humankind was hunter-gatherers. There were strangers around. A wandering tribe might stumble across something different, with odd, ugly faces, bizarre customs, strangely colored skin—and new and useful tools, or new and fearsome weapons.

   People who couldn't deal with aliens had to fight when they met. People who could, had their choices. They could trade, they could make agreements including treaties, they could postpone a fight until they had the advantage, they could set rules for war that would allow more survivors. And . . . a man who can talk persuasively to aliens, can also talk persuasively to his own tribe. A persuasive speaker was likely to become the chief.

   But even without the external aliens, there were aliens enough.

2) There were wolves. There were horses. There were saber-toothed cats. There were caribou and pigs and rabbits and woolly mammoths.

   A recent article in *Analog* pointed out that men are cursorial hunters.

Most predators sprint after their prey. Our ancestors didn't. They picked their target and chased it down over hours or days. A hunter had a better chance of feeding his tribe if he could learn to think like a deer.

So. Somewhere there was a man who found and kept a litter of wolf pups and raised them to know obedience. The tame wolves that didn't learn to think like men didn't live to breed. And somewhere there was a man who leapt on a horse's back and rode it to exhaustion. That tribe had enough to eat, so they didn't eat the horse. Presently they were riding horses.

So there were horses and dogs within certain tribes of men; but there were aliens closer yet.

3) We are a species of two intelligent genders. Men and women don't think alike, but we can learn to talk to each other. Some of us. When we choose our mates, we breed for certain traits.

Adults and children don't think alike. Successful human beings talk to their children. They teach their children to become successful adults. Successful children learn new means of hunting or farming and teach them to their elders. Where the generation gap is too great, that tribe or that family doesn't survive.

We have dealt with alien intelligences for all of history and prehistory. Wouldn't that hold for any extraterrestrial intelligence? Maybe not. Aliens may have taken other paths, paths that don't force negotiation upon them.

Parthenogenesis. Budding instead of sex: no opposite gender.

Children might have no intelligence. A human child's brain is big; it doesn't grow much while he's becoming an adult. An alien child's brain might be the last thing to develop. Or children might hatch from eggs and have to fend for themselves. An adult may never see a child until a young adult comes wandering back out of the breeding grounds. There would then be no intellectual contact with children.

An alien species may have radically divergent genders (as with most insects). If one sex is nonsapient, there is no negotiation. It doesn't take brains to mate!

Mating seasons are common enough in Earthly life, but look at the result. In mating season both genders might lose all intelligence. Intelligence might be a handicap as regards breeding, even for us, from the evolutionary viewpoint. An intelligent being is likely to think of reasons for not mating with an available partner, or for not having children just now, or at all.

But in mating season male and female *do not* negotiate before they mate. Males may negotiate with each other, but two males butting heads are very much alike. You might picture the elders of one gender arranging a mating before the season comes on. This could be done using cages. Lock 'em up together.

Humankind has been fiddling with reproduction for a long time. Before the Pill there were abortifacients and French letters. Technology may supplant our present modes of reproduction. War between sexes finally becomes a real possibility. One gender exterminated. Technology for reproduction from then on.

What I'm getting at is this. We assume that an alien intelligence will want to talk to us. Or to someone! But it ain't necessarily so. The evolutionary pressure may not be there.

II

Where are they?

The universe is far older than the oldest known intelligent species. Why haven't they come visiting? It's the most interesting question now being asked.

You've read tales of the interstellar commonwealth that has been ignoring Earth, or has made Sol system into a zoo or national park; but that won't wash. The kind of power it takes to cross interstellar space is difficult to ignore. Any decent interstellar reaction drive must convert more mass to energy than the mass of the payload; you have to get up to at least a tenth of lightspeed and back down! To take advantage of relativity you would need .9 lights or greater. There would be side effects on a cosmic scale. For laser-augmented light-sails, same remark. We would have seen *something*—something as powerful as the pulsars, which were assumed to *be* interstellar beacons until we learned better.

How long does it take to make an intelligent spacegoing species?

Our sample case is the solar system, Earth, and the human species. We'll stick with our only sample and generalize from there.

The human species seems to be within a thousand years of reaching across to the nearest stars. Our sample is a world big enough to hold a thin atmosphere, orbiting within the liquid water domain of a yellow dwarf star. If we want an oxygen atmosphere we must wait for the life-forms to develop photosynthesis. Our first guess is that it takes four and a half billion years for a planet of this specific type to produce thinking beings.

Keep in mind that other chemistries may form other kinds of life. Even so—

Nothing in our temperature domain works as well as water and oxygen and carbon. In hot environments, chemistries are probably too unstable. Within the atmospheres of gas giant planets there are conditions that might give rise to organic life: you find a *layer* of Earthlike environment. But escape velocity is very high, and what would they have for tools? In very cold conditions, on Pluto or Titan, or in the black oceans beneath the ice crusts of some of the moons of Jupiter and Saturn, there may be exotic chemistries that can support life. Then again, chemical reactions happen slowly at such temperatures. We might have to wait longer than the present age of the universe before anything interesting happens.

If we're looking for something that can build spacecraft, we can stick with our sample and not be too far off.

Four and a half billion years. Look again and the number goes up. To build a solar system we need gas clouds, galaxies, gravity, heavy elements, and stellar explosions.

The solar system condensed from a relatively dense interstellar cloud. Those aren't rare, they're all over the place. The cloud included supernova remnants, the materials that became the cores of planets and the elements of our bodies. The event that caused the condensation may have been a shock wave from a more recent supernova explosion. We need to allow time for previous supernovas, and time to make a triggering supernova.

The galaxies formed near the beginning of the universe. Supernovas have been occurring since a billion years afterward. It's fair to assume that it takes seven billion years to make an intelligent species.

The universe is generally given as fifteen to eighteen billion years old. Atoms didn't form for the first half-million years. Call it two billion years to spread supernova remnants throughout the galaxies. The first intelligent species should have evolved seven to ten billion years ago. Based on our own sample, they began exploring space almost at once: say, two or three million years after the taming of fire.

Large numbers of stargoing species should have been expanding though the universe for up to eight billion years. Somewhere a successful industrial species should have gone past the Dyson shell stage into really ambitious engineering projects.

We're alert enough to recognize Dyson shells now!

Where are they?

Something's wrong with our assumptions.

III

Maybe they're all dead.

We can postulate events that regularly destroy an intelligent species before it can reach out to Earth. What follows is likely to be depressing. Hang on. There are answers you'll like better.

Intelligences may tend to destroy the ecological niche that produced them. We do tend to fiddle. The Zuider Zee is still the world's biggest successful planetary engineering project, but the Sahara Desert seems to have been caused by goat herding. Rabbits in Australia, garden snails in Tarzana, mongooses in Maui.

We fiddle with life-forms too. Broccoli and pink grapefruit are recent inventions. There are hundreds of breeds of dogs shaped over tens of thousands of years of fooling around. It's a simple technique: what you don't like doesn't breed. But now we know how to fiddle with genetic coding. What are the odds of our making one irrecoverable mistake in the next thousand years?

Destroying one environment in this fashion wouldn't bother us much if enough of us have left the planet. But let's look at the energy considerations. Dogs were shaped by primitives who used the wheel if they were wealthy enough. Modern biological experiments can be run for millions of dollars, or less. A decent space station might be built for tens of billions. The odds are that your random ETI developed genetic engineering long before he thought of leaving his planet, because it's so much cheaper. Where are they? They made one mistake.

Here's another: nuclear war. Aha, you've heard of it. Nuclear war could certainly destroy an environment if it's done right.

Some nearby star might go supernova. The world need not be wiped clean of life, but a good many species would die or change, including the most complex.

The aliens' own sun may have turned unstable.

There's evidence for cycles of destruction on Earth, spaced around 26 million years apart. The causes are in doubt. Even the numbers are in doubt. The cause may be flurries of comets passing through the solar system. The nucleus of a comet is nothing you want to stand in front of. Read LUCIFER'S HAMMER, then multiply the numbers by a thousand. The event that killed the dinosaurs also wiped out most of the life on Earth, and half the species.

What are the odds that a comet or asteroid will intersect some random inhabited world during that brief period after fire and before the ETIs can get off the planet? In the three-million-year period of our existence our own odds are not terrible; but we may be luckier than most worlds.

So much for natural causes.

If you like paranoia, you'll love the Berserkers. Fred Saberhagen and Greg Benford have different versions, but both involve self-replicating artificial intelligences. Saberhagen's version is space-going forts left over from some old war, and they're programmed to destroy all life. Benford's version was built by old artificial intelligences, and they fear or hate organic intelligences. Both seem plausible, and either would explain our lack of visitors. If the Berserkers are out there, we must be just on the verge of attracting their attention.

These are the pessimistic assumptions. But let me give you the David Brin theory before you have to go looking for aspirin.

We know of two ways that otherwise Earthlike worlds can go wrong. Venus was too close to the Sun. Too much atmosphere boiled out, and the greenhouse effect kept the surface as hot as a brick kiln. Mars was too small to hold enough atmosphere, and too cold. There's evidence of liquid water on Mars at some time in the past, but never enough of it for long enough. Earth could have gone in either direction.

What about a third choice? Let's look at an Earth that's just a little larger. There's just a little more water. Astrophysicists are generally happy if they can get within a factor of ten. How much land area would we have if Earth was covered with ten times as much water?

Even twice as much would be too much. Life would develop, we'd get our oxygen atmosphere, but nothing would ever crawl out onto the land because it wouldn't be worth the effort. Not enough land.

We don't actually need more water than we have. Let's give Earth's core a little less in the way of radioactives. The crust grows thicker, circulation of magma slows down, mountain building becomes much rarer. We get shallow oceans covering a smooth planet.

Something might still develop lungs. A big-brained whale or air-breathing octopus might well develop an interest in optics. There's water and air to show him how light behaves. He might even find tools for telescopes—breed jellyfish for the purpose—but what would he *do* about the stars? He's got no use for the wheel and no access to fire.

There are less restrictive assumptions that could still keep visitors at home.

Our would-be visitor may have evolved for too specific an ecological niche. One lousy lake, or one lousy island, or the growing area for one specific plant, as Koalas depend on eucalyptus. Our ETI may not have the means to conquer large parts of a planet, let alone venture outward. This is certainly true of thousands of Earthly species. Even where some rare species has spread throughout the world, it was usually done by differentiation of species.

And it was done slowly. Our ETI, when we find him, may be subject to biorhythm upset. Even where a planet has been conquered, there may be no contact between parts of it. No airlines, no ships, nothing that moves faster than the speed of a walking alien, because jet lag kills.

A population of ETIs who have conquered their planet and are already suffering from population pressure, may not be able to breed with each other, let alone gather for a summit meeting. But they won't have wars of conquest either. An invading army would be dead on arrival.

IV

Where are they? Why haven't they come? We have answers now, though they may not be right.

First: Something kills intelligent beings. It may be natural or artificial. It may be some time bomb ticking away in their own genes. These are the pessimistic assumptions, and they imply that we too are doomed.

Second: The sky may be dense with water worlds, a thousand water worlds for every Earthlike world where land pokes through. But water worlds don't allow a technology that would lead to spaceflight. They might allow telescopes. Intelligent whales and octopi may be waiting for us all across the sky.

Third: The ETIs may have no interest in talking to us. Even where the interest can be generated, they don't have the skill for dealing with other minds. The evolutionary basis for that skill may be unique to humankind.

Fourth: The aliens may have adapted too specifically to their ecological niches. They may suffer from extreme biorhythm upset.

If these guesses are right, we have lost something precious. We lose the Draco Tavern and the Mos Eisley spaceport. We lose all of *Star Wars*. We lose Ensign Flandry and Nicholas Van Rijn and the Kree-Lar Galactic Conference. The only interstellar empires left to us are all human: *Dune*, and *Foundation and Empire*, and Jerry Pournelle's Codominium and Empire of Man before the Moties were found.

But we lose all conflict too, until interstellar war can be waged between human and human.

What's left? The picture is peculiar precisely because it was so common in science fiction forty years ago. Human explorers cross interstellar space to find and communicate with native wogs. Misunderstandings with the natives may threaten ship and crew, but never Earth.

Water worlds will not be a problem to us. We could build floating bases. The water-dwellers would not perceive us as competitors. Species restricted to one ecological niche would also pose no threat. On the contrary, they might have things to tell us or show us—art forms or philosophical insights if nothing else—and they would likely be glad of our company.

There is hope in the fact that dolphins like us.

As for aliens with no impulse to talk to us—we can give them reasons. We have done very well by talking to aliens. If we manage to settle the worlds of other stars, it will be because we can talk to aliens, and get answers.

● ● ●

• • •

"... But I carried away some magic. Watch: I put a half-twist in this strip of paper, join the ends, and now it has only one side and one edge ..."

"Talisman" (with Dian Girard), 1981

SPACE

Twenty-five years ago, my ambition was to tell stories.

It wasn't long before I decided I could save civilization too. I was about to blame that on Jerry Pournelle, until I remembered:

San Diego, the Starlight Motel, the Bouncing Potatoes Westercon in 1966. They put me on a panel alongside Harlan Ellison and a handful of other contributors to his forthcoming anthology *Dangerous Visions*. And I was talking about a short story, "The Jigsaw Man."

I told fandom assembled that the situation was desperate: that executing criminals by disassembling them for public organ banks would be feasible *now*. The argument that allows any convicted axe murderer to save a dozen lives in this fashion works just as well on a political dissident or a litterbug. The inertia of politicos would not hold back *the organ bank problem* forever. We had to be prepared!

Harlan was not trying to keep a straight face. Well, maybe he was.

I meant it, of course.

Barnaard performed his heart transplant a little before *Dangerous Visions* hit the stores. Next thing I knew, several study groups had sprung up to study the ethics of organ transplants and donor rights.

I stopped worrying. I kept writing on the subject, but then, it's a natural basis for stories.

I remained ready to save civilization.

When Apollo 11 left lunar orbit and began its descent, Marilyn and I were on our way to a Watch-the-Landing party. We were at a traffic light with the radio on. For just that moment my whole nervous system surged with fear. I wanted powerfully to shout, "Wait! Let me think this over. This is going to change all of the future, the consequences are beyond our control—"

It never crossed my mind that we would go to the Moon, and come back, and *stop*! Or stop the program early, stop building Saturns, and even attempt to burn the plans. Why? They worked!

For us fanatics there were a couple of wonderful years of lunar exploration, then an endless time spent planetbound, marooned. Then Jerry Pournelle told me that we could save civilization.

The Citizens Advisory Council for a National Space Policy has met five times over five years, for harrowing three-day weekends. The attendees include spacecraft designers, businessmen, NASA personnel, astronauts, lawyers. Adding science fiction writers turns out to be stunningly effective. We can force these guys to speak English. For those who can't, we can translate. Jerry does the yelling and gives us our directions. In each case we have spent a weekend designing a proposed space program for the nation, including costs and schedules.

It's weird to think that we are (or were) the only ones doing costs and schedules. Didn't we hire a government to do that? But the Council came about because Jerry realized that nobody else was doing it, in Washington or anywhere else.

When he talked me into this, and Marilyn into holding local civilization together while it happened, and forty or so pro-space types into attending at their own expense, Jerry could make only one promise. The President would see what we produced.

The pattern established at the first Council meeting was the one we followed thenceforth. It was absolutely new to me; I have never held a job in my life, except for one summer working in a gas station.

The science fiction writers (me, Jerry, and Poul Anderson on that first occasion) would take notes and turn them into English later.

After it wound up, Jerry asked me to write up my impressions, quick, while they were still in my mind. They're not too coherent, but here they are.

• •

NOTES ON THE SPACE POLICY SEMINAR

FRIDAY AFTERNOON

Activity started at noon and centered mainly around the doorbell, which never stopped ringing. Dr. Pournelle spent all of that time making introductions. I welcomed people without worrying about their names; I've learned there's no point.

We tried gathering round the poker table to get started. The poker table got overfilled quick. Marilyn had put the leaves in the breakfast table, making it our largest. We continued trying to organize, and did fairly well at it, though our ranks continued to swell until the crowding became ridiculous.

Consumption of coffee reached record levels. I reluctantly gave up trying to monitor that myself. Also trying to help Marilyn *and* contribute to the policy-making. From that moment she was on her own.

The need for Dr. Pournelle, or *any* single authority-figure with a loud voice and no neurotic fear of offending people, became obvious Saturday and stayed that way throughout. We thirty-six or so managed to continue in the direction we were pointed, mostly. I don't think it would have worked on as many science fiction writers; but then, we *did* convene for one stated purpose.

When the breakfast room got jammed, we broke up into groups, as directed.

The group I joined tackled the question: "How do we get free enterprise into space?" Suggestions and pro-huckster arguments came thickly and rapidly. Forty percent tax break on investments in space (that specific figure was never questioned). Ten year tax moratorium on salable products from space (instantly extended to 2000 A.D.). Starbase I, the permanent space station with huckster-room for rent. Incorporation rules. Present restrictions on business, some of which now make any small business almost impossible, let alone a space enterprise, should not apply unless Congress specifically says so.

I remember participating, but I don't remember adding anything specific. When the group disbanded I went to write up our decisions in tentative fashion. Art Dula had material to expand it; Bjo Trimble typed it in, after I showed her how. She *loves* Electric Pencil.

After dinner Art Dula and I seriously tackled our group's position paper. I titled it "How to Save Civilization and Make a Little Money," expecting that that would drop out along the way. We polished the bejesus out of it. Dula does know how to cut and polish, as well as I did ten years ago, and he developed the same hyperenthusiasm I was working under. It helped that there had been no serious disagreement about any major points. But he uses tremendous sentences bristling with clauses. I'd stare at some damned tangled paragraph, often reduced to gibberish by a crucial misspelling via Bjo; then yell "Trrrust me!" and slash it apart into little words and short sentences.

All the time we were working, raucous laughter rose from below. I was missing all the fun. We got our copies downstairs late in the evening, and I found myself passing them around and demanding that people read them . . . and thinking that a lot of this must go on during such symposia. Lots of people working through the fun time to produce paper, then watching people fail to read the damn paper.

SATURDAY

Marilyn's new chairs arrived, and were needed.

Without the volunteer help, *nothing* would have worked. There were three, and they made a good many trips for supplies. Marilyn was exhausting herself keeping us fed. Coffee vanished as fast as it appeared. I tried to ignore all this, because I was expected to contribute as a participant.

Some of these memories have gotten blurred . . .

Morning: a general session discussing progress. We had produced a fair amount of paper, and that seemed good to Dr. Pournelle. He kept insisting that we stay *specific*: that we should not restrict ourselves to general statements about how getting into space is a Good Thing. We should build thus-and-so? Fine. If you can't tell me what it costs, then what does it *look* like?

Lunch.

Dr. Pournelle broke us up into groups. I'd have loved to sit in on the Moon Project group, but thought I was more badly needed in Blue Sky. I took 'em outside—it seemed appropriate.

Discussion ranged all over the map. At one point Dr. Pournelle came out to be sure we weren't restricting ourselves too much. He found it wasn't necessary. We tossed in a few favorite far-out ones, like the orbital tower and esoteric means of propulsion, and the interstellar light-sail . . . but quickly dropped the subject of interstellar flight. We came up with short-range stuff too, and that was what got used.

Put seven crew aboard any Shuttle that isn't mass-restricted or already full. Have a lottery for the extra seats, or reward politicians, news commentators, and aging hard science fiction writers who jog. An astronaut in every village! Build a windowed pressure can with seats for the Shuttle bay. Accept that the Shuttle will be used to make movies.

SATURDAY EVENING

The volunteers went out for Chinese food for forty. (We've still got far too much of it.) Came back much later, telling tales of the restaurateur's shock as he realized they were serious. I made a cheese omelet for B.J., a woman on a very restrictive hypoglycemia diet.

We *liked* each other, almost universally, all thirty-odd of us. We were all gathered for a larger purpose. I failed to notice that the science fiction writers were being treated as absolute equals, because I expected nothing less; I had to have it pointed out. How times change.

After dinner Dr. Pournelle split us into groups. I got drafted for the discussion re: "How can the Space Program be made to help underdeveloped peoples?"

Chuck Gould stated our conclusion at the outset. *Every comsat that goes up should be overdesigned and flexible. We should be able to sell, lease, or give away comsat capability to any nation that finds a use for it, and instantly*. Fine. We then traded anecdotes and philosophic generalities for an hour or two—I had some of my own, but found it difficult to interrupt—after which we repeated the original statement again. I tried to hand in my notes. I was told, diffidently, that I (as wordsmith) was expected to produce the copy.

I said, "There's a problem. I'm not inspired."

"Why?"

I explained. I *know* how to help the underdeveloped people. I produce new wealth via space conquest and new technology, and expect a great deal to spill over. The rich get richer and the poor get rich too; it almost always works, as long as *new* wealth is being created. [I'm not sure that got into our final missive. Dr. Pournelle, it should.]

I/we worked on the position paper afterward, starting with my sparse draft and continuing Sunday, photocopying every draft. It was like pulling teeth, but we've produced a good, readable paper.

I got into the drinking and conversation earlier Saturday night. Dave Griswell and I started trading wild ideas. If any serious bureaucrat knew how his mind *really* works . . . well. He wants to collect the solar wind and mine it for resources, mainly iron. I offered him half a Dyson shell, saying you'd be able to move the sun too. He worked out the numbers, and it's just no good. But he likes my flux tube. (That became *The Smoke Ring*.)

SUNDAY

We didn't convene till eleven. But we convened like a flash flood! Everybody running in all directions. I never stopped except right at the beginning, when Dr. Pournelle convened us. He had a draft of the two papers to be sent to the Administration. It was pretty good. There was some discussion, including both nits (which got sarcasm) and important points (on the level of "Sure this is true, but do we hit 'em with it *now*?")

When that broke up, the havoc began.

Alan Trimpi showed me a position paper he'd first-drafted. It had all it should have, but it wasn't well written. By now I'd noticed the amazing range of writing skills among the attendees. I scribbled all over Alan's paper ("It's only marks on paper," he reassured me), then other papers while someone typed Alan's paper into a computer, then did a lot of (x + 1)-drafting in Electric Pencil . . .

I spent all three days feeling (a) hyperkinetic; that is, eager to speak or write or rewrite, unwilling to rest; and (b) irritated. I don't think the irritation ever got out of hand. It's normal. A writer correcting a bad or hasty draft *is* irritated. Bad writing becomes an irritant. It's worse when the draft is by a collaborator. I had *thirty-five* collaborators, and some couldn't write coherently, let alone concisely and without vagueness. I'd have to stop to ask the author, "But what were you *trying* to say here?"

Not unexpected. I was prepared to find shop-talk where the authors thought they were speaking English, and I did, I did, from the "dedicated satellite" level (but a dictionary *will not* tell you what that means) to a compulsive use of initials. (That is *not* being concise. It makes the text read *slower*.)

I moved at a dead run for most of two days. I never bumped into anyone, not quite, but with that crowd it was bloody likely every second. And they were all running too.

And always I felt I was accomplishing something!

"Read this." Okay, and I made chicken-marks as I went. Ruined one once and had to reprint the page. "Have you read—?" "No, who's got a copy? Find it." "How do I save copy on the machine?" I did that over and over. "The copier's jammed—" "How do I print something out downstairs?" People who found Friday's paper kept telling me they *loved* "How to Save Civilization and Make a Little Money." It'll stay on as a subheading. Maybe someday a bumper sticker?

Things slowed down late in the afternoon. It was bewildering. The first paper (what to advise the Admin to do instantly) is nearly ready. The second, more comprehensive treatment of a viable space program isn't quite so urgent. Both are in Dr. Pournelle's hands.

A few of us finished in the spa, pool and sauna.

The house is a disaster area. We've got leftovers everywhere, despite giving away what Chinese food we could and throwing away anything transient.

Marilyn collapsed at 9:00 P.M. and is sleeping like a brick.

I'm still hyper.

We still like each other, all thirty-odd of us. I particularly like Dave Griswell. And maybe we've actually accomplished something.

CONCLUSIONS

I have nothing to compare this experience with. There's little I can offer as advice on how to improve the experience. But—

We had two computers, a Diablo printer and a slower printer, a correcting typewriter, and a copier. I couldn't replace the ribbon or correcting tape because I only address letters with it; Bjo did that. One of us imported a computer-link and another Diablo. And the copier never got a chance to cool down! For this kind of seminar we needed anything that would write, but particularly the copier.

The volunteer gofers and typist were worth their weight in gold. It particularly helped that they had brains. Getting gofers with brains and dedication will not always be possible.

A huge coffee maker would have saved effort, but the coffee wouldn't have been as good. This may well be crucial.

Our house (I was told repeatedly) was perfect. What counted was the arrangement of rooms: we could gather everyone or isolate them.

I had reference materials on hand, though most such had to be brought in.

How much of this was crucial? I have no way of knowing.

In the Free Enterprise symposium I voiced few opinions of my own, but I was able to understand a little of what was going on. The reason for a tax moratorium on stuff manufactured in space were clear enough. Space is expensive enough without taxes; the United States pulls no taxes now from that source, so would not lose anything. Another point needed explaining: The law was murky. This need not bother a government—they could adjust the laws to fit whatever they're doing—but a corporation lawyer wouldn't be able to tell his employers how the law stood if they did thus and so. If we wanted corporations in space, the laws would have to be made unambiguous. (And in general, this has been done.)

We wound up with a lot of notes. Bjo Trimble, another volunteer, typed them into my machine upstairs.

That night Jerry told me he wanted those notes rewritten. I said, "Sure. Tomorrow." The party was just starting. These were some of the brightest people around; I wanted to probe their minds.

"If I wanted you to do it tomorrow, I'd have said, 'Do it tomorrow,' " he said.

Weird.

To make this work, some single entity had to go through all of the paper produced, get every attendee to ratify it, then run a lot of it through a typewriter to finish turning it into English or to make it concise enough to read. Jerry found a volunteer: himself. He probably never considered *me*. He knows I couldn't do it, and wouldn't.

The report was loosed upon Washington in January, 1981.

• •

HOW TO SAVE CIVILIZATION AND MAKE A LITTLE MONEY

Report of the Free Enterprise Committee

RECOMMENDATION

The most important goal is to make space self-sustaining, which means economically profitable.

We begin with the assumption that we wish to maximize freedom, in space as well as Earth; and that a fundamental human right is the right to have and use property.

FREE ENTERPRISE SHOULD DEVELOP SPACE RESOURCES

1. The President should make two clear statements of intent:

    "The United States of America must commit itself to extending free enterprise into space."

    "The Soviet Union has, and has repeatedly demonstrated, a **direct** interest in preventing free enterprise from entering space."

2. Various international treaties (in particular, the Moon Treaty) concerning the exploitation of space, must be carefully reviewed. The intended thrust of many past treaties has been to bar free enterprise from space.
3. It will not forever be necessary to subsidize space enterprises. Private investment in space industry should be encouraged by:
    3.1 A 40% tax credit for all space-related investments.
    3.2 A moratorium on taxes on the initial sale of goods and resources produced in space, through at least the year 2000 A.D. The tax credit and moratorium should cover techniques and hardware designed to **support** activity in space. Such incentives have been used in the past, by many nations, to good effect.
    3.3 U.S. patent, copyright, and trademark law should be extended to cover space-related hardware, software, and products.
    3.4 A good many present regulations bid fair to cripple most small businesses on Earth, let alone a company trying to gain a foothold in space. We need new, simple, specific laws to cover space activities.

WITHDRAW FROM PRESENT SPACE LAW AGREEMENTS

In 1967 the U.N. accepted a *Treaty on Principles Governing the Activities of States in the Exploration and Use of Outer Space, Including the Moon and Other Celestial Bodies*. This proposed treaty would have required that "all activities in space be conducted exclusively by states." The U.S. properly rejected this attempt to forbid private development of space resources. Note that the Communications Satellite Corporation, which is not an agency of the U.S. government, was created to operate for profit in space. The proposed treaty would have left its status in doubt.

In 1967, compromise between the U.S. and Soviet Union on the Treaty on Principles placed two limitations on private companies. First, "activities of nongovernmental entities in outer space, including the Moon and other celestial bodies, shall require authorization and continuing supervision by the appropriate state party to the treaty." (Treaty Art. 6) Second, "each state party to the treaty that launches or procures the launching of an object into outer space, including the Moon and other celestial bodies, and each state party from whose territory or facility an object is launched, is internationally liable for damages to another state party to the treaty or to its natural or juridical persons by such object or its component parts on the Earth, in air space, or in outer space, including the Moon and other celestial bodies." (Treaty Art. 7)

This treaty has chilled the investment environment for private corporations interested in financing space activities. The treaty's requirements are without parallel in the private sector. For example, if a Pan-American Airways 747 crashes and damages foreign property or persons, then Pan-American and its insurers, not the U.S. government, are liable for the damage. However, if a space object owned by a U.S. corporation does exactly the same damage, the U.S. government is internationally liable to the government of the state in whose territory the damage occurred. The result has been government control where none is needed and extensive regulation where none is required.

Additionally, many important provisions of the 1967 Treaty on Principles are extremely vague. This vagueness does not affect investment by a government in space, but no potential investor could meaningfully predict the legal and economic risks of private space operations.

After the Treaty on Principles was ratified in 1967, about half the nations of the world acceded to it. Far fewer nations have ratified three later treaties passed by the U.N. These include a Convention on Rescue and Return of Astronauts, a Convention on International Liability for Damages Caused by Space Objects, and a Moon Treaty. Like the 1967 Treaty on Principles, each of these treaties is an academic exercise in international law made far in advance of the reality it purports to control. These treaties do not, and cannot, take into account the rapidly changing nature of space technology. They cannot be amended to reflect a nation's changing economy. They fail to address the legitimate needs of private corporations to own space resources and exploit them for profit. They are really more political statements by the Third World and the USSR than a workable set of legal rules for the initial development of space resources.

For example, these treaties declare that all space resources in the Solar

System are ''the common heritage of mankind,'' a phrase interpreted by most nations to mean ''common property.'' This term is also found in the Law of the Sea Treaties. It is an example of how less developed nations are attempting to limit U.S. access to natural resources. This ''common heritage'' clause has already been used by the United Nations to impose an indefinite moratorium on deep sea-bed mining.

The U.S. should immediately act to withdraw from the 1967 Treaty on Principles and the 1972 International Liability Convention. The U.S. should carefully review the desirability of remaining in the Registration Convention and the Rescue Convention, and should consider, after thorough study, whether to withdraw from these international agreements.

The Reagan administration has several specific opportunities to reverse the recent weakness in U.S. international space policy. The following events in 1981–1983 are critical:

(A) The U.S. should ask *United Nations Committee on the Peaceful Uses of Outer Space* that the ''Moon Treaty'' be returned for renegotiation to safeguard private enterprise and human freedoms in space. The U.S. delegation should maintain constant vigilance over space activities at the United Nations.

(B) In 1982 the U.N. will host the *Second Conference on the Exploration and Peaceful Uses of Outer Space*. This meeting will be a trial run for at least the next decade of treaty negotiations and radio frequency allocations. The U.S. must submit its National Position Papers to the United Nations. The Reagan Administration should form a task force of space law experts who are known supporters of private enterprise and human freedoms in space to prepare these papers.

(C) In 1983 the Region 2 (Americas) of the *International Telecommunications Union* will hold an *Administrative Radio Conference—Space Broadcasting*. The Reagan Administration should resist the territorial claims of nations over geosynchronous orbit, stand up for U.S. rights to have direct broadcasting over any area of the Americas, and insist that solar power satellites be allowed to beam power back to the Earth.

POSITIVE STEPS TOWARD PRIVATE SECTOR INVOLVEMENT

In *Wealth of Nations* Adam Smith pointed out that South America has greater economic potential than North America. North America is more economically advanced because of the structure of its economy. This illustrates the need for a favorable matrix to foster a flourishing economy. The Reagan Administration should submit legislation to the Congress to create a favorable economic climate in space.

Favorable tax policies and a clarification of the legal conditions in which space ventures occur would be an important step forward and would require no governmental expenses beyond the costs necessary to enact the necessary legislation.

First, a 40% tax credit should be allowed on all high technology investment, including research and development, to direct our national strategy toward the creation of new industries, which could be expected to provide new sources of employment, taxes and foreign exchange. Naturally space industries would be included within the high technology sphere. Since this result would be at least as desirable as the production of power from solar energy, the 40% investment credit enacted to encourage solar energy investment should be expanded to include many other high technology research and development efforts.

Second, space is presently an **economically underdeveloped** environment. Many underdeveloped terrestrial nations have enacted tax moratoria to promote industrial development. Profits from the initial sale of space-produced goods and services, including **data** as a salable commodity, should be exempted from taxes. Similarly, no customs duties should be assessed on products from space. This provision already applies to less developed nations on Earth. This moratorium from taxation and duties should last at least until 2000 A.D. to facilitate the founding of a wide spectrum of space industries.

Private space industry will require clearly defined laws. Private space activities under U.S. jurisdiction should be exempt from all federal and state regulations except for those specifically enacted to control space activities by the Congress of the U.S. on a case by case basis. For example, U.S. patent, trademark and copyright law should apply to U.S. business activities in space.

None of these moves are guaranteed to **create** American industries in space. The most the United States government can do, is to make the risk less fearsome, the profits more attractive.

There have been six meetings of the Council. Five took place at our house. The last was held at the Pournelles', because Marilyn was half-paralyzed with a worst-case ruptured lumbar disk. (The operation worked. She's in good shape now.)

We have frequently heard our phrasing worked into the President's speeches.

Star Wars went through the Niven household.

Arthur Clarke and Robert Heinlein were present during that session. They were on opposite sides: Clarke opposed all of the Star Wars approaches. In this he was hampered: In greeting Max Hunter, he announced that Max had taught Arthur everything he knew about orbital mechanics.

This is typical of Arthur: give credit where due.

Max replied, "I didn't teach you enough, Arthur." (After all, there *was* an argument going.)

Jerry gives Marilyn and her team of volunteers credit for the *Treaty of Tarzana.* Marilyn is a wonderful hostess—a nitpicking Virgo—and her team of volunteers were as fanatical as any of us.

Saturday afternoon of the second meeting, proponents of various approaches surrounded our breakfast table. Each had his own idea of how to stop a flurry of incoming nuclear warheads . . .

General Danny Graham favored impact devices, "High Frontier," the logical heir to Arthur Clarke's original notion: take out a missile by firing a shotgun shell in retrograde orbit. Impact: ten to eleven miles per second. Max Hunter and others favored ground-based lasers: catch 'em incoming, or even loft a mirror and bounce the beam off that. Lowell Wood, Edward Teller's deputy, favored orbiting gamma lasers. Quarreling had already been reported in the news.

Afternoon became evening. They sat about the breakfast table, trying to work out some compromise . . . while smells from the kitchen surrounded them. No door there, just the edge of a wall. They heard Marilyn ask, "When shall we serve dinner?" and they heard Jerry answer, "When this team comes to an agreement."

We starved them out.

The Treaty was basically an agreement not to rain on each other's parades. In public, "All of these techniques should be tried; all may be necessary."

We're calling it SSX now: a small, wingless ground-to-orbit spacecraft that uses everything NASA learned before they ossified. The sixth meeting of the Council ratified a strong appeal for an SSX.

But the Citizens Advisory Council has seen several shapes for what Gary Hudson calls the Phoenix rocket design. They're truncated cones. They're small. They use densified fuel (you keep chilling the hydrogen and oxygen until they become slushy), aerospike engines (a ring of them around a cone, and you fake the cone), spindly little legs used for landing only, no wings, a selection of peaceheads for cargo or fuel or passengers . . .

And they're private enterprise (though Gary has finally compromised and accepted a government contract for a big dumb booster rocket).

If he ever builds a Phoenix, Marilyn and I will be aboard the first flight of the corporate rocket. We bought our way in early.

And now Jerry's claiming that we tore down the Berlin Wall at Niven's house!

It's hard to disprove. The argument goes:

1) The National Defense Initiative went through the Niven household before it was loosed upon the nation.
2) Opponents kept having their facts shot out from under them—and always came to the same conclusions—until their position started to look a little silly. Meanwhile, it *was* being funded.

3) The Soviets couldn't compete with the expense of Star Wars techniques.
4) They went to *glasnost* instead.

If you ask me, the Germans (both sides) ought to pick some sturdy, not too ugly section of the Wall and keep it. Build a museum with the Wall as its major support wall! The Wall is not a part of history that should be forgotten. Hell, they could even have races: over the wall, any technique is legal, a paint bullet disqualifies you . . .

. . . What do you mean, nobody asked?

Nobody asked us to form a committee to design a national space policy either. What a selling author learns, what Jerry Pournelle seems to have known from birth, is this: *You don't have to wait to be asked.*

• •

DEFENSES

Anything worth doing in space can be turned into a weapon.

I add in haste that that statement also holds true in your own neighborhood. Nobody will ever count how many victims of the elderly and wealthy persuasion have fallen to the lowly pillow. Anything with heft works in a bar fight: a glass ashtray, a bottle and a hard surface to break it, even the bottle alone. An automobile makes a fine weapon; so does gasoline. All of these things are universally available.

But in space the situation is entirely different. The energies necessary even to reach orbit, let alone to accomplish anything once we're there, are matched only in the field of weapons, and generally not by them.

The most efficient reaction motors are those with the highest exhaust velocity. A Saturn booster hovering over a building would reduce it to flaming slag; a fusion rocket would certainly do the job faster; a light-pressure drive would melt and boil it.

A mass in low orbit carries tremendous kinetic energy. What gives a spacecraft destructive power also gives it vulnerability: any undefended orbiting spacecraft can be killed by a bucket of sand in retrograde orbit. In higher orbits the velocities may be less, but the potential energies are even greater—which is why lifting the mass is so expensive—and the higher the orbit, the less retrothrust it takes to drop the mass back to Earth.

The distance between L5 and the Moon is the radius of the Moon's orbit. Between L4 and L5 the distance is nearly twice that. A signal laser powerful enough to cross such gaps would be lethal at close range.

Rocks thrown from the Moon by any kind of mass driver would impact the Earth as guided meteors, at seven miles per second.

Any nation that can return a piece of asteroid to Earth orbit, to mine its millions of tons of recoverable metals, could also drop it on an enemy with similar incoming velocities.

The United States should encourage *any* space enterprise involving its citizens. The more thoroughly we can establish ourselves in space, the safer we are. We must establish a presence in space, before someone can tell us not to.

If the Soviet Union is Number One in space, will there be a Number Two?

• • •

BIBLIOGRAPHY OF LARRY NIVEN

OPUS # TITLE and publishing history

1) **THE COLDEST PLACE**. *Worlds of If*, December 1964
collection, TALES OF KNOWN SPACE (#84)

2) **WORLD OF PTAVVS**. *Worlds of Tomorrow*, March 1965
Expanded to novel length, 1966 (#10)

3) **WRONG-WAY STREET**. *Galaxy*, April 1965
anthology, THE NINTH GALAXY READER, edited by Frederik Pohl, 1966
anthology, VOYAGERS IN TIME, edited by Robert Silverberg, cloth and paper
anthology, FIRST FLIGHTS TO THE MOON, edited by Hal Clement, cloth
collection, CONVERGENT SERIES (#113)
Portugese anthology, VIAJANTES NO TEMPO, as RUA DE SENTIDO UNICO, from Galleria Panorama
anthology, DIE MORDER MOHAMMEDS, as FALSCHE RICHTUNG, Marion von Schroder Verlag, 1970
as TWEERICHTINGSVERKEER, in ALFA EEN copyright 1973 Meulenhoff Nederland bv

4) **ONE FACE**. *Galaxy*, June 1965
collection, THE SHAPE OF SPACE (#40)
collection, INCONSTANT MOON, Gollancz (#60)
collection, CONVERGENT SERIES (#113)
French, *Galaxie*, Juin 1967 as LA FACE CACHEE DE LA TERRE
paper, anthology, SCIENCE FICTION-VERHALEN, Meulenhoff, Amsterdam, as DE SCHADUZIJDE

5) **BECALMED IN HELL**. *Fantasy and Science Fiction*, July 1965
anthology, WORLD'S BEST SCIENCE FICTION: 1966, edited by Donald A. Wollheim and Terry Carr, 1966
anthology, NEBULA AWARD STORIES 1965, edited by Damon Knight (cloth and paper)
anthology, TWENTY YEARS OF FANTASY AND SCIENCE FICTION, edited by Edward L. Ferman and Robert P. Mills (cloth and paper)
collection, ALL THE MYRIAD WAYS (#54)
collection, INCONSTANT MOON, Gollancz (#60)

collection, TALES OF KNOWN SPACE (#84)
Dutch anthology, DE SPEEKSELBOOM (NEBULA AWARD STORIES I) as DOBBEREN IN DE HEL ed. Damon Knight, Uitgeverij Luitingh—Laren N.H.
anthology, DER GIGANT, as PANNE IN DER HOLLE from Science-Fiction-Erzahlungen

6) **THE WARRIORS**. *Worlds of If*, February 1966
collection, THE SHAPE OF SPACE (#40)
collection, TALES OF KNOWN SPACE (#84)

7) **EYE OF AN OCTOPUS**. *Galaxy*, February 1966
collection, TALES OF KNOWN SPACE (#84)

8) **BORDERED IN BLACK**. *Fantasy and Science Fiction*, April 1966
collection, THE SHAPE OF SPACE (#40)
collection, INCONSTANT MOON, Gollancz (#60)
anthology, SF:3, AUTHOR'S CHOICE, edited by Harry Harrison
collection, CONVERGENT SERIES (#113)

9) **BY MIND ALONE**. *Worlds of If*, June 1966

10) **WORLD OF PTAVVS**. novel, paper, Ballantine, 1966
hardcover, MacDonald
paper, Sphere
French hardback, LE MONDE DE PTAVVS, 1974 from Editions Opta. Glorious interior illos.
as KZANOL DE RUIMTEPIRAAT, from Prisma, Het Nederlandse Pocketboek. Copyright 1970 by Het Spectrum.
as EL MUNDO DE LOS PTAVVS, paper, Edaf, Madrid, 1976
German, as DAS DOPPELHIRN, paper, Bastei Lubbe, 1977
Italian, as STASI INTERROTTA, 1976, Fanucci Editore, Eddie Jones cover
paper, as DE WERELD VAN DE PTAVVS, 1979, Elsevier SF Elsevier Nederland B.V., Amsterdam/Brussel

11) **HOW THE HEROES DIE**. *Galaxy*, October 1966
collection, THE SHAPE OF SPACE (#40)
collection, INCONSTANT MOON, Gollancz (#60)
collection, TALES OF KNOWN SPACE (#84)

12) **NEUTRON STAR**. *Worlds of If*, October 1966
collection, NEUTRON STAR, Ballantine (#26)
anthology, WHERE DO WE GO FROM HERE? edited by Isaac Asimov
anthology, THE HUGO WINNERS, edited by Isaac Asimov
anthology, THE ARBOR HOUSE TREASURY OF MODERN SCIENCE FICTION, compiled by Robert Silverberg and Martin H. Greenberg
French, *Galaxie*, Mars 1968, as L'ETOILE INVISIBLE

in GALACTICA, Hungarian, with (15)

13) **AT THE CORE**. *Worlds of If*, November 1966
anthology, THE SECOND IF READER OF SCIENCE FICTION edited by Frederik Pohl (cloth and paperback)
collection, NEUTRON STAR, Ballantine (#26)
French, *Galaxie*, Avril 1968, as JUSQU'AU COEUR

14) **AT THE BOTTOM OF A HOLE**. *Galaxy*, December 1966
collection, THE SHAPE OF SPACE (#40)
collection, INCONSTANT MOON, Gollancz (#60)
collection, TALES OF KNOWN SPACE (#84)

15) **A RELIC OF EMPIRE**. *Worlds of If*, December 1966
collection, NEUTRON STAR, Ballantine (#26)
anthology-textbook, THE GREAT SCIENCE FICTION SERIES, with commentary
in GALACTICA, Hungarian, with (12)

16) **THE SOFT WEAPON**. *Worlds of If*, February 1967
collection, NEUTRON STAR, Ballantine (#26)
as L'ARME MOLLE, in *Galaxie*, Septembre 1971

17) **THE LONG NIGHT**. *Fantasy and Science Fiction*, March 1967
collection, INCONSTANT MOON, Gollancz (#60) (as CONVERGENT SERIES)
collection, CONVERGENT SERIES (#113) (as CONVERGENT SERIES)
anthology, MATHENAUTS, edited by Rudy Rucker (1987) (as CONVERGENT SERIES)

18) **FLATLANDER**. *Worlds of If*, March 1967
collection, NEUTRON STAR, Ballantine (#26)
anthology, SEVEN TRIPS THROUGH SPACE AND TIME, edited by Groff Conklin

19) **THE ETHICS OF MADNESS**. *Worlds of If*, April 1967
collection, NEUTRON STAR, Ballantine (#26)

20) **SAFE AT ANY SPEED**. *Fantasy and Science Fiction*, May 1967
collection, THE SHAPE OF SPACE (#40)
collection, TALES OF KNOWN SPACE (#84)
anthology, 100 GREAT SCIENCE FICTION SHORT SHORT STORIES, edited by Isaac Asimov, Martin H. Greenberg, and Joseph D. Olander

21) **THE ADULTS**. *Galaxy*, June 1967

22) **THE JIGSAW MAN**. anthology, DANGEROUS VISIONS, edited by Harlan Ellison (Doubleday).
paper, DANGEROUS VISIONS (volume #2, Berkley)
paper, DANGEROUS VISIONS, Sphere
one volume DANGEROUS VISIONS, Signet

collection, ALL THE MYRIAD WAYS (#54)
collection, TALES OF KNOWN SPACE (#84)
anthology, THE ROAD TO SCIENCE FICTION #3, edited by James Gunn
French anthology, DANGEREUSES VISIONS, J'ai Lu, 1976, paper

23) **THE HANDICAPPED**. *Galaxy*, December 1967
collection, NEUTRON STAR, from Ballantine, as HANDICAP (#26)
anthology, WORLD'S BEST SCIENCE FICTION 1968, edited by Donald A. Wollheim and Terry Carr, as HANDICAP

24) **SLOWBOAT CARGO**. serial, *Galaxy*, February, March, and April 1968

25) **THE DECEIVERS**. *Galaxy*, April 1968
collection, TALES OF KNOWN SPACE (#84) as INTENT TO DECEIVE
German anthology, GALAXY 13, 1969
as BEDIENUNG INBEGRIFFEN from Wilhelm Heyne Verlag, München

26) **NEUTRON STAR**. collected stories, paper, from Ballantine
cloth, from MacDonald (British)
paper, from Sphere (British)
Italian, abridged and filled out with cartoons. as RELIQUIA DELL'IMPERIO, from Urania.
German paperback, from Wilhelm Goldmann Verlag
As NEUTRONSTER, paper, 1970 & 1979, Meulenhoff, Amsterdam

27) **GRENDEL**. first published in collection, NEUTRON STAR, #26

28) **DRY RUN**. *Fantasy and Science Fiction*, May 1968
collection, THE SHAPE OF SPACE (#40)
collection, CONVERGENT SERIES (#113)
Portuguese, as TENTATIVA SIMULADA, in *Magazine de ficcão cientifica*, Julho 1971

29) **THE DEADLIER WEAPON**. *Ellery Queen's Mystery Magazine*, June 1968
collection, THE SHAPE OF SPACE (#40)
collection, INCONSTANT MOON, Gollancz (#60)
collection, CONVERGENT SERIES (#113)
Swedish anthology, ARETS RYSARE 7, Forlags Ab Semic

30) **THERE IS A TIDE**. *Galaxy*, June 1968
collection, A HOLE IN SPACE (#74)
collection, TALES OF KNOWN SPACE (#84)
Nederland anthology, as ER IS EEN GETIJ in HET HEELAL VAN DER DROMERS

German anthology, GALAXY 12, as DAS GLUCKSSPIEL, Wilhelm Heyne Verlag, München, 1969

31) **WAIT IT OUT**. *Future Unbounded*, Program Book, for Westercon 1968
(revised) anthology, TOMORROW'S WORLDS, edited by Robert Silverberg (cloth and paper)
collection, ALL THE MYRIAD WAYS (#54)
collection, INCONSTANT MOON, Gollancz (#60)
collection, TALES OF KNOWN SPACE (#84)
anthology, THE SCIENCE FICTIONAL SOLAR SYSTEM, edited by Isaac Asimov, Martin H. Greenberg, and Charles G. Waugh
German anthology, ABENTEUER WELTRAUM, paper as GESTRANDET AUF PLUTO, 1981, Bastei Lubbe

32) **FOR A FOGGY NIGHT**. *Decal*, fanzine edited by Donald A. Cochran, July 1968 issue
collection, ALL THE MYRIAD WAYS (#54)

33) **LIKE BANQUO'S GHOST**. *Worlds of If*, September 1968
collection, THE SHAPE OF SPACE (#40)
semiprozine, ALTERNITIES, Autumn/Winter 1980
collection, CONVERGENT SERIES (#113)

34) **A GIFT FROM EARTH**. novel, paper, Ballantine, 1968
cloth, MacDonald (British)
cloth, SFBC (British book club)
cloth, Walker (American)
paper, Sphere
paper, from Bastei Lubbe, as PLANET DER VERLORNEN, 1972 & 1982
Italian, as UN DONO DALLA TERRA, from Futuro, 1973
as EEN GESCHENK VAN DE AARDE, paper, Meulenhoff Amsterdam, 1976
paper, 1979, Hayakawa Publishing, Inc.

35) **THE MEDDLER**. *Fantasy and Science Fiction*, October 1968
collection, THE SHAPE OF SPACE (#40)
collection, CONVERGENT SERIES (#113)

36) **ALL THE MYRIAD WAYS**. *Galaxy*, October 1968
anthology, WORLDS OF MAYBE, edited by Robert Silverberg
collection, ALL THE MYRIAD WAYS (#54)
graphic, PSYCHO, November 1972 (as ALL THE WAYS AND MEANS TO DIE)
anthology, GALAXY: THIRTY YEARS OF INNOVATIVE SCIENCE FICTION, with memoir
cloth and paper, Wideview Books

37) **THE ORGANLEGGERS**. *Galaxy*, January 1969

collection, THE SHAPE OF SPACE (#40) as DEATH BY ECSTASY
anthology, WORLD'S BEST SCIENCE FICTION 1970, edited by Donald A. Wollheim and Terry Carr, as DEATH BY ECSTASY
collection, INCONSTANT MOON (#60) as DEATH BY ECSTASY
collection, THE LONG ARM OF GIL HAMILTON (#88) as DEATH BY ECSTASY

38) **THE THEORY AND PRACTICE OF TELEPORTATION**. *Galaxy*, March 1969
collection, ALL THE MYRIAD WAYS (#54), as EXERCISE IN SPECULATION: THE THEORY AND PRACTICE OF TELEPORTATION

39) **NOT LONG BEFORE THE END**. *Fantasy and Science Fiction*, April 1969
anthology, NEBULA AWARD STORIES FIVE, edited by James Blish (cloth and paper)
collection, ALL THE MYRIAD WAYS (#54)
collection, INCONSTANT MOON, Gollancz (#60)
anthology, THE GOLDEN ROAD, edited by Damon Knight
graphic, UNKNOWN WORLDS OF SCIENCE FICTION, May 1975
anthology, THE MAGIC MAY RETURN (#127)

40) **THE SHAPE OF SPACE**. collected stories, Ballantine 1969
as LETZTES SIGNAL VON ALPHA CENTAURI, paper, Wilhelm Goldmann Verlag, München

41) **MAN OF STEEL, *WOMAN OF KLEENEX***. *Knight*, December 1969
newszine, *Ad Astra*, issue three (British)
graphic underground, dramatized: MORE EXISTENTIALIST FUN COMICS
anthology, SUPERHEROES, edited by Michel Parry
Heyne Science Fiction Magazin 12

42) **PASSERBY**. *Galaxy*, September 1969
collection, ALL THE MYRIAD WAYS (#54)
collection, INCONSTANT MOON, Gollancz (#60)

43) **GET A HORSE!** *Fantasy and Science Fiction*, October 1969
anthology, THE BEST FROM FANTASY & SCIENCE FICTION, 19th series, edited by Edward L. Ferman
collection, THE FLIGHT OF THE HORSE, #64 (as THE FLIGHT OF THE HORSE)
The Saturday Evening Post, June–July 1974
graphic, QUESTAR, Golden Press

graphic, STARSTREAM, edited by Roger Elwood

44) **THE MISSPELLED MAGICIAN** (with David Gerrold). serial, *Worlds of If*, May–June and July–August 1970
expanded, THE FLYING SORCERERS (#56)
French, DROLE DE MAGICIEN, in *Galaxie*, Mai and Juin 1972

45) **BIRD IN THE HAND**. *Fantasy and Science Fiction*, October 1969
anthology, WORLD'S BEST SCIENCE FICTION 1971, edited by Donald A. Wollheim and Terry Carr
collection, THE FLIGHT OF THE HORSE (#64)
anthology, PHOENIX FEATHERS, edited by Barbara Silverberg

46) **UNFINISHED STORY**. *Fantasy and Science Fiction*, December 1969
collection, ALL THE MYRIAD WAYS (#54), as UNFINISHED STORY #1
AMERICAN JOURNAL OF PHYSICS, February 1975

47) **LEVIATHAN!** *Playboy*, August 1970
anthology, LAST TRAIN TO LIMBO, no listed editor, Playboy Press
collection, THE FLIGHT OF THE HORSE (#64)

48) **NO EXIT** (with Hank Stine). *Fantastic*, June 1971

49) **THERE'S A WOLF IN MY TIME MACHINE**. *Fantasy and Science Fiction*, June 1971
collection, THE FLIGHT OF THE HORSE (#64)
anthology, ZOO 2000, edited by Jane Yolen (as THERE IS A WOLF IN MY TIME MACHINE)

50) **THE FOURTH PROFESSION**. QUARK 4, quarterly anthology, edited by Samuel R. Delany and Marilyn Hacker
anthology, THE BEST SCIENCE FICTION OF THE YEAR, edited by Terry Carr
anthology, THE 1972 ANNUAL WORLD'S BEST SF, edited by Donald A. Wollheim
collection, A HOLE IN SPACE (#74)
Yugoslav magazine, *Sirius*, broj 61, as CETVRTA VJESTINA

51) **RAMMER**. *Galaxy*, November 1971
anthology, BEST SCIENCE FICTION STORIES OF THE YEAR, edited by Lester del Rey
anthology, THE BEST FROM GALAXY, VOLUME ONE, no specific editor
collection, A HOLE IN SPACE (#74)
(included in A WORLD OUT OF TIME, novel, #91)
anthology, THE BEST SCIENCE FICTION STORIES, no listed editor and no date restriction.

German anthology, SCIENCE FICTION STORY-READER, from Wilhelm Heyne Verlag, München

52) **WHAT GOOD IS A GLASS DAGGER?** *Fantasy and Science Fiction*, September 1971
collection, THE FLIGHT OF THE HORSE (#64)

53) **THE FLYING SORCERERS** (with David Gerrold). novel, Ballantine
as DIE FLIEGENDEN ZAUBERER, Wilhelm Heyne Verlag, München, 1976 & 1982 Paper.

54) **ALL THE MYRIAD WAYS**. collected stories, Ballantine
German, as MYRIADEN, from Bastei Lubbe, 1973
Japan, paper, 1979, Hayakawa Publishing Inc.

55) **INCONSTANT MOON**. collection, ALL THE MYRIAD WAYS (#54)
anthology, BEST SCIENCE FICTION FOR 1972, edited by Frederik Pohl
collection, INCONSTANT MOON, Gollancz (#60)
anthology, THE BEST OF ALL POSSIBLE WORLDS, edited by Spider Robinson
paper, anthology, HEYNE SCIENCE FICTION, JAHRESBAND 1982, as WECHSELHAFTER MOND 1982 by Wilhelm Heyne Verlag, München

56) **UNFINISHED STORY #2**. collection, ALL THE MYRIAD WAYS (#54)

57) **WHAT CAN YOU SAY ABOUT CHOCOLATE COVERED MANHOLE COVERS?** collection, ALL THE MYRIAD WAYS (#54)

58) **RINGWORLD**. novel, paper, Ballantine
paper, Sphere
cloth, Gollancz
cloth, Holt, Rinehart and Winston
Spanish, as MUNDO ANILLO from Ediciones Martínez Roca, S.A.
as BURATTINAI NEL COSMO, from Andromeda (Dell-'Oglio)
paper, 1972 & 1976, as RINGWELT from Bastei Lubbe (West Germany)
hardback, as L'ANNEAU-MONDE, from Editions Opta, Paris, 1973. Nice interior covers.
paper, as RINGWERELD. 1972 Elsevier Nederland B.V., Amsterdam/Brussels, reprinted 1980
cloth, 1978, Hayakawa Publishing, Inc.

59) **FLASH CROWD**. anthology, THREE TRIPS IN TIME AND SPACE, edited by Robert Silverberg (cloth and paper, Dell)

collection, THE FLIGHT OF THE HORSE (#64)

60) **INCONSTANT MOON**. collected stories, Gollancz, hardcover
paperback from Sphere
anthology, THE HUGO WINNERS, VOLUME THREE, edited by Isaac Asimov

61) **CLOAK OF ANARCHY**. *Analog*, March 1972
anthology, BEST SCIENCE FICTION STORIES OF THE YEAR #2, edited by Lester del Rey (hardcover)
anthology, 2020 VISION, edited by Jerry Pournelle
collection, TALES OF KNOWN SPACE (#84)
anthology, ISAAC ASIMOV'S WONDERFUL WORLDS OF SCIENCE FICTION 5: TIN STARS, edited by Isaac Asimov, Martin H. Greenberg, & Charles G. Waugh

62) **RECIPES**. collection, COOKING OUT OF THIS WORLD, edited by Anne McCaffrey

63) **PROTECTOR**. novel, paper, Ballantine
paper, Futura (British)
as IL DEFENSORE, hardback, dall'Oglio editore 1975
as DER BAUM DES LEBENS, Wilhelm Goldmann Verlag, München. Paper.
as PROTECTEUR, Editions Albin Michel, 1976. Paper
paper, as BESCHERMHEER. Elsevier Nederland B.V., Amsterdam/Brussels, 1977.
paper, 1979, Japan, Hayakawa Publishing Inc.

64) **THE FLIGHT OF THE HORSE**. collected stories, paper, Ballantine
paper, Orbit (British)
Italian, as IL TEMPO DI SVETZ, Futuro
paper, Japan, Tokyo Sogensha Co., Ltd.
German, paper, as DER FLUG DES PFERDES 1981, Wilhelm Heyne Verlag, München

65) **DEATH IN A CAGE**. collection, THE FLIGHT OF THE HORSE (#64)

66) **THE THEORY AND PRACTICE OF TIME TRAVEL**. *Vertex*, April 1973
anthology textbook, LOOKING AHEAD: THE VISION OF SCIENCE FICTION, edited by Dick Allen and Lori Allen

67) **THE ALIBI MACHINE**. *Vertex*, June 1973
anthology, ANTIGRAV, edited by Philip Strick
collection, A HOLE IN SPACE (#74)

68) **ALL THE BRIDGES RUSTING**. *Vertex*, August 1973
collection, A HOLE IN SPACE

69) **THE DEFENSELESS DEAD**. anthology, TEN TOMORROWS, edited by Roger Elwood, paper

collection, THE LONG ARM OF GIL HAMILTON (#88)

70) **THE HOLE MAN**. *Analog*, January 1974
collection, A HOLE IN SPACE (#74)
anthology, THE BEST SCIENCE FICTION OF THE YEAR #4, edited by Terry Carr
anthology, THE HUGO WINNERS, VOLUME THREE, edited by Isaac Asimov
anthology, BLACK HOLES, edited by Jerry Pournelle
textbook, with commentary: SCIENCE FICTION: CONTEMPORARY MYTHOLOGY, the SFWA–SFRA anthology

71) **$16,940.00**. *Alfred Hitchcock's Mystery Magazine*, February 1974
collection, A HOLE IN SPACE (#74)

72) **BIGGER THAN WORLDS**. *Analog*, March 1974
fanzine, SPECULATION, as ALTERNATIVES TO WORLDS
collection, A HOLE IN SPACE (#74)
anthology, THE ENDLESS FRONTIER, edited by Jerry Pournelle

73) **A KIND OF MURDER**. *Analog*, April 1974
collection, A HOLE IN SPACE (#74)
anthology, FEAR, 1982, Davis Publications, edited by Alfred Hitchcock

74) **A HOLE IN SPACE**. collected stories, paper, Ballantine
paper, Orbit
as DIE LUCKE IM SYSTEM, paper, abridged, Wilhelm Goldmann Verlag, München

75) **THE LAST DAYS OF THE PERMANENT FLOATING RIOT CLUB**. collection, A HOLE IN SPACE (#74)

76) **PLAYTHING**. *Worlds of If*, August 1974
anthology, THE BEST FROM IF, edited by James Baen
anthology, 100 GREAT SCIENCE FICTION SHORT SHORT STORIES, edited by Isaac Asimov, Martin H. Greenberg, and Joseph D. Olander
collection, CONVERGENT SERIES (#113)

77) **NIGHT ON MISPEC MOOR**. *Vertex*, August 1974
collection, CONVERGENT SERIES (#113)

78) **THE MOTE IN GOD'S EYE** (with Jerry Pournelle). novel, cloth, Simon & Schuster
cloth, Weidenfeld & Nicolson (British)
paper, Orbit
Japanese, paper, 1974, Tokyo Sogensha Co. Ltd.
Italian, cloth, as LA STRADA DELLE STELLE Cosmo
as DE SPLITTER IM AUGE GOTTES, paper and hardback from Wilhelm Heyne Verlag, München, 1977
as DE SPLINTER IN GODS OOG, paper, 1978, Elsevier, Amsterdam

as LA POUSSIERE DANS L'OEIL DE DIEU, paper, Albin Michel, 1981

79) **THE NONESUCH**. *Fantasy and Science Fiction*, December 1974
collection, CONVERGENT SERIES (#113)

80) **THE BORDERLAND OF SOL**. *Analog*, January 1975
collection, TALES OF KNOWN SPACE (#84)
anthology, BLACK HOLES, edited by Jerry Pournelle
German anthology, IM GRENZLAND DER SONNE Wilhelm Heyne Verlag, München
in SIRIUS broj 55 (Yugoslav) as TU NEGDJE BLIZU SOLA
anthology, THE HUGO WINNERS vol. 4, 1985

81) **SINGULARITIES MAKE ME NERVOUS**. *Stellar*, original anthology edited by Judy-Lynn del Rey
collection, CONVERGENT SERIES (#113)
Italian anthology, STELLAR, as ME COSE STRANE MI INNERVOSISCONO, from Longanesi & C., Milano

82) **INFERNO** (with Jerry Pournelle). serial, *Galaxy*, August, September, October 1975
novel, Pocket Books, paper
cloth, Allan Wingate (British)
cloth, Gregg Press
paper, Tokyo Sogensha Co., Ltd.
cloth, as QUESTO E L'INFERNO 1978, Armenia Editore, Milano

83) **GALAXY STARS** (BIO OF JERRY POURNELLE). *Galaxy*, July 1975

84) **TALES OF KNOWN SPACE**. collected stories, paper, Ballantine
Japanese, paper, from Hayakawa
as HISTORIAS DEL ESPACIO RECONOCIDO, paper, 1978, Edaf, Madrid

85) **TIMELINE FOR KNOWN SPACE, AFTERTHOUGHTS**, and various remarks preceding and following the stories. collection, TALES OF KNOWN SPACE (#84)

86) **MY UNIVERSE AND WELCOME TO IT**. collection, TALES OF KNOWN SPACE (#84)
fanzine, SPECULATION, October 1971

87) **ARM**. EPOCH, edited by Roger Elwood and Robert Silverberg
collection, THE LONG ARM OF GIL HAMILTON (#88)
anthology, THE 13 CRIMES OF SCIENCE FICTION, edited by Isaac Asimov, Martin H. Greenberg, and Charles G. Waugh

88) **THE LONG ARM OF GIL HAMILTON**. collected stories, paper, Ballantine
as DE LANGE ARM VAN GIL HAMILTON, Dutch, from Prisma Science Fiction

89) **AFTERWORD**. collection, THE LONG ARM OF GIL HAMILTON (#88)

90) **DOWN IN FLAMES**. fanzine, *Trumpet*, 1969

91) **BUILDING THE MOTE IN GOD'S EYE** (with Jerry Pournelle). *Galaxy*, January 1976
collection, A STEP FURTHER OUT, by Jerry Pournelle

92) **DOWN AND OUT**. *Galaxy*, February 1976
(included in A WORLD OUT OF TIME, novel, #95)
anthology, THE BEST FROM GALAXY, VOL. IV, edited by James Baen
anthology, THE BEST OF MY YEARS, edited by James Baen

93) **MISTAKE**. original anthology, *Stellar* #2, edited by Judy-Lynn del Rey
anthology, 100 GREAT SCIENCE FICTION SHORT SHORT STORIES, edited by Isaac Asimov, Martin H. Greenberg, and Joseph D. Olander
collection, CONVERGENT SERIES (#113)

94) **THE MAGIC GOES AWAY**. *Odyssey*, summer 1976
expanded (#107)

95) **WORLD OUT OF TIME**. novel, cloth, Holt, Rinehart and Winston
cloth, Holt, Rinehart and Winston (1)
paper, Ballantine
as BUITEN DE TIJD, Deltos Elsevier, Amsterdam
Italian, as MONDO SENZA TEMPO, 1977 from Editrice Nord, Milano
Argentine, paper, as UN MUNDO FUERA DEL TIEMPO Buenos Aires, 1978
Japanese, cloth, 1979, Hayakawa Publishing, Inc.
as UN MONDE HORS DU TEMPS, Editions Albin Michel, 1978, Paris
Israel, paper (data not in English letters)

96) **CHILDREN OF THE STATE**. serial form of A WORLD OUT OF TIME, *Galaxy*, September, October, November

97) **THE WORDS IN SCIENCE FICTION**. anthology, THE CRAFT OF SCIENCE FICTION, edited by Reginald Bretnor
anthology, ANTIGRAV, edited by Philip Strick

98) **LUCIFER'S HAMMER** (with Jerry Pournelle). novel, cloth, Playboy Press
paper, Fawcett Books
paper, Futura
Japanese, paper, 1980, Hayakawa Publishing Inc.
as LUZIFERS HAMMER, paper, 1980, Wilhelm Heyne Verlag, München

as DE HAMER VAN LUCIFER, paper, 1980, A. W. Bruna & Zoon Utrecht/Antwerpen
Israel, paper (data not in English letters)

99) **CRUEL AND UNUSUAL**. *Cosmos*, May 1977, as THREE VIGNETTES
collection, CONVERGENT SERIES (#113)
anthology, ALIENS! edited by Gardner Dozois and Jack M. Dann (as FOUR VIGNETTES)

100) **THE SUBJECT IS CLOSED**. *Cosmos*, May 1977, as THREE VIGNETTES
collection, CONVERGENT SERIES (#113)
anthology, ALIENS! edited by Gardner Dozois and Jack M. Dann (as FOUR VIGNETTES)

101) **GRAMMAR LESSON**. *Cosmos*, May 1977, as THREE VIGNETTES
collection, CONVERGENT SERIES (#113)
anthology, ALIENS! edited by Gardner Dozois and Jack M. Dann (as FOUR VIGNETTES)

102) **ROTATING CYLINDERS AND THE POSSIBILITY OF GLOBAL CAUSALITY VIOLATION**. *Analog*, August 1977
collection, CONVERGENT SERIES (#113)
Japanese, *Isaac Asimov's Science Fiction Magazine*, 1981, along with an extensive interview with photos.

103) **THE LAST NECRONOMICON**. fanzine, APA-L 315 #4

104) **CAUTIONARY TALES**. *Isaac Asimov's Science Fiction Magazine*, July–August 1978
collection, CONVERGENT SERIES (#113)
ISAAC ASIMOV'S SCIENCE FICTION ANTHOLOGY
Japanese, *Isaac Asimov's Science Fiction Magazine*

105) **TRANSFER OF POWER**. coffeetable book, ARIEL BOOKS, VOLUME THREE, Thomas Durwood, editor; 1978
collection, CONVERGENT SERIES (#113)
paper, anthology, NIRWANA, as MACHTSOVERDRACHT 1981, Meulenhoff Nederland bv, Amsterdam

106) **FLARE TIME**. anthology, ANDROMEDA, edited by Peter Weston; first printing
Amazing Science Fiction Stories, November 1982
collection, LIMITS, Ballantine (#151)
anthology, MEDEA: HARLAN'S WORLD. Trade paperback & cloth, Bantam, 1985.

107) **THE MAGIC GOES AWAY**. illustrated novella, trade paperback, Ace Books, 1978
cloth, Ace
paper, Ace

cloth, 1980, Tokyo Sogensha Co., Ltd. with illustrations (maybe augmented?)
German, paper, as WENN DER ZAUBER VERGEHT . . . 1981, Bastei Lubbe, with illustrations
In Japanese, Tokyo Sogensha Co., Ltd.

108) **ASSIMILATING OUR CULTURE, THAT'S WHAT THEY'RE DOING!** *Destinies*, November–December 1978, edited by James Baen
collection, CONVERGENT SERIES (#113)
anthology, ALIENS! edited by Gardner Dozois and Jack M. Dann (as FOUR VIGNETTES)
anthology, THE BEST OF DESTINIES, edited by James Baen (see also #111)

109) **THE SCHUMANN COMPUTER**. *Destinies*, Jan.–Feb. 1979, edited by James Baen
collection, CONVERGENT SERIES (#113)
French anthology, paper, UNIVERS 1980, as LE CHIRPSITHRA, J'ai Lu

110) **SHALL WE INDULGE IN RISHATHRA?** (with cartoons by William Rotsler). *Science Fiction Review*, March–April 1979

111) **SPIRALS** (with Jerry Pournelle). *Destinies*, April–June 1979
anthology, THE ENDLESS FRONTIER, edited by Jerry Pournelle
anthology, THE BEST OF DESTINIES, edited by James Baen (see also #108)
Collection, LIMITS (#151)

112) **THE LOCUSTS** (with Steven Barnes). *Analog*, June 1979
anthology, THE 1980 ANNUAL WORLD'S BEST SF, edited by Donald A. Wollheim
Collection, LIMITS (#151)

113) **CONVERGENT SERIES**. collected stories, Ballantine, paper, 1979
paperback, Orbit

114) **INTRODUCTION** for CONVERGENT SERIES (#113)

115) **IN THE CELLAR**. *Isaac Asimov's Science Fiction Magazine*, February 1979
Japanese, *Isaac Asimov's Science Fiction Magazine*

116) **THE RINGWORLD ENGINEERS**. serial, *Galileo*, July, September, November 1979, and January 1980
novel, inbound signatures, limited edition, from Phantasia Press
novel, cloth, Holt, Rinehart, and Winston
goatskin, issue of 26, Phantasia; I have "Q"
paper, Ballantine
cloth, Holt, Rinehart and Winston
paper, Orbit (British)

Japanese, cloth, 1981, Hayakawa Publishing, Inc.
cloth, as LES INGENIEURS DE L'ANNEAU-MONDE 1982, Nouvelles Editions Opta
paper, as DIE RINGWELT-INGENIEURE 1982, Bastei Lubbe

117) **FUTURE HISTORIES**. article for the *SFWA Bulletin*, special issue on Future Histories

118) **THE PATCHWORK GIRL**. trade paperback, illustrated, Ace, 1978
Japan, cloth, illustrated (no data in English).
Japan, paper, from Tokyo Sogensha Co., Ltd.
Hebrew, with THE LONG ARM OF GIL HAMILTON. Data not available

119) **FROM MACROSTRUCTURES ENGINEERING: PROGRESS REPORT**. Lunacon '80 Program Book

120) **THE GREEN MARAUDER**. *Destinies*, February–March, 1980
anthology, DREAM'S EDGE, edited by Terry Carr (cloth and paper, Sierra Club Books)
anthology, BEST SCIENCE FICTION STORIES OF THE YEAR, TENTH ANNUAL COLLECTION, edited by Gardner Dozois
Collection, LIMITS (#151)
anthology, TOP SCIENCE FICTION, ed. by Josh Pachter, from Dent, cloth.

121) **RETROSPECTIVE** (with Steven Barnes). Section from DREAM PARK (#126). *Destinies*, summer 1980

122) **ON THE MARCHING MORONS** (with Isaac Asimov). *Isaac Asimov's Science Fiction Magazine*, January 1981

123) **THE REAL THING**. German first publication, TOR ZU DEN STERNEN 1981
Isaac Asimov's Science Fiction Magazine, November 1982
Collection, LIMITS (#151)

124) **OATH OF FEALTY** (with Jerry Pournelle). section in *Omni*, Oct. 1981

125) **THE ROENTGEN STANDARD**. *Omni*, "Lastword," October 1981
Collection, LIMITS (#151)

126) **DREAM PARK** (with Steven Barnes). novel, cloth, limited edition with inbound signatures, from Phantasia Press
trade paperback, Ace Books
cloth, Book Club edition, Ace
paper, Ace

127) **THE MAGIC MAY RETURN**, edited by Larry Niven. Ace Books, trade paperback

128) **WAR MOVIE**. *Stellar* #7, paper, edited by Judy-Lynn del Rey
collection, LIMITS (#151)

129) **LIMITS**. *Isaac Asimov's Science Fiction Magazine*, September 28, 1981
anthology, paper, ALIENS & OUTWORLDERS, 1983, Davis, edited by Shawna McCarthy
collection, LIMITS (#151)

130) **THE THEORY AND PRACTICE OF INSTANT LEARNING** *Herald-Examiner*, Sunday, October 18, 1981

131) **OATH OF FEALTY** (with Jerry Pournelle). novel, limited edition with inbound signatures from Phantasia Press
cloth, Timescape Books (Simon & Schuster/Pocket Books)
paper, Orbit (British)
paper, Pocket Fiction (Simon & Schuster/Pocket)

132) **TALISMAN** (with Dian Girard). *Fantasy and Science Fiction*, November 1981
collection, LIMITS (#151)
collection, MORE MAGIC (#153)

133) **THE LION IN HIS ATTIC**. *Fantasy and Science Fiction*, July, 1982
collection, LIMITS (#151)
collection, MORE MAGIC (#153)

134) **THE WRISTWATCH PLANTATION** (with Sharman Di Vono and Ron Harris). *Houston Chronicle*, March 1 thru July 17, 1982. A newspaper comic strip set in the *Star Trek* universe, it seems doomed to die unsung.

135) **THE NOTEBOOKS OF MACK SIKES**. *SFWA Forum*
fanzine, *Science Fiction Review*

136) **THE DESCENT OF ANANSI** (with Steven Barnes). segment in *Analog*, October 1982
Tor, 1982 (paper)
British: Orbit (Futura, Macdonald & Co.), 1984

137) **REFLEX** (with Jerry Pournelle). novelet.
anthology, THERE WILL BE WAR, edited by Jerry Pournelle.

138) **DE STRANDEN VAN SERIUS VIER**. Dutch. Collected stories taken from various sources. Meulenhoff Science Fiction, 1975

139) **A TEARDROP FALLS**. Short story set in the Berserker universe of Fred Saberhagen. Part of a multi-collaboration novel by Fred Saberhagen. *Omni*, June 1983
Collection, LIMITS (#151)
Novel by Saberhagen, BERSERKER BASE, 1985.

140) **THE INTEGRAL TREES**. novel, serial, *Analog*, October 1983 through January 1984.
cloth, March 1984, Del Rey (Ballantine).
paper, February 1985

paper, Futura Publications, 1985
as DE INTEGRAALBOMEN, paper, from Meulenhoff, Amsterdam, 1985

141) **NIVEN'S LAWS**. Collected stories and articles. Small hardback. Principal Speaker's book published by Owlswick Press for Philcon, 1984.

142) **TABLE MANNERS**. collection, NIVEN'S LAWS, 1984 (#141)

143) **NIVEN'S LAWS**. article. collection, NIVEN'S LAWS, 1984 (#141)

144) **CONVENTION STORIES**. article. collection, NIVEN'S LAWS, 1984 (#141)

145) **STAYING RICH**. article. collection, NIVEN'S LAWS, 1984 (#141)

146) **THE THEORY AND PRACTICE OF INSTANT LEARNING**. article. collection, NIVEN'S LAWS, 1984 (#141)

147) **IF IDI AMIN HAD HAD THE BOMB**. article. collection, NIVEN'S LAWS, 1984 (#141)

148) **IN MEMORIAM: HOWARD GROTE LITTLEMEAD**. poem. collection, NIVEN'S LAWS, 1984 (#141)

149) **WHY MEN FIGHT WARS AND WHAT YOU CAN DO ABOUT IT**. article. collection, NIVEN'S LAWS, 1984 (#141)

150) **COLLABORATIONS**. article. collection, NIVEN'S LAWS, 1984 (#141)

151) **LIMITS**. Collected stories. Del Rey Books, February 1985, paper.

152) **EQUIPMENT, METHOD AND THE REST**. Short article for *The Science Fiction Source Book*, by David Wingrove.

153) **MORE MAGIC**. collection, Niven as editor. Trade paperback, June 1984. Berkley Fantasy (Ace). (#132, #133)

154) **THE TIME OF THE WARLOCK**. Collected Warlock stories. illus. Dennis Wolf. SteelDragon Press. cloth, limited.

155) **FOOTFALL**. Del Rey (Ballantine), May 1985. Novel. cloth. Michael Whelan cover.
cloth, Victor Gollancz Co., 1985

156) **LIMITS**. collection, Ballantine Books, 1985, cloth & paper.
"The Lion in His Attic"
"Spirals" (with Jerry Pournelle)
"A Teardrop Falls"
"Talisman"
"Flare Time"
"The Locusts" with Steven Barnes
"Yet Another Modest Proposal: The Roentgen Standard"
"Table Manners"
"The Green Marauder"

"War Movie"
"The Real Thing"
"Limits"

157) **TELL ME A STORY.** Advice for writers, in WRITERS OF THE FUTURE, Volume II, 1986.

158) **THE SMOKE RING.** Serial in *Analog,* January–April 1987. cloth, Del Rey Books. June 1987.

159) **THE LEGACY OF HEOROT.** (with Jerry Pournelle and Steven Barnes). Cloth, Simon & Shuster, July 1987. Paper, Pocket Books. Maps by Alexis Wolser.

160) **THE TALE OF THE JINNI AND THE SISTERS.** Short story, *Argos SF & F,* Penrhyn Publishing. *Arabesques 1,* ed. Susan Shwartz, July 1988, Avon & Pan Books.

161) **THE DREADFUL WHITE PAGE.** "Postcard Story" for *Surplus Wyvern Press.*

162) **BRENDA.** Novella, *Warworld,* anthology edited by Jerry Pournelle. *New Destinies,* Spring 1988.

163) **THE GRIPPING HAND** (with Jerry Pournelle). Novelette, first section of *The Moat Around Murcheson's Eye.*

164) **CURSE.** Short story, unsold.

165) **NEXT TIME.** 100 words (a "drabble") for *The Drabble Project.*

166) **THE PORTRAIT OF DARYANREE THE KING.** Short story. First American rights unsold. Sent to ARGOS. ARGOS collapsed. Anthology rights promised to Susan Shwartz for *Arabesques 3.* Sold to Titan Books (England).

167) **THE WISHING GAME.** Short story, the final tale of the Warlock's companions. *Arabesques 2,* edited by Susan Shwartz, Avon Books, 1989.

168) **AUTOGRAPH ETIQUETTE.** 600 words of tips for writers and seekers.

169) **REVIEW of THE PRISONER** for *Reason* Magazine, 1987.

170) **REVIEW of AGAINST THE FALL OF NIGHT and GREAT SKY RIVER** for *Reason* Magazine, 1987.

171) **THE ALIENS IN OUR MINDS.** Anthology, *Aliens: The Anthropology of Science Fiction,* edited by George E. Slusser and Eric S. Rabkin, Southern Illinois University Press, 1987.

172) **INTRODUCTION to MAN-KZIN WARS.** Edited by Larry Niven, Baen Books, 1988.

173) **REVIEW of HORROR STORIES FOR BRIGHT PEOPLE** for *Reason* Magazine, February 1988.

174) **INTRODUCTION to BRING THE JUBILEE.** The Easton Press, 1988.

175) **READ THIS.** Essay, *The New York Review of Science Fiction,* September 1988.

176) **BULLETIN SYMPOSIUM: THE WORST MISTAKE YOU EVER MADE.** *Bulletin of the SFWA,* Summer 1989.

177) **CRITICISM.** Essay, *New Destinies, Vol. VII,* edited by Jim Baen, Baen Books, 1989.

178) **RINGWORLD RETROSPECTIVE.** *The Best of the Nebulas,* edited by Ben Bova, Tor, 1989.

179) **THE RETURN OF WILLIAM PROXMIRE.** Short story, *What Might Have Been? Volume I: Alternate Empires,* edited by Gregory Benford and Martin H. Greenberg, Bantam Spectra, 1989.

180) **THE MURDER OF HALLEY'S COMET.** Short story, *The Fleet, Book 3: Breakthrough,* edited by David Drake and Bill Fawcett, Ace, May 1989.

181) **READ THIS.** Essay, *The New York Review of Science Fiction,* May 1989.

182) **INTRODUCTION and ANTHOLOGY to MAN-KZIN WARS II.** Paper, Baen Books, 1989.

183) **THE BARSOOM PROJECT.** Novel, Ace Books, 1989.
hardback, SFBC (British book club), February 1990.
trade and hardback, Pan (British), April 1990.

184) **RESPONSE TO "THE NEW GENERATION GAP."** Essay, *The New York Review of Science Fiction,* September 1989.

185) **READ THIS.** Essay, *The New York Review of Science Fiction,* November 1989.

186) **BLIND ALLEYS.** *Bulletin of the SFWA,* Spring 1990.

187) **MOM AND THE KIDS.** Short story, paper, *The Fleet, Book 4: Sworn Allies,* edited by David Drake and Bill Fawcett, Ace, March 1990. paper, *All the Way to the Gallows,* edited by David Drake, Baen Books, 1996.

188) **MADNESS HAS ITS PLACE.** Short story, *Man-Kzin Wars*

III, Baen Books, 1990.

collection, *N-Space,* A Tor Book, published by Tom Doherty Associates, 1990.

anthology, *Isaac Asimov's War,* edited by Gardner Dozois, Ace, 1993.

collection, *Three Books of the Known Space,* Del Ray Books, 1996.

anthology, *Man-Kzin Wars: The Best of All Possible Wars,* edited by Larry Niven, Baen Books, 1998.

189) **N-SPACE.** Collection, A Tor Book, published by Tom Doherty Associates, September 1990.

190) **REVIEW of GOOD OMENS.** *The New York Review of Science Fiction,* August 1990.

191) **A.R.M. A TALE OF KNOWN SPACE.** Comic book, *Adventure Comics,* Malibu Graphics, September–November 1990.

192) **MY FAVORITE STORY.** Essay, *The New York Review of Science Fiction,* October 1990.

193) **INTRODUCTION to MAN-KZIN WARS IV.** Edited by Larry Niven, Baen Books, 1991.

194) **THE DEFENSELESS DEAD: A TALE OF KNOWN SPACE.** Comic book, *Adventure Comics,* Malibu Graphics, February–April 1991.

195) **ACHILLES' CHOICE.** Novel, A Tor Book, published by Tom Doherty Associates, March 1991.

196) **WORLD OF PTAVVS/A GIFT FROM EARTH/NEUTRON STAR.** Collection, BOMC/QPBC, June 1991.

197) **FALLEN ANGELS.** Novel, Baen Books, July 1991.

198) **READ THIS.** Essay, *The New York Review of Science Fiction,* September 1991.

199) **PLAYGROUNDS OF THE MIND.** Collection, A Tor Book, published by Tom Doherty Associates, October 1991.

200) **GREEN LANTERN: GANTHET'S TALE.** Graphic novel, D.C. Comics, 1992.

201) **WHERE NEXT, COLUMBUS?** (with Jerry Pournelle) for *Smithsonian Magazine,* 1992.

202 **REVIEW of COSMIC TIME TRAVEL: A SCIENTIFIC ODYSSEY.** *The New York Review of Science Fiction,* January 1992.

203) **THE CALIFORNIA VOODOO GAME.** Novel, Ballantine, 1992.

204) **READ THIS.** Essay, *The New York Review of Science Fiction,* October 1992.

205) **THE GRIPPING HAND**. Novel, Pocket Books, 1993, hardcover and paperback.

206) **BRIDGING THE GALAXIES.** Collection, San Francisco Science Fiction Convention, 1993. "Introduction," "Procrustes," "Where Next, Columbus?," "It's Only a Story," "Tabletop Fusion," "The South Los Angeles Broadcasting System," "The Color of Sunfire," "Intercon Trip Report," "The Lèshy Circuit," "All the Bridges Rusting," "Bibliography."

207) **CRASHLANDER.** Collection, Del Rey, 1994. "Ghost," "Neutron Star," "At the Core," "Flatlander," "Grendel," "The Borderland of Sol," "Procrustes."

208) **REVIEW of THE MILLENNIAL PROJECT.** *First Foundation News!,* June 1994.

209) **FOREWORD to WOLFF & BYRD, COUNSELORS OF THE MACABRE: FRIGHT COURT.** Exhibit A, Press, 1994.

210) **FLATLANDER.** Collection, Del Rey, 1995. "The Organleggers," "The Defenseless Dead," "ARM," "The Patchwork Girl," "The Woman in Del Ray Crater," "Afterword: Science/Mystery Fiction."

211) **SONG OF THE NIGHT PEOPLE.** Novella, *Sisters of the Night* (anthology), edited by Martin H. Greenberg and Barbara Hambly, Warner Books, 1995.

212) **BEOWULF'S CHILDREN.** Novel, A Tor Book, published by Tom Doherty Associates, November 1995.

213) **REGULATING THE BODY BUSINESS.** *Scientific American,* March 1996.

214) **THE RINGWORLD THRONE.** Novel, Del Rey Books, 1996.

215) **CATFISH AND RED MEAT FLAVORING.** Collection, *Serve It Forth: Cooking With Anne McCaffrey,* edited by John Gregory Betancourt, Warner Books, October 1996.

216) **THREE BOOKS OF KNOWN SPACE.** Collection, Del Rey Books, 1996.

217) **DESTINY'S ROAD.** Novel, A Tor Book, published by Tom Doherty Associates, June 1997.

Mass market paperback, Tor Science Fiction, May 1998.
paper, Orbit, May 1998.

218) **CHOOSING NAMES.** Short story, *Man-Kzin Wars VIII,* 1998.

219) **WISDOM.** *Altair #4,* 1999.

220) **RAINBOW MARS.** Collection, A Tor Book, published by Tom Doherty Associates, March 1999. "Rainbow Mars," "Get a Horse!," "Bird in the Hand," "Leviathan!," "There's a Wolf in My Time Machine," "Death in a Cage," "Afterword: Svetz and the Beanstalk."
hardcover, Orbit (British)
paper, Little Brown/Orbit.

221) **GETTING YOUR DIME'S WORTH.** Introduction, *Mystery in Space,* DC Comics, September 1999.

222) **MISSION TO ABISKO.** Report, *Mission to Abisko: Stories and Myths in the Creation of Scientific "Truth,"* Anthology, edited by John L. Casti and Anders Karlqvist, Perseus Books, 1999.

223) **LOKI.** Short story, *Analog,* January 2000.

224) **SMUT TALK.** Short story, *Playboy,* January 2000.

225) **AN INTERVIEW WITH LARRY NIVEN.** Interview, Space.com, 2000.

226) **THE BURNING CITY.** Novel, Hardcover, Pocket Books, March 2000.
British hardcover, Orbit, April 2000.
Mass market paperback, Little Brown/Orbit, January 2001.
Mass market paperback, Pocket Books, June 2001.

227) **MARS: WHO NEEDS IT?** Article, Space.com, March, 2000.

228) **HOW TO SAVE CIVILIZATION AND MAKE A LITTLE MONEY.** Article, Space.com, April, 2000.

229) **TRAVELERS.** Article, Space.com, May 2000.

230) **ROCKET MEN.** Article, Space.com, June 2000.

231) **SATURN'S RACE.** Novel, A Tor Book, published by Tom Doherty Associates, July 2000.

232) **THE WISDOM OF DEMONS.** Short story, *Analog,* July/August 2000.

233) **WET MARS (LARRY NIVEN TALKS TERRAFORMING).** Article, Space.com, July 2000.

234) **MAKING SOMEBODY PAY.** Article, Space.com,

September 2000.

235) **FLY-BY-NIGHT.** Novella, *Asimov's Science Fiction,* October/November 2000.

236) **SURPRISES.** Article, Space.com, November 2000.

237) **THE MISSING MASS.** Short story, *Analog,* December 2000.

238) **ICE AND MIRRORS.** Short story, *Asimov's Science Fiction,* February 2001.

239) **THE HEIGHTS.** Short story, *Analog,* May 2001.

240) **SSOROGHOD'S PEOPLE.** Short story, *Redshift: Extreme Visions of Speculative Fiction,* edited by Al Sarrantonio, Penguin/Roc, December 2001.

241) **CHOOSING LIFE.** Short story, *Analog,* January 2002.

242) **FINDING MYSELF.** Novelette, *Analog,* June 2002.

243) **THE CONVERGENCE OF THE OLD MIND.** Short story, *Analog,* July/August 2002.

244) **FREE FLOATERS.** Novella, *Asimov's Science Fiction,* August 2002.

245) **CHRYSALIS.** Short story, *Analog,* September 2002.

246) **NIVEN'S LAWS 2002.** Article, *Analog,* November 2002.

247) **THE ONES WHO STAY HOME.** Short story, *Analog,* January 2003.

248) **SCATTERBRAIN.** Collection, A Tor Book, published by Tom Doherty Associates, January 2003.

249) **THE DEATH ADDICT.** Short story, *Analog,* May 2003.

250) **THE INTEGRAL TREES.** Collection, Ballantine Del Rey, July 2003, trade paperback.

251) **THE TRELLIS.** Novella, *Analog,* November 2003.

252) **INTRODUCTION to THE RACKHAM FILES.** Baen Books, February 2004.

253) **STORM FRONT.** Short story, *Analog,* March 2004.

254) **CHICXULUB.** Short story, *Asimov's Science Fiction,* April/May 2004.

255) **RINGWORLD'S CHILDREN.** Novel, A Tor Book, published by Tom Doherty Associates, June 2004.
British hardcover, Time Warner UK/Orbit, July 2004.
Mass market paperback, Tor Books, April 2005.

256) **BOOMERANG.** Short story, *Flights: Extreme Visions of Fantasy,* edited by Al Sarrantonio, Penguin/Roc, June 2004.

257) **RHINEMAIDENS.** Short story, *Asimov's Science Fiction,* January 2005.

258) **BURNING TOWER.** Novel, Hardcover, Pocket Books, February 2005.
Mass market paperback, Pocket Books, September 2006.

259) **THE MAGIC GOES AWAY COLLECTION.** Collection, trade paperback, Pocket Books, February 2005.

260) **BUILDING HARLEQUIN'S MOON.** Novel, A Tor Book, published by Tom Doherty Associates, June 2005.
Mass market paperback, Tor Science Fiction, April 2006.

261) **KATH AND QUICKSILVER.** Novella, *Asimov's Science Fiction,* August 2005.

262) **BREEDING MAZE.** Short story, *Analog,* September 2005.

263) **THE HUNTING PARK.** Short story, *Man-Kzin Wars XI,* Baen Books, November 2005.

264) **THE SLOW ONES.** Short story, *Analog,* December 2005.

265) **THE DRACO TAVERN.** Collection, A Tor Book, published by Tom Doherty Associates, January 2006.
Mass market paperback, Tor Science Fiction, November 2006.

266) **THE SOLIPSIST AT DINER.** Short story, Paperback, *Elemental: The Tsunami Relief Anthology,* edited by Steven Savile and Alethea Kontis, A Tor Book, published by Tom Doherty Associates, May 2006.

WORKS IN PROGRESS

SCATTERBRAIN II (Collection)
BURNING MOUNTAIN (with Jerry Pournelle)
BOWL OF HEAVEN (with Gregory Benford)
FLEET OF WORLDS (with Edward M. Lerner)
JUGGLER OF WORLDS (with Edward M. Lerner)
INFERNO II A.K.A. PURGATORIO (with Jerry Pournelle)
DREAM PARK IV (with Steven Barnes)
THE MOON BOWL (with Jerry Pournelle and Michael Flynn)